Where Your Treasure Is

Where Your
Treasure Is

M. C. BUNN

WHERE YOUR TREASURE IS
ISBN: 978-1942209799

Copyright © 2021 by M. Catherine Bunn

Cover art: *The Woman in Red*, by Giovanni Boldini
Ⓒ This painting is in the public domain.

Bellastoria Press
P.O. Box 60341
Longmeadow, MA 01116

To Gregg

TABLE OF CONTENTS

THE CAST
Part I

London

Hampstead
Sir Percival de la Coeur, uncle of Miss de la Coeur
Paul Morrant, a butler and manservant
Winifred de la Coeur, an heiress
Bettina Dupree, a lady's maid
Richards, a groom and driver
Doctor Frederick Frost, a physician
The staff of the Hampstead house
Detective Randal Owens of Scotland Yard
Constable Robert Clive, London Police

Cheapside
Amelie Barron, cousin to Miss de la Coeur
Delilah Barron, mother of Miss Barron
Bert Barron, cousin to Miss Barron and Miss de la Coeur
Natasha Barron, mother of Mr. Barron
Gretchen Burns, cousin to Miss de la Coeur

...and about town
George Broughton-Caruthers, heir of Hereford Hall
Black Diamond, his mount
Rigsby Archer, a baronet's son
...a Very Important Person

The City
Mr. Graham Buckner, a bank officer
Selway Adams, a secretary
Mr. Kent Darby, a clerk

Southwark
Court Furor, a driver and prizefighter
Eglantine, a cab horse
Geoff Ratchet, a friend of Mr. Furor
Hezekiah Boors, a friend of Mr. Furor
Seamus Todd, a friend of Mr. Furor
P. Lili Piani, a gang boss
Fanny Merton, a barmaid

Sam Merton, brother of Miss Merton
Beryl Stuart, half-sister to Mr. Furor
Rosie Cartwright, friend of Miss Stuart and Mr. Furor
Zeke Odom, a sparring partner and dogs-body
Jeb Davis, a trainer
Billy O'Connell, a trainer
Grynt Spivey, a traveler
Jasper, Mr. Spivey's cart horse
Detective Inspector James Patterson
Detective Sergeant Nicholas Peele

...and of the Turf
Berserker, a racehorse

Part II

London

Southwark
Bess Montague, a madam

...and about town
Horace Greystone, a barrister

...and of Tattersall's
Sweet Little Banshee, a racehorse

Richmond
The Earl
Mrs. Harris, a former actress
Jarvis Perrot, a journalist
Nancy Whyte, a lady's maid

Cheapside
Latimer Kleinfeldt, a jeweler

Norfolk

Holloways
Elizabeth Pettiford, a housekeeper
Mrs. Lumley, a cook
William, a groom
Struthers, a butler
Jakes, a footman
Molly Striker, a housemaid
Oliver, a hall boy
John Burns, husband of Mrs. Burns
The little Scots, children of Mr. and Mrs. Burns
Reverend Fontaine, a vicar
The villagers and tenants of Holloways and Hereford Hall
Tulip, Miss de la Coeur's mount
Puck, Mr. Barron's mount
Flora and Meriwether, a mare and her foal

Hereford Hall
Charles Broughton-Caruthers, brother of Mr. Broughton-Caruthers
Hotspur, Mr. George Broughton-Caruthers' mount

Cairo, Egypt
Colonel Andrew Perth, resident of Mena House
Amr, a manservant

Part III

Venice, Italy
Herr Steinwicz, a tourist
Frau Steinwicz, Herr Steinwicz's wife
Gianni, an artist

London
Cheapside
Fabrizio Bertollini, a shop clerk

The Old Bailey
Jonas Worthington, a judge
Mr. Humphrey Whitehouse, a barrister
Arabella Bertollini, fiancée to Mr. Ratchet

PART I
November 1892 – March 1893

CHAPTER 1
A Spinster Reflects

Winifred de la Coeur was not a traditional beauty, but she was one of a kind. Or so George had whispered while they played cards. He had won the hand and taken hers in his. After all these years, she ought to know better than to trust him.

She stood with her maid in the hall before the pier glass and examined the result of their morning's work. They had begun earlier than usual. Bathed, combed, powdered, and perfumed, Winifred wore underlinens trimmed in lace a duchess would envy. Her dress was the latest fashion. The crowning achievement was the hat, an enormous concoction of absinthe silk covered in black tulle and ostrich plumes.

"Morrant is right. I do look frightful!" Her hands flew to her head.

"Pooh! What does he know?" Bettina scoffed, none too quietly. She adjusted the veil and shot a sour glance at the butler, who strode past them into the breakfast room.

"Dr. Frost arrives at ten o'clock," Morrant announced. He scooped the brandy bottle from where it rested by Percival's feet then read aloud from the daybook in which the older man penned his thoughts. "'*CAN A MAN ALTER HIS CHARACTER?*' Not before breakfast, sir."

"I'm not hungry," Percival grumbled.

"Up late? 'The unexamined life is not worth living,' and so forth?"

"More like 'Lions prowling about the door'!" He pushed away the coffee and toast Morrant set by him. "Tea with Tasha and Delilah yesterday nearly finished me. Like battling hydras!" He peered into the hall and spoke to Winifred. "Plans today?"

"The bank and luncheon with George at Simpson's."

"You'll take Morrant with you? I don't need him."

Winifred yanked on her gloves and lifted her chin. "Nonsense! They read the Irish bill tonight, don't they? That'll take ages."

"Long after midnight probably. All I shall think of the entire time are smoked oysters on buttered toast, a good cigar, and you. Blanchard holds forth like a hailstorm whenever he thinks we're eager to get away. Worse than my old school master. I'm too old for this sort of thing."

"Precisely. I'll be at the opera with Amelie and Bert. You'll stay at your club, so of course you'll need Morrant!"

In the breakfast room, her uncle tried to deflect his manservant's attempt to get him to eat. She watched with affection. Two bachelors, just as she and Bettina were two old maids. While her uncle's bad lungs had aged him prematurely, Morrant's physique was still trim, his black hair touched with grey along the temples. She frowned at her reflection, tugged the tight bodice, and wished she was going riding on the Heath with her cousins Amelie and Bert.

Neither man had hidden his astonishment as she twirled into the breakfast room in her parrot green ensemble. Her uncle shaded his eyes. "Good lord, you're bright as a Christmas cracker! Are we to have the Highland Fling?" He squinted at the skirt's purple tartan trim while she kissed his cheek. "My dear, you look ready to pop!"

"It's not Guy Fawkes 'til tomorrow, sir," Morrant said.

"It's so tight, I might explode!" She had inhaled against her stays. "It is vulgar. I feel like Gloriana gone wild. Add seven ropes of pearls, and call me the Virgin Queen."

Morrant coughed.

It was impossible to tell whether his eyes expressed disapproval or suppressed amusement.

About his opinion of the idiotic tea gown she had worn while she and George played cards the prior evening, there could be no mistake. Morrant and Bettina had had words over it. In spite of the man's usual equanimity, the recent changes to her toilette had put him in a permanent state of alarm. His opinion of George had already involved the use of horsewhips. Though Bettina asserted that a woman dressed for herself, and Winifred inwardly argued that a servant's thoughts about her wardrobe or the way she lived should not matter, Morrant's opinion did.

She grimaced at her hat and reached for it. "Ce chapeau, est-ce que les femmes françaises appellent la Catherinette?"

Bettina caught her hands. "Poof! Do not tease about old maids. I work hard to dress you beautifully! The hat is très chic et vous êtes une femme de la mode, a fashionable lady. We want people to notice!" She adjusted Winifred's jabot. "The cut of the jacket is so modest, so cunning!"

"I suppose it makes me look less fat." In the long mirror, she critically regarded her hips.

"Madame Gretchen is all skin and bones, so our cousin can get away with no corset." She pushed in Winifred's waist. "We are not so!"

Bettina Dupree was a dark, exacting young Frenchwoman of martinet nature who was perpetually at war with the laundress and chamber maids if they so much as breathed on Winifred's dressing table, or touched her perfectly turned kid boots and gloves.

Almost purring, the woman shook a deep grey cashmere cloak over Winifred's shoulders, fastened its silver buttons, and bent to straighten the silk of the dark purple lining. "After lunch with Monsieur George, we will meet at the dressmaker's, n'est-ce pas?"

More shopping. Winifred was already bored by her birthday resolution to attend more to her appearance, but Bettina read the society pages and took the notices seriously. She looked forward to the grand fashion houses and complained that all Winifred wanted to wear was a riding habit. "Richards will drive you. À bientôt!" She smiled radiantly for her maid's benefit and kissed both her cheeks.

Richards sat on the brougham's high box, bundled against the cold. Leaves danced along the street in a gust of wind. Morrant walked down the steps, a blanket draped over his arm. Winifred quickly followed, glad of Bettina's insistence she wear the warm cashmere.

Morrant handed her up, checked the foot-warmer, then decorously spread the blanket over her knees. She watched his hands smooth the material. Their faces were very close.

"Morrant!"

"No, Miss, let me—if I may, speak first."

His tone was so serious; she prepared herself.

"Though you're not in the best spirits this morning and worried about your uncle, you appear fit to face any challenge, even in that dress and—," he hesitated. "If one might hazard a guess at the identity of that object upon your head—that hat!"

The hint of his smile and the kind expression in his dark eyes were a relief. He returned her hand's pressure, then closed the carriage door.

Richards cracked the reins.

Winifred twisted about to catch a last glimpse of Morrant, who stood on the steps and watched after her. The carriage turned the corner.

Hampstead's quiet streets gave way to those of Regent's Park. As traffic increased, Winifred's spirits rallied. Never fond of London, this morning she welcomed its energy and activity, an astringent if not a completely palatable medicine for her nerves. Richards' whip handle tapped her window.

"Still going to the City, Miss?"

"Yes, straight to the Royal Empire Bank!"

George's letter with its bold cursive had arrived in the morning's post. Morrant laid it between her and Percival. She had torn open the envelope and felt her cheeks flush. "It's only about that piece of land he wants to sell me." She threw the letter on the table, pushed away the nearly finished plate of kedgeree that she already regretted, and pretended to read the newspaper's financial section.

"That detestable piece land," Percival had snapped. "I wish the earth would swallow it!" And their owner George, she had thought. Her uncle added that he was sorry if she was disappointed. She knew he was relieved.

During a shooting party that September, George had proposed the sale of a twenty-acre wood that separated the de la Coeur and Broughton-Caruthers estates and where the game warden encouraged the foxes. Winifred said that she was not interested. George replied that she made an art of playing hard to get.

How it must gall him, she had gibed. The first son in five generations obliged to sell off parcels of land rather than buy them! His brother Charles lived in Scotland in an enormous castle with his wife and two little girls. He had a steady character and was happily matched. They had acres of hunting grounds and no mortgages in sight. Charles had little money of his own but did not owe any either. Nor did he share George's lavish habits or the propensity for ennui that drove Hereford Hall's heir into low company and reckless deeds.

George smirked. "But he's boring, and neither as good looking nor as popular as I am."

On the day before she came up to London, she rode her horse Tulip across the fields to inspect the wood. Beyond it lay Hereford Hall's brick towers, graceful lawns, and chestnut-lined drive. She had given Tulip a smart kick and galloped down the sandy lane that led to the sea. In spite of her elder cousins' warnings, she and George had raced one another on it many times. She bent over her mare's neck, urged her to go faster, and pretended to outdistance her neighbor. She was Queen Bess, who ruled a kingdom of her own. No need of any man!

Her pride could not bear that George, or even her family, might suspect that while she had won the battle against her suitors, she had lost the war. At summer's end, once the field cleared and the dust settled, she discovered she was tired of holding up the increasingly heavy standard of her virginity. The other debutantes of her year had long retired from the lists on their fiancés' arms or were preoccupied by their confinements. She had attended so many weddings she lost track of the sprays of orange blossom Bettina cleared from her dressing table or the number of silver rattles that she and Amelie had wrapped. Her freedom was not the triumph she had imagined it would be.

At the first touch of sea breeze, Winifred had reined in Tulip and started for Holloways. Her uncle's country house lacked the Hall's Tudor grandeur. Its rustic parks and woods were a bit unkempt, like Percival in the morning before Morrant got hold of him. Yet local legend had it that Elizabeth I had favored Holloways over the Hall for reasons that had little to do with its fine trout streams and more with her host's golden-brown eyes. His portrait hung in the library. Elderly servants claimed he resembled a young Percival. Winifred gazed on the pale, handsome face with its halo of red-gold hair and wondered why her uncle had never married.

At the dressmaker's, she had confronted the mirror and her own prospects. Her ayah always said that she had her mother's high cheekbones and graceful movements. The rest was like her father, according to Percival; high coloring, blonde hair of the type called strawberry, a strong chin and full, labile mouth, and the de la Coeur eyes. Once too often, George had teased her about her taste for plain skirts and blouses. Bring out the most daring creations, she commanded the designer, no matter how outrageous. Determined to make George choke on his words and torment him with her wealth, she had written to the bank for her mother's Indian necklace.

That was before Morrant's distressed glances at the tea gown.

With only Bettina to see the flimsy article, how daring she had felt. They played cards before the fire. Morrant had entered. Never had she been more aware of her body, bare beneath the sheer folds of the garment the seamstress promised would afford "freedom" at home. As if she had not understood what the woman implied!

Bettina, who was proud of their bold choice, scowled at Morrant. "Your deal, Mademoiselle," she coaxed.

Winifred wanted to sink beneath the floor but had dealt the cards. To complete her misery, George strode in, unannounced as usual.

With enough dresses for a lifetime, she did not need to go to another fitting. The necklace was so valuable, she ought to leave it locked up. She'd never actually seen it, only the insurance drawings when the lawyers reviewed her father's estate. Its fiery opulence had reminded her of him. Rare, singular. Until recently, she wouldn't have dreamed of wearing it.

Like her ridiculous new wardrobe, that was George's doing as well.

Driven indoors by late-summer rain, he had promenaded with her and Amelie in the Hall's long gallery. Beneath portraits of his ancestors, they talked of the Queen's legendary sojourn in the neighborhood. Amelie mentioned the old monarch's love of jewels.

George laughed. "I can't tell one from another. They're all alike to me."

"What about your mother's necklace, Winifred?" Amelie cried. "The one with the big orange diamond like a bird's egg! I saw the drawings when she chose her presentation jewels. All that gold, big pearls, and yellow diamonds too!"

"A Moghul's hoard! Tonight, let's play dress up, like our Christmas romps. Win shall wear all her jewels and be our sultana. No, Gloriana! Bert and I will carry her in on a palanquin! Come on, Win! Amelie, be our Diana! Hail to our Virgin Queens!" George winked at Amelie, who turned bright pink and walked quickly ahead of them.

"Oh George, do be quiet!" Winifred scolded. "I'd never take it out of the bank!"

The jewels were a shield to raise before fellows like him. They were also a reminder of the love that brought her into the world. Her mother never had the opportunity to enjoy her husband's gift. Hours after Winifred's birth, she was dead.

"I'll never wear it—ever!" Winifred had said on the ride back to Holloways.

"If I had such lovely things I certainly would," Amelie had sighed.

Going without Morrant to the bank was a stubborn gesture, just as buying the clothes was a grandiose one, and meeting George for lunch was a foolish one.

Tears filled her eyes.

She stuffed the tulle veil onto the brim of her hat. Its net was like a cloud of smoke. Waving her hand at the ecstatic saleswoman, she'd proclaimed that she would take the lot, and now she hated all of it! No more silly hats! No more succumbing to maids and cousins! The jewels could stay in the vault. By Sunday, her dreaded birthday would be over. She'd be at Holloways and would ride Tulip alongside Amelie. They would race across the field behind the house under a sunny sky. Clouds would billow over the sea, and startled rooks would rise from the frosted grass.

George could eat lunch by himself.

Richards jerked the reins.

An omnibus forced them to the left of the thoroughfare as they passed Haymarket and turned onto the Strand. Cabs clustered thickly and propelled their slow but steady progress east.

In spite of the cold, the carriage interior felt close. She pushed down the window. Boiled cabbage and wet manure; rotting offal and greasy soot; the sour, sharp tang of horse urine. She pressed her handkerchief to her nose and silently urged Richards to drive as quickly as possible.

When the carriage stalled again, they were caught in the City's crush of traffic.

A flower girl darted into the street and pushed dangerously close to a neighboring hackney's wheels as it attempted to roll ahead of Richards. Apparently indifferent to being smashed, the girl thrust a nosegay of violets at the hackney. Her fingers were blackened, her shawl thin, her teeth rotten. From the cab's interior, a gloved hand shot out and waved her away.

Winifred hoped the girl would not approach her carriage next. Her emotions about the poor were never more keenly alive or conflicted than when she was in London. In Ahmedabad, she and her father swayed above brown faces, over bright dresses, veils and turbans. A naked man sat cross-legged, smeared with ashes. Her father explained the caste system, the chasm that separated Brahmins from Untouchables. In the shade of temples to foreign gods, the street sweepers and beggars made her sad but were part of an ancient, foreign system. On her first London visit, she'd been appalled that poverty existed there as well, only stripped of its romance.

The flower girl's shrill Cockney accent repelled her. Had such squeamishness in the village tailor's wife for an unbaptized brick mason been called to her attention, she would've condemned it. She knew all her tenants' names as her father had in India. London's poor were different, an unruly mass governed by no law but survival of the fittest. Crowds of red-faced men and women hurried through the cold. Only streets away from the bank lay terrible slums where the real Untouchables lived.

A slatternly woman and a well-dressed man turned furtively into an alley. A boot black strolled past, oblivious. A fat man's stentorian voice shouted, ham rolls for sale! He waved a greasy sign at passersby while his competitor's placard advertised a chop house. An organ grinder sang, his pitiful, tiny monkey atop his shoulders. The ragged maiden wove between them, in and out of the traffic, and waved her bouquets. Her ruined smile never wavered.

There were so many, too many like her. Outside the safety of Hampstead, of Holloways, this was the world; a pullulating, stinking, indifferent tide of humanity heaving against her carriage and about whose wretched lives she dared not think. The flower girl was almost squashed by the wheels of a passing omnibus. Winifred rummaged desperately in her reticule for some coins.

The hackney's driver tossed some coppers. Winifred blessed him. The girl caught one and thrust up her flowers. A brace of urchins descended on the rest of the coins. The boys rolled in a heap. A bobby furiously prodded their backs and heads with his stick, shouting for them and the girl to clear off.

Winifred turned away. After visits to the poorest cottages, cousin Delilah said it was best to put what one saw out of one's mind. Winifred couldn't. It was difficult not to ask why others weren't as fortunate. Those first, heady days when she came of age had been accompanied by a wonderful expansiveness. Percival's solicitors informed her that she was a woman of substantial property; deeds and shares, houses and farms. All her father had earned. There were no inherited titles appended to her name but no entailments or debts. The Hampstead house, the vast farm in Gujarat, more acreage in Norfolk, their revenues! Parliament's latest laws ensured these would remain hers unless a disgruntled husband sued her in a divorce claim.

George's invitation to lunch had to be about more than selling her twenty acres.

Half the horror of her debut had been suffering flattery for a beauty she was clear-sighted enough to observe wasn't hers. Yet as Arthur de la Coeur's daughter, she was inclined to a high amount of self-regard that might have been called vanity if it hadn't had some substance to bolster it. Like him, she was strong-minded and intelligent and proud of it.

Her self-esteem was capable of being rattled, however. The night of her last ball, Bettina had helped her into in a low-cut gown of pale gold satin. Delilah fastened rubies and pearls around her throat. Finally, they crowned her with a matching tiara. A young woman of glowing blonde looks like hers should make the most of what there was to make the most of, Delilah said for what felt like the thousandth time. Winifred wished the woman would give this grating advice to Amelie, who gazed dreamily at the elaborate toilette's progress.

A marquess' son partnered her during the first waltz. She was miserable. Her dance card was full, but no one suited. No wonder George called her Gloriana. A baronet's son asked her to stand up with him twice. To her relief, he finally stopped chattering. Like so many others, he'd probably given up when she refused to make small talk. Then she realized it was because his glance had strayed down to her bosom, to take in what she had to make the most of.

At least George made no bones about flattering her. When her suitors began their campaigns in earnest, he'd retreated and mirthfully watched her discomfiture. He finally emerged from the card room and came to her aid. They sat in the moonlight, mocking the men. "Why do they bother about my eyes and my dress? Why don't they simply compliment my money?"

"It's difficult to make love to a bank account."

Winifred smiled. "You've some experience of it."

"Too much! Now, that woman over there. Very good-looking, but have you heard that she and our hostess—?" George leaned closer. He always knew embarrassing tidbits about guests, or made them up. He enjoyed straining the bounds of decency as he recounted such tales.

"*Monsieur George, il est vraiment le Diable lui-même!*" Bettina cried when Winifred repeated what he had said about the women.

For all his buffoonery, George helped her through an awkward adolescence. When she was sixteen, he returned to Norfolk as a captain of twenty-four and made sure she was not left a wallflower. At hunts, they strayed from the company. He treated her with the flattering, coy, slightly aloof attentions of a worldly older brother. Like her, he preferred the country. His slightly risqué, masculine anecdotes of army life, or the antics that led to his rustication were thrilling. Because of his frank, relaxed manner, it was easy to confide her frustrations and fears. Though he laughed, other times he didn't. Suddenly, he would break into his Cheshire Cat smile, challenge her to a race, and take off like the devil was at his horse's heels. Unable to resist, she would tear after him.

Natasha and Delilah chastised her behavior and obliquely warned about its consequences. This was intriguing, for George enjoyed a romantic reputation, like a dashing highwayman of old. Friendship with a man who so jauntily flaunted the rules was a sort of freedom by association. Whispers of his affair with an actress made his light-hearted attentions all the more flattering.

When he lifted her onto her horse or grasped her waist in the waltz, his hands lingered or his eyes gazed into hers a second too long. Invariably, she stumbled on his toes, and their encounters ended in merriment. But as she lounged in her bath or curled up in bed, she indulged in flights of fancy. What would it be like to be the lover of such a man—if not George himself, at least one so lively and spirited? Not that, at sixteen, she had been apprised of what being a man's lover actually entailed.

His behavior at the last summer ball more than disappointed her. She relied on his companionship to get her through the season's trials. After shaking off the baronet's son, she found Percival busy in the card room, so she fled onto the veranda. A few feet away, obscured by an arrangement of ferns and palms, two men smoked.

"What the confounded deuce are girls about these days?" The baronet's son's voice complained. "What a block of ice that de la Coeur woman is!"

George chuckled. "Come, Archer! A man might put up with a great deal for her."

"Granted, she's rich as the Queen of Sheba and quite an armful but dashed difficult!"

"She's rather jolly once you get to know her."

"I beg your pardon. You should've stopped me. I hope I don't offend."

"Not at all." George's voice was smooth. "Next time, don't be put off by a little ice. Drive in your spike. She'll melt."

There was a long silence.

"I say, this is dashed awkward, George. Are you and Miss de la Coeur—?"

"As I said, once you get to know her, she's very—." George let the rest of the thought hang in the air, like their tobacco smoke.

That he would discuss her in such a way with another man; that he would speak of her as quarry, as one conquered. Foxes indeed! In the carriage home, she hid her woe from Percival. In her room, she'd torn off her dress and trampled its satin folds with such fury that Bettina wailed. She flung her tiara and reviled herself for being so naïve.

If only he would ask her to marry him! She'd have the pleasure of refusing in front of all the patrons at Simpson's. Never mind that the neighborhood had buzzed about their probable match for years. She could afford to ignore him, even if he could not afford to ignore her.

Her mind raced with figures, pounds, and shillings. They sprouted willy-nilly like garden weeds and blossomed with compound interest. Mr. Buckner had reported that her German bonds' percentages were rising. Mr. Bartles was about to close on a purchase of land adjacent to Holloways that promised access to a future branch of the railroad's main line. She'd make a loan on easy terms to Bert so that he and Amelie could finally afford to marry. They'd waited so long. Of course, she'd cancel it as a wedding present. Their first housekeeping would be at Hampstead. As soon as the upstairs plumbing and renovations were complete, she'd tell Bert about her surprise. There were plenty of rooms, so many she and Percival didn't use. A study for Bert, a pretty sitting room for Amelie, and a nursery!

Richards rounded the corner. The bank rose before them. She forgot the pedestrians struggling in the cold. She made plans that had nothing to do with George and grew excited.

The hackney she'd seen earlier pulled alongside them at the curb. A bright spot of purple in the cabby's hatband, the flower girl's bunch of violets, caught her eye. Bunched beneath his dark chin was a plum-colored neckerchief, gaudily spotted. His profile was partly hidden under his hat's brim, and his long, dark hair was pulled back in an old-fashioned queue.

Involuntarily, she sat forward.

Morrant!

The resemblance struck her as delightfully funny. Her old friend would've found that absurd tie a worthy mate for her hat. She called to Richards to see if he had noticed the man, but her old groom did not seem to hear her.

Their vehicles drew nearer, and her first impression was corrected. The man was a very rough type. His scarred, square jaw was peppered with beard, his profile classical but not quite. The resemblance to Morrant was so marked as to be interesting, but the driver was definitely not in her friend's league. His deep voice and Cockney accent were audible when he spoke to his horse. He was not the sort one would want to meet in a dark alley.

Two other carriages jammed before theirs. A bobby waved his hands. Men shouted. Both the cabby and Richards worked to restrain their horses and keep their trappings from tangling.

Winifred studied the cabby once more.

He was dapper in a down-at-heel way, a real London character. He wore a top hat, heathery-grey checked pants, and fingerless gloves. His worn velvet coat was a garish purple almost as gaudy as that which adorned her tartan flourishes. Its cut was fanciful and old-fashioned, more like a gypsy costume than livery. The coat was likely a dandy's cast-off from years ago, its survival into the present era miraculous. Its previous owner had probably been a rake. She wondered if its present one was. Like George.

George again! Go away! She craned her neck to see the rest of the cabby's face.

A hawker cried out, "Chestnuts—hot—chestnuts!"

Winifred only half heard him. The cabby leaned toward the open window of his vehicle, shouting unintelligibly to his fare. She stared at the wilted violets and his broad shoulders. The resemblance to Morrant was uncanny. She hastily drew back as the man straightened on his box.

How happy Amelie would be when Bert told her the good news. How Natasha would cry, though she always cried these days. Amelie would be married at St. George's in Hanover Square and have as many flowers as she wanted. Winifred would host the breakfast and assemble the trousseau with Bettina. Inwardly, she already argued with Delilah over details. Perhaps there'd be another, happier trip to the dressmakers' shops for Amelie's wedding gown and touring clothes.

The cabby pulled at his horse's reins, making way for Richards. One of the bank's liveried footmen held a spot for their carriage. Winifred tossed aside her blanket. Forget George! Morrant was right. Whatever the next hours might bring, she was ready.

CHAPTER 2
A Fool and His Money
Are Soon Parted

Approaching the right turn that would take him to Swift Street and the Royal Empire Bank, Court Furor concentrated on traffic. Cold bit his cheeks and hunger gnawed his belly, but he ignored both through force of habit. The soles of his boots were thin and his gloves pointless. He hunched more deeply into his coat and wished he hadn't tossed his last coppers to that flower girl. But when she had thrust her wilted violets at him and smiled—those black teeth of hers—Jesus, Mary, and Joseph! Of course, she could've stained them for effect. At her age, he'd already had quite a few similar tricks up his sleeve to elicit the pity of potential targets. Early on, he'd known how to get by. Only because of that girl's need—or her guile—he was now officially without a penny to his name. What did that say for the wisdom of experience?

No point worrying about what the day would bring, never mind the next one. At Beryl and Rosie's flat he'd read in a pamphlet the doctor had left that the life expectancy of men from the East End was only—it wasn't worth repeating. At twenty-four, he was living on borrowed time. No one had to tell him that.

People down his way didn't celebrate birthdays, mostly because there was nothing to celebrate, but he was doing all right for a boy born in the Old Nichol. That is, he'd opened his eyes another day. If he opened them tomorrow, he'd be twenty-five. He even had a job, sort of. Dear old Mum would've felt, not proud, exactly. She couldn't feel much these days. Wound in a dirty sheet and dropped into a pauper's grave. How old had she been? He'd no idea. But she'd known his birth date to the hour and the minute. Baptized and registered, he was!

Look up lad, she used to say. "You have to look up to get up." So far, the highest he'd managed was a carriage box. Screwed to the lowest rung in the social ladder, Court kept his eyes on the traffic and minded his horse. If he raised his sights too high, he might run over one of those boys who kept darting out into the street, begging coppers he didn't have any more of.

He was the last son of Mick and Sadie Furor. His four older brothers had given up in quick succession during their infancies. According to Beryl's pamphlet, his miraculous survival beyond the cradle was another statistical anomaly, though no one had taken note but his dear old Mum. By the time he was delivered, Sadie was completely worn out. She'd lost her good looks and her patience with her heavy-handed, fast-talking, skirt-chasing mate. Mick Furor saw his new son as another gaping mouth to feed and acted accordingly. He eschewed all responsibility for Court's upbringing except to provide him with a bad example and an early education in how to pick a pocket or take a blow. Meanwhile, Mick continued to populate the neighborhood with his dark-haired progeny, supplying Sadie with interminable heartache and Court with a half-sister, Beryl, among others. For all he knew, the rest of Mick's children had suffered the fates listed in the pamphlet and died young of various fevers, neglect, or starvation.

Then again, one never knew. One of the louts in the hackney, Geoff Ratchet, was from the old neighborhood and the same approximate age as Court. People said there was a resemblance. Court didn't see it. The Methodist pastor who headed the school they'd briefly attended preached that all men were brothers. If that included Geoff, Court hoped the pastor was wrong.

On the eve of his quarter century, Court felt it incumbent upon him to reflect. Since it would be ages before he'd be able to get some sleep, he might as well. His survival was both a mystery and a wonder. He was a man of no prospects and no property but preferred to think of it as freedom from responsibility. Both of his parents had survived much longer than Beryl's pamphlet indicated was normal for folks of their ilk. Court supposed he might too but wouldn't bet on it. Mick was stabbed in a brawl while Court was yet a boy. Sadie had recently succumbed to gin poisoning after a series of abusive liaisons. Her last paramours came from the list of Mick's compatriots: cardsharps, pickpockets, and opium addicts. Court's company was not much better. But he was inclined to gambling, horseflesh, and women.

It was no secret he fancied himself a bit of a lad though he wasn't overly tempted by long, romantic entanglements. An hour or two with a willing girl would suit. Truth be told, he was too poor to maintain a woman in a manner that would satisfy his pride. He'd lost too much at the tracks recently. He had done a fair bit of prizefighting to make ends meet but currently avoided the ring like the plague since he hadn't done too well there either. He didn't like the beatings he'd been recently forced to endure in the fixed fights set up by his employer, P. Lili Piani.

Today was a sort busman's holiday, driving Geoff and his friends to the bank. He sensed commotion within the hackney. He rapped on the roof and was answered by a thud. Idiots, the lot of them! That big bear Seamus couldn't help it, but Hez had more sense. Except that Geoff had appealed to his sense of honor. That always did it with Hez, being an ex-army man. As for himself, he would've never agreed to drive if Geoff hadn't promised to forgive a quarter of the interest on Court's debt to him and to loan some more money at a better rate so Court could placate Piani. Money—it was the usual tangle, as Beryl always said. He was tired of Piani breathing down his neck. After today they'd be square. Driving was one of his few skills besides fighting. So far this morning, it had been easy.

Flicking the reins, more by way of communication than impatience, he urged the mare forward but was in no particular hurry. Again, the cab shook. Jesus, Mary, and Joseph! Better to look at a horse's ass than inside the cab. There sat the three biggest ones this side of the Thames.

Given a choice, he preferred equine company. Horses were easier to talk to and never asked for money. This old girl still had lovely legs, fore and aft. If only she'd been bought by someone who knew how to use her properly. A waste, that's what it was. At the tracks, it wasn't the betting, it was speed and beauty that fascinated and thrilled him. A horse going full tilt, her soul afire—that was pure magic. It was the spectacle of a fine creature running for all she was worth, giving it all she had that kept him going back. It certainly wasn't his meager winnings. He ought to know better than to think he'd ever have any luck that way. Geoff told him he was a fool to waste his time. He leaned forward and spoke lovingly to the mare.

There were all sorts of ways to waste a life. Beryl said that he was good at most of them. Gentlemen spent all day at the tracks, he argued. Nobody said they were loafing! If he'd dared believe there was any truth to Sadie's tales, his pedigree would've inclined him to a pride his friends couldn't own. But he placed no credence in her family stories. His mother claimed her side descended from Britons who trafficked in stolen horses and whose scions found their way into the Roman families who chose to stay in Britain after the main force withdrew.

Didn't she mean Normans? Raving, when she talked like that. Court would mop his mother's forehead with his neckerchief. Romans, she had argued, shaking her finger. No one could possibly remember that far back. Well, she did! Heroic blood flowed in his veins, the finest. Latin! Anglo-Saxon! A family tree, a coat of arms! Court had peered at the dirty wall, the empty spot where she pointed. Ah, the old family pride, loose on the hoof! He'd hidden her gin bottle.

If ever there had been horses, they were lost long ago. In her last hours, Sadie was still telling tales. Her people had ridden armored into battle during the Hundred Years War. No foot soldiers, them! Knights! Parish records proved it! In the chapel where she had been christened! Where was that? She stared with wild, feverish eyes. The details of her own life eluded her. Give her the Bible! It was all there, the family tree! The only Bible he'd ever seen was at the Methodist school. The only book in their room was his copy of the *Arabian Nights*, so he put that in her hands. By the time the pastor arrived, she didn't know anybody and had no more need of Jesus, Mary, and Joseph. Poor Sadie, she'd not owned one pretty ornament he could pin to her dress. It would've been stolen before she was cold.

No use crying about it.

What mattered was getting some grub and how much he owed his boss Piani; ergo, his involvement in this fool's errand. Whether his ancestors had ridden in Aquitaine or not, he was bound to be in a mess before the day was out. Geoff's plan had seemed sagacious to the trio in the hackney when he rehearsed it with them in the yard of the Boar and Hart after a moderately successful day at the racetracks and over a second order of very strong rum punch. It had sounded cock-eyed to Court but he knew better than to argue with Geoff when he was drunk. Sam, the young brother of the barmaid, Fanny, had been eager for a part to play and hung on Geoff's words. Enjoying the relaxing effects of the rum, Court had pulled his battered top hat over his eyes.

It was not meant to be a robbery per se. Geoff produced a short iron pipe from his boot and a plan of the bank's first floor from his coat pocket. Where the hell had he gotten that? Hez asked. Never mind, Geoff snarled.

"I drew it," Seamus said proudly, "after I went 'round there the other day to have a look."

"It's very nice," Hez hiccupped. "Is it accurate, to scale I mean?"

Geoff thumped the man's head. "Ain't goin' to 'ang in the Royal Academy is it?" The point was to make it look like their victim, a bank clerk named Selway Adams, had taken his superior's strong box.

Hez was confused. "It's a bit complicated, ain't it? Couldn't we just invite him 'round for another card game and rough him up a bit?"

No! Geoff had a reputation to maintain, a score to settle. He was going to ruin Adams!

"He'll lose his job," Hez said thoughtfully and gave a yearning glance to Fanny who was inside behind the bar. "What if he has a wife— or a child?"

"Nobody cheats me!" Geoff raised his iron pipe and smacked it against his open palm. The son of a bitch would crawl—bleed! He ground his teeth and smacked his palm with the pipe again.

Hez grew uncomfortable. "It was only a few pounds."

Silently, Court agreed. It was much less than he owed Geoff. He'd lost all his bets that day at the track.

Geoff imbibed more punch. Adams was the lowest! "A cardsharp, a cheat!"

"People has some choice names for you, too," Seamus offered.

Geoff snapped at him to shut up. "A gentleman requires retribution!"

"No, that ain't what they call you," Seamus corrected.

Court smothered a laugh. Hez and Sam didn't. Geoff banged on the table.

Fanny came out into the yard. "What's all this? Sam, put down that pipe."

"Come on, Geoff! It's only money," Seamus said soothingly. "Right, Courty?"

Geoff was unaffected by their mirth. His successful courtship of Piani's niece, Arabella Bertollini, had puffed him up. Like an adder, he still felt tender in his new skin. "We need firepower."

With a sigh, Hez produced an army-issue pistol. Fanny rolled her eyes at him.

The sight of the gun had made Court queasy.

"I can 'elp too!" Sam cried.

"Now Geoff, come on! It's only money," Seamus repeated. He looked worried.

Court couldn't afford to feel disinterested in Geoff's plan. He'd worked for Piani since he was a boy, so it wasn't the first time that obstreperous individual had promised to cut his throat. This go-round, he'd threatened to have one of Court's ears, too. There was also a creditor to whom he still owed several shillings, with interest, for his claret-colored velvet jacket and some other matters that concerned room and board at the Montague Hotel. More importantly, he must make good on a bill he'd signed for the equally spendthrift Hez. Admittedly, he and Hez had been a bit drunk the night he offered his signature, but he could've sworn the paper said five quid, not fifty. Oh well, Hez and Fan needed a bit to live on. He was fond of Sam, and dear Fan was a former sweetheart. The assumption of Hez's I.O.U. was a sort of wedding gift. If the ceremony ever came off. She hadn't forgiven Hez for that bad night when he and Old Swank got into it. Five shillings or fifty sovereigns, any money was a fortune. Thanks to that beggar-girl, he hadn't a penny!

The wind whipped through his coat, a last extravagance from his days of feeling a bit flush. It wasn't warm or even that smart. It would be worn out before he paid for it. Or if today went like he expected, it would outlast him. As for the money he owed Piani, it seemed a paltry sum to become so violent about, given the man's deep pockets and his stranglehold over just about everyone Court knew in Southwark, but he wasn't inclined to argue with a man of Piani's lack of principle. Plus, he was tired of touching his friends for the odd bit of cash so as not to starve.

After Geoff and the boys finished with Adams, Court was to drive the nag away from the bank at better speeds than the jockeys who'd so recently and sorely disappointed him. Given the risk and his recent record at the turf, the odds weren't in his favor. Yet in spite of hugging the shores of the barely legitimate and mostly illegal for the majority of his life, he'd managed to avoid trouble with the law. Incredibly, he'd never seen the inside of a prison. Hard labor held no particular terrors. Where his next meal came from was more pressing.

As he rounded the corner and drew alongside a very fine brougham, he heard a hawker cry, "Chestnuts—hot—chestnuts!" Their aroma momentarily disturbed his otherwise stoic response to a perpetually growling stomach. He might get more to eat if he went to prison.

Inside the crowded hackney, his friends grew rowdy again. Seamus, a much bigger man than Geoff and Hez put together but who had less brains than either, demanded to stretch his legs. Court bent to the window. He was amused but not reassured by Geoff and Seamus' risible interchange.

In addition to Hez's pistol, there were three sticks of ersatz dynamite in a carpetbag. The glorified firecrackers were Sam's enthusiastic contribution. He had also produced a small pad of detailed drawings, incendiaries copied from various homemade, safe-cracking guides, the sort commonly circulated amongst Piani's cronies and most likely pure Greek to Adams or to anyone else other than the police.

What was that? Fanny had snatched the pad from her brother. She grew angry, and when she was roused, her Cockney was flavored with her native Norman accent. With Guy Fawkes on the way, the boy had lately made and tried out some small firecrackers, startling the Boar and Hart's patrons and setting fire to some flour sacks Fan had saved for her knickers. Sam refused to tell her where he got his supplies. He snatched back the pad and passed it to Geoff. The man stuffed it in his trouser pocket.

"Masterminds indeed," cried Fanny derisively, but for the first time, she looked worried. Hauling up Sam by the collar, she smacked the back of his head. "This 'ere lot ain't no example to you! Bone idle when there's real work to be done! Get inside! There's potatoes to peel!"

"I ain't peelin' no taters! I'm in the gang!"

"I'll gang you!" Fanny cuffed Sam. "Hez—ooh! Do-nothin'! Loafs, the lot o' you! Get out!"

At that point, Court had felt it necessary to intervene on Sam's behalf. Fanny had a heavy hand, but she was right. The child was only eleven and ought not to be involved.

When Court picked up the trio at dawn, he was more relieved than ever that Fanny had held firm. Sam was nowhere in sight. Geoff arrived with his iron pipe hidden in his greatcoat and a jackknife strapped to his waist. Hez wore his military pistol inside his vest. Seamus had a ham sandwich stuffed in his pocket, but he needed no other weapons than his corpulent fists. Judging by the thuds and muffled shouts in the hackney, Geoff and Hez were completely drunk. The morning promised to descend into mayhem.

He directed the horse to a slow walk, trying to secure a place in the queue for the curb. In the gleaming brougham beside him sat a woman, her face hidden under an enormous, bright green hat trimmed with black ostrich feathers. Her driver signaled, and Court tugged his reins. Her carriage cut in front of him, taking a spot held open by a waiting footman in the bank's livery. Court philosophically picked the grime from his fingernails while another footman helped the woman descend and took her small case. Though a thick veil covered her face, Court caught a glimpse of golden hair, coiled in heavy masses on her shoulders. The wind lifted the edge of her mantle, and he was briefly amazed by the brilliant green of her dress.

The chestnut seller and his cart caught up to the line of vehicles. The aroma was delicious. What he wouldn't give to go to that chop house advertised on the other man's boards. Court's stomach ached. He felt a twinge of resentment toward the woman. She'd obviously never missed a meal in her life.

As if in response to his thought, she pointed to a group of dirty little boys who trailed after the chestnut vendor. She gave one of the footmen some coins, and he purchased a whole tray of nut-filled paper cones. Wrinkling his nose, he quickly distributed them and wiped his hands with distaste. Meanwhile, the woman and the footman with her case mounted the stairs to the bank. The boys tore open the cones, spilled hot chestnuts onto the pavement, and began pelting one another with what they did not cram into their mouths. A bobby ambled toward the group; the vendor moved on; and the other footman followed the woman and her companion.

While Court observed this little drama, Geoff and Hez tumbled out of the hackney, almost as ill-behaved as the children and shouting oaths at one another. On his way to break up the boys, the policeman admonished Geoff and Hez to watch their language and be sharp about it. Geoff scowled at the bobby, but Hez blanched and made an involuntary gesture, almost a salute.

Court wished he could melt into the traffic. He turned up his frayed collar and tipped his hat over his eyes, avoiding the policeman's. It had been a good idea of Seamus' to smear some boot blacking over the cab's number and give it a run through the mud as well. He rapped smartly on its top. Seamus climbed out, stretching luxuriously. He peered up at Court, who jerked his chin meaningfully in the direction of the bobby and then at Geoff and Hez.

Seamus mumbled, "Well, I never," extended his long arms, and unceremoniously collected Geoff and Hez into a whirly-gig of variously patterned pants, waving limbs, and shouts of "Oi, get off! Let go!"

Under Seamus' influence, Geoff and Hez more or less calmed down and quietly mounted the steps, the big man stalking behind them. The bobby had plainly concluded the trio was not made of City men.

He finally turned away. Whistling, he walked to the corner and joined another policeman.

Court exhaled. Another day in his haphazard, hungry life. This poor old nag, that flower girl's black teeth, those spilled chestnuts, and the woman in the green hat with her coins—Jesus, Mary, and Joseph! What could a fellow do but look up and forget about all of it? He resisted the urge to glance over his shoulder at the policemen, flicked the reins, and told the mare to walk on.

The Royal Empire Bank's lobby was designed to crush the customer with the institution's irreproachability. Its rotunda soared three stories and surrounded one immediately with echoing balconies of roseate marble along which darted junior clerks or walked with stately mien secretaries and officers of the august, old firm. Like ravens, they strode purposefully in black morning coats and crisp white shirts with collars that raised the wearer's chin to a sharp incline denoting the loftiness of his work. The clerks' high desks leaned over Winifred in ponderous, uniform rows, and the constant murmur of masculine voices was dreadful with the secrets of high finance.

She took off her gloves and smacked the leather against her palm. At the bank, she felt sure of herself. She marched to a towering desk. A dry, bespectacled man glowered down at her. "Good morning. I am Miss de la Coeur. I have an appointment with Mr. Buckner."

As though she had turned a key in a gigantic windup toy, all the men within earshot stopped and faced her. The clerk almost threw himself from his perch and begged to assist her progress to Mr. Buckner's office. Another man pushed him aside and, raising his eyes in wonder to her hat, introduced himself as Mr. Darby. He said his name as though he hoped it sounded important enough that she'd allow him to accompany her upstairs. She stared him down. "Well?" she asked in the tone she used on men who already bored her. "What are you waiting for?"

"This way," Mr. Darby said breathlessly.

As their group sallied forth, the tone of the other clerks' murmurs distinctly changed and was punctuated by the sound of her name going on before her. Heads bobbed in deference. One footman followed; the other hastened ahead, opening doors. Clerks peered over their desks to catch a glimpse of her. Winifred swept along, elated. She loved visiting the Royal Empire Bank.

Their little party climbed the grand staircase to the first floor, crossed the rotunda balcony, and traversed a short corridor. The footman threw open a tall, paneled office door, and she was announced. Mr. Darby, who had accrued a stack of papers and a long black portfolio during their trek, padded hastily after the second footman.

Mr. Bucker signed documents at his desk while another man read a report from a portfolio much like Mr. Darby's. Mr. Buckner rose, smiling with the beatific self-assurance of one who bears good news. "Welcome, Miss de la Coeur," he said in a plummy voice. "A pleasure to see you again. Many happy returns on your upcoming birthday. This is my new secretary, Mr. Adams."

Mr. Adams offered Winifred a chair. Mr. Buckner gestured to the footmen. One retreated to the back of the room where he busied himself with a tea tray. It held a steaming pot of China oolong, coconut macaroons, and a vase of yellow and coral tinted roses—all her favorites. The other footman offered to take Winifred's cloak.

"Thank you, no. Now, Mr. Buckner, show me how well my accounts are doing."

"Ah! We'll get to those German bonds. Also, as requested, your mother's necklace." He set a red, heart-shaped box on his desk. "There are some papers to sign for it. As soon as we do that, we'll talk about our progress. The last quarter went very well. Fortune smiles on us!"

She took the jewel box but did not open it. Her poor parents. Uncle Tristan—none of his recent investments had worked out. He must sell Claremont and sail for India as soon as his daughter and new husband settled in Germany. The young woman had ruined her reputation to such an extent, Delilah doubted she'd be received anywhere. Running away with that notorious lady author and living openly as—what had George called it? It sounded like the Greek island. And Percival's health was shattered. What would Dr. Frost say to him this morning? Almost certainly, he'd have to leave for Alexandria before the month was out.

Mr. Adams handed her a cup of tea. He smiled. "Miss de la Coeur?"

Seamus Todd yawned. Hez had woken him early and the tot of brandy in the cab made him sleepy. He leaned against a rear column in the ground floor lobby, a tall potted palm providing scant cover. A frock-coated man passed and cast him an uneasy glance. Though he was used to creating a stir in the ring or as a bouncer at one of Piani's soirees, he wasn't at the bank to attract notice. He thought he'd better go upstairs to Adams' office and check on the fellows.

Meanwhile, Geoff and Hez, having quickly consulted the bank's directory, and having left the usher who had shown it to them rather harried, had climbed the stairs in the wake of a female who was attired like a peacock and attracting everyone's attention.

Hez couldn't get over the woman's hat. "Blimey! Have you ever seen the like?"

Geoff had no eyes for the woman or her astonishing apparel, though he generally took an interest in fashion trends. He was glad for any distraction from their presence. On the first floor, her group turned down a hallway. He and Hez slipped into a smaller corridor that fed off the hall.

Hez lightly tapped the glass of Adams' door, heartily wishing he was in bed and wondering when Fan would let him back into hers. Geoff shoved by him. "We only have to wait, you know." He followed his partner into the room.

No one sat at the two desks.

Geoff kicked a dust bin. "Getaway Adams! What'd I tell you? Tipped off! 'E must've seen Seamus! Damn it!"

Hez opened another door on a smaller room that contained a file cabinet, greatcoats, hats, and an umbrella stand. He closed the door and sank behind a desk, resting his head on the carpetbag. "Maybe he's down that other hall." Geoff didn't seem to be listening. "Maybe he didn't come in today. I say we go back to the Boar and Hart."

Geoff fumed. "'E may 'ave done me like a girlie before, but not this time! 'E ain't gettin' away! We're 'ere because Fanny saw that card under 'is chair. If she'd spoke up sooner, we wouldn't be. I'd 'ave got back me own that night and 'e'd be under the river! So, don't complain! We're 'ere because of 'er!"

Hez didn't like the way Geoff put it but supposed it was true in a way.

At their last game, early on Fanny had spotted Adams slip an extra ace of hearts under his chair. Hez didn't want his favorite pub destroyed in a brawl, so he found no fault with his sweetheart's judgment. She was usually right. Since the mock explosives were Sam's suggestion, he felt sentimental about being in charge of them and hugged the bag closer. "She's a woman who knows how to hold her fire."

Geoff grunted. Behind a baize curtain was an alcove sheltering a safe, just as his diagram showed. His blood boiled. He craved extreme violence. Even before the alcohol he'd drunk in the cab, his thoughts about Adams had become somewhat circumscribed. He experienced them as one might the universe in a nutshell. In short, he was obsessed with vengeance. Until he got his hands onto Adams and his money, he could think of nothing else. "Damn it! I wanted to force 'im to get out the strongbox and bring it to me on 'is bleedin' knees!" He kicked the safe.

"Well, that's that then. We can't get at it. Let's go!"

"Don't just sit there! Go through them cabinets! There's got to be a key." While he spoke, Geoff yanked open drawers and dumped their contents onto the floor.

Hez crossed his arms. "I doubt it. We could wait a bit. I'm telling you, if he's even here, he's down the other hall."

"Does I look like a man what's got time to wait?" Geoff flung an inkpot.

Hez barely avoided being hit. "Oh, all right," he hiccupped. He retreated into the room with the file cabinet and slowly opened and closed the drawers. "What am I looking for?"

"A key to the strongbox, you ass!" Geoff set to with the iron pipe.

In the office, papers flew, glass shattered, contents spilled, but no box and no key revealed themselves. The safe did not respond to the application of the iron pipe, except to produce a metallic clanging like a furious blacksmith's anvil.

Hez peeped into the office. "Watch that racket! You'll have the whole place down on us!"

The door to the office burst open, and Selway Adams stood in it. "Who the devil's making this row? We've a very important client in Mr. Buckner's office!" At the sight of the destruction, his jaw dropped. Then he saw Hez. "Boors, what in hell's name—?"

"Hello!" Hez casually waved his pistol to indicate his partner's presence.

Geoff straightened and twirled his iron pipe. "Well, well! Good old Getaway Adams. Only 'e's goin' nowhere today! What about it, 'Ez? Shall we show 'im what's what? Let's 'ave some fun!"

Adams turned white and stepped backward.

Geoff grabbed Adams by his lapel. "You cheatin' sharp," he hissed, poking him with the pipe. "Open that safe and give us your strongbox."

"Get off!" Adams ordered. He struggled to undo Geoff's fingers. "You're drunk, Ratchet!"

"Aw, let him go!" Hez said. "You've made your point."

Geoff ignored him. "What about the other night, the ace o' 'earts? Fan saw you! Cheat!"

"Fanny Merton?" Adams laughed. "That cow?"

Hez rounded the desk. "What did he say? What did you say, Adams?"

"You're a fool to cross me," Geoff continued. "I've promised meself your whiskers. Maybe a bit else for all me trouble." He gave Adams' groin a poke with the pipe. "You ain't man enough to need them little jewels! You won't even be the man you was when I'm done with you!"

Adams lurched for the door. Hez quickly blocked him. "I don't like the way you talk about Miss Merton." He hoped Geoff only meant to scare their victim, but Geoff's eyes had a nasty gleam.

"Want to know 'ow it feels to be fleeced? 'Old still, lambkin and give me that bleedin' key!" Geoff seized Adams' waistcoat and thrust his hand into the man's trouser pocket.

Adams emitted a high-pitched squeal.

A terrific scuffle ensued. Hez fell backward and a cabinet crashed to the floor. Adams and Geoff rolled next to it, pounding on each other.

"Aha!" shouted Geoff, brandishing a small key. He tossed it to Hez.

Hez threw himself onto his knees before the safe and tried the key. "It doesn't work!"

"Use the dynamite, you ass!" hollered Geoff.

Adams shrieked. "There's no strongbox, you bloody fools!"

Hez grabbed his bag. Inside it was a note, the letters cut from a newspaper or a magazine. Some of Sam's foolery, so he didn't read it. The three big firecrackers had long fuses. His heart hammered and his fingers prickled uncomfortably as he lifted one. It certainly smelled convincing. So long as Geoff didn't take out his knife—. Hez set his gun on the desk and found his match box while Geoff beat Adams' head against the floor. Hez shook a firecracker at them. "Tell me how to open the safe or I'll do it!"

"Get stuffed!" Adams yelled, rising to his knees. He threw Geoff off.

Geoff fell onto a wheeled chair that ricocheted into the hall. He sprang up and threw himself, knife drawn, across the path of an oncoming and very surprised clerk.

Mr. Darby, who was much put out and in over his head after being left alone with Mr. Buckner and Miss de la Coeur, wondered what on earth had become of Mr. Adams. Ahead, he heard a commotion. He stared in surprise at the destruction of his office. There was a flash of metal. Mr. Adams rolled beneath another man who wildly slashed at his back with a knife. A third man knelt before the office safe, holding a stick of dynamite under his arm and fumbling with a box of matches. Mr. Darby exerted the prudence of his twenty-one years and set off at a run.

Seamus ambled into the corridor that led to Adams' office. Glass broke. Voices rose. He bumped into a very frightened young man.

"Help!" he cried. "Get help! They're killing Adams!"

"What's this?" growled Seamus. He shook off the man. "That's not right. That wasn't the plan. It's not businesslike. This is a place o' business, ain't it?"

"Knives, guns—dynamite! They're killing him!" Mr. Darby hopped up and down, his voice rising to a squeak.

Seamus was worried. Geoff had been riled before he even got out of the cab. "Oh, I doubt that. They're just having a bit o' fun, like." He patted the man with an enormous, paw-like hand. "It's a joke, see? They don't mean nothing. It's a game. A card game was what did it. We'll go back, see how they're getting on."

"Go back?" Darby shrilled. Incredulously, he looked the man up and down. He took in the giant's yellow-checked trousers, the coat strained over a bulging chest, and the bowler hat set far back off the man's greasy, pockmarked brow. "You're with them!"

"No, I'm with you!" Seamus said in a friendly tone. He grabbed the man, lifted him off his feet, and carried him back down the corridor.

"Help, help somebody!" Mr. Darby cried. From over his captor's shoulder, he saw one of the footmen enter the corridor. He struggled violently and yelled at the top of his lungs, "FIRE!"

Seamus held the squirming clerk as he would a puppy, more intent on the voices up ahead.

"What have you done?" Hez yelled.

"What were you doin', gettin' in me way?"

"Trying to stop you, you mad dog!"

"Quit cryin'! 'E's just winded! Adams? Wake up! Ah, never mind! Soft, you lot! What's that burnin' smell?"

"Sam's firecrackers, I forgot!"

Geoff laughed wildly. "They ain't no firecrackers!"

"Bloody hell," whispered Mr. Darby.

"Well, I never!" Seamus agreed.

A rumble and a blast, followed by a rain of shattered glass, powdered plaster, and shards of wood put an end to all further conversation.

Winifred, as well as everyone else in that part of the bank, heard a muffled roar.

There followed what seemed an unimaginably long pause that in reality took only seconds. Then, there was a groan of timber, another rumble, and a tinkling of glass. Silence followed. The footman stared uneasily at the swaying gas chandelier. A smell of plaster and acrid smoke filled the room. No one moved.

"I thought Guy Fawkes Day is tomorrow," the footman whispered.

Everyone let out a breath. They laughed uneasily.

There were faint voices, groans. Distantly, someone shouted, "Fire!"

"The gas lines, good lord!" Mr. Buckner gasped.

Everyone began to move. The footman dove for the door. Mr. Buckner leapt with surprising spryness from his chair and grabbed Winifred's arm. The hall was already full of clerks and bank officers who jostled in the direction of the blast and carried fire pails. Her hat was knocked off. Mr. Buckner pushed Winifred in the opposite direction toward another hall. Others crowded ahead of them.

"Down the back stairs!" he shouted.

There was another ominous rumble. With a crash of broken glass, a plume of fire shot into the corridor, blocking their exit. Everyone who could stampeded back the way they had come.

Mr. Buckner pulled Winifred closer to keep her from being knocked down. A panicked mass of clerks surged between them. A man slammed into her, and she lost hold of her protector. She stepped back into what she thought was Mr. Buckner's office to avoid the crush. Little flames licked the walls and the ceiling of the corridor where she had just been. Winifred considered running through them but realized she didn't know where she was. Before she could decide what to do, a hand clapped across her face. A small, blunt object drove against her side.

"Don't move, girlie," gasped a man's voice close to her ear. "I've got a gun."

Somehow, she knew it was the man who had run into her. His breath reeked of alcohol and stale tobacco. The gloved hand pressed over her mouth smelled of plaster and brimstone. She grabbed at her assailant's arm. The gun barrel pressed painfully against her stays.

"Don't think I won't use it! This place is 'bout to blow sky 'igh! Do what I says! Go!"

Black smoke poured into the hall. Winifred struggled, hoping the pin from her hat was still in her hair. She felt for it. The man grabbed her arm. He shoved at her legs with his knee.

Winifred kicked wildly. The man lost hold. The corridor was filled with smoke. Flames danced at her feet. Disoriented, coughing, she searched for an exit. The man grabbed her wrist and twisted her arm. With a cry, she faced him in a vain attempt to relieve the pain.

Their eyes locked.

The man snapped the arm he had caught behind her. Winifred moaned. Her shoulder felt like it might pop from its socket if she struggled. He pressed his other arm across her chest and held the gun in front of them, pushing her into the thickest part of the smoke. Winifred closed her eyes. There was another rumble, a roar. The man bent the two of them double. They moved fast. Behind them, there was more breaking glass, more groaning timbers. The office was collapsing.

Court waited as patiently as he could in the alley a few yards from the stairs that led to the scullery of the bank's kitchen. A refectory at one's place of work seemed a wondrous luxury, and he tried to identify the offerings on the day's menu. As the minutes passed, however, he grew less preoccupied with mutton and more intent on ignoring the churning in his stomach. Geoff and Hez ought to be outside by now.

Unable to sit still, he climbed down from the box. The old mare grew restive too, stamping and jingling her harness. He stroked her velvety nose and fed her cabbage leaves that had escaped some sacks on a pallet. She was probably distracted by the butcher boy's cart, whose nag was tethered nearby. Soon, he promised, it would be over. He'd get her back to her mews. A nice warm box, a good rubdown, and some decent feed was what they both needed. He'd explain her absence somehow. From between her blinkers, her great brown eyes gazed into his. All at once, she lifted her head and flared her nostrils. Court also looked up.

Winifred and the man stumbled down a flight of narrow stairs. He kicked a door. Before them a deserted kitchen gleamed. Pots steamed unattended. The man pushed her toward the scullery. In a moment they would be outdoors. She redoubled her efforts to break free of him.

In a corner, a scullery maid and a butcher's boy kissed. At the sound of Winifred's screams, they broke apart guiltily and stared open-mouthed at her. Her captor swore and pointed his gun at the couple.

The girl screeched, and the boy snatched up a dripping pot lid in defense of his paramour.

"Fire!" the man shouted at them. "Run for your lives!"

The boy threw down the pot lid, grabbed his girl, and they fled outside.

Gasping, the man pushed Winifred after them. Stairs, fresh air—she gulped at it. Then she saw a hackney waiting in the alley and the driver in his purple coat.

Court's horse remained wary, her ears up, and swung her head toward the stairs that led down to the scullery. All at once, the butcher's boy and a shrieking scullery maid clambered up the steps. They raced down the alley and took off in the boy's cart at top speed. There was another rumble like the one Court had heard a minute ago. It sounded like distant thunder. He was vaguely aware of a rattle of bells in the street at the other end of the alley. A fire brigade passed. He smelled smoke.

Suddenly Geoff and a woman appeared at the bottom of the stairs. They were covered in white dust and coughing. A bright, wet, bloody streak covered half of Geoff's face. Their progress was impeded by the woman's wildly kicking little boots. Her struggles and the flashes of her bright green and purple silks made her look like an exotic bird thrashing in Geoff's arms.

"What in 'ell 'appened to you? Where's 'Ez?" Court shouted and ran forward to help.

"I don't know!" Geoff coughed. "Forget 'im! We've got to get out 'o 'ere!"

"What about 'er? I saw a fire truck! Is she 'urt?"

"She's comin' with us!"

"Bleedin' 'ell! 'Ave you lost your mind?" Court shouted. "Put 'er down!"

Geoff coughed and swore. "No! She saw me! Open the door!"

Geoff did not wait for Court to comply and thrust the woman at him. While Geoff bent over in another fit of coughing, the woman struggled and kicked, fanning dust all over Court, and cried for help. Involuntarily, he clapped his hand over her mouth. She only screamed louder.

"Shut up, you fat sow!" Geoff swatted her across the temple with Hez's pistol.

The woman's eyes rolled and she went limp.

Court howled in dismay and caught her.

Unconscious, her face took on an even sicklier pallor than the dust already gave it. In his arms, she was a mountain of soft cashmere and folds of velvet. Her mantle fell open, and her scent hit him. Lilies and some dark, exotic spice. It was so unexpected and heavenly that the alley and the hackney disappeared. Even his panic was gone.

"Give 'er 'ere!" Geoff grabbed the woman and hauled her into the cab. The hem of her skirt caught on the door and ripped. "Give me your tie," Geoff ordered.

Court removed his neckerchief, thinking Geoff wanted to wipe the blood off his face. Instead, he gagged the woman then removed his belt in order to bind her wrists. This was too much. Court grabbed the woman's ankles. "Put 'er 'ands in front o' 'er at least!"

"The bitch tried to stab me with a 'atpin!"

"Do it, or we ain't goin' nowhere!"

Geoff scowled in disgust but tied her hands in front. "Soft!"

From above came another low rumble. The mare lunged. Court let go of the woman to steady the horse. Another fire truck raced past the end of the alley. There was a distinct odor of smoke.

Geoff dumped the woman onto the floor of the cab. "The gas lines is goin'! Go on, drive!"

In spite of the horse, Court made another attempt to extract the woman from Geoff's clutches. "We can't leave 'Ez! We can't take 'er!"

Geoff clicked off the safety and waved the pistol under Court's nose. When Court did not let go of the woman, he pointed the pistol at her head. "I ain't arguin'! Drive!" He slammed the cab door.

His heart hammering, his head whirling, Court untied the horse, swung up onto the box, and grabbed the reins. As he turned the cab into the street behind the bank, yet another fire truck raced past.

Jesus, Mary, and Joseph! They were in for it now.

CHAPTER 3
To Virgins, to Make Much of Time

Court drove across Blackfriars Bridge into Southwark. The streets were crowded, but he kept the mare at a good clip, and finally eased the spent horse into a narrow, cobbled lane near the river. Geoff jumped out of the cab and smashed its number plates with his iron pipe. He seemed determined to take out his frustrated violence on some object, if not the woman. Court reined in the startled horse, which jumped and whinnied at the clanging.

Geoff announced that he was going to get his head mended. "Mind the woman 'til I come back."

"That could be 'ours!'"

"Me mates is a bunch of bleedin' girls! You got somethin' better to do?" Geoff sneered.

"Why couldn't we 'ave left 'er? She won't remember nothin' after that crack you gave 'er. Believe me, I been knocked out enough times. The shock alone o' seein' your ugly gob up close...."

Geoff turned on him. "Yeah, what about that? Why couldn't you 'ave taken it on the chin and gone down nice and easy the other night like Piani told you instead o' flattenin' O'Leary's face? I lost a lot o' money because o' you!"

"I ain't goin' down no more when I can win!" Court yelled.

"It don't pay!" Geoff yelled back.

"Neither do you!"

"Just do what Piani tells you next time, or I won't answer for it!"

"It ain't your worry!"

"What about me money? I ain't goin' to lose no more because o' you!"

"What about Adams?"

"What about 'im?"

"Come on, you said we'd be straight!"

"I said nothin' like. 'Alf the interest forgiven, and only IF I got me money, which I ain't!"

"Well, that's nice! A whole morning's work and nothin' to show for it! What a cock up! What a bleedin' mess! Same as always, you get an idea in your 'ead and won't let it go! Just shake it to death! So, what did 'appen back there with Adams, and what about 'Ez?"

Geoff wearily waved the pistol. "No more talk! I'll get me money. Right now, I wants a drink."

Court jumped off the box and tethered the horse, too exasperated to argue. The pistol was unnerving, and the gleam in Geoff's eye as he glanced inside the cab at the woman meant his blood was up.

Winifred lay on the cab's floor. The men's harsh Cockney was so thick they were almost unintelligible, except when they swore. The gist was clear, however. She tried to remember what had happened. She'd come to lying on her face, her captor's heel placed between her shoulders, her bones shaking with the cab's movements. She'd a sensation that they turned corner after corner, as though the driver was in a maze. Before that, she vaguely remembered an alley, a flash of stars, and dropping down a well. Down had been up; up had been down. She still felt light-headed. Between her knees, her cloak lay bunched and within it, her purse and her mother's jewelry box. At once, her mind sharpened.

Having grown up on a diet of novels, she knew what happened to ladies taken by highwaymen. They were robbed or ravished, or both. Knowledge of barnyard animal habits had supplemented what books merely suggested. She twisted about to get a look at her kidnappers.

There was the driver in his purple coat and top hat. His hair was black and his face dark, almost swarthy. His nose was a bit crooked, and his cheek deeply scarred. He bore another mark above his brow, but his hat covered most of it. The other man came briefly in and out of view, pacing and swinging an iron pipe. Winifred drew back.

Finally, Geoff seemed to wear himself out.

"Go on! Give us a quid," Court coaxed. "I ain't eat since last night. I'm starvin'."

Geoff gave a snort, turned on his heel, and walked toward the river.

"'Ow the 'ell am I goin' to feed 'er?" Court shouted.

"There's a purse in 'er coat. I'm too tired to mess 'er about for it now!"

Court followed Geoff. "Look 'ere, I done what you asked! I ain't doin' no more!"

Geoff aimed his pistol over his shoulder and pretended to fire.

Court threw down his hat and kicked it. "GEOFF RATCHET, YOU'RE A CHEAP, BLOODY, NO GOOD 'ARE-BRAINED SODDIN' SON OF A BITCH!"

Court punched the air and swore again. His echo bounded weakly off the alley walls. He grabbed his hair, then snatched up his hat and mashed it onto his head. Fingers twitching, blood pounding, he was tempted to chase after the bastard, wring his neck, and toss him in the river! He looked helplessly at the tired mare and the defaced cab. He threw back his head and stared at the grey sky. A sting on his cheek was followed by another and another. It was sleet.

Jesus, Mary, and Joseph!

He untethered the mare and smacked her lightly on the rump. "Go on!" he shouted and waved his arms. She did not move. Cursing, he turned his back on the cab and took a few steps in the direction Geoff had gone. The mare whinnied and jingled her harness. Court walked back to her. "Good old girl, you're the only part o' this business I'm sorry about." He unhooked the horse from the cab and slipped off her bridle. "I was only tryin' to make a few bob. Try not to 'old it against a fellow."

The mare clopped away. What a life! Not a penny to his name, and hell's bells but it was cold! If only he could slap the woman on her backside and send her on her way too.

Winifred shrieked as the man leapt into the cab. She had witnessed his performance in the street and heard every word. She wriggled as far from him as she could and drew up her knees. The man did not move. She raised her shaking fists. His hand shot out and grabbed them. He spoke in a quiet, rough way, like he had to the horse.

"Don't scream, or I'll slit your throat."

Court untied the gag but held it ready to slip on again if she began to holler. Her eyes met his. "What're you lookin' at?" he demanded.

"You bought the flower girl's violets," the woman whispered.

Geoff was right; she looked point blank at a fellow. Her eyes were a strange color, light brown or pale amber, like whiskey. They had a similar effect. Their appeal went straight to his head. His resolve to appear brutal faltered. He swallowed uncomfortably. "Don't you run. There's blokes much worse than me out 'ere 'o'd be glad to get 'old o' you."

The man backed out of the cab and drew her after him, helping her down more gently than she expected. An arm like iron slipped through hers. She could barely keep up with his long strides. They turned into another lane, and another. Briefly, she saw the river and the dome of Saint Paul's far way on the opposite bank. Empty windows and high walls loomed over them. Icy wind whipped around corners. Sleet stung her face. A few more yards, and they stopped in front of a once-fine house. Derelict and dark, it huddled amongst the warehouses, lost. Winfred tried to hang back, but he swept her up the steps.

Court was relieved his threats had worked. He didn't fancy playing the bully, though he was prepared to do so if that was what it took to keep the woman quiet. All the way to the house, however, she didn't make a sound. Once inside, he hoisted her in his arms and carried her up a flight of stairs. He had no plan except to get some rest. Later, he'd go through her cloak and see if she had that purse. He set down the woman, kicked open the door, and called out. Hopefully, no one was dossing. When there was no noise within, he poked his head into the room.

It was no more than a bolt-hole, but lately he'd had to make too much use of it. Pale light shone through its one dirty window onto a washstand and a stained mattress of striped ticking that lay on the floor. A horse blanket and another bedroll sat in the corner. He kicked aside a few burned rushes and empty cider bottles and shoved the woman forward. He felt above the lintel, hoping the nail he used to secure the door was still there.

As the room's details emerged from the gloom, Winifred gasped. Even the poorest cottagers of the parish didn't live in such squalor. She took in the crumbling plaster and the empty grate, the trash and the stained mattress. The man shut the door and slipped a nail through the staple of a hasp lock, high up near the lintel. He unhooked the belt from her wrists and hung it on a nail next to a washstand. Then he opened its cabinet and peered into the slop jar. In spite of her terror, a lifetime's habit of ordering servants exerted itself. Winfred set her jaw and clenched her fists. The man messed about with a water bucket, ignoring her. Finally, she stamped her foot. "I can't stay in this—this sty! Take me back, now!"

Court set down his bucket and replaced the slop jar. Her back against the door and her great, golden eyes ablaze, the woman looked very grand for all her trembling. "Oh, yes ma'am, whatever you say ma'am!" He tugged an imaginary forelock and spread the second bedroll. "I'll call up me six white 'orses straight away! Wave everybody! It's the queen 'erself!"

It was all Winifred could do not to scream.

"We ain't goin' nowhere Miss La-di-dah. Flatten your feathers! I'm 'avin' a nice, long lie down after me mornin's efforts. Now shut up and sit down before I uses that belt on you again."

The man removed his fingerless gloves, put them in his hat, and tossed the lot onto the washstand. He pulled the ribbon from his queue and rubbed his hair. His gestures' unexpected grace was almost charming. As it was, it unnerved her, like his strength. With a groan, he dropped onto the mattress and stretched out. Though she didn't want to turn her back on him, Winifred tried to reach the nail in the hasp lock.

"Oh, that'll work!" he said blandly and pulled the horse blanket onto him.

The woman jumped and clawed for the nail. Court closed his eyes. "Don't mind me."

Her feet thudded on and off the floor. The cries that accompanied her efforts smote his conscience, but her tenacity was worrisome. Having gotten her indoors, he felt a bit more confident though by no means cavalier. Hop! Hop! went her little boots. He opened his eyes. Apparently, the only way to deal with such a woman was to subdue her the way Geoff had. But binding and gagging her again was out of the question.

Finally, she stopped and faced him, her bosom heaving. It was like a scene from the worst music hall melodrama ever. He couldn't help but laugh. Fanny Merton could've told her that he wasn't worth such a display of fear. "Come 'ere," he ordered tiredly. "That coat looks warm." He tweaked playfully at the garment's hem. "Plenty big too. Bet there's room for both o' us."

She drew its folds nearer. "How dare you!"

The man gave Winifred's cloak a sudden, sharp tug. Stumbling over his outstretched feet, she fell to her knees. There was nowhere to flee but the corner, so she scurried into it.

Let her keep her nose in the air, then. Court was tired and extremely hungry. The combination made him churlish, and the temptation to take her down a notch was irresistible. He made as though he would crawl toward her. "What've you got in there? You're 'idin' somethin', ain't you?" Their eyes met, like they had when he got into the cab.

A tussle quickly followed.

Pinning her was the work of seconds, though it hadn't actually been his intention. Shrieking, she drummed her heels frantically and struggled as though her life depended on it. He tore open the cloak, determined now to make her share it. Silk and velvet, spotless linen and rich lace; but it was the scent of her that nearly overwhelmed him. It was enough to drive a fellow mad. Wild roses and lily of the valley, like a big bouquet in Covent Garden. She was a dream of springtime, her dress as green as wet turf after rain, her skin soft and creamy. There was a lot of her in all the right places too. Easy to imagine her making similar noises if they were occupied in a much more pleasant way. He closed his eyes, bent closer to her, and breathed deeply.

The man's face drew nearer. Winifred froze. Against her, she felt a great deal of very firm proof that his intentions were no good. He opened his eyes.

Hers wasn't exactly a pretty face, but he liked it. It was regal, very fine, like her clothes, like her. He grasped her hands to help her rise. Their fingers twined. He was uncertain which of them had done it first. Suddenly hopeful he might rule her yet, he bent close again. "I knows what a filly like you needs," he teased gently, "tamin'!"

He might as well have lit one of Sam's firecrackers.

She flailed wildly, clawing at every word. "How dare you!"

Plenty of girls he knew liked a bit of racy talk and even some vigorous horseplay before getting down to it, but not even good old Fan had half this woman's spunk. Hellcat or honey pot, he knew how to rein in the second enough was enough. That was the point. It was all for fun. Except in the ring, he'd never raise his hand to a living creature, let alone a woman. Under more genial circumstances, he would've played with such a good-feeling girl for hours but never against her will. But he held on to this one. She had to wear out eventually, so they could both get some rest. Otherwise, she'd make herself ill.

Court jumped to his feet, and so did the woman. Before she could get to the door, he grabbed her. She tried to push his hands from her bottom. They struggled in a posture that was half dance, half battle.

"Don't touch me! I'm not some harlot!"

The man laughed.

"You're a brute, fighting a helpless woman!"

"You ain't 'elpless, and this ain't fightin'!"

Writhing gained Winifred nothing but closer, even more immodest contact with that part of him she feared she was about to become better acquainted with. "Let me go! Thief! Beast! My grooms live better! Talk better! And they know how to treat horses! That old nag in the alley—!"

Finally offended, Court dropped her. "What'd I do? I didn't lay a 'and on 'er!"

"You drove that poor darling within an inch of her life!"

"I let 'er go!"

"In the sleet and cold! You won't get a penny from me—nothing— you or your nasty friend Geoff Ratchet!"

"What's that? What'd you say?" Quick little thing. What else had she heard?

"You—you'll do anything for money! The sort of men—beasts you are!"

Winifred's eyes darted to his belt. Her voice rose in terror. "You! Ratchet! Your type! You'll never have anything! Amount to anything! You're a brute! Vile and violent and DIRTY and STUPID!"

Abruptly, the man turned away. Winifred was too afraid to move, except to hastily straighten her skirt over her petticoat. She felt dizzy and hardly knew what she'd just said.

Those golden eyes, he wished they wouldn't stare at him. It was as if she'd read his whole, sorry life story, like she'd ridden on the hackney's box with him or stood at his elbow as he knocked on the door of some poor sod like himself, ready to do no better by them than Piani would soon do to him. There was no way she could know about all that or his recent, less than illustrious activities in the ring, but she'd got the measure of him and Geoff right enough.

But even toss-pots like Geoff and Hez had their own girls. He walked to the window and stared through its grime. Money was always changing hands. Why was there never any in his?

It was what she'd said about the grooms that hurt most. It wasn't her words; it was the memory they evoked that ached, as though it was yesterday. When he was Sam's age, he'd worked for a few months in the mews where he'd slept before filching the mare that morning. No task had been too menial. He'd brushed and combed and mucked and curried with all the enthusiasm of first love. One day, he told Sadie, he'd buy as many horses as they could ever want. Like the old stories.

Instead, they'd purchased the return fare to go help with the hops harvest. It had been magic. Fields and fresh country air, and his mother's smile. Within weeks, his father died in a bar brawl. Court's job in the mews ended. He went to work for Piani, and Sadie never got any farther from the Old Nichol than Southwark.

"You thinks you knows me?" The man slowly faced her. "You thinks we been fightin'? We ain't even got started."

Winifred's hair stood on end. He reached for her, and she swung at him.

"That's the way! Give us your best shot!"

She ran to the corner, clutching the jewelry box in her pocket.

"I see you hidin' somethin'. Come on, give it!" He grasped her arms. "Now 'o's boss, eh? I'll 'ave you feedin' me grub and lickin' me boots and glad of it!" The terror in her eyes heaped coals on his shame, but his fury blazed against it. He was determined to subdue her. "I'll show you what're you're really afraid of! Come 'ere!"

What happened next was a frightful, crazed waltz. Without the least effort, he whirled and slung her this way and that. The room spun, and he squeezed her closer, dipping her backward. Her corset pressed against her ribs. Black spots danced before her eyes. His hot breath poured in her ear. She was a sweet little bit and a better one than most. The house was empty, so she could yell all she liked. Snarling, he drove his face against her bosom, and tore her jacket with his teeth.

Beast, she'd called him! Court spat and growled, relishing the woman's shrill cries. The villain's act had an almost hypnotic power. He was Geoff; he was Piani; he was Mick Furor. For the first time, he was dangerously close to succumbing to the part's temptations. Even wresting his day's wages from this proud woman's purse could not be sweeter than overcoming her. What terrible freedom, to do as he wished with a fellow creature, especially one so lovely and weak.

With the last of her strength, Winifred groped wildly for the door. Her foot slipped, skidded. The man suddenly righted and let her go. She toppled forward; he pushed her backward.

The woman fell flat on her back. Court was rewarded by an immodest and thoroughly enticing view of her shapely legs. With a hoot of triumph, he dropped to his knees. The woman did not move. She did not breathe. "Miss?" he called frantically.

Working swiftly, he loosened the buttons at the neck of her cloak and then what was left of the ties on her green jacket. He pulled it open and yanked up her blouse and chemise, exposing her stays. Pulling and tugging, he undid the hooks at the bottom, then at the top. In a burst of impatience, he finally tore the corset open.

At the raucous sound of the man's victorious crows Winifred came to. Her vision swam; her arms and legs were dead weights. The man straddled her, tearing off her clothes. She tried to scream. Nothing came out.

Against his knee, Court felt an object he supposed was the woman's purse.

Winifred felt the man's hand grope beneath her skirt.

Court pushed down the billowing material. There was so much of it everywhere. Cashmere and satin, linen and frothy lace! He wasn't sure where his hand was or her purse amongst all the folds. If he could find it, he'd get his money quickly and put the purse back and then—.

Winifred felt the man's fingers on a part of her that no one had ever touched. She sat bolt upright, grabbed his hand, and bit it as hard as she could. Stars shot before her eyes.

"JESUS, MARY, AND JOSEPH!"

Winifred's head hit the mattress. In all her life, no one had ever raised a hand to her. For the second time that day, a man had struck her. It was never going to end.

Blood welled in the teeth marks on Court's skin. "What'd you do that for?" The woman gave him a reproachful look, clutched her cloak over her ruined corset, and burst into tears. A red welt had already risen on her cheek. Her trembling shoulders and muffled sobs filled him with misery and remorse. He approached but dared not touch her. "Let me see it," he begged.

"NO!" She yanked down her skirt.

Shaking his throbbing hand, Court stomped up and down the narrow room. He had to get away from her, from himself, but he couldn't leave her alone. He didn't want to. He raked at his hair and pulled it. The lower he felt the louder he wanted to yell, so he did.

"What a day! What a cocked up, bleedin' waste! But get this straight! I ain't Geoff Ratchet! First, I ain't no idiot, and second, when was you ever at a fight? I ain't never 'it no girl before BECAUSE I KNOWS 'OW TO TREAT A 'ORSE!" He filled the washbasin and plunged his hand into the water.

"I feel sick," the woman whimpered.

At the sound of her dry retches, Court hung his head. It was exactly like home. All his anger ebbed away. It wasn't about her. It was the morning's disappointments, Geoff's brutishness, and his imminent maiming at the hands of Piani's henchmen. It was his life.

Once, he'd been like those little boys who chased after chestnuts in front of the bank. He'd begged pennies like the flower girl, or picked pockets. When he was older, he shook down opium addicts and old codgers for Piani. Next came sparring, then fights. A few times he won fair and square, but more often than not he had to lose to get paid.

Fine folks like the woman always thought the worst of poor people like him. Today he'd proved her right. He wished he didn't care, but did. From the moment he saw her on the bank steps, or looked into those eyes, he cared what a lady like her would think. That was his mother's fault, giving him ideas that were above him, giving false hope. She'd been a lady once, she'd say, and it always made him so sad. Look up, she'd tell him.

With a howl, the man flung the wash jug against the wall.

Winifred stopped crying. A mess of cheap, broken china scattered the floor. Water dribbled down the wall.

The man clutched the washstand, his head bowed. "I wanted to wear you out, so's I could get some rest. You're so pig-'eaded! I wasn't goin' to 'urt you. Couldn't you see that?"

"No," she answered in a small voice. "You're too rough."

The man nodded and offered a rag from the basin. She shook her head.

"I don't mean to be. I likes softness. I wants it, but it's roughness I'm used to."

Winifred considered what "softness" might mean to him. "Well, it's not the way I'm used to being treated."

Court heard the quiet defiance and liked her for it. She refused to be broken. He felt in his pocket for his neckerchief and dipped it in the basin. "Your face, let me see what I done."

"No, don't!" Her voice wavered.

Court knelt, holding out both his hands. He edged forward very slowly, coming at her from the side. She pressed as far back as possible into the corner and lifted her chin, grimacing and eyeing him with equal caution. Suddenly, he had her.

"Let me see," he said in his low, gruff voice.

"Oh, that stings!" Wincing, she tried to push away his hand. He ignored this. His touch was assured, his tone dry and matter-of-fact. He moved her jaw and asked questions. No, her teeth felt fine. Yes, her head ached. No, she wouldn't be sick again. Except for her bruises, especially those on her wrists, she didn't hurt. "You talk like old Dr. Frost."

"I've been in lots o' fights, so I've met a few 'o calls themselves doctors."

The backs of his hands were like leather, the knuckles scarred like his face. "You really are a prizefighter, aren't you?"

He sat on the mattress and leaned against the wall, resting his arms on his drawn-up knees. Like her, he seemed weary, even unhappy. How cold the room was!

He sniffed loudly and wiped his nose on his sleeve. "Don't no one tease you at 'ome?"

She frowned and folded her hands. "Not like that. He's a gentleman."

Court felt this was a fair shot. It was her right to remind him of his place. But with her finally quiet, he felt like a stand-in actor who'd lost his script. They would be together for hours, maybe all night, for it still sleeted heavily. He raked his wounded hand through his hair, then examined the bite marks. Had she wanted a cab for hire, he would have known how to act, what to say. Avert eyes, bow head, and await commands. "Yes ma'am," "no ma'am." A few coins later, the shreds of his dignity intact, he could've driven away with a tale to tell Sam and Seamus at the Boar and Hart about his brush with a grand lady. How strange, her being there with him at all. A fairy queen in her gorgeous emerald gown. It was like a story from the *Arabian Nights*.

"What about you?" she whispered.

Court was startled. "Me? No, there's nobody."

Winifred felt unaccountably embarrassed. Why had she asked him such a personal question? "I only meant it's getting late. What would happen if you let me go? Would Geoff be very angry?" The man's rueful laugh indicated her question's absurdity.

"We ain't goin' nowhere in this weather. I'm knackered. Me legs is blocks o' ice. Try to sleep." He pulled up the blanket and closed his eyes. Soon he breathed deeply, his face hidden on his arms.

Winifred drew the other blanket around her and huddled inside her cloak. Long minutes passed. A draft blew through the rough floorboards. Wind rattled the window panes and jiggled the door. To keep awake, she examined the room again. A shaving kit lay on the washstand. Perhaps it held a straight-edge. If she moved the washstand and climbed onto it, she might be able to dislodge the nail. Then what? Soon, it would be dark. They were south of Saint Paul's and the Thames, and miles from Hampstead. Her pocket was full of jewels and her purse was full of money. She would be on her own. Cautiously,

Winifred withdrew her arms from her cloak. When the man did not move, she pulled off her corset and stuffed it under the mattress. If she had to run, at least she'd be able to breathe.

The man's shoulders rose and fell with his deep, even breaths. Though he was dirty, he did not smell worse than any man who'd worked hard outdoors. It was only sweat, and horse. Even the blankets weren't so bad, only stale. Like him, she was dead tired; but she dared not sleep. Her mind roared. The words he'd shouted as he tore about the room like a penned-up animal; the fury with which he'd smashed the jug; the way his shoulders sagged as he clung to the washstand.

When she first saw him at the bank, he reminded her of Morrant. What if her friend had been in this man's place, or was one of the men in the soup kitchens where she'd served in the East End, or a brickmaker back home? But this wasn't Morrant. It was one of London's poor millions. How strange that out of that human tide, this one soul and hers had been swept together. She took off her cloak and tapped his arm

Court sat up. "What? 'Ere, don't cry! Geoff won't be back for ages."

She wiped her cheeks and held out her cloak. "I'm not! It's the cold. Here, take half."

Court was surprised, not to mention grateful. He felt in his pocket for his neckerchief. "You're not afraid o' much, are you? Too spoiled or too stupid, I'll be bound. Not many could've stood up to Geoff in that alley. And you gave me 'ell!" He smiled and touched the tip of her nose with the wet cloth, and she gave the smallest smile in return. "There now, that's better."

The woman raised her eyes. "You're not going to let me go, are you?" she whispered.

Court dabbed gently at the bright welt. He almost wished he had never seen those eyes—almost, but not quite. "I can't."

CHAPTER 4
Waiting, Games

Percival took out his journal. A day would come when all his private jottings would be Winifred's, sooner rather than later if he didn't slow down on the brandy and cigars. Perhaps in his unexpurgated papers she would find a truer portrait than the one he had so far chosen to show the public, or some experience that would speak to her.

Until then, the usual audience for his writing was a coterie of gentlemen of a certain age and ilk, all of whom had been at school together or in one another's regiments, and who in their twilight years took immense satisfaction ferreting out the lies in each other's memoirs. His specialty, armchair philosophy and reminiscences of his travels with Morrant, demonstrated his few insights into life and provided his audience the opportunity for self-congratulatory epiphany. Amongst these gems of sagacity, he threw in a good tale or two (adventure without consequences, by subscription only, limited editions with photographic plates). Morrant critiqued his drafts without mercy, but Percival had yet to write the book of which he was truly proud.

There would be no further adventures in his real life. He must join the invalids who wintered along the Nile. He would try to meet his doctor's sentence with appropriate steeliness.

Before a fellow died, he ought to traverse the baleful regions of his heart and face its most terrifying beasts. At Mena House, there would be ample opportunity to explore the labyrinths of memory. He had some ideas about the monsters he would meet. The root of all personal mythology was what one had attempted but failed to achieve, what one had dreamed of but dared not pursue. Were his tales what had happened, or what his poet's heart only wished had come to pass? Perhaps a future reader, a historian interested in the quaint, dry ruminations of an aged man of liberal politics and an epistolary bent, would uncover the truth.

His heroic days were past; yet more than ever he wanted, nay, it was necessary, to protect Winifred from outrageous fortune's slings and arrows. But Frost was adamant. Not another winter in England! Already he had idled too long in its autumnal damps and fogs. For the rest of his days, he must chase the sun. If he improved, there might be brief summer visits to Holloways. Winifred could accompany him to Cairo, Frost suggested. Percival hoped not. Morrant had gone out to book their passage. When Winifred returned from her big afternoon, he would break the news.

An end drew nigh to the season of their shared life. Time for another man to protect and cherish her. He would step aside. In his absence, she would make up her mind about George. For all he knew, they had settled it already at Simpson's. Lunch with George! That outré, artificial costume with its lurid, unbecoming color was not like her at all.

If she turned him down flat, he would be prepared with a countermove, unlike the unfortunate Rigsby Archer. A man of George's caliber would rather die a soldier's death than admit the disappointment of his best effort or fondest desire. It was unlikely that Winifred was George's supreme passion. But one never knew. He wrote quickly.

A man's motives may appear honorable. After he peers closely within and probes into (or quickly glances away from) his heart, he can deny its truth and adopt an apparently rational, publicly laudable pose that includes family, career, even service to his fellow man. Or, a man's motives may not be clear to him even after thorough examination. He may act with a gambler's abandon. In affairs of the heart, neither character is assured of success or doomed to failure.

Love must include a revelation of Truth. Truth bears a sword whose name is Love. Shall our man fall upon it? A time comes when Man (and Woman) must be Honest, especially with himself.

Tea the previous afternoon at Natasha Barron's had upset him. He usually avoided sequestration by the family's older females, but Natasha and Delilah Barron had cornered him. Natasha's faded beauty was that of a pressed flower, and her nature matched. Delilah was a termagant. Gretchen Burns was also there, preparatory to her and John taking

Amelie to Ben Venue. Winifred played the piano at the other end of the room where Bert and Amelie sat. George was seated with them.

Winifred was used to being taken to task by her older cousins' alternately wheedling or harping chorus, especially by Delilah, who acted as their primary mouthpiece. Yesterday, he was their target. In an effort to cut short their well-meant persecution without appearing rude, he reminded them that his niece had been mistress of her own affairs since she came of age.

Heads had turned toward her and George.

"It is high time she settled down," Delilah began.

Winifred was no fool, no matter how often they might throw up their hands in consternation at what appeared to be the folly of her choices. Settle for what, was more like it. He saw no need to justify Winifred's good sense.

"A grown woman has a right to her opinion," Natasha agreed hastily and winced at Delilah's disapproving scowl.

"And am I not surrounded by many charming expressions of feminine acuity?" Percival smiled at Natasha and wished she wouldn't always let Delilah take over.

"It depends on the opinion," that woman said.

"Well, we all know yours!" Gretchen's glasses flashed. The tall redhead rose with an impatient shake of her skirts and crossed the room to Amelie.

Gretchen's exit boded worse to come. More than a match for Delilah, Gretchen's retreat was a planned maneuver. A tear-down with Delilah would only upset Natasha, and Delilah might cancel Amelie's visit. He did his best to maintain a gallant tone. "I've never encountered a female of this family who allowed anyone the privilege of knowing her mind for her. Winifred is no exception. What do you think, Tasha? Is my niece wrong to remain single if she doesn't like the fellows she meets?"

Natasha blushed. "Oh, I rather liked her last conquest, that nice Archer fellow. If she gave him another chance...."

Delilah rumbled deep in her throat and ordered the maid to bring more hot water. "He thinks someone has beaten him to the quarry, I hear."

"That's what Delilah—what we wish to speak to you about." Natasha's mouth drooped. "You know Rigsby was with Bert at school and is studying law, too. They had lunch the other day and he told Bert about that last summer dance. She must've hurt his feelings. That or

George said something that made the young man think he'd better cry off."

Percival ground his teeth. When Winifred was a girl, these talks always took place at the beginning of the season. They were about to warn him for the thousandth time about the dangers of an intimate association with George Broughton-Caruthers. That, or there was another titled booby or a promising American cowboy with a railroad up his sleeve that Delilah had read about in the society pages and wished to insert in poor Archer's place. If bigamy was allowed, she would have Amelie married off to as many baronets' sons as possible.

It was always a disappointment that the genteel poor and those on the fringes of the middle class (a great deal of his extended family) were so prosaic about matters of the heart. The collected wisdom of the wives of second and youngest sons was always tinged with polite envy or hard-edged acquisitiveness. Overhearing them discuss ranks and titles and income with Winifred poisoned his tea and left him feeling mean-spirited. Of course, Delilah was eager for Winifred to make the best match possible, yet he found it hard to care about the glamor she expected a brilliant alliance would cast on Amelie, or the connections Tasha hoped it might bring her Bert.

Winifred would make the right choice unless she decided not to choose at all. "She needn't do anything." He only said that because Delilah annoyed him. With George in the room, he knew it was a tactical error. Why didn't they join the young people? He tried to rise.

Cries of dismay!

"But she must choose somebody, Percy," Natasha pleaded. "I thought Rigsby Archer...!"

"Not that again, Tasha! She won't see him, and I don't see why she should," he protested.

"Oh, yes you do!" Delilah intoned ominously and raised an eyebrow.

"Oh dear," Natasha murmured breathlessly. "Delilah, you promised not to be indelicate!"

"Desperate times call for desperate measures!"

Percival resented being taken in hand in Winifred's place but was too upset by the implications of Delilah's warning to be offended. That even Natasha, who was too modest to voice what all could plainly see was at the root of Winifred's increasing moodiness and impulsivity, should take part in such a discussion only underscored the situation's gravity. Gretchen would have spoken out plainly, only she was thankfully across the room.

Delilah saw him look in the woman's direction. "There was never a better illustration of what we all know can happen!"

"Delilah!" Natasha begged. "Percy, couldn't you simply bring Winifred here for tea. Bert will invite Rigsby. I know he'll come!"

Silks and taffetas rustled closer, hemming him in. Soft white hands wrested his empty cup away and refilled it; others piled his plate with cake. Their faces drew closer.

"A viscount tossed aside, a duke's heir, an earl's second son!" Delilah hissed.

Percival sputtered. "Chaff to the wind!"

"Bert says that Mr. Archer is still mad about her! Oh, Percy, please!" Natasha begged.

"He'd let her walk all over him! She'd be bored to pieces!"

Delilah ignored him. "Are we to leave it up to Winifred this time? Idealism in a man is romantic and reckless. In a woman it is fatal!"

"She's principled!" Percival protested.

"She's spoiled! What's worse, she's a romantic, and I blame you for it," Delilah continued. "Arthur was a sensualist. Tristan is absolutely quixotic! Look at the state of his affairs! At Giselle!"

The woman had really gone too far.

"Reforming a man isn't exactly like redecorating a house." Natasha uneasily glanced George's way.

"Nonsense!" Delilah tut-tutted under her breath. "She has no other choice if she won't have the Archer boy, the baronet's son," she intoned slowly. "She needn't reform George, so long as she has Hereford Hall as well as Hampstead before something happens."

The scales fell from Percival's eyes. "You're not serious! What of all your warnings?

"Because he wasn't serious, Percy." Natasha was obviously embarrassed. "Now he is."

"I doubt that!"

Delilah laid a firm hand on his arm. "As you said, Winifred is a de la Coeur and will know her own mind once she finds out she must. And she must before George changes his."

"Percy's right. George will never know his, whereas Rigsby," Natasha reasoned, "who may be a lamb, is a sweet boy, and I think....""

"You're too late!" Delilah leaned toward her sister. "BAA! BAA!"

Natasha slumped. "Well, maybe Winifred will know how to manage him." She turned her pinched brow and worried gaze on George. "I hope."

George was gloriously handsome and in perpetual need of money, precisely the sort of man Winifred prided herself an expert in evading. His amorous exploits were the stuff of neighborhood legend. When he was a youth, George's name was already a byword for gambling, skirt-chasing, and recklessness within fifty miles of Holloways and the Hall. He could drive a woman wild with one hand and crush her heart with the other, all the while maintaining a brilliant smile for his next willing victim. Since his army discharge, he had continued his career as an amusing, irresponsible scamp. No one in their right mind trusted George, but everyone liked him.

"So, you won't interfere. You won't stand in their way, or say something—heartfelt."

Percival was stunned afresh. "Delilah, you speak as though she'd seriously consider him! Suppose she won't?"

"Get her to! No one is suggesting tactics as barbarous, or in her case futile, as ordering her about. She must be guided. Reason with her. Make your influence useful for once."

"Hypocrites, both of you!" he sputtered.

"Oh, Percy, we've made you angry!" Natasha pulled out her handkerchief.

"Otherwise, George will go the way of the rest of them. I only hope it's not before he—or she...," Delilah glared significantly. "I will say two words!"

"Oh!" Natasha shook her head. "You promised!"

"JOHN BURNS!" Delilah rose, her nose wrinkled with disgust. "Stop sniveling, Natasha. I must go see what plots my daughter and Gretchen are hatching."

Taking Winifred abroad seemed a better and better idea. She would have no protection from this match-making cabal. He turned to Natasha. "I'm shocked, especially at you."

"It's not only George. Delilah's right. It's Winifred! Of course, she's the best girl in the world, but.... Why, when I met Albert, even I felt—there comes a point! She must get married."

Poor Tasha fanned her handkerchief, faint from her admission that even a nice young woman could be human. She was so obviously uncomfortable, and so obviously right. He had the same thought every time he knew George had visited Winifred while he was not at home.

The group at the piano was breaking up. Natasha held out her hand to her son. Amelie took a seat on the other couch beside Gretchen. Delilah sat erect in her chair, glaring at the woman, and the maid re-entered with hot water for the teapot.

Winifred and George put their heads together, whispering.

Abruptly, Percival stood and called to his niece.

That harpy Delilah's words about his brothers, about the de la Coeur nature, and about Winifred made his blood boil. To question George's character was one matter. It was another for Delilah to suggest Winifred might not have enough.

He took up his pen to continue the thoughts he had begun earlier.

Can we change? Can one's character be altered (little evidence to support continued optimism—none as regards myself)? His mind drifted. That new maid's dark hair: there was a similarity of shape in her shoulders and the back of her neck to.... *As one hurdles the last mile post of middle age or races toward threescore and ten, one only becomes more tenaciously attached to one's Habits of Body and Mind. One is more ONESELF than ever.*

The emergence of old-fashioned capital letters in his increasingly crabbed handwriting was always a bad sign, an indicator of his return to the boyish habits of the classroom. One of the best parts of his youth had been the omniscience of ignorance. Dreamed-of deeds had lain before him in a magnificent, luminous haze, and he would be the hero of the story.

Character (?) = Fate/Destiny; Reflex/Free Will. Or consider the alternatives. One: It's nothing to do with us. We are moved by Forces and Designs larger than ourselves. So much easier if that is true. Throwing up one's hands or hanging on for dear life becomes irrelevant. Someone or Something Else is to blame (God/god(s); Universe/Power). Two: THERE IS NOTHING. What we perceive as Character is merely the result of/reactions to a Curiosity to see what will happen next (Curiosity deemed pernicious in Female sex but lauded as Initiative in men. Why?). Whichever Alternative one clings to—.

Percival scratched out the last phrase. The weather had turned nasty. His joints ached and his phlegm tasted rotten. Oaks died from the inside, didn't they? Damn Frost! He couldn't leave England! Or Winifred! Invariably, as soon as he and Morrant set out for his club, George was sure to bound up the steps like some infernal jack in the box.

*Whichever Alternative one clings to, most of us close our eyes and
blindly grope our way forward, hoping for the best. ARE WE THAT
HELPLESS?*

Odious scamp! Why did fool George have to be so bloody amiable?

☙❧

One waiter took away the last of George's lunch while the other
presented cheese and fruit. George ignored these, and the man poured
coffee. He stared over the heads of the crowded dining area to the
entrance. He had not minded waiting a half hour before he ordered but
was damned glad that he hadn't mentioned his luncheon with Win to
any of the fellows back at the club. He did mind being treated like that
pup Archer, but would not let her know. Instead, she would pay for her
teasing. In a short-lived burst of acrimony, he read his letter from Lottie
again.

He chuckled. Win put on a good show lately. He would not
complain about that. How self-conscious she was in her new gown!
Delightful! She had no idea how to conduct herself like a true courtesan
and was so brave she would not send Dupree away for even a moment.
He laughed aloud. Those blushes when she looked between him and
Morrant. Charming!

About lunch, she had probably lost her nerve, afraid of what he
might say. Poor child! What did she think? He certainly wasn't going to
propose over roast beef. He finished his coffee and left. Maybe a walk
down to the Embankment or a cab over the river to see who was about.
He could decide later whether to ignore her tonight. The stakes were
higher in the game they played now. If she wanted to keep up, she
would have to learn the rules—his rules.

But that tea gown and all that lay beneath it. With her golden hair
and skin, she was like molten liquid about to overflow. She lacked the
delicate features of the most successful girls of her debut year, but her
figure was the sort at which men like Archer cast covert glances; and
many men had looked as she turned away. By middle age, she would be
inclined to more than plumpness if she was not careful. That too had its
charms.

Let her think he wasn't coming, that he was angry. Old Percival
would probably have to sit late at the House. He would stare at her
from his box at the opera and surprise her at home later. Yes, a fellow
had to have a bit of fun now and again.

There had been a small shooting party in September, the last time he unreservedly enjoyed himself even though Win had seemed angry with him. He had worries enough to let that bother him. Not that the figures his banker showed him felt exactly real. Nothing did.

Bert Barron and John Burns had been at Holloways, too. Win and Gretchen, along with all the little Scots, had just arrived home from the seaside. Win was intrigued at the sight of him wooing himself into her uncle's good graces. They talked about the land. He let her have her laugh and worked on her cousins as well. Once he got her alone, he spoke not quite seriously but in a way that left his intentions unmistakable. Win had been speechless.

She had reined in Tulip and made as though to canter back to the house. He caught up but stayed a little behind. For a while she had said nothing, her lips pursed in a pretty little pout. It was not a totally unpleasant revelation to think that he wanted to visit her more often, she finally said. "But if you have something particular to say, stop courting me by proxy. Write a letter!"

It had taken him weeks, but last night he had written her about the land. He chuckled again and imagined her tearing open the envelope, thinking he had finally popped the question. That's what had ruffled her feathers. George walked along the river, feeling fine.

A cab stopped by the Embankment. George got into it and lit a cigar. He told the driver to take him to the Langham. He would kill an hour. There was usually someone there he knew.

He and Win had had some good times since that hunt. Nothing that ought to make her blush. Mostly they talked about the land and their neighbors, and everything else in the world, like always. Never had they been so much alone, Dupree excepted. Win knew his amorous adventures were not confined to the barns and hayricks of their Norfolk neighbors, nor had all his paramours been as easy to pick as its rustic blossoms. In Switzerland and Germany, he had met many fine noblewomen: Russian princesses and high-born German Frauleins, French aristocrats and Italian contessinas. Real trophies but rarely challenges. Lottie had been the brightest and the most challenging of all. She had caused him no end of trouble. He was still not reconciled to the lady's final estimation of their liaison or of him.

In fact, it festered. He threw his cigar into the gutter.

For once, his cavalier attitude had not served him well. The lady let him know that part of his character had been, in part, a deciding factor. There had been more serious objections, but he was damned if he'd explain himself to any woman! After their last meeting, they had exchanged letters. Her latest was in his pocket. Though Lottie remained inflexible, George refused to give up.

Was Win playing, or was she seriously angry? It shouldn't worry him. It didn't. Her moods had never worried him before. Damn her, the little also-ran, to leave him hanging! The way she would have Archer. If his efforts with her came to nothing, it would not be for lack of trying.

Inwardly, he swore at this lapse of confidence. He shouted to the cab driver, "Blackfriars Bridge! To the Lancaster Arms!"

We are all of us close to the brink of either despair or insanity. It is always near at hand. All it takes is a little push to find the abyss was but inches and is now directly under our feet. One is unselfconscious and absorbed in the mundane, wholly caught up in the expectation of the next moment. Then, the present is shattered. A screech of surprise—our own—fills our ears. Down and backward from what seemed a secure and unimpeachable height we fall.

The question is how much of the "accidental" is merely an accident. Did we throw up our hands when we could have saved ourselves by a slight effort?

His brother Arthur had gone to India, served in the army, and married his colonel's daughter. They settled on the family farm in Gujarat, but their happiness did not last. Arthur never remarried. He threw himself into work, invested well, and managed even better. He doted on his child, but ignored his health and replaced his wife's love with a fondness for wine and rich food.

Percival wrote in his daybook.

All along, we knew this moment was bound to come. We let go of the reins. In all but a diseased mind or the most passive personality a plea of ignorance as to one's motives is inexcusable. The well-regulated individual must—.

From his breast pocket he took out, kissed, and stared at the miniature portrait. He glimpsed the end of this ritual in the wardrobe mirror and hastily tucked away the picture. Since his hair had gone completely grey, it grew wilder and bushier than ever, as did his brows. His reflection reminded him how many years had passed since he began to press his lips to a piece of ivory. With a scowl, he wiped his glasses and marked out the last phrase and the one before it.

Yet how can that be? As modern men and women, are we not paragons of Control?

Good that Morrant wasn't back yet with their tickets and reading over his shoulder. The man would not scruple to hide his mirth.

As for the Church, its teachings are of no use if one is not first honest with oneself. We can only look within and take the measure of our natures. Even so, Self-knowledge contains its own cul-de-sacs. One's Character determines one's Fate.

Slowly, hesitantly, he scratched out the last word, wishing it was Delilah's eyes.

Yet the idea of fate brought to mind the image of his elder sisters bent over their embroidery like the Fates in his boyhood's Homer. The issue of his father's first marriage was grown when he was a child. His half-sisters were strangers to him along with their many sons and daughters. The fruit of those tenuous branches of the de la Coeur family tree infrequently dropped on him, writing of imminent marriages and christenings, or informing him of circumstances meant to prick his conscience and open his purse.

The tone of his previous paragraphs belied a host of self-doubts to which he struggled not to succumb. Late autumn was always a particularly difficult time, especially since Frost told him that he could no longer ride on the heath with Winifred.

Since late summer, her meetings with George proved how terrifically he had failed Arthur's trust. There was so much he wanted to say to her, but the right words eluded him.

He opened Tristan's letter but did not read it. He dreaded more money troubles for his brother, or with Giselle or the house. He reflected on his own fate and that of his brothers.

As the eldest, he inherited all. Tristan, second in line, had their father's acumen for investment and the residue of their mother's wealth but had squandered it all building Claremont, which he was now about to lose to that upstart Anderson couple from Manchester. Arthur had to rely on luck. The entirety of his newly-minted fortune passed to Winifred, who was outfitting the Hampstead residence with all the latest amenities. Tradesmen, plasterers, pipe-fitters! There wasn't a quiet corner upstairs. The house kept her occupied though, so he let her get on with it.

Scribbling wasn't quite a profession, but it helped to pass the wee hours and would until she got back from her day's adventures. Where was the brandy? Under the table by his foot. Though his books sold well for their type, his jottings were correctly regarded by critics and reviewers for what they were, "the musings of an Amateur," which was how he preferred to see himself. A Lover for Love's sake, perpetually and permanently. He restrained the urge to kiss the portrait again. All he could do for Arthur's only child was worry, adore, and hope for the best.

There was a thud against the door. Back end first, the new maid entered holding a rolled eiderdown. She was a plump, hardy girl with curly black hair and bright blue eyes. Peggy, wasn't it? She colored and set down her bundle. Percival colored slightly too. With alacrity and an admirably graceful silence, the girl darted out of the room.

Not much amorous activity left in his old bones. Yet what tumults of heart still assailed him. Almost as bad as when he was a boy. What a lie it was, that one's yearnings grew less riotous with old age. The incidents that formed the basis of his worst regrets might as well have happened yesterday. When he opened his eyes, he felt hardly able to face the day. A longing to lie abed, to tell Morrant not to bother, and an even stronger yearning to return to a time before bitterness weighed him down. To dream, to float over the country of the Past! There he could alight and draw nigh to the Dead, like Arthur, or to Her of the portrait in his bosom.

Whatever happened this afternoon, he wanted to tell Winifred that time heals all wounds. Only, it did not.

Dearest Winifred. She would always be the child of twelve Arthur left to his care. A girl with heavy gold braids, dressed in black, alone in a huge sitting room, baffled by sudden grief. Not pretty (his pity had been stirred), but intelligent, lively, and so clearly Arthur's that he had loved her at once.

To his reckoning, twenty-five was still young, though society matrons might demur. Like him, she was a fixture at charity fetes, balls, and house parties. If there was an unpartnered male guest, she made up a number at dinner. An aging bachelor ought to be glad to have his niece all to himself, but he wasn't. She seemed content in his company, but a woman of her age and temperament, of Arthur's temperament, the de la Coeur temperament, could not be satisfied as an old man's companion.

One's Character determines one's Fate.

Damn Delilah! Damn Natasha! And all meddling, grasping half-sisters!

Character. Woman was not required to have one. The word, as it was generally applied to women, was too narrow in its scope to be taken seriously. What she was required to be was Pure. In addition, money was desirable, perhaps more so than all other attributes. With a sudden motion, he struck out the whole sentence.

CHARACTER vs. MONEY. He ruthlessly drove the pen's nib against the last word.

What they must have suffered, those half-sisters he had barely known. What efforts they made to secure places in the world for their female children while he, the de la Coeur heir, the usurper, romped about their feet and made drumheads of their embroidery hoops. They might as well be seated in the room with him (oh, but in so many ways they always were!), three silent, long-suffering matrons who wound skeins of colored wool, and whose scissors snipped with a bit too much energy and precision at their slender threads. Maybe they had cut Arthur's thread early out of spite, or tangled Tristan's out of jealousy.

He re-read Tristan's letter.

The Anderson couple visited Claremont again Sunday. The man's a bully but Manchester's First Scion. She's an American, a Jewess (half?), and a Southerner. More money between them than God! Very interested in the house as their first child is on the way. How I miss Lynette! How she loved this place! We discussed a possible sale while we lunched on the hill 'déjeuner sur l'herbe' as Mrs. A. so wittily put it (while she twisted the knife), above the orchard where you enjoyed our walks. They're so smug and self-satisfied. Dear Brother, it was like supping with one's executioners!

Percival wrote Mr. Buckner a note about another loan for Tristan. Not that it would make any difference. Claremont was a millstone, but Tristan enjoyed spending money on those he loved. He had been deeply in love with his wife and built her Claremont. Now he was deeply in debt. Perhaps the Andersons' offer would not disappoint him.

Money, why did it have to matter so much? What a slap it must have been to his father's first family, the heir larking about the Great Hall on his pony, and later afield on ever finer horses. The state of his rotten lungs would give his remaining half-sister Olivia the last laugh. She must be nearly one hundred.

A few more letters were stuffed at the back of his daybook. He never begrudged his family's constant, genteel begging. Except for

Tasha's request, none was pressing. *Not quite enough for B.'s next quarter's allowance. Frugal as B. is, the cost of room and board in Lincoln's Inn is so high. Not a word to his Papa! Bless you for your last gift to B. Ever, N.*

One of his mental cul-de-sacs opened. He could not retrace his steps or find a way out of it. His hand fumbled for the portrait. Old, he was getting old.

One must not give way to Bitterness or its more ruthless companion, Regret, he jotted in the margin of his daybook. *That vicious pair is one of encroaching Age's most fearful threats, adversaries for which I did not sufficiently prepare.* Would to heaven Winifred never met them! Meanwhile, he must get to work. Winifred would be back soon. Where had he been? Oh, yes.

...close to the brink of either despair or insanity.

George stood inside a grocer's shop in Southwark. Its window afforded a full view of the street, and the front doors of the Lancaster Arms and the Montague Hotel. As it had the week before, a brougham waited by the curb, and a footman opened its door for a dark-haired woman dressed in a riding habit. The carriage rolled into traffic and rounded the corner.

George left the shop, walked down an alley, and stood behind the two hotels.

From his pocket he drew a gold sovereign and flipped it into the air. The coin flashed. George caught and placed it on his forearm. He held his gloved hand over the coin.

Heads, the Lancaster. Tails, the Montague.

He uncovered the coin, frowned, and flipped it again.

And again.

George uncovered the coin, smiled, and pushed open the back door to the hotel.

Winifred was not a capricious person. If his niece had a fault, it was her overly idealistic nature. She was too generous and apt to give a second chance when it was not merited. But not to Archer, and hopefully not to George.

Outside the family, this characteristic had been overlooked or misunderstood. By the end of Winifred's first London season, she had earned the soubriquet the Queen of Fire and Ice. Her bright smile and lively eyes encouraged many like Archer to a second essay for her favors. When her smile faded and her eyes wandered, not a few suffered the chill. They complained of being led on, or in Archer's case, crushed most cruelly, according to Tasha. Winifred had yet to learn what did not come naturally, how to cut a man without shredding his pride to ribbons.

Percival thought she was far too easy on her followers. From the edge of the ballroom, he overheard the effrontery and arrogance of young scamps who nosed about maidens with soft white shoulders and bursting bank accounts. His niece's long-sufferance of her would-be paramours was regarded by her detractors as the patience of a tigress toying with its prey. The late Arthur de la Coeur's sole heir expected much in the way of intelligence and character from a man. By her second season, word was out that she didn't suffer fools, though she enjoyed making them squirm. The stakes were great, but there had still been fools aplenty to nip at her tossing skirts.

The Hampstead servants had their own opinions of her behavior. The minority thought Mistress played fast and loose with her chances of landing an earl; the rest said she was right to bide her time and might yet shock the world by marrying a duke. A third and a fourth season went by. Considerable dismay, if not embarrassment, rocked even her staunchest supporters. No one had yet lived up to Miss de la Coeur's expectations, but some worthy man would. Mistress would not let them down. By the end of her fifth season, battle weariness had settled in below stairs. Even so, suitors who did not fare well with Mistress were raked over the coals. They were measured, weighed, and vetted; their pedigrees combed for flaws. It wasn't her fault if London seasons weren't what they used to be. Still, it was a great house. Master was a baronet, an MP, and an author. One could take pride in the de la Coeur name. Mistress was firm yet fair. She was demanding but also quick to forget mistakes, and kind. If she chose to take the long view, they could as well. She was rich enough not to have to marry.

But Winifred also showed signs of fatigue. She still might entertain a brave man's notice for a quarter hour; after that, she froze the vapid or those who courted her money. The allurements of her fortune and figure notwithstanding, her sharp tongue could lash lesser mortals. Rigid reserve or flippant dismissiveness had become her habitual masks.

The servants who knew her best said the least, like Morrant and Dupree. Holloways' housekeeper, Mrs. Pettiford, summed up the general feeling: if Miss Winifred's standards appeared unrealistically high, a woman could not be too careful. Matrons who oversaw the marriage market were not so merciful. Winifred was getting, as Percival's bookie would say, rather long in the tooth. More than once, Delilah made it clear that between a fresh bud of eighteen and a nearly overripe woman of twenty-four there was a world of difference.

Delilah had been in full cry at that tea party yesterday. It still gave him indigestion.

"One hopes for the best," he had said vaguely.

"Hope is all very well," Delilah sniffed over her teacup, "but it is not a plan for a young woman's future."

When he considered the matches amongst the bevy of young ladies presented during Winifred's year, he wondered how careful parents' planning was. At the garden party after her presentation, she laughed over her white plumes. A man would blush to show a single white feather, so why was a woman expected to display three?

Unlike Delilah, Percival thanked heaven that marquess and matrimony were not synonymous to his niece. What he regarded as freedom and narrow escape, most of her peers and cousins acknowledged as a settled point: Winifred was a Spinster.

After the last summer ball, as their carriage rolled back to Hampstead, his niece's fine profile distorted with a frown that made her look ever so much like Arthur after a row with Mama. In repose, it was a haughty, sensual face. The nose turned up slightly, which added a bit of comedy. In happier moods, the smile was broad. But it was the de la Coeur eyes that always excited the most comment. Annoyed or angry, their expression was formidable. Among those his niece loved, they melted with unreserved tenderness. At that moment, they looked ready to cry.

She yanked off her long gloves and threw herself against the cushions.

Woman's lot! He sympathized. He raged on her behalf. In an evening, to face subterfuge, to constantly feint and parry with nothing but a scrap of silk and a bit of whalebone to cover her heart. She had put up a brave fight and a good show. No actress could have better pretended equanimity before so many strangers. Bravely born, my girl!

Winifred wrung her gloves and shook her head angrily.

Year by year, she retreated into a harder and harder shell. But underneath it, she was still tender. Like Tristan he felt helpless, watching her fight tears. How did one raise a young woman?

Delilah berated him. "No one but a French maid for constant companionship!"

What to do with a girl who came home from her first parties in storms of tears because there was no one to whom she could talk to rationally? Young men used to public school, cricket, and insipid, virginal conversation were left quite flattened by her verbal repartee. Dazed, bewildered, or simply angry, they gave up.

Archer! She swore he'd be her last suitor. "Sometimes I think I could marry anybody to get it over with." She pressed her hands to her eyes. "Only I can't!"

Delilah was right. Now was the moment to fear for Winifred. Percival was no prude. They were perilous waters his weary niece treaded. So far, she had been able to handle men of her age and class, or those from a better one. But how would she fare with men who were more of George's stripe? He did not want her to become the prey of such pirates—wastrels and middle-aged baccarat players who had stayed too long at the party and found their pockets empty. She was entering an uncertain era for a woman of her means and abundant natural warmth.

Bachelor life had its freedoms and acceptable dissipations. There were aged courtesans he still counted as friends. Such options for amusement and companionship were not open to most women. It was not any better for a woman if they were. While they had grown old together, the years had been less generous to the beauties of his era than they had been to him.

It was even more harum-scarum on the Continent. A host of temptations would twirl its moustaches and eagerly parade before Winifred on long, muscular limbs in spas and casinos. Gigolos, penniless Italian princes, adventurers!

On the side of gross debauchery, she was averse to the Prince's fast set. Winifred, some old rake's mistress? Preposterous! On the other hand, he foresaw a withered future for his lively, blooming niece if she cut off her existence from all the pleasures allowed (or at least tolerated) by the society in which she could afford to move. A nature as warm as hers could not live vicariously. A man with an excellent mind needed ambition's spur and intellectual challenge. A woman of a generous heart needed cultivation and fulfillment: the meaningful occupations of home, husband, and children. More than the absence of those, he mourned that she would never love or be loved the way a woman ought to be. What might boredom or loneliness drive her to?

That blasted tea gown! Venus rising from the foam scarcely wore less. Morrant was still scandalized. Was it a flag of surrender she waved at George?

Beneath its soft, Grecian lines and laces, Percival had detected the considerable swell of his niece's uncorseted bosom. The train rippled languorously as she sank onto the sofa. No, no, she had insisted, when he offered not to go out. She had her novel, some sewing, and letters to write. She waited for no one in particular. The information both relieved and depressed him. Poor Winifred, alone with her dreams, staring vacantly at the embers while the clock ticked. On his return well after midnight, Dupree told him that Monsieur George had just left and had spent most of the evening at the piano with Mistress.

While not everyone in the world was meant to be married, George had obviously noticed that Winifred was not designed for celibacy. At Delilah's, Percival overhead George tell Winifred that multitudes of men (and women) who joined the matrimonial estate would have made better ascetics and were not worthy of the conjugal comforts. They were completely inept at fathoming or pleasing the very mates whom they had so assiduously pursued. Meanwhile, there were a thousand bon vivants who understood women implicitly, habitual roués who roamed the London alleys but who might have been content to go home to a tame domestic tableau had they only been lucky enough to have found (or been found by) the right woman.

Then the scoundrel had winked at Amelie!

Or, there were the flotsam and jetsam like him, Percival had thought, as Tasha led him across the room to the couch—old shipwrecks unlucky at love (or too lazy or diffident to know their own worth and so had failed to exert themselves when the opportunity arose). The stream of years had rolled on and swept him out into the darkening waters of old age.

Percival felt his niece's vulnerability and sympathized with her sore need for male attention. There were masculine characteristics society did not encourage a well-bred young man to exhibit before the fair sex. Not that a young lady would realize the danger of these charms until she was ambushed by them. George unfortunately combined excellent breeding, good looks, and an appalling lack of inhibition. He exhibited an astonishing amount of straight-forward maleness any woman could be easily forgiven for finding attractive, even if she wasn't prepared for the consequences. Worse still, rumor had it that George had nearly run through his money.

He pulled out the man's letter. Winifred had left it on the breakfast table. A truthful man could not pen the usual lines about her features and possibly mean them. But George Broughton-Caruthers was not a truthful man.

Percival tore the letter in two and threw it on the fire. The crumpled paper opened like a flower, brightened, then burst into orange and blue flames. Other autumn days long ago, he had felt youth's joys and apprehensions. The scraps burned. The pieces withered, curled, and blackened. Their ashes twisted and floated up the chimney. It would not do to leave Winifred and George alone, where they could throw cushions at one another's heads behind Dupree's back and reminisce about hunt balls they had attended together. In spite of Winifred's reputation for knowing her own mind, after an evening's company with George, she might not.

There was a loud knock on his door. Voices raised in the hall. Percival threw down his pen. Morrant rushed in with Richards, both of them pale and visibly shaken. It took Richards several tries before he could catch his breath.

"Sir, something terrible has happened!"

CHAPTER 5

"Does you trust me?"

Asleep, the man's features were transformed. His head hung between his knees, and the dark, curling hair spilled onto his crossed arms. He was only a weary mortal, not a beast ready to maul her. At first, she had only seen what she expected in such a man. He was a ruffian, sallow-skinned and coarse, with rough language and rougher ways. Now she reconsidered. Though his collar was dirty and so was his neck, his dark eyes could be full of humor and his smile kind. His scarred hands were powerful and beautifully shaped, and his features were graceful if hardened and weathered. What would he have looked like cleaned up, wearing a cravat and morning coat, and standing in her parlor?

The thought was fantastical. Yet the likeness between him and Morrant reasserted itself. Winifred could not shake it off. The more closely she regarded the man's features, the more tumultuous her feelings. The floodgates of her sympathies threatened to overwhelm her better judgment, even her senses of self-preservation and propriety. In an effort to convince herself the impression was the product of her over-excited brain, she contrasted her captor's florid, wine-colored coat and gaudy neckerchief to the dignified figure of her uncle's valet. It didn't help. The image of one man slipped effortlessly into the other.

Winifred pressed her hands to her eyes and her back to the wall. Real or imagined, the likeness confused her utterly. She questioned whether or not she was going mad, affected by Geoff's and the man's blows and the day's shocks. Though he appeared to sleep, she still sensed danger, but was unsure of its source. He might yet surprise her.

She restrained an impulse to touch the scar on his brow, his broken nose. It was like wanting to thrust one's hand in on a caged wolf.

When she first came to Holloways, she had imagined a much freer, unrestrained existence between those of the lower classes than what she had observed between the castes in India. In the village or when she went to the tenant cottages, she overheard what she took for open conversations as men and women plied their trades or tilled the land. Later experiences as mistress of the house corrected this naïve view. Farming families jealously guarded their reputations and took pride in their old surnames with almost tribal ferocity. In Hampstead, her staff held one another to as rigid and unforgiving a pecking order as any she endured. At Holloways it was nearly as bad. Below stairs, maintenance of one's place was more than one's little all. It was everything.

As the man and Geoff swore at one another in the street, she saw this pattern repeated and realized who was in charge. It was not only Geoff's pistol that made the difference. How humiliating for the man at her side to beg for money or to admit to losing fights for pay. More than likely, his rough treatment earlier was to prove to her—or himself—that he was as dangerous as his partner and part of the struggle to keep his place in the frightful, violent hierarchy he inhabited.

She deeply regretted how she had spoken to him. After a life spent being kind to one's inferiors, or trying at the very least to forebear and behave in front of them, it was unforgivable to grind him down, no matter what the circumstances or the provocation. She expected more of herself; she was capable of more. Part of her duty was to inspire those below her to do their best. This was not merely noblesse oblige, it was what she had been taught to believe was right. God was in his heaven, and the de la Coeurs were at Holloways. While her current situation revealed the impracticalities, if not the absurdities, of this point of view, she had never met a fellow creature whose pride or lack thereof might make such a difference to her fate. Indeed, if she was going to get out of his room before Geoff's return, it was imperative that she inspire the man. She must appeal to his better side. He seemed to want her to believe he had one.

Though she might try to order him about again, she did not want to. It would be so much better if she could win him over. The hours since she entered the bank had shown her enough meanness to last a lifetime. It might be a matter of course for him, but she had no stomach for it. How he was bound to Geoff, she could only guess. To judge from his drawn expression when she asked what would happen if he let her go, he dreaded the consequences if he failed in his post. His predicament was clear. In that they were equals, at least for now.

Winifred's mind recoiled at the ease with which Geoff had meted out violence. For that alone she did not wonder at the man's acceptance of Geoff's orders. In the man's regretful laugh, she heard his certainty of bloody retribution for disobedience. If not to him, it might be directed against one he held dear. She saw Geoff steal up behind an unsuspecting woman, perhaps the man's sister or mother, and do his worst. Until today, such scenes only existed at the opera or in novels. There was nothing remotely romantic in Geoff's beastliness. The morning's deeds were not the foolishness of picaresque tales written to titillate a naïve young girl curled up in the safety of her warm bed. Winifred blushed at the idle hours she and Amelie had wasted reading such trash. By contrast, the man beside her seemed to have a conscience. The rough way he spoke and acted was all he knew, but he'd also confessed a yearning for softness and seemed capable of it.

A bit of softness might be exactly what was needed to get him to unlock the door. Given his strength and boldness, she couldn't expect to control the situation. Winifred hesitated, frightened of the possibilities. An experienced woman would know how to tempt a man to do her bidding while maintaining a semblance of virtue, but she didn't want to bait him in such an unfair fashion. Such feminine wiliness was also from novels, not life—at least, not hers. To think that she, who had been courted for her thousands and taught to jealously guard her chastity until the ink was dry and the ring was on her finger, might be forced to offer her purse, even her person, to bargain with a thief so that he would return her to a life she increasingly despised. He was capable of gentleness and remorse, so he might not do the worst. Again, she looked at the man. Morrant! If only she was kind, he might be, like her friend. It would turn out all right. It had to.

For her it might, but not him. If he let her go, he'd face Geoff and possibly others they mentioned as they had argued. When the man and his confederates were caught, as they certainly would be, he'd go to prison. No matter what he did his future was bleak. By comparison, even now her life felt charmed. Somehow, in some unimaginable way, she would escape the day's vicissitudes comparatively unscathed. The man's words while he checked her wounds, like Morrant's as she climbed into her carriage, had given her fortitude. For him, it would not be so easy. Surely nothing ever had been. Nothing she said or did could change that. This room, Geoff, his means of employment—it was a miserable existence. He was bound, cornered, and trapped like an animal.

And her life? Drawing rooms, young men in morning coats, stacks of calling cards, ball gowns, and parties. Morrant was there, diffident and perfectly dressed, playing his role as she played hers. Each said what was expected; each kept one's true thoughts hidden. All the horrible, awkward evenings of her debut; the men whose names filled her dance cards; the meaningless conversations with those of her age and sex. She was bound up, cornered and trapped, too.

She'd wanted more. A women's suffragist, the wife of a well-known philanthropist, had invited her to lunch. Winifred had gone, eager to meet people with other interests than the social round. The conversation was high-minded and persuasive. She went to a few rallies. Not quite brave enough to give her signature to the ladies' cause, however, she did not go to any more. Instead, she joined Natasha, whose chapter of the women's guild planned a charity ball for East End slum children.

They toured a Whitechapel school and a shelter run by Methodist missionaries, some of whom were not much older than Amelie. In the soup kitchen, she peered at the thin broth, lumps of bread, and pale turnip mash. She'd embarrassed herself when she asked if there wasn't any pudding for after supper. In the dining hall, the younger girls and even the female workers seemed more impressed by her clothes than the fresh vegetables and supply of cast-off winter coats donated by the league. Mortified to attract so much attention when she had hoped to do some good, she had nevertheless allowed her gloved hand to be pressed as the girls crowded around, peering at her new spring dress and hat and bickering with each other for a chance to open her parasol or try on her fringed shawl.

She couldn't forget them or the earnest young mission workers. They were almost as thin as their charges and not much better dressed. As she ladled soup, she felt as sorry for them as the children. The faithful spent the hours of their youth teaching children to read, visiting tenements, and helping in the clinic. She wrote large checks and played hostess at subscription balls.

Unable to get comfortable on the mattress, she shifted the jewel box and tried to close the bodice of her frightful dress, plucking threads where the frogs of her jacket had been. The man destroyed most of them, acting as though he would eat her alive. How they had fought, like two animals in a pen. One cage for another. He would end up in

Newgate prison; hers would have better appointments. She didn't want more clothes or jewelry or another fine house. What she wanted was not in the bank or her mother's heart-shaped box. What she wanted was the most precious treasure in the world but the most difficult one to find; it seemed to be everywhere and nowhere all at once.

Her parents had had it though their union ended tragically. So did Gretchen and John even if everyone—well, people like Delilah—laughed at her cousin's coupling with the much younger, hard-riding Highlander. Even Uncle Tristan, with all his current woes, had married the girl he loved and cherished the troublesome daughter she gave him. Amelie expressed the true de la Coeur sentiment best. "If Bert was a traveling cobbler, I'd go with him. So long as we're together, I'm happy."

Winifred pressed her hands to her eyes again. She would not cry anymore! No matter how sorry she felt for herself at this moment, she had no idea what it was to live each day on the edge of starvation or one's dignity, even one's sanity. She must make a plan, think of a way to appeal to the man's better nature. He would have to help her. Her eyelids grew heavy, and she fought to stay awake.

Finally, the woman was asleep. Court tried to find relief in the fact, but his mind boiled with worries. Today he had acted the villain's part none too well but had taken first prize for a fool. She might have enough money in her purse to mollify Geoff, but he still had to deal with Piani later. If she knew how desperate he really was, it would only add to her contempt for him.

His stomach rumbled so loudly it was sure to wake her. How wonderful to be a finely dressed gentleman with lots of money in the bank and as much to eat as he wanted three, even four times a day! What a heaven of riches! He read Rosie's illustrated magazines whenever he could get to her and Beryl's flat for a real bath. The pictures fired his imagination, and he populated his fantasies of high life with a confusion of music hall images and tales from the *Arabian Nights.*

The woman was exactly like a bird of paradise captured from that glittering world. Gaslights blazed on jewels and mirrors reflected men in silk suits as they waltzed with gorgeously gowned partners. And the food—ah, what he would give for endless food and drink! Tables heaving with meat pies, ham rolls, and gallons of cider didn't quite seem up to scratch for her lot but would've suited him fine. Once, he'd actually tasted strawberries and cream. Rosie had been ill, so Beryl had bought some for a treat. Court thought he'd die with the pleasure. How Beryl and Rosie had laughed when he told them it was almost better than having a girl. The woman probably ate such dainties every day.

In her world, a fellow dined at his club. He couldn't remember when he'd last sat down to a good bit of rare beef or woken up between crisp sheets with an armful of clean-smelling woman. Before he began to lose his money and live so grubbily, he'd had his share of sweethearts, mostly whores, but friendly girls he'd known since childhood. Grateful as he was for their kindnesses, he wondered how it would be to lie down with a courtesan. There were always plenty at the Lancaster or at the race tracks, approximations of fine ladies in expensive dresses who rode in shining landaus with liveried drivers. They had all the trappings of wealth and respectability, but they were counterfeits. Not like this woman.

If he were from her world, he'd travel to distant shores for leisure and have a valet to dress him. He'd wear fine clothes and sport a rose in his buttonhole, not a bunch of rag-tag violets and an old coat from the pawn shop. He brushed its frayed cuffs. Once, it had made him so proud; now the velvet seemed cheap and tawdry next to her brilliant silk. It was a shame to think he owed money for such a futile attempt to appear smart. It would be in the rag-picker's bag before he could pay for it. Piani's henchmen would tear it off his back when they dumped him into the river.

Before Geoff came back, he had to get out of his room; but there was nowhere to go. Down his way, if a man wasn't an artisan or a skilled laborer, he begged for decent work, did errands for the gang if none was forthcoming, or starved. When a fellow got paid, he spent his money on gin, lost it at cards, and borrowed from Piani. When he couldn't pay him back, he got a slit nose or was beat to pieces. Court supposed he could always go back to picking pockets, like he did when he and Mick were in the game, but it was so low. If he counted all the pockets he'd emptied when he was a boy, he owed half this side of London. Funny how there had never been enough money, no matter how much he brought home.

Poor Sadie! Mick had never tired of pulling the wool over her eyes— or thinking he did. Court did not equate women with children, not in the sense that his father had considered them inferior, like animals. Court's experience raised a woman higher than any man he knew and deserving of better treatment. Most living creatures appreciated a gentle touch, especially the neglected ones. They just generally didn't get it.

That's what he'd meant by softness. While it might not be the just desert of a man like Geoff, Court still wished the world had more tenderness, if not more understanding between folks in it.

Truth was that people wore him out. They had problems he couldn't fix, like his own. That's why he loved horses. They were rough but honest. They required control but responded to firm, gentle hands. They never told a fellow's deepest longings or darkest secrets. A fellow had only to listen, and he'd know what went on inside their great, beating hearts. A horse would run its legs off for the sheer joy of it and give a man wings like the ones in Sadie's stories. Most of all, he'd never met a stallion who came home drunk and beat his mare or knocked his colt upside the head. Jesus, Mary, and Joseph!

Given the choice, he'd spend hours amongst them and never notice the time. Arriving early at the track, he'd roam about the stables and chat with the grooms and jockeys. He had a soft spot for lead ponies and rooted for horses that had yet to win a race. All that power and heart harnessed, waiting to explode and show what it was made for—that was courage. That was beautiful.

The woman slept. How good she'd felt beneath him—so soft and round, and that maddening scent! Sitting next to her was like being at the edge of much-longed for though unfamiliar territory he yearned to enter but couldn't. From the first moment he held her, he'd been transported, much as he was by the horses at the tracks. It was hardly gallant, but touching her face reminded him exactly of how he felt when he stroked a filly. He could almost forget his troubles for wonder that such a perfect creature lived. Surely this woman was the finest one—human or beast—he'd ever been near. He wanted nothing more than the pleasure of touching her again, pure and simple.

Winifred opened her eyes. The man was dabbing her cheek. It was soothing. It was so long since anyone worried over her but Bettina. Except for her uncle's chaste embrace or the restrained pose of a dance, she'd never been properly held by a man. The man continued to stroke her face, and her eyelids dropped. Not even George had tried when he might've…. If only Morrant was…. All her yearning for her old friend's quiet sympathy overtook her.

Court thought his heart might stop. She'd drifted off again. Her head bent forward; their shoulders touched. Though she trembled with cold and nerves, her breathing was easy. He held very still, frightened she would shy away when she felt her cheek graze his. If he took her in his arms, she wouldn't be able to resist his strength. He wasn't sure he could resist hers either.

Amongst the dripping firs, Winifred rode behind Morrant. They were almost there. Only where did they fly? He ought to help her. Out of decency, he ought not to press her too much when she was willing to be generous, if only she could be sure of him. If he was going to be so bold he ought not to—or he ought only to....

Her mind went blank. The man's fingers moved very gently, very lightly over her hair. The overwhelming urge to sleep was replaced by another. Winifred opened her eyes and sat up.

With a look of apology, the man held out a large piece of tortoiseshell comb.

"Oh!" Winifred cried, and reached into her hair. She was wide awake. As she found the comb's other half, she also felt Bettina's careful handiwork tumble down. "Oh!" she said again in real frustration. She began to yank out her hair pins and throw them onto the mattress.

Court wished he knew how to soften his voice into genteel accents. "That's me fault."

"Yes, it is!" Winifred said with some petulance. She sighed at her dirty clothes and lifted one of the ruined frogs on her jacket. "This is how you treat all your—your girls?"

"Yeah, I got so many I don't know 'ow I does it!" he snapped and was instantly ashamed.

The woman ignored him. She certainly knew how to dry up a fellow.

Winifred struggled with her hair. She must look a sight, not that it mattered. But what sort of woman pleased a man like him? What was she like? It was an uncomfortable thought.

Court knew he mustn't stare at her. Back in the Old Nick, what had happened between them would've been an incident unworthy of notice no matter how loudly the woman screamed. Thick golden coils of hair fell onto her shoulders. He hated her to think him so low. In the unlikely event Geoff came back that night, Court decided he would do his utmost to protect her.

Of course, he'd wanted to protect his mother, and that didn't turn out. Whenever Mick was jailed, the two of them shared a bed for warmth, for company, and because of her fear of what lurked in the tenement's dark halls. When Sadie's mind unraveled from gin, her tattered, faded love for Mick made her maudlin. Each night, Court lay between his mother and the door, and urged her to read from the

Arabian Nights or to tell the stories of King Arthur that seemed to make her happy. "It's because they're true, my Little Argus! Because they're about us!" she'd say.

After his father was killed, Court spent many nights on the landing, listening to the sounds within the flat while Piani or one of his men came to call on Sadie. Once, her wails made him kick in the door. What he saw on the bed, and his mother's vitriolic defense of her new lover, broke his heart. It broke many times thereafter, even when he knew she only accepted the men's attentions because she needed the drink. He roamed the streets down to the river and found Beryl also seeking oblivion in alcohol. They shared heartaches, but he dared not share her bottle. There was not enough water in the Thames, he told her, or enough gin in London to wash away what he had seen. That was when he agreed to start fighting for Piani.

"If I wanted to 'urt you, I'd 'ave done it already," he told the woman.

She did not answer. With an expression of sorrow and dismay, she held the pieces of her broken comb together. Court rose, took off his coat, and hung it over Geoff's belt. In spite of the cold, he plunged his hands into the washbasin. He was terribly conscious of his soiled, grey linens, his unkempt hair and blackened nails. He badly needed a shave, too.

Geoff wouldn't lay another finger on her, nor would he. He took out his shaving kit, checked the straight edge, and set up its mirror. He lathered as best he could with a chip of soap and scraped painfully at his chin. Soon he gave up and watched her in the mirror. Badly as he wanted to protect the woman, he didn't think he had it in him to be as virtuous as a knight of old. If only he was another sort of man and they had met another way.

"You ever worked in a soup line? Fine ladies often does."

"I have," she said and looked almost hopeful.

"Otherwise, the likes o' you would never sit down with the likes o' me. But I ain't no charity case!" He scrubbed his neck and wrists and rubbed water into his hair.

Winifred had never seen a man at his toilette. He took down his braces, unbuttoned his shirt, and reached inside it with the cloth. She glimpsed a great deal of black hair on his broad chest before she averted her eyes. "I did notice you this morning before I went into the bank."

"Damned purple coat," he said glumly. He turned away.

"It was also the violets you bought and—your face."

Court stopped washing down inside the front of his union suit and stared at her.

"So, if you weren't going to hurt me," she hesitated, "what were you going to do?"

Could she understand the difference between what he supposed she dreaded and what he felt? He didn't know how to say it without being blunt, even crude. The color rose to his cheeks. "Take me own sweet time, I 'oped."

Her cheeks flushed too and she stared at her lap. Suddenly, she threw down the pieces of her comb. "I'll be twenty-five tomorrow! Twenty-five years old!"

Court tried to make sense of this exclamation, which was made with no small amount of passion. Birthdays could be touchy subjects, especially with women. "It's me birthday too. Now what's the odds o' that?" He pulled up his braces and sat. This time he left more space between them. "What I meant to say is any man with blood in 'is veins would want more than a kiss with a body like yours so near. Make no mistake! I'd never take nothin' a woman didn't give freely. I might go off me 'ead at times, but you're a lady! If it 'appens between two people, friendly like, it's all right. You does see the difference?"

The woman stared at him as though he was a wild animal, or as though she was. He tried to be more reassuring. "It's not courteous to say so, but it ain't wrong. It's natural. It's meant complimentary in every species, I should think." He couldn't find the right words but hoped she understood. Her face was inscrutable, but at least it wasn't angry. "It's the intention what counts."

If George or a suitor had ever spoken to her in such a way, it would've been beyond insult. Yet she immediately forgave this man. He probably didn't know any better and was doing his best to explain that he wasn't without some sense of her honor, and equally important, his own. In a way, his frankness was the greatest compliment she had ever received.

Though it might offend the man, she drew away. Otherwise she was going to act rashly, not only because a few minutes earlier she had feared that she would die at his hands. Now she wanted to rest her head on his shoulder as she would have Morrant's, but after his words she couldn't reasonably expect him to respond in her friend's innocent manner. It would be asking too much.

"Doesn't what you say make it all the more necessary to let me go? Take me home, please! I won't make trouble." She thrust her hands into her coat pocket and pulled out her reticule.

Wistfully, Court estimated the worth of the beaded bag and its contents.

"Take whatever you need, all of it! Only let me go!"

Her words rang hollow, like an ill-prepared stage piece spoken unconvincingly. Under the blank look her plea elicited from him she became desperate. She threw down the purse. "Take it! I know you're hungry!"

"No Miss, I won't!"

His voice rose sharply, and a new thought occurred to her. She was Geoff's prize, both her money and her person. No matter what she offered, as long as the man was under orders, he wouldn't take it. Almost faint with horror, she stared at the locked door. She wasn't ready to admit defeat just yet.

"All my life I've known men like you. Good, decent men I can count on and trust. You're right. You're not like Geoff. You didn't hurt me, not really. You're a gentleman at heart. Your better nature shows you the honorable course. That's why you have to let me go! If there are others to protect, I'll help!"

"There's nobody!"

"Then take this and pay your debts!" She thrust her bag at him again.

"Not that way!" Court seized her wrist, an apology already on his lips. With surprising vigor, she closed her hand on his.

"You see, you are a gentleman! If we'd only met another way, at a party, you'd have told me what you really thought! No one ever has because of this!" She shook the purse. "I only want a man to be honest, to be brave! No one ever has been until now—until you!"

Court heard her plea, saw her quickly rising and falling bosom, and felt her hand on his. He fought to steel himself against this overtly bared arsenal of femininity. "I ain't none o' that."

"You are! Geoff had a gun, but you stood up to him. You were kind to that mare, and Geoff only cared for himself. Believe me, I know his type! You don't know the sort of men I do! They never say what they feel! But you're like my friend. You'd tell me the truth. At the end of the night, you'd bring me my wrap like he does and escort me to my carriage. We'd ride home together. Then we'd see the horses put away and stand in the yard under the moon and talk. Can't you see how it would be if you'd take me home?"

Court hardly knew where he was. Her sarcasm, her teeth had not been much; but her vulnerability, her rambling speech, and the picture of the two of them her words painted bewildered him utterly. The woman cried out for safety, for protection. Yet the longer he listened, the less certain he was that he could provide them. Her last question was a haymaker, surely, but it had found his weak spot. He was down for the count.

The man unwound her fingers from his hand. Her eyes followed his to the corner where the smashed remains of the wash pitcher lay. When he did not speak, she feared the worst.

Clearly the woman thought she was going to die or she wouldn't have spoken so unguardedly. But her instincts did her credit. It was a gamble. She could not count on what might happen when Geoff came back, for he might not come back alone. Court's odds were long as well. Among his crimes since the morning, he counted accessory to attempted robbery, assault, kidnapping, horse thievery—not to mention stealing the cab or the damage to that vehicle and the bank. He'd never be able to pay off Geoff or Piani, and heaven knew who else. He was glad Sadie wasn't alive. He'd probably join her soon.

When the sleet let up, he'd take the woman home. He'd brave it out with Geoff, make up some excuse. No, he'd give that jackass a taste of his knuckles. As for Piani, sod him too! Then, he was getting out of London. He didn't know how, but he'd figure that out later. Only, he didn't want to leave London with her in it.

The weight of her golden hair pulled against the two smaller combs on either side of her head. One was already coming loose. He tugged it, and a few strands spilled forward. She looked up, startled. "It might get broke, like the big one. Shame, all them pretty sparkles."

"They're only marcasites!"

Stupid of him! Geoff probably knew the difference between real diamonds and the stones, whatever marcasites were. Geoff was like a magpie. He loved jewels, gems, and shiny objects—like Hez's gun. Court couldn't quit thinking about it. "Put 'em up, or they'll get broke as well."

She pulled the other one from her hair and shoved the ornaments into her reticule.

"I am sorry about your jacket. That's a lot of trouble for somebody to mend."

"It doesn't matter. You weren't yourself," she murmured.

"Wasn't I?"

The woman's cheeks flushed, and she played with her bag. Disheveled and bruised, hardly what she was when he saw her on the steps of the bank, she was nevertheless lovely, even exquisite. Court's earlier estimation of her, that she was not pretty, had completely changed. She was beautiful.

Common sense screamed at him to raise her off his mattress, rush her to the nearest omnibus stop, and never think on her again. Those strange, amber eyes: he'd regret them for the rest of his life. He was charmed by her; he was perplexed with himself. It had all happened so fast.

For the first time, he heard his thoughts.

He sat up straighter. No, he wouldn't have it! He wouldn't be led about by the nose! He must assert himself, or he'd kiss her feet, which he badly wanted to do. The idea of unlacing her dainty kid boots and pulling down her stockings made him ready to roar and stomp about the room again. Batting her eyes, letting down her hair! She only wanted him to unlock the bloody door! It was bad melodrama, the worst, and he'd fallen into her trap! There was only one part he really knew how to play well, and he used it whenever his heart was under siege.

"You will help me? We still have some time before it gets dark," she pleaded.

The voice that came from him was Mick's. "No such chance, love. Me boots won't stand the wet."

She looked despondently at the empty grate. "How will we keep warm? What about food?"

His stomach felt cavernous, and the room was wretchedly cold. They'd freeze unless he got some coal. "You could miss a meal!"

At this unexpected turn, Winifred was crestfallen. Her mind had played her a trick, associating him with Morrant. Her initial assessment of him was correct. He was only a brute after all and Geoff's minion. She needn't make a fool of herself. As for his compliment, she would forget it. It was nothing but insolence. Always her money, never her! Well, let him have it! But her pride was deeply wounded. The worst of it was that she had wanted to repay what she thought was his honesty. She had meant every word she said to him.

Court waited for a scolding, but she had turned her face. Feeling a bit more in control, though his heart beat like a racehorse's, he pulled up the blanket. They would wait out the sleet. He'd take a few coins, only enough to buy coal, a bit of food, some candles. It was humiliating to take from her, but he must. He would leave the door unlocked. If she had flown when he returned—he wouldn't think of that.

She thoughtfully twisted the ends of her loosened hair.

He quickly looked away. Or, they could leave immediately, his heart and his pride intact and her person safe and untouched. He squeezed his eyes shut and saw the long strands of her hair fall over her face like threads of spun gold.

Far off, a church bell pealed three times.

The man's voice startled her. He was on his feet. Darkness came early, he said, so he had to leave soon to get food and coal. For how long? Just a bit, the shops were near. Blackfriars was to the north, only a right turn out the street door, then the next left.

"We ain't but two hundred yards from the river."

Uncertainly, slowly, she reached for her purse.

Winifred tried to appear calm. Was he suggesting she leave? The straight edge still lay on the washstand. But all alone! She was terrified. Hands shaking, she opened her bag.

How carelessly he'd slung her about earlier. It would take all his courage to leave her. When he came back, she'd be gone. He'd never see those amber eyes again. What happened to him afterward wouldn't matter. Nothing would ever matter again. All at once, he dropped to his knees beside her. "Wait a bit! I doesn't need your money yet. Let's not say nothin' about that no more, not for a minute or two."

She looked almost grateful, he thought. He pressed his lips to the cheek he had bruised.

"Why did you do that?" she gasped, holding her hand to her face.

He took her hand and kissed it. It was a leave-taking, like the knights gave their ladies in the old stories. He knew only too well how to make trite love talk, how to coax a girl until she was willing, but at present he didn't know what he said or did. "Why are you goin' back to 'im? 'E don't do nothin' for you, your gentleman, or you wouldn't've said all that about me 'n' you."

"No, he's not my gentleman! I don't have—! I've never had—!" Winifred pushed the man but not hard. His kiss and obvious excitement set her feelings in an uproar. It was useless to explain who Morrant was. But the man meant George, only he didn't know him either.

"Then what a pack o' fools you run with!" He kissed her cheek again.

"No, I only meant my—no, I mean my friend!" she finally managed to say.

"Friend? Show 'im 'o's boss! Give 'im the cold shoulder! That'll make 'im sit up and take notice what 'e's got to lose! Now me, I knows me place. You don't 'ave to worry. I'm down enough and all. Fine folks, even the ladies does what they likes these days. Don't you read the papers?"

The woman choked back a convulsive laugh, or perhaps it was a suppressed sob. Her fingers dug into his shoulders. He pulled her closer. "You're curious, ain't you? What it would be like? Nothin' wrong in that! I'll leave you safe as 'ouses and good as new. You'll 'ave somethin' to think about, and I'll 'ave somethin' to dream on."

"And if I do—what you want, you'll let me go?"

The hopeful gleam in her eyes pained him. He fought not to feel disappointed. Of course, she wanted to go home. Otherwise, she wouldn't allow him to be so free with her. Her tricks would never stop, but he didn't care. So long as she let him kiss her, only kiss her. He nodded, already unhappy.

She shook violently and gripped his fingers. "You won't tell your friends, or Geoff?" she pleaded. "You won't laugh about me with all your other sweethearts?"

That seemed a bit nice when he only meant to kiss and cuddle her for a while, but she was a lady and very well bred. "Me mates? Now, 'o'd believe it? This is between us!" She was flushed, almost breathless. He tightened his hold about her waist. He felt inept, a boy alone with his first girl. He wanted to do everything at once but had forgotten how. "Earlier, when I 'ad you down, was that you or me, did this?"

"I don't know." Winifred watched his fingers twine with hers. "It was me, maybe."

"Did you like it?" Court kissed her fingertips, her palm, and her wrist. "Do you?"

"Take me home," Winifred whispered, "please."

The man's dark eyes shone. He kissed her hand, then her cheeks again. He pulled her closer. His embrace grew firmer, his mouth more insistent. Bert and Amelie stole quick kisses, but theirs were not like this.

She felt his tongue, tasted him. He kissed her neck, her hair. Then he stopped, resting his head on her shoulder, trying to catch his breath. She tried to catch hers too. She touched his black curls, his face. He raised it, and his eyes were fierce. Winifred's heart beat wildly, but so did his. This time when he kissed her, she kissed him back.

His hand slid under her blouse and pulled up her chemises. His fingers brushed the bare skin of her breasts and his mouth quickly followed. Winifred gasped. She gazed down at his closed eyes, the dark lashes resting on his cheeks, his mouth tugging intently at her flesh.

When she gasped again, he looked up. "Is it too much? Does you want me to stop?"

Moaning, the woman pressed him to her again.

They fell back onto the mattress. Court pushed up her skirt and lay against her, working with his mouth and hands. From the quickened movements of her raised hips and the wet against his searching fingers, he knew what was happening to her but doubted she did. Grasping her bottom, he pulled her hips higher and moved his other hand faster. She shuddered, uttering a series of high-pitched, startled cries.

She was melting, flying, falling. Winifred clung to the man and wailed without restraint. She could hardly bear it, yet she didn't want the pulsing sensation under his hand to ever stop. When she opened her eyes, he was looking at her and smiling. In a rush of emotion, she kissed him. He left his hand on her, and the warm, beating waves gradually ebbed.

He drew back and ran his hand over her breasts. The woman panted, staring at him. He helped her sit up. "Didn't you like it?" He hoped she heard the gentleness behind his teasing. Grabbing his shirt, she kissed him so hard that he toppled backward. With ecstatic little cries she pushed her hands into his hair, frantically kissing his cheeks, his eyes, and his neck. Laughing, he rolled her to her back. "I guess that's yes!"

This time, her mouth opened for him like a hot flower. He helped her pull off her blouse and one of her chemises. They unfastened her skirt and got that off too. After that, they fell onto the mattress again. She was a fast learner and seemed to want more, like him. As with all else about that morning, it happened quickly. He pulled his shirt out of his trousers and started to unbutton them. He paused.

Winifred saw the man's uncertainty.

"You does know what 'appens between a man and a woman?"

Embarrassed, she admitted her ignorance. "Not really—only words— books!"

He gave her a quick kiss. "That's all right! I knows what to do. Like I said, you'll be fine, safe as 'ouses!" He unbuttoned his trousers and pulled them down.

Until the air hit her damp chemise, Winifred had completely forgotten how bitterly cold the room was. She had been so transported by what the man did to her, she didn't feel it. All her worries about Geoff, even her mother's necklace, had been obliterated. Tomorrow, the next minute, had not mattered so long as he was close, kissing and touching her. At Hereford Hall, she'd once become tipsy from drinking too much champagne punch, but this was different. Her head, her skin was still full of trickling bubbles from what he had done. The man pulled the blanket and the folds of her cloak over them.

He kissed her, slower, deeper. The world had turned upside down, and she knew it would never be righted. All she'd been taught by her aunts and older cousins, warned about, admonished to remember, had been told was wicked or sinful—it was gone.

As he dealt with the prosaic business of finding the ties of her petticoats, she stared at the cracked ceiling. He tugged the ribbon in the waistband of her drawers. The brickmakers' cottages outside Holloways were bad, but this place was much worse.

"How do you live?" the woman asked.

Court stopped kissing her neck, startled. Forming words was like coming up from deep water. "I gets by." He pushed her breasts together and suckled them the way that drove her wild before, hoping she wouldn't change her mind in the seconds it took him to pull down his union suit.

"But how do you?"

"By me wits, I don't know. I always 'as some'ow," he said impatiently. At the sight of her creased brow, he caressed her and spoke with more kindness. "Why should you care?"

"Because I do. I want to know all about you—everything." Lightly, she traced his brow, his cheeks, and his nose. Her touch was like the brush of a moth's wing.

Winifred took in the purple scars and the crooked bridge of his nose. She stared into his dark eyes and searched their depths. It was as though she'd never seen a man before. For the first time, she felt the mystery of another human soul. It was beautiful; he was beautiful.

Court saw kindness as well as desire in the woman's eyes, and his were suddenly wet. He hid his face against her neck. As unbelievable as was the fact that she was lying nearly naked beneath him, her statement was even more confounding, the most amazing moment by far in the strangest day of his life. What was happening ought to be impossible, yet it was absolutely real.

A golden star had fallen into his dark, dirty world. A goddess had spoken to a mortal. Someone like her wanted to know about someone like him. They weren't in a hospital ward or a missionary soup kitchen. She wasn't a dream or a picture in a magazine. She was a real woman sprawled sweating and almost totally unclad under him, and he was lying practically naked on top of her. The loveliest creature he had ever met wanted to know all about him. Him! He struggled to find his voice. "Tell me your name."

For a second, Winifred hesitated. "Winifred de la Coeur!"

It was delightful, like the rest of her. "It's pretty, genteel like." The woman laughed, and so did he. "Me name's Court, Court Furor."

"Court," she repeated and smiled. "Court!"

Slowly, he untied the ribbon at her waist. His slid his hand inside the laced cloth, over her damp skin, and down further where she was still wet.

Tears trickled over her temples and into her hair. She spoke thickly. "You were going to leave me! You wanted me to go!"

"No, Winifred, I could never leave you, not for long! I'll never want nothin' or nobody like this ever again, not like I wants you!"

Her whole life, she had waited for those words.

He got on top of her. There was nothing to separate them. A country full of light and hope that he had only dreamed of but had never really believed in lay before him. It was in her; it was her, and she would take him there. He wiped her tears and pushed his hand into her hair, stirring the springtime fragrance that so intoxicated him. "Does you trust me?"

Winifred nodded.

"It's all right to be afraid the first time."

She tried to smile.

"It'll 'urt for a bit, maybe more than a little."

She nodded and bit her lip.

He kissed her again. "Say me name."

"Court," she whispered.

"I likes 'ow you says it," he whispered back. "Say it some more. Say it while I—."

"Court!"

Nothing existed but his dark eyes, his eager mouth, and his insistent hands. At first, it did hurt but not for long. Soon, she was soaring, blazing. She had never felt so frightened or so free. There was nothing but his body and hers.

Court felt her move under him, heard her call his name. He could hardly control his joy and apprehension. He knew the fate of mortals who flew too near the sun, and he had tasted its fire.

It didn't take long for either of them. But they both knew what was happening was forever.

Afterward, they rolled apart, breathing hard. They had come back from a wild, undiscovered land to his cold, dirty room. There were no words for his feelings; only her name would do. She buried her face against his shoulder and prayed the sound of the sleet would last a long, long time.

He pressed his face into her fragrant, golden hair and tried to think of nothing but her. It wasn't difficult. She whispered his name. That was all, but it was everything.

CHAPTER 6
Bottom and His Mistress
Take Some Supper

Sleet drove against the window, making a sizzling noise. Winifred had put on all her clothes, but she was cold and hungry. The sound was tantalizing and made her think of frying bacon. Her eyes had gradually grown used to the failing light, but it was nearly dark. Pulling her cloak about her, she tottered stiffly to the washstand. Through the dirty window panes, Saint Paul's dome hung disembodied over the river. Water and sky were iron grey, the buildings on the far bank so murky she could barely make out their lights.

A frozen rime of yellow bordered the edge of the chamber pot. Gulping back her revulsion, she carefully set it on the floor and squatted, unsure where to empty it afterward. It was the first time she'd ever done such a thing, but it had been a day of firsts. Cautiously, she crept into the hallway. Damp rose from the peeling walls. She avoided the dark staircase where Court had disappeared. A large window overlooking the river was ajar, so she tipped the pot's contents over its sill. Court had also left a fresh pail of water next to the door. She lugged it into the room.

As she did so, she missed Bettina—all the homely services the woman had done for her over the years, especially when she was ill or it was her time of the month. She thought of the new chamber maid. It had never occurred to her until now that the lowly office of emptying her slops was that poor girl's job.

Unable to find the nail, she lit the tin lantern. The weak glow of its candle end would not last the hour. She scraped the trash into the grate and struck more matches. The paper flared but quickly went out. She tried the rushes, but they barely glowed and only smoked. The room felt colder than ever.

After trying to push the washstand in front of the door, she stopped. It was surprisingly heavy. Except for the whistling draft, the house was eerily silent. There seemed to be a thousand tiny holes in the walls, and the room was made colder by being on the corner of the house.

What if Geoff returned before Court? Or what if Court didn't come back? Trembling, she groped for the nail and tried not to let her imagination run wild. Such an eventuality seemed unlikely, for he had only torn himself away after several fits of kisses and a flood of promises to return soon with food and other comforts. The room grew dimmer and darker. The sleet hissed against the window. Finally, she gave up her search. Tucking her knees close, Winifred huddled under both blankets and pulled the second bedroll in front of her. She clutched her mother's jewel box and tried to think comforting thoughts. The wind howled, and the minutes crawled by.

Like the shadows of clouds that rushed across a broad Norfolk field, Winifred's memories of Holloways swept across her interior landscape. Not far from King's Lynn and the Wash, the medieval farm house was nestled within a grove of almost equally ancient oaks. Though sprawling, in comparison to its grander neighbors, it was a modest country manse around which had mushroomed a hamlet too tiny to be noted on any map. Locals knew the place by the house's name. Especially during hunting and fishing seasons and Christmas, the long corridors and cross-beamed rooms rang with the voices of her numerous cousins and their families when they visited en masse. Except for Terrance de la Coeur's renovations and the most recent Victorian additions—such as the wrought iron greenhouse at the edge of the wheat field—and some concessions to modernity—a new water pump and range in the kitchen, and a gas chandelier in the downstairs parlor and drawing room—the house was much as it had been when Elizabeth I visited.

At the Rose and Crown, house staff and farmers sipped their ale. Children gawped at handbills pasted to the notice board outside the church's gate and on the side of Barney's Mill. The shock the railway line had caused a generation or two earlier was still topical. Except for the pub, Saint Clement's was the scene of the village's most important social intercourse. In its hall, ladies gossiped about the new vicar while they planned the Christmas Bazaar. The bells in the church's Norman tower rang the hours and announced weddings, christenings, and funerals. Market days in larger neighboring villages or a nearby cattle auction, a trial, or a dance in King's Lynn added variety to Holloways' diurnal and unvarying seasonal events.

Within sight of the settlement's edge, there was the common and an enormous oak some said had been planted during the Restoration. The abandoned medieval castle and its earthworks hard by was the playground of local children and any de la Coeurs too young to ride to hounds. Until then, there were miles of muddy lanes to wander, stiles and brambly hedges to climb, and copses to explore. Grownup de la Coeurs fished, hunted foxes, and tramped the edge of the fens with their guns, searching for grouse. Tenants' cottages and farmers' firesides were familiar visiting places for charity and social calls. Hereford Hall was a short ride away, as was the Wash, and the Crown Prince had an estate a few miles east.

Holloways and its grounds could not compare to Hereford Hall's glory. One feature of note infrequently drew visitors, however. Winifred liked to play guide if her housekeeper, Mrs. Pettiford, was busy. The barnlike Great Hall boasted a quadruple-tiered stained-glass window honoring the Virgin Queen, constructed during the reign of Charles II. Its myriad, diamond-shaped panes depicted her as Diana in full hunting dress, along with her hounds. On sunny days, the hall's oak panels were strewn with wavering oblongs of red and yellow, blue and green while the Queen's golden dress and white face blazed beneath a diadem of moon and stars. In Tudor times, the hall had been the refectory and living area but was no longer used except at hunt gatherings, Christmas, or other special occasions. Those familiar with the house and the oldest tenants maintained that, as a harbinger of crises, or great changes in the de la Coeur family, the Queen would tread the Hall's blackened floors or the upstairs corridors on the way to the bed chamber she had used when she stayed at the house. Winifred amused visitors by admitting it was currently her room. She hoped to see the Queen's ghost but never had.

On rainy days when she was a girl, she had delighted in romping up and down the hodgepodge of staircases, sometimes with her many cousins but often alone. There were warrens of pokey upstairs rooms in which to play, and a dim, heavily draped library stuffed with books and maps, family heirlooms, and souvenirs from India. The oddest of these, a stuffed crocodile named Percy, had been brought back by an

industrious ancestor of the same name, an early investor in the East
India Trade who had gotten himself in the Court Lists for his energies
concerning tea and shipping. Ever since, someone or other in the
family, if not in India, always seemed to be in the House of Commons.
Winifred had re-christened the crocodile George.

In the months after they returned from Gujarat, Percival often
traveled to London to see to the Hampstead house and his
parliamentary duties. The first time she was left alone, Winifred had
tasted the full bitterness of her grief. The paneled bedroom felt like a
finely carved box into which she had been shut, never to see her father
or their farm again. Without her friends and her ayah, she would die!
The twisted bedposts towered; the canopy seemed ready to collapse.
Overwhelmed, she had shut her eyes and sobbed. Eventually she
stopped, and the faded Tudor roses embroidered on the underside of
her bed's canopy and along its curtains became interesting. She even felt
hungry. She got up and took stock of her surroundings.

It was a corner room, darkly paneled like much of the house; but
when she drew back the brocaded drapes, sunlight sparkled off the
facets of the mullioned windows. She opened one that overlooked a
large garden. Gravel paths crisscrossed between clipped boxwoods and
flowerbeds laid out in a grid. Beyond, there was a huge rose arbor and a
less formal planting, a hedged enclosure with a tennis lawn, and beyond
that, a lily pond. Breeze, freshened by sea air, blew against her cheeks.
A church bell rang, and birdsong came from the eaves. A clop of
hooves, a horse's whinny made her run to the other window and fling it
wide. A stable boy and a groom led a newly purchased mare—hers! At
once she forgot her sorrows, ready to fly downstairs.

But there were masculine voices in the corridor. It was her uncle's
valet and one of the footmen. She had met the black-haired Morrant on
her uncle's arrival to fetch her from the farm. While Percival
automatically put her at ease, his tall manservant had made her feel
unaccountably shy. She waited for him and the footman to pass. Her
father always praised her for being trusting and open, intensely curious,
even adventurous, like him. Even though he was gone, she was still
Arthur de la Coeur's daughter and would not be afraid. Winifred
washed her face and wiped her eyes. Plucking up her courage, she
decided to search for the kitchen.

On the way down to the servants' hall, she literally ran into Morrant.
In his deep, West Country voice, he intoned that it was not yet time for
tea. However, he had taken her by the hand, sat her down in the

housekeeper's room, and brought her milk, bread and butter. Would he show her to the stable? He would. Could she take her new horse a few lumps of the housekeeper's sugar? Look about for Mrs. Pettiford! Morrant had quickly dumped the lot into her handkerchief. After that, they were friends.

In her uncle's company, she met his remaining sister, Olivia, a very old and regal personage. It had been rather like meeting the Queen. With her elder cousins, she paid social calls, went to church, and followed them on their rounds as they saw to the needy of the parish. She took soup to the sick, crocheted blankets for babies, and distributed old shoes and clothes to the brickmakers' families or helped at the church jumble sale. She had her lessons to finish, the church organ or the sitting room's pianoforte to practice, and her poultry to feed. The gardener, Rogers, showed her how to tend the beehives.

Bert was almost her age and Amelie was a little younger. With Bert she could ride Tulip, and with Amelie she could play with her dollhouse. Though Gretchen was busy with her first children, the little Scots as she called them, the woman often entertained them in the nursery or helped sew doll dresses.

Holloways seemed like the uncle who had come to meet her, old and friendly, but also mysterious and full of history. Ramshackle and rambling, creaking and crannied, the house rewarded exploration. A thimble found within a crack in the wainscoting, an old strip of lace discovered in a drawer, or a linen press that had lost its key, these objects fascinated her almost as much as the house's many actual treasures. Doors swung open of their own accord late at night, especially during the rainy changes of season. Attic windows patched with waxed paper whistled when wind from the sea tore over the fens and roared in the oaks. Water pooled in the deeply pitted flagstones of the garden, mirroring clouds. The floor of the house's oldest room, unusable except to amuse children and visitors, was sloped and warped to such an extent that the wood had formed a concavity, like an enormous billiard pocket. Into this depression, Winifred and Bert rolled marbles and tennis balls, or slid with Amelie or the little Scots down the sloping floor.

Ever fanciful, Amelie said it was as though the boards had decided in their old age to become like young trees again, reasserting their right to grow into whatever shapes they'd dreamed of becoming when they were born. "Young trees are seedlings then saplings, and straight trees are stronger," Delilah would say. "But not as interesting," Amelie would answer.

On rainy or the coldest days, they chased each other and Gretchen's toddlers in the Great Hall, or Winifred played the jangling harpsichord while her cousins sang at the top of their lungs. Once their shrieks had frightened a huge barn owl from the rafters, and it stunned them to silence with its sweeping flight and white face, imperious and strange as the old Queen's.

It was also a house full of hiding places to read and draw, or daydream. Winifred had done her share of that. No amount of Percival's love or her cousins' boisterous company could ever completely assuage her lingering sorrow. At Holloways she discovered the depth of her inner resources. Though she didn't consider herself as imaginative as Amelie, her mind was prone to its own flights of fancy. In the library, inside a shadow box was a pair of riding gloves purported to have belonged to the old Queen. In somber and solitary moods, Winifred would open the box and pull them on. They fit her very well.

Quick footfalls came up the stairs. In spite of his prohibition not to, she opened the door.

"Get back inside, you little fool! I've got our feed! Go on!"

She called to him joyfully. A delicious aroma of baked pastry and meat wafted up the stairs.

All her loneliness, her fear he would not return, and her terror of Geoff were forgotten. Court shook snow off his coat, and she took his wet hat. He bustled about with a coal sack and handed her a basket. He set the washstand back into place and laughed at her effort. Her relief at seeing him was so intense she could not restrain herself and fell on his neck.

"I said I was comin' back. When I says a thing, I does it. You can count on old Court!"

"It was so cold and dark. I wanted you." She strained him close, pressing her face to his chest.

Court felt a rush of warmth. How wonderful to be greeted thus every evening. She raised her face to be kissed, and he bent his lips to hers. Like their earlier lovemaking, it was heaven to hold her. He couldn't help but be amazed she hadn't run away. He returned her embrace and kissed her more deeply.

When he drew near the house, he'd told himself not to be disappointed, to be glad even if she'd flown. But as he turned the corner, he saw that the new snow was unmarked by footprints. His heart had leapt. Joyously, he saluted the falling snowflakes, the millions of tiny, sparkling jewels that spilled down on him. He'd run the rest of the way and sprung up the staircase, unable to recall returning to his dismal room or to any room with so much gladness. The sound of her voice softly calling his name had been sweetness itself. Now, holding her, a sensation unfamiliar since boyhood and rare even then stole over him. He had come home safely to rest. He was a happy man.

For several moments, speech was superfluous.

Abruptly, Court thrust her away, full of instructions. He locked the door then darted swiftly about the room, stuffing wads of newspaper into the drafty holes in the plaster. Winifred helped. Court handed her a box of candles, and they worked for some minutes lighting and placing them in the lantern and empty beer bottles or onto the broken bits of crockery from his demolished water jug. Winifred set his shaving mirror behind the largest taper while Court piled coals into the grate and lit them. They tugged the mattress and bedroll near the fire, laid her green skirt on it for a sheet, and spread out the horse blankets. He pulled off their boots, his socks, and her stockings. As he set them near the fire, the shoulders of his coat steamed.

Winifred opened the basket. On untying a checked cloth, she found a large pork pie, a loaf of brown bread, a block of cheddar, chutney, two bottles of wine, one of spirits—even tea and a bag of candied almonds! She spread out their supper, exclaiming with delight over each of his purchases and praising his resourcefulness. Looking extremely pleased, he uncorked the wine. The firelight lit the walls and cast their leaping shadows. His cold, dark chamber had become their warm, secret grotto.

"Court, this is magical. It's wonderful! You're wonderful!" His eyes shone with pride, and she felt hers must show how extremely happy she was.

He knelt, hovering over their supper, and raised his finger. "Are you ready, set, and—!"

"GO!" Winifred shrieked.

The more Court ate, the more buoyant his spirits grew. There was no cutlery but his knife, so he shoveled food into his mouth, vaguely conscious of her gaze. She ate with equal enthusiasm, licked her fingers, and wiped her mouth on the checked cloth. They toasted the eve of their mutual quarter century. They cheered Guy Fawkes' downfall. They did it all again and grew merry.

Court drank from the wine bottle and admired Winifred delicately sipping tea from the lid of his shaving tin. Indulgently, Winifred watched him raise the bottle with a practiced but uncouth gesture. He wiped his lips on his sleeve, eying her in a way that made her blood rise to her face.

Prodding the fire, he spoke of his expedition. Privately, he recalled with amusement the shop owners' expressions as he counted out coins. No one ever expected him to have any money, but he didn't tell her that. He'd wondered if he ought to go further afield where no one would know him; but the cold had bitten at his boot soles, and the sleet had pricked wickedly at his cheeks. Besides, he'd been reckless with joy and eager to get back to her. He did tell her that part and how beautiful the snow was when it began to fall.

Seeing him so happy was delightful. If he was bothered that their supper was the result of her money, he didn't show it. With a conjuror's flourish, he produced two rosy apples from his pockets, and she quartered them with his knife. He took the pieces from her fingers with his teeth, nipping and snorting like a horse until she nearly screamed with laughter. He tossed candied almonds into the air and caught them in his mouth. Winifred attempted this but was unsuccessful. Her efforts earned his kisses instead.

After supper, he heated some water and shaved. Winifred watched, fascinated, while the straight edge scraped the soap and beard away. In a strong, pleasing baritone, he sang a song about a woman who abandoned her lord for The Wraggle-Taggle Gypsies, O!

"Was that how your parents met?"

"Me old dad rode with travelers and circus folk, jugglin' and doin' tricks." He demonstrated with his shaving brush, tin, and soap cup. He grabbed the bag of almonds and threw it into the air.

To Winifred's astonishment, it disappeared. She looked about. Court drew an almond from behind her ear and popped it into her gaping mouth. He pointed to her purse. The rest of the almonds lay loose within it among her coins. "How did you?" she asked, chewing. "That's not possible!"

The woman's amazement made Court grin with pride. "Now, remember 'o you're dealin' with, me lady!" No use to add how he and Fast and Handy Furor had worked the yokels on market days. He picked pockets while his father distracted the farmers with jests or shell games. "What about your folks?"

She told him about the farm in India and playing with her ayah's children. She described Holloways and her gallops to the sea on Tulip. "I'm never happier than when I'm riding."

Like him, she didn't say much about her parents except that she didn't remember her mother and that both had been dead a long time. Whoever was at home would be upset by now, wondering at her whereabouts, or even if she was alive, Court thought. He felt guilty but tried not to. She was alive and quite well, thank you! As for the gentleman who teased her, she didn't allude to him again, and he was glad of it.

He kissed her vigorously. "'Orses makes me 'appiest too." He recounted his most successful exploits at the racetracks, praised various beasts, and decried loutish owners who mishandled their charges. "If I 'ad a fine animal o' me own like Tulip, I'd know 'ow to keep 'er."

"Did you get those scars riding?" she asked shyly. She knew right well he had not.

Court sprang up and stripped off his shirt. He assumed a boxing stance, challenging an imaginary adversary. He demonstrated punches and footwork, elucidating the finer points of prizefighting. He bragged about his recent knock-out and gave her a detailed account of his victory. Her mystified smile inspired him to hop and dance about the room, reliving the contest and boxing with his shadow.

Winifred was amazed afresh by his grace. His torso bore scars like those above his brow and nose, but those on his back were the most terrible. She recognized immediately the marks of a horsewhip. The idea of him taking blows to his face was horrible enough. There must have been confrontations outside the ring that had not ended well, or he had been beaten as a child. Aloud, she pronounced him very brave to fight in the ring but silently wondered why any man would subject himself to such torments.

She supposed that, like her, parts of his life were difficult to speak about; perhaps those he did tell were only half true, much as she wanted to believe all of it. He was so charming that it was difficult to credit his assertion that he didn't have any sweethearts. A vision of his life on the streets rose in her imagination. It would take more than soup lines and religious tracts to help, much less change lives like his. "How much do you owe Geoff? That's what today was about, right?"

"Geoff's an ass!" he scoffed. Under her steady gaze, he stopped woofing and punching. "'E and this bloke got took by a card sharp, so they went to collect. As for me interest in the affair, I don't owe Geoff nothin' after today!"

"There are others, a Mr. Piani. I heard you arguing about it."

"Maybe I owes 'im a bit, too," he conceded, shrugging.

"I see. Geoff didn't get any money, so you didn't either. How will you pay this man?"

"Now look! Me and the capo's got a business agreement. If I drive for 'im and take a few more fights, we'll be square. Geoff can go—ah, never mind!" He smacked the crumbling plaster and tried to ignore the troubled look in Winifred's eyes.

"Is Piani dangerous? Does he charge a penalty? There must be a rate of interest."

Court threw himself onto the mattress and stretched on his side next to her. He wasn't used to women talking like that, nor did he like the idea of a woman worrying about his affairs, much less managing them. Plus, it was useless to explain his problems. It was impossible for her to understand a life like his. No one wanted to hear such stuff, and he wasn't going to talk about it, not on a night like this! He tugged the ribbon of her petticoat. "Don't think on it no more. I ain't! Tell me about one of them big parties where you dresses up fine and eats 'til you busts."

Winifred relented and lay down beside him.

There was so much to share before dawn broke the sweet enchantment. For a while longer a poor rough man and a rich haughty woman became two eager children curled together before the fire. They told their best stories. He scattered the happiest parts of his life before her, and she described foreign lands where she had traveled.

"My cousin Amelie would say we knew each other a long time ago. Court, what came between us? How were we separated, who once knew each other so well and now hardly at all?"

"I don't need to know nothin' else but what we got 'ere," he said, "and I won't let nothin' come between us."

He spread out her golden hair and pulled down her chemise. Bending closer, he kissed and adored each of his treasures: the amber of her eyes, the rubies of her lips, the ivory and coral of her breasts. He was dazzled by his riches and could not get enough of them.

Winfred's fingers wandered to the raised marks on his shoulders. She stared at the ceiling, wondering who Piani was and if he was a bad man. Court must never go hungry or be beaten again.

"Is you losin' interest? Now, 'ow can I send me lady over the moon?"

She forced a laugh. "I only wondered what you're thinking."

"Not much. I can't when I'm busy with all this." He nipped at her neck but saw she was preoccupied, maybe even worried. "All right, I was thinkin' 'ow beautiful you is, 'ow lucky I am, and 'ow we gets on so well."

"Yet we ended up in such different lives, until today," she said thoughtfully.

"I know, like somebody dealt us a bad 'and, like we was cheated." He sat up. "Now see what you done," he chastised quietly. "You got me thinkin' as well. That'll never do."

"In India, when I wanted to forget my troubles I snuck out with my ayah's children and pretended to be one of them. It didn't matter that we didn't speak the same language. When we were laughing, we weren't really all that different."

Court spoke quickly. "Well, you was. You could go back 'ome when you was 'ungry for your tea, and their mama served it to you." She frowned. "It ain't meant against you," he added without rancor. "It's just you're a lady. Your ayah's little girl wasn't. Don't listen to me. I thinks about food too much and what I ain't got. It's low, but I can't 'elp it."

Winifred felt indignant, remembering how Geoff had denied Court money when he said he was starving. "I'll bet Geoff never begs!"

This sounded like a rebuke, but he decided it wasn't. Still, the idea rankled. He stared at the remains of their dinner. Geoff always had cash. He could take Arabella to a fine restaurant and a music hall after. "We got no choice about where we ends up."

"Don't we?"

"Not where we're born."

"I meant, doesn't Geoff work for Piani too?"

"You must think money'll buy anythin'!"

"Not always! But Geoff would do what you wouldn't."

"You can't deny some folks got more advantages, or knows 'ow to get 'em."

"It doesn't mean they're happy. Do you think he is?"

"Don't know. Bellies don't stay full. People don't stay 'appy. A man's got to 'ave pride."

"I don't disagree. Court, look at me. I've been happy with you tonight, happier than I've been in years, maybe ever! You must be proud of that!"

Court had been happy as well and wished with all his heart it could last. But it wouldn't. As for feeling proud, no matter how he endeavored to skip the worst bits of his life, he suspected she guessed at the truth. A man didn't want his woman's pity; he wanted her respect. He wasn't used to talking about himself, certainly not about his feelings. Being so happy with her tonight, he realized how close to the brink of despair he'd often been. He stirred the fire. "Tell me some more about 'Olloways and them 'orses. It's 'appy, and I likes to 'ear you talk about 'em."

Winifred sighed and sat up. "We have a ghost, Queen Elizabeth, but I've never seen her. And I used to love going down to the servants' hall because—." He turned their shoes to dry and began to brush his coat. She struggled for words, thinking how Morrant looked after Percival's clothes. "They seemed freer, but only because I was young. No one is. But there's a longing for freedom, so it must exist somewhere, mustn't it?"

"I feel it at the tracks sometimes. Maybe you does when you rides Tulip."

"I'm not supposed to visit downstairs anymore, not like that. I miss it!"

"Winifred, don't cry!"

"I can't help it! Oh Court, you do make me feel free even if I'm not! Even if we're not!"

"Now, that's just daft," Court said gently. He put his arm about her. "Problem with you is you ain't never lacked for nothin' 'cept good sense. Everybody's got their place. It's just 'ow it is."

"I know and I hate it! I hate it!"

Her tears vexed him, and her words more. If such a one as she was didn't feel free, what could he possibly hope for? Staring at the glowing embers, his life passed before him, a series of dim, dingy days that crumbled to ashes. Hours of melancholy or boredom flared into short-lived pleasures, a few extra coins for a pint, maybe an hour spent with a willing girl. Their light-hearted petting and glimmers of affection always faded to nothing, mostly because he chose to make an end to them. He'd had offers, girls who wanted to be his only one even if they had to keep paying their pimps. He wouldn't tolerate that. If he couldn't support a woman, let alone a child in the manner he wanted, he'd just have to be on his own. A wise fellow would take his pleasures and not trouble about what came next, but he couldn't do that. Maybe he was a fool, but he wasn't going to be like Mick Furor. And his woman wouldn't end up like Sadie.

"So, you been 'aving downstairs time with old Court, is that it? You likes slummin', does you?" He gently dug at her ribs, tickling her until she squealed. His blood rose at the sight of her squirming and struggling. "You wouldn't make it two 'ours workin' in no servants' 'all.

But I'll set you free if that's what you likes!" He pulled her mantle over them. "Get on top of me," he urged.

She did. He circled her waist with his hands then slid them under her backside. Exposed to his eyes and the firelight, she felt self-conscious. Pressing her hands over her breasts, she regarded her body critically. "You were right. I could miss a few meals."

"Did I say that? Then I ain't got no sense either. Come 'ere!"

Court wanted to stay inside her much longer, but he was already so close. They had cast off her cloak and the rest of their clothes. She was on top of him, eyes closed and head lolling, her breasts shaking. He forced himself to slow down, but it was difficult. "I likes 'ow—you—lets go!" he gasped. "I wants to—oh, let go too!"

His hoarse whispers were far away, incoherent. Winifred rocked back and forth, needing to quicken her pace. His hands gripped her buttocks, and she bore down, her whole existence concentrated on a single point of her body and his. His grunts changed to short, quick breaths. Her movements grew more urgent, his as well. He grasped tighter, and while she moved her cloak twisted beneath their legs.

Suddenly the lid of her mother's jewel box buckled under her knee. Each time she rocked back the lid released, making a small but distinct click. Court did not seem to hear it over his moans. She glanced down. The red velvet was just visible. Her movements were working the box out of the cloak pocket. "Huh!" she cried in alarm. The necklace had already spilled onto the mattress. "Oh, no—stop! NO!"

"I can't! Ah, Winifred—I CAN'T!"

"OH!" she shouted, grabbing for the necklace. The box clicked—then clacked. "OH!"

"OH, WINIFRED!" he shouted happily. "DON'T STOP! DON'T EVER STOP—OH!"

There was a very loud, metallic pop.

"JESUS, MARY, AND JOSEPH! WHAT IN 'ELL WAS THAT?"

In one motion, he sat up and threw her off. Winifred grabbed for the necklace and the cloak. "My knee!" she gasped, frantically shoving the lot out of sight.

Howling with mirth and relief, Court collapsed onto the mattress. "I thought it was bleedin' Geoff, and me about to go off! Well, I never!" He dissolved into fresh hoots of laughter and rolled. After a bit, he was able to wipe his streaming eyes and prop up on his elbow.

Winifred snatched frantically for her disheveled clothes. Court threw his arms about her. "Red cheeks!" He slapped her bottom. "Don't be mad! Give us a kiss and a smile! If we can laugh about this on top o' everythin' else 'as 'appened today, ain't that all right? I'd call that bein' free!"

A coil of guilt wrapped about Winifred's heart. She was still afraid for him to see the necklace. It wasn't so much that he'd want to steal it; it was what he'd realize once he saw the jewels. Though he already thought she was rich, he had no idea how rich she was. She smiled weakly and declined the wine bottle when he offered it.

"Look 'ere, I'll make it up to you!" Court tossed aside the empty bottle, flipped her onto her stomach, and whispered what he was going to do to her next. He felt the pride of rajas, listening to her gasps and peals of delight as he got started. He dreamed his goddess would keep him by her side for a thousand and one nights. They would fly off together. They already were.

Winifred tried to make up for withholding the necklace by abandoning her body entirely to Court's. Nothing mattered but their limbs and mouths, their whispers and cries, and those parts of him and her which set her on fire. Tomorrow did not exist.

Boatmen called to one another on the river, their voices faint. A bell rang, tolling midnight. It no longer snowed, but the wind had picked up. Dim stars showed between broken clouds. Court turned from the window and took in Winifred's naked back, her hair golden in the firelight, and her expression, as peaceful as a child's. He pulled the cloak over her shoulders and piled on the rest of the coals to see them through the night. For now, he wanted to watch her sleep.

Winifred had felt him rise and heard the bells' doleful clang. Through her hair, she gazed at Court leaning against the wall, naked as Adam and surely as magnificent. There couldn't be enough days or years to ever grow tired of him; she'd never lived but to be caressed by this man or to return his kisses. Her heart beat hard over what they'd done before she fell asleep. She was spent but utterly fulfilled.

His endearments were crude, his compliments unrepeatable. He addressed and had words for parts of their bodies that she dared not name, for parts of her that she hadn't even known existed. The absurdity of his passionate expressions made them both shake with laughter, but his voice and eyes were expressive of affection that went beyond vulgarity or poetry. She forgot shame or embarrassment, and he seemed to know none. Not in loving, he had protested. Instead, he knew a hundred ways to take and be taken; and all of them were happiness and play. She felt as innocent as she supposed Eve must have when she woke after her first night with her new lord. She'd never imagined what it was to be so tumbled and rolled about, to be handled so roughly and so tenderly all at once. His restraint and his terrific strength amazed her. His imagination stunned her. She shivered with remembered pleasures.

The room had spun and flipped as Court's searching kisses fell between her thighs. Grasping onto him in an attempt not to leave earth, their topsy-turvy embrace put her face as near to his ardent, responsive flesh as he was to hers. This elicited a series of pleas so desperate she could hardly refuse him. Following his example, she kissed him in a similar fashion and was overjoyed by his enthusiastic yelps. Afterward, she rolled to her stomach dizzy, exhausted, and already wanting him again.

"Just look at you." He wiped his mouth with the heel of his hand and passed her one of her petticoats. Though a bit abashed, his smile was friendly, almost conspiratorial.

Hers was too. "That was going over the moon?" She wiped herself off.

He ran his hands over her. "And the stars! Ah, Winifred! Ain't we good together?"

She had pulled him close. After a while he took her again, very gently, like their first time.

Now she watched him at the window, and wished the bells would stop. At last, she sat up and fumbled for her torn chemise and drawers amongst the tangle of their discarded clothes. Court found his union suit and trousers and pulled them on. While he inspected the worn toes of his socks, she slid the empty jewel box under her end of the mattress. Court checked the fire and sat next to her. The flames curled, glowing blue and red. She lay in his arms, staring sleepily at fiery cities as they rose and fell; lights of castles winked among the embers; glittering armies marched, and molten rivers flowed down craggy slopes.

Court gazed drowsily into the fire, too. Here flickered the kingdoms of his mother's stories, heroic landscapes where he rode with Winifred, carrying her to his castle. She probably spent every night drifting to sleep before such warm, golden scenes. The unwonted presence of coals in his grate made him reflect again how different their lives were and how different they were. He pressed his lips to the crown of her fair head. He didn't want to think about it.

"There's another world in there," she said softly.

"There's a better world right 'ere." He tipped her chin to kiss her. It was not her fault if she had a warm place to sleep every night and he didn't. Her embrace made him hope she might learn to understand, even forgive him for what had lacked. It was more than manners, clean clothes, and bread. It was the absence of opportunities, good fortune, even Providence. It was what stopped a boy from the Old Nichol becoming the man he wished to be for her, the man he didn't know how to become. It was hope.

"Court?" she murmured. Her gaze was searching, deep.

Right then, he couldn't return it. "I was that far away, kissin' you."

"Dreaming? I almost was, too."

"Somethin' like that." He'd let her dream for them both.

Until the bells rang, she did. When she woke, she saw he had uncovered the remains of their supper that still warmed on the hearth. He uncorked a bottle, drank deeply, and passed it to her. "What we does down me way on cold nights. Might as well eat the rest, or the rats will get it."

Awkwardly, Winifred swallowed and coughed. The bottle smelled strongly of brandy or some cheap liquor like it. She set it aside and scooped up some of the pork pie, sucking the gravy from her fingers. While she made-believe they could stay in this room forever, she was more than content. She wiped her mouth on her petticoat and caught his eye. He winked at her and drank again. She was a fallen woman, but she didn't feel like one. What would Delilah have said? She didn't care. She felt like a queen, his queen. The man gorging on the last of their pie was a ruffian, a thief, and a kidnapper; but he didn't seem like one. He was simply Court, and he was hers. Even though the bells reminded her it would all soon end, she drifted among the stars a while longer.

The bells stopped. The river men were long gone. Except for the occasional coal that dropped through the grate or the snap of dry rushes when Court added them to the fire, the room was quiet. Their shadows stretched up the walls. Court watched them. He rarely drank spirits because they made him act stupidly or feel ravenous. He thought of Piani's men roaming the dark streets. He shoved an enormous slab of bread and cheese into his mouth and drank some more.

Winifred thought how lost he would be, seated at the table of her Hampstead house. Confronted with a shining phalanx of cutlery and crystal, stuffed quails in aspic and cerises flambés—or a lobster, what would he do? Would anyone see beyond his scars and ragged, outlandish clothes? Would they love him as she did? The thought stopped all her other musings.

She loved him.

Winifred tested this emotion the way she and Bert did the depth of a stream whenever they fished, or the way Gretchen's husband John sounded the meters under their boat when he and the little Scots punted on the lily pond. She compared it to her feelings for Percival and Bert, even Morrant. Its warmth and strength were similar, but it was very different. How odd to be so certain; but there it was—a fact, incontrovertible, solid. Her love was as real as Court was.

Out of all the men she had met, she had fallen in love with this one. The meeting of their bodies was undoable, but she did not want to undo it; nor was that when she had started to love him. It felt more like this Love had always existed and had only become evident—could only become evident—when her eyes met his. It took him to make it real, and it was theirs alone, impossible to find elsewhere or to replicate. Not that she had understood this, seated on the floor of the hackney when he grabbed her. She had been much too frightened. Or even as they made love the first time. She'd been too transported. It was simply him.

Court could see that she was thinking and perhaps worrying again. "What is it? Am I a sight?" He belched, hoping she would laugh. "Me sister says I eats like a dog."

"I wasn't thinking about that."

"Let's get some sleep. We're startin' early."

"I wish we didn't have to. I don't want to leave this room, ever! How will we see each other again? When will we?"

Court stared at the fire. He had no answer. If only she would rest her head on his shoulder. He would kiss her hair and watch her sleep. Actions were better than words, or at least easier. He took a nervous sip from the bottle. "I ain't makin' no promises I can't keep."

"Don't say that! You're not hard like Geoff! You bought those violets! You gave that girl all you had. That's the sort of man you really are! I have to know when because I love you, Court."

He was stunned. "Sudden feelings like that ain't possible, not for—a lady!"

"They must be! Do you think you're the only one who can feel it?"

Court blinked at the orange coals. She was right. He loved her too and couldn't hide it. But what did it matter? What did it change? For a night, Sadie's stories had come to life. The golden goddess had stepped out of the sun and seized his heart, but she had to return to her world and he to his. He tipped back the bottle and swallowed. He realized she was still speaking.

"...I don't want you to keep living like this."

"Like what?"

Winifred faltered under his dark, suspicious look. "Well, this room obviously. It's fine tonight." She gestured to the fire and their food. "But I can't bear thinking of you here, alone, or fighting again."

"Then stop thinkin' so much." He lifted the bottle to his lips and stared at their shadows.

The change in his tone made her skin prickle. "At Holloways our head groom Richards has his own cottage, a garden, even a horse! If you'd come home with me, you could—we could—." She stopped. With every word, she could see that he was becoming very annoyed, even angry.

"What?" he said sharply. He swallowed from the bottle again.

He didn't need her to remind him that his life was hateful and mean, or that his nasty room was only bearable because of her money. It was he who should help her, not the other way around. As soon as Geoff left, he should've seen her safely to an omnibus and gone his way. Instead, he'd bedded her like she was a common whore and taken full advantage of her yielding innocence. Geoff always teased him that he had no more sense about women than Seamus had brains. Well, he'd lost his head completely over this one. He couldn't tell her that he was already mourning her loss, was sick at having to let her go. But once the police or Geoff or Piani got hold of him, none of it would matter. He drank again.

"I don't know. We'll think of something. Only come back with me, Court."

"I don't need no lookin' after, 'specially by no woman. Thanks for me supper and me birthday present." He raised the bottle and winked. "You seemed to enjoy givin' it to me."

Winifred blanched. He was drunk. With each swallow, he seemed to grow more like Geoff. Suddenly, she was angry. "That was beneath you! Don't act like you don't understand me!"

"Oh, so now I'm ignorant?" he snapped. "I understands perfectly. I'm to be groom. You're to be mistress. We'll sneak off for a roll and a poke in the 'ay whenever your gentleman what you won't talk about ain't lookin' after you proper, right? Ain't that the plan?"

She blushed more deeply. "I told you there's no one! It wouldn't be like that!"

"Then 'ow will it be? Will we walk out together on Sundays? Go ridin' in Saint James's? I won't 'ave it, some woman orderin' me about, expectin' me to wait on bein' 'er fancy man! I don't need nobody's charity, Miss La-di-dah. I gets me girls for less trouble!" He bowed, making a sweeping gesture with the bottle.

He had to end this. If he looked at her seated so fine and regal like the queen she was, if he allowed himself one more glimpse of her eyes, he'd fall to pieces. If he had to, he'd make her hate him before the night was out.

Winifred watched him drink and grew increasingly apprehensive. She forced her voice to be firm. "Court Furor, give me that bottle!"

The bottle flew past her and shattered. Winifred scrambled out of the way. Court punched the wall and kicked the blanket. Heart thudding, she snatched the shaving kit's lid and flung it at his feet. "Here! Throw something else! You won't scare me that easily!"

"Leave me alone," he warned.

"No! Come home with me!"

"There's no way it'll work!"

"There's always a way!"

"NO THERE AIN'T!" he bellowed.

He stared numbly at the remains of their meal. He'd spent her money like a king, yet her purse was still full. All he could give her was trouble, and a man ought to be able to offer the woman he loved the moon and the stars. Couldn't she see that?

When he did not move or speak, Winifred righted the basket and put away their food. As she picked up the last of the pie, Court grasped her hand. He gnawed her fingers and bit her palm until she cried out. He spat out the pie and buried his face in her lap, pulling roughly at the folds of her petticoat.

"Ah, Jesus, Mary, and Joseph!" he moaned. "You've spoilt everything!"

Winifred's heart ached. His back heaved, and the sound of his weeping was terrible. "Come back where I can look after you, and you can look after me, and somehow it will happen. I don't know how, but it will."

"Don't be soft with me. Ain't nobody been so soft to me since I was a boy."

"We'll ride every day! The food's endless! Don't you want to? Don't you want me?" She smoothed his hot brow and gently tugged his curls. "I want to be with you so much, my love!"

Her kind words were torment. He'd never be able to tear them out of his heart. Couldn't she see that he ate like a dog and lived like one? He'd been treated like a cur all his life and would be until he died. He hated Mick Furor for making Sadie love him and ruining her life. He hated himself for being born. He sat up, red-faced and roaring. "Stupid woman, this ain't real, none of it! I'll show you!"

Winifred could not get away from him.

"'Ere's real!" He yanked at his trousers and got on top of her, ignoring her screams when he grabbed roughly between her thighs. "When Geoff comes, we'll show 'im 'ow it is, won't we?"

A battle followed. His hands were merciless, his language foul. She spat and fought, shrieking. "I won't let you! Not like this! Court, stop it!"

"Give up!" he shouted. He was so tired. He'd never been so tired. She fought on, wildly. He pulled her close, in tears again, like her. "Just give up!"

"No! I won't!"

If she didn't give up her dream, he wouldn't be able to either. In spite of the vision she spun, he knew how it would be. She and her gentleman would mount their horses, and he would muck out her stalls. He could already see her riding away with the fellow. The idea of the other man touching her was agony. His fingers looked so grimy on her white skin. He'd always be dirty, filthy. No matter what he or any man did to her, she would always be precious and pure.

Court lay still, so did she. They stopped crying and held one another under her cloak.

She was honey; she was gold; she was all the good things of the earth not meant for the likes of him. It was the same old story. He'd lose her as he did his fights, as he had lost everything else that he'd ever wanted or loved; and he'd have to learn to hate her for it, for being so far above him. Or at least forget about her. Only not right then. He strained her nearer. That could wait until tomorrow.

The boatmen called, and the bells tolled. It was tomorrow.

CHAPTER 7
Cold Comfort

The grate was full of ashes. Court mildly cursed the icy water in his washbasin, oblivious to Winifred's sharp sighs. She sat on the mattress struggling to button her boots. She had managed her torn stockings but given up on her hair. Unceremoniously, he offered the chamber pot. When she declined, he used it and set it on the shelf. He stood in the doorway, tying his neckerchief.

"I'll be downstairs," he mumbled. "Bring the food."

In her effort to fasten her jacket, she tore off another of its black frogs. She was twenty-five, a spinster, and a ruined woman. She had lost her heart and virginity several times over to a man—a criminal—who would not be admitted into the mud room of her servants' hall. She tossed the frog onto the floor. As an afterthought, she pitched the empty jewelry box onto the mattress. She stuffed the hunk of bread and the cheese into her cloak pocket. One last, wistful look at Court's room and she ran down the stairs.

They stuck to the alleys. He trudged through the snow a few feet before her, head bent and his hand clamped onto his hat. Through the holes in her stockings, her heels chafed against her boots' leather. They were stiff from Court's effort to dry them. In moments, they were wet through. Wind whipped about her ears, and her knuckles turned bright red. She clutched her cloak tightly, bending her head as well.

After their fight, they hadn't talked. Court restlessly shifted his weight on the thin bedroll. He must've thought she was asleep, however. As he straightened the cloak over her shoulders, he had found the necklace. Perhaps he felt it when he put his arm around her. While his hand searched her cloak, she held her breath. So deft were his fingers she didn't feel them when they entered her pocket or withdrew the jewels.

He knelt with them by the grate and turned the necklace slowly in the light. He sat like that for a long while. Finally, he noiselessly returned to the mattress and slid the jewels into her pocket. He lay down next to her on his back, but he didn't sleep. She lay awake a long time too.

When Court first carried her to his room, scenes from Bettina's penny romances and Amelie's novels had almost petrified her. If he found the necklace, he would slit her throat or drown her in the river. Instead, Court had put it back in her pocket and was about to take her home. Surely Geoff would not have acted thus. If only Court was the son of some well-off yeoman farmer with an old family name. All the barriers between them would've fallen away. She could've amused the neighborhood and married him.

What happened thoroughly shocked them both, so she could not accuse him of seduction. She'd gladly gone with Court into that wild wood where unmarried women were never to venture; it had been her choice to lie down with him there. Though he'd tried to thrust her away afterward, she wasn't fooled. She knew men who truly had no feelings, who were all swagger, the creations of their tailors and valets. They were their houses and their dogs and their clubs and their hunting rifles. When they married, their wives and children were additional trophies. In Court's attempt to act as though he felt nothing for her, he had shown an excess of passion, not its opposite.

It was difficult not to remember another such man. She would stand by her father's chair while he pored over soil maps and geological surveys. How godlike he seemed, not in his power but in his beneficence. Golden-haired and florid, comfortably paunchy, when he lifted her to explain their kingdom, his love had encircled her world in a magic border of warmth and safety. As she read the names on the map, he gazed at her with ineffable tenderness. No one else had ever looked at her that way or made her glad to be theirs so totally. Not until Court.

Gone were all the careful boundaries of class, even those of male and female. Like veils in a temple to a dead religion, Court had torn them away with the last of her fragile linens, challenged them by eliciting passionate declarations from her to equal his. The world would forever be different. She didn't regret the loss of the virginity that had once seemed so important to guard, but she did regret the loss of the gentle look that made her ready to let it go. The first time they lay together, his eyes were full of tenderness, wonder, and finally, an ecstasy that matched hers.

"Look at me," he had ordered, touching her as she had never been touched. "Say me name." She had until there was no other word. It was a plea for him to completely shatter her old self. They had been so close, one. Now he was twenty feet ahead of her.

With a catch in her throat, Winifred picked up speed, slipping and sliding. She wanted to be angry with him for ignoring her but only felt hollow at the sight of his bent, solitary figure. She wanted to summon her old pride, but it was gone. She would have to put on her bravest face to make it through this ordeal. She stopped running and called sharply. "I'll not be trotted through the streets like that old mare. Walk beside me, or I'll go no further!"

Court waited for her to catch up. "Come on now, or we'll miss our 'bus."

They turned the corner into an open market. For the first time, they met others who hurried along the pavement. Tradesmen unloaded vegetable crates from wagons; butchers in long leather aprons with sides of beef slung across their shoulders piled carts for delivery boys; red-faced char women bundled in shawls scuttled by on their way to warehouse offices; clerks walked purposefully toward their places of business. A milk truck rumbled past, followed by another and another. On either side of the street, young men emerged from shops, threw open shutters, or swept the pavement of snow. Court and Winifred approached an arcade where vendors uncovered long trays of silver-scaled fish, their mouths gaping rosily. A cloud of steam poured from a grated window near their feet.

Bread, Court thought dreamily. He hoped Winifred had brought the last of theirs.

He ducked his head and took her elbow, for she gazed about with unfeigned interest and exclaimed at every sight and smell. They'd already attracted a few stares. He should've shaved, and his claret purple coat and checked pants looked flash and outlandish amongst the workaday crowd. Winifred was nearly as much of a sight. No hat or gloves, her gold hair tumbled all about her shoulders—and that bruise on her cheek! The wind whistled through the arcade and blew her mantle behind her, exposing the unearthly absinthe green of her dress. He was relieved she seemed oblivious to the leer of a shop clerk they had passed or the outright disapproval on the face the char who scurried by, clucking like a hen.

At the end of the arcade, they joined a small crowd. Court helped Winifred refasten her mantle. The edge of the bruise was a yellowish hue. With partial success, he tried to obscure it by turning up her collar; but the wind continually lifted her hair. A stout woman trundled to the curb with her tea cart. A few people converged on her, blocking the steaming cans. Winifred craned her neck and eyed a basket of buns wistfully.

"I've never ridden in an omnibus," she said loudly. "What do we do first?"

Court shushed her. "Just give 'im your money! You knows 'ow to do that, I'm sure. 'Old still, blasted cloak! This 'bus goes to 'Aymarket. Get on and keep still."

"Then what? That's miles from Hampstead. Oh, Court I'm so hungry! I've got my purse! Let's have some of those iced buns!"

A youngish woman in a snug fitting coat stood close by. Through her veil, she glanced over her shoulder and looked Winifred up and down. Grinning, she batted her eyes at Court. He glared back, barely suppressing a snarl, and grabbed Winifred's wrist. "Don't show your purse! 'Old onto it in your pocket. Brought the bread and cheese, didn't you?"

Eying Winifred, the woman maneuvered through the crowd and told the tea vendor to give her four buns. "Plenty to share," she said with unnecessary volume. She sidled back toward them, licking the pink icing. Another grin at Court, and she shouldered her way past the throng to the curb as the omnibus rattled around the corner.

Court's face grew hot. A streetwalker, a very low sort from the look of her, had finished for the night and had sized up Winifred for exactly what she was, a lady who had lost her way home and slept rough. To leave her on the 'bus with a woman like that would be like handing a baby to a witch. He held Winifred's elbow until the woman climbed to the upper deck, then pushed Winifred onto the steps for the lower one.

The inside of the omnibus was stuffy but warm. There was nowhere to sit. As they jostled toward the back, Court held onto Winifred to steady her. The 'bus lurched. Court grabbed a hanging strap, and she swayed against him. After that, he held onto her more tightly. At the first stop, a man rose from the hindermost seat and pushed past. Winifred sat.

The straw on the floor was wet and filthy from the boots of passengers, most of whom looked sleepy and slovenly. The wooden slats of her seat were hard, and at each pothole, every bone from her buttocks to her teeth shook. As the 'bus jolted over the cobbled streets, she was reminded of how many bruises she had sustained from the previous day's adventures. Her temple began to throb; her neck and thighs ached. She shivered with a sudden chill and felt clammy soon after. As soon as the seat beside her became vacant, Court threw himself onto it.

He looked over the top of her head and would not meet her eyes when she glanced up at his. Brought together by the frequent halts and starts, he slid his arm under her cloak and about her waist. Winifred shuddered again and laid her cheek on his shoulder, a bit light-headed.

"You shouldn't do that 'ere," he said quietly. "It's ain't proper for a lady."

"A lady, me?" She smiled against his collar, taking heart at his softened tone. Her fingers found his, and he did not withdraw them. "Didn't you see that woman back there laughing at us? I'll bet she knew what we did last night!"

"Don't you start, not 'ere!" he scolded, but knit his fingers with hers.

"Go on, Mr. Furor, knock us about!" She mimicked his Cockney accent. "That'll convince 'er I'm already spoken for! Miss Iced Buns!"

Court pressed his face into her hair to smother his laughter. Incredibly, she still smelled heavenly. He closed his eyes and breathed her fragrance. He had meant to be firm, even hard with her this morning. He gently brushed his knuckles under her chin. "People don't talk on public transport. Don't you know nothin', you rude little chit?"

At the sight of her pale, upturned face, his resolve to leave her weakened. Though her brow was drawn and there were deep circles under her eyes, she was lovelier than ever. He wanted badly to kiss her. Soon, she was asleep. He stared without seeing the other passengers. He dared not close his eyes or he'd be dreaming of a big country house and horses, of open fields and wooded tracks that led to the sea, and a garden full of flowers that smelled exactly like her.

He pulled her closer, vowing silently that it would be his final gesture of affection. She sighed, and her drowsy eyes glimmered at him through her lashes. He plucked the wilted violets from his hatband and threaded their stems into a hole in her jacket. Then he rained kisses on her hair and cheek, oblivious to their fellow passengers. It was only a leave-taking, like the knights did for their ladies, like the one he'd meant to take of her yesterday before she stole his heart.

The omnibus stopped in Haymarket, and passengers disembarked. Court helped Winifred to the pavement and pulled her under the shelter of a theater's awning. Across the street at the opposite corner, a bobby was on patrol.

"Number 44 will be along shortly. Ride it to the other side o' Regent's Park. Someone'll know the next one what goes to 'Ampstead. It'll take a while, but you'll get 'ome before midday." He shoved his hands in his pockets, unable to look at her. It was almost over. That made him miserable, which made him angry. Number 44 rounded the corner. It was early.

Winifred grew desperate. "Court! Ride with me, please!"

"'Fraid not, love." He stepped from under the awning and away from her.

"You will think of what I said!"

"Thing about brandy is I never remember much after. Fact is I don't recollect 'alf the rubbish 'appened last night."

Winifred grabbed his sleeve. "Don't! Why are you doing this?"

"You got your place. I got mine. It's best we both get back to 'em."

"The only place I want to be is with you. Come with me, Court!"

With an impatient oath, Court shook off her hand and faced her. "You know what you are? A spoiled little girl what's always got 'er way. Now you can't 'ave it, so you're flummoxed." He waved at the 'bus. "Get back on your 'igh 'orse and ride 'ome!"

Several people hurried past on their way to the 'bus. Winifred did not move. He tapped his hat brim. "Good day, Miss de la Coeur." He turned on his heel and strode into the crowd.

Behind her, the driver clanged the bell. Winifred mounted the 'bus steps, stumbling as she looked over her shoulder. She searched for Court's top hat, the violets, and his purple coat. But he was gone, swept back into the human tide, the ocean that was London's early-morning populace.

The vehicle moved. She leaned across her fellow passengers and pushed down a window, scanning the crowded pavement. Number 44 rounded a corner, but still she craned forward. Voices protested her intrusive posture. She was forced to give up and took hold of a hand strap. Her vision swam with tears, and so did her head. Her cloak fell open. Air stirred against her damp skin. She pulled sluggishly at her jacket, surprised to find it unbuttoned and her thin blouse under her fingers. The 'bus rounded another corner, and she almost fell. A man offered her his seat. Shivering, she sank onto it and pressed her hand to her spinning head. A woman spoke.

Did she need help? Was she lost? Had she lost something?

Winifred gasped, wildly groping at her cloak. The necklace was in her pocket.

Was she hurt?

She shook her head but otherwise could not answer.

Much later or perhaps very soon thereafter—she wasn't sure—other voices rose around her. The omnibus had stopped. There was a general confusion, but it was of little interest and seemed far off. The driver was speaking to a policeman. The woman and the man who had offered his seat spoke rapidly as well. Winfred realized the policeman was asking her questions.

What was her name? Where was she going?

She didn't know. She didn't care.

She's hit her head, the woman said. Look at her face! Another policeman boarded the omnibus and spoke in the first policeman's ear. She's in shock, said another man. Perhaps she's been attacked, someone else offered. Her cloak, said a woman, was there a nametag or a dressmaker's mark? The passengers grew quiet. The policeman bent close, flicked the hem. His hand closed gently on her arm, and he helped her to stand.

"You dropped these, dear." A woman held out a nosegay of wilted violets.

Winifred stared at them, then at the policeman. As he led her down the aisle, she searched the passengers' faces. The one she wanted to see was not there.

Court had a pickpocket's knack for disappearing into crowds. From the safety of a lamp post, he watched until Winifred was inside the 'bus. After that he drew nearer, close enough to touch the vehicle's side, wanting to make sure she was all right. When she pushed down the window, he could've touched her. The bell had clanged. The 'bus eased into traffic and turned a corner. She was gone.

For a long time, he stared after the 'bus, heedless of the pedestrians who hurried past or the patrolling bobby who paced nearby. Finally, he started to walk.

As ever, he was hungry. While she'd slept on the first 'bus, he'd slipped two pippins into her pocket. He'd found some of her money in his trousers that morning and had also slipped that back into her purse. No food and not a penny. What he'd let slip through his hands in twenty-four hours! He thought dully of the necklace. She'd never know he'd found it or put it back either.

Those jewels! He'd never seen such fabulous wealth. But after holding her, what did he care for cold stones? A man couldn't eat them. They might as well have been fairy-gold, for all he could've sold any one of them to any toss-pot he knew. The unearthly object hadn't even tempted him and still didn't. The necklace was only a reminder of the chasm between them.

A wave of misery broke over him. He tried to take some comfort in the tears she'd cried as she searched the crowd for him. Their sparkle was far more precious than jewels, and they were his. He wouldn't part with their memory for all the diamonds in the world. That he was her first lover was his forever as well. He'd always have their night together, and so would she.

He walked aimlessly but finally made his way south along the river. By the time he crossed the bridge back to Southwark, he was footsore and dead tired. He picked up his pace, however, for he was back in Piani's territory. If he didn't get off the streets soon, one of his boss' henchmen might pick him up and slit his nose. He headed for the Lancaster Arms.

Bess Montague owned the hotel where his half-sister Beryl and her friend Rosie worked. It was an old-fashioned establishment that charmingly preserved the Regency period's urbanity. Court liked its style, and never went there without imagining himself as Dick Turpin or thinking of Lord Nelson. The Lancaster's women were like a stable of thoroughbreds. Young to youngish, milky white to mahogany, they provided entertainment and discreet companionship for gentlemen at evening card parties and late-night dinners. Beryl said its register read like Debrett's and was a guarded secret; its rooms were private and well-appointed. The food was delicious. Most important of all, Bess' girls were clean and regularly vetted by a doctor. There was a special entrance for a certain very important person. Court always used the kitchen door.

To his relief, Rosie was there, arguing with the butcher's boy over the day's order. Pink-faced, the boy sputtered while she corrected the bill, castigated the mutton's quality, and told him to tell his master not to send her any more offal. The boy protested, but she cut him off in her childlike voice. "Them sausages wasn't fit for the dustbin, so if your master wants what owin', 'e can make it right or there won't be no next order! Be on your way!"

Court leaned over the stair rail, tipped his hat, and prepared for what was coming.

"La! Look at you! You're filthy!"

In contrast, Rosie was the picture of cleanliness. Tiny as their Monarch, she was infinitely prettier. Her dark dress was trimmed with Belgian lace at its collar and cuffs. Brass keys shone at her waist, and her skirts rustled as she turned her back on him. He followed her to the housekeeper's room, her command post at the hotel. Rosie's light brown hair was swept up into a chignon fixed with black ribbons. Becoming ringlets shook about her temples as she put the receipt book back in her desk. She flipped open an account ledger, ran her finger along a column, and penciled in a figure.

"Can't a fellow get somethin' to eat?" Court hugged his arms across his chest and glanced longingly toward the kitchen.

"You can get a bath and a brush!" She grabbed his lapel and marched him to a side room filled with silver. She closed a knife box and turned a key on a ribbon which hung amongst those at her waist. "Think you're goin' in me kitchen in that condition? Rode 'ard and put away wet!" She wrinkled her nose. "What you been sleepin' with, a 'orse?" She left but soon returned with a tray. It held a pot of tea, a plate of eggs and ham, fried tomatoes and mushrooms, and a rack of toast.

"Oh Rosie, me love!" he groaned with pleasure. "Marry me!"

She swatted him. "I can't stay to talk. Come up for a bath after. You won't bother Beryl none if you needs the bed." Before she left, she tweaked his queue. "Look at that 'orse's tail! We'll do somethin' with that long mane later!"

Court felt better. Food always helped, and so did Rosie. When he had demolished his breakfast, he crossed the alley to the other house.

Bess also owned the Montague Hotel, where she rented rooms to a less pricey sort of working woman, and that was where he meant to lie down. It was an equally old structure, its charms in decay, but not without a shabby élan. He'd known many of the girls who lived there all his life, and his reputation amongst them chagrined him not a little. They howled with gleeful derision at his swaggering and refused to take him seriously as a "tough." Alone, however, it was usually easy to get one of them to give him an I.O.U. and a bit of a cuddle. He was always grateful for their favors but this morning wanted a bed to himself. If none was available, he'd take any amount of Beryl's scolding and Rosie's teasing so long as he could get a bath and a lie-down.

Yawning women in peignoirs and paper curlers or varying amounts of slatternly undress greeted him familiarly as he made his way upstairs to Beryl and Rosie's flat. Like Rosie, the two rooms were fresh and clean, a sort of domestic miracle to him each time he entered.

It was all Rosie's doing. His sister had no homely instincts. In the parlor was a round card table under a lamp, and Turkey carpets. His sister's crammed bookshelves overflowed onto stacks of her newspapers and bound editions of *Punch*. Above her disheveled desk lay Rosie's neat account books on a shelf he had made for them. Above that, a framed needlepoint of roses read "Our Home." Rosie's taste in art was decidedly sentimental: gilt framed angels and children with faces like sugar plums, a doe-eyed Jesus about to knock at a door. Before the glowing grate was a long sofa flanked by two stuffed chairs and their ottomans; one was leather, like the sofa, and the other was printed with bright flowers. More of Rosie's handiwork was evident on the embroidered fire screen. The mantle held a clock surrounded by a litter of seashells, trinkets, music boxes, and case-glass vases full of dried flowers and peacock feathers. In a corner cabinet were fans and cheap knick-knacks, mostly of a souvenir variety, more shells, and a blue Mandalay tea set, Rosie's prized possession. Along with the rest, Beryl had bought it on one of their seaside trips. He'd always envied them those excursions, though they only went when Rosie was ill. He'd only ever seen the Thames at low tide, and the thought of walking along the ocean's edge was fantastic.

Through the curtained arch was a large brass bed. On the room's bluebell colored walls, he and Rosie had stenciled sprigs of yellow primroses, and there were more pictures, mostly seascapes. The wardrobe and dressing table were very old. Lace curtains filtered the light, and on a marble-topped table, ferns and forced Dutch flowers grew in Chinese bowls. On Beryl's side of the bed were more piles of books and newspapers.

Court wound up one of the music boxes. He sank onto a chair by the grate and removed from its arm a teacup holding one of Beryl's half-finished cigarillos. The late edition of the previous day's newspaper was open to the racing schedule. After checking the last race's results, he turned to the front page. His breath stopped.

EXPLOSION ROCKS THE ROYAL EMPIRE!
The Royal Empire Bank was rocked by explosions this morning.
Authorities have not determined whether the initial blast was due to foul
play or the result of a fault in the gas lines. Streets around the bank were
closed to traffic for several hours while firefighters worked to subdue the
blaze. Casualties include....

Rosie entered carrying towels, soap, and a long-handled brush. She set these on the table and grabbed the paper. The hall boy entered, hoisting an enameled hip bath. At her direction, he pushed back the printed chair and set down the tub. Another boy carried two buckets of steaming water. Rosie brought a night shirt from the bedroom and spread it on the chair.

While the boys filled the bath, Court stripped. Rosie inspected the clothes, grimacing, and handed offending items to the boy. "Don't throw out me coat," Court begged as he lowered into the water. "Or me neckerchief! And put down me 'at!"

"Wash your neck." Rosie handed him the brush. "You ain't presentable to a knacker!"

"He looks as though he's already been to one," said a low, husky voice.

Beryl stood the door, smoking. In her long duster and riding boots, she gave an initial impression of height, but she was not that much taller than Rosie. She tossed a riding crop on the table. Rosie dismissed the boys, and Beryl shrugged off her coat. Her slender figure was clad in a black garter belt studded with metal brads, dark stockings, and little else. Rosie helped her into a red kimono. Clamping the cigarette between her teeth, Beryl squatted next to Court, lifted his wounded hand, and examined it narrowly.

Rosie bent and examined the marks as well. "Lor', what 'appened to you?"

"A mistake," he said ruefully.

Beryl smirked. "Was she a pretty one?"

"Not particularly."

Beryl raised an eyebrow, stood, and gave Rosie a resounding kiss on the cheek.

While Court scrubbed his back, the hall boy brought Beryl's breakfast. She protested, and Rosie admonished. He washed his hair while Rosie poured coffee and filled Beryl's plate.

"I can't eat all that!" Beryl shouted in alarm. She pulled off her boots.

Rosie snatched them away. "You will—every bit if you wants these polishin'!"

Court agreed with Rosie. There was not a spare ounce of flesh on Beryl.

Depending on whether she wore an evening dress for work or her habitual trousers at home, she resembled a youth who plays the maiden's part in a masquerade, or vice versa. She was modestly curved and wore her thick hair cropped short. It stood out in wild, disheveled curls after her night's activities. She raked her fingers through it with a gesture very like her brother's.

"That old goat was 'ere again!" Rosie indicated the riding crop.

"No, that's not for him. Some men are simply obsessed with their backsides!"

Court coughed uncomfortably.

"Should I be jealous?" Rosie teased, smiling at Beryl.

"Ha! My one and only, come here!"

Rosie eluded Beryl's outstretched arm. "Not until you eats at least 'alf them eggs!"

When they were children, Court had suffered violent crushes on both of them, but Beryl had no eyes for anyone but Rosie. The pretty little girl sat between them in chapel, doll-like and docile. So far as he knew, his sister had never cared for anyone else.

They first met when they all briefly attended school. The Methodists' mission was to feed and minimally educate—if not redeem— the children in and around the area between Shoreditch and Bethnal Green. Beryl had been the most obviously intelligent of the unruly pack. To Court, it seemed remarkable that he'd learned anything while he was there, but Sadie set her heart on his going. Her boy would read and write and "look up!"

Compared to Beryl and Rosie, he'd been lucky. Mostly, Mick had left him alone unless he was in his cups or Court made a mistake during their con-act. He didn't beat Court on a regular basis but had an explosive temper and a hard hand when he did. It was the erratic nature of Mick's rages Court had dreaded most. He and Sadie got the worst of it when they stood up for each other.

It had been different for Beryl and Rosie. In a neighborhood where drunken brutality passed as the normal state of affairs, Beryl's stepfather was known for his bestial treatment of her and her mother. After the woman was released from his chronic beatings by cancer, Beryl left home and school, removed Rosie from her own intolerable ménage with her alcohol-sodden father and lecherous uncle, and took up her profession. The two had been inseparable ever since. Court hadn't stayed at school much longer either, for Mick had died about the same time.

Beryl set down her coffee. "I'm going riding this afternoon."

Rosie threw down the boots. "Court, did you speak? Or am I mad? I will go mad!" She marched to the bed and turned down the coverlet, her pretty backside shaking as she plumped the pillows. She rounded on Beryl. "You ought to rest up for tonight, but does I care? Go ridin' with the old goat! Catch your deaths, both 'o you!"

Beryl dug a silver spoon into a jam jar, sucked it, and regarded Rosie forlornly. The woman brushed past her, grabbed a pair of stockings off the dressing table, and headed for the printed chair. Beryl picked at a piece of toast. "Are these your apricot preserves? They're awfully nice."

"Where're you ridin'?" Court asked.

Beryl glared and shook her head vigorously.

Rosie picked up a sewing box from beside her chair and turned her back on Beryl. "You might as well 'ave that breakfast, Court. You see what she thinks of me efforts!"

Beryl lit a cigarillo and stared morosely at Rosie. Suddenly, the woman threw down her sewing, ran to the bedroom, and snapped the curtains shut across the arch. Rolling her eyes at Court, Beryl followed.

Court dried off and put on the nightshirt. While the women bickered quietly, he devoured Beryl's dry toast and poached eggs. Rosie opened the curtain, and Court joined Beryl on the bed. For the moment, peace had been restored, and Court was profoundly grateful.

Rosie sat at the dressing table, polishing Beryl's boots. She giggled suddenly. "You should see Beryl's old goat. Rich as Croesus and one breath shy o' Bedlam!"

"There's no harm in him," Beryl said quietly. "He's just an old bugger."

Rosie stopped laughing. "Then why talk to 'im so much? Why ride with 'im every day?"

"It is not every day."

"It's most days!"

Before they could start arguing again, Court interrupted. "I wish I was a 'orse."

Rosie's eyes lit up. "Oo-ooh, a frisky black stallion, that's our Courty! We knows you likes a bit o' ridin'! Been up to no good with that 'and? Maybe you needs a good whippin'!"

"Well, I'm not going to do it," Beryl said wearily and faced him. "I'll get you a big fat lady, and I'll give her my whip. Up and down 'round London Town, she'll ride our Courty to market!" She dug a finger into his ribs. "Astride brother mine, no side saddles for you!"

They all laughed, but Court's heart wasn't in it. Rosie tended to his wound and tied up his hand. While she did so, the headline seemed to scroll across the walls. Words from the article danced about his brain as well. *Many wounded after explosion in clerks' offices on second floor...others missing...Officials at Scotland Yard state....*

Years seemed to have passed since the previous morning. He imagined Winifred on a horse in a beautiful riding habit, prancing along the walks of Saint James's. Then he saw her pull down the 'bus window, crying. Why hadn't he taken her hand? Why hadn't he gone with her?

"Court, what's the matter? Are you ill?"

In Beryl's dark eyes he saw concern and not a trace of her usual mockery. Rosie cocked her head like a little wren. It was difficult to look at either woman, and it was moments before he found his voice. His heart had been broken so often before he met Winifred. He'd learned to carry its pieces carefully. But if anyone cared for him, it was these two. "I met a lady."

Beryl rolled her eyes but spoke with some relief. "Why am I not surprised?"

"No, I mean a real one!"

Beryl groaned and pulled the quilt over her face.

"Shush, Beryl!" Rosie said. "Tell us about 'er, Court!"

He did but kept the most intimate details to himself. They divined the truth, however; he saw it in their eyes as they exchanged quick looks and listened breathlessly. "She wanted me to be a groom at 'er family's country place. Anyhow, we quarreled." He thrust his hands into his hair. "Jesus, Mary, and Joseph! She was so lovely! I'm such a bleedin' ass!"

There was a light tap on the door. A maid peeped in at them apologetically. "Mrs. Cartwright, Madam needs you to fix tomorrow's menus. The wine merchant's 'ere as well and the knife-grinder wants payin'. Cook's all a-dither about tonight and the flowers still ain't all delivered!"

"I'm comin'! Court, it's like one o' your fairytales!" Rosie bustled out behind the maid.

Beryl took another cigarillo from a silver box on the bedside table. "What else were you up to yesterday? Young Sam was here looking for you and Seamus. He was worried."

Court started from the beginning with Geoff and Selway Adams' card game at the Boar and Hart. He fetched the newspaper and Beryl read the story, whistling between her teeth as he described the kidnapping and Winifred's necklace.

"It must have been worth a packet!" she sighed.

"I wouldn't take what's 'ers! What've I got to give 'er worth that?"

"Your services apparently," Beryl smiled wryly. "Remember the mews? The drunk old groom who let us ride the horses he was supposed to exercise? We went all the way to Saint James's!" She threw back her head and laughed.

"Old Bobby, you brought 'im gin," Court smiled sadly. "Always was a little 'ell-raiser, you!"

"Look, don't make yourself miserable over this. There's nothing in the papers about a kidnapping. Geoff can go to the devil! I'll loan you the rest for Piani."

"No, that's for Rosie! You don't 'ave that much any road, not after Brighton."

Beryl's face clouded. "It didn't set us back much." She smoked thoughtfully. "Why not go to Holloways? Give it a go! It would get you away from your troubles here at any rate."

"Be 'er servant? No thanks! I declines the pleasure of shovelin' 'er shit! I got me pride."

"As do we all, after a fashion. But if I wanted a woman that much, I'd do anything. When I'm working, you think I worry about my pride? I do all sorts of ridiculous, atrocious—I can't talk about it. Long as Rosie doesn't have to go with a man again, I'd wade in shit up to my neck!"

They were quiet for a while.

"'Ow much longer before you two can get out o' 'ere?" he asked.

"I don't know. Someday! We'll be alright." She smoked, and her eyes grew distant.

"You're the best person I know." He lay his face close to hers.

"With friends like yours. Let me rest!" Beryl wearily stubbed her cigarillo and rolled over.

❧

As soon as Morrant withdrew, Bettina locked Winifred's door.

They didn't have much time.

Dr. Frost was on his way. Mademoiselle was in the bath. In the parlor, a policeman and a detective were talking with Sir Percival. The day before, the detective interviewed her and Richards. A policeman had met with Monsieur George at his club.

No wonder her lady shook as with ague when Morrant carried her upstairs. She had been nearly naked beneath her cloak. Only a blouse under her jacket and a pair of drawers under her skirt; she wore no woolens; her stockings were in tatters. Bettina had stifled a shriek as she helped her take off her boots and disrobe. The skin was rubbed clean off her heels and toes. As well as a bruise to her cheek, others marred her young lady's limbs, back, and buttocks. There were even more alarming blotches on her neck, breasts, and upper thighs. Bettina knew at once what these were but pushed from her mind the activities that must have caused them.

Bettina spread her lady's filthy garments on the rug. Over these insentient scraps of cloth, she quietly poured her tears, allowing the worries of the past hours to spill. The soft grey boots, whose soles were hardly longer than her hand, were already at the bottom of the rubbish bin. The brilliant green and black jacket was ripped beneath an arm and missing three of its four frog-fasteners; the condition of the skirt and blouse defied description. The cloak looked as though Winifred had rolled in a dust tip. Most disturbing was the state of her lady's culottes.

Wrinkling her nose, Bettina raised the underdrawers to the lamp and bent closer. She drew back suddenly.

Shaking with rage, she snatched up her mistress' cloak. From one pocket she pulled two pippins, a hunk of bread and cheese, and a woman's handkerchief she did not recognize folded around some wilted violets. Further inside the pocket was Winifred's reticule. Bettina weighed the purse in her hand and undid its clasp. It was full of notes, coins, and candied almonds. She threw down the purse and rummaged in the other pocket. Here was one of her lady's chemises, and a bundle within it. She unrolled the torn garment.

The necklace and its large pumpkin-colored diamond filled her with awe and superstitious dread. Crossing herself, she laid the jewels beside Winifred's underclothes. Behind her, water splashed. Winifred called for assistance. She wanted to wash her hair.

Bettina ignored her. The chemise and culottes bore similar stains. She knew her lady and what the state of her lady's underclothes portended. All night long, she had prayed to the Holy Mother for her mistress' safety. When the police brought Winifred home and she had first seen the bruises and ruined clothes, her mind had been filled with scenes of assault and rape. There had been one man, perhaps many. Her heart nearly broke. Now, she was uncertain what had happened. Muttering in Gallic, she marched into the washroom.

"I've a riddle for you, Miss! What sort of man steals a woman's virtue but leaves her purse full? Et ses poches plein des bonbons et les bijoux?" Her lady sank deeper into the water, covering the love bites on her breasts with the washcloth. Bettina thrust out the linens and the necklace. This was too much, even if she was French!

In spite of her concern, not to mention her compassion, Bettina's voice rose. It might mean her position to speak out, but she understood the dangers even if Miss did not. "What are you going to tell them, these detectives for the bank?"

Winifred flushed deeply. "That it's my necklace. I didn't take it. Why are they still here? I wasn't robbed! I'm fine. I've nothing to say. My water's gone cold. Run the tap, please."

Bettina stamped her foot and shook the stained linens. "Run it yourself!"

"You do jump to the worst conclusions. It must be from growing up in Marseilles!"

"Aha! What conclusions do I jump to?"

Winifred sloshed about uneasily. "Throw them away!"

Bettina had always been privy to the secrets of her mistress' chamber. "Was I born yesterday? This crust isn't piss! This is a man's— il est le sperme! Dr. Frost will examine you. What will you tell him? Bonjour, Monsieur le Docteur. Moi, je suis très bien! Mademoiselle, êtes-vous toujours vierge? Mais oui! Mais non!"

Winifred quailed under Bettina's mocking dialogue.

"What will you tell your uncle or Monsieur George if you must go far away to have a baby? What will you do with it, hein?"

"I don't know!" Winifred cried. "I can't think about it now!"

"You must! We are women, so we must always think! Plan!"

Winifred couldn't meet Bettina's flashing eyes. She rubbed the washcloth against her skin and winced. It burned where Court had entered her. The stricken look on Morrant's face as he had helped her to her room bespoke the household's fears and worst of all, his.

Behind her, Bettina continued to complain and chastise. Sir Percival had been up all night and was very unwell this morning as a result. Like Morrant and Richards, Monsieur George had been to the hospitals, the police, searching for her. "We thought you might be dead!"

Winifred wrung the cloth. Grey scum floated. The precious little bits of Court that were still on her were washing away with the dirt. When they were together it all made sense. Now, none of it did. "Maybe I won't have one. Women don't always—do they?" She stopped uncertainly. "You don't have to come with me if.... You don't have to stay if it's too scandalous."

"How can you think I care about that? I care only for you, Mademoiselle!"

The desire to tell the whole truth, to speak of Court and her love for him was a great temptation, but the police were downstairs. She wanted to unburden her heart but not tell Bettina details that might catch her maid in a lie later. She was frightened for Court and for herself, too.

Her mistress' tears made Bettina sad, but she needed more information to know how to help. She knelt next to the tub. "I heard the policemen. A woman on the 'bus in Haymarket saw you in the street with a man, a driver like Richards perhaps. You quarreled maybe, she thought."

"He only helped me find the omnibus and wouldn't take any of my money for it. Please don't speak of him to the police! It was nothing. He wasn't anybody!"

Bettina knew Winifred was lying, and her lady did not lie. She yet retained enough innocence not to know how to dissemble. This man was very important. She took Winifred's hand. "I am also a woman! I will do all in my power to aid you, but you must first help me understand. Those many hours, you were lost. Where did you go? What happened? There was a man, maybe not this one the woman saw, but someone. Downstairs, the police, they don't care for you—for him. They want answers! It is their job!"

Winifred felt like a child caught being naughty. Too exhausted and heart-broken to be defiant, she nevertheless shook her head. "I won't talk about it!"

Bettina smoothed the damp hair from Winifred's brow. Though there was only six years' difference between their ages, she felt so much older. Always, she was as jealous for her lady's virtue as she was proud of her appearance and the de la Coeur name. Winifred laughed at her older cousins' talk about propriety, but it was sensible and for a young lady's safety! Monsieur George, she had never worried about him troubling Mademoiselle. He would never lead her astray, for he was very old-fashioned. Some women were for men's amusement; others were for marrying. A mistress would not be the mother of his heir. The woman he treasured, her whom he would protect out of pride for his honor and name, would be.

Life had taught Bettina she must learn quickly. She had never dispossessed the de la Coeurs of the myth that she was from Marseilles. That was where Sir Percival had hired her on his way to Gujarat. In fact, she was from Normandy. Her orphaned girlhood was another life, and she never spoke of it. At fourteen she had married a fisherman of forty because she was homeless; he was very kind and let her remain une vierge until she was sixteen. She came to his house as maid of all work then personally cared for his mother until the old lady died. During a storm at sea, he drowned. She miscarried soon after and was greatly aggrieved, for she had liked her husband and loved his mother very much. Sometimes, she thought she had loved him too but did not like to dwell on it, or their lost son. Next, she traveled to Bombay as a governess for an English family. There, she pondered the difference between what was desired and what was necessary.

Une femme sole with no means and no family had to earn her living. She could not afford an affair of the heart or risk a man not worth his salt. The lot of her betters aroused no envy. The Englishwoman with whom she lived could not divorce her worthless mate. Like Bettina, she had no property or money. It all belonged to her brothers and her husband.

There were much worse fates than loneliness. Such had been Bettina's thoughts as the doctor instructed her on the proper doses of arsenic to treat her syphilitic mistress. Days and nights, monkeys chattered in the trees of the English families' compound. She sat beside the woman, listening to her fevered litany of heartbreak and neglect while her children cried piteously in the nursery for their mama. Meanwhile the husband continued to infect the Indian prostitutes of Bombay and, it came out later, his neighbor's wife.

With Mademoiselle and Sir Percival she began afresh. The de la Coeurs were a happy family. England was a welcomed change from the spa life she and her former mistress had led on the Continent before that woman's wretched end. Winifred's months in Germany and her debut had been good times. Bettina enjoyed the long visits to great houses where she met other servants. She always returned home with a sense of pride in Miss de la Coeur compared to other young ladies and a sense of satisfaction with the orderly running of her and Sir Percival's houses. Returning calls and sewing clothes, late nights waiting up after parties, mornings pasting cuttings into scrapbooks, and afternoons accompanying Miss in the carriage at the park or shopping for ball gowns. Even the seasons thereafter had their triumphs. Miss met the Prince and danced with him!

Yet Bettina recognized that such a life could not go on. Much as she loved her, Winifred was no longer a girl who needed the reassurance of her maid's companionship. For her own life to begin, there were decisions Bettina was most eager for Mademoiselle to make and to make well.

Since the end of summer, she had become more reconciled to the idea of Monsieur George as a prospective husband for the young lady. Never mind his past! First and foremost, his family was ancient, and he was un gentilhomme. As for his grand affair with the singer, she did not believe it was a real passion. A man who always mocks others does not easily open his heart. Yet he often laughed at himself as well, like a sad clown. The heart was so variable, so unevenly built.

And he so obviously enjoyed Mademoiselle's company. Of course, he would never be faithful, but Bettina could not imagine him being faithless. Once settled, he would never leave her so long as she gave him a long leash. He would not conduct himself any better than the next man but would set up Winifred like a queen in Hereford Hall. Yes, he would spend her money and keep a mistress, but when the children were born, he would tease and spoil them as he always had her lady. He would be good enough.

If only the past twenty-four hours did not prove catastrophic to all her hopes. Bettina thought that she must make an extra effort to keep in Monsieur's good graces, though she had never bothered before; and she must encourage Mademoiselle not to lose heart. It was Monsieur George or endless sun, sand in one's boots, and Egyptian servants! Morrant promised that Mena House had room enough for them to live as comfortably as they did at Holloways. Bettina loved Winifred but did not want them to have to grow old together beneath the Pyramids.

She had been to the British Museum with Winifred and Sir Percival many times. The Egyptian room was a chamber of horrors. The golden sarcophagi with their great, staring eyes made her shudder. She'd walked through enough temples and wandered among too many tombs with her former mistress in India. What was the point, glorifying the dead with gold and jewels? She wanted to dress Mistress in them now! Bettina liked London's hustle and bustle. She did not want to waste what was left of her youth in a country whose time had passed. The glitter of city lights was preferable to the desert's glare. She had been thrifty. Someday she hoped for a life of her own, man or no man by her side.

"Miss Winifred, stop crying and listen to me."

Bettina produced a pocket diary wherein she recorded Winifred's menses, which had just ended. She suggested how they would answer the doctor, police, detectives, her uncle, even Monsieur George. As she helped her lady from the bath and into her gown, she explained what they must look for during the coming weeks as signs of pregnancy, even infection.

What sort of infection? Winifred sank onto the pillows. Bettina was vague. Dr. Frost would know what to do. Winifred began to shake. The clamminess she felt on the 'bus was back. "I'm so afraid."

"I know," Bettina said gently. "But I will stay with you!" She turned down the lamp and took a seat by the bed. There was much to say but not now. She held Winifred's hand. "Close your eyes, rest!"

She would not talk about the shame of not knowing who one's father was, or the agony of losing one's only child. She would not speak of the grief when one is destitute and alone, the hunger or fatigue, the vexations of learning a foreign tongue, or the indignities of traveling in steerage. Nor of blind madness, tabetic ataxia, catatonic spells, night sweats, and crippling agony.

Bettina's experience of the world was much different than Winifred's, and though she wanted to tell Mistress that it would be all right, sometimes it wasn't.

CHAPTER 8
A Day at the Races

Selway Adams lay in a hospital bed, wishing the pain in his temples would subside and the stout policeman in the bowler hat and horribly cut great coat would leave him alone. His partner looked like the angel of death. An orderly stopped at his bedside to change out his water jug. The wheels of the cart squeaked and Selway winced.

Detective Inspector James Patterson had no intention of quitting Adams' side or relieving the constable at the door until he'd gotten the details of the Adams attack written down and spoken once more to the pretty nurse who attended the ward. He and his partner, Detective Sergeant Nicholas Peele, had been at the hospital for a couple of hours, but there was much more to do. He licked the end of his pencil and held it poised over a small but extremely full notepad. He waited until the orderly moved to the next bed. "Now, let's just go through your story once more to be sure," he coaxed. "Who else did you see upstairs?"

Adams swore. "That blasted de la Coeur woman! Why don't you question her?"

As far as Patterson was concerned, the man in the bed was a mess and a bad dog who had nothing to boast of but his pedigree, and Patterson had no high opinion of that either. Adams' head was wrapped in bandages; both eyes were blackened. His arm was in a cast, and one leg was raised in a sling attached to a pulley. He had lost a few teeth, had several ribs cracked, and almost been deprived of a kidney. Patterson ignored all this.

Adams had gotten what he deserved. He looked as though he'd fallen under a 'bus, but that was where he belonged. Patterson could not abide cheating of any sort, especially from those who already had a leg up in the world. He wasn't a prig but felt the devil was in the details. Once a fellow started to let the little ones slip, Old Nick had him fast and worse would soon follow. In John Bull England, even a beggar ought to be able to play a decent hand of cards and place a secure bet. No matter how low a man's circumstances, he should expect to see a fair fight on his night off. What happened in the ring should be a match of equals, a thing of beauty. A bloke's beer should not be watered in any sense.

He hadn't been particularly keen to take this case when it was first presented to him by his chief and still wasn't. A minute of conversation with his subject proved his worst suspicions. Adams was an annoying, spoiled twit who didn't know when to leave well enough alone. What was he doing associating with a known ruffian like Geoffrey Ratchet and a fast-dealer like Hezekiah Boors? Hadn't Adams a club and friends of his own level whom he could skin?

But that was the point, wasn't it? Adams liked to look down on fellows like Geoff and Hez. No, he didn't feel sorry for the man one bit.

Patterson knew the suspects well enough to feel that they were generally harmless so long as they kept their quarrels amongst themselves. He'd been locking up Geoff and letting him out for years. Hez had been in for drunk and disorderly on a couple of occasions but was otherwise clean. They knew the rules. Adams, on the other hand, was out of his league, slumming in P. Lili Piani's territory and rubbing shoulders with ambitious trouble-makers like Geoff. That was the danger of mixing classes. Folks wandered out of their ilk, didn't know the natives' customs, and got hurt. He glanced down the ward at the orderly. The little, wrinkled man methodically worked his way from bed to bed. Someone really ought to oil the wheels on that cart.

"Have a word." He nodded toward the orderly and Peele set off in the man's direction.

Back to business, Patterson thought. Rumor had it, Geoff was jockeying to extend his influence within Piani's turf, that the attack on Adams was more than the usual come-uppance. Piani certainly didn't want to handle the hornets' nest his minion had stirred up, the sort of trouble that made headlines. Nice, quiet graft was Piani's stock and trade: extortion, pimping, and keeping the neighborhood firmly under his thumb. Southwark wasn't exactly Whitechapel, and Piani's fiefdom

within it was well-defined. So long as no one got killed, the police didn't
bother him much. In return for their laissez-faire philosophy, the man
could be an excellent informant when his competitors' activities
encroached on his.

In the affair of the Royal Empire Bank, Hez had gone along with
Geoff for one joyride too many. He wanted a bit of the ready to fix up
matters with his sweetheart, Fanny Merton, the barmaid down at the
Boar and Hart. What that chap needed was to throw in his lot with his
old regiment and stop hanging around that den of thieves. He'd have a
word with Fan, who was no fool. Geoff, however, was not only an idiot
but slightly mad into the bargain, especially if he'd been drinking.
Patterson sighed. He'd let Piani manage his troops' discipline. If he
didn't, Geoff was bound to be more of a headache than usual.

Patterson hadn't seen Hez since the event but had an idea who
knew where he might be. His source was Fan's brother, young Sam,
with whom he'd been on speaking terms since he caught the lad setting
fire to a bale of cotton outside a warehouse. The boy had been playing
with matches and admitted a fascination with all combustibles. Patterson
asked him if he liked engines. After that, conversation came naturally.
He liked kids, but he and Mrs. Patterson had none. Much the way a
mother bear or a she-wolf has a protective instinct for her young, what
bothered him most about his job when he went home was what became
of the young people with whom he crossed paths during his
investigations. One didn't want to rile him by turning a child to crime.

He knew firsthand how slippery the slope was. He and Piani had
played in the streets together but on approaching man's estate had gone
their separate ways. Until this Adams mess, Patterson had recused
himself whenever he sniffed Piani's shit. Funny how a few bad choices
could chart out a whole life. It might have been different. Once set,
one's course was difficult to change, and neither of them was getting any
younger. He'd see what he could do about Hez and Fan, and he knew a
fellow in Leadenhall Street who might appreciate some assistance at his
boss' new business. Motor launches they'd tried out down at Putney last
spring or some such. It was time to get Sam fixed up before Piani's
offers got too interesting.

Adams groaned and fidgeted, calling Patterson from his
ruminations. The fact that this rotten apple seemed to think he deserved
special polishing was offensive. If Adams thought he was untouchable
merely for being an earl's natural son and chose to swim in shark-
infested waters, so much the worse for him. If one had any sense, one

certainly didn't dangle large purses before the noses of hungry curs like Geoff, who knew his way around.

Once more, Patterson applied his pencil to the pad to make sure none of the attack's minutiae had escaped him. He'd not have this case thrown out of court on his time. The missus wanted to know when his promotion was coming. "I've got the business at the bank all sorted," he said to the recumbent Adams, "but we need to go back over earlier events. Now what else can you tell me about this fateful card game?"

"I told you, man," Adams snapped.

"I've got Ratchet and Boors. Was there anyone else?"

"Some swank army friend of Hez's, but he left early. That brat, Fan's brother—."

"Sam!"

"In and out—always underfoot. Furor was there too. I told you before—the boxer."

"But he wasn't part of this particular game? You didn't see him at the bank?"

"No! Lazy son of a bitch mostly slept on the settle, like always, or played with the kid."

The orderly squeaked by on his way back down the ward, and Peele approached as well.

Patterson cleared his throat. Sadie Furor's son—he didn't know him personally but remembered Sadie well enough. Waste of a lovely woman. A good soul. Did what she had to after Mick's sticky end. Some said Piani'd set up Mick Furor in that bar fight. By the time he met her, Sadie was in a bad way. She must have been very pretty once. He appreciated a sweet face, but a bit on the side wasn't his style, not with Mrs. Patterson to think on.

There was justice to be meted out, but fidelity to one's own was precious too. Loyalty could outlive love; it was all sentimental twaddle otherwise. That's what Mick Furor hadn't understood. The goodness he'd got was worth more than its weight in gold: a kind wife to come home to and a son to hold on his knee and bring up to be a man. A fellow had to draw the line. He considered Court Furor's presence at the Boar and Hart, hoped he could discount it, but was afraid that would not be the case. Furor was a known driver and strong arm for Piani. What little information Patterson had on him was conflicted, but he hoped Sadie's son was more like her than Mick.

"That was the lot? There was no one else?"

"No man! I've told you already. My head hurts. My back is the very devil. Leave me alone and go do your job. I'm dying right now." Adams closed his eyes. "I want my nurse. Call her for me." He tried to turn on the pillow and groaned. "Get her!" he cried petulantly. "And tell someone to oil that bloody cart!"

Patterson slowly ambled to the end of the ward where the orderly placed a fresh jug of water beside the bed next to the door. He nodded to the fellow, and the man winked—or maybe it was a twitch. What tedious work it must be, Patterson thought, like his sometimes.

He spent a few pleasant moments chatting with the nurse at her desk. The whole time, however, he mulled over what Seamus Todd had told him and Peele in an earlier interview in the ward upstairs. Todd was a heavy for hire who occasionally did a bit of body-guarding and prizefighting. He was an enormous, bearlike fellow with an equally bearlike disposition. One had to go carefully with Todd, who, while stupid in the extreme, was very loyal—though often not too discerning—and took the code of the streets seriously. He did not snitch; he could keep a secret; and he would die for a friend. With care and a drop of whiskey, however, one could slowly extract information from him in a round-about way. But woe unto the impatient officer who tried to bully the man.

Todd had been confined to bed because he was at the bank the morning of the explosion. He had saved a clerk and gone back into the building multiple times to help the firemen with their rescues. When Patterson heard about Todd's activities, he questioned the clerk, who was lying in a bed some yards distant from the big man. Next, he paid Todd a visit. How had he gotten to the City? Opening an account at the Royal Empire, was he? Just happened to be on the floor where Adams' office was located?

Once he established Todd's conveyance was a hackney, he asked for details about it and the driver's appearance. Todd feigned forgetfulness, but Patterson had seen he was uneasy.

A cab had been stolen from a mews a few streets away from the bank. A groom remembered a black-haired fellow in a dark velvet coat who had hung about asking for work a few days before, but the groom had discouraged him, not liking his looks. "A bit too smartly dressed and too run down at the same time," he said. Scar over his eyebrow and along his cheek? Crooked nose? That was him. Damn and blast, Patterson had sighed, scribbling Furor's name in his note pad and following it with a question mark.

He had learned these facts slowly and in no particular order. He wanted a description of the driver's clothes, but here, Todd's meager intelligence asserted itself. When Patterson saw the crafty gleam in Todd's eye, he knew he'd lost his quarry's scent. But there was hope. When Todd clammed up, Patterson suspected that the driver wasn't only someone Todd knew but a friend, and the circle of Todd's close friends was small. He asked after a few of them, and Todd divulged that Furor owed Geoff money.

"Quite a lot actually, but he owes everybody, even me. Still, it's only money." An unpleasant thought seemed to occur to him. "Well, I never!" he exclaimed. He squinted dangerously at Patterson, tapped his nose, and growled. "Thought you almost had me there, didn't you, gov'nor?"

"Ah, but you were too quick for me."

A slow grin spread across Todd's face and he chuckled. Patterson smiled and chuckled too. He really did like the man.

It was scant information, but London was large. Todd could not know all its denizens. If one drew a circle around the gym where Todd lived and estimated the places he might stroll in an afternoon, one began to get ideas. Never mind the odd omnibus trip. Todd didn't like them and wasn't likely to hire a whole hackney for his personal use. The list of his intimates would be fairly small, as would be Geoff's and Hez's. Patterson felt sure the driver that morning was someone they all knew and that Seamus would trust, or he wouldn't have gone along. It was someone who badly needed money, too. Patterson could be patient.

If only Adams remembered who Hez's swank friend was. Fellow might be helpful.

He drew a stick figure of Todd and surrounded it with names. From each name he drew a line to another one. He would continue this process until he made all the connections, and he was certain he would make them. These fellows were dumb, and he was smart. That's why they eventually got caught and had nothing to show for their efforts but prison records while he took home his pay packet regular and bought Mrs. Patterson a new hat just to see her smile. They would go to Aberystwyth at Christmas to see her aunt, and he looked forward to all the singing about the Child in the manger.

That was what it was all about, the Child. A little fear of the law didn't hurt either. That was the beginning of wisdom. Them as was too proud and didn't admit a bit of nerves were generally fools who got themselves hard time or hanged, or were cut by another fool. He thought of himself and Piani as children at play by the river, of Geoff in his first lock-up at the same age and equally full of cheek, of Furor taking it in the ring. Young, impressionable Sam and slow wits like Seamus, the hopeful girl Sadie must have been before Mick Furor got hold of her. Suffer the little children...or take the millstone 'round your neck and go to the Devil.

"Oh, Sister," he smiled at the nurse. "Best see to that Adams fellow yonder. He's a might snappish at present, so mind your hands."

The older man bit his cigar and laughed good-naturedly. "Not my game tonight!" He tossed in his chips and raised his glass.

Court scraped the lot toward him. He'd never had such luck. He was walking on air. He was winning, and winning big. He toasted the older gentleman by his side.

When he'd woken in Beryl's bed, it was early evening. Rosie had laid a shaving kit on the dressing table and clean underclothes on its bench. The hall boy carried in a steaming jug and towels for his shave. A fresh shirt and a second-hand evening suit were folded neatly over Rosie's chair. While she gave him a haircut, Court inspected the clothes and spotted evidence of her clever mending. He ran his hand along the patterned silk necktie she'd chosen.

"For your birthday," Rosie said as she tied it. She re-bandaged his wounded palm and pressed three gold coins onto it. "They're from Beryl."

Court accepted them and kissed her cheeks. It was easy to see how Rosie kept his sister wound about her finger. She made a fellow feel he didn't mind what he owed or how many lies she told. "We won't tell 'er," he whispered. "I'll pay you back."

"Whatever does you mean?" She lowered her dark lashes. "Sit down so I can fix your 'air." She brushed what remained of his curls with scented pomade and smoothed them into long waves. She smiled at the effect. "'O's that dark, 'andsome man?" she teased.

Court flushed, pleased beyond measure by what a shave and a clean suit of clothes did for a bloke. He wished Winifred could see him. "I cleans up pretty well, don't I?"

Rosie kissed the top of his head and straightened his tie. "Beryl says you're to stay for the night's festivities, only don't drink any brandy and don't play baccarat!"

Snow had changed to heavy rain, and rain had changed to fog. It was thicker than pea soup, which checked Court's urge to strut across the street. Sounds floated disembodied from their sources. A celebratory bonfire burned at the end of the street. Guy Fawkes' effigy hung above it. A grand carriage emerged from the gloom. It stopped before the Lancaster's special door. Shoving his hands in his pockets, he did not wait to see the important men who disembarked.

He entered his usual way. His appearance was rewarded by the footmen's tweaks and the kitchen staff's hoots and whistles when he sat down in the servants' hall. Meals were always good at the Lancaster, but for Bonfire Night there was beef and stuffed chicken and deviled oysters, buttered peas and potatoes. He ate two helpings of strawberry trifle and custard. Afterward, he snuck upstairs and found a table where he could play cards well out of Old Bess' sight. He soon won enough to pay for his supper. He felt like a prince, knowing he could repay Rosie.

He bought a bottle of claret and followed Beryl to a secluded chamber for patrons who preferred high-stakes games. His luck at cards attracted the notice of an older man at the baccarat table who invited Court to join him. Beryl was engaged at the roulette wheel, her back turned.

The man had slightly protuberant blue eyes and a fine head of slightly receding hair. A huge cigar was clamped between white teeth which often gleamed over his pointed beard. He seemed to enjoy losing as much as winning, both of which he did often. As the night wore into early morning, he expressed pleasure at Court's continued good fortune and ate a great deal. He ordered cigars and Champagne, lobster and oysters. When the gentleman laughed and clapped Court's shoulder, his well-padded ribs shook like those of a slightly depraved Father Christmas.

"You bring me luck!" Court exclaimed. His pile of chips grew.

The man smiled as a bottle of brandy was set before them.

"Who is that dark little minx who's been watching you, some sweetheart?" He turned his light, prominent eyes toward the archway that divided their alcove from the next one.

Beryl was dressed in scarlet trimmed with black lace, her shoulders bare and her ruffled train swept behind her like a Spanish dancer's. To disguise its short length, her hair was adorned with velvet roses and black ribbons pinned at the nape of her neck. All night she sat at the elbow of a pudgy, bespectacled fellow in slightly rumpled evening clothes.

Her partner's ginger head bent myopically over his cards, and he paddled his fingers on them. Earlier, he had attracted knowing winks and nudges from spectators, but these had stopped long since. Before him were stacks of chips that added up to an amount much larger than Court's, and an air of suspense hung over his table. Only two other players still dared face him while the rest sat silent, watching. Beryl's hand rested on the back of the man's chair. She appeared perfectly composed, but Court thought she was excited.

He hoped she was having a good night. He raised his glass in salute and hiccupped. "That's Beryl. Once, I thought she'd be me girl 'til I found out she's me sister. That cooled us down a bit. Still, she's a corker." He hiccupped again.

The older man chuckled and stared appreciatively. A large, bright jewel sparkled on his finger as he lifted his cigar. "To some that might add piquancy to the romance. Everyone in my family marries their cousins, so the lines do get rather closely crossed. Nothing that racy though."

"It's like that 'round our way as well," Court said confidentially. "I've 'eard tales would raise your lid. The way folks carries on it gets right ticklish not knowin' 'o's 'o! Like in *Tom Jones*!"

The man seemed to find the reference extremely funny. "You're a reader then!"

"I likes a good story," Court said.

"As do I! Your friend has an interesting partner, a very successful barrister. They'd make a good subject for an artist friend of mine." The man sucked deeply at his cigar. "I'd pose them as a Dickensian Ganymede and Jove—charming!" The man caught Beryl's eye.

Blushing, she inclined her head and dropped a shallow curtsey. She whispered in her barrister's ear. He nodded but did not turn around.

"I don't know about charmin', but money maketh the man, at least for the night." Court regarded his chips with satisfaction. His older partner offered a cigar from a blue, enameled case, and Court glimpsed a gold crest before it disappeared back in the man's pocket.

"Look at you, my young friend! You're rich. Like Themis' disciple over there, you might yet find a partner with whom to enjoy your winnings. I hope she's as toothsome as his!" A footman pushed back the drape to allow another to enter with more food. Court's card partner shucked oysters and indicated the large open salon beyond. "Take your pick of Lizzie's blooms!"

The women all wore décolleté gowns of bright silk and satin, long gloves, and jewels or flowers in their hair. It was indeed Benn' showplace. Feminine examples of every size and shape were on display to satisfy every conceivable taste. Here were the Lancaster's most tempting nymphs, the young and gay to the older and knowing: china doll ingénues and sulky vixens, milky white Valkyries to dark and exotic Negresses, tiny Thumbelinas and towering Amazons.

Suddenly melancholy, Court shrugged his shoulder under the man's warm hand. "I couldn't." There was a friendly gleam in the gentleman's eyes that invited confidence. Court was tipsy enough to talk. "There is a lady, a real lady," he said dreamily, "so I won't utter 'er name!"

"Perish the thought!" The man poured Court more brandy.

"She's not 'ere. She would never be 'ere! We quarreled and 'ad to part. I won't never see 'er no more. She's out with 'er rich gentleman friend or 'ome at 'Olloways by now."

"Holloways, in Norfolk?" The man examined him with more interest. "Charming, very rustic, I know it and the family well. We've an estate nearby, near King's Lynn. You know it?"

"I've never been to the country much." Court gestured at the salon. "If you was to see 'er next to all them, you'd understand. I've never met anyone like 'er and never will again. Still, it was lovely bein' with 'er that once." Already, he was back in his room. Winifred's pale skin and golden hair gleamed in the firelight and under his hands. "Eyes like amber, like whiskey."

The man appeared lost in his own thoughts. "I've seen eyes that color once." He patted Court. "Take heart! Passion springs up in the most unlikely soils and sometimes even true love."

"She's proud, and I thinks better 'o 'er for it. No, I'll keep lookin' for me fillies at the tracks. Give me a mare 'o places regular anytime!"

Old Bess entered the salon.

The man offered Court his hand. "I have enjoyed our conversation tonight. The horses are a favorite pastime of mine too! Tell me your name again."

"Friends calls me Court. Court Furor."

"Good luck, Mr. Furor. Perhaps your mare will win and your proud lady will consent to come down a bit for the sake of romance. Your tale is one whose end I hope to hear one day!"

With that, the man crossed the crowded salon to Old Bess. At his approach, people made way. Men's heads bowed and women dropped curtsies. He extended his arm to Old Bess, and the pair slowly made their way toward the double doors that led into her private wing.

Court vaguely thought he ought to know the man's name. It was right on the tip of his tongue. That crest, perhaps he'd seen it on a carriage at the races. He'd seen the fellow's photograph in the newspaper—a business tycoon or politician who'd been knighted. The world's doings never made much difference to his circumstances, so he hardly paid attention to the headlines except for the racing results. Beryl joined him.

"So, how was Bertie?"

Finally, Court realized the identity of his evening's card partner. With a deep bow, a footman opened the door. Old Bess and the Crown Prince were gone.

ৡৢ

Natasha rose from Winifred's bedside and Percival took her seat. Dupree changed the flowers on the table before the window, another bouquet from George.

As soon as the women left, Percival took out the miniature portrait. A sloe-eyed, raven-haired maiden whom he had lost, irretrievably, to fortune's vagaries and perhaps youth's callowness stared into an eternal sunlight. In her rarefied lineaments he discerned the real young woman to whom he had so completely and quickly given his heart. The ivory's cool luster brought her back, the warm, breathing creature he had not forgotten or would ever leave off regretting.

After a day's fox hunting, he had met this dark-eyed beauty. He happened upon her as she toiled along a lane delivering dairy wares to the great house where he was a visitor. Percival set her on his horse and shouldered her burden. She had been intelligent and forthcoming, modest in manner and singular in expression. Her cousin Morrant should have been in her place, she said, only he was helping a gentleman at the hunt. Percival apologized for causing her inconvenience.

She was the loveliest girl he had ever seen, and he was smitten. His host encouraged the match, for the maiden's family was of an ancient strain, yeomen in that region since well before William the Conqueror, even before King Llewellyn. Chaperoned by her cousins, they met on fieldside paths and danced the quadrille at a church harvest fete. In company, she was charming and lively; alone, her blushes grew as deep as his. He pressed her hand. Her eyes were innocent but lacked discretion. Percival felt repaid for his boldness and dared hope he might win her.

He extended his stay and nerved himself to speak with her father. He told no one, not even his beloved, and sent no letters home about his plans. The girl's father was in Shrewsbury, so their meeting was delayed until his return. An uncharacteristic freak of rashness and high spirits led Percival to insist upon trying his host's newly-broken horse. The hunt began early. It was cold but not too frosty. Within sight of the fox, Percival's spirited mount obliged his interest by throwing him as they took a fence. Morrant found him unconscious in a ditch, his arm broken and his collarbone snapped. By nightfall he had a raging fever. It went to his lungs. He lay in bed a fortnight and knew no one.

Meanwhile, his sweetheart behaved with equal rashness. A child, not quite sixteen, she took a child's delight in tricks and gaudy show. The man was a gypsy, his lordship's servants said. Like Percival's horse, he was a well-built and extremely wild-spirited beast. Morrant confirmed the worst: his cousin had followed or been carried away by her demon paramour. No one knew whither, and no more was heard of her.

Late autumn leaves whirled against the windows of his niece's room. Similar patterns of red and gold had flown outside the room where he struggled not only with his lungs and broken bones but despondency and heartache. Those faded messengers of winter's approach foretold his youth's premature end. Unwilling to speak to anyone but Dupree, Winifred feigned sleep when visitors called. He had done the same in his grief, unable to tolerate any but Morrant's company. Youth is stubborn, if not always hopeful. He had lived, so would Winifred.

Dr. Frost's report to the police stated that she had taken a significant blow to her head and was concussed. That, along with the shock of the explosion, could have rendered her unconscious or amnesiac for hours. It was plausible that her recollections immediately before and after the event had been affected, if not erased. She might never remember, or there could be inaccuracies. A concussed person's judgment, as well as her emotional response, could be altered. "It may lead to depressed spirits, like hers," he told Percival.

Winifred had reason to be downcast. At Dr. Frost's recommendation, she saw a woman's specialist in Harley Street. The doctor was blunt. "We must wait. Signs of infection aren't always obvious in women, and the treatment is rough. It can cause sterility."

Dr. Frost warned of additional problems. "Physically, she's a very strong young woman. I only hope that when, or if, she recollects the most traumatic events, she will not keep them to herself. Nightmares, hysteria, even an aversion to marital intimacy can result."

Because Dupree had assumed the post of nurse, Percival relayed the doctors' information. He trusted the Frenchwoman's discretion and knew she would tell Winifred the doctor's diagnosis if she became ill. The Harley street doctor did not advise it, and Dr. Frost also advised caution. Percival agreed with Dupree's forthrightness but dreaded speaking to George on such matters and had no intention of doing so unless the man asked for Winifred's hand. Her state was not exactly what he had in mind when he hoped George might find a reason to lose interest.

For years Morrant had been his steadfast friend and confessor, but about this blow neither of them could speak. They never talked about his lost cousin either. Her family contended that she had been abducted, but the local authorities' search was ineffective. In spite of her seducer's low character, gossip was rife that she had gone with him willingly. Some in the family agreed and feared for the Morrant name and their daughters' prospects. There were arguments. The Morrants were proud people, however, and bore their collective shame with heads held high. When Percival asked Morrant to be his valet, the young man was glad to quit the neighborhood.

Life had a way of throwing one at the fence; no matter how tightly one held on, the reins slipped from one's hands. Since losing her, Percival had always felt old. If the woman lived, she was perhaps much changed. To him she remained ever young.

Why had he not searched harder for her? Because she left him for another? Had his pride, his vanity been so wounded he could not bear this humiliation? They had not been much, but did these outweigh his need for her? Or had he been frightened to confront her lover? Maybe she had never felt what he did. He did not know the answers to these questions or why he had gotten on that blasted horse. Or loosened his grip on the reins as it hurtled over the fence.

The bright threads of young lives pulled, dropped, tangled—cut!

Gretchen touched his shoulder. He had not heard her come in. She pulled another chair close to the bed. Percival kissed his niece and let Morrant help him to his room.

A race track on a sunny day is a wonderful place, especially on a false spring day stolen from the jaws of impending winter. The wet turf is still green in spots and smells greener; the sound of horses' hooves on the packed earth is like the drumming of a hundred happy hearts beating together; and the brass band plays. Ladies bob and sway like strawflowers. There is food and drink in plenty. The flags fly brightly and snap in the wind. The jockeys are resplendent in outrageous silks of lemon yellow and candy pink, robin's egg blue and silver, vermillion and sable. The bookies call out their bets over the heads of the eager crowd. And then there are the horses.

Court intended to store up all this joy to share with Winifred the next time they met. They would meet again; he felt certain of it. After an evening with the Prince, he felt charmed. Within forty-eight hours, he'd held jewels and Winifred; he'd won more money than he'd ever had in his life and shaken his future king's hand! She was right. There was always a way. Life was looking up.

He wore a second-hand suit Rosie had mended. His hat and brilliant green necktie were brand new. Feeling dapper, he winked at the ladies and got quite a few blushing smiles in return. His head and his heart were in the clouds. Heaven would be full of horses, like the turf was today. He leaned over the paddock rail, watching the grooms lead out the mounts that could be purchased before they raced that afternoon.

While Beryl got dressed that morning, Court sprawled in the bath, smoked one of the Prince's cigars, and made plans. Her barrister was taking her to the tracks. Excellent idea, Court agreed. Perhaps he'd see them there and this horse she was so excited about.

Rosie was uncharacteristically quiet while he ate breakfast. "If I was you, I'd lay low."

He gave her a kiss and four sovereigns. "No, take it all back—with interest! I'm ridin' a winnin' streak, and one's goin' to 'appen for you and Beryl soon. I can feel it."

"Put me down! I wish you wouldn't go," she answered. "You should take your money and pay Piani. You could buy a ticket to that lady's place and 'ave all the 'orses you want."

"Now Rosie! That's too small for a prince's mate. Let's be grand!" He danced her around the room. "We've got friends in 'igh places.

Piani can go 'ang! Before this day is out, I'll 'ave enough to 'ire me own 'orse, maybe buy one. Next time I sees me lady, I'll greet 'er proper."

By late afternoon he had placed two bets. On his first, Fireball came in second at ten to one. On the next, Prancing Poppy came in third at five to one. In both cases, he had bet to show, not win. The Prince's luck had held! It is amazing how quickly a man can build castles in the air when his pockets bulge with cash. Court furnished his and built its stables too. It was all appointed in luxurious style, a cross between the Lancaster Arms' most sumptuous apartments and Scheherazade's bedchamber.

In his daydream, he and Winifred entered the stable. He was leading her by the hand through the immaculate stalls and up to a loft filled with sweet, new hay when he heard the bookie's call. Last chance to place one's bets!

Berserker was a five-year-old of famed pedigree and growing repute. Sired by Canon Ball, he was two-time winner at Kildare's Curragh. Court shook off his reverie and put his hand into his pocket. The wad of notes gave him confidence. He pulled most of them from his wallet. The remains of his luck at the card table were in his other pocket. On second thought he pulled that out as well. Nothing small about him! He felt like a prince. His heart thudding with excitement, he placed the lot on Berserker to win.

It was ten minutes before the race, so he walked toward the refectory tent. A familiar voice hailed him. There was no point pretending he had not heard.

Geoff Ratchet pushed through the crowd. "You gave me the slip the other mornin'!"

Court extended his hand and Geoff took it, jerking him so hard that they stood nose to nose. To his amazement, he smelled no alcohol on Geoff's breath. The man showed his teeth, but it wasn't a smile. "I don't like it when I gets stood up. I don't like it when folks doesn't take me at me word. What 'appened to the bleedin' woman?"

"Easy, man!" Court shook him off. "Anyone'd think you're angry. 'Ave a pint on me."

Without waiting for an answer, he entered the tent. Geoff stood at the door. Court got their drinks and shouldered his way to a trestle table. He wondered how he could get away and assumed a nonchalant tone. "The woman was nothin' but a wailin' nuisance. What did we need 'er for?"

"For me money! Where's 'er bag?"

"Ah, come on Geoff. Let it be! I went to take a piss and she got out. Ain't nothin' in the papers about 'er, so we're lucky I reckon." He and Geoff sat elbow to elbow. "Look, we don't want to go down for kidnappin' no bird, do we?"

"She was a witness," began Geoff quietly.

"She don't remember nothin'. I told you!"

Geoff stared at him.

Court knew that look but laughed bravely. "Right, maybe your pistol whippin' and your belt. She was so scared, she don't know what she saw. She thinks we'll kill 'er in 'er sleep if she opens 'er mouth. I tell you, she won't say nothin'!" He laughed raucously and took a sip of beer.

"What 'appened to your 'and?"

"She bit me when I was lookin' for the purse. I didn't find it."

Geoff shook his head. "You never learn."

Court didn't want to talk about Winifred to Geoff. It felt like swearing in church. "So, where's 'Ez got off to, France?"

"I 'aven't the foggiest. Adams is alive, but in a pretty bad way. Todd saw 'im in the 'ospital."

"Seamus won't talk." Court was suddenly nervous. "Lucky for you Adams lived."

"You ain't out o' it! You're a witness. You 'ad motive. You 'elped with the woman and drove to and from the scene."

"Jesus, Mary, and Joseph! Let me know when you takes silk! 'Ow bad is Adams?"

"Much worse off, and we all might swing," Geoff muttered into his beer.

They were silent for a few moments.

Geoff glanced at the track. "I cleared ten bob on Silver Slippers in that last one. What about you?"

"I've done alright, got another on in a few minutes." Court finished his pint quickly.

Geoff eyed him narrowly. "I ain't placin' no more bets lest it's a sure thing. I got other business. I'd best get back to it." He drained his glass and stood.

A bell clanged. It was time for the horses to line up.

"By the way, this was in your room." With a smirk, Geoff tossed a red velvet box shaped like a heart onto the table.

Court picked it up. The box was deeply dented, its hinge loose. The metal was soft, so he pushed his thumbs against the satin interior. POP! Court's face flushed.

Shoving the box into his pocket, he strode toward the track. The wind grew colder, whipping the ends of men's coats and ladies' long veils. Court held down his hat. It was nearly twilight, so it would be the last race. The air smelled of rain. He hoped it would hold off.

The jockeys rode their horses to the starting line. In the distance Beryl and her barrister stood at the rail. She wore a nosegay of roses pinned to her wrist, a large pink and black hat, and a matching plaid coat. Court drew closer to the rail too, trying to remain calm, but the buoyant joy of the early afternoon was gone.

Winifred would surely be questioned, or already had been. She had seen Geoff, and she and Geoff might have been seen as they left the building. What about him that morning he put her on the 'bus? Unless she feigned amnesia, she wouldn't be able to get around telling what she knew. He didn't want Winifred to lie for him. And that box! Geoff knew he was lying about her.

Berserker was third on the inside. The horses pawed the ground. The crowd hushed. The brass band played in the distance. At the pistol's report, they were off! The ground shook. The horses lunged. Berserker was neck and neck with his neighbors, running as though possessed. Then he broke out of the starting lineup. Another horse strained forward too, a mare. She was about to catch up.

Suddenly Berserker seemed to decide that the track did not suit him. Or perhaps it was the company, or his jockey. Whatever the reason, the jockey was suddenly on his rump in the dirt. Berserker lived up to his name by jumping the inside rail and thundering across the center field. He jumped the other rail out in front of the approaching horses as they rounded the course, took the next rail, and careened into the pasture beyond the track. The far crowd rushed the fence after him. Berserker stopped and began chewing the grass.

Court stood with his mouth open. Hooting with laughter, Beryl strode toward him with her friend. Then, her expression changed. She shouted and frantically waved her hands. Uncertain what her cries and panicked gestures portended, Court looked about and realized who else she'd seen. It was Geoff. This time, he had company.

It was too late to run. His horse was gone; his money was gone; and the race was over. Two of Piani's henchmen grabbed him by the arms. The crowd flooded between them and Beryl. The last he saw of his sister was her horrified face. She yelled while her friend held onto her.

The men hustled him behind a shed. Court's back slammed against the wall.

His luck had run out. His castles crumbled. He'd never see Winifred again. When these fellows were done with him, she probably wouldn't recognize him anyway.

Piani leaned against a post, whistling softly between his teeth. After Court hit the gravel, the men pulled him up and slammed him against the wall again. Geoff reached into Court's pocket, took out the velvet box, and threw it on the ground. He opened Court's wallet and drew out ten shillings. "You're not bleedin' serious? This is all?"

Piani shoved Geoff aside and pushed his face up to Court's.

P. Lili Piani was a dark, furious little man who wore a bowler hat over his oily black hair and favored natty coats and checked pants. His breath smelled of stale whiskey and his brown eyes snapped. He flicked open a knife and held its point inside Court's nostril. "I'm bound to agree with Geoff. I'm a generous man. I lends to me boys out o' the goodness o' me 'eart, and this is 'ow you treats me? ME!" He pulled the tip of the blade forward.

"Well," Court began in a voice slightly higher than was usual, "if you 'as all your cake now, what's to eat later, as me dear old mum used to say? You knows I'm good for it." Frightened as he was, he was also furious with Geoff. He would not break down in front of him or Piani's men.

Piani's eyes started from his head. He backhanded Court.

Court licked his teeth to make sure they were all there and spat out blood.

Piani wiped his ring and thrust the soiled handkerchief at one of his men. "You're a nasty, grovelin', no count dog, a real son o' a bitch 'o needs to learn a bit o' respect. Take him, boys!"

For the next few minutes, Geoff held Court while the two other toughs beat him until he was almost senseless. Piani leaned against the post and cleaned his nails with his knife, whistling softly. The men finally stopped. Geoff let Court fall to the ground.

"No 'ard feelings," said Geoff. "After your last fight, I 'ad to get square. It's your own fault. By the way, me weddin' with Arabella's on for sure. Got me own business. It feels good to do an 'onest day's work. You ought to try it." He wiped his hands with Court's coat and walked away.

Court rolled on his side and vomited. The two toughs laughed, gave him a final nudge with their boots, and walked after Geoff. Court's head swam. He could still hear the band playing very faintly. The tune's words whirled nonsensically in his mind. A bicycle built for two, or two girls built a bicycle, or—

Piani squatted, bending so Court could see his face. "Listen to your friend," he said. "'E's gettin' on in this world. A store to run, a nice young woman to come 'ome to! Learn from 'is example. Reform! See, what a young man like you needs is guidance, rules—discipline." He dabbed delicately at the cut he had given Court's cheek. "Why can't you be more respectful?"

Court didn't answer. He couldn't. It began to rain.

Piani regarded him sadly, picked up the jewel box, and turned it. "You know 'o I misses, me boy?" he asked gently. "Your old mum! Sweet Sadie. Ah, 'er and me, now we 'ad some grand times after your dad.... Well, you don't want to 'ear none o' that." He tossed the box aside.

Court tried to raise himself. Piani pushed him down. He kept a vise-like grip on Court's neck, twisting it. Court's stared into the man's eyes, his heart seething with hatred.

"Now you're all quiet and tractable. I feel kindlier, like. Think I'll keep you close. Like Geoff. Police 'as been askin' questions 'bout what you boys 'as been up to. Takes up me time. I don't like it. But a good citizen does 'is duty and don't mind 'elpin' out the authorities."

"I won't fight for you no more!"

"You takes a blow and a kick pretty well, me young dog. You're ready for the ring again. Let's go 'ome. The boys are waitin', and I'm gettin' wet."

"I'm sick o' losin'! I won't do it!"

"But it makes me so 'appy." He pushed Court's face against the ground. "You ain't got no choice, no ways."

Gravel crunched under Piani's boots. He crossed the yard, whistling between his teeth. The sounds grew fainter. Court stretched out his hand for the battered jewel box, but it was out of reach. Finally, he lay still. The band stopped playing, and the rain fell harder.

CHAPTER 9
A Night at the Opera

Act I
The Seducer's Diary

In a private room of his club in Pall Mall, George Broughton-Caruthers admired his reflection as his valet dressed him for the evening. While he held out his arms so that the man could adjust his jacket and brush its shoulders, George indulged in an uncharacteristic bout of introspection. It was a mental state he actively resisted. Of late, however, when he rode in the park at twilight or sat in his armchair at the club before going out for the night, he had caught himself waxing philosophical more often than was his wont.

He had known Winifred almost from her arrival in England. How gawky she had been, bumping about the dance floor at Hereford Hall. On their first hunt, she had been too artless to hide the impression he made. He smiled at the memory.

George was pleased with what he saw in the mirror. His straw-colored hair was still thick, his tall figure trim and well-proportioned. Around his blue eyes were lines which ran in spidery creases over his high cheekbones, but his brow was relatively smooth, unmarred by excessive worry or thought. The years had been kinder to his face than his pocketbook. Recently, he had been forced to acknowledge not only the perks of being Hereford's heir but its responsibilities. He wasn't going to let it bother him. He straightened the pearl stud in his tie while his valet turned down the gas lamps. A half hour remained before his carriage would be ready. The man hovered, awaiting further orders. George dismissed the fellow and immediately forgot his existence, as he did most of those who served him until he needed them again.

A ring box lay on his dressing table, and beside it, corsages. For Amelie, there were blush-colored tea roses, not too imaginative. For Win, he had chosen more carefully: rosebuds of coral red, a white orchid, and yellow frangipani tipped in pink. The blooms' exotic fragrance filled the room. Their scent brought Win vividly to mind, as though she was beside him.

"Darling Win," he said aloud, "my, my, how we have grown up."

A vision of his long-time neighbor materialized, stretched voluptuously on the sofa. She raised her arms in a welcoming gesture that was at once feline and feminine in the extreme, purred his name, and laughed at him as she always did. Exhaling the flowers' odor, George opened his eyes. He lifted a glass of brandy and sipped. Glancing sidelong in the mirror at the debonair figure he cut in his evening clothes, he tried to imagine how she would see him tonight. Besides those incipient lines etched about his eyes, there were deep grooves on either side of his mouth; but such flaws lent a man's face character. They showed a fellow had lived.

Whether he had benefited from the lessons of experience was another matter. Charles maintained that he was a quick study in some areas but studiously ignored the implications of others: gambling and seduction versus management of one's finances, for instance. But damn, what was one's inheritance for if not a fellow's enjoyment? He had laughed off his brother's officious meddling but been extremely annoyed.

How had Charles got hold of that letter he had written to Pennington, or found out about that disastrous card game at the Boar and Hart? His brother's land manager owed enough to tide him over to next month, and he'd left the game when he realized Adams was, as usual, cheating. It hadn't seemed worth his while to call out such a bounder in such company, but he was glad Geoff Ratchet had. From which side of the family his younger sibling had inherited his puritanical thrift, the devil only knew; certainly not their father, who never missed a chance to place a bet, or their mother, who was eternally at her dressmakers. He'd write that juicy kitchen maid at Charles' who was so sweet on him. Braithwaite, wasn't it? She'd pass his message to Pennington.

No matter what happened tonight with Win, it went without saying that he would be admired and sighed over by every woman who caught sight of him. Poor little Braithwaite! Toppled as easily as a nine pin! He chuckled, remembering a delicious interlude behind Charles' kitchen shed with the dimpled scullery wench, then felt more somber. Since this time last year, he had let a debutante worth many thousands and even a marquis' daughter slip from his hands through sheer ennui.

After several disconcerting conversations with his bankers that spring, he had begun to think that if he wanted to continue his mode of living into his forties, he had better look sharp. Otherwise, he would have to retrench at a Continental spa with Mama and rent out the Hall. Tonight, he must broach negotiations with Win over more tender matters than mutual woes about property taxes and falling grain prices. Needing to sell the land had turned out to be a bit of luck.

He thought well enough of himself not to be disturbed by what "wealthy also-rans who received no serious marriage offers" might think of him for going cap-in-hand. Archer had been a bit worse for wear when he said that, so George had let it go. On the Continent, he would have challenged Archer to a duel. Not that Archer was worth his while any more than Adams. He knew how people gossiped about him and Win, but they always had. Anyway, Archer would not talk. He was too embarrassed at losing his chance. It was Win's fault. She might have had her choice of studs her first three seasons out if she had not been so damned picky.

The thought of marrying a woman for money, especially Win, was not distasteful. He was of an adventurous rather than a romantic nature. There were many roads to pleasure open to a man, and he knew most of them too well as evidenced by his shrinking assets. A wife would not be an encumbrance to a fellow who knew how to handle his private life.

George snapped open the ring box and critically observed the sapphire and diamond ring he had ordered from Kleinfeldt's. It was one of a dozen or so trifles he meant to shower on Win if she behaved herself. She had a chilly side, but there were volcanic depths beneath all that ice. Archer would never have known what to do with her. He poured more brandy and stretched out on the couch. This evening he would have to call upon all his resources. He was taking her to the opera and meant to make the night count. He took the ring out of the box and pitched it in the air. The jewels flashed and spun.

Charles accused him of carelessness, not only in money matters. For instance, this past summer when he and Mama had been in Scotland,

Charles asked him what he meant to do now that he was so low on cash. "You can't continue to throw away your life. I know why you haven't married," he said. "You mustn't let—certain problems—stop you." George had told him to mind his own business and go to the devil. He had drunk quite a lot up there for something to do besides torment Charles, play cards, and tease the delectable Braithwaite. He would not let that hypocritical prig comment on his private life. He and Charles had not spoken since, and successfully avoided one another for most of Charles' visit to the Hall a few weeks back.

George decided he was not really bothered by Charles' words. He had his own way of explaining the various chapters of his history to himself. His life story was a tale constantly written, revised, and purged of inconvenient details. It contained some exaggerations and outright lies of which he was perfectly aware; other scenes were vague and more difficult. Whenever possible he preferred to shine, at least by his own standards, in this picaresque narrative.

With Win, for instance, thus far he had behaved blamelessly, even beneficently. Unlikely as it might seem to Charles, it was not a role he wished to relinquish. In fact, it was a picture of himself he cherished. His brother's promptings aside, had the discomfiting reality of his attenuated finances not forced him to act, George doubted he would have ever proceeded thus with his neighbor. The state of flirtatious limbo in which he and Win had always floated was not tethered to earth by domestic details and their inevitable boredom. While familiar, it lacked the familiarity which bred contempt.

He put the ring back in its box and tossed it on his dressing table, along with unopened creditors' letters from London and Vienna, I.O.U.'s for gambling debts, bills from his tailor and saddlers, and worst of all, the latest querulous letter from his mother. She was at Bath, her habitation for most of the winter since his father died, and rambled on about her water treatments and sessions with a medium. There was nothing wrong with her joints, and her letters were tiresome. When he eventually wrote back, he would hint for a few pounds and touch upon the details of her spoiled, pointless life that so engrossed her.

The autumn his father died, the month he was expelled after his sole year at college and had joined the officers' cavalry division of the army, he had met Win. Though he had been too drunk to remember most of his time at school except for the sport, he had collected enough stories and spun enough fabrications to amuse her. Win's golden eyes and ringing laughter had seemed justification enough for his wasted hours. They became regular visitors at one another's homes, and met during the intervals of her finishing school holidays and his leaves. They hunted and dined together, partnered for croquet at garden parties, walked and rode with her cousins, and played duets on the piano. At the social apex of their neighborhood, they had developed a good-humored understanding that never strayed beyond the fierce public flirtation or barbed jesting that was the provender of much teatime gossip amongst the virgins and spinsters of the parish. In spite of being closer to her age, Charles had hardly existed for her, and she was amusingly oblivious to his mother's dislike.

Alarmed by his reputation but tempted by the glories of Hereford, Win's elder cousins mingled discomposure and hopefulness regarding a possible match. As she grew older, he encouraged Win to ever more immoderate behavior, yet he had also enjoyed his role of protector and confidant. No longer an ugly duckling, yet not quite a swan, Win was good company. He commiserated with her yearning for the liberty he enjoyed and answered her curiosity about his free, masculine life. Her naïve coyness inspired him. He made up adventures or confided in her almost to the point of indecency, all the while refraining from outright seduction. At that age, she would have been too easily overwhelmed, and he had liked her too much for that.

In this very comfortable fashion, they had carried on until the weeks before her debut. Quite suddenly, he had judged it prudent to withdraw his attentions and rejoined his regiment, lest he be thought ready to plight his troth. During her first season she had written often, amusingly, and candidly; but he divined that she was dismayed by the giddy social carousel and had found no real friends amongst her feminine peers. She very much wanted, was terribly impatient to grow up. *...but I cannot see marrying or raising a family with such men as I've met. Is this what Delilah means by a young woman's 'Fate'?*

His mother had also written on the subject of family in her last letter. She wanted to see a Broughton-Caruthers heir before she died. So far, Charles had produced only daughters. When, in the long Highland evenings, the nursemaid had brought down the gurgling bundles to be displayed and Charles had proudly fetched up his eldest to be kissed, George excused himself and searched out Pennington. He imagined Win dandling a child on her knee someday.

Win's long-ago letter lay with her others in his desk at home. Feelings, how funny they were. He could never quite catch hold of his. They blew about like the dried-up leaves in the park.

At the end of her school days, and before her debut, Win had gone to Bayreuth for the Festspiele with the family of a school friend. His regiment had been on the way back from Burma, and he was tempted to meet her. Instead, he stopped in Vienna. At the Weiner Hofoper, he saw Lottie for the first time. Afterward, he went backstage and invited her to supper. She refused, but told him she would be at home the next afternoon.

Win had returned to Holloways after a Grand Tour with Sir Percival full of rapacious good health and inconvenient German literature and philosophy, sheaths of Beethoven's music and Schubert's Lieder. Her waltz was much improved but still boisterous; her appetite was as robust as ever. Her cousins threw up their hands in horror as Win devoured yet another custard bun at tea and joined her lusty contralto with his tenor. Delilah bemoaned Percival's choice of school. Why not France or Switzerland? She was more forthright than ever, and she had ideas. For once, George agreed with the dreaded Delilah. No eighteen-year-old needed ideas, especially when she didn't believe a one of them.

There were many other letters from her after her debut and during his protracted stays in Vienna and Egypt. He laughed at Win's enthusiasms. Philanthropies, charities, women's suffrage even! If she was bored, he wrote back, she ought to spend more time at the dressmaker's like his mother. *Only remember,* he wrote, knowing it would exasperate her, *that blue stockings do not suit you.* He read the descriptions of her rejected suitors with even more amusement. Sometimes, he hoped he would return to England to find her safely engaged; at others, he had opened her letters dreading that very announcement.

When he rejoined his regiment, he had thrust from his mind the idea that all might be changed when he returned to England. From her debut photograph, he could see that even in her presentation gown, Win was still more of a hedge blossom than an English rose, but her childish plumpness had redistributed itself into soft shoulders and a generous bosom. He came home for the hunt. No woman wore a riding habit better, even when hers was spattered with mud. She was equally attractive in her garden smock and straw bonnet. Five minutes waltzing with Win kept a fellow's head spinning for the next half hour. Riding with her exercised his stamina and made him consider leaving off cigars. In spite of her admonishments that he read more serious books—*Faust* and *The Sufferings of Young Werther*—she had still been as sweet as Turkish delight and ready in her laughter as ever.

The years passed. He came home for the big hunts and went back to Vienna. She struggled; he sympathized. Other times, he secretly rejoiced. Arm in arm, they walked in the gardens at Holloways and Hereford Hall. They tramped the heath at Hampstead and rode in the London parks. He amused himself by alternately flirting with her in a more openly erotic fashion or drawing her into his ironical view of their neighbors. She followed his lead and was always a quick, if naïve study of character. They corresponded. She still thought the best where he suspected the worst, excepting her suitors, about whom they were in complete agreement. He grew used to thinking of her as being not exactly his, but certainly no one else's.

This new reticence on her part was the result of her recent ordeal. It had taken several visits before she acknowledged it, and he assumed that, in time, they would return to their old, playful confidence.

"Did you speak with Uncle Percival?" she asked from her bed.

George had taken her hand.

"I'm afraid you can't call me Gloriana anymore. It wouldn't be—accurate."

"Dearest Win, darling, we don't need to talk about it."

So, they had not.

He was grateful Sir Percival had waited to speak with him until both the Harley Street specialist and Dr. Frost were satisfied that she was neither with child nor syphilitic. Of course, he had obliquely considered both these possibilities and the brutalities that might have led to them, but gone no further in his musings. What mattered was that Win was alive. She was still rich. The energy and frankness which dismayed her aunts was only subdued by her present troubles. When her health and spirits returned, she would require a firm hand or she would lead a fellow on a merry chase. Once she got over her shock, her body promised hours of pleasure to the man who caught her and went to the trouble to treat her well. He would be that man. She had no idea of half her worth and he had never allowed himself to feel for her a tenth of what he might.

Yet as fetching a picture as Win presented the other afternoon, lying on her pillows and letting him hold her hand, he had not lost his head and wasn't going to lose it tonight, or ever.

There were reasons he did not want her to fully engage his heart that he could not think about for very long without their becoming insupportable. Years ago, these reasons made Win's company imperative on his visits home. If she had not been his friend, inasmuch as he allowed another into his bosom, he might have drunk himself to death or gotten shot on the least pretext.

His double life began shortly after he joined the army. In London, he would steal away from the Boar and Hart where he and his fellow officers played cards and search the dark, foul smelling alleys, half hopeful and half afraid, until a ragged girl called to him through the fog. How he had come upon her that first time as he walked alone, slightly drunk, he hardly remembered. He had been recently at Hereford for the hunt ball. He and Win had been much together. On a whim, he had gone back to town.

It was no use saying he thought the child was lost. When the girl took his hand, there had been no mistaking what she was or the meaning of her words. His mind screamed that she was too young to be on the streets, her body obviously immature and not ready for a man's, yet she was just as obviously experienced at her trade. When he hesitated, she sank against him, weeping. If she didn't earn her keep, she'd be beaten.

He offered to take her home. In his arms, she was light as a feather. Laying her head on his shoulder, she told him the way. They neared the river. A shop shuttered and closed for the night, a dim flight of stairs within, an attic room, barely furnished. Once there, she presented a small foot, a shapely ankle. Could he unlace her wet boots? As he sat, she slid onto his lap and whispered in his ear. George thrust her away, appalled by her suggestion but extremely aroused. If he didn't want to do that, then perhaps he might want to—. She raised her skirts a little, whispering; then she raised them even more. She was naked beneath. He tried not to remember the rest.

He promised himself he would not see her again, but whenever he was in town, eventually he would excuse himself from his fellows. His heart hammering, he would walk the opposite direction of the shop only to find that his feet took him there. She always seemed to be waiting nearby, her light brown hair falling in ringlets about her doll-like face, singing to herself. As soon as she saw him, her slender arms reached out, and her eyes filled with joy. He would catch her to his breast in a whirl of release and gladness, taste her kisses, and run with her up the stairs. From the slightness of her frame, the translucence of her skin, and the indescribable delicateness of her secret parts, he had known that she was much, much too young.

Her face looked so pure and sweet, and her voice was equally childlike, but her practiced caresses had been anything but, and of a nature he was unable to resist. For all his experience, he trembled at this new depravity and told no one of their meetings. He became obsessed not only with the delights of her body, but also with her. He cared for nothing else. Under the sloping roof of the vile attic room where they resorted, her bed became his paradise.

There, they clasped one another for hours. Later, walking hand in hand by the river, he sang Schubert's Lieders. The girl mimicked his songs in her high, hopeful soprano and stood on tip-toe to be kissed. He swept her up into his arms, bought her supper, and half jealous of her enjoyment of each morsel that entered her mouth, he watched as she gorged on roast beef and jam tart. He gave her presents and made promises. Each time he left, he told himself he must end it.

George listened to his heart's quick beats and remembered the madness of those hours. In battle, one must be ready to respond quickly, to move. It was crucial to find terrain over which one could traverse in speed and safety. One must also constantly plan for an orderly retreat.

His brain was arranged in a series of pigeon holes like the ones in his desk at Hereford Hall. Usually, he had the facility to open and shut these compartments wherein dwelt his memories, some of which, like those of the girl, were a hodgepodge of confusions and vagaries whose tangle could overwhelm him unless they were kept under lock and key.

Once shut, some drawers he rarely if ever peered inside again; girls from the parish, for instance, or the whores of Cairo, and various courtesans from his travels on the Continent. Depending on how much he had drunk, he might subject himself to the bittersweet pleasures of looking within others: certain memories of Win, for example. More dangerously, he might pull them open all at once. He could observe some past amours and feel next to nothing or amusement at others' folly and perhaps his own; or he flirted with regret and experienced the brief rekindling of an intense passion, as with Lottie. But no matter how consuming these erotic flights might be, les histoires de son coeur were safe, done, and clearly marked finis.

Why then, as soon as he left Kleinfeldt's with the ring had he felt, as he did now, his heart's unquiet knock against his ribs? While the jeweler showed him the stone, George had barely attended. He had pulled open his little darling's drawer and searched the mess within; but for what? These long months it had been slammed shut, its key firmly jammed into the keyhole but not turned, not locked, not yet.

All the way back to the club, he reminded himself of his objective: Win and his plans for tonight's campaign. One's lines of demarcation must be firmly drawn; one's battle plans ready. He had not been a soldier for nothing. She remained a challenge when so few women bothered to try. Autumn evenings, they had played cards by her fireside or resorted, as always, to the piano. He admired her frothy tea gown; she ignored his compliments. While she poured tea and discussed property law, he pretended to listen and uncovered her body in his mind. These assertions of her feminine and financial independence always aroused his need to wound, to conquer, and to subsequently comfort, verbally and otherwise.

All of that was at an end, for now. Sir Percival made it clear that though Win had not suffered the worst consequences that could have followed her abduction, she nevertheless suffered deeply. In her uncle's voice, George had heard deep sorrow, and his own usual composure was momentarily shaken.

"You two have seen so much of one another since last summer," the old man began hesitantly. "It was like old times. I'd begun to wonder if the two of you—if you might think about—."

Morrant had entered and announced that Win was ready to see him. On their way up to her room, George watched Sir Percival's valet with extreme distaste. Why she and the old man were so fond of him was unfathomable. Black as a Moor! There was African blood in him, he'd bet his best mare on it! The sooner Percival decamped with him to Egypt the better. They entered Win's bedchamber. Dupree hovered about too. Her eyes and ears missed nothing. George had felt a sudden, obdurate need, such as he had never experienced before, to get Win away from them all, to possess her utterly.

Finally, they were alone.

Holding her hand, he realized he preferred for her not to speak of what any woman could be forgiven for wanting to take to her grave. Neither of them had said much.

Afterward, George had ridden over the heath, hard as he could, feeling that he had irreversibly cast his lot. They had not talked of the future, but it was a presence he wished had left the room along with Morrant and Dupree. George had reined his horse. The horizon glowed through bare branches; stars and planets winked in the eastern sky. He had carried two letters into the Hampstead house. While Sir

Percival spoke to him, he briefly considered consigning both to the flames. Sitting with Win, he changed his mind. Hers lay under his latest offering of flowers.

He still carried Lottie's.

A desire to flee far away seized him like it had that first time he escaped to the Continent; but he waited. Slowly it grew less intense, fading like the light. It was an ineluctable moment, watching another day in one's life die. He was tempted to calculate how many more twilights there would be until the final one. But what did it matter? What did any of it matter? After stabling his horse, he dressed and ordered dinner at his club. Instead of eating it, he had hired a cab and told its driver to head for Southwark.

That was less than a week ago. George breathed the odor of roses and frangipani. In the shadows cast by the lowered lamp, his reflection looked haunted, haggard, and middle-aged. Amongst the bills and haphazardly discarded neckties on the dressing table lay the ring box. He picked it up. "Tonight," he said out loud.

Act II
"... you will do nicely beside him."

Clothes lay in piles on Winifred's bed and chairs. The contents of her jewelry and glove boxes were mounded in a heap on one side of the dressing table. Since mid-afternoon she had tried on one outfit after another, but finally conceded to Bettina's original suggestion, the gown of sherry-colored satin she had bought the same day as her ill-fated green dress. Their choice hung on the wardrobe door. Her mother's necklace sat on a velvet tray with the pearl and diamond earrings from George. After enduring Bettina's brushes and curling irons, she fretted while her maid fastened several jeweled, star-shaped pins to her hair, another of his gifts.

In spite her mistress' ill-humor, Bettina refused to be put out, greeting dresses and cloaks and her lady's jewels like long-lost friends. Beaming, she fastened the back of the gown. After weeks of nothing but peignoirs and bed jackets, Mademoiselle looked so much better and like she ought to, si un peu pale. She stepped back, admiring her handiwork. "Eh, enfin! C'est trop belle! "

"It's the color of mud, and much too décolleté."

"C'est magnifique!" Bettina lightly touched a powder pouf to her mistress' shoulders.

Winifred regarded her reflection. The last of her scrapes and bruises had faded. She agreed that her skin was good, her eyes and hair splendid. If only her bosom didn't make her look like a puffed-up hen! She already dreaded the owlish glint of opera glasses trained on her and George. She smoothed her bodice. Her stomach flipped. "If people spy on us, which one will be judged fairest?"

"Monsieur George est trop beau, but you will do nicely beside him."

Winifred grasped Bettina's hand, and the woman squeezed hers.

Except for a few carriage rides to the Harley Street specialist and walks on the heath with Bettina, it would be her first public outing. She missed her uncle, who had been unable to delay his departure any longer. Dr. Frost was adamant, so he and Morrant had sailed the week prior.

What would she and George talk about all night? Each time he visited, they sat quietly in her room. She admired his latest bouquet, or he talked about the weather. Her new-found knowledge about love, about men and women, made her regard him differently, more shyly. It seemed better to remain silent, unless it was to talk about matters personal to them both. But neither of them said anything of consequence.

"It was awfully nice, you going to all the hospitals, looking for me," she had told him.

"Why wouldn't I?"

"You don't have to come every day."

"Don't you want me to?"

"No, well, I mean, if you want! I do get so—. Anyway, the flowers are lovely."

"You're pale."

"George, I'm fine really. I'll be all right."

"You've never been lovelier."

Maybe they had nothing in common except their shared past.

Only that was not true. George loved the hunt and she loved to ride. That everyone thought she enjoyed hunting was her own fault. The sight of an animal cornered made her sick, but she never let on. Even without George, she joined her family riding to hounds and supported the events that brought the neighborhood together. That was why Charles had sent Percival that letter. The game warden had written Charles that he was afraid George was going to clear the land between their houses and sell its timber. He'd heard rumor of offers while he was at the Rose and Crown. Charles remembered how Winifred loved the foxes. It was entirely up to her, George replied in answer to her letter. He suggested she buy him out.

Why couldn't she simply tell George the truth? She'd never realized what a liar she was. She had lied to Bettina about Court; then to Dr. Frost and the Harley Street specialist and the men from Scotland Yard. She lied to her uncle and Morrant, the servants, and her family by letting them all think she had been ravished. And tonight, she would lie to George. It would never end. If she married him, she'd have to lie to everyone for the rest of her life.

She tried to reconcile her present feelings with past ones. Years ago, when she and George were apart, she rarely missed him. Like his company, his correspondence was a source of pleasure; but she never tore open his letters with a fluttering heart or tucked them under her pillow. The cream-colored envelopes with his bold, slanting cursive were neatly tied with green ribbon and stowed, like her cousins' letters, in their own spot in her desk. Lying in bed after her doctor's appointments, she'd reread these light-hearted epistles from the era of his torrid and much publicized affair with the opera singer and wondered if they contained a hidden message that he had been unable to share openly; or a meaning in the lines that she'd been too naïve to interpret.

She re-examined the image she'd had of him in those years. His letters only enhanced it. He'd been the sort of man whose valet made him, and his tailor was a genius. In uniform, he had no equal. Handsome in the extreme, tall and straight, perfectly proportioned and flaxen-haired, his moustache and sideburns were of a silky texture, and his languorous smile had a world-weary turn most women found irresistible. It was rumored his opera singer had nearly died of grief when George abruptly ended their affair. It was not hard to imagine why.

She had always suspected George's character, not least because he used his ability to charm indiscriminately. He could be haughty in a way that did no justice to his station, though he inspired loyalty in many of his tenants. While he was every inch the gentleman, from her girlhood she'd sensed an unquantifiable taint that emanated from him, like the fogs that seemed to come out of nowhere and settle over London's streets. Her unease couldn't be explained away as a mere reaction to his or others' stories about his conquests. What he did to other women was deplorable, but she could hardly feel guilty for other people's gullibility or stupidity. At times it was even comic. Yet a darkness surrounded George each time she re-read his letters.

A part of him was always hidden, a shadowy palimpsest beneath his facile turns of phrase. She'd never heard anyone else, not even Delilah, allude to this, but she trusted her instincts. His high cheekbones and erect carriage gave him an air of nobility, slightly tarnished by the rumors of his excessive hedonism; and the beauty of his bright blue eyes was only marred by their slightly bored expression. Amongst his peers, his lips were often ready to curl into a sneer, usually before his derision's recipient had turned away. None of this got to the heart of what she dreaded.

In the years before George's return the previous spring, he was consumed by his army career, his travels, and his amours. During that time, they had seen each other not much above half a dozen times, and always at Christmas fetes or house parties, dinners and hunts balls, as in the old days. Had she felt a little let down when their talk never rose above the light banter of her early youth? Yes and no. As two of the most eligible catches in their county, there was still the tacit understanding between them that, while it was all very tiresome to know that people still tried to match the two of them after all these years, they would publicly continue to play the game. Neither had minded when they were younger because nothing had been at stake, especially their hearts.

The letter under his latest bouquet had been a surprise. Not only was it an invitation to the opera, to include Bert and Amelie, it contained the suggestion—not at all veiled, that he hoped the evening would be a memorable one. *Let us not forget how deep the currents of our friendship run, what we have shared in the past, and what we could share in the future. These weeks have taught me what is precious and enriches my life beyond measure.*

Reading the letter, she almost forgot his behavior at the ball, how he'd spoken so crassly to her exasperated dance partner. She heard their voices again, the low laughter, George's insinuations about her, about them. She would not chance such a betrayal again. She could not endure it, not when she needed his friendship more than ever. For all his fine words, she didn't trust him. She wouldn't be one of his little fools, one of his stories!

Bettina protested as she tore the star-shaped pins from her hair. Winifred threw George's earrings onto the table. "I'm not going!"

Moments later, Bettina fastened the necklace's clasp. "Better, maintenant? We are calmer, n'est-ce pas?"

Winifred nodded, hand to her throat. Her mother's necklace was heavy. From its chased braid of gold depended yellow gems, each large as a man's thumbnail. Clusters of smaller topazes were set amidst fat pearls, and it was finished by an enormous, pumpkin-colored diamond. When Mr. Buckner placed its box in her hands, her wildest imaginings couldn't have conjured the next few hours, the extremes of fear and joy such as she'd never know again. Once, the necklace made her think of her parents. Tonight, it made her think of Court.

If Geoff had found it first, she'd be dead, maybe Court as well. When he held the gems before the firelight, she'd pretended sleep, like she did when Percival or her cousins kept vigil at her bedside. Court had taken nothing she didn't give, and he'd saved her from Geoff, no doubt at great risk. In spite of that, his final words informed her that she was a spoiled, rich girl who enjoyed a ragged holiday when it suited her, that she was a selfish creature to whom objects such as diamond necklaces were mere toys that could be overlooked when she was distracted by other trifles, such as him. That she had her place and he had his. When Court and Geoff met again—if they hadn't already—it would be violent. If she ever found Court this side of the grave, it would be a miracle, but what then?

"Monsieur George will not be able to resist." Bettina patted Winifred's hair into place.

"He'll be as charming as the Cheshire Cat if he thinks I'll sign a check."

"You must try to be encouraging! You must be ready for romance."

"I must be ready for George," sighed Winifred, "and one never is!"

Pulling aside the curtain, she searched the snowy street for his carriage. Nervously, she slapped a pair of long gloves against her palm until Bettina put them on her. It was unfair that George be kept in the dark. To think, like everyone else, that she'd been raped. But could she rely on his broad-mindedness to the point that she could admit she'd taken a lover, if only for a night?

In regard to George's relaxed relations with the fair sex, when it concerned his future wife, whoever she turned out to be, Winifred was not sure how far George's sang-froid would take him if he knew the truth. She could easily imagine him challenging a gentleman like himself to a duel, but a groom? A man so desperately in need of money might happily forego deflowering his bride if only he could plunder her coffers, but she hoped George had more pride.

On the eve of her birthday, he'd found the house in an uproar over her disappearance. Every day thereafter, he returned whether she'd see him or not. Bettina would bring his lavish bouquets and often a gift of equally lavish jewelry. Bettina arranged each morning's floral offerings in a crystal vase. Today's were orange chrysanthemums, coral and ivory roses, and creamy yellow carnations. They stood on a table before the window where Winifred watched for his carriage.

"Ces sommes très charmantes. Regardez-les, Mademoiselle," Bettina sighed. "And the earrings, so beautiful! He is getting thin, like you! He sincerely cares, I am sure."

"He is presumptuous, I am sure," Winifred had rejoined, putting down the newspaper and settling more comfortably onto her pillows. The long-stemmed bouquet was the most enormous and extravagant one yet. In spite of herself, she had admired it, and the earrings were lovely. "I don't have the slightest interest in George. As far as I am concerned, he is a piece of land; and as far as he is concerned, I am a bank account." Bettina's gave her a look of disbelief and disapproval, so she'd raised the paper again and made a show of reading the stock figures.

Bettina had huffed. "Mademoiselle, you have become hard-hearted. Monsieur George knows what you need after your—." She waved her hand in the air, pulling a sour face. "He is trying to be good for once. Let him be, for heaven's sake!"

"I doubt it. We'll find out tonight, won't we?"

Bettina had left the room spouting Gallic proverbs, which Winifred roughly translated along a theme of "waste-not; want not." She set aside her newspaper and slid out of bed. She had stroked the wax-like roses, gently parting their moist, ivory petals and inhaled. She gathered the flowers to her breast and closed her eyes, thinking of Court's lips, of where and how they had lingered, kissing her flesh in places she'd never dared imagine a man's lips pressed. She had abandoned all shame and returned his caresses. The dark waves they had ridden together beat beneath the skin he had touched.

She pressed her hot forehead to the windowpane, watching the light snowfall. An occasional pedestrian passed through the pool of lamplight. She waited for the next figure, dreaming it would be Court and not George's carriage that would stop before her door.

What if George did ask her tonight? What would she say? If Court had walked into her room, she would've flown with him to the meanest hovel or to the end of the earth.

Her gaze traveled over bare branches and up to the rooftops which enclosed the square. London was so large. Court was in it somewhere, on a street driving a cab or raising his fists in a ring, doing whatever it was he had to do to stay alive. Every day she scanned the papers, hoping for details in the Selway Adams case or more information about the explosion, but there was nothing.

Court! Court! Court! She traced her finger along the pane.

Her family, the servants, they all thought she lay in bed day after day to recover from her shocks. It wasn't that at all. It was because when she was alone, her eyes closed and the curtains drawn, she could fly back to Court's room, that night, and him. She had to stop dreaming, to accept that he had let her go. Of Court, of what they had done, she must force herself not to think, though she often found herself staring blankly into space and realizing too late that she was doing just that, like now.

He was "gone for good and all" as he would've said, and George was on his way. Winifred breathed on the glass. The letters she had written appeared: C-O-U-R-T. She rubbed them out.

Act III
Doctors and Detectives

Bettina waited in the parlor for Monsieur George. Miss Amelie and young Mr. Barron would arrive presently. The footman set out sherry and glasses then stoked the fire. While he worked, Bettina read her diary. Over a month had passed since her lady's return.

In a cipher of her own devising, she kept track of her lady's social calendar and made notes. In the past this also included seasonal events, family holidays, dressmakers' fittings, and her menses. Until she went missing, Mademoiselle's were always regular as clockwork. More recently, the diary recorded visits from Dr. Frost and those to the Harley Street specialist, their instructions, and the state of her lady's health.

The day Mistress was brought home by the police, after his first examination, Dr. Frost had stood over the washstand in her lady's bedroom, scrubbing his hands. He packed his microscope in its box, his tools in his bag. Earlier, while he had gently examined Winifred's various bruises, his look was impenetrable. While Mademoiselle lay on her back, her eyes squeezed shut and clasping Bettina's hands, he took samples, smeared them on glass slides, and set them carefully on a tray.

Bettina had tried to appear calm as she helped her lady rearrange her nightgown. Because of her last mistress' fate, she had many nightmares. In comparison, pregnancy was manageable. Only pray the child would not be infected or deformed! Bien sur, if her lady wished it, she knew of certain herbal compounds. Bettina was religious, but not superstitious and had no fears for her soul. In these matters, she was practical and trusted no one but herself. Had she ever met a priest who hired himself out as a nanny? Non! She liked Dr. Frost, but did not think he would break the law. Even a well-performed procedure could result in infection or death. Her way was better.

She had shown Dr. Frost the underclothes, the jewelry, and the purse. She told him what Winifred said about the man's precautionary method against pregnancy. One man, was she certain? Oui! Bettina affirmed.

The doctor was an old gentleman who had worked in fine houses most of his career and had seen enough of people both high and low not to be shocked. Yet he was as baffled as Bettina by the untouched purse with its candied almonds, the necklace, and the wilted violets. How her lady had cried when she tried to throw those away!

While Winifred went to the water closet, he had instructed Bettina in great detail about her duties. She must check for discharge, rashes, sores, and fever; she must note Miss de la Coeur's diet, sleep, and state of mind. If the young woman was with child, he knew a house in the country, very discreet, where she might wait out her confinement. "Of course, she could miscarry. You'll tell her exactly what not to do in order to prevent this." He looked at her significantly.

Or, if Winifred chose to go with Sir Percival to Egypt, he would write to a doctor he knew in Alexandria and another in Cairo. Mrs. Burns and her husband were ready to host her mistress' accouchement if it came to that, Bettina answered. "Madame Burns said they would gladly raise the child, ill or not. They have five already!"

For the first time, the doctor seemed almost moved. His voice remained, as usual, gruff and quiet. "What an energetic couple they must be."

The rest of that day had been terrible. Two policemen remained at the house. Sir Percival declared to the detective that his niece would be unable to answer any questions until after she had rested. He didn't care how long the man had to wait—weeks! Forever! While Morrant quelled the downstairs staff and issued orders about how to address the police or what would happen if they dared so much as blink at a reporter, the detective had waited in the parlor.

Before he went downstairs, Dr. Frost spoke to Winifred about her examination and what he would say to the police. Bettina excused herself, but Winifred asked her to stay. Whoever the man was, whatever the circumstances of his congress with her lady, Bettina wanted retribution, preferably a sound thrashing. But she dreaded the police and the newspapers.

"They're bound to ask me if you've been interfered with," the doctor said. Given the stains he had seen on her underclothes and what he had seen of her, "you were."

Winifred stood at the fireplace. She picked up a small jade box George had given her and set it down. "Is this how the police will talk to me?" Her voice had been calm, but Bettina saw she struggled to hide both her fears and her temper.

Dr. Frost knit his brow. "I speak as your doctor and an old family friend, if I may presume. It seems yesterday Sir Percival introduced us. You were such a self-possessed little girl."

"That was grief, not poise. What about now?"

"Only you know that. You're grown up. I don't doubt you've told Miss Dupree and me the truth, but not all. You've a variety of bruises and some very singular marks, not sores exactly, that were made by—," he hesitated, "a human mouth. But you've denied outright rape. I'm as intrigued as your maid. You're deep. I like you for it. I only hope it will turn out well."

"I don't know what you mean."

"In light of your misadventure, you are very cool."

"Why is it men don't have misadventures? For you it's a matter of course. If I won't say what happened, perhaps I'm too shocked or tired. What would you or any man know of what it's like to be carried off against your will and so frightened you were willing to—? Wasn't I supposed to be out of my wits, the weaker sex? Should I be now? Shall I swoon, the outraged ingénue?"

Dr. Frost fixed his eyes on hers, like an old hawk about to swoop down on its prey. "I wouldn't risk such a performance with the men downstairs. That policeman who brought you home has bitten off a chunk of the world. You've only had a bite." He held out the candied almonds. Winifred averted her face. "You do remember, don't you?"

"The detective, what will he ask me?"

"That depends on what I tell them. Ah, now you're shaking." He snapped shut his bag. "As to the rest, listen to Dupree. You're extremely lucky to have her. Let her look after you."

"What should I do?"

"You could tell the truth."

Winifred covered her face with her hands.

The doctor spoke more gently. "I'll not insult your intelligence by talking to you as though you're a child. You show very definite signs of having been used rather roughly by a man or men. However, you were also treated with some care as evidenced by a lack of bruising or abrasions where I would most expect to find them after a sexual assault, and from what Dupree found on your undergarments. Whether those stains belong to one man or more, I can't say."

"The police won't ask me about any of that, will they?" she asked, coloring.

"They might ask me. I'll hold them off as long as I can. You're a grown woman with a mind of her own. I don't know what you'll choose to tell them. I'd say as little as possible. To them, you are merely a piece in a puzzle they need to solve quickly. They're concerned with the interests of a much larger institution than you or the other insignificant young person involved."

"Who?" Winifred's face paled.

"Adams, Selway Adams," the doctor said. "What they'll probably ask is whether this man, or men," he glanced at the pile of underclothes, "was part of what happened at the bank or witness to it. Or did this person or persons prey upon you afterward as you made your way home? The first is all the police really want to know. But you may be compelled to give evidence at some point. If you wish to call for an investigation or press charges against whoever is responsible for your physical injuries, that's your affair."

"It would cause a scandal. Poor Uncle Percival!"

"He'll soon be in Egypt. I'd go with him if I were you—if they'll let you. Whatever happened, it's an ordeal you must put behind you." The doctor looked unhappy for the first time and shook his head. "Assault, rape, seduction, loss of virginity by force or sheer fecklessness. It does happen to women of your class. You'd be surprised how often and at whose hands."

As though to herself, Winifred whispered, "What will I do about George?"

"Rest assured that if he really wants to marry, he won't let this come between you."

"Money covers many sins, Doctor, the lack of chastity, or a pretty face."

"Those are melancholy thoughts, my girl. Don't give in to them." Winifred thrust out her hand, and the doctor took it. "I can only envy the energy of youth and the man who claims you."

At Winifred's insistence, Bettina was present while Detective Owens from Scotland Yard and a policeman came upstairs and took her statement. Mademoiselle lay against the pillows and maintained that she had lost consciousness after the explosion. The detective cleared his throat. Somewhat abashed, the policeman with him read from his notes. Miss de la Coeur had been positively identified by several of the bank's staff as having been forcibly taken at gunpoint from the bank by a dark-haired man. Her hat had been retrieved from the rubble in Mr. Buckner's office, and the torn hem of her skirt had been recovered in the alley behind the kitchen entrance.

Winifred stared at the fire.

A cab was seen behind the bank, the policeman prompted, and its driver. Could she describe either man, the fellow in the bank, or the one in the alley?

The gas lines blew. She lost consciousness, Miss de la Coeur had repeated stolidly.

"You might be called as a witness for the prosecution," Detective Owens said drily. "Mr. Buckner has confirmed that the other victim was with you in his office. You met him, Mr. Selway Adams. It'll be a mess if he dies."

Winifred raised her eyes to the man's. He stared at her, unblinking.

"Oh yes, Miss!" the policeman added. "Bloke's in hospital in critical shape, terribly concussed. Horribly beaten, he was. Stabbed as well, almost lost a kidney. He could as easily die of sepsis or pneumonia as from his injuries. He's already named his attackers: Geoffrey Ratchet and Hezekiah Boors."

As he said the men's names, Winifred's eyes glazed over.

Detective Owens continued to watch her closely as he spoke. "Frequenters of the Boar and Hart. Common card sharp and a former soldier. Boors has a record, minor offenses, and isn't violent. Ratchet's a different story, a heavy for an Italian gang. Don't you worry Miss, we'll catch them. Another bank clerk identified one of their confederates. We brought him in this afternoon."

Winifred sat forward. "Which one, who is he?"

"Seamus Todd," the man said.

Winifred collapsed onto her pillows. "I only hope poor Mr. Adams doesn't die."

The policeman spoke up, brightly. "Like the governor says, we'll bring 'em all down. Rats in a barrel. Adams is top brass, son of an earl, so it'll be a proper inquiry. It won't end 'til we get to the bottom of it, not 'til we've got every man jack of them!"

"We've got another man on it at our Southwark branch. Miss Dupree, your mistress looks unwell." Detective Owens rose. "Sorry to trouble you, Miss. Routine, you understand."

⚬⚬

Mr. Broughton-Caruthers' hired brougham rolled to a stop before the house. It was not as fine as the old carriage he kept at Hereford Hall, but Monsieur always had a smart vehicle at his disposal in town. Right behind it a cab held Miss Amelie and Mr. Bert, come from his mother's. Winifred's menses had returned two days ago. A little late, peut être, but never had two women wept with such joy at the sight of so much blood! Bettina put away her diary, exultant. The worst was behind them.

Monsieur George climbed the front steps, followed by the young people. They clung together, shivering with cold and excitement. Monsieur glanced up through the falling snow at her lady's lighted window. Once inside, he thrust his hat and coat at the footman.

Bettina took the box of gorgeous hot-house blossoms. The scent of frangipani smote her, and she shuddered. Indian evenings! She restrained the urge to cross herself. Amelie danced across the foyer, eager for her corsage, and Mr. Barron greeted her in his kind way.

Monsieur turned to the footman but did not look at him. "Tell Miss de la Coeur I'm here," he said dismissively. "She knows I don't like to be kept waiting."

Act IV
"La ci darem la mano"

George and Winifred sat side by side in his box at Covent Garden with Amelie and Bert seated in front of them. He paid no attention to the actors or the young couple's excitement, thoroughly absorbed by what he would say to Win later, once they were finally alone. If he were to throw himself at her feet then and there, no one would question his motives. Tonight, she was a fit prize for the proudest, most vainglorious of her former suitors. She had risen from the flames.

From head to foot, Win was every inch the goddess, all polished marble and burnished bronze, aglow in silk, a dazzling milky white from her neck to her breasts. She was as distant and regal as ever, or suddenly girlish when she turned to her cousins with an observation about the performance or a person in the audience whom she recognized. The simplicity of her dress and hair were perfection, a testament to Dupree's genius. And she wore his presents. Good girl!

Win's apparel seemed designed to enhance her matchless eyes and the much richer jewels at her throat. Around it rested a necklace the likes of which he had not seen outside Burma. Part of a splendid bridal set, probably. Moghul gold, delicate yellow gems, fat pearls; the heavy, faceted pendant glowed bright orange, like a coal about to drop between the dark cleft of her breasts.

Amelie turned to question him about the libretto. "What does Don Giovanni mean? 'La ci darem del mano. La mi dirai la si.' Then Zerlina says, 'Vorrei et non vorrei. Mi tremo un poco il cor. Felice, e ver, sarei, ma puo buriami ancor.'"

Teasing chit, George thought. She knows right well what it says. What in heaven does stupid Bert do with such a little flirt? Probably nothing, like the good boy he is. Those bright eyes, flitting between him and Win every few minutes. He'd teach the little vixen a lesson. "Oh, he only wants to take her for a walk and show her—something of his." He smiled ferociously at the girl.

Amelie colored and concentrated on her program.

"It means he's a bad man!" Winifred rapped George's arm with her fan. "Like George!"

"Only because the writer made him the villain of the piece," Bert said.

"No, because he chooses to be wicked," Winifred argued, glancing at George.

"He can't be that bad, can he?" Amelie fidgeted with her fan, but she smiled.

"You never think anyone can be wicked!" Bert said.

"You're the one thinks everybody's innocent until proven guilty!" she shot back.

"That's only fair play!" Winifred said.

"No, it's the law!" Amelie said, with mock severity. "You'd better uphold it, Bert Barron!"

"I know what he'd like to hold up to her!" George suggested under his breath.

"What did you say?" Winifred asked sharply.

"Stop it, Bert!" Amelie laughed, pushing his hand away. "Here! Hold my fan!"

They bent over her program, shaking with secret laughter, and clasped hands.

Winifred watched them, smiling indulgently, and George watched her.

Inviting Win's younger cousins had been an inspired choice. It seemed to please her as much as anything he could have done. His flowers had been a triumph as well. As Amelie's fiancé, Bert was allowed the intimacy of pinning the corsage to her lace shawl. His hands shook so badly, anyone would have thought he was about to make love to her right there in the foyer. Amelie had simpered, obviously pleased at his discomfiture. With a wink at the girl, George had slipped Win's flowers over her wrist.

While the four of them rode in his carriage to the opera house, George considered the other couple's delight at the prospect of an evening together. *Don Giovanni!* Were there ever two such obvious virgins? What sport his old barracks mates would have made of Bert. He was a pretty fellow, his features a dark, masculine version of the lovely girl who sat beside him. No more than a puppy, his passion for his cousin was surely overgrown puppy love. What of the girl? Amelie had the porcelain fairness of many blondes, and still carried baby fat in her pink cheeks; but she only played at being shy. In her alert glances at him and Win, George detected some of her cousin's spark and more than a hint of her mother's perspicacity. What a shock George could have given that sly baby, left alone with her for a quarter hour. Amelie thrust out her fan and withdrew it quickly whenever Bert tried to take it.

Oh yes, George knew lots of games to play with the likes of her. Bert would have his work cut out, keeping up with his sweetheart's demands. Unless the fellow pleased her, he'd find himself yoked to another Delilah when his Amelie hit middle age.

It was another matter entirely to bring such a fine, proud creature as Win to heel. She was no tease, in spite of her tea gown performance. Here was a real woman, a charming enigma, a tangle of pleasing contradictions. George recalled the fantasy that had so inflamed him earlier. Win on his sofa, stretching like a tigress. The picture changed into a vision of ripped lace and linen, of tormented and bared female flesh. It was also very arousing.

For what felt like the hundredth time that evening, he turned his gaze on her necklace and tried to estimate the worth of its various components. He had always known that Arthur de la Coeur left Win a packet, but these jewels were worthy of a Moghul queen. The fire of the largest pendant stone was hypnotic. He counted the pearls, weighed the gold, and wondered how many carats the yellow diamonds were. The money even one of those would raise could keep a fellow going for ages out East.

He'd like to shove the necklace in Lottie's face. The singer had made his career, ensured his reputation abroad, and opened doors to him during his travels, but she'd also thrown him over. In spite of her relationship to the Bavarian prince, they had not bothered to hide their affair. It was a point of regimental pride that he was her preferred lover. What days and nights those had been! At the hunt, in salons, and on dance floors, how he had preened and strutted; his boastfulness knew no bounds; and in bed, she had let him rule her like a pasha. He had spent her money like water, and she had laughed at his antics. What was a prince but a bound and collared creature that could make no decisions on his own? What was a crown if a man must wait for the imperial mandate to stock his bedchamber? It was beyond contempt. He had been on top of the world, rollicking, crowing to high heaven at his luck.

Then without warning, Lottie brought him crashing to earth. Her letter came the same day as the one Win wrote about her frustrations that she would never find the appropriate mate with whom to start a family. Lottie's prince had finally taken a wife; she too was engaged. A match arranged years earlier; her intended was a banker, a middle-aged Pole of irreproachable reputation. So, she would rather be a Hausfrau than a celebrated soprano? She would give up her brilliant career and him? Such a lack of imagination! He had never suspected it of her. His debts had forced her hand, he wrote. There could be no other reason.

It is not only the money, her next letter explained. Though George would always be her grand amour, it was not to be. *My fiancé's family name must live on. I must have sons. They must have security. What was it you once told me about yourself? You are not "a safe bet." After so many careless months, I know what that means.*

George tore her letter to shreds and took his gun to her apartment with the intention of blowing out her brains, then his. At the spectacle of his desperation, she begged him to forgive her. He would not, ever! A violent, passionate scene followed. At dawn, he left her. The story went around that the day before her wedding, a doctor was called to pump her stomach. George heard the tale and rejoiced. Lottie knew her mistake. Let her always regret throwing him over every time she let her Polish banker into her bed! Sons! She would turn into a fat Frau with a dozen brats.

Poor Lottie! He did not want her anymore, but missed her after his fashion. He missed his life abroad; or maybe he missed—who knew? He could never name it. He blinked at the gem's elusive fire. Old Percival was a screw but had the right idea. Keep traveling, keep moving. George dreamed of ranging farther east to the Himalayas, Japan, the Pacific islands; even to California with its gold, or Mexico. There were so many places a fellow could lose himself.

Winifred felt George's gaze and tried to concentrate on the music. As always, he was sizing her up, his eyes wandering up and down her body. He was always sure to make some remark about her frock or hair, usually provoking, sometimes complimentary, generally amusing. No matter how hard she tried to play it off like a woman of the world, the words made her uncomfortable. Make him wish to touch, Bettina would say. Then make his hand burn if he tries! Earlier that evening, she had almost shrunk before his frank stare, and it was her cheeks that burned. As he put on her corsage, she'd smelled brandy. "You're drunk!" she had hissed.

"Not yet." He rolled his eyes at Bert and Amelie. "But I'll try!"

In the carriage, George had talked of the evening's coming pleasures and praised Amelie until she was the color of her rosebuds. He offered Bert use of his new shotguns. There was to be a shooting party. George had invited some fellows from the City he wanted Bert to meet. There was also a particular horse that belonged to one of his neighbors that Bert ought to consider. Like Amelie, Bert had been flustered, not having funds to purchase mounts or much else, but apparently flattered to be spoken to as though he did. Winifred gave George a reproachful look but took note of the horse's name. Bert's mount Puck was a good-tempered but woefully old beast they had all ridden as children that was stabled at Holloways.

So far, in spite of the brandy, George had behaved beautifully—for him. Yet that roving stare, which he turned from her to the other boxes' inhabitants, was worrisome. George glowered when he was in an ill mood. There was no other word for it. Other telltale signs of boredom reared their heads. That vague sneer, his lightly drumming fingers. At longish dinners with his mother or teas with tedious cousins and loquacious vicars, she'd seen George turn venomous with those who weren't quick-witted or able to keep up with him. Regardless of age or rank, he had a talent for finding people's sore spots and picking at them. He'd practiced on Charles for years. George bored was George vicious. Yet how readily people forgave him, especially Charles. It was like Saint Sebastian apologizing for not offering his tormentors enough of a target.

For the rest of the act, George's expression settled into a vacant moroseness. The singers fluttered to and fro. He yawned volubly. Then Bert and Amelie caught his attention as they passed her opera glasses back and forth. George's gaze focused on Bert as he straightened Amelie's shawl over her shoulders. "Touching," he mouthed, his lips twitching with suppressed laughter.

Winifred would not let him taunt Bert in front of Amelie. Her fingers wandered nervously over her necklace as she searched for a way to divert him. "George, now I'm having as much trouble as Amelie. I've lost my place in my program. Translate for me."

George took Winifred's program but did not look at it. "We're in Act II. *Don Giovanni.*"

Winifred snatched it back. "You're going to be beastly, aren't you?"

"Beyond redemption! Poor Bert, he ought to watch our hero at work and learn, but he can't take his eyes off Amelie. She has him wrapped around her finger."

"I believe the sentiment is mutual. You let Bert alone!"

"Pity his sufferings. How does a man talk to a woman whom he has known for years but finds he knows not at all, Miss de la Coeur?"

"If he's only interested in himself, Mr. Broughton-Caruthers, he'll never learn a thing. The woman's hardly to blame! I disagree with you about *Don Giovanni.* Your hero is a fool. In my play, the hero would be direct but not brazen and tell the truth about his feelings—if he had any—and see what the lady says."

"Boring, prosaic! You'd close after the first night!"

"Well, he could ask her about her tastes in music and poetry, or what she wants for her next birthday, or about her favorite horse, or her best-loved novel...."

"Cross examination? Much too clumsy!"

"Then he might be kind, like Bert. He'd have her in the palm of his hand."

"You'd like that?"

Winifred heard the sudden change in George's tone.

They both stared at the stage.

"Win, the other afternoon, we were getting on so well, but tonight you've been cold as ice."

"George! I'm like I always am with you. I was irritated about the brandy earlier."

"I thought we understood one another. Why do you toy with me?"

"You're a fine one to talk!"

"You don't take me seriously."

"You're always playing."

"Am I playing now?"

Winifred was not sure.

"After these past weeks, all my efforts! I thought you'd see I can be counted on. But never mind!"

Winifred was stung. "I thought you only counted on me buying your twenty acres."

"That's not fair."

"It's the truth! George, when have I ever toyed with you?"

"Always, I think, or I might have spoken seriously to you years ago!"

Winifred was unprepared for the vehemence of his exclamation. George's eyes were thoughtful, almost melancholy. She felt confused. Her friend had only grown better looking with the years; he was as dangerous and amusing as ever. With regret, she admitted that she'd always liked those qualities in him very much, maybe too much. Only now she understood what they led to, and he knew she did.

She was surprised by a flush of warmth, of passionate arousal. In an instant, his hand wrapped about hers. He flashed the smile she knew so well, his eyes glittering. Already, she regretted her lapse. "George! No wonder the village belles weep as you go by. You are heartless!" She tried to pull her hand away, but he held it fast.

"So are you. That's why we'd be so good together."

"Everything you say is a lie." She faced the stage and tried to wrest her hand free. It was beginning to hurt. "At least that's certain. Let me enjoy the music."

"I'll not be kept waiting forever."

"We've kept everyone in suspense so long. What would the neighborhood talk about?"

"They'll never stop talking about us, Win. They'll always say I wanted you for your money and wonder why you'd have me when you know what a bounder I am. But you will have me." He drew her gloved hand to his lips.

So, he'd finally said it, sort of. Winifred's breath came quickly as his fingers probed the orchid petals of her corsage. He brushed them ever so lightly back and forth before he pushed the flowers further up her arm. Slowly, he unfastened the buttons along her gloved wrist and inserted his index finger into the opening. Her pulse leapt beneath his touch as he finished with the buttons and pulled the glove from her hand. His were beautiful, with manicured fingertips as fine as the pink petals of Amelie's roses. Their faces drew close together, and she could smell the bitter, though not unpleasant scents of tobacco and alcohol.

With a sudden motion, he bowed over her wrist and kissed it. The tip of his tongue flicked against her bared skin, once, twice. A little cry of alarm but also delight escaped her. In the music's crescendo, Bert and Amelie seemed not to notice. George slid his arm about her waist and tipped her chin. She struggled, dismayed by the tightness of his hold. "George, don't. Not here."

"Ah?" he breathed. "Then where, when?"

His hard, blue gaze traveled slowly over her breasts and lingered on the necklace. The angle at which he held her face made it hard to swallow. "I don't know. Soon, maybe."

"I'm getting very impatient with all this waiting and playacting, mia cara!"

She gave him a shove. "Acting is all you ever do! It's your creditors who are impatient!"

George threw back his head, laughing so loudly that several spectators in the boxes nearby turned their opera glasses on them with censorious frowns. Amelie and Bert, who sat dreamily with their heads together, jumped apart and looked behind them.

Winifred pressed back against her seat. Her blood tingled bewitchingly, and it frightened her. Was she so changeable, so easily won? Court was a dream. Even if he wasn't, she couldn't have him. He had told her goodbye because he had his pride, whereas she apparently had none.

A small leather box landed in her lap. With trembling hands, she opened it. Inside was a large sapphire and diamond ring. The heat in her cheeks was replaced by a sudden coldness.

George put the ring onto her finger, laughing until there were tears in his eyes. His voice rang over the music. He'd never appeared more godlike. He kissed her, this time on the mouth.

Bert and Amelie had twisted around completely. The people in the next box learned over to get a better view. The actors looked up, and the conductor glanced over his shoulder.

"Oh, Win, the look on your face! I could fall in love with you, only don't make me! It would be the end of old George, and then who would you make miserable besides yourself?"

CHAPTER 10
Hobson's Choice

After Piani's thugs beat him behind the outbuilding at the race course, a very lean time of it opened up for Court. He had known lean times before and hard times, but these were definitely the leanest and the hardest. Boxing matches were one of Piani's many entrepreneurial ventures, amongst which dog races and cock fights also figured prominently. His gyms were ad hoc, informal spaces, such as the storeroom of the empty shop where Court worked out. The venues for the fights were set up in a similar fashion. Piani's toughs handled the door and kept watch, ready to shut down the proceedings at the first whiff of the law. He fixed the outcome, set the odds, paid off the bookies, and raked in the cash.

Some fighters benefitted but knew when it was time to get out of town. This was not an option for Court. Piani took every penny he earned. His debt was subject to a varying rate of interest which seemed to rise and fall according to his boss' irascibility or short-lived benevolence. While Court had rarely had two coins to rub together in his life, this new twist on his impoverishment worked him down in a way that being poor never had before.

He was fed enough to get him back on his feet and in training but no more. Mornings were spent conditioning and reviewing techniques. Nights were passed lying in the back of a stable wishing he was dead. He'd hoped he'd never have to fight again, not like this. In desperation he walked out one night and was halfway across Blackfriars Bridge when he was picked up by Piani's footpads and hustled into a pub. When he woke up, he was back in the stable. He had a vague recollection of having had his jaws forced open and whiskey poured down his throat. He rolled over and was sick. Davis, his trainer sat on an overturned feed bucket. The man tossed him a rag and told him he was a fool. Court did not disagree.

The companionship of horses continued to be preferable to that of men, though on the coldest nights, he resorted to the office where Davis and Zeke, his sparring partner, snored next to the stove.

His blistered knuckles slowly calloused and his striking improved. There was nothing else to do but practice, shovel shit, sleep, and practice hitting some more. Bread and boiled potatoes appeared at intervals. "Lean and hard, that's what we want," Piani leered appreciatively, inspecting Court's muscles. Court thought that it was not beyond the man to starve him slowly for sheer amusement. The man liked to stick around while his henchmen beat his debtors. Afterward he would flip over the unconscious bodies with his boot tip, his face lit with a connoisseur's delight.

One day, Piani had showed up with a lady friend, and she brought along another woman. They participated in Piani's inspection of Court's muscles. When his boss and escort turned away, the other whore batted her eyes at Court's and ran her finger down his abdomen. "Won't they let you cut your hair, Sampson?"

Like food and shelter, Piani would add to his long list of debts any other comforts Court chose to avail himself of. He had withdrawn from the soft, full bosom pressed against his arm and tried not to return the woman's smoldering glance, but she felt good. There was a lot of her to hold, and an abundance of blonde hair curled over her shoulders. But her eyes were completely wrong. It was all completely wrong.

"Our prize stud is conserving his energies, aren't you, boy?" Piani chuckled; the women laughed too. Giving Court a final caress, the blonde flounced away and took a seat by her host.

Court was only too relieved to turn his back on the group. He and Zeke began to spar.

As Piani said, he seemed to have a natural ability for taking a blow but had yet to give one with any gusto. His heart was not in it. It wasn't in anything. Once, the ring had provided an outlet for his frustrations and often his rage. Fighting offered hope, even when it only lasted until the end of a round. Court had learned, if not how to escape Mick Furor's fists, at least how to endure them for Sadie's sake. He could credit his father with an ability to withstand pain but little else. During practice matches with Zeke, Court had yet to knock down his partner, but that morning he made a show of trying to for Piani and his women. Though he might have to go down on the night, he would let them all know that he could give as good as he got. In a burst of fury, he hailed blows on Zeke's gloves. The man retreated, muttering in surprise, and spat. Court hopped back, twitching and snorting.

Piani chewed his cigar and grinned at the blonde. "I'll bring you along more often, puss!"

While Court pummeled the bag and the women cheered, he promised himself that someday it would be Piani's face. He would bring him down. Down! DOWN!

"Last minute of the sixth," Piani whispered on his way out. "You knows what to do."

The first fight was a nightmare. Waiting to square off with a big Irishman, he'd felt like one of the cats Geoff used to tie together by their tails. Davis clanged the first bell. The referee waved them in. The bawling crowd, the stale odors of cigar smoke and beery piss, of cheap feminine scent and sweating bodies, the red and drunken faces of the spectators, and the taste of his own blood, all swirled together. He must keep on his feet under stinging pain until Geoff's signal. Then he would hesitate, lower his gloves an inch, and take a blow to his head or an uppercut to his jaw. His knees would buckle, by his own will or involuntarily. He tried not to think that far ahead and focused on the moment.

Puffing on a cigar and swaggering, Geoff worked the crowd. It mostly consisted of Piani's thugs, the very lowest class of whores amongst whom Court recognized his golden-haired siren, and hard-core gamblers, some of them obviously well-off slummers. This kind of evening was the preferred entertainment of louses such as Selway Adams and the worst swells that showed up at the Boar and Hart. He recognized one such at the bar, obviously making a night of it. Old Swank was an army friend Hez had brought around many times until they fell out over Fanny. Court swung at his opponent.

The night wore on. Davis took out his watch. They were better than halfway through the sixth round. The blonde had snuggled up to Geoff, who gave Zeke a nod. Court took a jab to his stomach and a swipe to his head. He staggered but didn't go down. Zeke chewed a wad of tobacco and glared significantly, but Court ignored him. The Ulsterman took another swing at his head. Court bobbed back, then forward, parrying. Desperately chewing, Zeke pulled his ear. The crowd roared approval as Court let go a volley of blows on his opponent's chest and ribs, plowing like a steam engine. The surprised Irishman dropped his fists for a fraction of a second. Court's left landed on his nose. The bell rang.

Davis and Zeke rubbed Court down in his corner. "Didn't ye see me?" Zeke called through the din. "Did ye forget what round it is?"

Court's ears buzzed. In the crowd, money changed hands. The fat blonde wiggled with delight. Geoff looked disgusted. From the bar, Old Swank cheered him. Court felt light, sharp. Across the ring, his opponent fumed and swore, raising his gloves threateningly. The man's nostrils poured blood. His handlers did their best to staunch it with cotton wool. The crowd roared. Geoff lit another cigar and, like Davis and Zeke, shook his head like one who washes his hands of the whole affair.

The bell rang.

Court barely had time to get to his feet before the Paddy rushed him. The man turned loose a left uppercut to Court's chin. The sounds in the room were suddenly muffled, like wind flapping against canvas. Dazed, Court blinked at the referee. He tried to sit up.

Zeke was on his knees next to him. He spat his wad of tobacco on the sawdust. "Lie down, ye knot-headed bastard, or ye'll get yerself kilt!"

Court grunted. His eyes rolled and he was out.

A further corrosive to his spirits were Geoff's boasts. As Piani's protégé, he had risen in the man's good graces at a meteoric rate. Once he became officially betrothed to Signorina Bertollini, he was intolerable. At Piani's celebration dinner for his niece, Court helped stand guard at the restaurant's door. Piani announced that he had turned over his late brother's shop to his future nephew-in-law. He tearfully joined Geoff's hand with Arabella's, toasted their new relationship, and embraced the couple. Court had never nursed hatred in his heart, except for Piani, but began to feel it for Geoff. At every fight, he prowled near the ring in his smart suits and ties, flashing his diamond tie stud, champing a cigar, and counting his winnings as Court took a hit. At least Geoff had never known about Winifred's necklace. All that wealth had been right under the son of a bitch's nose. It was meager comfort while one's face was being smashed in, but it was some.

Other nights, Court continued in his job as driver for Piani's agents or the man himself. With the cold rain pattering on his old top hat, he stared straight ahead at the horse's ears. Sitting on his box, he waited at the curb and wished his eyes wore blinders like the mare's. Piani's thugs covered the entrances of whatever private house or business Piani visited, or disappeared into the shadows to keep watch on the street.

After Piani entered the establishment, windows darkened or someone drew the curtains. Maybe Geoff, who often joined his future in-law. Court suspected that his erstwhile associate, who had always been the most prone to violence of all his friends, now had hands that were permanently stained with blood.

The minutes crawled by. The mare's ears twitched. Eglantine, her name was. Still a fine-looking nag for her age. It wasn't right to use the good old creature thus, as an accomplice to human wickedness. She ought to pull children on a dog cart, not take assassins hither and yon. And her reward from Piani? The glue factory. Court felt a surge of anger. If he moved quickly, he could unhook her from the hackney. A kick and they'd be off and at the city's edge before dawn. Out of the corner of his eye, he saw a guard's cigarette flare. He pulled down his hat.

Working for the devil was the result of walking a slippery slope. The Methodists had preached that when he and Beryl and Rosie had sat in chapel, waiting impatiently for some grub. Geoff probably hadn't heard. He usually slept through the sermons. Court wished he could truthfully say his long slide down had been as inevitable as the hunger that rumbled in his belly, but he couldn't. He'd made his choices, like he did in the ring. Few turned out as planned.

The mare raised her head and snorted. He smelled it too—death. Piani returned to the cab. Court shuddered as though he witnessed Satan's approach. Geoff strode behind him, his long coat flapping, and wiped his iron pipe, grinning and licking his teeth. The cab door slammed. Court told the horse to walk on. They had some dark secrets between them, him and Eglantine.

Two days later, Court drove Piani's finest carriage and pair, its equipage draped in black crepe and feathers, to the funeral of the man he and Geoff had recently butchered. The widow owed Piani for the drive.

The dreary days of November and December flowed into one another, like sewage into the Thames. It was nearly Christmas. As he drove down Bow Street to the opera house, he stared dully at its lit facade. The days before Piani got hold of him seemed another life and his night with Winifred a dream. Snow fell. He held the reins while Piani waited for his lady friend to be handed down from the cab. The courtesan and Piani mounted the steps with the crowd. Her dark velvet cape made Court think of Beryl. Her rich old gentleman probably enjoyed opera. Court scanned the throng for her scarlet and sable. They hadn't met since Berserker's mad dash. If she was there, he hoped she wouldn't see him.

Recently, Sam had started to turn up to watch him and Zeke spar, and no amount of threats could keep him away. Better get back to the Boar and Hart or he'd lose his place. Sam shrugged at Court's warnings and punched the bag he and Zeke used. Maybe he wasn't at the pub no more. Maybe he had a new employer. Court was horrified. Not Piani? With nonchalance, Sam presented a neat pink handkerchief tied around four sovereigns. Court's heart had ached with remorse and gratitude. "Take that right back where you got it," he commanded.

Sam lolled against the ropes and pocketed the money. "Maybe I will, and maybe I won't. Can't no one tell me what to do, now Fan's gone!"

Rosie's warnings to him hadn't worked much better. Playing the gentleman and riding a fine horse! How ludicrous his fantasy of surprising Winifred as she drove in the park seemed now. Instead, he imagined her in the stands with him sprawled and defeated in the sawdust or shivering on the cab's box in the falling snow. He hated to feel sorry for himself, but did. Rosie's soft pity and Beryl's bracing good sense would be unbearable. His night with Winifred, his card game with the Prince, the money he'd repaid Rosie the next day; it might as well have all been a dream.

"Tell 'er not to send me no more," he told the boy.

Never again would he take a penny he hadn't earned, especially from a woman. Geoff scoring off his coming marriage to Miss Bertollini was low. Gentlemen did it all the time, Sam argued. That was different. Why? Sam asked. Because they were gentlemen, Court said.

Sam snorted and sounded just like Geoff.

Court decided he'd get on in this world by his own efforts, or he wouldn't.

Snow piled on his shoulders. He waited in the line of cabs for his turn to set off into the traffic. There was a mews close by. Time to get Eglantine out of the weather. Beneath the grand colonnade, Piani and his courtesan joined the throng of furs and hoods, silk evening suits and top hats. The parade of finery aroused only the faintest rankling of envy. Clothes definitely didn't make a man, not Piani anyway. No matter how expensive his suits were, Old Bess would never allow him inside her establishment.

He wouldn't have minded the sight of Winifred in all her finery. Seated in one of the gilded boxes near the stage, she would be dressed in shiny satin and lace, her bare white shoulders aglow in the gaslight and her heavy hair elaborately piled and held in place by jeweled combs like those he had pulled down. She was born to be set up high; and this was where he was meant to be, down in the street on his box.

No point looking up. No stars on such a night.

With a shake of the reins, he and Eglantine set off for the mews, leaving the opera's lights behind. He followed another cab and crossed the square, breathing deeply of damp horses and muddy pavement. In the flower stalls, there were Christmas smells, cut evergreens and holly sprays, but they left him indifferent. He longed for colorful bouquets and the scent of spring blossoms. He hung his head. Snow slipped off his hat onto his lap. He cursed it quietly.

That night as on many others, he lay in the stable, exhausted but wakeful. Over and over, he relived the moments Winifred had been his. Her back arched, her face transformed by an expression he was sure no one had ever seen but him. His hands moved relentlessly on his flesh. Afterward, he turned his face to the straw and was glad only Eglantine was there to hear his heart break. He thought of the blonde whore and rolled restlessly. He wouldn't. He was done with that. Winifred had not only given him something to remember but much to ponder. Whether it was a blessing or a curse, he didn't know.

Christmas came and went, and it was the year's end. He lay in Eglantine's box with a whiskey bottle, listening to the bells ring out midnight. From the storeroom came the sounds of carousal and singing. It was some of Piani's men, Davis and Zeke, and Sam, whose childish voice struck the only hopeful note in the darkness. He hated the lad to be in such company but knew that the boy missed Fan. No one had seen her or Hez since the bank blew up. At first the caroling was boisterous; but after a while, a maudlin note crept in. Sam tottered into the stable, hiccupping. He dropped down beside Eglantine and began to snore. Court pulled a blanket over him. He raised his bottle, wished Hez and Fanny well, took a deep draught and shuddered.

He hated whiskey. He forced down another swallow.

A dark ribbon of sky and stars showed above the alley alongside the stable. Court stared at it for a long time. There were three choices, he said to Eglantine. He could take Rosie's money which Sam had offered him again that night. This he rejected, firm in his resolve not to touch her cash. That left two. The horse blinked. He could work for Piani until he got killed in the ring. "Or I could walk out again. 'Course I'd take you and Sam. Tonight's as good as any." If they didn't starve or freeze on the road, they might find their way to Holloways. "Then I'll get down on me knees and beg 'er for a job, any job."

Court had very little pride left to swallow, but what he had stuck in his throat. "Oh, Jesus, Mary, and Joseph, what am I goin' to do?" He leaned against the wall of the box and looked up. One of Piani's men stumbled into the alley behind the stable, relieved himself, and lit a cigarette.

Court raised his bottle and drank again.

Three fights later, Court won by referee's decision. The outcome came as a total shock not only to him, but to Davis and Zeke.

At the end of the night, Geoff introduced him to a new trainer, a Dubliner named Billy O'Connell. He said Piani had wooed him away from the Paddy who knocked out Court in his first fight. "Rough and ready, I likes the look o' you!" He grinned.

Court didn't like O'Connell's face, but the man knew his job. He not only expanded Court's conditioning regimen but made sure he ate better as well. So did Davis and Zeke. Court tasted decent beef for the first time since his stay at Old Bess'.

"Do as you're told for once!" Davis growled between mouthfuls of roast and gravy.

"Aye, listen to sense, ye great crazed arse!" Zeke sawed at his chops.

Court was also relieved of his driving duties and devoted himself solely to training. Sam hung around to fetch water and carry towels while O'Connell honed Court's strikes and foot work. He also made Court concentrate on balance and flexibility, and forced him to stand on one leg and to adopt absurd poses that made Sam and Zeke double over with laughter. But they worked. Davis spotted him at ever-heavier barbells, and Court made Zeke sweat. In the next match, his opponent was slightly taller than Court's five feet, eleven inches; the difference in their reaches worrisome. O'Connell was confident. All the new moves and Court's increased lung power kept him on his feet until the last bell. To his amazement, he got his first knockout.

"Not pretty, but a fair start," O'Connell said while Davis rubbed him down.

Sam was elated and followed him everywhere.

Piani was building Court's reputation in order to increase his drawing power, Davis said. If his next fights were fixed, no one said so, and nobody told him to take any more knockouts. When his opponents hit the ground, he took grim satisfaction. Davis rubbed him down afterward. Zeke took tender care of him the rest of the time. But for days after a fight, a dreamy torpor would overwhelm him, followed by nausea and attacks of nerves. All his new-found confidence disappeared, and he could hardly raise his head. There was an ache above his eye but no bruise. Because Geoff informed him that his performances had significantly reduced what he owed, he kept his worries to himself. Zeke caught him vomiting and told O'Connell. The man's lack of concern convinced Court that Piani didn't intend for "The Whitechapel Fury" to live long.

If that was the way it had to be, Court intended to go down fighting.

Meanwhile the boss and his women came to Court's practices, and the food was good. Geoff attended as well, sleeker and also much better fed. Davis always eyed him uncomfortably and was nervous in his presence. While Court and Zeke sparred, Geoff rocked back on a stool, settled against the wall, and cleaned his nails with his jackknife. He admired his many new rings, then glared at Davis, who made himself busy. Piani told Court that it was time to begin the next phase of his development. "Seamus Todd, three rounds and a knockout, that's the bill of fare."

Court listened in disbelief, wondering at Piani's game.

Todd was a heavyweight, Davis gasped. The bastard was a bloody great giant, Zeke said in awe. "And dumb as an ox," Geoff added with quiet satisfaction. O'Connell guffawed. Sam quickly left by the back door. Geoff watched the boy go, caught Court's eye, and blew on his knife.

"There's a career could take off with right management," Piani said. "I told Todd to look on it as an audition. The papers will be there. This fight'll be an exhibition of me newest talent."

"An exhibition of insanity," Davis mumbled to O'Connell. "Todd'll kill him."

"Seamus won't work for you," Court said to Piani.

O'Connell spoke. "Todd's out o' your class. No problem. You're ready. We'll put on a real show. It'll be a big draw. The purse and your cut, that's the point!"

"Ah girlies, ain't we goin' to 'ave fun?" Geoff muttered to no one in particular.

Piani went on. Todd would drop a few pounds; Court would add a few. "You boys 'as enjoyed the food. How 'bout more?" He smiled at Zeke, who appeared hopeful.

Todd had agreed to the terms of the fight, O'Connell said. There would be a rematch in three weeks during which he knocked out Court. "Then we'll trade him." He had connections in Dublin, and he and Piani intended to profit by them. "Plenty for Todd to do up north."

Piani clapped a heavy hand on Court's shoulder. "Todd might enjoy a bit o' time away. Circus traveler when 'e was a boy. Told me about it. Talkative chap. Means well, but talkative."

Geoff flung his knife into the wall.

"'E'll never do it," Court said, as Geoff wrested the blade free.

"Oh, 'e's takin' this opportunity quite serious, I assures you." Piani sneered. Geoff threw the knife again. "Asked what percentage 'e'd get from the purse and tickets. Regular man o' business, our Mr. Todd!" There was laughter from all sides.

That didn't sound like Seamus, Court thought. None of it did.

Piani withdrew with O'Connell. The women waited near the door. Geoff flung the jackknife into Court's punching bag, wrenched it out, and followed.

Zeke shot Court an aggrieved glance and picked up the empty water buckets. Davis grabbed Court's arm. "Todd was took in for questioning by the police. Geoff too! That bank what blew up a while back. I don't want nothing to do with that! I ain't involved! Ye hear?"

Court freed himself. Davis gathered the boxing gloves and spat in disgust.

That evening, Court and Sam walked along the river. Since O'Connell's arrival, Court made it a habit to take an after-supper perambulation. So long as he did not stray beyond the boundaries of Piani's turf, as indicated by the presence of his thugs who lounged on various street corners, he could wander at will.

While Sam pitched stones, Court puzzled over the new information. Zeke was frightened, sure to flee or squeal if he was put in a tight spot. Davis was doughtier but unwilling to stick out his neck, and obviously knowledgeable about more than he let on. Though Zeke and Davis were on easy terms, it was their current job that brought them together. They knew as well as Court that Piani routinely pitted people against each other and was no respecter of relationships. It didn't pay to make friends. Trust was a risk. Court couldn't argue with the wisdom of Davis' attitude of every man for himself; nor did he resent Zeke's cowardice. His would confront Seamus directly.

"Geoff thinks you're both stupid," Sam said. "Todd'll never see any o' that money!"

Court resisted the urge to pat the boy's fair head. Fanny's tongue was in it. That was sure.

Sam shoved his hands in his pockets. "Police didn't 'old Geoff long. Oho, that got you! Didn't tell no one they took 'im in the other day, but I got me ear to the ground. Told Davis, and 'e gave me a shillin'!"

"Don't you do nothin' to get in trouble," Court said. "Spyin'! Fanny'd never forgive me."

Sam chucked a stone. "Don't worry. I'm one o' the gang!"

The boy flashed a sly grin then tore off down the sand, chasing gulls.

Court climbed the stairs to the street and approached a corner. Sam followed. The broad shoulders of one of Piani's men appeared in a doorway. Court took a hard right into an alley and doubled back. Sam walked on with a jaunty air and whistled. As Court slipped down the next steps to the riverbank, he heard outraged shouts. Sam flitted by on the pavement above, the fellow at his heels. They disappeared into the alley. Court untied the first small skiff he found and rowed against the current. A few hundred yards later, he saw the Tower across the Thames. He climbed an iron ladder to a loading dock and entered a warehouse. On the other side of a clothesline, a shrill voice sounded.

"Come on, move your feet! Move 'em!"

Seamus Todd stood in a sawdust-filled circle tapping the gloves of a wiry man who barely stood high enough to eyeball his sternum. The elfin being danced about kicking up dust, yelling epithets or encouragement each time Seamus made contact with his mitts. Seeing Court, they stopped. "Well, I never," Seamus said wonderingly. "Look Grynt! It's Courty!"

"Don't call me that!" he pleaded, embarrassed by the presence of Seamus' companion.

"Court Furor, me old mate!" Seamus lolled his head in Court's direction but peered down at the man. "I told you all about our Courty!"

"Aye, you did! You did," the man said quickly. "Grynt's the name." He untied Seamus' gloves and unwound the tape from his charge's hands.

The man's accent was impenetrable, his age impossible to guess. He was gnarled and knotty, nut brown, and crooked as a twig. If he'd had a few dry leaves in his hair he could have easily passed for an animated thorn tree. Yet for all that, his ugliness was compelling, and his eyes had an intelligent twinkle. Court could not help but stare at him, as he would a particularly interesting plant at Kew Gardens.

"And there's Sammy!" Seamus pointed at the door.

Panting, Sam flourished a cigarette case. "Stupid bloke thinks I threw it in the river!"

Court was more than relieved to see the boy safe but had to laugh at his cheek.

Grynt clapped his hands, winked meaningfully, and called Sam. A bright gypsy wagon was parked near the ring. Beside it boxes and boards acted as a table. The boy dashed to a portable hob, lit it, and set a kettle on. A tray and cups were in another box. Court was only half surprised the lad knew his way about. While Sam was busy, Grynt opened a tin canister and took out a loaf of bread, which he sliced and set in a toasting rack. Seamus took command of this with an air of delicacy. Sam ducked into the box and retrieved a honey pot, a bottle of anchovy sauce, and a jar of pickled eggs. From the wagon, Grynt produced an oilcloth, plates, and cutlery. The kettle sang.

While Grynt played mother, Seamus browned the toast. "Sam's a wonder. Keeps me like a regular valet since I came home from hospital. You could use some tidying, Courty."

Court's top hat was suddenly on the floor. Seamus held him in an affectionate headlock. The toast and tea cups lay scattered. The small man grabbed the hat and waved it at Seamus' face, like a tamer with his lion. Seamus let go, and Court got his breath back.

"Tea first!" the fellow growled, poking Seamus' chest. "Pick up that lot! Bacon, Sam!"

The boy disappeared into the wagon. At Grynt's gesture, Seamus docilely followed. As Court joined Grynt at the table, the clothesline caught his attention. Among socks and shirts and union suits was pinned a broad painted canvas, partially complete. Paint pots sat near it on a small deal table. The canvas bore a roughed-in sketch of a strong man in a circus ring surrounded by equestrian acrobats, showgirls, and dancing clowns. Trapeze artists flew above.

Shackleton's Seven Mysteries and Perpetual Shows United, read the elaborate lettering.

Sam emerged, loaded with victuals. He followed Court's glance. "Seamus did it."

"It's a beauty. Sounds very grand," said Court. "When's it to be?"

"When it's needed," Grynt answered vaguely, passing the tea. "It comes and goes."

Seamus came from a family of tumblers and performers. His father was a strong man, and his mother could lift a bloke clean off the ground. "Grab him 'round the thigh, she'd tell him to step on her knee, and up!" Grynt demonstrated, balancing the bread tin on the end of his knife. When Seamus was a baby, his pa and ma tossed him like a ball. There was nothing wrong with his brains but what happened to them after he took a bad spill. "Got it in him to do his dad's act, only it's not his calling." He gazed proudly at the painted canvases. Court agreed they were very good. Seamus always made quick sketches of patrons' faces and street scenes at the Boar and Hart, he told Grynt. Then he thought of Seamus' map of the Royal Empire Bank and fell silent.

"I used to mind 'Little Hercules,'" Grynt chuckled. "When he telegrammed about his trouble last autumn, I decided it was time to volunteer, do a bit of light orderly work at hospital."

"What's your usual line?" Court asked.

"Theatricals mostly, the mystery plays." He gestured at yet another canvas on the floor that Seamus had not finished refreshing. "I make a game Pirate King in the pantomime."

"What about this match up? Geoff made it sound like Seamus wants to do it."

Grynt screwed one eye shut and placed a finger alongside his crooked nose. "All part of the act, Mr. Furor. 'Three rounds and a knockout,'" he said in an unnervingly accurate imitation of Piani's voice. "Let's give 'em five. Put on a real show!"

Before Court could respond, Seamus emerged from the wagon with a salted ham and helped Sam dispatch it at the cutting board. "Courty's a lover, not a fighter," he said placidly.

"Move your big arse!" Grynt said firmly and opened a pot of sweet gherkins. "Can't strategize on empty stomachs. Sam, Gentleman's Relish!" The boy dashed back inside the wagon.

"Well, Grynt? You two have a nice chat? What do you say?" Seamus asked.

"Thinking!" The little man sliced savagely at the cheese and bread. He produced a dry onion from his pocket and ate it like an apple between slurps of tea.

Seamus piled a plate with food and handed it to Court. In happier times, they had dozed on benches in the Boar and Hart's yard, mere spectators to the machinations of worldlier men such as Geoff and Selway Adams. How often, when he hadn't a penny, had Seamus lent him money, split a pasty or a pint, or invited him to share the bed of a nice, friendly girl?

Watching Sam within the wagon, Seamus reminisced too. "Before Hez came along, we had some laughs with Fan, didn't we?" He grinned and thrust an elbow into Court's side.

Court coughed on his tea.

Sam joined them. He gave Grynt the relish and made a face. "Our gang don't need girls."

"That's right," Grynt said. "Concentrate! Keep your mind off women." He stabbed his bread and cheese onto a toasting fork and intently oversaw its bubbling progress.

Seamus pulled a postcard from his pocket. It was addressed to Sam, care of the Boar and Hart. "Honfleur, Normandy! Sounds like pretty girls' names." He sighed deeply, gazing at the picture of the seaside town. "Fan writes, 'Artists live there year 'round and paint the sea and sky.'"

Court read the card. Fanny was a cook in a big house. No mention of Hez. Was that to protect her brother from her troubles and maintain her lover's cover, or had she ended the relationship? That didn't seem likely.

Seamus agreed. "Lucky Hez will make an honest woman of our Fan." He turned to Sam. "She'll send for you when it's best! How you and her understand them froggies I'll never know! BUNJUR!" he pronounced forcefully, as though the boy was deaf.

"Parce-que ma sœur et moi, nous sommes français, mon ami!" Sam bowed.

Seamus delicately lifted his teacup. "Ain't he a wonder?" His eyes took on a wistful expression as he chewed his food. "If I got that purse, I'd go to Paris and take up me paints serious like. First, I'd send some of it to Fan for a wedding present."

How was Beryl, he asked. Still very much taken, Court assured him. Seamus sighed and saluted with his cup. "Oh well! Here's to pretty dark-haired girls, Honfleur and Normandy!" Court raised his mug, as did Sam.

After that, they ate in silence. What else did Seamus remember from their days of weak beer and fast women? The early era of their friendship seemed a bygone, innocent age. Seamus had left the circus for London, hoping to make his way back to Paris and become a painter but never had. Sam and Fanny were more late additions to Court's youth. Fanny had shown up at the Boar and Hart with her baby brother a few years back. He'd often wondered if Sam was hers. Her recent disappearance seemed to negate that possibility. At least, he hoped so. Seamus' wiry friend was equally mysterious. Was he trustworthy?

Careful of his handlebar moustache, Seamus wiped his mouth with a prim gesture and stood. He made a gentle jab at Sam, who also hopped to his feet and happily raised his fists. "Come on, Sammy. Let's clear up."

Grynt quickly finished his eggs. "Knockout in the first fight, we'll walk through it. Careful choreography's the ticket, Mr. Furor." He winked a beady eye. "I've seen you fight. You're a mad man in the ring. You act like you want to get yourself killed!"

Seamus could kill him without half trying, Court answered. Mystified by another of Grynt's winks, he gave his coat and shirt to Sam. They decided to block out the end of the fight.

"Tap here," Seamus indicated his jaw, "kinder light. I'll fall back easy. Run me against the ropes a few times. We'll struggle a bit like I'm off balance. I'll push you to the middle o' the ring and mess you about. When you've had enough, land one on my head right here. Down I'll go!"

Grynt hovered close by, his shoulders hunched and one eye on Seamus. Sam sat down to watch, clutching Court's clothes under his chin. Court raised his hands and stepped onto the sawdust. Seamus danced forward, feinting light punches at Court's head and shoulders.

Grynt muttered, "Make it look good ladies. Make a good show."

"All Piani knows about fightin' is 'e likes lots o' blood," Sam said.

"Pacing's important. Keep it simple, watch for me now!" Seamus commanded.

He was an artful fighter for a man so dumb and a graceful one for one so large. Naturally sedate, his initial punches appeared slow until he exploded with economical precision, only to melt away before Court could get his bearings. Though he was taken for an idiot most of the time, in the ring Seamus was nobody's fool.

"What'd I tell you?" Seamus said to Grynt of Court. "There's real artistry in those hands."

Barely able to follow Seamus' lead, Court did not think he deserved the compliment. He might improve under his friend's tutelage, but Grynt's presence distracted him. None of Seamus' motions were wasted nor was he predictable. His swings were elegant, his aim worthy of a sharp-shooter's. Piani was a fool to want to trade him.

They tried once more. Grynt kept time. After three minutes, the huge man hardly seemed to breathe while Court panted. Do it again,

Grynt shouted. Seamus swatted at him. Court dodged, swearing. He lobbed a neat left on Seamus' chin but felt the effort it took to reach so far.

"Very nice," Seamus chuckled. "Don't overextend. Always could use both hands well. Speed's good, but pace yourself! All heart and not enough lungs, that's what Fan used to say!"

Swinging with his right, Court made contact with Seamus' ribs. It was like hitting the side of a house. The impact shivered up his arm into his shoulder. Suddenly, he felt the futility of his actions. All the energy drained out of him. The spot over his eye throbbed. Grynt threw himself between them with a slashing motion of his arm and urged them both to drink. Sam darted to Court with a towel. Out of breath, he gratefully plunged his face into a bucket of water.

"What's the matter with you lad?" Grynt shouted. "Where's all this heart Seamus brags you've got? You're not focused! You're everywhere! You can't go on like that for three rounds, never mind five! What's your game?"

"I ain't got none!" Court shouted back.

"Well, we've got to get one because Geoff does!" Sam hollered wildly.

"Bloody Geoff can go to the blazes! I'm sick of Geoff!" Court yelled back.

"Ah, he's got inside you!" Grynt drove his finger into Court's chest. "Him and Piani's like big cats, playing with you, working you over for your debts. Piani's tired of it! Well, so are you! This business about you and Geoff and the bank has him worried, has him scared! Use his fear!"

He knocked the man's hand away. "Piani ain't scared o' me! Geoff ain't got no worries! What's me money to 'im now 'e's Piani's boy? 'E wants me! I'll die in the ring someday!"

Seamus hung his head. "Courty, Grynt and me knows all that."

Grynt spoke to Sam. "Lad, fetch that bottle of wintergreen oil so we can give our friends a rubdown. It's in the trunk." The boy took off. Grynt waited until he was inside the wagon. "Selway Adams is in a bad way. Geoff stabbed him above the kidney, and he ain't healing proper."

"'Ow do you know that?" Court was mystified.

Grynt sat down on his tea chest. "If I had to bet whether it was Hez Boors or Ratchet who'd stick a knife in a man, I know where I'd put my money! I've been on Adams' ward every day since Seamus was in hospital and heard the nurses talk. If Adams dies, Geoff's going to go after anyone who could tell what he—or she—knows about it. The police are breathing down Piani's neck for information. He don't want to know what Geoff does or how he does it so long as he cleans up his mess. That's their deal, or he loses Signorina Bertollini, the store, the lot!"

"The police talked to me. Geoff knows it," Seamus said glumly. "Fellow called Patterson, he asked lots of questions about a driver. I didn't say nothing, but he could tell I knew. Then, Geoff collared me. Patterson had asked him the same thing."

"I don't understand. You don't work for Piani, or Geoff. Why would you agree to this?"

Seamus smiled at Court and tapped his arm. "Like Sammy always says, we're a gang."

Grynt spoke very quietly. "I told Seamus to let Geoff think he was all lathered up, to act like he thought you'd betray them straight away if you got caught. That's when Geoff offered him a cut of the purse. 'Accidents 'appen in the ring,' he said. Yes, Mr. Furor, Seamus tells me everything! What he don't, I see!" He widened a beady eye. "I know all about what you two—all of you—did at the Royal Empire that morning!"

Not all, Court thought. He was grateful but didn't see how Seamus' loyalty would help either of them. "Even if Geoff is convinced, you really wants to do this?"

"If Seamus doesn't take you on, someone else will," Grynt said. "I was for getting out of town soon as Seamus came out of hospital. Not him! He had to talk with you, but you're a hard man to get to these days. Then Geoff made his proposition. Now it's too late. Police are watching Piani, and he's watching all three of you. Geoff has to make this right. There's a lot more than money riding on these fights for both of them."

"'Ow are we goin' to pull it off?"

Sam appeared at the wagon door with the bottle, and Seamus quickly went to him.

Grynt whispered hurriedly. "First of all, like you said, you're going to die, Mr. Furor."

⚭

It poured rain and had all afternoon. George turned the pages of the early evening edition. *The Flower of Youth* .... Selway Adams' obituary stated that he died in hospital after a brief illness. The club barman heard it was pneumonia. George turned to the society pages. The columnist for *Today's London: Acta Diurna* reported that torrential rains had fallen on the funeral cortege. *The hearse was gorgeously bedecked in ebony ostrich plumes and pulled by six black horses, also adorned with sable feathers. The length of the line of mourners was a testament to a life cut off in its prime.* The Earl's name was not mentioned. Nor was it explained that the line of mourners mostly consisted of a small group of harried newspapermen, competing society columnists, and plainclothes police clustered under the church portico. George closed the newspaper and felt for his cigarette case.

Funerals were usually a bore, but it had been an interesting afternoon. A gathering afterward had been hosted by Mrs. Harris of Richmond. Not a formal wake, one understood. Not Society either, just the outermost fringes of the Smart Set. Guests were numerous. George was among them. He ate many prawns and drank deeply of the punch. The scandal was delicious, and he had savored every morsel.

His hostess held court. His Lordship and "Selly" had not spoken in ages. "The de-ah boy, Selly always wrote his papa every month, and the Earl wrote him back."

"He wrote Selly a monthly check," quipped a woman on George's right. He recognized her from the stage.

"Dah-ling Selly" had been the offspring of the Earl's liaison with Jenny Blythe, a showgirl of notoriety in an earlier decade. "Back when the Earl and Miss Blythe were bold, gay, and reckless, like the rest of us," a venous-nosed gentleman on George's left explained. He signaled to the footman who served the wine.

"The Earl's tears will dry soon enough. They did after Miss Blythe's morphine overdose. He left her for—ahem—a younger actress." She nodded at Mrs. Harris.

"Not so young anymore," the man whispered with a smirk. "Not so many monthly checks for her either in the near future, I hear."

In a steady monologue, Mrs. Harris confided to the small crowd gathered around her while they sipped champagne punch and consumed caviar. "My dah-lings! His Lordship was always so lavish with Selly! He spoiled him." She shot a freezing smile toward the bereaved parent who stood on the other side of the room with a group of men.

"But he never legally acknowledged Sedgie," the venous man hiccupped to George.

"'De-ah Selly!'" the woman corrected. "The only son, but three daughters by his wife!"

"So, no heir apparent, but I've also heard that Mrs. Harris...."

"But speaking of monthly you-know-what," the woman interjected, "my maid says that Mrs. Harris' maid says that she's at least three months along."

"At her age? Why didn't she...? Is it really the Earl's?"

"Ah, there's the rub!" The actress smiled. "Look at him, lecherous old fool! If I was her, dah-ling Selly would've had more to do with it!"

George abandoned the chuckling pair and crossed the room. The bereaved father was in deep conversation with a middle-aged, sandy-haired man whose suit was so poorly cut and out of place among all the frock coats that George was both intrigued and amused. Next to them stood a younger man, also badly dressed.

"Justice must be served," the Earl had sputtered, wiping his eyes. He was more than slightly inebriated. "Bottom-dwellers, scum of the earth! I'd lock them all up, like we did the Boers!"

"We're assisting inquiries with the Yard, my Lord," the sandy-haired man answered patiently. "Peele here, my best man, is on it."

A reporter materialized at George's elbow. He was always at parties, eating as much as he could and sniffing out morsels for scandal sheets. Private detectives perhaps, he speculated about the bad suit and his partner. "Damn," he growled, as one of his competitors, a roundish, effete man with a monocle, approached.

"No, it's Detective Inspector Patterson, Southwark Branch." The man with the monocle smiled moistly, and the reporter made a quick exit, looking anxious and annoyed. "Jarvis Perrot, *Today's London: Acta Diurna.*" He gave George his card and sniffed at the retreating reporter. "Poor fellow, I sent my boy to the paper with that a quarter hour ago. Now, Ratchet is the name that ought to be on everyone's lips." He licked his. "Only it won't be. I've already tried and was warned off by my editor. So far as I can make out, he's no one—yet. But he definitely knew Adams. The police clammed up tight when I asked if Ratchet was at the bank or if he might be charged, so I'm staying on it. *The Times* will give me a byline if I crack this. The doctor would only confirm Adams' kidney was damaged, and not by the explosion. But I talked to a bank clerk named Darby who saw a dark fellow with a jackknife. What do you make of that?"

George shrugged and stared vaguely toward Patterson. Peele stared back at George and Jarvis Perrot with equal vagueness. "Perhaps you'll create a cause célèbre."

"Not I, said the fly! This Ratchet is rather a success down his way. Drumming up sympathy for or ire against the lower classes is hardly worth my while. But my instincts tell me it's going to be 'the story.' The fellow's engaged to the niece of a sort of small-time, Italian kingpin. Someone will be the goat. Adams was running with a rough crowd. It's always big when there's an aristo involved, but what if it's about more than the money? A love angle perhaps? No one at that service gave a damn about Adams, certainly not the Earl, in spite of his best performance. He'd as soon see the matter over and done with. He'll have enough of a scandal if Mrs. Harris decides to publish his letters. Do you play cards?"

George did not look at Perrot. "You know of a good game?"

"The Lancaster, you've heard of it?"

George suppressed a smile. "You have, apparently."

The man sniffed. "What with Patterson getting involved, I only wondered if you'd ever been down that way. You might've heard some tidbit about this Ratchet fellow. Ratchet, the Tool of Crime! How I'd love to meet him. He sounds so deliciously low!"

On his way to the billiards room, George listened to the couple who walked ahead of him. There had been a terrific row between the Earl and Mrs. Harris. "Those pearls she had on at the service are the last gift she'll get from him. He's gone back to his wife!"

At the church, George had taken a good look at Mrs. Harris. A bit too dark and thin, and too made up. But about her swanlike neck a string of enormous South Sea pearls had shone lustrously, black as ink. As soon as she got back home, the woman had thrown them into her newly installed flushing toilet.

He knew this because when he first arrived at the house, he had gone in search of a water closet. On a tour of the bedrooms, he noticed a lady's maid cross the landing. She opened a door. Raised voices issued therefrom. Mrs. Harris buzzed briskly into the hall, spitting invectives, then the Earl, fagged out and red-faced. The maid did not emerge, however. As soon as the unhappy couple started downstairs, he ducked into their room.

"Just what I wanted," he teased the maid, who was bent over a toilet bowl.

She straightened stiffly but did not rise. She pushed a strand of greying hair behind her ear, looking as tired as the Earl, and much more put out. She was trying to retrieve her mistress' pearls, so he'd have to go elsewhere. George fished the necklace from the U-bend. Afterward she stoked the fire and knelt before it. "The knots will have to dry before I can put them away."

George sat on an ottoman beside her. "Why not keep them?" The woman laughed ruefully. "It's hardly your affair if your mistress chooses to throw away a fortune!"

"Stupid bitch!" the maid said suddenly.

George sized up the woman. Late thirties, probably a country pastor's daughter. Or maybe her father had been in a low-level profession. It would be a large family, and she had a Midlands accent. He asked and was confirmed. Did she hate her life so much? A woman had to work. It wasn't so bad except when it was, she said. And then it was very bad, George supposed. Was the baby really the Earl's? What did it matter? Mrs. Harris had played it all wrong, she answered. "His wife is smart. Left him to his own devices. Now he's found out what this one's really like. He's sick of her. She takes it out on me. I'm sick of them all."

George made a suggestion. "You'd feel better for it, and I won't tell a soul about the pearls." He had a nerve, she said. "I like to think so," he answered. "What about it?"

The woman stared at the fire. Suddenly, she rose, draping the pearls around her neck. She sat on the edge of Mrs. Harris' bed and gave George an arch look. "Why not, dah-ling?"

He stripped off his coat and loosened his tie. The woman flopped onto her back, threw her arms overhead, and laughed.

George came out of his reverie. He had finally found his cigarette case. One of the old boys of the club, a veteran, asked him if he was finished with the paper. George passed it to him. The man sank with a grunt and snap of knee joints onto the chair opposite. Outside the window, rain poured on Pall Mall. In spite of the wet weather, it had been a lovely afternoon.

The first fight between Court and Seamus was in the middle of February.

O'Connell instructed Court. "Todd'll work you over good. Stand your ground. Don't go down too early in the second. It's got to look close 'til the end. Piani wants a spectacular finish, a lucky shot, not a rout."

Court knocked out Seamus a minute into the fourth. Piani scheduled a rematch.

O'Connell kept him busy, and Court was glad. After he read about Adams' death, he gave up newspapers. Even turning to the racing results made him nervous, for he dreaded more bad news. Whenever he went out, he examined any new face he didn't recognize as one of Piani's men. He put his head down and walked faster.

They had another meeting to work out the second fight's details. Grynt deemed it too risky for Court and Seamus to be seen together. "If I say come at four o'clock, be here at two," he said quietly, looking askance at Sam. Court understood. The boy was not part of it. The man took complete charge and wouldn't tell more or his plans. Seamus didn't seem to know much either.

"Just fight me like you mean it all the way to the end, Courty."

Several events further unsettled him. His old purple coat and top hat disappeared. Then Sam stopped coming to watch him and O'Connell. In spite of his better judgment, Court snuck to the warehouse to see if the boy was there. Grynt's wagon was gone. There was no sign of anyone. Zeke said Geoff had stalled Seamus in his old room at the Boar and Hart. For days Court waited for word from Grynt, but the man had severed his cryptic communiqués.

The Boar and Hart was off limits, so he accompanied Davis and Zeke to the Golden Goose. Seamus showed up with Geoff and his growing entourage. The fat blonde was with them, clinging to Seamus' arm. Zeke suggested they ought to leave, but Court thought it would be all right. While Seamus ordered drinks, the woman squeezed next to Court, bent over the bar, and displayed a generous glimpse of her bosom. Zeke hastily raised his beer.

Seamus took note and approached. He picked up the blonde and passed her to Geoff. "What are you looking at?" he challenged, tapping Court's shoulder.

"We're off!" Davis set down his beer.

"What're you lookin' at?" Court asked Seamus.

Chairs scrapped the floor. The row that followed nearly cleared the pub. Geoff finally subdued the roaring Seamus and left with him. The blonde bounced after them.

"I've never seen Todd like that!" Zeke was clearly shaken.

"You got to be more careful!" Davis yelled. "If this fight ends in just a knockout you'll—we'll all—be damn lucky!"

Court laughed it off. In fact, he was impressed by Seamus' dramatic capacities. That much of Grynt's plan, he'd been prepared for. But that night he woke with a start, sweating and clutching at the air above his face, certain that Geoff had come for him with his jackknife. He lay shuddering until the thunder of his heart subsided. He left Davis and

Zeke snoring in their beds and went to sit with Eglantine. In her box, he waited for the ambiguous reassurance of another cold, grey dawn.

The rematch was set in a cotton warehouse far down the Thames in a neighborhood unfamiliar to Court. He was taken by boat. Piani's men were everywhere. From the dressing room where he sat with O'Connell and Zeke, he heard the crowd. He could also smell it. The pocket of his robe felt heavy. Rosie's pink handkerchief tied around four gold sovereigns! When had Sam put them there? He still hadn't seen him or Grynt.

Davis scouted the crowd. Lots of expensive suits, he reported, big gamblers, and some blokes Geoff claimed covered contests for papers as far away as Dublin and Calais. "You and Seamus will be famous!"

Zeke rubbed Court's shoulders. In the past weeks, he'd bulked up in a truly impressive manner. He weighed more than he ever had in his life. Every bit of it was muscle.

"You'll be fine! You'll be fine!" Zeke intoned breathlessly, over and over.

O'Connell grinned. "Rough and ready, right Furor? Show 'em Whitechapel's fury!"

Court nodded but his stomach flip-flopped.

He emerged from behind the curtain to the roars and jeers of the crowd and stepped into the ring, trying to remember all that Grynt had told him. He hoped he would be as convincing as Seamus at the Golden Goose. He wanted to go down doing his best, fighting like he meant it. On Seamus' side of the ring, his friend listened to Geoff. Court didn't know the other men with them and looked for Grynt. In the stands he saw Old Swank, the soldier from Hez's former regiment. He turned away, quickly. Otherwise, except for Piani and his gang, he didn't recognize a soul.

O'Connell took his place with Zeke in Court's corner and nodded to Seamus' group. Geoff was seated, trimming his usual cigar, and wore rings on every finger. The number of his hangers-on was almost as numerous as Piani's, only much better dressed. Piani was seated high up in a specially roped off stall, talking to the fellows Davis had said were newspapermen. Piani would pay attention when Seamus really got going on him, Court supposed.

The first two rounds were awkward, though he and Seamus had rehearsed their moves. He put it down to nerves. At first, he came out strong, appearing to keep Seamus on the defensive until Seamus hit him over the eye. When he fell onto the ropes, O'Connell bellowed in his ear for being slow. The strike was a surprise, but Court decided not to worry. Davis cut him. Zeke wiped him down, shouting encouragement. Throughout the second round, Court's head pounded mercilessly. His arms seemed to shoot out in slowed-down motion while the crowd's actions appeared to speed up. Seamus smacked his nose. After that, he felt drunk.

A man reacted and struck, bobbed and wove, and he guessed it was him. He shook his head, trying to clear his vision, to get back inside himself. His glove made contact with Seamus' face. The big man staggered. The bell rang. Suddenly it was all over. He was back in his corner. O'Connell talked rapidly and waved his fingers in front of Court's eyes while Davis and Zeke hovered, wiping his face and exchanging worried looks. He didn't understand a word they said but nodded. He licked his teeth and tasted blood.

In the last seconds of the third, Seamus chased Court about until he was exhausted. The crowd booed. The referee rushed into the ring. Court fell away heavily into his corner and swore aloud at Seamus, waving his glove. He'd done his best to make a show as Grynt had instructed but felt giddy and confused. The ache behind his eye pulsed. To make matters worse, Seamus had developed a mind of his own, abandoning their choreography. For the first time, Court wondered if he'd made a mistake. Perhaps Seamus' fury in the pub was real; perhaps the meetings with him and Grynt were part of a setup, and he'd fallen for it. Geoff had nothing to do with this; or maybe he did. Or perhaps it was all Piani's scheme, as he'd suspected from the first. Court glanced at the top tier of seats and caught Piani's eye. The man smirked.

The bell rang.

Seamus' blows rained on Court with a ferocity he'd never endured before. His inhaled the hot smoky air. He couldn't think or move his arms fast enough to block. He stared up at Seamus for reassurance or a shred of recognition; there was none. The big man's eyes were blood red, like a bull's. Seamus' glove landed on his stomach. A rib caved. If the fight ended in a knockout and nothing more, he'd be lucky, like Davis said.

The bell rang. In what seemed seconds, the bell rang again. Fifth round.

"Once more into the breach!" The yell came from the stands. Old Swank! Geoff and his cronies heckled and whooped. Newspapermen wrote furiously. Piani grinned, grim but satisfied.

Davis helped Court stand, and he stumbled forward. Seamus came on strong, then slackened his blows and took several jabs to his face. Court drove his opponent to the corner and whipped him rapidly around the sides until Seamus threw him off again. They took the center of the ring, pushing against each other like bulls. Court rapped at Seamus' kidneys while Seamus pummeled his ears. The crowd cheered its approval over a few derisive hoots.

Court didn't know when the bell rang or how he got to his corner. He sat gasping while Davis pressed the swelling over his eye. From behind O'Connell, Court saw Seamus roar incoherently while his team worked on him. His vision swimming, Court took in Zeke's and Davis' worried faces. They expressed his thoughts. Something was amiss. Geoff leaned forward, feral and excited. Piani opened a champagne bottle and passed it to the swells and big newspapermen.

Finally, it was the sixth round. In spite of the swelling over his brow and the ache behind his eyes, he staggered off the stool, weirdly detached. Once more, he searched for Grynt. Instead, he spied a sandy-haired man in a bowler hat and an ill-fitting suit. The man's eyes met his.

The bell sounded. Propelled by Davis and Zeke, Court launched at Seamus. His breath came in short gasps. His lungs burned. The throb behind his eyes was the devil, and the muscles in his right arm seized up. There was a terrible pain in his left side where Seamus hit him in the second round. His knuckles were raw. Seamus' body was a slab of stone. Thirty seconds into the round, Court gave Seamus an uppercut to the jaw with his right.

The giant reeled backward. The crowd drew a collective gasp as his legs gave under him. The man collapsed to his right knee. Geoff started forward, disbelief on his face.

Seamus glared blackly through his brows at Court. Then he rose, shaking his head. He swung wildly. Court danced back. Seamus swung again. Court parried with his left and came in under Seamus' jaw. The man went down again. The crowd drew its breath. So did Court.

Had this happened at the beginning of the fourth round, it would've made sense. It was part of their plan. Now, Court didn't know.

Geoff broke the silence. Jumping up and down, he spat foam and screamed at Seamus to get up. The crowd came back to life.

So did Seamus. He slowly heaved his bulk erect. There was nothing human in his eyes.

Court tried not to clench his teeth. He kept his hands up and had already struck out when Seamus pulled back his right. With a monstrous growl, he returned the uppercut to Court's jaw.

The impact jolted through his skull and every bone. Pain was a room, far away but terrible, and he was locked inside. The mob of jeering faces swirled and pitched sideways. The floor rushed to meet his cheek with a sickening smack. All was blackness.

PART II
March – June 1893

CHAPTER 11
Night Thoughts

A fire glowed in the grate. Beryl lounged on the sofa, staring at the embers and smoking her cigarillo. She was dead tired from riding with Horace that afternoon and stretched her sore legs on the ottoman. Rosie's head was nestled on her lap. The woman's eyes were closed, her breathing easy. On the small table beside Beryl was a bottle of whiskey and a crystal tumbler. Behind them, the large round table beneath the shaded lamp held the remains of their supper. A romantic volume from which Beryl had read aloud earlier lay face down on the sofa's back, but stuffed beneath the cushions was reading material of a more immediately compelling nature, an R. S. Surtees novel on loan from Horace. Though Beryl would have liked nothing more than to lose herself in its scenes of hounds and hunting, she dared not move, lest she wake her girl.

It had been a while since they spent a quiet evening at home. They had not felt much like going to the music hall. Usually, it was Rosie's favorite outing, but neither of them had the heart for its frivolity since the news about Court's fight.

Horace had accompanied them to the morgue. There, they were thrown into confusion when the attendant said firmly that no corpse identified as Court Furor's had been delivered.

"There must be a mistake," Horace said.

"Body snatchers!" Rosie gasped.

Beryl had not been so easily alarmed. "Stop it, Rosie! You sound like Sam. It's the usual cock-up. Labeled wrong. He's somewhere. We simply have to find him."

"Surely a doctor was there on the night?" Horace had asked when they went to the police station. He produced his card and placed it before the officer. "We'd like to speak with him."

The man lifted an eyebrow as he read the pasteboard. He checked his records. "Your guess is as good as mine, Mr. Greystone, sir! You're the second party today what has come. First it was deceased's brother. Very unpleasant that was. My condolences for your loss." Beryl scowled. The man seemed to realize the awkwardness of his statement. He swallowed against his high collar.

On the way back to their flat, Horace said that he had found out the name of the senior officer who had been called after the fight. "A detective inspector, James Patterson of Southwark branch, you know the man?"

Neither she nor Rosie had ever heard of him.

As for Seamus Todd's whereabouts, reports conflicted. Several of the Montague Hotel's customers who attended the fight said Todd had been taken into police custody after Court's knockout. The Lancaster Arms' hall boy had an older brother who worked at Saint Pancras' ticket office. Todd was seen on a northbound platform in the company of "a big, sandy-haired man wearing a long, brown coat."

"That would be Patterson," the same policeman told Horace when he returned to the station. Court's death had yet to be formally recorded. His body had yet to be sent to any morgue.

Sam had also disappeared.

In the pocket of Beryl's kimono was the boy's note. Exasperating scrap of paper. Its pasted-on block capitals would tell her no more than they had when she first saw them. She took it out and read it anyway.

APPEARANCES DECEIVE!

Beryl stuffed the paper back into her pocket.

Rosie slept. Gently, the woman's bosom rose and fell. Her girl did look a treat in the warm, new dressing gown embroidered all over in gold chrysanthemums and pink peonies. Her hair spread over Beryl's thighs in thick damp coils, still darkened from washing. Beryl ran her hand gently over them and marveled, transfixed as always by the sight of her Venus' glory. It should be ever thus: quiet, still, the world far away. Her own eyes grew heavy.

Tendrils of seaweed brushed her fingers. She and Rosie rested on a boat, a sleepy gondola adrift on a sunset lagoon.

The vision did not last. Pictures of other, harder times intruded. Faces of men and youths crowded about, twisting in various expressions of lust and abandon. She and Rosie sprawled on their hands and knees or knelt before the men. One face in particular stood out. Not the usual punter's, but a gentleman's, a soldier, handsome and cruel.

Beneath her grip, Rosie stirred. Beryl relaxed, lifted the whiskey to her lips, and applied the cigarillo again. That was a long time ago. While the coals hissed and Rosie slumbered, it would not be too difficult to return to the warm, trancelike state she had almost achieved. Another swallow of whiskey and their boat would slip its moorings.

Beryl set down her glass. That was the point. They would never get anywhere unless she quit dreaming. They were never going to get out of this room or out of London.

Though they made her flinch, she sought out the darts of her old familiar anxieties, so astringent and ennobling. Anger was even better, like the pure air that smote her cheeks while she and Rosie walked along a winter's seashore, Brighton or Devon. Give her obstacles, enemies—monsters! She was ready to fight them all. Left alone with her memories, she became muddled in dark, murky shoals and foundered in deep waters. There, she would sink. She would drown.

In spite of her best resolve, Beryl seized her glass and drank all of it. Whiskey was her oracle. It was the only way she dared slip beneath the surface of waking memory to meet her worst nightmare, that soldier. If only he would stop coming back. She almost knew how to defeat him. It was difficult to remember afterward what her tears revealed so clearly when she was drunk.

While she cherished every minute alone with her girl, Beryl was not sorry that Rosie was asleep. She poured more whiskey. She needed to think. In fact, as Horace kept reminding her, it was imperative. Her mind struggled. First Court and the doctor; then Seamus and Sam. Where had they all gone? It was like a magic trick. It didn't make sense.

"You'd drive Christ off a cliff!" she had snapped at the boy. The evening of Court's fight with Seamus, Sam lurked about the Montague's entrance. It was the first they had seen of him in days. When she spied the note, she tore it from the boy's hand, opened it, and burst into laughter.

All the way back from Tattersall's, Beryl had silently rehearsed how to tell Rosie about the agreement that she and Horace had finally reached that afternoon. She would have to admit that Horace had reviewed their household accounts. Beryl was already nervous about Rosie's reaction when she and Horace stepped out of their cab.

At the sight of the boy, she was annoyed, but his note brought some relief. Its melodrama would distract Rosie from what she had to say. Small comfort if the pasted words referred to Court. Though she put on a brave face for Rosie's sake whenever the subject of Court came up, she trembled inwardly lest Sam's next visit bring bad news. The note only indicated that the lad had crossed the border between reality and fantasy. His perseverance, if not his misplaced creativity, was marvelous. It must have taken an age to cut out all the letters of his message from his volcanic periodicals. If Sam had time to play like that, maybe Court was all right. Wishful thinking. Nobody ever helped Court.

She had grabbed Sam's arm and shoved him ahead of her and Horace into the foyer.

They were met by a bevy of slatternly, half-clad women who laughed at Sam's predicament. From parlor and stairs, they crowded around or leaned in for a better view of the commotion. Beryl's annoyance grew. She kicked Sam. "Why were you poking this through the door? Just give it to us! No more cloaks and daggers!" She crushed the paper in her fist and threw it at his face. "Tell us where the fight's to be! NOW!"

"Sam!" Rosie called from the door of their flat. She pushed between the whores and made her way downstairs. "Beryl, stop it! You'll knock 'im sideways!"

Onlookers were divided as to Sam's fate. A few protested on his behalf, but most of the women encouraged Beryl. There was general agreement that Sam's drubbing was a good precursor to the evening's upcoming contest between Court and Seamus. Bets were shouted as to how many cuffs Sam could take before going down. The boy grimaced in real pain as Beryl boxed his ear, but also appeared pleased at his note's dramatic effect on Rosie. She clasped the paper with shaking fingers and peered at it until Beryl blushed. Rosie was a wizard with figures, but everyone knew she couldn't read a word.

Horace gently took the note. Sam shook like a rabbit in Beryl's grasp but stared with mingled curiosity and suspicion at Horace's thick glasses, his beautifully cut but rumpled coat, and the thinning red hair that showed as he removed his top hat.

"What's 'e?" Sam asked Rosie while Horace pondered the note.

"What's Lincoln's Inn!" she hinted significantly. "What's the Inns o' Court?"

"What's Newgate?" Beryl threatened. She wished the crowd of women would go away. She stabbed her finger at Sam's note. "What's evidence?"

The boy struggled but remained defiant. "What do I care?"

"You'll care when you're hanged for wasting our time and taking Rosie's money! He might be clever if his head wasn't stuffed so full of bosh!" she complained to Horace.

"I'm sure he's an intelligent lad." Horace handed the paper to Beryl. He aimed his thick lenses at Sam. "My name is Horace Greystone. I'm a barrister."

"Coo!" Sam said. "Samuel Merton, personal assistant to Mr. Seamus Todd and pyrotechnical specialist with Shakleton's Seven Mysteries and Perpetual Shows United."

Beryl shook him. "Scrounger for easy pickings, that's you!"

Horace spoke. "Miss Stuart tells me you like reading adventures. I enjoy Stevenson."

Sam seemed to derive courage from the respectful address. "Conan Doyle's for me! I'm goin' to China to see where they first made gunpowder. 'Ave you ever defended a known criminal, like in them Whitechapel murders?"

"Privy paper and penny dreadfuls!" Beryl smacked the boy across his head. "Horace, don't listen! He thinks he's Guy Fawkes and blew up the Royal Empire Bank!" She smacked Sam again. "Gentlemen don't defend blackguards!"

"Let 'im be! You'll 'urt 'im!" Rosie begged.

Beryl hit Sam again. "Useless! He's a born liar!"

"That was make-believe about the bank, wasn't it, Sam?" Rosie cried.

Her intervention before so many onlookers seemed to offend him. "I ain't no child!"

"Then feed yourself for a change!" Beryl taunted. "Don't look so sorry for him, Rosie! Bloody scab's off to Geoff's next. See what he has to eat, little spy!"

"Maybe I will!" Sam howled back at Beryl, suddenly red-faced.

"Go to the devil!" Beryl threw up her hands, and the boy scampered off.

"Sam!" Rosie ran into the darkening street after him.

"Ignorant little beast! You're just like Geoff Ratchet!" Beryl yelled.

Rosie spun to face her, eyes snapping furiously. A hush fell over their audience. Abashed, Beryl turned on her heel and pushed between the women. A few titters of laughter followed. Horace remained downstairs with Rosie. Cries of sympathy for the boy went up once

Beryl was at their flat's door. "Stupid lot of gaping cows," she had muttered.

Maybe she hadn't been fair. Beryl's fingers drifted through Rosie's curls.

"You terrify 'im, that's why he don't speak open!"

"Worse than useless!" she complained, but had not thrown away the boy's note. After the fight, its significance grew and troubled her. The accounts of what happened after Court's knockout must be mistaken. But what had become of him, or Sam and the rest?

The novel lying open on the sofa's back threatened to slip. Beryl caught and set *Evelina* on the table next to her whiskey bottle. Rosie loved books with pictures. The smell of Moroccan leather covers and the sight of marbled end papers delighted her, too. Mostly, she loved it when Beryl read aloud and performed the voices. When Rosie spotted *Evelina* at a used book stall on their last daytrip to Brighton, Beryl had made much ado about its exorbitant price, but been secretly pleased. The novel was one of the first they ever shared, long ago when they were still girls. As soon as Rosie's disappointed back was turned, Beryl had bought the book and been more than richly rewarded when she presented it before they went to bed.

No hope of any of that, not with Rosie's present mood. It had been a long time, too long. With an unsteady hand, Beryl groped for her whiskey. The glass tipped, slopping liquid onto the table, and splashed the cover of *Evelina*. She snatched for the book. What had been perfect was marred forever. With an impatient gesture, she flipped the novel onto the carpet where it lay before the grate like a wounded bird.

Even the best stories were nonsense. Court's beloved *Arabian Nights* and old Ali Baba: now there was a pack of lies. How often did anyone outwit such brutes, like Piani? King Arthur and his crew, another great, steaming pile. Except Mallory got it right about Lancelot and Mordred: best friends and family were only too apt to do one in. Take Geoff, for instance. Guinevere was a traitorous whore, as well.

Rosie shifted against Beryl's lap, murmured, and drifted off to sleep once more.

Poor Court, that woman had turned his head. Rosie still berated herself for giving him money. Beryl tried to comfort. Court met the Crown Prince because of her generosity. Who knew what might come of that? Privately, she agreed that Rosie had been foolish. Any cash in Court's pockets was temptation to act rashly in the presence of a pretty piece of flesh, equine or human.

Rosie wept at the news of Court's capture as though it was a death sentence. Beryl had paced about the flat, outraged and shamed by her impotence in the face of his tormentors. The sight of him dragged away by Piani's men almost killed her, but she begged Horace not to involve the police. Rosie's tears made her angrier with herself. She had thrown down Horace's latest gift, her pink and black hat, and kicked it. She tore at her jacket's buttons and cursed her tight boots.

Rosie automatically stooped to unlace them. Then, she gathered up the smashed hat. Her own little fingers had trimmed its veil and fashioned its velvet roses. With downcast eyes, she got out her sewing basket and began to repair the damage.

Beryl had burst forth with an oath. "I'll kill that bastard Geoff Ratchet! See if I don't!"

"Why're you so surprised?" Rosie sighed. "'E's actin' no more than 'imself. If you'd seen Court when I said not to go out—." Her tears flowed while she worked. "Champin' at the bit! Ready to make somethin' grand o' 'is life 'e was with all that money 'e'd won, or—."

"Or throw it all away on something grander?" Beryl finished. "Like that fool woman!"

Rosie spoke with equal vehemence. "'E got a right to dream! It ain't the money! What about pride and 'avin' somethin' o' your own?" She cried harder. "'E ain't cared what would 'appen to 'im since Sadie was laid in 'er grave. Only today 'e did!"

"Then he's a fool!" Beryl shouted. "What was he thinking, risking it all like that?"

Rosie let the hat drop to her lap. "I'm tryin' to tell you! All your brains, you're thick as a post! Court's ripe for the pickin' and the woman got 'im! It's the same with Sam. If somebody don't look after 'im, no tellin' what that boy'll get up to—or 'o 'e'll give 'way to."

Beryl rolled her eyes and voiced her wonder at Rosie's capacity for soft-heartedness, especially for the undeserving. But Rosie's talk made her uneasy. Even before Court and Fanny's brief and extremely light-hearted fling, her brother had always tolerated Sam's puppyish need for attention, and went out of his way to be good to the kid. She was under no such obligation. "Sam's got to look out for himself."

Rosie didn't argue. Instead, she hired Sam to carry her messages to Court and bring them news. "What's the 'arm? It makes the lad feel needed. It makes 'im feel important!"

"That's what I mean. It puts ideas in his head!"

"What's wrong with that?"

"The day he sticks out his palm and you don't have a penny to put on it, you'll see."

The boy was an erratic reporter, arrived unannounced at all hours and, if other women were present and he was out of Beryl's reach, pocketed Rosie's money with an arrogance worthy of Piani's most hardened collectors. Rosie seemed impervious to his insolence. Reeking of tobacco, he slouched into the Montague's foyer or appeared at the Lancaster's kitchen door to wait for her. Unless prompted to a private conversation with Rosie by a coin whose value he respected, he treated anyone who would listen to minutia of no consequence and talked by the hour.

The whores were entertained by how many raw eggs Seamus Todd ate for breakfast. Sam stood on one leg and imitated how Court swore during his conditioning regime. Donning a hat and shawl, he described the color and cut of the dresses worn by the tarts who accompanied Piani to training sessions; and with an air of great secrecy, he told them about a fat, bosomy blonde on whom Court was sweet. He dropped his voice to a stage whisper, screwed up one eye, and laid a finger against his nose. The Montague's women roared with laughter.

Only slowly, when it was the three of them, did he unfold the grimmer details of Court's daily living arrangements. Sitting before the grate on Rosie's footstool, he ate and talked all at once. For Rosie's sake, Beryl endured Sam's twaddle and resisted the urge to strike him. She did not like what she heard, but hid her concern. Rosie could not. Sam was maddeningly offhand and at his most heartless when he could see that she suffered.

"It's all me fault!" she cried.

"Oh, 'e gets on well enough!" Sam polished his shilling and bit it. "They feeds 'im like 'e'll die tomorrow. 'Course 'e probably will, fightin' Seamus Todd."

"You're getting fat, too," Beryl said. "Who else feeds you besides Rosie?"

Red-faced, Sam clutched his coins and took off. Beryl wished him good riddance, but like Rosie, she was sure he carried some of their misery with him.

Later while they lay in bed, Rosie asked, "What'll become of 'im?"

Beryl feigned sleep. She would not say what Rosie wanted to hear or encourage the woman to open her heart and their flat to an orphan. If Fanny and her beau saw fit to leave a stray pup behind, so be it. Rosie shifted and sighed.

Beryl had stared into the dark. Neither she nor Rosie knew their exact age. A lifetime ago, they squashed with Court and Geoff onto the same pew in the Methodist chapel, their faces and clothes rendered less filthy by the mellow colors that poured from the painted glass window. She had been willing to risk petty crimes or a boring pastor to get a bite to eat and out of her stepfather's way.

"Sam will scrape by, same as the rest of us," she mumbled, turning on her side.

It was all the dreaming that did one in. Dreams were the beginning of hopes and the end of them. She had run to the mission, driven by hunger, but mostly hoping the angel with light brown curls, the one Court called Rosie, would be there. Seated in chapel, trying to catch the girl's eye before Court did, Beryl began a career of dreaming and making plans for her love that were far more elaborate than all her brother's *Arabian Nights.*

Winter mornings, they waited impatiently for the young pastor's interminable prayer to end and the soup kitchen to open. As always, she and Rosie were flanked by the boys. Court sat by Rosie, stifling yawns but obediently squeezing his eyes shut during the benediction; Geoff slouched by Beryl, audibly snoring and ready to drool. Rosie opened one eye to peek at him. Beryl's eyes were already open since she used every available occasion to stare at the pretty face beside hers. Their eyes met. The girl's smothered giggles brought the blood to Beryl's cheeks. She turned away. A little finger brushed hers. Their eyes met again.

Time stopped.

They sang the blessing. The minister, the altar, the painted banner of Jesus the Good Shepherd that hung behind the platform: they were the same old objects but different, transformed, and lit from within like her. In a flash, she understood. Nothing would ever be the same. Life wasn't just moments flitting by; it was the means to an end, to her goal, her mission. Not that she had been able to convince Rosie to run away with her until many days afterward; and while the physical pact between them that was to confirm what Beryl had always known about herself was months off, she was already bound, body and soul, to Rose Cartwright.

Youth's passions were the only ones that mattered. One ought to forget them, but never did. They kept one alive. She had mourned her mother's death, but was mostly relieved for an end to the woman's pain. Until Court's fight, she never considered how his loss would affect her.

Most of all, she could not imagine life without Rosie. Without her girl, nothing would matter.

Over the weeks, Sam's assurance grew. Beryl blamed Rosie's indulgence and seethed when she returned from riding with Horace to find the two cozily seated by the fire. Rosie always laid out a spread: iced ginger cakes, a huge plate of corned beef sandwiches. The gilt on her Mandalay tea set glinted in the light. Beryl had shut the door with unnecessary force.

Sam stuffed the last of his cake into his mouth.

Rosie calmly wound a skein of wool. "I'm going to make Sam a jumper."

On Beryl's desk, a cigar butt swam in one of Rosie's china saucers.

Recently, Sam had begun to smoke. Geoff's cigars, he'd bragged, coughing and a bit green. At Beryl's scowl, he put it out. "Braggadocio! Broad hints! A bigger liar than Geoff! A more hapless romantic than my brother!" she had complained to Horace. "What's to trust? There's some sort of plan for this fight, but the brat won't say. I'll wring it out of him!"

Beryl dumped the slop of cigar butt, ashes, and tea into the dustbin by her desk.

Warily, Sam took another sandwich. Between mouthfuls, he addressed Rosie. "Like I was sayin', 'Ez'll protect Fan." The woman filled his plate and handed it to him along with a ball of wool. "I got me eye on things 'ere."

Beryl pored over Rosie's account book, trying to make sense of the month's expenses. As usual, she had overspent. This put her in an even fouler mood. The smell of food or what was left of it didn't help. She was hungry but needed to lose more weight. The sandwiches did not look like those that came from the Lancaster's kitchen. Rosie must have bought the meat especially for Sam and made them herself.

"So, Fanny writes you all the time, eh?" Beryl growled. "She and Hez get on pretty well, I'll bet. The two of them, no one else in their way, eating them out of house and home."

"Don't drop that wool, Sam," Rosie said. "You're doin' it just right."

"How is Fanny?" Beryl pressed. "What news from France?"

Sam stared at the woolen threads Rosie had wrapped about his hands.

"Get on with what you was sayin' about the bank," she prompted.

Sam cleared his throat, importantly. "It was all Geoff's plan. Seamus stood guard. 'Ez carried 'is army gun. Plus, they 'ad dynamite," he whispered dramatically and tapped his nose.

"Watch me yarn," Rosie scolded gently. "The papers said it was the gas lines blew."

"Don't you believe it! There's more 'o the stuff. It's Piani's! I could get it! Geoff knows. I could go to the police and drop 'im in it. That's why you don't need to worry none 'bout Court."

"BOOM!" Beryl said under her breath.

"What about Court?" Rosie asked. "Does 'e know about all this?"

Sam gave Rosie a pitying look that indicated it was beneath him to hold a charming woman accountable for her ignorance. "Court don't know nothin'! 'E slept through preliminary discussions! 'E only 'ad to drive 'em away from the bank. Geoff owes Court for savin' 'is neck."

"I doubt he sees it that way," Beryl said.

"Blood's thicker than water," Rosie retorted.

Sam continued. "That's right! Geoff's on the way up. Piani's on the way out."

"Not if he's got an arsenal, which he hasn't," Beryl said.

Sam addressed Rosie. "Court's safe! I can take down Geoff and Piani at one go."

Beryl slammed Rosie's account book shut. "Then do it! Go to the police! Save Court now, before this idiotic fight! Have my attorney's card!" She made a show of searching her pockets and glared at the pair before the grate. "Nothing but lies, stories! Don't waste your money, Rosie! But Sam, I'll grant you this, you're a great teller of tall tales!"

"'E's got to think of Fan and 'Ez, don't you?" Rosie said. "'E can't go to the police!"

"His own skin, that's all he thinks about! And his belly! And his bloody stories!" Beryl raged. "Bet Fan really misses those, hey, Sam? Be sure to send her my regards."

Sam stared at the fire. "We was a real gang at the Boar and 'Art! Geoff and Court fell out, is all. They'll set it straight. They're brothers. That's what's important, not the money. That's what Seamus says."

Beryl grunted and tried to catch Rosie's eyes, but they were fixed on Sam's face.

"Fan's not mad at you, Sam. She only left for 'Ez's sake," the woman soothed. "Your name was on that postcard what she sent."

Sam shook his head. "She wasn't thinkin' o' me."

Beryl bit her tongue and set the account book on the shelf. Aloud, she wished Geoff Ratchet dead. No one answered. She had pressed her face against the window, feeling mean-spirited and low. What was hidden in the boy's head or heart was anyone's guess. What was in hers didn't bear close inspection. What went on inside Rosie's these days, heaven only knew.

"I don't care what you does or 'o you does it with!" Rosie had shouted from atop the stool by Beryl's wardrobe. She stuffed the newly-repaired black and pink hat in its box. "What's this?" She shook the last R. S. Surtees novel, a loan from Horace. Beryl had hidden it in the box's tissue paper lining. Rosie flung the book. Beryl ducked. "Say somethin'! Or ain't I worth the effort?"

Beryl picked up the book. "I told you I'd be late. We were looking at a horse. Horace found the right one, a real beauty. Come along next time and see her."

"What do I care about an old nag? Nasty brutes what breaks necks. No thank you! Ride to 'ell with your fancy man!" Rosie paused for breath. "So, that's it? That's all you got to say?"

Beryl had felt perilously close to jerking Rosie off her perch. She was dreadfully tired and needed to change clothes for work. She grabbed her whip. "I told you. We were talking about—."

"Books, 'orses, important topics you can't discuss with me!" Rosie scoffed.

"I asked you to come!"

"You thinks I'm stupid! That I don't see what's 'appenin'!"

"Rosie, I've told you! It's not what you think."

"You don't need to tell me nothin', 'specially what I thinks! The only person you talks to these days is 'im. Not that I care." Rosie clambered off the stool and thrust her face up to Beryl's. "I ain't cared for ages! What's talk to me? Words won't change what you can't do nothin' about!"

Rosie brushed by Beryl, grabbed a pair of dirty riding boots, and threw them into the far corner. "Don't think I'm doin' these no more! Tell your gentleman from me, 'e can lick 'em clean when you're done kissin' 'is fat old arse!"

The door slammed. The Mandalay tea set rattled.

Beryl wandered into their sitting room. The flat was always so quiet and empty after Rosie left. Familiar objects sat in the corner cabinet.

Shells and fans, china dogs and cheap little trinkets her girl set such a store on. She wound up a music box.

Their first room had been over a chandler's shop. A fetid mattress, a make-shift screen fashioned from a tattered Japanese shawl that had belonged to Rosie's mother, and a sunken cane chair. Though they could rarely afford coal to fill the smoking grate, a greasy smudge darkened the sharply-sloped ceiling. In Beryl's memory, it always rained or was foggy. Thick, dun-colored air perpetually obscured the twisting alley and clotted one's lungs. After the men who followed her or Rosie upstairs pulled up their trousers and departed, Beryl lay with Rosie clasped shivering in her arms and peered at the skylight, mentally counting their money, calculating the price of their freedom. No more violent step-fathers or depraved uncles to fend off!

The line of men who came upstairs seemed endless. At least they paid for their offenses.

Above the dirty skylight, a pale disc shone whitely from behind ragged clouds. Beryl blinked at the sun and tried to pray. In chapel, the pastor said Jesus stood at the door and knocked. Beryl listened. Except for a mouse scratching in the wall, the room was quiet. Beyond the circle of her girl's arms, she could not feel Him at all. If there was a God, what did He think of them for what they did in order to eat? She didn't think about it for long. She was too exhausted.

People had always told Beryl she was clever. That meant eluding police, pulling one off, getting one over. The naïve and gullible took what they got down her way; laughter was the least painful consequence for one's follies. By Sam's age, she had already learned that taking advantage of another's credulity had an especially sweet savor when her dupe assumed that he was more intelligent than she was. Her stepfather, for instance, or Rosie's vile sire and monstrous lecher of an uncle. Evading Piani had been equally rewarding, but Beryl never made the mistake of thinking him stupid. While she and Rosie lived above the chandler's shop, she had to exert her utmost efforts to frustrate his pimps, and finally fled with Rosie to Bess Montague.

"How much do you still owe this Madam?" Horace asked. "Don't think of this as a loan." He reached for his billfold, his milky blue eyes searching hers. "Take it! You and Rosie could be quit of this wretched place and in your little seaside cottage in no time! Isn't that what you want?"

It was all she had ever wanted.

Beryl had risen from the couch in Horace's room, buttoned her shirt, and coiled her whip. She didn't want to talk about it. Were they going to ride or not?

Horace brushed his thinning hair. Probably, he was one of those fellows who had always looked middle aged. He carefully fixed thick-lensed glasses on his snub nose and grunted as he struggled to pull up his braces. She helped him into his riding jacket and brushed dandruff off his shoulders. He was so unassuming he did not require a manservant. It was difficult to imagine him striking terror into anyone's heart in a court room.

New girls at the Lancaster Arms laughed behind their hands at their first sight of Bess Montague. Some whispered that she was a man. If she was, Beryl assured them that Madam was the most strangely put-together male ever. Because Bess had personally trained her in pleasure's blackest arts, Beryl had seen her statuesque mentor in various odd, prickly costumes and states of dramatic semi-undress. Bess received alms-seekers from amongst her girls during her bath or evening robing sessions, and there the laughter died. She exhibited an unflappable aplomb as she donned her work attire that never failed to unnerve guests. Her oval, moonlike face had no distinguishing features until her maid applied makeup. From her imperious height, Bess' pale, almost colorless eyes stared down petitioners while her maid finished the lurid toilette, crowning her mistress' scraped skull with one of her many elaborate, hennaed wigs.

"Perhaps" and "maybe" were her favorite words.

Bess Montague was clever. She had no fear of P. Lili Piani. She knew too much about him. She knew much about a great many, powerful men.

"I wouldn't think of interfering with Mr. Greystone's particular requests," Bess had said to Beryl while her maid laid a rope of pearls and metal links on her boney shoulders. Other clients, important ones, might not take kindly to being ignored. "But that is your business." Madam didn't like to mention it, but Beryl's next payment and the balance of her last one was due.

If she needed time, Madam would grant ten days after the first of the month sans interest so long as Beryl was ready to join the girls for another photographic session. Sales of the last set of prints had proven extremely popular.

Beryl protested. "They were for a private client!"

"Not the original plates!" Madam showed a row of small, yellow teeth.

Beryl didn't need Rosie's help to calculate the punitive rate of Bess' compounding scale of interest if she missed another payment. Madam had rules. There was not a woman at the Lancaster Arms who did not understand the consequences of transgressing the Code of Conduct.

No walking out with a particular fellow. No visitors above stairs who were not in the register. No extra time off unless the doctor ordered it. No clients until the doctor pronounced a girl clean. No cash under the table.

Until she met Horace, Beryl could truthfully state that she had not strayed. She would be ready to pose for the next set of photographs.

Rosie was correct in one respect and justified in her anger about Horace. Beryl never completely confided all her troubles, not even to her girl. Yet somehow, she could talk to him and told him about their lives.

It was only after she had been in Bess' employ a few months that Beryl wondered if she had made a mistake. Rosie's work in the hotel's scullery was too much. She fell ill. Beryl borrowed money from Madam for a week by the seaside. The week turned into a month. Beryl spared no expense, hired a nurse, and Bess covered their bills. Too desperate to refuse, Beryl never questioned Madam's generosity.

Back in London, Madam explained her terms. Beryl countered, demanding that Rosie be made a parlor maid. It paid more and the work was not as strenuous. "Do it if you're serious 'bout us payin' you 'cause Rosie can't slave in a kitchen no more!"

The woman showed her teeth. "You're not afraid of anything, are you?"

Ever wary, Beryl answered. "Not much."

"You'll do anything, too. I know about you and your pretty friend. Such soft hands! Such sweet mouths! What wouldn't Piani do for me, I wonder, if he could have you both to himself?"

Beryl froze. "Rosie can't take no more. But I'll do whatever you—or 'im—wants."

Madam stared through her. "I don't like Signor Piani. No, I've a different scheme in mind. Your little Rose shall be a maid, and you shall be my darkest star." Bess flicked her cat o' nine tails next to Beryl's cheek.

Well into middle age, or perhaps older, Madam professed satisfaction that she no longer needed to wield the exacting disciplinary techniques she had honed for decades and for which she was so celebrated. She began to train Beryl that very hour.

Had she been quite sixteen or seventeen? She couldn't be sure.

At first, the work was a relief. She didn't have to go with men in the regular way or be touched unless she allowed it. Violence did not bother her when she was not its recipient. What she did to the men and with the girls left her numb. She slept by day, rose at dusk, and learned to think of herself as a performer. Hearts beat. Bodies climaxed. Lusts were satisfied.

One's inner life or who one was, these were less than inconsequential. They were meaningless. What mattered was money. Their goal. Rosie. Believe in the moment absolutely. Then set aside the whip and the night's memories. Otherwise, all was lost.

It took two years to pay back all she owed to Madam. Rosie kept strict household accounts. The money was good but never quite enough. Rosie's lungs became inflamed. They returned to the seaside. It happened again and again. Each time, Beryl swore she would not accrue more debt.

Horace shook his head at their history. "Rosie is asthmatic and always will be. She must have a more healthful climate. What do you owe this dreadful creature for the last treatment?"

Not much, she lied. Beryl faltered as she described her part in Bess' new business venture, what Madam called her "erotic tableaux." It was only after the first session that she realized how thoroughly Madam had cheated her and the other girls. "We only got paid for posing. I didn't think to ask for a share of the profits if she reproduced the pictures." She tried to make light of it. "Masks and costumes, it's all total make-believe, not even like a real session."

"It's Hell's merriment!" he cried. "My dearest girl, this must end! Let me help!"

"Don't!" Beryl cut him off. "I—we—have to do this, Rosie and me, no one else!"

Beryl turned deaf ears to Horace's remonstrances and pleas. His concern for their plight pained her but not nearly so much as the mission clinic's angry young doctor. They had only been on the streets a few weeks. After examining their sores, the man had pulled Beryl aside. "Your ignorance is an outrage!" Had she never wondered why the most seasoned whores shuddered to perform the perversions she and her friend stooped to? While a nurse cleaned and dosed Rosie, he explained the danger of their work. Worse than his outright condemnation was the compassion in his eyes. Beryl was stricken. She had let Rosie down. It was her fault Rosie was ill.

But back in their room a bag of coins lay under the floorboards. Her way, in spite of its risks, there would be no babies to feed. If what the doctor said was true, there might never be. She and Rosie tried to keep clean and continued to whore in earnest in the room above the chandler's shop. Their bag of coins grew.

Then one night, Rosie met a tall, blue-eyed, golden-haired soldier. Her gentleman.

"Nothing like you." Beryl raised her glass to Horace.

"What happened to the sack of money?" he asked.

"It's under the rug at the Montague Hotel."

Beryl had always read to Rosie. An excellent mimic, she strode about, acting the parts. She deepened her voice, its pitch already low and raspy from smoking. Over the years she learned many foreign phrases and cultivated a refined accent by listening to her well-heeled customers. Before Bess' training, she had delighted a client by reading long, profane passages from de Sade in French without knowing what they meant.

But it was the way Rosie had rewarded her on the bed in their little room that made Beryl ache for love's first, sweet taste. In her arms, the girl was a rare bird captured, innocent and wild. Almost too readily, she had succumbed to Beryl's caresses. An unnatural, early exposure to male brutality was the cause, Beryl had reassured herself; but the knowledge her darling could not say no made her uneasy. After Rosie's honey kisses, Beryl tasted the bitterness of jealousy.

She would not share her girl. Not with anyone, not ever.

"I shares you!" Rosie teased.

Work was different, Beryl argued. "You knows I don't care 'bout nobody else!"

"If I sees too much of me gentleman, it's only 'cause he pays so well!" Rosie argued with another kiss and handed Beryl a gold sovereign.

From behind the Japanese shawl, Beryl spied on the pair. Her darling lay with the tow-haired soldier and listened to his promises. Adoration lit her girl's face. Rapture filled Rosie's cries. Too late, Beryl understood the truth of the words she had read to Rosie in chapel. Jealousy was crueler than the grave. She crept off to sit by the reeking

Thames. She lifted a gin bottle and forced herself to swallow. It was not only to escape Piani that she took Rosie to Bess Montague's.

Her youth passed. Customers steadily flowed from Bess' personal roster of celebrated clients. Beryl's assistants never lasted long enough to get to know them. Bess chose pet names for them, always the same ones: Pearl and Ruby, Diamond and Opal. Only Beryl used her real name. Though when she tied on her mask, she often wondered who she was. It didn't matter. She knew what she had become. She was weary. At the thought of continuing until she was Bess' age before passing on the whip, Beryl felt the ground slip beneath her feet.

"So, I agreed to the pictures," she told Horace. "Posing seemed easy at first."

"My protégée!" Bess had said after the first session, stroking Beryl's dark curls. "Clever girl, you've always had such talent, such passion! Play your cards right, and one day all this might be yours." She tapped Beryl's whip handle against the vault that held the client roster.

"We'll be rich!" Rosie exclaimed. "If she makes you Madam, we can go anywhere in the world. We'll be free!"

Rosie didn't understand. Beryl didn't want any part of Madam's schemes. Even when she retired to her villa on the Riviera, she would expect Beryl to pay her tribute: a monthly check and copies of the balance sheets. The Lancaster Arms would always belong to Bess Montague.

"My dear, I'd never hold you here against your will," Bess said. "It's a matter of your priorities. It's your choice. All my girls are free to go, so long as we've settled our accounts."

Horace was right. The place was Hell.

Beryl's fingers groped for the whiskey. Maybe Court had slipped out of London. Maybe he lay misidentified in a morgue or in an unmarked, shallow grave.

Firelight shone on the sleeping Rosie. To survive, one needed craft and guile as well as others' greed and stupidity. One needed reptilian instinct. Humanity, a soul, was expendable, especially one's own. So long as she had Rosie, nothing else mattered. She had always known she was damned. Like death, that was also a sort of freedom. If one wasn't afraid, one could do anything. Except escape London.

Or Rosie's gentleman. He always knew where to find her. They didn't talk about him—and lots of other things. Beryl's days of feeling clever were long over.

APPEARANCES DECEIVE!

She read Sam's note, balled it up, and threw it on the fire.

CHAPTER 12
My Kingdom for a Horse

White stars danced and doubled. A soft metallic jangle accompanied their movement. Under Court a pallet shook and bounced. Every bone ached, yet he felt remarkably peaceful. Gradually, he realized that the stars were points of light thrown from a pierced lantern. Pots and pans swayed from hooks and clanked against one another. Outside, Grynt's reedy voice sang in an unknown language, maybe the gypsies' tongue, or Gaelic, or one more ancient. Like the wind. Court listened and wondered. At his side, Sam breathed deeply.

The next time he opened his eyes, all was still. A pink patch of sky showed through the Dutch door near his feet. He smelled wood smoke and frying bacon, and heard Grynt and Sam talking. Court rolled onto his side and carefully and sat up. He checked his mouth with his tongue for loose teeth. Miraculously, they all seemed to be in place.

"I 'eard you moanin'!" Sam wore Court's top hat and purple coat. "Oi, Court's awake!"

"We've ham and eggs," Grynt said as Sam helped Court to a camp stool by the fire, "and a lovely bit o' fresh bread." The man sat on another stool, chewing a willow stick and brewing tea in a big can.

The caravan was parked in a clearing. While Sam draped the coat over his shoulders, Court listened to a stream babble and wondered if its waters ran to the sea. Grynt handed him a mug of very strong, sugary tea and a plate laden with eggs. The grass sparkled with dew. Birds chirped and rooks cawed. Court searched for them amongst the pale silver fuzz that betokened new leaves. He bit into the bread, chewed slowly, and closed his eyes in pleasure. He drank greedily from a jug of cold water that Sam held. As for the trees that arched overhead, they spoke. Look up! A catch in his throat, he stared at their slender bodies and spreading arms. He had never been in a wood.

Sam's voice pierced his reverie. "Yesterday, you slept through Cambridge! All them tall white buildings! The river! This mornin' we're for Ely, right Grynt? Fine day for travelin', ain't it?"

"Aye, lad! Edge of spring it is and cold, even for March," the man commented.

Court tried to remember what had happened but couldn't. His hands looked like someone else's, strange and swollen, their knuckles skinned. His head ached. He felt odd, like he wasn't all there. It was all right about Cambridge he told Sam, and stared at the waving branches again.

While Sam shaved him, Grynt explained. "Seamus hit you, and you blacked out. Sam fetched a surgeon from the nearest public house. Quarter of an hour later, he announced you'd suffered a hemorrhagic stroke from the blow and died."

He had other details. Geoff quickly retired from the scene but was later seen dining handsomely on oysters and champagne at Baglioni's with Piani. "O'Connell and Davis left town, but not together. A police bloke named Patterson collected Zeke and Seamus and took them to the Boar and Hart. They both got very drunk and wept about your passing. Patterson locked them up for the night."

"For all rights and purposes, you're dead," Sam said cheerfully.

"What'll Seamus do now?" Court asked Grynt.

"When I was a little toad, me old dad took the lead in our theatricals: Solomon the Wise, King Herod, the Second Shepherd. Mum often played boy's roles. I learned all their tricks." His eyes narrowed to slits. His shoulders shook with mirth. "No one but you three ever got a good look at me once I came to town. Geoff and Signor Piani haven't the wit between them to realize no doctor ever saw you. It'll take Patterson some time as well." He tapped his nose. "Don't worry, lad. I'll see to Seamus."

Court returned to his pallet and slept a long time.

When he woke, Grynt had headed farther north. Court climbed beside him and Sam. Woods gave way to open horizon. Flat expanses of farmland bisected by occasional windbreaks stretched for miles. The road was straight and empty. A more seasoned traveler might have found the landscape dull, but Court was not seasoned. In spite of his sore ribs, he breathed deeply of freshly tilled earth. Its rich odor and the light blue sky reminded him of the race track. It also brought to mind his and Sadie's one country outing, and he wished she could be with him. In the distance, church bells pealed.

Sam leapt down from the box and ran ahead.

Grynt smiled as the boy danced down the road. "Bit of the colt's still left in that one."

"I wish I'd never got mixed up in this Adams business! I wish I'd never met Geoff!"

"You were being a mate to a mate. Only Ratchet's the wrong sort," Grynt answered.

They rode without speaking.

The older man finally broke the silence. "Shackleton's Seven Mysteries and Perpetual Shows United is on the road again!" he exclaimed merrily. "The world's stage is wide, and a change of scene helps now and then. We're going to catch up with Seamus, maybe in Hull or York, perhaps Scotland. You're welcome to come along."

"I don't know where I'm goin'," Court said. "I don't know what to do."

Grynt appeared to consider this. "Well, we're in Norfolk, near Holloways. No, I don't read minds, lad. You talk in your sleep." The old man grinned. "Girls! You're as bad as Seamus!"

"Jesus, Mary, and Joseph!"

"Now, don't take on! You may have said more than the lady would like, but not enough to make her blush too deeply. I gather your intentions are honorable?"

"As if that would make any difference for 'er and me! Did Sam 'ear?"

"Can't say. Hasn't let on if he did. Who is this lady? It sounds serious."

"She was at the bank. Geoff and I—we took 'er!"

"Whoa!" Grynt gave Court a sideways glance and slowed his horse. They approached a crossroads and its mile marker. A delivery man on his wagon rested there, talking to Sam. Grynt squinted and raised his boney finger to the side of his nose. "That changes things quite a bit, lad. Speak nothing of these matters before the boy."

The child waved and skipped toward them.

"Geoff is the only other person 'o knows 'bout me and 'er," Court said.

Grynt spoke without moving his mouth. "Signorina Bertollini aside, I doubt Mr. Ratchet has the capacity to appreciate your finer feelings and might consider your lady a liability. I'm not concerned about more than your nocturnal ramblings have already divulged, though I suspect there are some details of interest about the bank. Does the lady return your feelings?"

"I thought so. Now, I doesn't know. It was a mad night. She was...! It was...!"

"Like a dream? I know lad. If the lady offered you a place in her stables, that's friendly enough for the nonce. Ah, spring and young, lively things!" He snapped the reins and called to his horse. "Giddy-yap, Jasper!"

Sam grabbed the side of the wagon, panting. Court helped him mount. "Man said a village and a big old 'ouse is over yonder. The other way's King's Lynn."

Grynt directed his horse to the village. They entered a spinney. In the distance rose a tall, wrought iron gate between very old brick pillars. Sam pushed aside the ivy that covered a brass plate inscribed "Holloways." The gate was open. A sandy lane marked by fresh cart tracks lay beyond. Court caught a glimpse of a wagon turning a bend. A thicker wood spread to their right, and a huge tract of land opened out to their left on the other side of the spinney. Church bells clanged faintly. Wind rose and brought an unfamiliar smell that stirred Court's blood.

"Salt air!" Grynt breathed. "'Tis the Wash and the sea. This is where we part. We're off for King's Lynn tonight, then north. Wait for my letter."

Court was about to take his hat, but on second thought let Sam keep it. He bade his companions a farewell. Long, slanting shadows fell over his path. It seemed he walked for miles. The pain above his eye throbbed, distant but worrisome. In spite of the brisk wind, he wiped his brow with his neckerchief. Under the worn soles of his boots, he felt the rising damp and turn of every stone. He hugged his old purple coat around his aching ribs and was hungry. The sun sank lower, streaking the horizon with orange. The church bells pealed louder. The first thatched roofs and curls of smoke from their chimney pots appeared between the trees. He saw the wagoner and ran, hailing the driver. A place in Winifred's stables! He'd be lucky if he got one in a pig sty.

Richards had an excellent memory. He was sure he had seen the man before who now sat in the mud room, but couldn't place him. The fellow chewed a large slice of buttered bread, his eyes vacant. His ragged purple livery must have been twenty years old at least, and he wore his stringy black hair in an equally old-fashioned queue. As for the man's wounds—raw knuckles, freshly cut cheek and brow, and the yellowing bruise above his eye, Richards didn't like to say to Mrs. Pettiford that the fellow had been in a fight, but there it was.

"He's asking for a job," the housekeeper had whispered to Richards as she led him from the servants' hall where everyone was gathered for tea. The man had arrived on the back of the shopkeeper's delivery cart, dozing between sacks of flour and two large bolts of grey and pink stripped cotton cloth Mrs. Pettiford had ordered for the maids' new spring skirts. "He slurs his words a bit, but doesn't smell of drink. He says Mistress offered him a place—with you!"

As head groom, Richards felt he ought to have had some say in the matter. If it was left up to him, he would send the man packing. The fellow raised a mug of tea with scarred, shaking hands. The sympathetic expression in Mrs. Pettiford's eyes dismayed Richards not a little.

He cleared his throat and spoke in as amiable tones as he could muster. "Ahem! Well now! I'm Richards, the head groom."

"That's right!" The fellow nodded. "You're the man I wants."

"I don't know what you've heard about jobs, but we've grooms enough already."

The young man wistfully examined his diminished hunk of bread. He cast a hungry glance toward the kitchen. Behind Mrs. Pettiford, a merry burst of laughter issued from the servants' hall. "I understands, sir, but you don't. Miss de la Coeur said if I was ever in these parts I should look in and ask for groom's work."

Richards heard the man's unmistakable Cockney accent. He sniffed, but as Mrs. Pettiford said, the fellow was not drunk. He peered more closely at the man's face. He was not ill favored, only extremely rough. "Haven't I seen you somewhere?"

For the first time, the stranger's mild expression grew wary. "I don't know, maybe."

Dupree joined the group, glancing at the man. "What is this?" she asked Mrs. Pettiford.

"A vagrant," Richards said firmly.

"A tramp? Ouf!" Dupree wrinkled her nose. "The maids are getting silly. Shall I tell them to get back to work? Shall I call for Jakes or Struthers to help Mr. Richards move him on?"

"He's asking for work," Mrs. Pettiford whispered. "Let him rest a bit. He says he met Miss de la Coeur in London, but I can't see how!"

To Richards, the answer to the mystery was obvious. It must have been at one of those charity establishments in the unsavory parts of the East End where Mistress helped, a soup kitchen or clothes closet. He disliked the town and disapproved of such efforts. Young ladies did not need to expose themselves to such, and heaven knew Mistress had been exposed to enough! The Hampstead servants always made him feel a bit out of his depth, and driving in London's traffic was nerve-wracking. The horrors of the last visit had only confirmed his prejudices. The city's indigents were not like the parish poor, who knew their place and were appropriately grateful. They didn't come begging at Miss de la Coeur's door. What might this fellow expect or be up to? He and the young man eyed each other uneasily. "What's your name?"

The man stared at the floor, seemed to struggle to come to a decision, then met Richards' eye. "I 'ad a bit o' bother in London. I owed...," he hesitated, "bad sorts o' people. She knows all about it." He held out his rough hands. "I 'ad to take up fightin' again. She knows all about that, too. I don't want nothin' from 'er, 'cept work. I'll muck stalls, walk beasts, mend 'arnesses, brush 'em or whatever she—you asks—anything so's I can be 'round a 'orse and out o' the ring! Tell 'er I ain't fightin' no more!" He tore savagely with his teeth at the last of his bread and butter.

Mrs. Pettiford drew a deep breath. She was a stern but kindly woman. Her son Jim was at sea off the coast of Brazil. She constantly prayed that he would not be imperiled by rum, gambling, or the vices of wicked women. Her Christian sensibilities were roused, but so was her caution. "Do you still owe these bad people?"

"I've paid me debts several times over. Tell 'er I don't mean to get no more."

"I'll tell her nothing until we know your name, young man!" she said.

The man tapped his brow in apology. "Tell 'er 'Aymarket, Number 44 'bus. She'll know!"

Mrs. Pettiford pulled Richards into the alcove between the mudroom and the hallway to the kitchen. Out of the corner of her eye she saw Dupree scurry past the servants' hall and mount the stairs at a run. The scullery maid, the younger female staff, and Richards' nephew William took turns peering into the hall, craning their necks for a look at the man. The animation which had lit his features as he explained himself was extinguished. His eyes were vacant again.

In Mrs. Pettiford's estimation, he was not at all bad looking, though he was appallingly dirty. He had dark fine eyes and would have had a classical profile if his nose had not been obviously broken. His cheek was pitifully scarred. Yet he reminded her of a much younger.... No, she suppressed the thought hurriedly. Sentimental foolishness! Nevertheless, she searched his features with more interest. Uncanny how they took her back, but that was years ago. It couldn't be. Still, she was inclined to treat the young man with more care.

"Perhaps we could get him a bath," she said. "When Mistress and the others come in from their ride, I'll speak to her. Maybe he could spend the night in the stable? We'll send him on his way in the morning. Poor lad, one doesn't want to think the worst of one's fellow creature."

Richards cleared his throat. "I suppose it isn't Christian to judge a man for being hungry." Privately, he did judge him. If the man wanted a job in a stable, there were plenty in London. Getting into debt with bad sorts was his problem, not Miss de la Coeur's, and the stables were his province, not Mrs. Pettiford's. He'd rather she locked the fellow in a cupboard or that he sat out the night in King's Lynn police station. "Will can help me get him to the tack room."

"Mr. Richards, I do believe that would be best. I'll send out some hot water." Mrs. Pettiford bustled back to the servants' hall.

Richards and Will walked the stranger to the stable. Mrs. Pettiford soon followed with soap. Oliver, the hall boy, carried hot water. While Will set up a cot, the man washed his face and neck. He sank onto the thin mattress and was instantly asleep. With a sudden gesture, Mrs. Pettiford fitted a blanket about him. She hurried out of the tack room.

Richards had known the woman for years and never seen her so worked up, not since her son went to sea. It was very odd. He stared at the man's tranquil features. Maybe it was not at an East End soup kitchen where he had seen him. That purple coat, he could almost place it. A carriage, no. A cab, maybe?

"Keep an eye open, Will. Lock the door when you leave to look to the horses." He gave the man a final glance. He was getting old. His memory wasn't what it used to be.

꧁

Winifred let go of the bell rope. She sat behind Percival's desk and stared at the household account book but didn't see it. There were Mrs Pettiford's menus to approve for the rest of the week and Carlson's farm supply inventory to check. Rents were in another ledger. A cottage roof had fallen in. She closed the account book. She didn't like to trouble her uncle with such details in her letters, but he seemed to enjoy them. Usually, she did too, but today she'd put off these matters and gone riding instead. She still didn't want to think about them or dress for dinner either. She was tired and not the least bit hungry. In fact, she only wanted to be alone. But she ought to apologize for putting off Mrs. Pettiford all day. It had probably upset her schedule. From the desk drawer, she took out her uncle's latest letter and read the caption on Morrant's post card.

Mena House—View of Pyramids at Sunset.

She wished she had gone with them.

The room where she sat was her uncle's study. It was across the hall from his bed chamber and dressing room, a sanctuary where he retreated and read the sporting news and wrote, especially when his sisters' families or Delilah visited. No one ever entered uninvited. Unlike him, she did not expect to be left long to herself, not with her cousins and George in the house.

She opened the box that contained Percival's beloved cigarettes, banned by Dr. Frost. Inhaling the mild aroma of tobacco, she re-read her uncle's letter.

...The mignonette outside the chapel smells delightful and reminds me of you. It bloomed all winter. They were working on the links last week so had to pass the time in swimming baths instead. Stuck! Cornered! Interminable conversations (one-sided, his) each day with arthritic colonel (Boer campaign) who has nothing good to say about locals. Am sending home four Moucharabieh panels/you and cotton/Gretchen. Let me know if she wants more. No plans to return to Holloways until June unless you change your mind about G. and wish to come out here. Most people take steamers to Aswan, but the company is ghastly (more colonels). We could hire a dahabiya, just the four of us. Very pleasant, don't you think? You dressed as Isis. Spent yesterday aboard a felucca, endlessly tacking. You would enjoy the birds. Morrant and our one crewman fished (enclosed sketches). Jolly boat-chap, most

obliging. Does Dupree fish? Not a word about baksheesh from boat's captain (colonel is proved an ass). Sunset today was sublime. P.

There was a sketch of Morrant with his fishing pole and the crewman with a net, a photograph of Morrant and others on horseback at the foot of a pyramid, and finally a caricatured self-portrait of Percival swimming away from a walrus-like creature who wore a huge moustache and military medals. She wished Percival would not be so brave so that she didn't have to be either. She re-read Morrant's card too.

Answer to your Question: Lungs still v. bad. P. sleeps a Great Deal, SMOKES on sly. Your Letter cheered Him (us!) up no end. M.

The tears came suddenly, and she wiped them away. She would not break down. She shut Percival's cigarette case, put it and her correspondence back in the drawer, and gazed out the window and across the yard toward the stables. It was a lovely evening.

If Percival dreaded the onset of autumn, for her the birth of spring had been particularly terrible this year. She could not remember ever feeling like this. The lengthening days, the odor of damp earth, the restive activity of her poultry or the baby rabbits John had gotten for the children were her private torments. She held Gretchen's infant and pressed the other small, warm bodies to hers. To do so only intensified her restlessness.

It made her blush to think of the liberties she'd allowed George since that night at the opera and how much she enjoyed him taking them. Only this afternoon, they had stolen away from Bert and Amelie. He touched and kissed her, and she did likewise to him. It was an intense relief, like slaking a burning thirst. She was dismayed at how often she needed this succor, once George showed her it was within his power to give. Each time, her ache returned with more intensity until George ended it.

She tried not to compare those intimate scenes to her hours with Court; but it was impossible not to do so. Though Court had been cruel, she'd never believed in his parting performance. Even so, his farewell had broken her heart. As she lay in bed after the police returned her to Hampstead, that wound had been more painful than the rest. It had never properly healed.

At Christmas, the news had already spread around Holloways that George had spoken to her while they were both in town. They were not officially engaged. No one in the family listened. In London, her elder cousins, usually so careful of her virtue, seemed unaccountably ready to turn a blind eye to her and George's tête-à-têtes and abandoned her to his company. Bettina was even removed. After one hour alone with him, she understood too late why they had always been so vigilant. Maybe because of their new closeness, or perhaps because he felt he had been remiss on his first attempt, George had finally offered her his ring properly, without mockery; and she had taken it with, if not exactly a glad heart, a grateful one.

It happened while they sat at the piano, playing from her old book of Schubert's Lieder. Gretchen had suddenly remembered she left her embroidery next to the baby's crib, and Delilah had dragged Amelie from the room. George ignored the exodus. He commiserated with Winifred on the worsened state of her uncle's health and complained about wheat prices. When talk turned to renovations at Hereford Hall, he glossed over the severity of his old money troubles even as he enumerated new ones.

"I can't let the house fall down, after all. Mother's never satisfied unless it's Charles' idea."

"He says the same about you."

"God, how I wish she'd die sometimes, or go to live with him."

"Maybe she will. She doesn't like me." Winifred smiled.

"Mama doesn't like anyone! We'll stay in London or travel."

"I don't know if I'd like that, not all the time."

George shrugged. "Only if she's at the Hall then. We'll visit all the great opera houses, then go east, around the world! Let's go to California!"

"Was Charlotte really mistress to a Bavarian prince?"

"Now there's someone of whom Mama really didn't approve." He imitated his mother's voice, whispering loudly. "George! She's a Jewess!"

"But that didn't matter because you loved her."

"Nothing mattered! I was tired of the army, of being on my own, of home. So, I took up with Lottie. Our affair was like playing a high-stakes game—exciting! One day, we were both played out. It wounded my pride a little when it ended. That was all. We weren't close. Not like us."

Gone was the bantering tone with which he'd teased her when she was a girl. Winifred was flattered by his confidence but incredulous. "If there had been a child, would you have asked her to marry you?"

George had smiled his most charming smile and played a few desultory notes. "I saw a lot when I was in the army, Win. I learned not to care for much. A fellow pays for that."

"Isn't that's what everybody thinks I'm going to do for you?"

"Don't make it sound as though it's only about the money."

"Isn't it?"

He played the piano some more. "Darling Win," he spoke almost to himself, "Hell's a pleasure palace whose rooms are full of every sweet. A fellow wakes one day and sees it for what it is. He doesn't want to stay there forever. He'd go mad!"

"Would he? But if he did stay, I'd understand. We'd still be friends," she offered.

He gently struck a melancholy chord. "We've always been a bit more that, haven't we?"

"I don't know."

"That's my fault." From her finger, he withdrew the ring he'd given her at the opera. "Do you remember our first Christmas dance? You stepped on my boots and made me laugh."

"I ate too much cake, got it on my dress, and cried!" She shook her head at the memory.

"I told you then I wouldn't forget you. I want to love someone, Win. I want it to be you. A man can keep a harem, but he should only have one wife." He stopped smiling and knelt. "I only want one. I'll never marry anybody else but you, Win. I swear it!"

No woman had ever looked long or deeply into George's eyes without feeling their narcotic force and hoping vainly that there might be some truth in them. Winifred was not sure what she saw in George's.

"Marry me, Winifred," he whispered and slid the ring on her finger. "Be my wife."

The sapphire and diamonds on her finger sparkled. At the memory of George's kiss, tears surprised her as much as the pleasure she had taken from his touch that afternoon. She felt confused and unhappy. How ready she'd been to betray Court, to forget her heartache and let George pet and caress her. She pulled off the ring and shut it in the drawer with her letters.

Bettina's voice called breathlessly from the hall. "Mademoiselle! Oh, I have been looking for you all over! A man is downstairs with Mrs. Pettiford and Richards asking for you!" She grasped Winifred's hands. "It is 'Aymarket, Number 44! Mademoiselle, it is THE MAN!"

Mrs. Pettiford entered the room. "Gracious, Dupree, you must have flown up the stairs. How dark it is!" She turned up the lamps. "Come this way young man!"

Court followed stiffly after the housekeeper, glanced briefly at Bettina, then around the room. Winifred took in his bruises and skinned knuckles, the new scar on his cheek. His hair, sleek and damp, curled over his collar. He was more ragged than ever but much better fed. When they'd met, his coat almost hung on him. Now it was tight in the shoulders and arms.

Mrs. Pettiford spoke. "I heard your bell but had to fetch this man from the stable. I took care of those menus. Otherwise, I couldn't get the orders in on time. We'll dine at eight-thirty as you said. Did Dupree already tell you about Mr.—?"

"Mr. Furor!" Winifred managed to say. "Yes!"

"Oh, oui! Yes!" Bettina nodded vigorously.

"Thank you, Dupree. I'll leave you to manage." Mrs. Pettiford nodded at Court. "Good evening, Miss and good luck, Mr. Furor!" She gave Court a small, encouraging smile before she closed the door.

Winifred's eyes followed Court's from the Indian rugs to the leather-bound books, the damask chairs and couch, and the scrolled ceiling. His gaze finally rested on a painting of a horse that hung over the fireplace. All the while, Bettina watched her.

"It's a Stubbs," Winifred said.

"I know what it is," he said quietly.

"What happened to you? Was it Piani?"

He touched his brow and looked uneasily at Bettina.

"Bettina, fetch my shawl." She motioned at her maid desperately.

"Oui, Mademoiselle!" In a whisper she added, "The others are coming upstairs!"

Winifred waited until Bettina was gone. "Court! I can't believe it! How did you get here?"

He stared at the picture, slightly shaking, and clenched his hands by his sides. His face was a mask of barely contained rage. "Does you still want a groom or not, Miss?"

"Court!" It was hardly the declaration of love she'd dreamed of. When he did not look at her, Winifred lifted her chin and spoke with hauteur to match his coldness. "That depends on you, Mr. Furor."

The tension seemed to drain from his body. He held his brow and raised his eyes to hers. "I shouldn't 'ave come," he burst out, miserably. "It's a mistake for me to be 'ere."

"No, it isn't!" Winifred rushed from behind the desk, holding out her hands. "Oh Court, of course I want a groom! I want you! How could you think that I'd change?"

"Miss!" It was a warning. He drew back from her, jerking his chin in the door's direction. Bettina had not closed it all the way.

There were steps outside, a smell of cigar smoke. George entered the room. He was dressed for dinner. As he entered, he briefly glanced at her and Court. Then he looked at Court again, raised an eyebrow, and poured a brandy. He stretched out on the couch and picked up a newspaper.

"Anything new, darling?" he asked. "Did you read your letters?"

Court's eyes followed George, blazing.

Amelie and Bert came in next, followed by Gretchen and John. Everyone was dressed for dinner. They all stared at Court except George, who continued to read.

"Who is this?" Amelie asked.

Winifred's mouth was dry. "This is Mr. Furor, our new groom."

"I'll go Miss," Court said.

"Are you all right?" Amelie asked him. "He's sweating, Winifred. Isn't he sweating, Bert?"

"I'm fine!" Court said sharply. "Miss," he added.

"He doesn't look fine," Gretchen said. "He looks ill. Are you ill?"

"Maybe he was kicked by a horse," George offered from behind his paper, "or knocked out by a big, dumb ox."

"That is a terrific bruise," Bert said with admiration.

"You've been in a fight," John said. He poured some brandy, tasted it, and filled his glass. "Look at that nose! He's a boxer. What do you say, Bert? He's from the South, heads or tails, and give us a quid, eh?"

"Tails! Make it two!"

"Done! Damn!" John chuckled and passed the notes to Bert.

"He's a prizefighter out of London. Did he tell you that, darling?" George folded his paper. "Didn't he tell you that while he begged a job?"

"He wasn't begging!" Winifred said quickly.

"I spoke with Mrs. Pettiford on the stairs. Am I right, man?"

"Somethin' like that." Court clenched his teeth.

Winifred bit her tongue but was ready to lash George with it. His announcement and the certainty that he was enjoying a private joke at Court's expense rattled her.

"Good lord, Winifred, you didn't lose your ring while you were riding?" Gretchen asked.

"Again? Not your engagement ring!" Amelie cried.

"I put it in the drawer!" Winfred exclaimed impatiently.

Gretchen went to the desk and took out the ring. "If you keep taking it off, it's going to get lost. The baby found it in your sewing basket this morning. I had to take it out of his mouth—again!" She looked significantly at Amelie while she handed the ring to Winifred.

She thrust it on. "My fingers swell!"

Gretchen raised her eyebrows, stared over her glasses at Winifred, and sat on the window seat. "Mmm! Mmm! Now where did I put my wedding ring? Aha!" She held up her hand.

Court's expression grew thunderous. "I'll just go to the stable. Evening, Miss."

"Not until you're dismissed, man!" George whispered sharply from behind his paper.

Winifred saw him bite his lip and shake with silent laughter.

Bert picked up one of the lamps. "I'll light your way, Mr. Furor."

As soon as the door closed, George threw down his paper and burst into a loud laugh.

"What is so funny?" Amelie asked.

"It's not a joke!" Winifred sat next to George. "The man needs work!"

Gretchen called to her husband. "Richards doesn't need another groom, does he? Is the man here for the foaling?" She turned to Winifred. "Why did you put your ring in the drawer? It's a silly place. One of the little Scots will find it."

"Is he good?" John took the racing section from George and flopped onto an armchair.

Bettina entered with the shawl. "Will you dress, Miss?"

"I'm too tired!" Winifred snapped. "There isn't time. I'm sorry. I won't be up late."

"Of course, Mademoiselle." Bettina did not appear offended. She glanced from Winifred to George, raised an eyebrow, then left.

"So, he simply turned up, or did you know him already, too?" Amelie asked.

Winifred did not look at George, who peered over his paper at her.

"Darling?" he prompted. "Amelie asked you a question."

"He looks as though he walked all the way!" Amelie went on. "He looks like a character out of Dickens, doesn't he, Gretchen?"

"Maybe he followed her home from London like a smelly black dog," George chuckled.

Bert re-entered looking excited. "John, your mare's definitely going to foal tonight!"

From behind his paper, John gave a contented grunt.

"How do you know him?" Winifred quietly asked George.

Instead of answering, George addressed John. "You ask whether Furor's any good? Hit and miss! I've lost money on the blighter! Fellow from my regiment, Hezekiah Boors, and I used to play cards with his mate Adams at the Boar and Hart. Furor's usually there. Den of thieves! He and Hez sparred for a lark. Fellow's second-rate. Maybe he'll make a better groom."

Winifred was alarmed. She had not heard those names since the detectives questioned her. "Selway Adams? You never said you knew him. Who else do you know from this pub?"

Amelie whispered, "Bert, isn't that the clerk who died after the bank explosion?"

Bert whispered back. "It's not been proved there's a connection. That's hearsay!"

"It could be anarchists!"

"Amelie, Winifred doesn't want us to talk about that," Gretchen warned.

"Then it's still being blamed on the gas lines?" Amelie whispered to Bert.

"It's under investigation!" He widened his eyes and mouthed for her to be quiet.

"What? Why?" Amelie asked innocently and bent nearer to Bert.

"I only know what we talked about because the brother of one of the fellows I went to school with is at the Yard," he whispered, "and the last time we had lunch he told me a bit, none of which is worth repeating. So, it's only hearsay at best, and rumor at worst!"

Amelie giggled at this report. "Counsel will sit down!" she said in a mock-low voice.

"It was ages ago," George explained to Winifred. "We'd both already spoken to the police, and I didn't have any information. It seemed best not to talk about it anymore. I didn't want to upset you." He smiled sweetly, then returned his attention to the racing results.

"How did Furor find his way here, I wonder?" John asked no one in particular.

Amelie spoke to Winifred. "Was that how you met him?"

"What?" Winifred asked sharply. "Who, Adams? He was Mr. Buckner's secretary."

"No, Mr. Furor!" Amelie said. "If George knows him from the pub where Adams played cards, then Mr. Furor might also know the men who went to collect from him and started the fire. George said it was a den of thieves."

"Speaking figuratively, I'm sure," Gretchen said.

"In this case, literally!" George laughed again. "By Jove Amelie, that's good thinking!"

"Amelie," Bert begged, "that's precisely what I mean by rumors. They don't know who went to the bank."

Gretchen looked out the window to the stables. "Poor dear, first foal! I do feel for her. Though I don't like to sound like your mother, Amelie, for once I will. Enough has been said on the topic of the Royal Empire Bank. Lord, I'm hungry!"

"John, what's this horse, Sweet Little Banshee? Do you like her?" George asked.

"Never heard of her," John answered. "What's she carrying?"

From afar, there was a metallic cacophony.

"The supper gong, thank heaven!" Gretchen sighed, dropping the curtain.

Bert rose and extended his arm to Winifred. "I say well done, giving a man who's down on his luck a job. I think Mr. Furor's a brick!"

"Mistress Bountiful!" George murmured and finished his brandy.

"You ought to know," Gretchen murmured back.

"What was that?" he asked pleasantly, rising and offering his arm to Gretchen.

"Winifred's so good to all of us and everyone at Holloways," Amelie said, taking John's, who gulped down the last of his drink. "And now she'll be good to Mr. Furor, won't you?"

Everyone went downstairs to the dining room. George seemed utterly undisturbed by Court's arrival. In fact, they all seemed to forget him very quickly and fell on their food with good appetites. Winifred could barely stand the sight of her soup and was ready to scream by the time Jakes brought out the last course. Finally, the men retired to the smoking room. She and her cousins sat in the drawing room where Struthers served coffee. Gretchen crocheted baby booties while Amelie played the piano. They talked about Flora, the mare who was ready to foal. Amelie wondered aloud again how Mr. Furor had found his way to Holloways. Winifred pretended to read but watched the clock in agony. The men rejoined them. Everyone played cards. Winifred could not concentrate, and John admonished her for overlooking several good tricks.

Across the table, George sat with his cards and his cigar, barely suppressing yawns. Bert talked to Struthers, who acted as butler during Morrant's absence, and had just announced the vet's arrival to John, who excitedly fortified himself with more brandy. He was very fond of his mare, he said with a wink at Gretchen.

"What do you say, George?" he asked. "We're still taking bets. What'll it be, colt or filly?"

George reached into his coat, and handed John a few coins. "Flora, is it? I'd say a colt."

John pocketed the money, and called to Bert and Struthers. More money exchanged hands. George stifled another yawn.

The whole fraternal order, the secret brotherhood wherein men drank alcohol and bonded over blood and sport and gambling and loose women open up before Winifred in George's sleepy, bored face. She rose abruptly. "I'd like to wait up, but the day's done me in."

"It was rather a long ride." George smiled indulgently and bade everyone goodnight.

As Bettina helped her undress, Winifred begged her not to ask any questions. The woman folded the clothes with great sighs. Winifred held firm. Alone, she tried to think but was too upset to do so. She tossed and turned. If George knew Court, Court must know George. Only, how well? For a long time, she lay imagining Selway Adams and Geoff playing cards with Court and George in the Boar and Hart. For all that she'd shared with both her lovers, the men were strangers to her. She didn't really know either one of them.

<hr />

The mare paced restlessly. It was well after midnight. Mr. Burns, Richards, William, and Court stood nearby. He had always wanted to witness a birth. He didn't tell the men it was his first.

Mr. Brown, the vet, washed his arm with soap and water. "Feet first, then the nose, it's a straightforward presentation." He obviously enjoyed his work. The men's relieved murmurs showed that they were ready to enjoy themselves too. "She's gone on a bit longer than I would've liked, sir, but she's about there."

"All in good time, my beauty," Mr. Burns crooned to his horse. "We're all with you."

Richards admitted that he would be glad of Court's extra hands the next day. "It will be late by the time she's finished. William will have enough to do afterward, and there are all the other beasts to look after in the morning. You said you didn't mind mucking out."

Mr. Barron appeared in the doorway. He had changed out of evening clothes into worn old tweeds. "How is Flora doing? You're looking much better," he said to Court.

Court didn't feel it, but thanked the young man.

When Mr. Barron left Court at the green baize door that led to the servants' hall, he'd never been angrier. The last few months' trials were nothing to those of the quarter hour he'd endured upstairs. Old Swank was Winifred's gentleman! That cad her intended! Not only was it a blow to his hopes, it was an abomination. If he stayed in the house a moment longer, he'd have to go back and crush the man's face. He pushed open the door and ran downstairs. He'd walk out and keep on until he dropped in a ditch. It didn't matter whether George saw him fight Seamus because it didn't matter what happened to him. Nothing mattered. He came to a standstill at the foot of the stairs, head throbbing, overcome by the image of Winifred and the man's leering face.

Mrs. Pettiford sat in her room and had invited him to join her for a cup of tea. Court barely listened as she explained the layout of the house and the most convenient stairways to use when he helped the hall boy to carry bath water or firewood. The servants' quarters had their own rules and schedules, as well as curfew. On and on she rattled, but it had soothed his nerves. She poured more tea. Voices came from the kitchen, and a footman rushed past the door with an empty tray, calling to the cook for the next course.

"You'll get used to our ways," the woman said. "Always lots of people coming and going. A large family, the de la Coeurs. There were three older sisters who had several children apiece, and there were three younger brothers. Mr. Arthur—Mistress' father—is dead. That leaves Mr. Tristan and his daughter, but they haven't visited in years. Sir Percival was the heir. He has no children, but Mistress runs the house well enough. He's in Egypt for his health. It's her cousins who are here now, Mr. and Mrs. Burns and their children, young Mr. Barron and his cousin Miss Amelie."

"What about the other man? Is 'e a cousin?"

Mrs. Pettiford laughed. "Mr. Broughton-Caruthers? Dear me, no! He's our nearest neighbor at Hereford Hall. He and Miss have been friends since she was a girl. Now they're engaged!" She sighed. "I can tell you the announcement came as a bit of a shock, though there's many have said for years it was bound to happen."

Court set down his cup and forced himself to speak. "It'll be a big weddin' then?"

"The biggest in these parts for many a year. When I think how soon June will come 'round, and all there is to do! Thank goodness she wanted to wait 'til her uncle could come home. Then there are all the arrangements for the London house and plans for the Continental trip. They'll be gone months and live at Hereford afterward, of course. Mr. Furor, are you alright?"

"It's me 'ead," Court said through his teeth. "It 'urts fierce sometimes."

She surveyed his brow with motherly concern. "Small wonder. Take one of these!" She unlocked a cabinet and took out a bottle of pills. "I heard you on the stairs. I saw you in the hall."

Court couldn't speak.

"London's a long way to come for a job. How did you meet Mistress?"

He shook his head. "It doesn't matter now."

She stared at him thoughtfully. "It'll be a different sort of life from now on Mr. Furor, if you'll let it be. A better one, I hope. No more money trouble and no more fights."

Court heard the gentleness behind this indirect reproof. "I doesn't want no more trouble."

Lying on his cot in the tack room, he thought about her words. It would be extremely difficult to let matters be. It wasn't merely that Winifred was engaged to George, it was what Court knew about the man.

Along with Hez, George Broughton-Caruthers had once been an irregular patron of the Boar and Hart. Everyone called him Gentleman George, or Old Swank. Court never gave a thought to his real name and hadn't seen him much in the past year, which suited him fine. Selway Adams had been a conceited cheat, but George was much worse. He was arrogant. He treated people, especially women, as though they were playthings.

One night, George and Hez had come to blows over Fanny. Even dull-witted Seamus had seen that George only flirted with her to get a rise out of Hez, who was in his cups. Worse still, Fanny's head had been turned by George's good looks and flash ways. When Hez caught Fanny letting the scoundrel kiss her, George made light of it. "Every man of us has ridden her a few miles before you got in the saddle. Haven't we, ma Cherie?"

Fanny was not easily insulted, but at this she burst into tears. Hez demanded satisfaction.

At low tide, George and Hez met beside the Thames. Fog threatened. It grew dark. Court agreed to act as Hez's second. Geoff volunteered to stand with George. Seamus tried to comfort Sam, who had followed them and refused to return home to his sister.

The men advanced to their marks and faced off. Hez drew his gun. Helpless with mirth, George drew his and aimed it at his own head.

Seamus clapped his hand over Sam's eyes. George pulled the trigger. He staggered. No one moved. Then he began to laugh. The air rang with the eerie, maniacal sound. It went on and on. When Hez did nothing, George flung the gun to the ground, pulled a whiskey bottle from his coat and toasted Fanny. He spread his arms, offering himself to Hez.

"When you're ready to prove your undying devotion for that WHORE, I'm ready to oblige!" George saluted and drained his bottle. "Damn all whores!"

Hez lowered his gun.

Muttering, George threw the bottle onto the sand. "I knew you couldn't do it! I don't give a tinker's damn! It's not worth it!" He stumbled away. Geoff snatched up the gun. He ran after George. The two of them disappeared into the thickening fog.

Court was disgusted. He didn't trust a person who didn't give a damn. He trusted even less one who enjoyed making others miserable for his own amusement. The man was a wretch. Sam snatched up George's bottle, ready to do what Hez refused to, but Seamus restrained the boy and took him home. Hez sat on the sand and buried his face in his hands. Court sat down with him. Through the fog, Court caught intermittent glimpses of Geoff and George. The man reeled by the river's edge, singing in a foreign tongue while Geoff grabbed at his coattails to keep him out of the water. The unearthly sound made Court's skin prickle. What in hell did the words mean?

"Damned if I know," Hez said wearily. "It's always that infernal German song about the trout when he's drunk. Think there were any bullets in his gun?"

Court didn't know.

Hez threw his onto the sand and clutched his head. "A child! How could he do that in front of the boy?" He hoped Sam was too young to understand what he'd seen.

Court had been startled by the soldier's naïveté. Perhaps Hez genuinely believed an Englishman—a gentleman—was incapable of such behavior. He didn't answer. Geoff had told him some nasty stories about Old Swank, and what he knew of Beryl's misery and infrequent retreats into alcoholic torpor confirmed them. As for Sam, he already knew much more about his sister's relations with Hez, and the opposite sex in general, than was good for a boy.

No one should be above caring for someone or something, Court thought. In his lowest moods while he was in Piani's clutches, he'd known his life mattered to Beryl and Rosie; and though his friends could do nothing for him, he knew they hadn't forgotten him. George's behavior smacked of a selfishness that Court had never experienced in his own breast and couldn't begin to comprehend. Even Mick Furor, who lived as though life was cheap, would never have put a gun to his own head.

Until he met Winifred, Court hadn't thought it possible to care so much for another person. The strength of the desire that swept through him when he saw her in the lamplight, the joy he felt as she held out her arms took his breath away. He'd pictured her so many times as he lay alone that he'd assumed he'd be prepared when he was finally confronted with the real woman. He wasn't.

Her golden hair had lain on her shoulders in thick, braided knots, and her color was up. In her close-fitting riding habit of dark brown velvet, her waist appeared so small. He could smell her lovely scent from where he stood. And her eyes! They expressed as clearly as her shouting it that she still loved him. How could she be with a man like Old Swank?

As George and one after another of her family had entered the study, all he could think was that he knew exactly what she felt like under her velvet and crisp white linen. He knew exactly how to make her melt in his hands, and she knew what to do to him. If her thoughts were like his tonight, she was miserable. He could feel her skin, even taste her. That a rogue like George might already have touched her made him blind with rage. He'd seen George at work on many a woman, always with an eye on his competition, savoring the other's jealousy, reveling in their heartache.

Like Hez, Winifred had been taken in. That was the only answer and surely that was the only reason she'd have accepted him. It didn't matter how the man acted here among decent folk. She couldn't conceive of what Old Swank was capable of when they weren't about. No, he could not, would not leave her to George no matter what the bastard threatened. Let him do his worst. She wasn't married to Gentleman George yet.

"There she goes!" William cried happily.

Mr. Barron stood by Court. The young man's face expressed the others' quiet excitement. "Come on, old girl!"

Court's heart beat rapidly as the mare's body heaved once, twice. She stopped.

"Easy my beauty, easy!" Mr. Burns coaxed. He leaned forward, completely focused.

The mare strained. A bit of slick, greyish membrane oozed between her hindquarters. After several minutes she tried again. There was more of the shining sack and within it, the distinct outline of tiny hooves, a muzzle, and the slit of a closed eye. The mare dropped down to her forelegs and rolled onto her side, breathing heavily. The men were hushed. She strained again, huffing and blowing through dilated nostrils.

Richards knelt and stroked her head, his voice low and encouraging. The mare's eye rolled at him. With a final convulsive heave, she pushed again. The slick, shining sack slid free from her vulva. The gangly foal kicked free. It lay inert, its eyes still closed. Then it sat up, blinking and shivering.

"It's a colt!" Mr. Barron said with excitement.

"Can we call him Meriwether?" William asked Mr. Burns.

"Flora's Meriwether, I like that." The man shook everyone's hand. He took out his flask and drank to Flora and her colt. He passed it to the veterinary. "Well done, Brown!"

The little colt's legs folded beneath it. It lay stunned but watchful as its mother swung her head about and licked it all over. After a bit, she nudged him to his feet. The men all laughed appreciatively as the little creature tottered forward to William and then backward to its mother. He stuck his head between her forelegs. She shook him off and nudged him back, and he began to suck lustily. The men all laughed again.

"I'm glad you were here for this," Mr. Barron said to Court.

Court took the flask from the young man and drank, feeling a bit awkward but honored.

"I don't ever get tired of it!" Richards said, resting on his heels.

"Mayhap it'll be a good beginning for you, Mr. Furor," said Mr. Burns, taking the flask from him and raising it with a wink.

Court stared at the colt, unable to respond. A lump rose in his throat. The mother nosed and licked her newborn while it continued to suckle. When Court sat in chapel as a boy, listening to the pastor's stories, he'd always enjoyed but not made much of them. This night, to whatever or whomever He was that had brought him to this stable, Court inwardly bowed his heart and gave thanks.

CHAPTER 13

Such Stuff as Dreams Are Made On

Colonel Perth had complained of backache since he came down to breakfast. At first, Percival hadn't paid much attention. Andrew always grumbled about his various afflictions or the abysmal service of the hotel's (excellent) staff. The man could be so unpleasant, truly insufferable, especially to locals. Out on the golf course, however, he had seen the man was uncomfortable. Morrant noted it as well, but neither of them alluded to it while the man swore at his caddie, Amr, and cursed his swing. By lunch, he was in real pain. Morrant suggested they call a doctor, but the colonel refused.

No reason! He wheezed, alternately laughing and wincing. He'd have a nap. Right as rain he'd be! Down for drinks by five o'clock! His body servant, the long-suffering Amr, followed him.

At supper, the portly man had hardly touched his food. Conversation went on. The other diners were oblivious. Suddenly, the colonel rose with a preoccupied grimace. The woman next to him inquired of her dining partner opposite whether she'd spoken amiss or offended. Before the words were out of her mouth, Colonel Perth's right arm shot out stiffly as though he was about to salute or address the company. His face almost purple, he pitched forward heavily and writhed on the floor.

It was his heart, the doctor told Percival and Morrant. Would he recover? His kidneys weren't good, Percival said. Any family they could contact? The nurse waited with her pen poised.

There was (supposedly) a daughter in Bristol and a son in Plymouth, and grandchildren scattered about at school and university.

None of them had much to do with Andrew. Though he always had some story to tell about one of them, Percival wondered if they actually existed. "Free as a bird, that's me!" the man liked to boast as he whacked at his golf ball. He also liked to brag that he'd raised a family that was perfectly independent of him. So much so that Colonel Perth never got any mail, Morrant had observed, and passed Percival his club.

No family as such, Percival told the nurse. "We're his only friends." He'd find out what he could from the Mena House staff or the embassy the next morning.

Andrew Perth and his wife "Teenie" (Percival had no idea of her real name and had never seen a photograph) had come to Egypt for his health, but she had been the first to take ill. A malaise had slowly overtaken her. This turned into a fever which led to a necrotic infection. "All from a mosquito!" Andrew held up his index finger and thumb and squeezed them together. "This big!" Thirty years of marriage done, just like that. He snapped his fat fingers.

Go back to the hotel, the doctor advised. He'd see to it the colonel got some rest. If any significant changes occurred, the nurse promised to contact the front desk. Amr drove them back.

At Mena House, Morrant set up Percival's portable desk on the porch outside their rooms and lit the lamps. He sat down to his book, *The Compleat Angler* (how many times had he read it?) while Percival took up his latest letter to Winifred (why couldn't he finish it?).

The life of the Heart is lived mostly in Secret, its landscape a terrain at once so unfamiliar to many as to be terrifying or traversed so often as to become a waste land where almost nothing can be felt. We are creatures of Extremes, yearning for Adventure and Excitement on the one hand and the Safety of Habit on the other. For days I have trembled to write the letter I should (must) if I am to fulfill my promise to your father, my dear brother Arthur.

As the hours draw nearer to your wedding day, it is clear that it will be impossible for me to make the trip. Yet every moment you are with me. I hold you close in my love. What I write is what should have been said before I left.

A moth flew beneath the lampshade and fluttered about the chimney near the flame. It crawled up the glass, hovered on its lip, then dropped inside and began to walk the burner's collar.

Delilah had remonstrated against what she called his "interference." He did not know what Winifred felt for George, he had argued. That was what bothered him. If it was love, it should be plain to everyone.

"But it isn't always plain," Natasha had answered. "I was terribly shy."

"You've always been a mouse," Delilah said quickly. "Your case required interference, or nothing would've ever happened! Winifred's does not. If she'll have George, it will definitely be for better or for worse."

"I can't see her making a decision she doesn't mean. Or, I hope not." Natasha sighed.

"I'm afraid it will be for the worse," Percival said. "As for what she means, Delilah, you were the one who thought she didn't know her own mind."

"She knows it in one way, to the exclusivity of all other points of view!"

"I ought to shepherd her toward George, you said. I'm glad I didn't, but I hardly congratulate myself. I didn't do anything! I should've sent her away, like you do Amelie!"

"Perhaps Winifred's not meant to be happy. Some people aren't." Natasha clapped her hand over her mouth with a look of horror and gave Percival a melancholy smile. Dear Tasha, she always reminded him of a wilted flower.

Percival dipped his pen and wrote. *If you do not know for certain, if you are not absolutely sure, put off this irreversible step. Darling girl, do not think you must take any action that goes against the dictates of your heart. Let Love Be Your Only Law and your Lodestar.*

The moth climbed up the inside of the lamp's chimney, its wings beating dangerously near the flame. Percival took out his handkerchief, swiftly pulled the shade and chimney off the lamp, and blew the moth back onto the table where it staggered in broken circles before flying away.

He held the letter's edge near the flame, then drew it back.

⚬

Beryl sat on the wall by the river. Her thinking spot, her trouble spot. It was near one of Piani's buildings, where Court had trained for his fights. It once held the old chandler's shop where she and Rosie had started out. She lifted the gin bottle again. Sam had followed her here a couple of times. She'd run him off. Court used to follow her too, to make sure she was all right.

Beryl wished she had explained about Horace to Court that day at the track. Only she was not sure she could, even to herself. Horace was different from any man she had ever met.

From her and Rosie's earliest days, she struggled to separate her work from their private life. Though one constantly threatened the other, Beryl managed a division of sorts, however flimsy, by dreaming of her and Rosie's future.

"Our Home," Rosie's needlepoint sampler read. Her girl sewed it in their first room, and its words were sacred. Beryl took them literally. Their flat was their inviolable space. In it, they rested and ate, argued and loved. One day, Rosie's sampler would hang in their seaside cottage.

From the first, Horace understood her need to dream. He'd examined her sable boudoir at the Lancaster. "I find an element of fantasy is essential to shore up one's personal life."

For instance, his purchasing the horse at Tattersall's was an absolutely fantastic and foolish gesture of true love. "It's a ridiculous, exorbitant expense," he had said excitedly. It had always been one of his most cherished dreams to own a race horse. "I'm not a gambling man," he told her, "but you make me feel I could chance anything."

The night Court had played cards with the Prince, Horace had staked such huge sums it made Beryl's knees turn to water. "I am completely and utterly alone in the world," he said. "There is no one at home to whom I must justify the risks." But she had trembled for him. As mistress of his many secrets, her heart galloped while he calmly placed higher and higher bets.

Horace had dreams of justice and fast horses and dark, strange love. Except for Beryl, there was no special friend with whom he had ever entrusted his desires. Like her, he prayed to a God in whom he believed, but whose ways challenged the limits of his courage and tested the boundaries of his credulity. Like her, he did not understand how or why he was made as he was, but hoped his Lord would go with him when he had to answer for his life and troublesome thoughts.

That a fellow creature such as Horace existed was a revelation. She'd never met anyone so unique or complex. Her response to him was complicated and new in her experience of men.

They had met in the Lancaster's darkly-draped boudoir. Horace sat in his shirt and underdrawers on the side of the couch, his paunch exposed, his knees knobby. "Pride is a peculiar sin, the cardinal one. I wondered if my prolonged celibacy might be a species of it rather than a blessed state. I have studied many texts on the subject as well as Eastern writings and their illustrations, but I felt nothing. In Paris I visited a very good maison de tolérance. The ladies were extremely kind, but to no avail. So, I thought I would try this, a more robust form of stimulation."

Beryl had passed him her whip. "If it's flagellation for your sins you want, help yourself."

"My dear, you've no idea of my visions of Hell." He glanced at the room's least severe accoutrements; leather straps and dangling harnesses, spiked masks and chains. He regarded the obscenely-shaped handle of her whip and laid it aside. "This is merely theater, or in my case, comedy."

"If you're a virgin," she said quietly, "I don't take that lightly, not at any age."

"I have always admired beauty, but never desired to possess it." He blinked at her and smiled sadly. "Well, almost never. You really are the most extraordinary creature I've ever seen."

An uncharacteristic flush overspread her cheeks. "Get undressed if you're going to."

Perhaps it was his spectacles that had made her let down her guard. He was nearly blind without them and asked for his lenses once he was trussed up. Trying not to laugh, she placed them on his nose, then worked on him for a bit. She tried a variety of techniques. Nothing happened. She laid down her whip and unwound the velvet cords from his wrists and ankles.

"I am not wholly disappointed. Perhaps we made some progress. You make me feel the thorn in my flesh I have chosen to deny. How I wish you were a boy."

"Agreed," she had answered morosely. As a member of the legal profession, his position was delicate. She respected his religious upbringing. Still, he was a customer. His second visit yielded no better result. Her professional pride was at stake. "Shall we try something else?"

"I won't break the laws of both man and God. I cannot live against the rules of the Brethren nor against the rules of my heart. I certainly don't expect you to live against your inclinations, either. I see we're of like mind, but you are nevertheless a woman. For these reasons," he continued apologetically, "a continued attempt at a physical liaison will not do. It would be absurd, ludicrous, and painful. Neither of our hearts could ever truly be in it."

Beryl was taken aback. She had only meant that if he wanted, there was a footman who didn't mind helping out for a few extra bob. With a tenderness that startled her, he pulled her peignoir over her naked skin.

"I suspect that is the root of my problem as well as yours, Miss Stuart."

The man who sat by her side was freckled and pasty and pudgy. His ginger hair was thinning, and his gestures nervous and awkward. Yet he spoke as though he knew her. Usually, she would have recoiled from such familiarity and refused to see him again. What he recognized in her and she in him was solitude of heart. He was the saddest yet merriest person she had ever met.

"When I'm working, my heart is never in it." She threw down her cigarillo and stomped it out with her boot. "What you want, it's not the end of the world. You're not the first, only it's not my usual line."

"I want clarity," he said with determination. "My heart and my actions must be of a piece, one! I cannot live a lie. Nor can you. I will not be divided in that way." He pulled up his trousers. "My Lord has never soothed my yearnings, not these, anyway. I wouldn't expect Him to. But He helps me bear the beasts that prowl about my door at night."

During his next visits, they only talked. They began to ride together, and he showed her his rooms and books. What a pleasure their conversations were! Horace was a hard-working, punctilious, immensely rich, and terribly lonely man who could have no more allowed himself an intimate physical relationship with another human being, male or female, than she could have fallen in love with the Crown Prince. For Horace, the only intimacy possible was abandonment of his will to dominion by another's—his God's. She admired his faithfulness. She accepted the honor of his regard and treasured his trust.

One afternoon after a ride in Saint James's Park, Beryl coaxed him back to her boudoir. Horace had barely to unclothe his privates and brush them against her raised buttocks before he uttered a strangled, surprised cry and she felt the full effusion of his release. He rolled onto his back, panting heavily. Beryl sank forward, her own heart beating quickly.

Horace stared resolutely at the ceiling's Grecian fresco. Beryl did too. Venus subduing Mars, she said. I see, he said, and they were quiet again. He seemed genuinely shocked to take gratification in a woman's, or anyone's, flesh. Beryl wasn't sure what she felt. As though nothing had occurred, they got dressed and talked about horses. It never happened again.

By day, Horace donned the wig of the barrister and drafted his water-tight legal briefs and stood before the courts of men. Yet he was a dreamer. He yearned for flight, for freedom, for a power beyond that which his body allowed. "A youth running, or a horse! There are no more beautiful sights." He was enslaved by his dream of a particular mare: Sweet Little Banshee. He met her during a client's shooting party and attended her first races, pursuing her thereafter with a lover's ardor. Unlike some men, his passion did not abate once he felt assured of acquiring her.

From the moment Beryl laid eyes on the Banshee, she understood his need and wanted to ride her. And the Banshee! Those sleek, trembling flanks and that bright brown eye! She could sense the animal's intelligence. Like Horace, she fell madly in love.

The day Geoff betrayed Court, the Banshee placed sixth after breaking out of a melee. No mistake, the creature wanted to win. The jockey had barely worked her. Berserker cut right across her path, but she had held on, the little trouper! While the other horses ran helter-skelter, she had seen her opening. She simply flamed up.

At Tattersall's, the groom walked the winsome, sleek animal before them. Horace tightened his hand on Beryl's. The Banshee was beautiful, perfect. From her alert eyes to her powerful hindquarters, her shining bay coat and sturdy fetlocks, the vet pronounced her sound, her conformation nearly perfect. Horace was ready to buy her. "She's the one. I see us winning with her. Can't you see it?"

Beryl returned his hand's pressure. Here was the extension to her physical power that she so yearned to realize. "Let me ride her for you!" she pleaded. "Or do you think I'm mad?"

His gloved fingers twined with hers. "My dear, we both are."

Beryl opened her eyes. It was very late. She heard bells and the cries of boatmen who dragged the river. The tide had changed. Had she slept? Her dreams were so real....

She was back at the race track, dressed in a jockey's bright uniform of scarlet, white, and black, like a playing card. Place your bets, ladies and gentlemen! The wind rose. It whipped the silk against her skin and pushed dark clouds, heavy with rain, flashing with lightning. Beryl wanted to fly to them, seize their electricity, and lose herself in the storm. Instead, she crossed the green to a dais. Court's woman sat high up, enthroned. A ray of sunlight broke through the clouds. Her golden hair shimmered like a halo. Beryl knelt and presented her whip. The woman bent, kissed Beryl's forehead, and Beryl was transformed. She was Court. She pulled the woman off her throne and kissed her back. The woman was transformed, too. Rosie!

In precious hours alone with her girl, Beryl dispensed with reality. They hired a carriage, drove around the park, or went to the music halls. Pounds and pence, the ongoing struggle to keep within their budget, all cast to the winds! Mostly, she spoiled her darling whenever possible, not only because she loved her, but because of the terrible interims of Rosie's illness. While the moments crept by and she watched the woman struggle for breath, Beryl's guilt crushed her.

In spite of Rosie's courage and probably because her work ethic was equal to Beryl's, there were days the woman could not rise from bed. Weeping in terror, she gasped for air. Beryl put out her cigarillos and opened the windows, but Rosie still complained she was being smothered. All the doctor could do was order fresh sea breezes and complete rest.

During her attacks, Beryl was always terrified Rosie would die. As soon as she was better, Beryl shook off Rosie's reflex to hang on to their few extra pounds. They sat beside the sea. While Rosie lay wrapped in blankets on a lounge chair, Beryl read to her. They walked Brighton Pier. If Rosie saw a cheap, sentimental print or parasol, or wanted another ice cream, Beryl bought it. She never voiced her dread, that Rosie would not live long enough to see their dream come true.

Beryl shouted at the nurses and hotel staff. Without regret, she added to their bill any extra comforts Rosie required. Clinging to Beryl, Rosie stared wistfully at the breaking waves. Beryl delayed the date of their return to London another day. These prolonged idylls consumed most of their savings, or it was frittered away. In London, Beryl bought a set of turquoise earrings because her girl was better and so fetching in her new silk frock as she twirled about their room. Before curtain time at the music hall, they dined out to celebrate. Beryl made believe that they were already independent, that the flat they rented for an exorbitant rate from Bess was their dear cottage by the sea. They bought another watercolor of the waves and hung it by their bed, little windows onto their dream world. Wrapping Rosie in a new cashmere shawl, she made believe her girl would never get sick again.

Because of Horace, Beryl increasingly forbore to service any but her highest paying customers. In order to have more time to ride, she fobbed off the rest to her assistants. Except for the violence, the pure physicality the appointments required, she didn't miss it. Men's pleasure in its run of the mill or its most perverse expressions struck her as ludicrous.

Court's latest term of servitude under Piani had caused her much uncomfortable reflection. "I never thought my work with Bess would last so long," she told Horace. "It would only be until we could get this amount of money, or until Rosie had seen that doctor, or until we paid off a merchant for those needful household objects." One must pay Bess' rent or get out.

Horace had agreed to check Rosie's bookkeeping. He found no fault with her accounts but gently admonished Beryl. "My dear, she's as thrifty as a Scot! When it comes to Rosie, you've a hole in your pocket. You don't know the value of a pound. You're profligate!"

He had introduced her to property law and taxes. In his company she gained access to establishments she would never have dared enter without him. During the course of a week, they were in and out of his or his colleagues' rooms at the Inns of Court, the Royal Empire Bank, Tattersall's, and the offices of various estate agents. Though she had always congratulated herself for being a quick study and managing her financial affairs much better than her father ever did, under Horace's tutelage she admitted that she had barely kept her and Rosie's heads above water. He explained investment, a concept that had been, heretofore, an abstraction.

"You have a several-headed hydra to contend with, my dear. One, your significant debts to Bess Montague; two, immediate living expenses, which Rosie's excellent budget will help rein in; three, her health—we must make plans for that; four, your old age."

"I'm not going to get old," Beryl said.

"Finally, we have to save for a mortgage, or in the short term, at least a renewable, long-term lease on a home in some coastal area that suits you both. You haven't the cash at this point for either. That is where I could assist."

"No," she said firmly.

While it might fulfill her personal sense of vengeance to whip men's backsides to ribbons, there remained a massive divide between people who grew up as she had and those who called themselves middle class, Horace said. "Additionally, in the eyes of the law, a woman can never get the upper hand." There were real, solid barriers she could not kick down: office doors and bank vaults, to name but a few.

"I wish I had some of Sam's dynamite." She had stretched out on Horace's couch and put a pillow over her head.

The institutions were guarded by men who resembled him and many of her clients. There were armies of them; phalanxes of scribbling secretaries, hunch-backed from leaning over desks; harried law clerks grown thin with overwork; hollow-eyed solicitors in ill-fitting, grizzled wigs.

"I'd like to see them strung up, stripped naked, and writhing under my whip!" she shouted.

"Pitiful creatures they may be, but they've the whip hand of you!" Horace demurred. "You've got no credit and no collateral, and aren't likely to get any!"

The futility of these outings and her powerlessness filled her with an extra measure of ferocity when she returned to work, but she could barely hide her despair from herself. It wasn't that she wanted to brutalize men per se, but she needed to express her rage at a world for which men seemed to be mostly responsible.

Horace argued that was putting it too simply. "It does you little credit to feel so much contempt for half the human race." They had mothers and fathers. They had been children once.

Beryl snorted. She could tell him a thing or two about kids—and fathers!

"Shall I tell you about mine? I've no one, nothing I can go back to— not as I am. My family cannot accept me. There is but one Father who waits, one Brother who never fails me."

"How can you believe that if the people who are supposed to love you won't prove it?"

"Men's hearts, like men's laws, are imperfect. There is always forgiveness. There is always love. Even if many of my prayers had not been answered these recent months, I'm not alone." He smiled at her. "We are who we are and what we are, but we need not be damned by it."

They had returned to the Royal Empire Bank. A gentleman named Mr. Buckner reviewed the terms of a loan. It sounded hopeless, so Beryl daydreamed about the Banshee until the words "various coastal properties in Devon" attracted her attention. The talk devolved into the season's hunting prospects. Beryl's mind wandered again. Her friend's usually nervous fingers spread over his knees and grew still. His eyes sharpened behind his glasses. Beryl was disappointed by Mr. Buckner, but Horace seemed invigorated by their chat. They took a hackney to a surveyor's office and left it with a map.

In his rooms at Lincoln's Inn once more, Beryl had poured whiskey, and tried to swallow her frustration and resentment. She sifted through the other maps and leases they had already collected, crestfallen at the rents of even the most modest houses in second-best locations. Horace unrolled their new map. There was a cottage in Cornwall, a small holding that was part of an estate where the banker had hunted. Its proximity to a village and its remoteness from a large town with a rail line seemed to meet the limitations of her finances. Horace pointed to the spot. "Mr. Buckner has stayed there himself. It overlooks the ocean, right up against a cliff's edge.

"We mustn't waste time. The owner is very eager to negotiate a lease. I could be your bank," he suggested excitedly. "A quarterly schedule at no interest—you could defer paying me for, say, the first two years. That way we—you and Rosie, I mean—could move on this now and set aside the rest of your money for a doctor. It's not so far from London we couldn't sometimes meet."

"I'd always owe you for that first two years. I can't do that."

"I see. Perhaps we can come to terms—some form of security. Yes, that's it! You could purchase a share of the Banshee, that way if she won you can...."

Beryl raised her hand to cut him off. "No good! I'd still owe you."

Horace rolled up the map.

It was their dream—theirs alone. But such an opportunity might not come again. Her and Rosie's sack lay under the floorboards. She was sorely tempted. What would Rosie say? To ride the Banshee for Horace was one thing; to buy part of her was another. Rosie had never told their plans to a soul and probably assumed Beryl had not either.

Of course, Court had known. Except for that woman's offer, he'd never had his chance. If only he'd taken it.

"You'll discuss this with Rosie of course. You have told her about all this, haven't you?"

"She doesn't know you've been advising me."

Horace was shocked. "I'd have thought—. You share everything! You're equals! Don't you want to know what she'd think? You must tell her about this today!"

But she didn't.

She had watched Rosie sleep instead. Her parted lips revealed the slightly ridged tips of her front teeth. Her lashes lay against the hollows under her eyes. She looked like a child. An ache, not happiness exactly, but one Beryl recognized as love, wrung her heart. She tipped the bottle and drank. In front of her, the Thames lapped the pebbled shoreline where Sam had liked to play.

Childhood had been a blur of tears and rages, sleepless nights at home and hungry days on the streets. The only bright spot had been her girl. "Maybe today you have nothing," the young minister had promised them in chapel, "but God is in His heaven, and there your treasure is!"

Beryl had known better. Rosie sat between her and Court, prettier than a Bible story angel, singing hymns more sweetly than a sparrow. All might not be right with the world, the pastor exhorted, but everyone had their place in it. Beryl had found hers by Rosie. She vowed to make their world the best place she could.

Geoff seemed to have found his place early as well. With Court, she and Geoff had regularly pilfered from the offering basket and stolen food from the mission's pantry. Her brother never instigated the raids, but gladly followed their lead. She wanted to pray for him but couldn't.

God! She liked His pillar of fire, His thunder and lightning, but didn't much believe in Him. Not the way Horace did. The fact of Him and His judgment—yes; but His mercy, or that He would help Court, or her and Rosie, or anyone else—no. Horace told her not to give up. They were too close, he said. To what, she wondered. Maps and cottages! Cornwall! It was only while she was on the Banshee's back that what he said seemed possible.

Horace talked about answered prayers. She knew better than to ask. God made the world right and good; men made the world wrong and bad. "It's up to you to choose to do right or wrong," Horace said. Or had that been the Methodist minister?

The world, with all its agonies and injustices, would end. She must simply get through her allotted time. If what followed was no more than unconsciousness and dirt, so be it.

What made life bearable was having Rosie to come home to after her nightmare job in the Lancaster's black boudoir. Those hours didn't matter as long as she could provide and live for and protect her girl from the wretchedness men had made. But she hadn't. Her nerve had failed. When Horace offered her their chance, she'd given him no answer. When Rosie asked what was the matter, she shouted at her to mind her own affairs.

The Thames rolled in front of her. A skiff bumped against its mooring. Fog rose.

She violently wished she were a man, for physical power her slight frame could never give her. She envied Court his time in the ring, even if he had died there. How she longed to smash Geoff's teeth with her fists. If she were supreme ruler for a day, she'd mount that dais in the middle of the green and pitch her lightning bolts. Heads would roll. She would enjoy spilling blood! As for Piani! They used to draw and quarter traitors, and stick their heads on pikes along London Bridge. Her fingers tightened.

"Oi! That's me 'air you're pullin'!" Rosie gently protested. "Talkin' in your sleep again. 'O's you takin' to London Bridge?"

"Rosie!"

Beryl started to her feet, stumbled, and sat down hard on the pebbled shore. She was alone, shouting at the air. Her bottle was almost empty. Time to open another. Like Horace said, a bit of fantasy was essential. If she couldn't have that, she'd take gin.

❧

Morrant opened the curtains of Percival's room. They had an excellent view of the Pyramids, and the morning air shimmered like polished glass.

He directed the young man to set down the breakfast tray while the boy went into the bathroom to fill the tub. On the porch, Percival had left his letters from the evening before, stacked for the morning's posting. He must have burnt several others before going to bed. There was a mess of ashes on the blotter. Morrant cleared them and blew from the lamp's chimney the remains of a moth that had incinerated itself. On top of the letters was a postcard of the Sphinx that Percival had written his niece.

Great OAF Col. Perth fell in his soup last night. M. and I had to fish him out. Must have some Company on the Links. Will spend day in hospital defending his man Amr (nice lad) from the Walrus' tusks. Still undecided re: coming home your Big Day (extremely large package arriving Holloways soon). Greetings to G. My Love to you, P.

Morrant frowned and replaced the card on top of the stack of mail. Percival had said he was going to write a letter to Miss Winifred. Morrant searched for it then considered the ashes on the desk.

"Something is the matter, Mr. Morrant? Something else?"

He handed the mail to the young man and gave instructions to order a driver. They would be gone for the rest of the morning but back by midday. Golf? Perhaps, it depended on how they found the Colonel. They might require the driver to take them to hospital after lunch as well.

As soon as the young Egyptian closed the door, Percival stirred in his bedroom. Morrant took down his master's fresh suit, set out the shaving kit, and set the breakfast tray and newspaper on the card table.

Another day in Cairo.

CHAPTER 14
Trout

Detective Inspector James Patterson sat at his desk. Detective Sergeant Peele sat next to him. Beside the door, a constable stood. Geoff Ratchet sprawled in a chair. It was not the first time they'd brought the man in for questioning, and it wouldn't be the last. Patterson wanted to send the officer away, lock the door, and wipe the grin off the son of a bitch's face. Instead, he mulled over his notes.

On reconsideration of their contents, he was intrigued more than ever by the outcome of the fight between Todd and Furor. From information he had gathered about Furor's and Geoff's movements in the days prior to the business at the Royal Empire Bank, he was sure he'd identified Geoff's driver; but that was neither here nor there if Court Furor was dead. If he was alive, however, that was another matter. They couldn't find a body. They also couldn't find the doctor. He hadn't ruled out any possibilities yet and wondered if Geoff had similar thoughts.

Dumb as Seamus Todd might be, he was a skilled and even gifted boxer who didn't make ham-fisted mistakes. Todd as part of a conspiracy to premeditate murder, especially of a friend, was difficult to imagine. Todd being coerced if he was sufficiently afraid that someone near and dear might get hurt if he didn't comply with orders was a possibility. Fearsomely bearlike in nature, Todd also had a she-bear's fierce protectiveness.

Sam Merton had been spotted in both Todd's and Geoff's company quite a bit before the fight, moving back and forth between Todd's and Furor's training quarters. The boy also went frequently to Bess

Montague's establishments. Furor had a sister and a friend who both worked at the Lancaster Arms. Todd had waxed sentimental in Peele's presence about the women, the sister, Miss Stuart, especially. Todd also spoke in affectionate tones about Sam, feeling in loco parentis since the boy's sister and her fiancé had left the child on his own. Todd would lay down his life for the right person. Only, which one of them was it? And what or who had come between the men if, in fact, Todd had delivered a fatal blow?

There was an easy answer to that last question. Geoffrey Michael Ratchet. Now there sat a scoundrel who'd find a way to get a fight going between a saint and his mother. Zeke Odom had said that Furor and Geoff were family, cousins or half-brothers; he wasn't certain. Patterson narrowed his eyes and clipped off the end of a cigar with especial vigor.

"I've been thinking how you've been getting on in the world, Geoff. Your fortunes have looked up recently. Piani's niece, is it?" He lit his cigar and puffed a large cloud of smoke.

Geoff was impassive. "The banns is bein' read."

"Signorina Bertollini's uncle has set you up in one of his tailoring shops."

"A gentlemen's haberdashery and outfitters," Geoff corrected, brushing a new bowler hat.

Patterson puffed luxuriously on his cigar. All those gaudy new rings of Geoff's. Flashy! He was willing to take his time to reel in his man. "I worry about you sometimes, Geoff. I truly do."

The man cut his eyes at Peele. "I prefers Mr. Ratchet."

"To think I remember you before you wore long trousers, Geoff. A young man on his way up can make a false step. Down he comes a-crashing. We wouldn't want that, would we?"

"You wants somethin'."

"Let's go fishing."

The officer guarding the door smothered a laugh. Peele gave him a warning look.

Geoff made a motion to rise. "Bugger that! I gots business to tend."

The officer stepped forward. Patterson raised the hand that held his cigar. "All work and no play? You will get on. Another time maybe. But before you go...."

Geoff drew an impatient breath and settled back on his chair.

Patterson tapped his bulging notepad. "Let me relate a cautionary tale, something to think on while you're minding the shop. Always remember to take time to think." He did not give Geoff the opportunity to respond, though the man had opened his mouth. "Imagine you're this history's protagonist. Scene One: two men vandalize a bank office, assault a clerk, and set off a round of dynamite which hits a gas line. The clerk is the natural son of an earl who has friends in politics that would like to make the case into, say, a rallying cry for cleaning up our slums."

Geoff appeared bored.

"Scene Two: as a result of complications from his wounds and lying in hospital so long, the aforementioned clerk develops pneumonia and dies. Three: our hero takes a woman hostage, threatens a scullery maid and her beau with a deadly weapon, and assaults his hostage. With the help of yet a third man, a driver, our hero kidnaps her."

"Fascinatin'. Are you done?"

"It gets better! Scene Four: our hero arranges for the driver's death in a boxing match. It's a fixed fight, so now we can add conspiracy to murder and fraud to our protagonist's crimes."

"Are we at Scene Five?"

"The final act has yet to be writ," Patterson said. "There's more. Our protagonist has engaged in multiple extortions, assaults, and I'm willing to bet my mother's life on it, murders in the employ of Signor P. Lili Piani, who if I'm not wrong, had better watch his back. This young fellow has designs."

Geoff crossed his legs and brushed his hat again. "There's nothin' you can substantiate and no witnesses to what 'appened in that office. As for Piani, your imagination's run riot if you thinks I've done aught for 'im but collect rents. All that's in the past. I'm me own man, now."

"Now, who's telling tales?" Patterson asked. The man remained maddeningly self-assured. He put his elbows on his desk and leaned toward Geoff. "You're wrong. There is a witness."

Geoff shook his head. "'Ez? Me and 'im 'ad a drink that day. I ain't seen 'im since."

This was old ground. Fanny Merton—and maybe Hezekiah Boors—was in Normandy. Geoff might know their exact whereabouts, or maybe not. After the fight, Patterson found Fanny's postcard to Sam when he searched Todd's coat. *Harbor View, Honfleur.* He'd kept the card and the information from his fellow officers. He had his reasons, one of which had been recently confirmed when Peele intercepted a letter Todd sent to Miss Stuart. Amongst other interesting information, none of which was advantageous to Geoff, Todd wrote that he was on his way to a hamlet called Holloways, near King's Lynn. "Ah, Geoff, didn't your days on the streets teach you better? A woman, I'm talking about a woman, lad."

Geoff wondered if the man meant Fanny Merton or—. A slightly queasy sensation burned in his stomach. Extremely unpleasant, especially in the presence of a man whom he grudgingly acknowledged was more intelligent than he was. Up until that point, he'd almost enjoyed Patterson's story. He rather liked the hero. He sounded daring and powerful. Suddenly, Patterson had the air of a man who carried a noose in his pocket and liked the feel of it. Peele's face was stone cold as Judgment Day. Sweat started under his collar. He resisted the urge to pull at it.

Patterson sat very still. Fear was a dangerous emotion to inspire in a man like Geoff Ratchet. If he couldn't dress it in contempt, he was apt to rage like a cornered beast; yet he'd recently shown himself capable of reptilian calculation. Both would likely lead to the same outcome: a compulsive desire to eliminate the discomfort's source. If Geoff couldn't throttle the man who sat complacently across from him, he might turn his destructive tendencies on a more defenseless object. That was a chance Patterson was willing to take, that Geoff's fears would propel him to contact a witness that he and Peele could use to clinch their case. He didn't know if Geoff knew the name of the woman he was accused of abducting, a Miss Winifred de la Coeur.

Geoff struggled to think without letting Patterson see the effort. His thoughts tore back and forth. Which woman did Patterson mean? The bank's scullery maid, maybe, or Fanny, or—.

"Something bothering you, Geoff? Room's too hot?"

An inferno blazed. Flames crackled about Geoff once more. He smelled smoke and dust and stared into a pair of eyes that were equally full of fire. The woman! The feel of her. Not skinny but a nice, healthy girl. Expensive clothes. Very expensive. That green dress!

He'd returned to Court's room with the ransom note the next morning, just as he said he would. Court, on the other hand, had not kept up his end. In addition to the wine bottles, Geoff had found a corset, stockings, and lacey underlinens, all of very fine quality. Fast and Handy Furor, they used to call Court's old man. Like father, like son! Geoff snorted in disgust. At the race course, Court's excuse about the woman had been feeble, even for him. From the first, Court handled the woman like she might break. What annoyed Geoff most was the empty jewelry box. Court had surely pawned its contents and lost the money at the track. He almost regretted Todd had killed the luckless sod. He wished he'd done it himself.

Disappointed as he'd been, both by Court's disloyalty and in the knowledge that he'd never get back the money the bastard owed, Geoff had quickly ceased to worry about him after the knockout. The man was rotting in a pauper's grave, like Sadie. As for the woman, during Patterson's prior interrogation he'd steadfastly refused to admit her existence. There'd been nothing about her in the respectable newspapers. So, he let it go. Only the potboilers speculated on the more exciting possibilities, rape as well as abduction, accompanied by salacious illustrations. They got the woman's appearance all wrong. Darker and thinner, like his Arabella. He bought the papers anyway and meant to save them, only that stupid Sam had cut them up.

Patterson's voice continued. "Maybe she saw you before the blast, when you got out of the hackney. Or maybe it was after the explosion. Either way, she saw you, didn't she? She'd know you in a heartbeat, wouldn't she?"

Geoff didn't betray the acid rage that rose in his gorge. Patterson might mean one of the others. It was a bluff. But what if it wasn't? If he could've leapt across the desk and strangled the man he would've. When he was first brought in, he'd admitted only the most cursory details about his whereabouts that day. Patterson had let him go. At the time, he hadn't bothered to ask himself why the officer seemed satisfied with so little.

Geoff turned his head slightly, his eyes indicating the constable's presence.

Patterson nodded and the man left, closing the door.

"What do you want?" Geoff said.

Patterson's face was impassive. "A really big fish, that's what. You're still small fry. In the grand scheme of things what you've done may not matter much. Adams is dead and buried; we can't undo that. But the Earl is an influential man. On behalf of his son's memory, he's willing to work with anyone who can do the public at large some real good."

Geoff's brow furrowed.

"What you want is room to expand your operations," Patterson continued.

A light seemed to dawn in Geoff. He looked uneasily at Peele. "What's this? You wants a cut o' the profits? What's it to me if some lord wants to knock down a block o' tenements and Piani pockets a bit o' the swag? Talk to 'im about it!"

Damn profits! Could the man not think but one step at a time?

Peele leaned forward. He stabbed the desk with his finger. "Adams is dead!"

Patterson held up his cigar, conciliatory. "Cooperation, Geoff, that's what's wanted."

"She's willin' to come forward then?"

"Maybe."

Geoff snorted, but it was not quite a laugh.

Patterson wondered which woman Geoff had in mind. The man seemed sunk in what, for him, was deep thought. Fear, craftiness, or maybe greed glinted in his eyes. Patterson hoped his bluff worked. The de la Coeur heiress was thankfully beyond Geoff's reach. If a hair on Fanny Merton's head got harmed, he'd hunt Geoff down like a bad dog.

"So, what's this about goin' fishin'?" Geoff growled.

⚛

Bert was happy. It was a fine May afternoon. He waited in the stable yard for Furor and William to bring out the horses. Mr. Greystone's letter had arrived by morning post and confirmed the date for his qualifying examination. He could hardly wait to tell Amelie. In private, it was almost all they talked about.

"After I pass, we can be married!" He had pulled her close.

Amelie's eyes shone. "Perhaps by Christmas!"

His rooms in Lincoln's Inn were small, but all he could afford. Perhaps within a year they could rent a proper house. Before the words were out of his mouth, she had kissed him. What a kiss! Her boldness shocked but also excited him. One room would be enough for them, she said, as breathless as her embrace had left him. It wouldn't be enough for her mother, he laughed, and swept her off her feet. He might have already taken silk. He was that elated.

Of course, he ought to shut himself indoors and read, but was too worked up to concentrate. Instead, he had scribbled a hasty letter to Amelie who was in Norwich with her mother. He could not share his news with Winifred, for she was in King's Lynn paying a call on the ancient Olivia with Gretchen and the little Scots and would not be back until well after tea. He'd be on the train to town by then. He thought of riding to Hereford Hall, but George was probably too busy, arguing with the builders over renovations.

George had his own wedding to think of and his arrangements to ready the house for Winifred. So far, he was only satisfied with the dovecot, his special surprise for her, and some of whose bricks he had laid with his own hands. When George swore him to secrecy about it, he had for once envied George's wealth. How he would love to set up Amelie in a grand place like the old Hall. The idea of her cooped up alone in a tiny flat on winter afternoons while he worked made him more determined than ever not to relax his schedule after the afternoon's break.

The unfinished dovecot had also made him somewhat melancholy. Its rafters had yet to be roofed and shingled, but as soon as George paid the builder, the structure would be completed. Bert had stared through the open beams into the blue sky. A happy chapter of his youth was about to close. It would be an adjustment, visiting Winifred at Hereford Hall instead of Holloways when she and George returned to the country that autumn.

William walked Puck into the yard. Bert's mount was a fifteen-year-old dappled grey. The cow-legged old gent was fat but patient as Job, a good companion for the little Scots. Puck had never been a real hunter. Mostly, he liked to canter, but surprised everyone by taking a fence now and again. Bert hoped he sometimes surprised Amelie and gave her a little thrill, the way her kiss had thrilled him. She seemed to appreciate his return of her ardor when they parted.

While William checked Puck's girth strap and bridle, Furor rode Tulip into the sunshine. "I hope you don't mind my stealing your help for an hour or two, Will," Bert said.

William winked. "If Uncle asks, Mr. Furor's giving Tulip a bit of exercise."

Bert and Court set off down the lane that led into the village. As they rode beyond the church and the Rose and Crown, Bert explained his plan. "We'll go 'round the edge of the estate. There's a lovely stream we've always fished with the Broughton-Caruthers family. You can manage my tackle. I've brought an extra rod."

Court did not mind being conscripted for such a job on such a day. Mr. Barron chatted amiably and unselfconsciously about his prospects. The young man was not always so voluble. In the presence of most men he was not exactly shy, but quietly alert and watchful. Around Court he became much freer, though he was never vulgar. After Mrs. Pettiford, Court liked Mr. Barron as much as anyone he'd met at Holloways.

He'd made plenty of comparisons. Most of the neighbors in Mr. Barron's social sphere were decent enough. Court observed the squires and their families at church or when they visited. He had attended Mr. Burns and his wife during the season's final hunt and liked them. But in spite of the excitement of riding to hounds for the first time, he'd found the general company of ladies and gentlemen dull on the six-mile journeys to and from the meet. The interests of Mr. Burns and the local gentry were circumscribed to other thorough-going sportsmen, or their dogs and horses.

Mr. Barron liked the hunt, but was more like Winifred. He was a good listener and enjoyed a wide range of topics. Today's self-absorption had a charming frankness that was not the least arrogant and encouraged Court to a similar candor. Not for the first time, he wished he could be more forthcoming.

The first and most obvious barrier to total confidence between them—or with anyone else at Holloways—was the criminality and low circumstances of his former life. In those days, except when he considered Sadie, Court was never burdened by shame. With Mr. Barron, he suffered its full weight. Second, there was the vast difference in their stations. Court had observed, appreciated, and quickly adopted his fellow servants' formal manners around their employers and one another. As curious as the staff was about him, they were too polite to pry unless he let a detail slip. A person on Mr. Barron's social level wasn't obliged to even know a servant's name. Third, Winifred was the gentleman's cousin. Fourth, Court's feelings for Winifred were such that he wouldn't have uttered them to a soul.

Happily employed as his days and evenings were, beneath the contentment work supplied, Court was miserable. Proximity to Winifred made him want her more than ever. Her engagement to a man of George Broughton-Caruthers' character only underscored life's injustices. That the wedding day fast drew nigh made him want to get roaring drunk, ride to Hereford, and beat George to a pulp. He reminded himself of his own unsuitability as a suitor to Winifred and did his best not to dwell on it.

Though George was often about, they'd managed to avoid each other. Only once had George personally addressed him. They were in the stable, alone. Court shoveled manure.

"Like your job, Furor? Then keep your head down!" He winked and threw a couple of punches at Court's face. "Heard from Todd lately?"

He'd been tempted to knock off George's hat, but didn't for Winifred's sake. He made no reply. Old Swank didn't deserve one.

In the house, there were few chances to cross paths with Winifred. It was more difficult outdoors, for she rode nearly every day. Though he made sure to stay busy and in company, if William was unavailable, he helped her mount. As she and Tulip pranced out of the yard, he swallowed his mortification and frustrated desire. Winifred's heavy, braided hair shone like a golden crown under her smart hat. The spread of her skirt over her fine seat and along the horse's body, the turn of her booted ankle in the stirrup were regal elegance itself.

"I already assist Mr. Greystone. After my examination, if I pass, I'll be able to try cases alongside him," Mr. Barron said. They stopped by the stream.

While Court secured the horses, the young man prepared their rods and reels. He folded Mr. Barron's jacket, and laid it over the wallet that held their refreshments. Mr. Barron pulled on a pair of gaiters and waded into the stream, flicking his rod. Court sat on the bank with the tackle and basket. His knowledge about a lawyer's training was as scanty as that of fishing, but he didn't doubt Mr. Barron would pass his test. His mentor was a barrister whose rooms, like his, were in Lincoln's Inn. Except for Sundays, the young man spent his time holed up in London reading or drafting briefs, or seated in a courtroom alongside other aspirants to the bar. Otherwise, he read legal history, analyzed judicial opinions, and stayed up late to vet all sorts of documents and contracts for his employer. In idle hours, he studied for his exam and wrote to his fiancée.

The young man gracefully cast his line onto the water's rippling surface. The peaceful sight of Mr. Barron fishing was what was meant by the expression a rest truly earned, Court thought. Yesterday had been Whitsunday, so today was a holiday. Except for the young man's good news, Court was surprised that Mr. Barron took the extra day of rest and was not already back in London. Mrs. Pettiford had explained that though certain family branches were wealthy, Mr. Bert's was not. He had no money except a very small annual income, all of which went to cover his domestic and educational expenses.

"Ain't all lawyers well to do?" Court had asked.

"Aren't, Mr. Furor!" She poured their tea. "When families have as many children as those Mr. Bert and Miss Amelie came from, especially girls, it's as much as they can do to get the sons clerkships in reputable businesses or a place at Oxford! Both Mr. Bert's and Miss Amelie's fathers were younger sons to boot."

"Down my way, there's naught to pass on to younger sons or older ones!"

"It was so in my family as well, but that's another story," she said grimly. In lieu of her own history, she was only too happy to tell Court that of the de la Coeurs.

"Miss Gretchen's—that is, Mrs. Burns' father was a silversmith and knighted for it, and she married well. Don't let anyone tell you otherwise about Mr. John, especially Miss Amelie's mother! He's the second son of a distiller and very well off. The age difference caused quite stir, with him so much younger, but never mind. Terrance de la Coeur's family farmed these lands for generations, well back before Tudor times. He didn't marry Rosalind Bunting until he was middle-aged. They had eight children, but only three daughters lived to adulthood: Cordelia, Hermione, and Olivia. Cordelia had no children and is long dead. Mr. Bert is descended from Hermione, who is also dead, and Miss Amelie is Olivia's youngest grandchild.

"The old man married again, this time to an heiress from Cardiff named Gaenor Gruffud. They had three sons: Percival, Tristan, and Arthur. Sir Percival was the eldest but never married. Next was Mr. Tristan. He wed a girl he met during his travels in Germany, a tanner's daughter. Since she died, he's fallen on hard times. Their only child recently married a German nobleman. Mr. Arthur was the youngest and found a wife while he served in India. She died right after Mistress was born. His London house and all his property in Gujarat went to her. Mr. Tristan has gone out there to live, and I'll hope he'll make a better go of it this time. Miss Winifred is Sir Percival's heir, but I can't say that Holloways will be hers. There's no entailment, but there's a family tradition. It will probably go to her and Mr. Broughton-Caruthers' child if they have a boy. If they don't, Percival may pass it on to Mr. Bert's father."

Whenever Court helped Oliver carry water to the bedrooms, he studied the portraits that lined the staircase. To greater and lesser degrees, he saw Winifred's features, coloring, and amber eyes repeated in them. The resemblance of Terrance de la Coeur's descendants to one another brought to mind Mick Furor's prodigious efforts to populate the Old Nichol with his black-haired progeny, only not to such a grand effect.

Mr. Barron stood in the water, gazing after his line. "My old man is as generous as he can afford, but it doesn't go far! The pay will make a world of difference once I begin to practice."

Court reflected on the disparity between what straightened circumstances meant to the young man and what they meant to him. "You'll be on your way at least."

"True! Amelie's ambitious for me and thinks I ought to go into politics. Running requires more money than I'll earn for years. There's lots of hard work ahead. I could use more than a bit of luck!"

Court admired the man's attitude. To have struggled so hard to come so far and find it was only the beginning of the journey was daunting. Yet it was second nature with Mr. Barron to count his blessings. Each Sunday after the banns for Winifred and George were read, Court resolved to emulate Mr. Barron's example. If he didn't, he feared he'd take to the bottle, like Sadie had.

The horses always raised his spirits. In addition to mucking their stalls, there were so many animals to feed and exercise, clean and comb. In the tack room, there was a never-ending list of tasks: saddles to mend, brass to polish, and the carriage and old phaeton required endless maintenance. The pasture must be kept clean as well. Before bed he read an equestrian sporting and medical book and an old stud register that he'd found on a shelf in the store room. When the farrier and the vet saw his interest, neither had been dismissive. Richards was dour but fair, and Will was always quick to show the way when Court erred.

After some minor faux pas, as Mrs. Pettiford gently called them, at table in the servants' hall, he gradually improved his manners. He was often vexed by the local accent's burr and had to have words repeated. His own uncouth speech and Cockney twang elicited grins. For all his embarrassments, he joined the laughter at his mistakes.

He couldn't quite shake off the uncomfortable parts of his past, however. Will and Oliver were intensely curious about the life of a prize fighter, gyms and equipment, and the latest training methods. Oliver read the same sort of trash Sam consumed and passed the rags on to Will. The slender lads quizzed Court about conditioning and diet and thirsted for stories about London street life and low haunts such as the Boar and Hart. He dreaded such talk and was circumspect when he answered their questions.

To the male staff's amusement, the pair of youths lightly sparred behind one of the barns. Court carefully supervised, anxious they not hurt one another. He hung up a bale of hay in a canvas sack and demonstrated the correct stance and form. Struthers and Jakes took their turns at the bag. Even Mr. Barron gave it a go. Soon, Court supervised an ad hoc gym. He'd been especially impressed with Mr. Barron's natural ability. "We could build up that left 'and. Only lead with your right. That way, when you bring on the left for more than a parry, BAM!"

"They'll never see you comin' Mr. Bert!" William shouted.

Finally giving way to his pupils' encouragement, Court beat the bag to pieces. Amidst their cheers, Mrs. Pettiford's shadow fell across the barn floor, her arms crossed and her brow dark. "I heard the noise!" After that, they only boxed on Mrs. Pettiford's afternoon off.

With the exception of Richards, who still maintained his professional distance, Court felt accepted by the male staff. The feminine ranks were a trial, however. In the servants' hall, he strove to be silent or monosyllabic unless it appeared rude. He avoided the under-housemaid Molly's saucy flirting and Dottie the scullery maid's blushing glances. Unless the questions were Mrs. Lumley's, whenever possible he shied from elaboration in response to feminine queries about his life. The cook's delight was to quiz him about London fare. She was incredulous at his lack of acquaintance with green vegetables. If information was forthcoming about what was served at the Lancaster Arms, she rewarded him with extra helpings.

Mr. Barron waded ashore, holding a trout aloft. "I'll fix a rod for you. Or would you rather read? You've brought one of Sir Percival's memoirs, I see!"

"Oliver was showin' me 'ow to lay a fire in the library. Mrs. Pettiford said I could borrow it. It's almost as good as me mother's old stories."

"*Along the Silk Highway,* that's a good one." Mr. Barron flipped open the book's frontispiece. "Percy's years in Afghanistan and India. When I was a boy, I'd have given my eyeteeth to travel with him and be in battles! More than half the tales are probably made up or cribbed from another fellow's lies, but it makes ripping yarns! Mother says he was disappointed in love. That's why he went abroad. Difficult to think of the older generation that way, but I suppose my children will say the same of me! Now he's in Egypt for his lungs. Not much adventure in that. He cut a rather dashing figure in those days. You look more than a bit like his man."

Court expressed surprise.

"Your coloring or some such, or so Amelie says. Women notice that sort of thing. Maybe you'll meet him. Percival's been a good master, or I guess he wouldn't have stayed on so many years. Greystone certainly has been to me. Funny old stick is standing my exam fee. Father knows him from years ago. Old fellow did some legal work for the firm where Pater clerked."

"Men needs good masters, same as 'orses. You'll be a good 'un, too, one day."

"I'll try. Winifred has helped me no end for Amelie's sake. Once she makes up her mind, there's no refusing her. We can never repay her generosity. She wouldn't want it, anyway." Mr. Barron handed back Sir Percival's book. "Richards has eased up?"

In a bad temper, Holloways' head groom was a tyrant but obviously took great pride in the stables and loved the horses like they were his children. Only Mr. Burns was more devoted. Court spoke easily of such matters. Old Puck and Tulip, or Mr. Burns' and his wife's spirited mounts, two lovely bays named Mackie and Colleen.

The afternoon wore on, and he and Mr. Barron both fished. As the sun lowered, they packed their gear and rode back to the village, discussing the merits of various hunters for sale in the neighborhood. Their way took them by a field where a man plowed. Court admitted a special fondness for Holloways' working animals, especially the great, gentle shire beasts. Mr. Barron spoke admiringly of Mr. Broughton-Caruthers' stallion, Hotspur.

"He keeps a mount in London too, a gelding named Black Diamond."

Not even Gentleman George disturbed Court at that moment. The long shadows of the man at the plow with his horse rippled over the furrows. Warm air blew in delicious draughts, scented with tilled earth and freshened by the sea. Winifred had wished for freedom. Tulip beneath him and the sky above were almost as good. "I 'ad a 'orse, not mine really. I only drove 'er. Eglantine was a good old girl. She'd like it 'ere. I do miss 'er."

"A cab horse, was she?" Mr. Barron asked.

Court nodded, and they rode in silence.

Bert surreptitiously eyed Furor. To dissemble, to not come right out and ask what he wanted to know felt dishonest; but he did not want the man to put up his guard. Even before Amelie pointed out Furor's resemblance to Morrant, he had seen it. Like Percival's manservant, Furor had a melancholy streak. Bert was almost certain he knew why.

Another man might be quick to judge Furor's aspirations, but he was not such a man.

His legal training had taught him to be watchful, if not suspicious of his fellow creatures. In Furor's case, such skepticism was not only unrewarding, but uncharitable. Even as an intellectual position, it simply did not hold up under closer acquaintance with the man who rode by his side. Bert was not sentimental unless it concerned Amelie. While Gretchen might ignore Amelie's flights of fancy, and Delilah might disagree with his betrothed's sympathetic interest in Holloways' latest addition to the staff, he could not. Like his fiancée, he had theories about Furor that he hoped to substantiate. But first, he needed more information.

Furor had been concussed in a fight. The man's taciturnity might stem from other factors; for instance, there were the conditions under which he had mysteriously arrived. The man did not have to say much to gain more than Amelie's notice. Any stranger's arrival was an event in Holloways, but Furor had much about him to stir interest. There were the obvious attractions of his splendid physique, physical strength, and grace. He drank but little. His native intelligence and curiosity about the world did him credit. His pleasant baritone gained him a seat in the choir. Horses responded well to him, as did people.

"In combination, these traits prove purity of character," Amelie concluded.

"Not if he stares at Winifred during prayers, like you say!" Bert had teased.

Amelie pinched his arm. "You look at me, too!"

Their conversation took place the prior afternoon in Holloways' garden. Winifred had ridden out with George. He and Amelie, Gretchen and John sat with the Burns' spaniels. Amelie colored in a sketch of Gretchen holding the baby. John snored while the dogs panted at his feet or snored as well. The little Scots roamed the yard. The boys chased one another with cricket mallets and the girls tramped in the flower bed, destroying peonies. The newest Scot crawled at a yawning Gretchen's feet, yanked fistfuls of grass, and shoved them into his mouth.

Bert grabbed Amelie's hand. "You heard what George said of him and his pub associates. I'm inclined to agree with Gretchen. You're too romantic!"

"Winifred's losing weight. Dupree says so. Ask her!"

"It won't hurt her," Gretchen said acerbically.

"I'd rather face Medusa!" Bert said of Dupree.

"She never used to ride every day. She practically ignores her poultry. Why, we looked after them all last week!" She indicated the little girls seated amongst the flowers. "She nearly bit Molly's head off this morning while Dupree dressed her. Afterward, the air was so thick with Mr. Furor's name you could cut it with a knife!"

"Amelie, this is trying!" Gretchen pulled the baby onto her lap and brushed a wad of slobbery grass from its dress. "Winifred asked after Mr. Furor's health. The girl would go on about him, rather like you do!"

"Yes! 'How well Mr. Furor looks when he serves at table! How handsome he is with all that wavy black hair. He's as healthy as a stallion!'" Amelie mimicked the maid.

John opened an eye, peered in mock alarm at his wife, and chuckled. "Poor Will!"

"Precisely," Gretchen agreed. "Winifred can't have her maid or her cousin being silly. Mr. Furor's mysterious past makes him a figure of romance below stairs. That's not your affair. If Mrs. Pettiford won't keep discipline among the ranks, Winifred is correct to be firm. Really Amelie, when Delilah isn't here, I'm almost inclined to—!"

"Oh, please don't send me to Mother! I won't stay in Norwich 'til Winifred's wedding!"

"Then you'll go to Cousin Olivia's tomorrow! Your imagination's more than I can manage. The sooner you're married, the better. Or John, could we take Amelie back to Ben Venue? I'll lock her in the nursery. You can help me with the girls or read improving books to Olivia!"

John stretched and yawned, rousing the dogs. "Why not," he said affably. "Amelie, come to Ben Venue." He rose stiffly and ambled on his bowed legs after his children. While his elder daughter grabbed onto his coat, John lifted his younger one briefly and yelled at his sons to stop clobbering one another. The little girls broke away, flopped about on the lawn after their brothers, and then all the children ran screaming in circles with the barking spaniels.

Gretchen sighed and handed Amelie the baby. Her shawl slipped and dragged in the grass as she joined her wayward family. Gretchen towered a good five inches over her husband, who lit his pipe and scratched his belly. They stood close together in friendly silence and watched their children and dogs run.

Amelie bounced the baby on her knee. He burped contentedly. She wiped the child's chin with Bert's handkerchief, and tucked a gold curl behind her ear. Never had she looked lovelier.

Her observations about their cousin's behavior were astute. His gaze followed Gretchen and John as they collected their dogs and cavorting offspring from the lawn and herded them indoors. He suspected that Gretchen would agree with him.

Taking his cue from George's comments, Bert had investigated Furor's prizefighting career. The result was most intriguing, but he did not share the details, not even with Amelie.

Furor was dead.

Inexperienced and with small knowledge of the law compared to his mentor, Bert had already heard some extremely strange cases. Clients of all classes came to Horace Greystone's office. Stratified as London's society was, the citizens who confided their troubles to his mentor were often exposed to higher or lower company than they were used to keep. The reasons for their associations might or might not begin with amorous entanglements, but all of them generally involved money. While this entertained courtroom spectators, it was almost always ruinous or heart-breaking for the defendants' families.

In addition to clients' characters, Bert closely observed and judged his own. Even a decent man might be tempted into situations outside his control. By his reckoning, he had never been unfaithful to Amelie, at least in his heart; but to his abiding regret a few of his contemporaries' misplaced generosity and a night's unaccustomed inebriation ensured that he would not lie down on the nuptial couch as innocent as the hour he was born. At their expense, he had sampled a prostitute's delicious, forbidden fruits. He owned the shame for his moment of weakness and strove to restrain the appetite his experience had aroused.

What bothered him more than his absence of chastity was his and his fellows' lack of compassion for the woman. He would never forget her face. If Amelie had been under the influence of spirits, found a fellow, and partaken in similar fashion, he would have been outraged at both of them. Not only would it have broken his heart, it would have been unforgivable.

Bert questioned the fairness of his response. It was not a matter of honor, merely.

The woman with whom he and his friends had lain was without doubt, drunk; given the horrors of her profession, why wouldn't she be? Yet even without the aid of alcohol or hope of compensation, could not

Woman as well as Man feel curiosity about the physical act, be inflamed by desire, or overcome by passion? Medical writings were at odds with one another on the subject, but what he had seen in Mr. Greystone's office taught him he must be more broad-minded about the female sex. Otherwise, he stood in danger of dismissing or misunderstanding half of humanity's motives. Carnal appetite was natural to both sexes, as were all passions. What if violence or force was involved? From the moment he learned of Winifred's disappearance and the visits afterward to the gynecologist in Harley Street, he had struggled with these thoughts. He sympathized with Percival's anguish and felt a measure of it. Dr. Frost's frequent visits, Winifred's low spirits, and Dupree's vigilant nursing assumed an even weightier significance when he imagined Amelie in his older cousin's place.

A woman's virginity, her innocence, was not a virtue for which she was to be admired. It was her birthright; but thereafter, an accident of circumstance. The prostitute was likely born with no advantages, or denied them. For a man to treat a woman's loss of virginity as her fault in any sense of that word showed not only a lack of charity but imagination. Virginal or not, into whatever high or low estate she was born, a woman must be cherished for herself. She must be protected from the worst impulses of her fellow man.

While Amelie dandled Gretchen's baby, he ached for Winifred. Even if George was good to her after they married, her dreadful experience had not left her unscathed. He wondered at the extent of her injuries or whether Dr. Frost's visits included arrangements to terminate a pregnancy. Perhaps she had miscarried or been infected with venereal disease. Surely George was privy to these details. In spite of their neighbor's reputation and need of money, Bert had come to regard George's constancy to Winifred with a degree of respect he hoped the man would not disappoint.

Any of the grim scenarios he imagined, not Amelie's insinuations about his cousin and Furor, might be at the root of Winifred's moodiness. In spite of his fiancée's taste in reading material, he hoped she remained naïve about the grosser details of Winifred's disappearance. Given Delilah's diligence, it seemed likely. As usual, Amelie was more concerned with romance.

Her newest and almost constant question was, "What must George think of Mr. Furor coming all the way from London to be near her?"

Bert chided her. "George is the one person who takes no notice of Furor whatsoever. Frame your questions correctly or not at all. You've no evidence to support your fairy-tale conjectures. Take Furor at his word. He came to Holloways because Winifred offered him a job!"

"You don't really believe that," she said.

He didn't. As he sat up late over his studies, he often prayed. Irresistibly, like Amelie, he linked Winifred and Furor in his meditations. Along with a rather lax Anglican upbringing, he had absorbed enough of his employer's sterner Calvinist morals to develop a strong belief in man's fallen nature and to hope for his redemption. He did not understand Election, but felt lucky not to have been born into a life like that of the woman with whom he had lost his virginity. To repent meant to turn around, to cast off the old life and begin afresh. He hoped to make Furor understand, as a fellow man, or as a child of God who had made his own mistakes.

"Midsummer is only weeks away," he said. "The banns will all be read soon, Winifred and George shall be married, and the neighborhood gossips finally vindicated. They'll be very rich and start a family as quickly as possible, I suppose. They'll have heaps of land, even though George has sold off I don't know how much. She'll pay his infamous debts."

The man who rode beside him said nothing.

"I shall have to look about me. My Amelie will be impatience itself once Winifred and George tie the knot. Have you a sweetheart or a family back in London?"

"Only me sister. I guess Christians down our way marries in church but mostly babies come and folks just gets on with it." He rubbed his scarred cheek. "It must be fine 'avin' a profession and knowin' Miss Amelie will be your lawful bride one day. You'll be proud."

"I shall be more than proud, Furor. I shall be the luckiest man alive. Do you plan to stay on at Holloways?"

"I like it 'ere very much, but that may change."

Bert considered how best to pursue his questioning. Over and over, he'd seen Mr. Greystone gently wheedle the most appalling personal details out of clients. He spoke abruptly. "Perhaps the wedding won't come off. Amelie thinks our cousin is preoccupied in a way that does not accord with her current state as a bride-to-be. A jolly fellow like Mr. Broughton-Caruthers, the wedding and all that, she ought to be happier!

"I say it's only nerves. You've heard about her ordeal last year. Servants will talk, and the whole village! She never speaks of it, naturally. In fact, Sir Percival and the unfortunate bank secretary's father, the Earl, made sure it was all hushed up as much as possible. Guy Fawkes prank gone wrong or some such. Gas lines ignited, or that's what the papers said.

"She went missing and was very low afterward. She seemed to recover her spirits for a while, especially with the engagement. But Amelie says there's been a change these past few weeks. Woman's intuition, perhaps. What she must have suffered during those hours she was lost, a woman on her own in the city! Surely, it haunts her. You did hear about it, the Royal Empire? Supposedly a ruffian held her at gunpoint, but he and the driver escaped. We know none of the details. As I said, she doesn't speak of it."

The man pulled Tulip's reins and fell back behind Puck.

Bert pretended not to notice. "I hope you don't mind my saying so. Winifred's not only a cousin, but my dear friend. Except for our parents, she's done more for me and Amelie than anyone, so her happiness is my—our—concern. You don't much like Mr. Broughton-Caruthers, do you? I saw it the first night. He said you'd met."

Under his late-afternoon's growth of beard, a flush spread on the man's cheeks. He did not speak immediately. "A while ago. 'E and another soldier came regular to our local, card playin' mostly. They was no wilder nor worse than most."

"George has always had a reputation!"

"Maybe Mr. George 'as changed, or maybe 'e ain't. It's not me place to say."

Bert pulled Puck alongside Tulip. "But you would speak out if you knew anything that might—you know! I only want my cousin to be as happy as I am with Amelie."

The man rubbed his forehead and wrinkled his brow.

"So how did you meet her?" Bert asked.

"She fell into my way, sort of."

The man's voice was so low Bert could hardly hear it. Furor's discomfort was plain enough, however. Bert's skin prickled. "Yes, but was it that morning she came home or the day of the blast? If it was then, why not return her at once? I'd never seen Sir Percival in such a state, like a hen who's lost its only chick."

The man bowed his head, breathing heavily.

"Of course, she may have been out of her senses," Bert added, conversationally, "the blast and so forth. The doctor said she suffered a blow to the head, and she was very badly beaten up. She might not have been able to tell you who she was or where she lived."

"It wasn't like that," Furor gasped.

"Then how was it?"

"I—I don't like to say, sir."

"There's no need to be mysterious, man. What harm can it do? What happened?"

"You probably know I was in a 'eap o' money trouble."

Bert did know, but he waited.

"I was—workin' on that. Your cousin was an inconvenience I didn't anticipate."

Bert did not challenge this ungallant statement. His mind whirred with possibilities, for he believed he had found the key to his difficulty. His friend with connections to the Yard said that the police were still on the lookout for a driver, and Furor had admitted he drove a cab. "Sorry, I'm muddled! Was she with you the whole time? From the moment she fell into your way until you helped her onto the omnibus?"

"I left 'er in me room for an hour for coal, and to go to a bakeshop."

"Then she could have left at any time? She was at liberty?"

"It was snowin' and bitter cold. Night was comin' on. It's a dangerous neighborhood."

Court wished the man wouldn't ask him about Winifred, but felt bound to answer. Mr. Barron was a gentleman, a million times more worthy of the title than George Broughton-Caruthers. He was also a barrister, almost. It was important to speak respectfully and truthfully to such a man and useless to do otherwise. His father and his kind thought they could outsmart the law. He entertained no such delusions. He didn't want to be caught in a lie, or for Mr. Barron to think him lower than he already felt. But it was difficult. He would not betray Winifred's honor.

Bert changed tact abruptly. "The people you owed, you paid off your debts to them through your fights. Is there anyone else who might be interested in your current whereabouts?"

"People like the ones I've known 'ave a way of circlin' 'round. They won't quit pickin' at you 'til there's no more to be 'ad. About her and that day at the bank, we was—."

"Carefully, Mr. Furor," Bert warned. "I only meant to ask whether your family knows where you are. Would they wish to find you?"

Court nodded. "That's 'o I mean. There's somebody else besides me sister, but 'e's part o' what all I'm tryin' to leave behind. Your cousin was the biggest surprise of me life. 'Is too, I reckon. That's what I was tryin' to say 'bout the bank. She wasn't meant to be part o' nothin'."

The pieces finally clicked together, but Bert needed to hear the rest of the story from the man's own lips. Though his hands trembled on Puck's reigns, his voice remained calm. "Why did you come here?"

"I needed the job!"

"Come now, man!"

The abrupt coldness in Mr. Barron's tone made Court look up. The gentleman's face was a mask of ice. His eyes were full of fire, like a true de la Coeur's. The countryside seemed to disappear. Mr. Barron was donned in a wool cap and robes, all his mildness of manner gone. Court stood in the dock, trapped. "You thinks I wants more than me wages, or that I means to blackmail 'er because we was alone for a night?" His voice rose. "She'd send me packin' and rightfully. 'Ow could you think so little o' 'er? Miss de la Coeur's a lady! I'll swear to that!"

"Mr. Furor, there's no need! Calm yourself!"

"Tell Mr. George, there's no man alive good enough for 'er, or could love 'er like she deserves! If me presence at 'Olloways ain't right, if I'd bring danger or make 'er un'appy, I'll go!"

The man rocked in Tulip's saddle, gritting his teeth. Sweat poured off his brow.

"Gentleman George! Old Swank, tell 'im this! I'll 'ave me references with 'is signature! Before Miss de la Coeur, I ain't never 'ad a good word from nobody nor no luck. She's the best thing ever 'appened! Too good for the likes o' 'im!" His voice broke. "And she's too good for me."

All the energy drained out of Court. He clutched his throbbing brow. A wave of nausea threatened, and he slumped over Tulip's neck.

A hand gripped his shoulder. Fingers wrested the reins from him. The darkness before his eyes faded to a mist. White sparkles resolved into tiny crescents. At first, he thought it was the Wash, but it was the farmer's plow blade multiplied. Sunlight flashed off metal as it drove through the dirt. It was a strangely beautiful sight, full of a hidden meaning he strove to grasp before it escaped him. A farmer plowed a field and found a treasure and hid it and sold all he had and bought the field. That was it! He'd heard that story, long ago, in a room full of golden light. From far away, then from suddenly quite near, Mr. Barron's voice penetrated his reverie.

"I take it then that my cousin offered you this job out of gratitude for looking after her that night and helping her find a way home."

Court stared after the farmer and his horses. "I 'opes not!"

"Can you tell me why then?"

"That's between your lady cousin and me."

Bert let out his breath. Amelie was right. Furor had as good as told him he worshipped Winifred, but what could the wretched man do about it?

"Mr. Furor, I know more than a bit about what it is to want something very badly, to wait and wait and to feel that it's always just out of reach. A man should have his chance, a bit of luck, and a friend. Everyone can use a little help at times, especially a good, decent man."

It felt strange to think Mr. Barron might mean him.

"Thank you for your candor, Mr. Furor."

Court blinked with surprise at the hand extended to him. He shook it and groped for the right words to show his gratitude. "You don't 'ave to be kind, not to somebody like me."

"Kindness has nothing to do with it," Bert said quickly. "We both have a great deal of hard work to do. I want Winifred to be happy, like Amelie and I are. And for you I want justice." He smiled. "No, more! I want what's right!"

⚜

Latimer Kleinfeldt peered through his loupe. Pincer-like, delicately, his fingers opened and closed around the sapphires and pearls. Years earlier, he had reset jewels owned by Mr. Broughton-Caruthers' grandmother to make the necklace. Since then, it had lain in Kleinfeldt and Sons' vaults along with other expensive adornments that belonged to his customer's family. Such beauty, such fine craftsmanship needed to be brought into the light. "The settings appear sound."

The gentleman in front of him did not answer. Of the brothers, he preferred Mr. Charles. One knew what to expect, whereas Mr. George could be so changeable.

"What shall I do with the necklace, sir?"

"What are you looking at, man?" George snapped. "Box it up!"

After he left the shop, George decided to walk from Cheapside to Pall Mall and dine at his club before he took the last train home. He had come to town late in the afternoon, and all the way was preoccupied by troublesome matters. The figures from the previous year's wheat harvest meant he must borrow money again. For the second month in a row, his steward badgered him to raise rates on the cottages, but George had balked. They were not charging nearly enough, Mr. Ellis argued, and several of the old cottages desperately needed repairs. George liked his tenants and knew that Smyth, whose roof had caved in, poached and had a daughter who was a slut. Pimm, Hereford's carpenter, was lame after a fall, and his wife was nearly half blind from taking in sewing for extra cash. The couple tended to her widowed sister as well.

On Sundays, George tossed his bit into the offering plate, but didn't trust the parish council. There were no friendly societies for men like Smyth and Pimm. He'd repair the cottages out of his own pocket and deal with the rest. Such had been his thoughts as his housekeeper accompanied him on an inspection of renovations to the chambers for his and Win's use. She might not know much, Mrs. Stafford complained, but she was sure the builder cut corners and stuffed his purse by selling some of the lumber. He had certainly dragged his feet, George thought, examining the unfinished plaster work.

Win was making trouble as well. Of late she had decidedly lost some of her spark. He was not exactly angry at her, but might become so if she didn't straighten up. He would not be treated in this fashion. When they first announced their engagement, she seemed satisfied enough. She had been affectionate, to say the least. Damn it, she had been warm!

What a delight to discover in her the sensual appetite he had always suspected, an unabashed readiness for pleasure to match his own. It was also a relief that, after that business at the bank, she was not put off by the earthier, more ribald enjoyments of courtship. Until recently, she had behaved admirably. There was no reason for her to play the coy maiden now.

⚭

Geoff watched George through half-closed eyelids.

George's boot caught the table leg as he stumbled into the inglenook. Geoff stopped it from toppling over. How much had the man already drunk? Before George interrupted his dreams, he had been leading a mighty host through parted waters. Then George crashed into the pub, singing at the top of his lungs. George elbowed him. Geoff moved a little farther down the settle. Just in time, he saved his bowler hat from the man's lowering backside.

"The Boar and Hart!" George's eyes swam. "It doesn't change."

Neither did George, except he looked rough. Geoff despised the man who plopped down next to him as a dandy and an arrogant son of a bitch, but was more than ready to cultivate his company. He was a catastrophe, a walking disaster, but in his way, George was extremely amusing, especially when he wound up another punter. Also, he usually needed money. Geoff was glad to oblige. He knew all about Old Swank, his shilly-shallying, his perverse tastes, and his errant habits, having trailed him many times after he left the pub. Men like George always thought they could hide. Men like Geoff always found them out.

Point of fact was that few people actually knew what they wanted. That was their problem. Money or maybe a woman or power. He'd followed George enough times to know the fox's dirty secret. Back and forth, 'round and 'round, up and down the streets of Southwark. Sometimes, just for a laugh, Geoff bypassed his quarry and went straight on to the hotel. Sure enough, George would eventually end up on its steps, gazing at the flat's windows.

Easily distracted or jerked about like puppets, most people whined about their lot. They fancied themselves the victims of crossed stars. Mostly, they were victims of idleness, or their passions, or their obsessions, like Old Swank. They allowed their lives to happen to them.

Not like him. Geoff sat up straighter, wide awake. After his chat with Patterson, he'd seen the breadth of the possibilities that lay ahead. The promised land was for him, Geoffrey Michael Ratchet. The inspector was practically in his pocket. Piani was getting old. As Patterson said, he wanted room to expand operations. Let a man know his own mind, and the waters simply parted. The planets circled the sun. The sheaves of wheat bent to the larger one, like they did in the Bible story. In Geoff's experience, a lesson he had learned well from Piani, it was best to make that sure some who bent over never stood up again.

"'Asn't seen you in these parts for some time," he ventured.

"I've been busy. I'm getting married." George slurred his words.

Geoff contained his skepticism. "Night on the town, is it?"

"I hear you're going to tie the knot as well."

"Miss Arabella Bertollini, niece of Signor P. Lili Piani," Geoff said proudly. "Me intended." He showed George a small photograph. The man gave a sharp, derisive laugh. Geoff was piqued but let it go. "I'm in business now, men's haberdashery, gentlemen's outfitters." He put away the picture and pulled out his card.

George stared at it without interest. "Well, that's a way to kill time! Look here, I want some capital of my own, too. Farming isn't what it used to be."

"Tsk! Tsk! Land rich, cash poor, all you gents," Geoff scolded in vaguely mocking tones. "Now, if you needs a bit to tide you over, I'm more than ready to—."

"What? No, not that again, man! I'm talking business. My girl's generous to a fault, but I can't go to her cap in hand every time I want to buy a horse, can I?"

Whatever Old Swank had in hand for his intended did not interest Geoff. "Good luck with that 'orse!" He made ready to leave and bid his companion good night. George pulled a slender box from his breast pocket and set it on the table. He gestured for Geoff to open it. The man was an ass, Geoff thought. He opened the box.

George watched in satisfaction as Geoff lifted the necklace and let it dangle from his fingers. He sank back onto the settle, his eyes glazed over as if he was hypnotized.

"Pretty isn't it?"

Geoff licked his lips. They had gone dry. So had his mouth. In earlier times, he would've cudgeled out George's brains, or his own mother's, to get his hands on such an object.

"For my fiancée. If you like it, she has another, far more fabulous one we can play with."

Geoff hardly listened. The sapphires' facets winked at him in the firelight, glittering like the eyes of nocturnal creatures. The braided pearls and platinum links felt smooth and cool as the skin of Arabella's shoulders, only the gems were much more desirable than any woman, their spell far more potent. Theirs was a siren's song, a speaking silence of rare, rich colors.

George swiftly withdrew the necklace from Geoff's hand. The man's covetous glance followed the jewels into their box and his coat pocket. Geoff wiped his mouth on his cuff and appeared startled to see George still seated beside him. "Whets your appetite, doesn't it?"

Geoff gulped at his beer. He knew he should leave, but wanted to stay.

"This is a trinket compared to the one she already has. Her father brought it back from India. Gold, pearls, yellow diamonds! An orange one big as a robin's egg. It's insured for a king's ransom! I'm breaking it up and want to transport some of the stones to Vienna."

Geoff was almost sick with longing for the jewels. Worse, he knew that George could see his lust. He lounged against the settle, took out his jackknife, and picked his nails with it. "Why not keep 'em 'ere? Don't she want it?"

"It's gaudy, barbaric! Unfortunate associations, her dead mother and so forth. We'll get a copy made. Jewelers do it all the time. Women never travel with the genuine articles. Of course, if the real ones were stolen, there's the insurance."

Sensing danger, Geoff drew back. "A mad scheme's up your sleeve. Cock-up's a-brewin'!'"

"You'd know about that!" George leaned close. "You've had a few! That fight was a beauty! You'll never guess who's working in my fiancée's stables. A friend of yours, Court Furor."

Geoff failed to see the humor in George's smile. It was like being at the zoo, counting the tiger's teeth while it ate supper. His eyes darted. He almost expected Patterson or his man Peele to spring from the shadows. At the sound of George's laughter, he finally understood. He shook with rage. "You will have your little joke. Court Furor's dead! I saw it with me own eyes, so did you!"

"I left early because I knew how it would end. Furor's a loser, but he got lucky for once. He's very much alive and quite well, I assure you." He took out the necklace again and twirled it around his finger. "Come on, Geoff. Not even you could get this one wrong!"

Geoff's ears buzzed. That empty jewel box in Court's room. That fat blonde. If he ever saw either of them, he'd kill them. But first, he'd gouge out George's bright blue eyes. Conceited ass! He seized his hat and crammed it on his head. George could find another bloke to take the piss out of. "For all I knows them jewels is fakes! Court Furor ain't me affair."

George lay back on the settle, chuckling. "Oh, but he is." He carelessly swung the necklace, then gave it a kiss. "You'll be back, man. I know you will. You can't help it!"

Like you, Geoff thought, cursing George with all his heart. No one had any dirt on him! No one ever would! But he knew more than a bit about George. It would keep. He walked quickly to the door that led into the yard and pushed it open. They'd see who had the last laugh.

"If Fast and 'Andy Furor's in your lady's stables, best make sure 'e stays there and out o' 'er knickers. I'd never be such a fool as to leave me Arabella with that randy sod for twenty minutes, let alone twenty hours!"

CHAPTER 15
Worse and Worse

Business in the Lancaster Arms gaming rooms had been brisk. Around the card tables, men moved like automatons; others sat still as statues. At the roulette wheel, observers bent at each spin with ever-more feverish, agitated expressions; others stared, red-eyed and weary. George played cards in a careless fashion and won, but wanted to exercise his will in a more concerted manner. His conversation with Geoff had not quite satisfied his need to tease and torment.

Jades of every age and description attended the other late-night habitués, providing a feast of bared shoulders, bosoms, and shadowy décolletage, whispering promises of pleasures to come. Most of the women nodded in their chairs, as sleepy or bored as George. Fair hands languorously plucked at cards. Dark fingers traced long-stemmed glasses. Lips parted and lashes fluttered. Eyes occasionally met his, registered his indifference, and turned away. George took his brandy bottle, found an unoccupied couch, and lay down.

Near dawn, he opened his eyes. A woman in Spanish lace caressed him, and he sleepily accepted the motions of her prowling fingers. Finally, she gave up, slumped against him, and yawned hugely. Except for two old men who still played bezique, everyone else was upstairs, she said. "Everyone," George repeated but meant it as a question. Her knowing smile answered his feigned nonchalance. He gave her a kiss and left her with the brandy.

George crossed the alley and climbed the stairs of the Montague Hotel. On the first landing, he paused. The door to the flat was ajar. A woman's high, sweet voice came from inside. At his touch, the door swung open.

She was bent over the fireplace polishing the brass knobs on the andirons and whistling between her teeth. Around her, the carpet was covered with open newspapers, and she wore a smock over her usual dark dress. Everything else in the flat was exactly as it always was.

When George was at a brothel, his appetites were generally straightforward and devoid of emotion; but the sight of this woman threatened his usual sang-froid. His heart beat harder. As she vigorously pulled the cloth back and forth over the brass, her round backside shook. Perspiration stood on her brow. The combs that held back her hair were almost completely loose from her exertions. Light brown curls spilled over her temples and down her neck.

"Hello, darling," he called quietly.

The woman started, glanced at him, and resumed polishing.

He threw his coat onto the sofa and kicked aside an ottoman. He sat on one of the two armchairs that flanked the grate. When she didn't speak, he unknotted his cravat, shoved the tie in his pocket, and stuck a long leg in front of her. "Take off my boots. There's a pet."

She sat back on her heels and threw one of her rags into a bucket.

George stretched his other leg beside her. "Where's your girl? This isn't your job."

The woman grasped the bucket, stood, and stared down at him without expression.

"Never mind, I like you grubby, the dirtier the better."

Two pink spots formed on the woman's cheeks.

"Sit on my knee."

"I ain't got time for games, George."

"Just one!"

The woman tried to step over his leg. He kicked the ottoman in front of her.

With a sudden, furious gesture, she flicked her dust cloth at his face.

George let the woman get to the door. In one swift motion, he was up and caught her around the waist. She grabbed for the doorknob. He turned the key in the lock and flung it. With a little cry, she tried to catch it. The key clattered on the fireplace tiles. George let her go. She tripped on the rug and fell to her knees. George grabbed her from behind. Her hands scrambled for the key.

She sprawled on her stomach, struggling under his weight, and grunted. He reached over her and flicked the key farther into the fireplace. Her heels kicked vigorously against his shins. He was oblivious. "Where are my flowers, my sweet rosebuds?" He felt of her breasts, ignoring her whimpers of protest. He buried his face in her hair, found the nape of her neck, and bit it.

The woman struggled harder. George kissed her ear and began to croon softly. She waved at the key, trying to push forward with her toes.

"'In einem Baechlein helle, Da schoss in froher Eil'. Die launische Forelle, Vorueber wie ein Pfeil ...'"

Finally, she lay still.

While he sang, he slowly lifted her skirt and stroked her thigh. Stealthily, he reached around, inch by inch, and felt inside the front slit of her underdrawers.

"No! No!" she gasped, kicking again.

"The door's locked!"

"She's got a key!"

Hot, venomous spite shot through him. He sat up. "Then she'll come in, won't she? Pathetic half boy! Repulsive, unnatural bitch! Why you stay with her is beyond me."

The woman's eyes lit up with their earlier fury. She rose to her knees. George pushed her onto her stomach. He yanked up her skirt and pulled open his trousers. "Let her see how a real man goes about his work."

"Don't! George, don't!"

George ignored her pleas. He slid his hand between her legs. Her kicks were much less annoying than her cries for her friend. He didn't really mind, so long as she didn't scream.

Then he almost shrieked himself. On the carpet beside his hand lay a serpent. Reflexively, he seized the coal shovel and struck it. Panic gave way to relief, and he snickered. In their struggle, his brightly patterned tie had worked its way out of his pocket. Still laughing, he dropped the shovel onto the tiles. He pulled the woman, who was trying to catch her breath, back to him.

"What was it, a mouse?" she asked, panting.

George had already forgotten his fright, inspired by a new idea.

The woman glanced over her shoulder. At the sight of George winding the silk about his hands and pulling it into a taut line between them, her eyes grew huge. He snapped the tie.

"Isn't this what she does? Well, I can do better! It won't take long," he whispered hoarsely, almost beside himself with excitement. "But not unless you ask sweetly!" Straddling her waist, he snapped the cravat before her face, then drew it between her teeth. She began to cough and claw at him. "No, no!" he admonished gently and kissed her hair. He pulled down his trousers with his free hand. "It mustn't do that! It's only a game, our little game!"

The woman moaned.

George began to sing again.

∽✧∾

The rank odor of tobacco was strong. Horace thought whoever had enjoyed the cigar must have recently left. He stopped on the landing, took off his hat, and wiped his brow. He wished that he and Beryl had gone to his rooms first to change out of their riding attire. It had gone extremely well with the Banshee. Her timing had improved. Beryl hurried ahead and pushed open the door.

"Rosie?" she called.

When he entered the flat, she was pulling back the curtains. Horace blinked at the light. The odor of cigars was even stronger in the women's parlor. Newspapers were spread over the carpet before the cold grate. He righted an overturned bucket of rags and glanced about. Usually, the coal was lit and Rosie would have laid out the tea. Instead, the table was covered with dirty dishes and trash. Beryl went to the archway that separated them from the women's bedroom. Its curtains were also drawn. She yanked them open.

Rosie lay between the dressing table and the unmade bed. Her hair spread over the carpet. She was naked except for Beryl's dressing gown.

"Heavens, she's fainted! She's ill!" Horace cried.

Beryl did not move.

Horace rushed past his friend and helped Rosie sit up. She looked about, groggily. The area around her mouth appeared bruised. So was her neck. A quick inspection showed that her arms and legs were covered with small, dark wounds. "Child!" he cried in dismay, helping her onto the bed. "Beryl, have you any water? Don't just stand there! We must get help!"

Rosie's eyes focused on Beryl. She began to sob.

"Leave her alone." Beryl had already turned away.

Horace could not believe his ears. "She's been attacked! We must get a doctor!"

Beryl stood by the table. Amongst its detritus were two empty wine bottles and glasses. On the stacked plates were the remains of a meal; crumbled cake, apple cores, an overturned bottle of cream. Beryl flicked the end of a cigar from one of Rosie's Mandalay saucers. "He was in our room," she said in a dead voice. "You brought him to our room—our home!"

Her last words were uttered through clenched teeth. He had never seen such a look in his friend's eyes; but he had seen it before in some of his clients'. The ones kept locked in solitary jail cells who required twenty-four-hour guards or strait jackets. Her brow was dark, murderous. The hair stood up on his neck.

"No, I didn't!" Rosie clung to him. "I wouldn't never bring 'im 'ere!"

Horace put an arm about her frail shoulder. "Whom do you mean? You know the man who did this? Beryl, what is this about?"

"Shut up both of you!" Beryl snarled. She bent over the table, clutching its edge.

"The door was unlocked!" Horace said quickly to the woman.

Her eyes streaming, Rosie nodded hopefully, obediently. The shield of Horace's arm seemed to give her courage. She faced Beryl. "I thought 'e was you comin' 'ome! Only you didn't!"

"Beryl, she's shaking. She needs a doctor! I'll fetch one!"

"No!" Rosie shrieked.

"Leave her alone!" Beryl snapped. "Don't listen to her!"

"'E was too strong!" Rosie shrank closer to Horace, and dissolved into tears. "You didn't come! Why didn't you come 'ome?"

"This is insupportable!" he shouted. "Your friend is hurt!"

The ragged noise Beryl made was not laughter. She sank onto the other side of the bed and covered her face with her hands.

Horace addressed Rosie. "She was with me, riding, training on our new horse. They're brilliant together. The Banshee broke her own record today. We're going to race her. Beryl's going to race her." He shook Rosie's shoulder gently. "And we're going to win!"

Rosie stared disconsolately at Beryl's back. "I waited. I thought it was you. Cross me 'eart!"

Beryl jumped to her feet. She pulled a valise and a carpetbag from under the bed and opened the wardrobe. Without discrimination, she tore clothes from hangers and drawers.

Rosie wailed. "No! Don't let 'er leave me!"

Beryl stuffed the valise and slammed it shut.

"Beryl, your friend has been attacked! Stay with her while I send for a doctor!"

"She doesn't need a doctor!" Beryl hissed. She pushed a chair against the wardrobe.

"This is unforgivable!" Horace shouted.

"I don't want forgiveness!" Beryl grabbed her hatbox. A stack of Horace's Surtees novels fell with it. She cursed, hopped off the chair, and kicked the clothes and books that had fallen to the carpet. She dumped her hat and a gin bottle onto the bed.

"She'll murder 'im!" Rosie choked out. "She'll 'ang!"

"Does it matter how I break my neck?" Beryl stuffed her bag with the bottle and books.

Rosie wailed against Horace's shirtfront. Beryl continued to pack. Horace was at the end of his patience. "I'm sending for a doctor!" As soon as he rose, he realized his mistake.

Rosie scrambled across the bed to Beryl. She dove at Rosie and grabbed the woman by her hair. Rosie did not even cry out. Beryl fell on top of her, savagely beating the woman about her head with one of the books. "Stupid bitch! Lying whore!"

Horace wrested the book from his friend. "Stop it! Have you gone mad?"

Beryl clutched the woman's throat. They rolled over the bed and onto the floor. Beryl shoved what Horace took to be one of the smutty rags from the cleaning bucket in Rosie's face. "Never again! You swore it! YOU SWORE IT!"

He pulled his friend off Rosie. Beryl flung aside the cloth and stumbled back around the bed, breathing heavily. Rosie thrust out her hand in mute appeal. Horace took the cloth. It was a man's soiled handkerchief embroidered with the initials G B C.

"Don't you pity her!" Beryl's voice was full of disgust. "She don't need no doctor!"

Horace was mortified to hear Beryl mock her friend's accent. He was about to give Rosie the handkerchief when he saw that his fingers were covered in soot. So were Beryl's. She wiped them impatiently on the sheets. He looked at the marks on Rosie's face and neck.

She climbed back onto the bed and lay limp, watching while Beryl took her bags into the other room and dropped them. She rifled the desk drawers, snatched out a drawstring purse, counted the money within, and put the purse back. Next, she shoved aside the table. China and bottles crashed to the floor. She kicked these away along with the rug, and dropped onto her hands and knees. After lifting one of the floorboards, she groped within the space below. There was a clink of coins. She shoved a sack into her cloak pocket.

Without a word, Rosie rolled onto the pillows, softly weeping.

"There's money enough to keep her a while." Beryl pointed at the desk.

"Where are you going, my dear?" Horace asked.

Beryl hesitated. "I don't know—to the devil."

"You'll not do anything foolish?"

"That's what fools do!"

She descended the stairs in a determined fashion but did not rush. The hotel's front door closed. He returned to the flat. Rosie stood at the bedroom window overlooking the street.

Not once in his life had he ever been rocked by such passions as those he had just beheld. Even in their torment, he envied the women their ability to participate in the drama of their lives with every fiber, body and soul! They suffered deeply because they loved deeply. He picked up his remaining Surtees novels and stacked them.

"Perhaps Beryl's and my friendship is partly to blame for your present trouble." He held out the handkerchief.

Rosie glanced at it and turned to the window. "You ain't her friend. You're a customer."

Horace returned to the sitting room and straightened the rug. He placed the table in its wonted position and cleared bottles and broken china from the floor. He knelt before the grate and gathered up newspapers and rags and set these outside the flat's door. Behind him, he heard Rosie fill the wash basin. He went downstairs with the rest of the trash and the wine bottles and dropped the refuse in a bin in the alley. A meager patch of blue showed between the buildings. He stared at it. The sky paled to violet, the clouds to pink. A star came out.

When he returned to the flat, Rosie had lit the grate. Water boiled on the hob. The bed was made and the table laid for tea. She had arranged her hair and donned her usual, polished cotton dress of deep grey with its snowy lace collar. There was not a mark on her skin.

"That's a lovely print," Horace commented as he sat in Beryl's chair. He wasn't sure Rosie listened, but he talked on, very quietly. "*The Light of the World* by Holman Hunt, have you seen the original? It's at Keeble."

Rosie turned a key in her fingers. She set it on the mantle amongst the seashells.

"'Behold, I stand at the door and knock ...'"

"That's just it, sir, 'e didn't!" She faced him, weeping. "'E never knocks! 'E just comes in!"

After a quick inspection of the Boar and Hart's patrons, Beryl hired a cab. It drove her to Cheapside. Near St. Mary le Bow, they turned onto a shop-lined street and stopped at Bertollini and Ratchet – Gentlemen's Haberdashery and Tailoring. The name gleamed in newly painted, gold block letters on plate-glass windows. Inside, newsprint covered them. From around the papers' edges, light shone.

The shop door opened with a jingle of bells. Except for a floppy-haired, mustachioed clerk who stood on a ladder arranging long, shallow boxes on a shelf, the room was unoccupied. The young man stared down at her, first with surprise and then with impatience. He spoke with a stilted, almost theatrical Italian accent. "We're not-a open yet, signora! Not until-a Monday week."

Ahead was a door with its shade pulled down half way. On its single long pane of glass was painted the word "Private" in the same gold letters as those on the store's front. Beryl scowled and strode past a counter piled with bolts of cloths and between tables stacked with hat boxes and silk neckties, gloves, and shirt collars. A pile of boxes fell. She waded through them toward her goal.

Protesting, the young man clamored down the ladder and ran around the counter, endeavoring to block her. "No, no, signora! We're not-a open! Signora will be pleased to wait until-a Monday week!"

"No, signora won't. She'll bloody well see Geoff Ratchet RIGHT NOW!" Beryl yelled over his shoulder at the door. The young man blanched but did not budge. Beryl made a feint to her right and then her left. The man twitched side to side but held his ground, and appeared extremely embarrassed. "I know he's in there. Get out of my way, you slimy little—! OI, GEOFF! IT'S BERYL!"

The young man waved his hands and held a finger before his lips in a gesture at once pleading and indicative of horror at such uncouthness in a signora. Beryl jutted out her chin. With a withering look, he turned on his heel and slipped behind the door. Its lock clicked and the shade was hastily yanked down.

Time passed. The clerk did not return. Beryl paced back and forth. "RATCHET," she bellowed. "GEOFF, I KNOW YOU'RE IN THERE! I'M COMING IN RIGHT NOW!"

Almost immediately, the door opened. Looking harassed, the clerk explained that his employer was with a customer. He led her down a dim hallway, holding up his pleading forefinger for quiet as Beryl stomped behind him. They passed a men's fitting room on one side and another opposite. Additional rooms held sewing machines and fitting mannequins. At yet another door with a lowered shade, they stopped. Beyond it, masculine voices rose in laughter.

The clerk opened the door an inch and peered inside. She tried to push by. He backed into her, knocking her arm sharply with his elbow. "Oh-a, signora, mi dispiace!" he cried loudly in exaggerated concern. "You drop-a your hand bag!"

"What? I don't have a—. What are you doing, oaf?" Holding her shoulders, the man turned her to face the wall. Quickly retreating footsteps sounded in the passage. She glimpsed a roundish man in a homburg. He turned his monocle briefly to them and was gone. The front door bells jingled.

The clerk let out a deep breath. "O.K. signora, now you can-a come in."

Geoff Ratchet sat with his feet propped on a big desk, staring at a calling card. Compared to his clerk, he seemed the soul of equanimity. He smoked a very large cigar, and the remains of an enormous supper of spaghetti and beef filets filled a tray laid atop his desk blotter. The clerk whisked this away. With an elaborate lack of haste, Geoff let first one and then the other of his feet drop to the floor. He closed a set of ledgers and stroked them. The clerk whisked these from the desk as well and locked them in a cupboard.

Geoff showed his teeth. "Beryl, me love! I don't know when I've 'ad the pleasure."

Beryl took the only other chair. Its seat was still warm from Geoff's other visitor.

Geoff waved his cigar at the clerk. "Bring the lady some tea. You're lookin' well, luv."

"Forget the tea," Beryl scowled. She pulled off her hat and rubbed her hair.

"No more visitors," Geoff ordered in a firm, quiet voice, "and lock the bleedin' front door this time." He showed his teeth again to the clerk, who nervously danced in place and tossed his hair. The young man closed the office door with a bang.

Geoff pushed his box of cigars toward Beryl and spoke with a combined air of apology and indulgence. "Me fiancée's nephew, 'er favorite. 'E's a good lad, but not used to takin' orders. 'E gets peevish with the long 'ours, what with our openin'."

Without success, he tried to read Beryl's expression. Contrary to his compliment, she did not look at all well. Her face was pale and her brow pinched, as though her guts ached. Always slender, she was rail thin, even gaunt. Trouble at home. Rosie was probably ill again. Even so, he had no idea why Beryl would come to see him. They'd never liked each other, had barely tolerated one other's company when circumstances threw them together as children, and in adulthood had adopted a strategy of avoidance.

Yet he was ready to appreciate Beryl's dark charms while she collected her thoughts. Her apparel was eccentric, but so was she. The long cloak of lavender worsted that she shrugged back and the cockaded hat that she had impatiently pulled off belonged to the latest women's fashions. The men's riding breeches and muddy boots seemed more apropos to her trim figure. When they were children, he'd tease her about her boyish looks or pester her about Rosie until she'd take a swing at him. Excellent fun, but today he felt no such inclination.

Amongst the valuable prizes recently confiscated from one of Piani's more unfortunate clients was a series of lurid, pornographic prints. Almost at once, Geoff had recognized Beryl in spite of her mask. In her violent postures and leather corset she was so lively and sharp, like a wasp. Perhaps those pictures were her problem. Geoff's tastes tended to dark, small-breasted vixens, such as his Arabella. A bit of temper added spice. He was a desultory connoisseur of light pornography, the sort available in certain gentlemen's periodicals, but the freakish goings-on between Beryl's female companions and their male victim had made him shudder.

Nevertheless, his erotic fantasies had been infected by the voluptuous violence of those dark images, and he wondered what it would be like to spend an hour in that Venetian boudoir. Behind his need to tease Beryl was an unsatisfied curiosity born of the rumor that she was, like him, one of Mick Furor's children. He'd always professed skepticism, but was privately angered at the thought it might be true. If it was, joining in with his half-sister's sadistic antics was one line he still hesitated to cross, yet it was tempting to think she might owe him a favor one day.

A set of photographs of his own, perhaps. A private session.

He leaned back in his chair and put his hands behind his head. "'Ow strange you should appear 'ere at this particular 'our. We 'asn't talked in ages."

"We never talk," she said flatly. She clutched at the sack of coins in her coat pocket. Geoff had handed Court to Piani's men. This was madness. To her extreme annoyance, the clerk entered with a tray that held glasses and a decanter, a teapot and cups. He set it down and bustled about, fussily arranging napkins and a plate of almond cake and nougats.

"Events o' the last forty-eight hours 'as been so oddly 'armonious, so strangely serendipitous, a man begins to wonder about 'is life." He snapped his fingers. "Get along, Fabrizio!"

The clerk banged out again. Geoff could sense Beryl's mounting impatience. He bit luxuriously into a nougat. Since his latest chat with Patterson, he had cut back on alcohol—must keep the old wits sharp! He was fast becoming a devotee of sweets. He served a plate and set it before her. He took a slice of cake and sniffed it.

Beryl glanced at the decanter. She badly wanted a drink. Clutching the bag in her pocket, she hesitated. In the cab, she told herself that it was dangerous to involve Geoff, that he might blackmail her until she died. But she needed his help. Since she didn't intend to live much longer, Geoff could threaten her all he liked. What she was about to do would break poor Horace's heart if he ever found out. She pushed this from her mind. It didn't matter. Nothing mattered.

Geoff chewed, closing his eyes to slits, and watched Beryl. He had already had two visits before hers, both of which boded well for his future. First came Detective Sergeant Peele. What did he know about Piani's rumored arsenal? Geoff was startled by the question. Until he came into possession of Hez's pistol, he'd always carried a knife or his iron pipe. The rest of Piani's men were similarly armed. Though he still claimed ignorance about what set off the gas lines, Peele's interest, combined with Sam Merton's never-ending supply of homemade firecrackers and the dynamite he had given Hez made him think Piani might indeed have a cache of weapons, or was buying matériel to exchange for other contraband.

If he had any information, Peele suggested, he was the man to contact. Patterson's not interested? Geoff asked carefully. Piani's days were numbered, Peele said. The man had spread himself too thinly and gotten involved over his head. "I know what side my bread's buttered." He set a packet on the table. Inside it was a wad of bills. Geoff pushed it back to Peele. "Don't think if Patterson brings Piani in, it'll be over for you, Mr. Ratchet," the sergeant warned.

"Patterson's always let Piani get by, but can't afford to anymore. Soon it'll be your turn. Nobody'll care what you do so long as Piani's been bagged. You'll need some new friends."

During that last round of questioning, the day Patterson joked about fishing, the inspector showed him a map of London on his office wall. It was full of multi-colored threads and push-pins. Geoff had hidden his shock at how much work the police had done, the extent of what they already knew about Piani's various local activities. More surprising still was his recent involvement with several criminal syndicates whose tentacles reached beyond London. About these, Geoff had no inkling. His mind whirled with ideas for how to assert his own interests, once he was married to Arabella and part of the family.

Patterson spoke. "In a better world, I'd have the right piece of evidence to clinch all this information together into a grand charge that would topple Piani's entire kingdom."

That the work of Piani's lifetime might come to nothing the instant he was about to expand, or before he, Geoff, got to enjoy the spoils, was worse than a shame. It was unjust! Unfair! Criminal! Hadn't he bled money, courting Arabella for a place at Piani's table?

Why didn't the police arrest Piani if they knew all that? Such cases took years to build, Patterson told him. With local elections coming up the following year, the pressure was on his department to clean up the neighborhood. "That's just politics, Geoff. It doesn't usually make a lot of difference to the likes of us, but because of Adams' father being an earl and having so many friends in the government, this time it does.

"What the force needs right now is a crime big enough to bring Piani in for a while, say until after the next general election." He looked wistfully at his map. "Then he'd be out again, and I'd just have to keep on fishing. But someday.... Someday Geoff, we'll get the big one. He'll be out of our way for good."

Patterson had taken Geoff for a drink and professed being tired of his superiors' bending over for favors from above while they did nothing but put heat on him. "Wouldn't I like to tell the missus it's Chief Inspector Patterson? But is that likely with this Adams business? What wouldn't I give for an end to it?"

They took a hackney to Geoff's new store. Patterson came inside, and admired the freshly painted lettering and the fine quality of the stock. As he looked about, he spoke in a fatherly way, reminding Geoff of the first time he was charged with petty theft. "It was me took you in.

A watch, wasn't it? And now all this! You've come on." He set his hat on his head and went to the door.

"Think about it, what we talked on earlier. In this world there are two sides. You're on one or the other. There's some will make it sound like you can be in the grey, but that's just wandering in a fog. I think you know better than that, Geoff. You're a man knows where he's going."

Geoff had indeed considered Patterson's words as he looked into Peele's eyes. They were the only part of the young man's face that seemed alive. They peered back at Geoff intently, coldly, but burning with ambition. He put the money in his desk drawer and poured Peele a drink.

His next visitor came while he ate supper. The well-fed man wore a monocle and an expensive, but several years' old suit. He lifted a re-blocked homburg from his curled grey hair. "Jarvis Perrot." He handed over a card and peered a little fearfully at Geoff's bloody steak knife.

"*Acta Diurna: Today's London*–Chief Correspondent, 70 Kew Street, Belgravia," Geoff read and was no better informed than he had been. He did not ask the man to be seated.

"I'm an independent journalist." The man quickly retrieved his card. "I've been covering the Adams affair. He was an acquaintance of yours, I take it."

Geoff was ready to show the man the door, but he continued quickly in his fruity voice. "I attended the funeral and spoke with his father afterward. I did a follow-up story about current regulations surrounding the use of gas in public buildings. Perhaps you saw it." Geoff couldn't say that he had. He took out a cigar and trimmed it. The man grabbed the other office chair and squeezed his big backside onto it. "You're about to be married to Miss Bertollini, I take it. My congratulations! Her uncle, P. Lili Piani owns a great deal of real estate between Quickwater and Riverside streets. There's been a great deal of rumble about renewing the area. I wondered if Mr. Piani has any thoughts of selling any of his properties to...."

"'O wants to know?" Geoff puffed smoke. The man handed him another card. This time the man's hand shook slightly. It was printed with a name Geoff did recognize, that of a retired actress. "Miss Mary Harris, 12 Pemberfield Place, Richmond. That's posh!" He took a small volume of *Shakespeare's Quotations*, a gift from Arabella, out of his breast pocket, slipped the card inside it, and replaced the book in his coat. "If I 'ears somethin', maybe I'll call on 'er."

Mr. Perrot watched the disappearance of the card with some trepidation. "I am—ahem—acting as her agent. It might be better if you contacted me." They were disturbed by the sound of Beryl's voice. The nerves that the man had thus far been able to control seemed to suddenly get the better of him. He laughed nervously. Pink tongue, bad teeth. Geoff laughed too. Fabrizio poked his head in the door and indicated someone was in the hall. "If you don't mind, I'd rather not be seen! Awkward! Thank you!" Mr. Perrot sprang up like a jack in the box.

Geoff had shown the man the side door from his office into one of the fitting rooms.

What a rum old world it was. The planets sang in their courses, and the gods danced 'round him. He had connections to high places. Slight as they were, he knew the strength of silken threads. Now Beryl's arrival when they hadn't spoken in years! It all felt so fortuitous.

"Does you believe in destiny?" He sucked his cigar, took the book of quotations from his pocket, and opened it to his favorite, marked with Mrs. Harris' card. "'Be not afraid o' greatness. Some are born great. Some achieve greatness, and some have greatness thrust upon 'em.'"

Beryl gripped his desk and spoke in a rush. "I want you to kill someone. Beat him to a pulp, cut his throat and throw him in the river, so long as it's done!" She pulled out a bag, heavy with coins, and set it on the table. "I want to be there when you do it!" Looking even more ill and pale, she fell back in her chair.

Geoff stared at the bag. He stared at her. Peele's money, Perrot's real estate scheme, and last night, George's jewels! What did it all mean? It meant his star had risen. His hour was at hand.

There was only one person on whose behalf Beryl would be so upset and that was Rosie. There was only one man with whom he had ever known Rosie to be more than professionally involved, and that was Old Swank. He had known the man was headed to the Montague when he saw him in the Boar and Hart. Geoff coughed in an attempt to smother a fit of elated sniggering.

"What's the matter with you?" Beryl snapped.

Still shaking, Geoff poured two glasses of whiskey. "Me, I'm fine! But you're in a bad way."

Beryl pushed the bag at him. "Do it! Or get it done!"

"Not me line." He gestured expansively at his new office. "You see what all I've got to do!"

"What about Court? What about that fight with Seamus Todd?"

"Idle gossip!" He snapped his fingers. "Any road, ain't you 'eard? Court's in Norfolk, a village called 'Olloways, workin' in a fine lady's stable."

Beryl sank farther back in her chair, her face paler than marble.

"Remember Old Swank, our Gentleman George? 'E told me last night on 'is way to a little pre-nuptial celebration. 'E's to marry Court's new mistress!" He sniggered again.

The woman raked her hands through her hair. It was some moments before she spoke. "Why are people like us even born? Do you ever think what lives we might've had if we'd only grown up anywhere else? Oh, Court! Court!" She covered her face.

Geoff heard her despair. It was time to close in. He poured more whiskey into her glass. "Such imponderables ain't worth our time, me girl. We can't do nothin' about 'em. Our business is with the possibilities at 'and. You was brought 'ere tonight for a reason, and I don't mean 'cause you 'ates George Broughton-Caruthers." He tapped his glass against hers. "Destiny's afoot! There's a master plan, me girl, and we're goin' to be the masters of it!"

It was still an hour before the dressing gong, so Bettina would not return for a while. George adjusted the gas jets that flanked the mirror. He lifted Winifred's hair so that she could fasten the clasp of his latest gift. As usual, he was right about such matters. Its sapphires would complement her gown's peacock hues; and it was a perfect fit, closely encircling her neck like a collar. He sat beside her and turned his attentions to her shoulders.

On the tennis court, Winifred had pleaded a headache from too much sun, come indoors, and told Bettina to draw a cool bath. She'd no idea what excuse George made to their hosts. She was uncomfortably aware of her nakedness beneath her dressing gown and was certain he was nearly naked beneath his. His lips worked against her neck, and he slid his arms around her waist. Voices and laughter from the other guests who came upstairs to rest before supper passed her bedroom door. She arrested George's wandering hands.

He let her go and picked up her mother's necklace. "Wear mine tonight instead. Good girl! I'll take this old thing back to town when I go."

Winfred caught his fingers. "I'll do it eventually."

"It shouldn't be left lying about, and you're not going back to that bloody bank."

"I'll write to Mr. Buckner that you'll come then."

"Don't bother. I'm going up to town on Monday." He walked to the window.

Winfred began vigorously brushing her hair. "Why? You just came back."

"The usual stops: my bookie, horse trader, my suit-and-tie maker."

Winifred brushed harder. She was surprised at how quickly he let her alone and was vexed that part of her felt not only disappointed but denied. Since their engagement, she'd allowed George more and more favors, succumbing to his caresses but faltering to make the final step. Initially, the addition of physical intimacy to their relationship had been a source of hope and even some comfort. He hadn't suggested that they go so far as sleeping together. If she gave in to him even a little bit, they usually found other ways to pleasure. It had been weeks since their last encounter. Putting him off left her in a state of feverish lassitude.

Nearly certain she would never see Court again, it was pointless to wonder why she had done what she had with George, or deny that she enjoyed it. George was more patient with her skittishness at being caught in flagrante delicto than she'd dared hope. He never put her in danger of exposure and seemed satisfied with kisses and prolonged caresses. But of late, he'd become more persistent in his demands, even a little reckless. She was already weary of them and of herself. Over and over, her body betrayed her heart. It was like wine; a little and one could stop. A little more and one didn't want to. When they had children, she hoped her needs would not be so intense, that she would settle down.

Then out of nowhere, Court reappeared. He'd taken the measure of George, and of her. No wonder he wouldn't speak to her when they met. His presence was a torment, yet she feared he might leave. Once again, Court had turned her life upside down; or maybe he'd set it uncomfortably right-side up.

At the engagement party, Winifred had been terribly nervous. Gretchen pulled her aside. "Buck up! Do you know the best part of my decision to marry John? Absolutely no one could offer me a bit of advice on the matter!" She kissed Winifred. "I knew what I wanted. All my life my mother and or some maiden aunt had told me what to do. Now they couldn't. This was about the two of us, no one else."

"Yes, but did you know he was the right one?" Winifred had asked.

"My dear, I never gave it a second thought. When he asked me to marry him, it was exactly like we'd run up on the edge of a cliff. I wanted to jump! John said let's do it together, so we did!"

Home from her first year in school, she had been a bridesmaid at Gretchen's wedding. Like everyone else, she'd ignored the slight bulge under the bodice of her otherwise rawboned cousin. She regarded the tall Gretchen and stout, bow-legged John Burns with a mixture of amusement and a young girl's fastidiousness. Falling over a cliff with, never mind falling into bed with such an unlikely lover, seemed incredible to her at that age. As she approached the altar behind Gretchen, she'd wondered what in the world her cousin saw in the man's pock-marked, ruddy face. John was wealthy, but Gretchen had plenty of her own.

Time proved them right and the family wrong. The couple was rarely out of one another's company. They argued equally over politics and rode to hounds as competitors. Their conversation was inane and peppered with private jokes. She scolded and he grunted indifferently. Their cheerful brood, and the likelihood that another baby was on the way, set at naught the initial mystification with Gretchen's choice of mate. Not even Delilah denied they were a happy pair.

Winifred recollected her first impression of Court seated on the box of his cab. How quickly he had begun to look quite different to her. It was like John, for whose snub-nosed features she now felt nothing but affection; she did not doubt that they inspired passion in Gretchen's thin bosom. She tried not to think of Court's scarred cheek resting on her breast, or the topsy-turvy embraces they had shared only hours after their meeting. Whatever feelings he may have had that night, his conduct since his arrival at Holloways more than demonstrated they were conquered.

The old fears assailed her. There was nothing about her that could sustain a man's attraction for long except her wealth. In spite of the yearning in his eyes the instant before George surprised them, perhaps Court really had come to Holloways for the job or to get away from London. She was embarrassed by what she used to laugh at, the gossip that George would one day marry Miss de la Coeur for her money. The pre-nuptial documents were filed; money had been transferred from her account to his; and she had signed the deed for his twenty acres. It was too late to turn back, so why not go forward? Neither Court nor George had ever once said that he loved her. Who had she been to laugh at John Burns? She threw down her brush with a clatter.

George didn't seem to notice. He continued to describe the hunter he wanted to buy. Hopefully, George was unaware that her retreat into more maidenly behavior coincided with Court's arrival and put it down to an attempt on her part to make him more eager for the wedding night. She rose to get his attention. If she felt this way now, how would she act on their trip, or feel after a decade or two of marriage? "George, my head is pounding. Go away and let me rest!" She went back to her dressing table. "Where's Mother's necklace?"

"You gave it to me." He held it up.

"Did I?" She regarded it, and him, in some confusion. She sank onto the bench and rested her head on her hand. "I suppose I must've."

George studied his fiancée's agitated state and unhappy expression. In spite of her recent coldness, he refused to give credence to Ratchet's insinuation about Court Furor, though he did increasingly find it more than a bit strange the man had showed up. Why hadn't it bothered him more? Because Furor was nothing; he was nobody; he barely existed. His Win, allow such a fellow to touch her? Geoff didn't know the woman, or he would never have made such a laughably idiotic suggestion. If Furor was at the bank and arrived at Holloways with ideas of frightening Win or getting more money out of her or some such nonsense, he'd obviously seen sense after his dressing down in the stable. The man hadn't stepped out of line once.

The thick-headed Ratchet was obviously unaware of Furor's escape after Todd's knockout. Otherwise, he might have thought Ratchet and Furor were still in league, plotting mischief. Furor hadn't the initiative to do so much on his own. Perhaps his arrival was only a coincidence, though an odd one. Furor was a loaf and a lay-about. He only needed to hide from Geoff, and would be on his way eventually. Or he'd get rid of him. It was simple. George dismissed the whole affair.

Whatever bothered Win came from a different quarter. Until recently, she never seemed worried about the consequences of extended foreplay. Her behavior indicated that at some point before the Royal Empire debacle, she had taken a lover. It was intriguing but difficult to imagine his imperious, unapproachable Win surrendering to any of the men of their acquaintance, but she must have.

This realization had initially shocked him more than Ratchet's lewd remark. When her lack of inhibition continually surprised him, he reminded himself that he was not one of those old-fashioned, bearded ladies who thought that only whores were capable of a full response. He did not particularly care that he was not the first to unleash Win's fire, but it was a bit disconcerting after all these years when he had thought he knew her so well. Not one of the fellows she had met was up to her standard. But if it wasn't one of them, who was it? He joined her on the bench and set her mother's necklace amongst her other jewels.

"So, you like your gift?" She gave him a wan little smile. "And me?"

Winifred let George take her in his arms. He stroked her hair and kissed her brow, fondling and teasing her breasts, and whispering how much he had missed her. He knew what she needed for her headache. They moved to the bed. While he untied her dressing gown, she lay perfectly still and stared at the ceiling. The necklace was snug, and she swallowed uncomfortably. For a while he caressed her, slowly kissing first one part of her, then another. She stroked the top of his head as he bent over her lap and shoved a pillow under her buttocks. He wrapped his hands about her thighs. His breath on them was warm. "George! You will be careful!"

"Aren't I always?"

He kept kissing her, and she squirmed. "No, I meant with Mother's necklace!"

"Oh, that." He propped himself on his elbows, picked one of her hairs from his tongue, and flicked it away. "It's not something else, is it?"

"No," she lied.

"Well then." He untied his dressing gown.

After that she willed herself not to think. George guided her hands onto him and bent over her again. When he lifted his face, his eyes had the impatient, determined expression that meant he was deeply aroused. When he climbed on top of her and raised her legs, she did not protest. He began to kiss her deeply, possessively, and shifted himself closer. Darling Win, he said over and over. Clasping him tighter, Winifred raised her hips a little, and the deed was done. From now on, it must be George, always George, only George. Tears rolled down her cheeks.

George tasted their sweetness and smiled.

CHAPTER 16
Low Comedy

Act I
Shakleton's Seven Mysteries
and Perpetual Shows Reunited

"It's all about balance," Grynt said, "give and take."

A pair of tight-rope walkers carefully approached each other. The line beneath their leather slippers wavered slightly.

Though it was evening there was still plenty of light. It was nearly midsummer. On the road by Grynt's cart, other travelers drove brightly painted wagons. All were bound for the common to set up the fair. Grynt let Sam hold Jasper's reins, for they drew near their campsite under the shadow of an oak grove. A medieval castle rose behind it. The Wash lay close by to its east and Holloways to its west. Seamus had already gone ahead to pitch their tent. He stood juggling three colored balls in the light of their cooking fire, to the delight of a group of little boys.

The man and the woman teetered, inching forward, their arms outstretched. The rope shuddered almost imperceptibly. The man knelt. The woman raised her leg behind her in arabesque, slowly tipped her body, and took the man's hand.

"'Ow does they do it?" Sam gasped. "What's the trick? Does 'e 'old 'er up, or does she 'old 'im?"

"No trick but hard work, lad. They have to learn to hold themselves steady before they can make it look that easy when they're on the rope together."

They approached a fortune-teller's tent, its purple canopy painted with golden bulls and silver stars. For Grynt, the heavenly bodies were guides for dark nights, though he would not gainsay the man who earned his living by persisting that he saw portents in their patterns. Unlike Sam, he was not tempted by crystal balls and Tarot cards. He did not expect much and was hardly ever disappointed, nor was he ever lonely. "Not when I've got Jasper." He clucked affectionately at his horse. He preferred to be a bystander to affairs of the heart. "All I require is what's in me wagon and another day on the open road, but I'll let you down if you'd like to consult Mithras the Miraculous." Sam declined but looked wistfully over his shoulder at the fluttering canopy.

After they left King's Lynn in March, Grynt and Sam headed north, always in the hope of catching up with Seamus. Grynt would stop in a village, throw down his cap on a street corner and saw on his fiddle while Sam smacked a tambourine and collected coins and local gossip. Along the way, Grynt stopped to pick up his mail. Some of it was from Court, to whom Grynt had written to inform him of the various villages along his and Sam's route. Their final stop was to be Edinburgh.

Just beyond the Scottish border, they found Seamus at a pub, hauling beer barrels off the back of a wagon. He wore false eyeglasses and sported a bushy red beard. Since Patterson put him on the train, he had taken odd jobs like the one at the pub or roughed it. Like Court, he had written to Grynt. He also wrote Beryl Stuart about their setup. Sam was horrified.

While Seamus explained, his eyes filled with tears. "It wasn't honest what we did. I couldn't let her worry. It must've broken her heart thinking I killed him, that our Courty was dead!"

"She ain't got one!" Sam protested.

"Well, it's done," Grynt said philosophically. "What will be, will be."

At the beginning of summer, they journeyed south. Each night as they sat about their campfire, Grynt read aloud from Court's latest letter. Sam stargazed and Seamus smoked his pipe. Holloways' staff names became familiar, from Mrs. Pettiford the housekeeper to Oliver the hall boy. With Court, the trio of friends rode to hounds with Mr. and Mrs. Burns and showed Mr. Barron how to box. Court was even more eloquent in his description of Richards' stables and especially enthusiastic in his lists of menus and praise of Mrs. Lumley's cooking.

Mrs. Pettiford had taught him much: the ways and history of the fine house, the proper protocol for entering and exiting a room when gentry were present, even the mysterious order of guest presentation at meals. She had also given him elocution lessons and strove to correct the worst faults of his speech in an undertone so that the other servants would not hear when he blundered. *But they always do, and it makes for a good laugh.* The footman Jakes and stand-in butler Struthers showed him how to wait at table when one of them had his half day off, or what to do when an extra valet was needed. *I can tie a gentleman's cravat proper and brush Mr. Barron's frock coat without shredding it. But I'd rather harness his old horse.* There was also the mistress' lady's maid, Mademoiselle Dupree. *Tell Sam I've finally got the correct French for most of the entrées and rattle the names of all the serving pieces right off, though the parlor maids still find my Cockney twang while I do so a scream.*

Once he thought he had seen the ghost of Good Queen Bess when he played hall boy for a night. Oliver had gone home to help his brother with the plowing. *In the Great Hall, there was a tinkly sort of music. A lady dressed in white came toward me. I was so frightened I almost dropped, but when the ghost laughed, I saw it was only Jakes in a sheet, with flour on his face and an old periwig on his head. Will was in the corner with a music box, and we all fell out.* Richards even let him drive the carriage on Sundays to and from church. London and its troubles were a world away.

"He'll be as elegant and knowledgeable as Beryl soon enough." Seamus sighed. "He always could tell a good story. Had loads of them when we was lads."

"Like 'ow the thief o' Baghdad proved 'isself a prince and won the princess in the end," Sam sighed. He pushed Court's top hat back from his brow. "I don't think I'd like all that muckin' out and lightin' stoves before dawn, or carryin' kindlin' and water up all them stairs. Sounds too much like the Boar and 'Art, 'cept Mrs. Pettiford don't make 'im peel taters! All 'e used to 'ave to do was drive Piani."

"And fight in all them fixed contests!" Seamus puffed on his pipe. "No Sammy, not bein' honest, that's what puts a man down. Service is respectable."

"Aye, a man always serves somebody." Grynt folded Court's letter into his waistcoat, then took out the pieces of a flute which he screwed together. He began to play softly.

"Not me!" Sam countered. "You don't answer to no one either, Grynt."

The little man frowned. "I know who my Master is and no mistake."

"Why'd you bring Court 'ere in particular?" The boy nodded in Holloways' direction.

"It's far out of Geoff Ratchet's way," Grynt mumbled.

Sam stared at the fire.

The next day, many more painted wagons had parked beneath the oaks or pitched camp near the castle. There was a din of hammering as menfolk set up the main dais and game-of-skill booths, the puppet theater, and the concessions tent. Smells of hay and large animals, smoke and stew pots mingled in the air. Children's shrill voices cried out, and women called after them. The church bell rang four times. Court rode up the lane that led by its yard to the common.

He was mounted on an old, dapple grey horse. He wore a sky blue checked shirt, dark corded breeches, and a pair of aged, but very fine riding boots. His clean-shaven cheek still bore the scar from Piani's ring, but his color was much improved from outdoor work. His queue was gone; his dark hair brushed neatly back. About his neck was a brightly patterned, purple cloth.

Sam stuck two fingers in his teeth and expressed his appreciation with a piercing whistle. "You're a regular country gent! Is this your 'orse?"

The animal belonged to Mr. Barron, Court explained, and the boots had once been his.

Though Grynt was not of a nature to be so dazzled by Court's transformation, he screwed up an eye and peered at him in satisfaction. "I'm that glad to see you!" He shook Court's hand.

Behind the wagon, Seamus lathered his jaw from a soap cup. On a clothesline strung behind him were several freshly painted canvases depicting acrobats and performers. Others for game booths flapped in the breeze. An unfinished banner lay draped over a folding table, weighted down by a paint box. He threw down his razor and pumped Court's hand. "Courty! Well, I never! Look at you, a new man and risen from the dead to boot!" He clapped a crushing arm around his friend's shoulders.

"We should celebrate," Grynt said. "Seamus, you and Sam get us some refreshment. Tent's ready by the look of it." He waited until the pair was nearly halfway across the common. "All's well then, is it?"

"She's to be married to the biggest blackguard 'o ever lived!"

"I wondered when you wrote naught about her," Grynt said. "You'll not stay on then?"

"The weddin's in three days. They'll be on the Continent the rest o' the summer and come back for the shootin'. If Mr. Bert takes me on as manservant, I'm bound for London again."

"I'm sorry, lad." Grynt reached into his pocket and withdrew an envelope. "Seamus went into King's Lynn this morning for me mail. I've a letter you should see."

It was from a man named Peele. "He was set over Adams in hospital, a detective sergeant. He'd seen me talking to Seamus. Maybe he heard a bit more than he let on at the time. Sharp, that one!" He chuckled and tapped his nose. "But maybe I heard him and Adams say sommat as well. The woman that was taken from the bank, the name of your lady love, Miss de la Coeur! Anyway, this letter! Peele asked me to keep an eye out, let him know if I heard sommat of interest."

"'Owed 'e know you'd be 'ere?" Court asked.

Grynt nodded at the concession tent. Seamus and Sam crossed the green with a box of bottles. "Seamus sent your sister a letter. Something tells me Peele's had a close eye on her."

"Bloody Seamus," Court muttered, but without rancor.

Their friends joined them. They drank the ale while Sam bragged of their adventures on the road. Court admired Seamus' canvases and lifted the corner of the unfinished one. It was an announcement for an all-comers boxing competition.

"What d'you say, Courty? It'll be over yonder under that great oak. I'll be doing some exhibition lifting and bend the iron bar. Some o' the locals have already signed up for a lark. Put your hand in for old time's sake. Grynt's recording the bets. You'll have no trouble, long as the village blacksmith ain't handy with his fists!"

"A bit o' the ready might come in useful soon," Grynt said.

Court laughed ruefully and untethered Puck. "Mrs. Pettiford'd 'ave me 'ide, but we'll see."

Act II
News from Home

Bettina sat down to her tea beside Mr. Furor. Mrs. Pettiford passed out mail. Everyone who had a letter eagerly opened theirs or was already reading. An envelope sat by the man's plate, untouched. She'd never seen the writing before.

The appearance of a second communication from London in one day made Court very uneasy. He wished Mademoiselle Dupree would not stare. He tore open the envelope.

Bettina feigned an interest in her teacup but peered through lowered lashes at Mr. Furor. He stuffed the letter and its envelope in his pocket. She made a pretense of attending to the bread and butter on her plate. The man picked up his fork then set it down. Jakes passed him the beer pitcher. Mr. Furor's hand shook slightly as he filled his glass and drank.

"News from home, n'est pas?"

"Miss Dupree, I need a favor."

His voice was low. Mr. Furor was always polite but never went out of his way to talk to her. She took the pitcher and passed it to Jakes. Interested as she was, she did not want to attract the others' attention. The under-house parlor maid Molly already eyed their tête-à-tête with curiosity, but the girl always simpered and stared at Mr. Furor. She narrowed her eyes at the girl. The little flirt should pay more attention to Will.

"Of course," she whispered back to Mr. Furor.

"Tell your mistress I got to see her. It can't wait. I'll be in the stable." He pushed away his untouched plate and left.

If Jakes or even Struthers dared speak to her so sharply, she'd have told them where to go and no mistake, but she'd watched Mistress very closely since The Man from Haymarket 44's arrival. Bettina finished her beer and waited a full minute. "Will, if I was you, I'd tend the horses and let Molly kick up her heels by herself!" Amidst laughter, she drank the rest of Mr. Furor's beer and rose. Then she climbed the servants' stairs to her lady's bedroom to deliver his message.

Act III
"Don't Do It, Miss!"

Inside the storeroom it was so dark Bettina had to blink several times to adjust her eyes. Feeling along the wall, she pushed open the door. Mr. Furor's and Mistress' voices were nearby. Quickly, she crouched behind some feed sacks. The man's back was to her, but she could clearly see Winifred pacing before Tulip's stall.

"Oh Court, do stop calling me that!"

"But it's 'o you are!" He put down his bucket and began to brush the horse.

"You never fail to remind me, Mr. Furor!" She slapped her gloves on her palm. "Three months! Never once have you deigned to speak to me. I told you, I don't care what people think!"

"Well, you ought! You're a lady!" When she laughed, he went on. "You are to me and these people 'o knows you! Bloody 'eadstrong!" he muttered, stroking Tulip's flank vigorously.

Winifred played with her gloves. "What did you have to say that can't wait, then?"

Mr. Furor stepped out of the stall and set down the brush. "You're really goin' to marry that man?"

"How dare you remind me of our places, then ask such a question?"

"I'm speaking as a friend."

"I don't want to be your friend!" She stamped, then looked down, cheeks afire.

"There's no way but to be plain. Don't do it, Miss!"

She faced him, eyes snapping. "Have you an alternative in mind, Mr. Furor?"

"'E'll worry you for money all your live-long life."

"I don't care about the money! You could have it! All of it!"

"Not from a woman!"

"Not from me, you mean!"

"I've got a chance to earn me keep 'onest for once!" He returned to Tulip's stall. "This ain't about me! It's about you throwin' yourself away on a man what treats people, women 'specially, like they ain't real. They're toys, like 'is guns and 'is 'orses!"

Winifred stared at him incredulously. "You come here and act like nothing ever happened between us! Like the worst a man could take from a woman is her money! All this time you wait to speak to me, and this is what you have to say?" She walked back and forth again, beating her gloves against her skirt. She laughed but sounded close to tears. "Three days before my wedding, when you've had three months! All you had to do was—. I know all about George!"

"You don't know nothin'." He pulled the letter from his pocket and held it out to her. "This came today from me sister. Read it!"

Winifred took the letter and read. Slowly, she folded the paper.

"The man you marries ought to be worthy of you. He ought to be a man like Mr. Barron."

"He is worthy, but I can't marry him unless he asks me. And I won't ask him!"

Mr. Furor put the letter away and picked up Tulip's brush.

Winifred leaned her face against the rough post of the horse's stall. After a while she spoke. "For so long, I'd made up my mind to be single and independent. I love my family and they love me. It should be enough, but it isn't. When I came out, I wasn't a success. I wouldn't let myself be. It didn't matter that I wasn't beautiful because I had money! You've no idea what fools people act when they learn how rich I am. They'll do anything, say anything. They'd perjure themselves before God or take vows they don't believe in. You're no better! You won't tell me the truth, even when I know how you must still feel."

Mr. Furor worked on Tulip's flank. "I told you. I won't make promises I can't keep!"

"At least George and I are old friends."

"That man ain't nobody's friend."

"You've only yourself to thank. I wouldn't have accepted him if I'd thought—."

Mr. Furor stood still. His shoulders sagged.

"Do you remember I told you about those terrible parties?" she continued. "George used to be the only one could make me laugh. You said he didn't look after me, but he did in his way! He still does. He will, I suppose, once we're—." She pressed her forehead against the post. Tulip poked her head out of the stall and nuzzled her mistress' shoulder. Winifred stroked the beast and gently tugged her mane. "Oh, Mr. Furor, why did you have to come here? Please go away!"

Winifred began to cry.

"Miss, don't! Bear up! I likes you proud. Or angry! That's 'ow I first saw you, fired up 'as 'ell, and it's what brought me 'round. You was like a fine, sleek mare, all kick and teeth! It's just I knows Mr. George gets pleasure from breakin' soft things, and I won't see you broken."

Winifred cried harder. "You've broken my heart!"

Laying his hand next to hers without quite touching it, Mr. Furor whispered, "When a man wants to bring a mare 'round, it takes firmness. She's frightened 'til she sees it's not 'er spirit 'e wants to break. Then she's 'is and 'e's 'ers, forever and all. Nothin' on this earth will change that. I'd never break you, Miss de la Coeur, or your 'eart. Don't say that to me, please."

Their eyes met.

"Once, you said you trusted me. Does you trust me now?"

"I'll always trust you, Mr. Furor."

He stepped away. "Then there's somethin' else we got to talk about. That night in me room, the necklace that was in your pocket...."

She smiled for the first time.

"Did you lock it up some place?"

"I gave it to George to return to the bank almost a week ago."

"I 'ope 'e did. It ain't safe for no one to 'ave." He drew near her again. "Geoff saw Mr. George with some jewels at the Boar and 'Art that night before 'e went lookin' for Rosie."

"He gave me a different necklace before we...!" Her face was stricken. "Oh, Court, I wish I'd never...! Shh!"

They both turned toward the stable yard.

Mr. Furor spoked hurriedly. "About two weeks ago, Geoff was seen going into a Cheapside jeweler's right after George came out!"

Winifred waved her hands at him frantically.

There was a sound of steps and voices. Richards and Will were back from their tea. Mr. Furor slipped into Tulip's stall, and Winifred ran toward the feed sacks. Bettina scrambled out of the way and hid behind a box. Her mistress ducked through the door into the storeroom.

Act IV
"BUNJUR!"

Bettina wiped her eyes on her shawl and quickened her step down the lane that led to the common. At last she understood enough, if not all. Sadly, she thought of the recent house party Miss Winifred and

Monsieur George had attended. Bettina had known when she went to help Mademoiselle dress for supper that her lady had not taken a nap. As she straightened the damp, twisted sheets she found Monsieur's gift, a beautiful sapphire necklace, under the pillows. The odors of male sweat, her mistress' perfume, and the musk of lovemaking were fresh. At the time, she only sighed, relieved not to have to worry whether Winifred missed her menses or not.

But after listening to her lady and Mr. Furor, her heart pounded. It hardly mattered to her what his sister's letter contained about Monsieur George. Miss Amelie had been correct all along. Miss de la Coeur was in love with Mr. Furor! And why not? Was he not honorable? What if they had been lovers? He had also saved her; and now he wanted nothing more than her happiness, only he was too poor to declare himself. Bettina's sense of injustice was roused.

In the servants' hall, she never corrected the assumption that her own people had been in service for generations. Whose business was it if she did not even know her parents' names? The English were so obsessed with one's status, one's place! But she was a Frenchwoman. Liberté! Fraternité! Égalité! Vive la Révolution!

She hurried along the green's perimeter to the concessions tent. She bought a half pint of shandy and felt she had definitely earned it. As she took her change, a very tall, muscular man with a glorious moustache eyed her from where he and a boy sat at one of the long tables. The man smoked his pipe while the boy played with a deck of cards. She sauntered to the table, sat down a few feet from the pair, and sipped her drink. She assumed a distant air. The man remained appreciatively watchful. The boy pushed his top hat well back on his fair curls and continued to turn over his cards.

"The Mighty Mithras showed you how to read them? What do they say?" the man asked.

The boy stared at his deck with disgust. "They says you're goin' to meet a lady!"

Bettina stared at the beer advertisements and livestock posters that hung behind the boy's head. "What are you looking at?" she asked the man.

"A fine sight, if I do say so!" He bit at his pipe.

The boy turned over another card. "They says you're goin' to travel!"

"Who says so?" Bettina tartly asked the big fellow.

"Seamus Todd's me name, and this is Sammy."

"We've got to get back to the ring," the boy said curtly. "Let's go Seamus." The big man ignored this. The boy furiously turned over more cards. He darted a glance at Bettina, gritted his teeth, and raised the corner of his upper lip.

"May I be so bold as to ask your name?" Seamus shifted closer and faced her. Huge muscles rippled beneath his sleeves, which were rolled above his elbows. His fine dark eyes twinkled merrily.

"You might. Je m'appelle Mademoiselle Dupree."

The boy regarded her with sudden interest. "You're lady's maid to Miss de la Coeur up at the great 'ouse yonder!"

Bettina was surprised at the boy's accent. "Mais oui! Êtes-vous français aussi? But you also sound like east London. How do you find out about me? Am I in your cards?"

"French, are we?" The big man's eyes lit up even more. "Well, I never. BUNJUR!"

Bettina laughed.

So did the boy. "We got a friend what works for 'er in the stables!"

Seamus leaned closer. "That's right, our Courty! Shall I buy you some cake to go with that? Sammy, go get us some tarts. Sam and his sister are from Normandy. 'Tis lovely country, I reckon. Me and Courty go back years in London town." He flexed his arm. "Did a bit of prizefighting!"

The boy's laughter died. "Seamus! It's time for your next act!"

"Maybe Mr. Furor will not be with us so much longer, I am afraid," Bettina said.

"Your mistress is gettin' married," Sam said, "and 'e's goin' to be a valet."

"You know more than me! She will lose a good man, I think."

"Ever see him fight?" Seamus gestured proudly at a poster behind them. "I painted that!"

Centered over a silhouette of a rearing black horse was an unmistakable likeness of Mr. Furor raising red boxing gloves.

"FURIOUS FUROR—CHAMPION BOXER!"

"Ça c'est magnifique!" Bettina was truly impressed. "It's very good!"

The man regarded his work and then her with satisfaction. "We've been in some tough spots, but I trust him like a brother. He's a good bloke, just been unlucky." Ignoring the boy's widened eyes, he beamed down at her. "I like your accent and your voice, Maddy-moy-zel. It's husky, like when a lady first wakes up and rolls out o' bed."

"Oh! La! La!"

"BUNJUR!"

The big man leaned further over her, and she felt a bit awed.

The boy gathered his cards, stood, and straightened his top hat. "Seamus, you're on in five minutes! Don't mind 'im, Mademoiselle Dupree." The boy mouthed the word "simple" to her.

Oblivious, the big man stared down at her. "You go on, Sammy. I'll catch you up."

"Five minutes!" The boy glared at the two of them, then turned on his heel.

"Now, where were we? I can't hardly think, lookin' at them pretty brown eyes and all them dark, rich curls!"

"Can't you?" Bettina felt a bit breathless. His forwardness had a boyish quality at which she could not take offense. She searched the crowd for Sammy's top hat, but he was well on his way to the old oak where a crowd had already gathered. The man next to her sat closer than he ought, his hip brushing hers, but she didn't mind. Such a big, handsome fellow, was it possible he had only a child's brain? Was the boy being mischievous, or was the man?

"Sammy seems very protective. Does he look after—um—out for you?"

The man blinked slowly. "Wee! But that's what friends are for, and we're old friends."

She slid closer and ran her finger around the rim of her glass. "If Monsieur Furor is such a friend too, may I ask a question about him?" She fluttered her lashes at the big man.

His chest swelled. "Ask me all the questions about Courty or whatever else you like!"

Act V
"You Know Her..."

"Did you take my mother's necklace to the bank?"

George sat on the window seat behind Sir Percival's desk, staring down onto the stable yard. He had been seated there a long time. Earlier, as he mounted the stairs, he had seen Furor go into the stable. Winifred followed at a run, face flushed and lips parted. George had gone into the study, poured a drink, and taken up his post at the window. A quarter hour passed. Richards and Will crossed the yard.

Shortly thereafter, Winifred ran back to the house. A minute more and her quick steps sounded in the hall. She burst into the room. At the sight of him, she turned pale. She busied herself with her ledgers, and he'd left her to it. At the moment Furor was walking toward the village with Will. Distant lights from the fair twinkled.

George supposed he should have taken matters in hand from the beginning. The night of Furor's arrival, when he surprised Win and the man during their cozy little interview, he should have paid off the good for nothing lay-about and sent him packing. He hadn't been bothered because the louse was only Furor, after all. He'd never given the son of a bitch a second thought unless it was to regret betting on him. But more than once he'd heard the maids whisper of Furor and Win in the same breath. Even at the Thorn and Crown, or in the servants' hall at Hereford, voices fell silent as he entered, and guilty eyes met his. At the Thorn and Crown, his entrance interrupted a half-finished jest. The farmers' greetings were muted, their eyes shifty. As they raised their glasses, or when his staff nodded—did he imagine it—or was he mocked?

"It's at my jeweler's," he said.

"What on earth for? There's absolutely nothing wrong with it."

"You didn't have the settings checked after that day at the bank?"

"No," she said shortly and turned back to her ledgers.

Of course, she didn't like to talk about that day. Who could blame her? But they were going to talk about it. They were going to talk about a lot of things. The quarter hour she had just spent alone with Furor in the stable, and the twenty hours she'd gone missing until he put her on an omnibus in Haymarket.

Since the house party, he had grown ever more careful in his observations of Win; her gestures and expressions as various people entered a room, for example; what she said and did not say. Most importantly, he kept abreast of the company she kept when he was not there. The maid, Molly, had not been difficult to enlist. Along with Geoff's parting words, Molly's lay coiled in a dark corner of his mind.

The first night he had Win's necklace, he kept it in his dressing gown pocket and tried to treat it with no more concern than a pocket watch. By day, he had left it lying on his desk. Feeling this might be too careless, he stuffed it into his jacket. This did not quite satisfy either. Until he delivered it to Kleinfeldt, he found that he needed to touch it often to reassure himself of its presence. Even in the jeweler's vault, it gnawed at his brain and troubled his dreams. Once, he dreamt he lay paralyzed on a bed in his old barracks, or perhaps an attic. A gold serpent slithered between the bedclothes; its bright orange eyes stared into his.

There had been other nightmares. Phantoms stalked him through foggy streets or whirled out of reach before dissolving into the shifting air. He turned a familiar London corner and was in a vast desert. An old crone wrapped in ragged widow's weeds stood solitary as an obelisk, waiting. Certain it was Lottie, he tried to run to her. Sand filled his shoes and dragged at his feet. The necklace lay heavily against his breast. He clutched at it, his hand gnarled and mottled with liver spots. He was an old man! He tore the jewels out of his pocket. Shards of worthless, brightly colored glass spilled through his fingers.

"You don't want to take the original when we travel," he said.

"I thought you didn't want me to wear it. George, you said you'd take it to the bank."

"My jeweler can make a copy. It's more valuable than I realized."

"I don't want a copy. I want you to do what you said you would."

George swirled his brandy. It clung to the sides of the glass. The liquid was not only reminiscent of the color of Win's eyes but other parts of her. The hair at the nape of her neck when it was damp, the warm cleft between her breasts, the shadows beneath her buttocks and under her arms, or the secret places between her thighs; there were some hues of a woman that were fugitive and unforgettable—irreplaceable.

Kleinfeldt had been eager, yet fearful, as he pored over the necklace with his lens. He wouldn't promise the diamonds' yellow could be achieved exactly with semi-precious stones. Diamonds of lesser quality perhaps, but it would still be approximate. The pearls were not any easier. If done properly, the job could take weeks and much of his time. It would be extremely expensive. Recreating the brilliant fire of the pendant stone, the color of a blood moon, was impossible. It was one of a kind.

George started to take back the necklace.

The jeweler grasped the gems and fondled them once more. "I only want more time!"

The two of them had stared at the fiery diamond and its companions, lying on their velvet bed. George thought of Win, how ravishing she was when she let herself go. There were letters he could write to a jeweler he knew in Vienna and another in Budapest, but he had not. Was it worth the risk? Win had trusted him, after all. How lovely she had been as she lay stretched naked beneath him with only his sapphires about her neck. Her capitulation had not only been a surprise. It was a revelation.

It had been exciting to think of the other guests in their rooms getting dressed, fussing with their maids and valets over gloves and studs, worrying which of the supper's entrées would ruin their digestion, or even if their own assignations would be successful while he and Win had been.... He still couldn't quite believe it. Then the dressing gong clamored, and Win was off the bed like a shot, struggling into her dressing gown and breathless with fear lest Dupree catch them. She had practically shoved him out the door, like they were in some farce, when moments earlier she had been so warm and yielding, so quick and eager, like ivory melting against him or honey pouring between his lips. He had stumbled into the hall, almost drunk with her.

She had been cross and tetchy all that evening. During supper, she barely attended to her partner's attempts at conversation, the old fellow's endless story about a property dispute. She took a bite from each course as though it pained her to open her mouth. When the men rejoined the women for coffee, she hardly looked at him. Once everyone had gone to bed, he came to her. He had hoped to hear her call out to him as she had that first time. She had been compliant enough but quiet. She fretted about another headache afterward and quickly sent him on his way.

As for the necklace, there was the issue of re-cutting the largest stone. Geoff had gone with him to Kleinfeldt's that time. To George's horror, the man had shown up at his club and he couldn't get rid of him.

"You said it yourself, that I'd be back." He showed his teeth, took off his hat, and helped himself to a cigar.

The die was cast. Once they got to Cheapside, he and Kleinfeldt had argued. The man was stalling, and his anxiety had begun to make George nervous too. The usually subservient jeweler absolutely refused to touch the pumpkin-colored gem. Its size and unique color were the least of his concerns. His eyes darted uneasily at Geoff as he spoke. It was from India, Kleinfeldt protested. Many such stones were stolen from idols! There were curses! Geoff had snorted. George accused Kleinfeldt of being unnecessarily fastidious, not to mention stupidly superstitious, but the jeweler was resolute.

"It's geometry, a stone! Cut it!" George had shouted.

"It's not so simple!" Kleinfeldt exclaimed, almost hysterical.

Geoff gripped the man's shoulders and shook him. "Yes, it is! Understand? Simple!"

George spat at Kleinfeldt's idiocy but thought that it might be better to chuck the whole affair. The necklace meant so much to Win, and Geoff was a fool. Though the ass hadn't been drinking, he'd seemed off. There was bound to be another cock-up, not that he had any real plan.

All this had been on his mind when Win ran out of the stable. He had come upstairs by the staircase Old Bess was said to walk in her nocturnal rambles, playing a game with himself. If Win smiled at him at supper or teased him in her old way afterward, he would go back to Kleinfeldt tomorrow and call off the whole affair. Geoff could go hang.

Then he saw Win follow Furor into the stable. Not that there was anything odd in that. She often went to check on Tulip after a ride, or she might have left her gloves in the tack room. As he paused on the stairs, the little Scots scampered past him in dress up clothes, bearing wooden swords and dolls, the spaniels yapping at their heels. Their nurse followed, ordering them to the nursery and their tea. The shrieks of laughter and the dogs' barks echoed in the upper passage. A door at the top of the stairs closed. It was quiet once more.

Sometimes he hated not only Charles, but John Burns, too.

"Why don't we go back to my farm in India?" she asked.

Win stood next to him. He set down his glass and drew her closer. "You'd hate it. You'd miss Amelie and the wretched little Scots. You'd cry all the time to come home. It's only nerves," he soothed. "Have they fitted the dress? Am I not going to marry the most glorious bride this county has ever seen?"

Winifred fiddled with his collar. He let her go. She wandered to the fireplace and stood before the Stubbs. "George, the last time you were in London—."

"I saw you leave the stable. Did Mr. Furor upset you?"

It was time to tell him the truth.

Until today, the rumors that surrounded George had only been exciting stories. The actual fates of those girls about whom she heard gossip were no more real to her than the heroines of romantic novels. Yet even as she excoriated him for his wanton destructiveness and her heart broke for the woman that he had lately wronged, she missed the playmate of her girlhood, the dashing soldier who had entranced her and everyone else. Too late, she realized she had loved that George with all her girlish heart.

Rosie! How she wished she'd never read Court's letter.

She wanted the George who would whisk her into the cupboard during Christmas night's romps. Beautiful and fair-haired like the storybook prince who wakes the sleeping beauty, he struck a match and presented her with sugar plums which he would relinquish only when she agreed to kiss him beneath the mistletoe. He never collected on her promises with more than a peck on the cheek, but he whirled her on the dance floor afterward until she was giddy. Year after year, as Percival lit the tree, George would toss a gift box onto her lap. It always contained some trifle, but she had kept them all. She wanted the George who played the devil in the children's pantomime, hopped about the furniture like a frog, and slid down the banisters, hooting like a mad man. It had all been so much fun and no harm done!

Somehow, she'd confused that George with the complicated man whom she'd agreed to marry. As she read the letter from Court's sister, she finally understood this. She didn't know George and never had. She suspected no one did. She wondered if anything he'd ever told her was true. The pain she felt at her realization, at her loss, was more dreadful than she would've thought possible. A part of her she hadn't known existed or mattered so much was gone. What she'd read in the letter destroyed it. No, she corrected herself; George had.

He set down his glass and rubbed his hand over his eyes. "Ah, Win. Don't look so confoundedly disappointed in a fellow. It's not as bad as that."

"It's true then?"

George sank onto the couch behind her. "That I don't want to go to India to live?"

"No, that you—," she stopped. If she went on, it would be the end between them. She didn't see how it could be any other way. "You said you knew Court before he came here."

"It's Court now, is it?"

"His sister wrote to him."

George felt his impulse to good will curdle. He waited for her to go on.

"You know her and her friend, too."

With a move that startled her, George was on his feet. He gripped her arm.

"You'll have nothing to do with them! You're to have nothing more to do with him! Damn, but this has gotten out of hand! I should have known better!"

"He doesn't want money! It isn't blackmail."

"What else could it be? You trust the word of a man like that? You are a baby! He's the driver for an Italian gang boss. I'll bet he's been at the scenes of more crimes and murders than you could count. He collects money for the fellow. He's a card sharp and a thief, as well as a second-rate boxer. And his sister, that unnatural bitch belongs in a freak show!"

"What about Rosie?"

"These people live in packs. Beryl Stuart and her little friend are whores, lovers! Frankly, Furor isn't much above their cut. How do you think a dog lives when its vomit dries up? Furor would bed down with any bit of skirt, so long as there's grub and a place to lay his dirty head for the night!"

Winifred tried to wrench her arm away.

George yanked her closer and pressed his lips to her ear. "When I think of a man like that talking with you alone, even thinking of you, I don't know what I might do. I used to think you proud, Win, and you were. You were so far above all the others, a goddess!"

"I'm not proud!" She struggled in his arms. "Not like that!"

"As my future wife, I expect you to know your worth."

Winifred shook him off. "You have to help her! What if she has a child?"

"It won't be mine!" George roared and flung her away.

Winifred stumbled against the sofa and grabbed it for support.

He filled his glass and forced himself to speak calmly. "This is madness! Furor's sister wants money, darling. That's what this is, nothing more. The sluts!" When she did not respond, George felt his anger rise again. "I'll see to it he's thrown out."

"I engage and dismiss the servants in this house!"

George's fury broke. "And I look after what's mine! I'm going to the police."

Winifred's eyes widened.

"It's what should have been done as soon as he arrived. You're right. I do know Furor and Hez Boors and Geoff Ratchet and Selway Adams, Beryl Stuart and Rosie Cartwright, all of them! I know where Ratchet and Furor were the morning the Royal Empire blew up, and I know where you were when you didn't come to Simpson's or back to Hampstead that night. So, you're not to have anything more to do with Furor! Understand?"

"You don't frighten me!"

George gulped down the rest of his whiskey and grabbed his jacket. "Don't I, darling?"

CHAPTER 17
The Ring

It was a lovely Midsummer's Eve. Light lingered in the west. A half
disk of moon waxed among scattered stars. Amelie and Bert walked
arm and arm toward the torches and colored lights. As they
approached the carousel, he took her hand, and they broke into a run.

Winifred held onto George's arm. Neither one of them spoke. She
and Amelie had taken his carriage to Hereford Hall for supper. George
seemed to have forgotten the stormy scene of that afternoon and had
never been more charming or attentive. Bert had joined them at the
common, having been busy with the legal affairs of the old gentleman
with whom she'd dined at the house party. Winifred was desperate to
speak privately with her cousin, but didn't know what to say without
incriminating Court.

Of law, she knew little but what concerned her own interests. Of
criminal law, she knew even less. George might be bluffing, but his
suspicions showed her that she must be careful for Court's sake. She
remembered his troubles with Piani and his furious conversation with
Geoff about the fixed fight. She heard Inspector Owens' words and
those of his man from the Yard, their certainty that all involved in the
Adams investigation would be brought to justice. George seemed to
suggest what Court had done for Piani before his involvement with the
Royal Empire Bank was enough to get him hanged as an accessory to
multiple murders, not to mention Adams'. Though she did not see how
Bert could help, she must try.

But George's recent activities were equally terrible. Under what
circumstances or why he and Geoff Ratchet frequented the same

jeweler's, she could not divine. It might be blackmail. Beyond doubt, the secret life wherein George incurred his debts ran like a foul river beneath the men's relationship. Then there was Miss Stuart's letter about him and Rosie. Whenever Winifred thought of the woman, she felt morally indicted for George's unforgivable indifference. Court's words, that George enjoyed breaking soft creatures, did not worry her on her own account. The way Miss Stuart and her friend conducted their private lives was none of her affair, but their welfare was. Court had laid their plight at her doorstep. She would not betray his trust.

They reached the center of the common. Youths and maidens piled wood and broken furniture to make a bonfire. A throng was gathered under the great oak about a dais and a make-shift boxing ring. Bert and Amelie had finished at the carousel and were on their way to the stalls for pitch-the-ball and sling-the-penny. At the sight of the towers of china and glassware, Winifred thought of all the wedding crystal and Limoges plates piled on the long table in the Great Hall. George maneuvered her toward the crowd.

"Look, darling! Furor's name is on the board. He may do well for once. The locals are more in his league than the professionals Piani used to match him against."

People made way for them. Amongst the faces of villagers and farmers she recognized many from George's estate and others less familiar whom she supposed had come from King's Lynn. On the dais, a nut-brown, boney little man cawed out names in a voice like a raven's and took bets. Behind him flapped various banners. One sported a rearing black horse and Court's likeness. She turned from it. As they drew nearer the ring, she heard what she realized must be the sound of a man's bare fist making contact with another's body. Then she heard it again. Her gorge rose at the crowd's corresponding roar.

In the ring stood Court, stripped to the waist, his taped fists raised. Blood flew to her cheeks at the sight of his bared torso and the muscles that stood out on his chest and his arms. The scars on his back and face were purple from his exertions, and his black hair clung to his temples. Before him stood a farmer, a powerful man named Patrick Nye, who already sported a bruised cheek from Court's ministrations. The man was gigantic next to his opponent, but Court seemed calm and focused. Nye took a rather wild swing at Court's head, even to Winifred's inexperienced eyes. Voices rose, cheering and booing. Court bobbed and danced backward. The men circled one another, lunged, pummeled each other with short, convulsive jabs about the ribs, and sprang apart. The crowd cheered again.

The wizened man clanged a bell and shouted the odds for the next fight. Around her and George, people grabbed for their purses and exchanged money with astonishing speed, and a fair-haired boy who carried a top hat ran about, handing back coins from inside it. Court and Patrick Nye shook hands and shared a bucket of water. The little man scribbled in chalk on a slate board as people shouted out their bets. The boy ran about the crowd once more, collecting money in his hat. He stopped by her and George, but she shook her head. George pushed by the child, tugging her toward the dais. Behind them, the crowd howled as two more farmers took their positions in the sandy ring. Their shadows leapt in the torch light and broke apart on the oak leaves.

"George, I don't want to watch this. I'm going to find Amelie and Bert."

He tightened his grip and shouted to the little man, who winked and took his money. "I bet on Furor to win his next fight. Let's see what he's really made of. It could be his hour of glory!"

Winifred wanted to close her eyes as George pulled her to the ring. There were some surprised looks on the spectators' faces at the sight of her so near such a rough scene, and she felt George was exposing her unduly. There were a few women by the ring but not many, and none of her class. The crowd included most of the men from the village and many of her and George's male tenants. Even in their excitement, they nodded or touched their caps.

In the distance, Bettina walked the earthworks with a man who made Farmer Nye look puny. Bettina would never stand for such nonsense! How she wished for a sharp Gallic tongue to cut through George's quiet bullying. She hated him. If she and Bettina packed tonight, they could leave from Gravesend for Alexandria before anyone discovered where they'd gone.

The big man drew Bettina's arm through his. The pair descended on the other side of the earthen mound and dropped out of sight. Never in all their years together had Winifred seen the woman step out with anyone. A twinge of the old forsakenness that used to drive her to the stable or Morrant's pantry made her eyes grow wet. Where were Bert and Amelie? She couldn't see over the heads of the crowd. Her heart sank.

The bell clanged. The farmers stepped from the ring, laughing and rubbing each other's bleeding heads. The gnarled little man shouted Court's name and that of another farmer. George yelled to her that it was one of his men. The little man jumped from the dais, and the boy took his place, furiously tugging the bell rope. The crowd cried out and lurched forward as one; Winifred and George were carried with it. At first, she could see nothing. Then a man stepped out of her and George's way.

Court delivered a powerful right to his foe's jaw. The fellow went down, spread-eagle on his back. Winifred was shocked at how quickly it was over. The crowd burst into raucous laughter. The little man stood over the farmer counting and sawing the air with his arm. The crowd joined in. The man tried to stand, but his legs buckled. Cheers went up nearby for Court. Winifred saw not only Jakes and Struthers, but Will and Oliver and many of her other servants, male and female, gathered and cheering too. A few of George's tenants jeered their disapproval. Court raised his taped and bloodied fists in the air and smiled at the crowd.

When he saw Winifred and George, his smile faltered. He touched his finger to his forehead and walked to the opposite edge of the ring. He'd entertained the possibility Winifred and George would come to the fair that night, but had hoped the ring would be too rough for Winifred's taste. Though her face was impassive, her eyes were full of concern. He suspected that she was there only because of George's coercion.

After Court plunged his head into a bucket of water, Sam wiped him down and bawled in his ear. "Old Swank is 'ere! Ain't that the de la Coeur lady with 'im?"

"You said he'll take all comers?" George's voice cut through the crowd's noise. He called to Grynt. "You there, man! That open spot on the marquee next to Furor's, I'll have it."

Grynt shot Court a quick look but replied to George. "That's right, sir! There's not a one too big or too small, but London's Fury will take them all! This is your night if you want to fight!" He spun in a circle, flapping his hands at the crowd and whipping them up.

"Well, then. He'll have to take me," George shouted, pulling off his coat and handing it to one of his young tenants. He tore at his cravat and unbuttoned his shirt. When he had those off, he handed them to a mortified Winifred. The young farmer relieved her of them. Several men from the Hereford estate began to hoot and make their way in his and Winifred's direction, shouting their master's name. Others in the crowd took it up until there was a chorus of GEORGE! GEORGE! GEORGE!

"George, don't! Please stop! Why are you doing this?" She followed him to the edge of the ring as he waved to his supporters. He seized her about the waist and kissed her, to the crowd's delight. There were shrill whistles, and the young farmer shook George's clothes overhead.

"We're going to see what your Mr. Furor is made of, once and for all!" He seized his cravat from the young man and tied it about her left wrist like a gauge. "Glad to see you're wearing my ring for once! Take care you don't lose it!"

Before she could stop him, he raised her arm for all to see, his eyes ablaze. Their imperious gleam reminded her uncomfortably of the way he looked when he meant to have her.

Across the ring, Court splashed his face from a bucket of water and wiped some through his hair. The boy rubbed his shoulders and arms while the little man bent near, hurriedly talking and pointing at George. Court shook his head violently and shouted, but she couldn't make out their words over the noise.

George grabbed her hand. The change in his expression was startling, and for a second, she had the wild hope he'd changed his mind.

"Darling Win, if only you could...!" The crowd drowned him out. "I would! I want to!"

"What?" Winifred shouted back at him, unable to hear. "George, oh, for heaven's sake!"

He dropped her hand, seemingly master of himself again. The young farmer helped him into the ring. A fife and drum began to play. Amongst the cheers, Winifred heard low growls and laughter. She smelt not only beery breath but stronger spirits. She was on her own in an increasingly rowdy crowd. The words "spitfire," "hell-cat," and a few other coarser appellations about the female sex were uttered nearby. She ignored them. George stepped to ring's center, and the crowd's roar was deafening.

Bert and Amelie sat holding hands. The strong man, Seamus Todd, straightened out the iron bar he had bent into a hoop. Dupree was seated on a bench nearby. The man lifted a set of weights and invited two thrilled boys to grab onto the ends. There was a smattering of applause as he hoisted the lot with one hand.

Molly ran across the grass with Will close at her heels. Amelie looked in the direction they had gone. Others walked or ran toward the oak, where there was a growing noise from the crowd. Oliver ran by, holding a banner from the concessions tent. It ruffled and snapped above his head. A black horse and Mr. Furor! Amelie turned to Bert.

"It's the boxing ring. Something's wrong. I know it. What's happened?"

"Stay here with Dupree. A fight is no place for ladies. I'll find George."

"Be careful, Bert! Where's Winifred?" Amelie called to Dupree.

The woman shook her head, then seemed to see the crowd for the first time. Pointing at it, she spoke rapidly to the strong man. He put down his barbells and set off with long strides.

Bert glanced over his shoulder to make sure Amelie was safely with Dupree. As he neared the oak, he could hardly make his way through the seething mass, much less catch a glimpse of the fight already in progress. He finally managed to shoulder his way to a spot near the ring's edge. Furor and George were in the middle of the roped off patch of earth and sawdust, circling and jabbing one another. On the other side of the ring, Winifred was being buffeted by a group of men who had clearly spent too much time over their ale in the concessions tent.

The crowd had already sorted itself into distinct factions, some calling for Furor and others for George or Hereford Hall. The painted banner depicting the black stallion was hoisted near him, and across the way, someone else had raised a pole from which flapped George's coat. A few yards to Bert's right stood Will, but the youth was too distracted by Molly's hysterical dramatics to notice Bert's waving hands. John and Struthers attempted to approach Winifred from her left, but were having a rough time of it. A hand grabbed his shoulder. It was Jakes.

"This doesn't look good!" He nodded at the crowd.

Bert agreed.

George was at least half a head taller than Furor and had a much longer reach. While George was slender, he was powerfully built. He moved with assurance and more than a touch of arrogance. At first Jakes said Mr. George had played the crowd, but after taking some neat jabs from Furor was getting down to work. He obviously had some experience of boxing, though Jakes doubted he was used to fighting bare-fisted.

Furor had already, obviously, tasted George's power. The bell rang and he jogged to the other side of the ring. A swift stroke to the swelling over Furor's left eye, and the wrinkled man who stood before him wielding the razor was spattered with blood. The man slapped Furor's torso all over with a wet sponge. A fair-haired boy who wore a top hat stood near the bucket, red-faced and bawling encouragement. The little man rang the bell. Furor sprang up and danced back into the ring, head down and hands raised high. George sauntered forward, languidly raised his bloodied fists, and looked down upon Furor.

Bert was more concerned for Winifred, of whom he had lost sight. He frantically called up to the tall Jakes, who pointed. Bert finally spied her again. She was hard pressed to keep to her feet as the men were joined by a group of red-faced women who jostled her from side to side. Jakes' efforts became more aggressive. There were protests and some shoves, but they were getting closer. Winifred shouted, her face dust-streaked, her hair loose. About the time he and Jakes reached her, John and Struthers also closed in.

"Bert!" she gasped. "This is horrible. We've got to stop this!"

"They're deciding who's the better man!" John yelled.

Furor's fists wetly smacked against George's stomach. He grunted and clipped Furor's jaw. A man elbowed Bert, and he elbowed the man back. Down with Holloways, yelled a drunken voice. Up with Hereford, howled another. Posh lot! Slummers! A woman cried. Struthers pushed a man off him, and Jakes was nearly knocked into Winifred.

"We've got to get her out of here," Bert said quickly. "John, take her other arm. Struthers, you go ahead. Jakes, keep behind us."

They tried to move. Bert glanced uneasily at the blood-shot eyes that met his on all sides. They were angry or indifferent, glazed by drink, or feral with mad exaltation. The crowd, for all its restless movement, seemed to congeal around them. They were hemmed in.

Winifred leaned close to her cousin. "George threatened Court! I have to help, or he'll call the police. Oh, Bert, I must tell you about that morning at the bank and what happened after!"

Though Bert heard perfectly what she said next about Mr. Furor, he pretended not to.

"George will get him hanged," she screamed. "If he doesn't kill him tonight!"

The man next to them wildly slashed the air with a pole sporting a white flag with a red dragon. John grabbed his cap to protect it. Bert and Winifred ducked.

"George won't kill him," he shouted back, and hoped he sounded light-hearted. He didn't want a full confession from her any more than he had wanted one the day he took Mr. Furor fishing. He knew enough already that he ought to turn in the man to the authorities himself. He wondered when the truth about Furor's part in the Adams affair and Winifred's disappearance had dawned on George, or that his fiancée and Furor were in love. A group of the servants from Holloways, including Richards, had managed to find spots to stand behind Furor's side of the ring. The strong man Todd had joined the boy in the top hat. "John and I will take you home," he cried. "Amelie's with Dupree. This is no place for you."

"I won't leave him!" Winifred shouted. She pointed. "And Amelie's over there!"

To Bert's dismay, Dupree was on the dais, and the strong man handed Amelie up to her. Her fists clenched and she jumped up and down, screaming like everyone else.

The crowd roared again. Struthers came to a standstill. Bert and Winifred did as well.

Furor delivered a left to George's jaw. He reeled. His supporters made a collective moan. George stumbled but regained his balance, blinking and shaking his head. His eyes were dark with fury, his hair matted with sweat.

"Furor's for it now and no mistake," Jakes said breathlessly.

"Aye, here we go!" John cried. He released Winifred's arm and pushed back his cap.

There is a moment in every fight when the audience can feel the advantage turn from one combatant to the other. There are also moments in some great fights when the conflict ceases to be merely professional and becomes personal. A man must prove himself. He must, at all costs, stand his ground. This was such a moment, Bert thought. The people of Holloways, Hereford Hall, and the parish, both great and small, saw this as well and awaited the outcome.

Whose heart and whose courage would win the fair prize? Many people in later years would claim to have witnessed the Midsummer fight and many would exaggerate its next moments or their part in events. Everyone, however, seemed to realize the stakes were high, perhaps the very highest. That was the way Bert would always remember it afterward.

Lunging, George grabbed Furor by the arms and slung the man away from him.

Court briefly kicked in the air, then hit earth with his feet and stumbled. In a moment, George was on him, seizing his waist. Court fell to the ground, the breath knocked out of him. George straddled him, but Court twisted away and scrambled to his feet. The cut over his eye reopened, and blood flowed freely onto his face. He shook his head, trying to see.

The crowd's blood was up as well. The boxing match was over. His confrontation with George had deteriorated into a brawl. He'd seen this sort of thing before, and it was always messy. Other people besides him and George could get hurt badly.

He raised his fists again in a final attempt to rein George in but to no avail. George came at him with his hands outstretched. Court ducked and charged George's midriff. He grabbed George about the waist. The two men fell heavily to the ground.

Winifred moaned. Everyone was yelling, even Bert, riveted by the spectacle of two men beating each other to pulp. Furor's banner was gone as was the pole with George's clothes. Around her, men shoved one other. There was a sound of blows and oaths. A bottle, then another flew over their heads. Glass smashed. A woman shrieked.

Sam ran alongside the ring, shouting at Court. Seamus grabbed him. Grynt paced the perimeter as well, scanning the crowd, then peering at Court and George. "The bell!" he bellowed at Seamus. "Be ready!"

For Court, the only way out of George's hold was to knock the man clear of him. George's sustained power over five rounds had been a surprise. He also obviously had some knowledge of wrestling, only he was rather free in his form and even more vicious in his technique. Court pried George's hand off his face, and they rolled. George probably didn't know exactly what he was doing, but he was doing well for all that. Court tried to flip George over and get on top of him, hoping to put the man in a strangle hold or twist his arm, but George hugged his ribs. Slippery with sweat and blood, Court worked his right arm free to return a blow to the man's face. He fought to get his hand to George's neck and press down on the artery. George's fingers groped for his eyes again. Court's knee worked its way up to George's groin. The man slid off just in time. Court was on his knees, and George was trying to get to his.

Court grabbed his opponent's right arm and twisted it. "Come on man! This is over!"

George winced as his shoulder strained but did not give in. He seemed to find where the center of his weight was and rolled, throwing

Court off. Court lunged and thought he had George, but he scrambled away. He sprang when Court was almost on his feet. The men grappled face down in the dirt. Court was on the bottom this time.

George gasped, "I want you out of here tonight! I know about you and Geoff Ratchet!"

Court struggled to protect his shoulder in case George tried to pull his arm behind his back. "I know what you did to Rosie!"

George snarled and bore down on his right shoulder. Court's head snapped back in pain.

They were face to face.

"Don't come near Win again. I'll break your neck. I'll kill you!"

George twisted Court's right arm. With a pop, his shoulder socket gave. He managed to roll to his back, swallowing furiously against the vomit that filled his throat. His arm felt limp and useless. George straddled him, grabbed his neck, and pressed his windpipe. His guts burned. The air waved before his eyes. With his left fist, Court beat as hard as he could at the man's face. The skin on his knuckles was gone, but so was the skin on George's cheek. His vision narrowed, darkened with small, dancing black points. The bell sounded.

Suddenly the ground fell away, and he was on his feet. The crowd booed and hooted. There was cheering too. His head swam, his vision doubled. The Herculean body of Seamus Todd stood between his and George's. His knees were water, but Seamus' brawny hand steadied him. His friend's other hand held his opponent in its inexorable grip.

George raised his arm to the crowd and shook his bloody fist.

Grynt held a speaking trumpet and cried in a sing-song cadence. "Ladies and gentlemen, due to the unorthodox nature of this fight, we call a draw. But what a show! A hand to Furious Court Furor, the Dark Horse, and London's white-hot Fury! And to the Champion of Hereford Hall, George the Dragon! Don't he blow smoke? Ain't he a terror? Well done me lads! Collect your money at the dais, folks! Line up! Line up!"

Seamus helped Court to Grynt's wagon.

A group of cheering men hoisted George to their shoulders and sang rowdily. Bert recognized most of them as gentlemen farmers or tenants with whom George hunted and played billiards, but there were some villagers and townspeople among them too, and a few of Winifred's tenants. One of George's eyes was blacked, the cheek below it wiped clean of skin, but his expression was elated. A group of the farmers' daughters and some country lasses of ill repute danced shrieking and laughing after the men to the bonfire. One of them raised a pole with George's shirt and a woman's bloomers tied to it and waved her trophy.

People collected their money, and the spectators slowly dispersed. John pocketed his and made his way to Amelie. The gnarled man and the boy with the top hat climbed down from their perch and walked to the campsite under the trees. Dupree stood with Richards at the edge of a crowd gathered by the painted wagon into which Court and the strong man disappeared. Will, Oliver, and Molly waited there too. Jakes and Struthers begged Winifred's leave to join the Holloways staff in their vigil.

On the other side of the common, George lit the bonfire.

"I'm going to him!" Winifred started for the painted wagon.

Bert caught her hand and held it firmly. "Not tonight!"

John helped Amelie from the stage, and she ran toward them. In her light summer frock, she fluttered like a pale moth under the torchlight. Bert thought how lovely she was, how he never tired of seeing her approach with eyes so full of gladness and innocent love; and all of it for him. He vowed never to take for granted his great luck and good fortune.

Winifred stood with her arms by her sides, staring at the painted wagon and the group surrounding it. The dust on her face was streaked with tears. As for his cousin and Mr. Furor, Bert had no advice.

❧

Peter Smith, the sexton of Saint Clement's, opened the doors of the narthex to dispel the damp. Sunbeams shone through the dust motes as he shook the rug. The ash leaves trembled under the weight of the rain that had fallen soon after dawn. On the common were the remains of the great Midsummer's Eve bonfire. Only a few of the painted wagons were left. Otherwise, the travelers had packed up and were gone.

The village had not quite settled down after the big fight. There were those who said Mr. Broughton-Caruthers had won while others averred that Mr. Furor could've gotten the better of Mr. George, even on his back and left-handed, if a draw hadn't been called. Opinions were not divided as to the conflict's nature. A personal grudge had been aired for all to see. Speculation ran high about its true source. Some said it was an affair of the heart, others money. Knowing Mr. Broughton-Caruthers' exploits, amorous and financial, bets were even. Mr. Furor was still a dark horse, so odds as to his motives were undecided. There were rumors about him and Miss de la Coeur. Likewise, hadn't there been rumors about her and Mr. Broughton-Caruthers for years? Folks always talked about the Gentry and the Weather! Both men had given and taken a beating; that much was certain. The crowd for the wedding promised to be large, and a few were disposed to believe there might be another scuffle. Money was already changing hands.

The night's chill clung about the interior of the sanctuary, fortuitous for the flowers which the women from the big house and the church matrons in charge of decorations had lifted in swags late yesterday and fastened at the ends of the pews with white sateen bows. The church was filled with the sweet, waxy smell of lilies and roses, orange blossom and stephanotis. The new vicar—he would always be new; old Greenways had lived so long—Reverend Fontaine, entered to inspect the arrangements, nodded to the ladies who had arrived early to make final touches, and withdrew to the vestry. The ladies continued their work, talking quietly.

In the choir loft sat the boy with the top hat who'd helped at the fight. The child had been asleep on a gravestone, curled up like a baby rabbit. Mr. Rogers' cart turned into the churchyard. Oliver sat in the back with the altar arrangement and the bouquets. Otherwise the lane was empty. Soon the village folk would arrive. It was almost time to light the candles. Mr. Pond spread out his music and tried the organ's pedals and stops. The dulcet piping of Bach rose to the sanctuary's vaulted roof. Smith spread the rug and called Oliver to ask if he was ready to check the bell ropes.

Sam wished the bells would stop. The scent of flowers made him queasy. Faithless Fan and Do-Nothin' Hez, Froggie-Frenchwoman and Stupid Seamus! The de la Coeur lady, and Old Swank twisting Court's arm! Sam rolled onto his face, grabbed a prayer stool cushion, and pressed it over his ears. The shoulder was dislocated, not broken. The vet had set it, as the only medical man available since the local doctor was at a woman's childbed. Seamus had stayed with Court. Sam left, unable to bear Court's moans. He had run across the green, his own heart feeling like it was barely strung together.

From the edge of the crowd in the refreshment tent, he had watched Gentleman George's well-wishers set him atop a table. To quote Rosie, the man had been "rode 'ard and put away wet." His hair stood on end; he was stripped of his shirt. Dirty, bruised, and bleeding, he was the men's hero, the women's darling, the mob's god. Their eyes shone as they gazed up at him. Girls thrust themselves forward, sweating and eager, most of them as red-faced with drink as the men. One waved George's shirt, jumping up and down. Every time George looked her way she shrieked and shook her big bosom. Seamus' beautiful banner was balled up in a fat woman's hands. George grabbed it, kissed her doughy cheek, and unfurled the canvas over his head. He ripped it in half to a deafening cheer. As its pieces fluttered to the floor, he bought a round for everyone.

While the beer was drawn and passed, he sang an old, bawdy song, a nasty tale about a knight who went a-pricking with his lance when he found a lady tied to a tree. Soon everyone joined in, laughing at the worst parts, even the women. A song like that could have twenty verses, so Sam found a place to sit and rested his chin on his hands. Next, George ordered a brandy punch, a night-cap to send his hardies home to their beds. More cheers and screams of laughter greeted this announcement. George started another song about a traveling laborer and how he plowed the field for the farmer's wife when her husband wasn't at home.

When the punch got to Sam, it was almost gone. Holding his breath, he tipped the pail and drank deeply. It was vile, but he repeated the dose. Hot and giddy, he wandered into the dark, stumbled up and over the earthworks, and wove toward the Wash.

The moonlight on the water made him miss home and the Thames. Hez had stood on its shore, raised his pistol at Gentleman George, and done nothing! Sam still couldn't believe it. That's why he had to slip his note and that stick of dynamite into Hez's bag with the firecrackers, so Hez could show Fan he had as much guts as Old Swank. Don't let her down, Sam had written. Don't let me down, he had hoped. If a fellow did a thing, it should be big, and the Royal Empire had been huge! But Hez didn't even say thank you. He'd run off with Fan without so much as a goodbye. They didn't even ask him to go along.

Sam stared at the altar and the stained glass, the candles and the flowers.

Court had gone mad too. What was so special about the de la Coeur woman? He wouldn't let Old Swank beat him up for her. She dressed fine, but was fat and had a face like a midshipman. A girl ought to look like Rosie, pretty and sweet enough to have her picture on a Valentine candy box. And the Frenchwoman! Snuggling up to Seamus with her questions about Court. Sharp, fox-faced vixen! He'd like to hand her a stick of dynamite. Women weren't to be trusted. They ruined all his plans! He would travel alone, like Grynt.

᪐

John helped Winifred into the carriage. Dupree gathered her veil and followed. Gretchen had gone ahead with the children and Bert and their parents to the church. Richards sat resplendent on the box with Will in gorgeous livery by his side. The under female staff wore new dresses and caps. Struthers had on a new waistcoat. Mrs. Pettiford had on her Sunday best and already wiped her eyes.

Amelie felt the high tide of the servants' hopes beat against her back. It was their day as well. She took her seat. Jakes firmly closed the door, stepped onto the footboard, and the carriage rolled onto the drive.

Taking Mrs. Pettiford's arm, Struthers led those servants who would attend the ceremony, and they fell in behind them. Almost as soon as they reached the gate, the first well-wishers from the village appeared. Amelie tried to smile at the frantically waving hands and handkerchiefs. Children flung flowers through the open windows. John took off his hat and collected some. Another nosegay landed on Winifred's train. Rosemary for remembrance; white violets for purity, or a gamble on love. In the absence of any movement from Dupree or her cousin, Amelie brushed it aside.

Her cousin was gorgeously attired in a gown by Worth. Heavy buttercream moiré silk and Alencon lace shot through with silver threads and gold beads glinted in the sunshine. As usual, Dupree had outdone herself in the arrangement of Winifred's hair, and it supported a tiara of sapphires and pearls, a gift from George that had belonged to his grandmother, like the sapphire and pearl necklace that encircled her throat. She also wore the pearl droplets he'd given her. Under the veil, her eyes shone with feverish brightness. Her skin was pale. Amelie recollected the story of the thief who went dressed in white like a bridegroom for the day of his execution and was cheered all the way to Tyburn.

"Does George think Mr. Furor insulted Winifred's honor?" Amelie had asked Bert once they got back to Holloways after the fight. Though she was thrilled her intuitions about her cousin and Mr. Furor were correct, she still liked George very much. "You wouldn't like it if I was in love with another man. You'd defend your claim upon my heart, wouldn't you? He has a right to Winifred's!"

Bert's brow clouded. "You mustn't talk like this to her. And don't ever discuss Mr. Furor with her, not after tonight. It would be very unkind and extremely foolish."

Amelie was affronted. "She shouldn't bear what happened tonight by herself. When I go upstairs, I'll ask her what we should do. We always talk!"

"Amelie!" Bert's voice was stern, and he looked almost angry.

He so rarely chastised her except in play that she fell silent, mortified.

"Our interference might make matters worse. It's very serious. You mustn't speak of it to anyone, especially not Winifred. When I told you about the Adams investigation, I shouldn't have. It was a grave error of judgment."

"Bert, we tell each other everything!"

"No, darling." He held her hands. "I'm not angry with you. Try to understand. When we're married and I'm a lawyer, there will be times I can't tell you much, maybe anything, about my cases. This is like that, I'm afraid. For her sake, please don't ask me to."

They kissed before parting, but Amelie was very unhappy and deeply worried.

Winifred didn't want to see anyone, Dupree had said. She shut the door to Winifred's room and held the torn and dirty dress her mistress had worn at the fight. "Monsieur Furor had a letter today, bad news from home, maybe. He talked to Mistress in the stable." The woman pursed her lips. "Perhaps Monsieur George thinks they talked about something else. Alors, he wants to teach somebody a lesson!"

"But Mr. Furor didn't—."

"Oui, he teaches him a lesson tonight, too!" Dupree walked away quickly.

Gretchen and John were already in bed, so Amelie sat up alone. As she always did when she could not sleep or felt dispirited, she wrote in her diary.

Perhaps because of her Trials last autumn, W. has changed. Dear B., I lied tonight! Like you, she does not talk to me anymore either. I don't think she talks to anyone. I've never known her so reserved. Concerning her Ordeal, Mother told me not to ask what happened. I heard enough of the servants' whispers and our mothers' talk to guess. Do they think I'm a child or deaf? I see Men in a new light, even dear you!

Amelie had set down her pen. How little she knew about men and women. Gretchen told her it was nothing to be frightened of, that Bert would be gentle and patient.

Bert, whom she regarded as her equal in friendship, was her superior in other ways. Like tonight, when he had been angry. She did not know how to talk to him. Whenever he professed to be charmed by her silences, she wanted to shout that she could hardly tell him what she thought, that she hated he knew so much more of the world than she did. Why was it that whatever her mother kept secret always turned out to be frightful? It wouldn't be frightful with Bert, Gretchen said. It would be very nice. "You might even learn to like it!"

John stared placidly out of the carriage window. Amelie considered the purpled pits on his pock-marked brow. "A bulldog and pea hen!" her mother called him and Gretchen. She thought of all the little Scots. She and Bert were so close to their own happiness, she could not imagine any woman settling for less.

After church the previous Sunday, she had asked George what he thought of Reverend Fontaine's sermon. George told her the only reason he ever went to service was to see if any of the ladies' hemlines had gone up.

She stared at Winifred's sapphires and touched the seed pearl cross Bert had given her for their engagement. She had always admired her cousin but often felt terribly envious. Not today.

Perhaps it was a blessing neither she nor Bert was rich. They simply needed enough to live; it was for that alone they waited to wed. Her mother said it was one matter for a man to run off with his cook; it was entirely different when a woman took up with a servant.

It was madness, Gretchen said, as they waited for the seamstress to finish fitting Winifred's wedding dress. "You must find your level and stick with it."

Gretchen was perfectly aware of the figure she and John cut when they danced the hunt ball's first quadrille. John was the son of a wealthy distiller and seven years her junior. He had been thought wild—not with women, but with horses and guns. Well-matched in stubbornness, they argued several times a day. In spite of some highland idiosyncrasies, Gretchen was at ease with her husband's people; and John never made too much of an ass of himself when they were in Sheffield, she said.

"Our fathers were both men of business, so John and I are on the same level, like you and Bert, or like your parents. You both grew up in Cheapside. Your fathers both work in shipping and insurance. Winifred and George are on a level, too. She has an old name, and he has an even older one. They both have estates in the country."

Amelie was rather disappointed. In the stories, such things didn't matter. What if the similarities Winifred and George shared were only superficial? "What about love conquering all?"

Gretchen shook her head. "Love is all very well. It can help with difficulties but doesn't stop them coming. You think your mother hard, but there are reasons to stay with one's own kind. Winifred has been very foolish. All those seasons, the gowns and expense! What was it for? So that she could meet a suitable man of her own station who'd give her a life in exchange for some of her money! What's wrong with that? If she's not satisfied to be Mrs. Broughton-Caruthers, it's her own fault. She could've had that Archer boy."

"That's what Mother says!" Amelie cried impatiently. "But she didn't love him."

"She wasn't in love, you mean. She didn't give young Rigsby a chance. He's a bit dim, but not a bad sort. She might've learned to care for him. She can't pick up a chicken without going mad over it! She's got that sort of heart."

Amelie couldn't contradict these observations. "What about George? She's paid off his debts! I don't see how he's done her any favors."

"As I can attest, or as everyone has attested for me, attraction is a mystery." Gretchen peered over her glasses. "But there may be more to it. Anyway, the differences we're talking about aren't a matter for concern unless one is climbing up the social ladder or falling off it."

The indignities of falling from the social ladder made Amelie squirm. Luckily, Bert would never disappoint her in that way. Faced with the dire prospect, she wondered what she would do. A husband who made the court list was wonderful, but no advantage could come to a woman enamored of her groom.

Yet if people wished to live their lives together, complications arising from differences in background or social proprieties seemed unjust. "It's terribly unfair that people might not be received based upon whom they marry. I wish it didn't matter what people thought. But it does."

"It's the way of the world," Gretchen agreed. "I don't think less of you for admitting it. You and Bert will struggle along until he has more money, but you needn't worry. Bert will take silk and be knighted like Papa."

Embarrassed that her hopes for Bert, and thereby herself, were so transparent, Amelie had grown quiet. Gretchen and John's first child had been christened barely six months after their wedding. Not even Delilah could explain that away, though no one ever alluded to it. If the Burns' invitations in London and Sheffield were limited because of their indiscretion, Gretchen never seemed to mind. They spent a great deal of time at Holloways or his family seat, Ben Venue.

Amelie had been awed by the life Winifred's money bought her. Ball gowns and jewels were wonderful, yet the contradictions inherent in a marriage to George would be no less daunting than being shut out of society had she loved beneath her station. As Mrs. George Broughton-Caruthers, Winifred's social place would be secure. As the wife of a man with a reputation such as his, her private life would always be subject to speculation. The whispering would never stop.

George would never reform, Gretchen said. "Men don't. Take them as you find them or not at all."

John yawned hugely. It was early yet, and his cheeks were already pink. Amelie caught a whiff of brandy. The buttons on his waistcoat strained over his belly. His light, curly hair was thin on his shiny, sunburned pate. Unless it was shooting season, she could clock his movements by the hours the family sat down to meals. He was provincial, boring, and unimaginative. He was also generous, loyal, and guileless. One look at him, whether he was settling down with his port after a huge meal or bickering with Gretchen over how to best educate their offspring, and Amelie could see he was a deeply contented man.

If he had a score to settle on his wife's behalf, he would have done so in private. He would never have led Gretchen to that ring or made such a spectacle of them both. The servants might laugh behind their hands at his and Gretchen's ear-splitting discussions, but that was preferable to what Amelie was afraid Winifred would be exposed to from now on.

Dupree sat beside Amelie, still as a statue, her expression unreadable. Winifred faced the window but seemed to see nothing. Except for the rapid drumming of her fingers against the seat, she was immobile too. Her ring flashed. Amelie realized that she had been listening to the sound for some time. John yawned again, and with difficulty she stifled her urge to join him.

For two nights, she slept brokenly. After the fight, Winifred had eventually knocked on her door. Side by side, they lay in Winifred's bed and talked about the Queen's ghost. Her cousin also talked of her father and India, of Morrant, and her first hunts with George. Amelie drifted to sleep in Winifred's arms, her dreams full of temples whose interiors were butlers' pantries heaped with Holloways' silver. The torches became those that surrounded the common at the fair. Mr. Furor and Bert walked the top of the earthworks and were swallowed by shadows.

When the distant crying of the littlest Scot woke her, she had not been asleep very long. Winifred was not in bed. She paced the hall outside her room. "Stay with me," she begged.

Arm in arm, they had walked. Winifred clung to her. Up and down stairs and corridors, around and around the Great Hall until at last the dawn lit Gloriana's diamond panes. Winifred raised her eyes to the light and shuddered. With renewed impatience, she paced faster, broke away, and raced upstairs. Amelie ran after her. On and on, Winifred walked.

Dupree brought breakfast, took in the situation, and relieved Amelie, who did not call for Molly's help, but dressed herself quickly and returned. Dupree sat by the untouched food, holding George's ring. Winifred walked up and down. Did she know the stories of Queen Elizabeth's lovers, brave Sir "Robin" Dudley and his step-son Robert Devereux? "She had him killed you know!" Winifred whispered.

Amelie knew but listened. Winifred rambled disjointedly about Elizabeth and Dudley's unrequited love, about her decision to execute Robert Devereux. "Of course, it was a crime, what he'd done. Not even her love could change that! But it was on her heart 'til the hour of her death."

"Mais c'était une reine, a queen, and did what she must." Dupree held up the ring.

Winifred stopped walking, then abruptly left the room.

Amelie followed Dupree to the Great Hall. Terrified for the maids to see her cousin's strange behavior, Amelie fetched Mrs. Pettiford. They managed to return Winifred to her bed. John went for the doctor. Winifred lay staring, her feet swollen. "Her bridal shoes, they will not fit," Dupree sighed, "and they were handmade!" John returned. The doctor was detained at a woman's childbed and did not arrive with a sedative until noon.

After church, Gretchen and John took turns sitting with Winifred. The young Scots were brought from the nursery to occupy their cousin. When her duties allowed, Mrs. Pettiford took a turn at the bedside.

"That Molly is so provoking!" Mrs. Pettiford exclaimed. Dupree and Gretchen exchanged glances. "I told a modified truth to the servants, so they wouldn't ask why you two weren't in church. With the fight, Mistress didn't sleep well, so you're resting." What part of that wasn't true, Amelie wondered aloud. Gretchen squeezed her hand, and Amelie said no more. The second night, she slept with Winifred. In her fitful slumber, she heard Winifred's soft laughter. Or maybe her cousin cried. Amelie stayed with her until it was time to dress for the wedding.

Winifred continued to drum her fingers against the seat. George's ring flashed.

CHAPTER 18
Cut and Run

The dear old cottages, the mill stream, the fields! It all slipped by so fast. The few hundred yards left before they reached the church were both too short and too long a distance. Amelie and Bettina sat across from her, and John by her side. Within the carriage, all was stillness; but through the window, it was the way she'd imagined a coronation. There was the grocer and his wife, Mr. and Mrs. Parker; the smith, Harrison Froggert and his son, Orson; the farrier with his new wife and their baby. Peter Took, the cobbler, and the miller's wife, Constance, and all their children. Prunella had turned out to be a beauty. The faces were like projections from a magic lantern.

Maidens ran under her window raising their flowers. Little girls were held up by their parents. Youths banged drums and played bugles. Boys shouted and chased the carriage. Everyone else waved handkerchiefs and hats, cast flowers, and cried out for joy.

She didn't mind the villagers' happiness. It was their right. This morning was the best day she could offer her neighbors until she presented them with Hereford's heir. That might not be many months off. The afternoon George finally took her, she had been within her cycle's most fertile days; but she had gone ahead. She missed her next menses and was sure that Bettina had noted the anomaly in her diary.

She tried to concentrate on the faces. There was Sally Pope and her old Aunt Hazel; the Misses Claire, and the whole Coggs family. Ten children, healthy and bright-eyed as the day, and alike as peas in a pod. Would George's all look exactly like him, as John's did?

During the fight, the crowd's great outpouring of devotion for George showed her that they would not admit a stranger's victory, no matter how much Court was liked. He could've fought any other man in the village or the county, beaten him, and been lauded as a hero. But when George stepped into the ring, Holloways' villagers and Hereford Hall's tenants closed ranks. Banner-waving and team cheering aside, whatever squabbles existed between the two groups were forgotten. They were united in this, that what happened in that ring had been for local honor and pride. George's victory was theirs. Blood had been spilled. No outsiders or strangers from London would take what belonged to them. Only the people who knew Court, and those among her servants who counted themselves his friends, cared what happened to him.

She and George might be small household gods, yet they were gods nevertheless. The joining of two great local families upon which so many lives depended was not about either of them. It was about satisfying the hopes of those who served them long and faithfully. They must appease those who paid their rents and plowed their fields, who gave the sweat of their brows to make their lives easy. Admiration and envy sat close, on the edge of a knife, but so did real need.

What she and George did with their lives mattered to these men and women because their livelihoods depended on the success or failure of their betters' decisions. The gods could have their whims, but let them finally get on with it! What was about to be performed before the church altar between her and George wasn't about them, or the verses the vicar would read from Corinthians, or the vows in the Prayer Book. It was a more ancient rite. The ceremony meant that no matter what happened or changed in the wider world, there would always be a Master or Mistress upon whom the tenants of Holloways and Hereford Hall could depend. The Loyalty of the Lowly must be satisfied by a sacrifice of Hearts on High.

George had not called on her since the fight. She didn't care what the motive for his absence might be. John had ridden to the Hall to see him. George sent back a note that said he would leave her to her rest. Her fiancé needed his as well, John said. When the crowd had exhausted the refreshments in the concessions tent, George had taken the party back to Hereford. It had gone on well into Sunday morning. The new vicar had not been pleased to learn to whom a good quarter of his parish paid their true homage.

Her ring felt tight. Winifred drummed her fingers on the seat.

Uncle Percival's last letter had been an apology and an invitation. *My lungs have betrayed me again. I must pay for my pleasures!* He and Morrant were ready to sail from Alexandria, but had returned to Cairo. *Percival has overdone it,* Morrant wrote, *and is too weak for the journey.* All of her and Bettina's trunks were packed for the wedding tour. Bettina had also filled one of her own small trunks with Winifred's older clothes.

A train, a boat, more trains, another boat. In a few days, she and Bettina could join Percival. Sunset would find them all together; her reading to her uncle, Bettina sewing, and Morrant fishing while the broad waters of the Nile slid by. White-sailed feluccas would approach their steamer with supplies and more fish. The desert would turn purple in the sunset. Men would wave, raising their day's catch, encouraging them to buy. After a few months, their group would grow by one. A tiny one. She would never come back to England. Or see Court again.

Or George. The cravat he had wound about her wrist was tucked inside her sleeve. What had he tried to tell her before he entered the ring? He had looked uncertain, like her. Didn't he love her? Of course he did in his way—whatever that was. And she cared for him enough.

If it hadn't been for Amelie, she would've done herself a mischief. Amelie, so beautiful and pure in her white dress and jacket; she was the one who ought to be queen for a day!

Gloriana at sunrise, her diamond panes at first pale and then brighter, her face dazzling; Winifred shut her eyes against the image. Light brought her nothing but pain, and her head ached. The old queen's ghost could rest. No need for her to haunt Holloways. Amelie and Bert's children would see Winifred's shade roaming the Great Hall in her wedding weeds, carrying her disappointed love locked up in her heart. She had become what she'd always dreaded.

In her last days the old Queen was so uneasy in her soul that she couldn't lie down for fear she'd die, for fear of Hell and God's punishment for what she'd done. Was it her dear Robin or Robert that she mourned? Who betrayed whom? Perhaps all of them were ensnared in a drama over which they had little, or maybe no control. She'd talk to Percival about it once they started down the Nile. It was the sort of conundrum that delighted him.

Percival's letter showed him of two minds. On one page he wrote, *One must give one's heart and hope for the best,* but on the next he said, *Faith, trust, or madness bring us to a chasm. Drawn by curiosity, repelled by fear! Like children, we dance as close to the edge as possible. There is much about our choices we don't understand.*

Exempli gratia, as soon as the doctor orders rest, I want more than blue blazes to play a round of golf. Now I won't be with you and G. on the day, but with the Colonel. You are in my thoughts every minute of every hour, and M's. We shall not return to dear Holloways until next spring, if then. How sad you will be if IT happens in Cairo, without a last farewell. I cannot lie on a chair awaiting my final trip down the Nile! M. is polishing our golf clubs right now.

The sound of rain dripping from the gutters had woken her. It was not yet dawn. Amelie lay close, breathing deeply. Drifting in and out of sleep, she suffered for Court's wounds and missed him. She worried over George and vainly fought not to. She rolled over and over, trying to find a way to fall back to sleep. Every time she closed her eyes, she was at the hunt. The horses ran pell-mell and leapt over fences. Bracken stirred—the fox! Hounds spilled over hedges and streamed across fields after the vixen in ecstatic chase, baying like hell's angels.

The clock struck in the corridor. Her fears, which had finally retreated into troubled, turbulent dreams, but otherwise left her alone while the doctor's sedative did its work, came howling back full force and tore around her brain like trapped, frenzied animals. She could not close her eyes again for fear of seeing the torn, bloody fox.

Court's jacket and cap on their peg in the tack room; the sound of Will calling his name in the yard; his cigarette ends mixed with Jakes' outside the kitchen door: these had been her talismans. So long as he was near, a chance remained that all might be made right. His absence made only too clear how illogical her hopes were, or how deeply she had drawn from this subterranean well. How had she come to believe all her happiness depended on one person when they had spent so little time together? Court was not coming back; nor was she going to him. He had gone, and so had hope. The clock had struck again. Bettina stood at her bedside with the wedding gown.

The carriage stopped.

They were a few feet from the churchyard gate. Jakes appeared at her window, somber as Bettina. Will dismounted the box. Gretchen waited beside the wall with her daughters, the governess, and the baby. Molly held the hands of the little girls, who were dressed in white muslin and ribbons, and swung baskets full of rose petals. Even the two boys stopped their play among the headstones and stood quiet, toy swords at their sides. Conscious all at once of the gravity of their office, they fell in behind William while their mother gave their marching orders.

Winifred trembled, and John's hand caught hers.

"My girl, the road goes right back where it came from, and so can you!"

"George doesn't like to be kept waiting."

John gripped her hand. "Let him! Richards will drive you straight to the station. I'll make the announcement. George can take a bite out of me if he needs a tough bit to chew on."

Gretchen thrust her head into the carriage. "John, did you ask? What did she say? Has she come to her senses? Winifred, listen to sense for once. John's right!"

"Winifred!" Amelie pleaded. "Whatever you do, wherever you go, I'll go with you!"

"But the village has gathered, and my dress!" Winifred stammered. She looked from one to the other of the worried faces around hers. "The breakfast! They've all worked so hard!"

"None of it matters!" Gretchen snapped. "I'll see to it!"

"Dupree, she's packed, isn't she?" John asked.

"Their trunks are in the vestry," Gretchen answered. "Winifred, now I must ask you a question. It's very important. Have you lost something?"

Winifred looked at her hand and George's ring.

"I didn't mean that!" Gretchen said sharply. "I meant, have you missed something?"

Their eyes met. The woman aimed her glasses next at Bettina. "Dupree, are you sure?"

"We missed—something." Bettina looked Winifred in the eye.

Winifred whipped a handkerchief from her cuff and handed it to Amelie. "Darling, wipe your eyes. Chin up. Isn't that what you always say, Gretchen?"

"I'll thank you to never remind me again what I say, and I'll try to return the favor." She stood aside. "Jakes, the door!" She marshaled her boys to gather up Winifred's veil.

William handed her out of the carriage, and John followed.

The churchyard was filled with the poorer parish folk and a few performers from the fair who had stayed on. The bent, wrinkled man who called the fight opened the gate to Gretchen with a flourish. The crowd parted. Men doffed hats and women dropped curtsies. Gretchen's little girls danced up and down, holding onto Molly. As

Winifred passed the man at the gate, he bowed deeply and screwed up one eye. Already, she could hear the organ's reedy voice. John took her arm, and his sons and Bettina lifted her veil so it would not catch on the sides of the tombstones or be marred by the wet grass. Amelie followed, shedding tears and holding Winifred's bouquet.

At the threshold, John tightened his grip and gave her a final, questioning glance. The music stopped. Winfred felt terribly cold. She was stunned by how many people packed the pews. They even stood in the side aisles. At the vicar's signal, everyone rose and turned her way. An appreciative murmur stirred; faces leaned into the aisle. She could barely see George and Bert standing at the altar below the vicar.

Amelie handed Winifred her bouquet and kissed her. Bettina stood at the foot of the stairs that led to the servants' balcony. She blew a kiss, then she and Molly went up. At the organ, Mr. Pond peered over his spectacles at the vicar, who nodded. The pipes boomed. Gretchen led her little girls inside. The youngest immediately emptied the contents of her basket. Amelie entered next. The wedding march thundered. Winifred and John and the boys started down the aisle.

Now she could see George in his army uniform, handsome in spite of his blackened eye and raw cheek. She and John arrived at the altar. Bert looked to John, who gave a barely perceptible jerk of his head. Bert faced the vicar, expressionless. John released her and stepped back. George held out his hand. It was taped, and his knuckles were scabbed.

Winifred took it. Like hers, his fingers were cold.

The next moments were like those just after she and Mr. Buckner heard the blast of the first explosion at the bank. The organist stopped playing. A hush fell over the room. Except for the occasional creaking pew or muffled cough, she and George might have been alone. In response to the vicar's instructions and what George said, she moved and uttered words as though she were asleep. George slipped a bright gold band onto her finger, above the engagement ring. She slipped a ring onto his finger. The scab broke open on his knuckle and bled. Bert passed George his handkerchief. The vicar spoke the verses about love that she had heard at many weddings in this same church. When he stopped, she realized she hadn't listened. She was dreadfully cold. George's lips kissed hers.

It was done; it was finished.

The organ played; the crowd stood.

Mr. and Mrs. George Broughton-Caruthers walked arm in arm up the center aisle.

The vicar closed the Bible and wiped his brow. He did not like weddings and was more than relieved that this particular one had passed without incident. The fellow Mr. Broughton-Caruthers fought, the groom from London, had been in the congregation with the strong man from the fair. A rougher pair he never saw; and a boy in a top hat stood up at the back of the choir loft at a most awkward moment, but he had ignored it. Surely the child meant no trouble and had only wanted a better view. There were the Misses Claire, lingering over Miss Amelie's dropped bouquet. He'd walk to the house with them.

In the bell tower, Peter Smith, Oliver, and William, who knew the changes for the wedding chimes, pulled gleefully on the ropes. The bells clanged noisily and joyfully, and the congregation poured out of the church after the groom and his bride.

The ceremony had been most satisfactory. Onto the big house and the wedding breakfast! It was a lovely morning. They were a lovely couple, though Mr. George was shockingly bruised; and she was noticeably pale and needed his arm's support. She hadn't been well. All the excitement.

A shame about old Sir Percival's not being there! But life goes on! Miss Amelie and Mr. Barron would be wed next and not a moment too soon to judge by the way she threw herself into his arms at the altar. Hadn't everyone always said Mistress and Mr. George would marry? Finally, they had—in style, too, and without a hitch! A country wedding was much better than if they'd done it in London. Hadn't St. Clement's fetched up fine with all the flowers? Reverend Fontaine hadn't done badly either, though he'd never be as good as Greenways and rolled his r's like he thought he was a bishop. The old must give way to the new! But the old ways were best, weren't they?

The church filled with the chatter of those who lingered to admire the flowers. Mr. Pond, aware of and annoyed by the noise, pulled out the stops. The organ bellowed the toccata full blast.

"Furor was here. Didn't sit with the staff though."

"Sure Mr. George sacked him after the other night."

"Here's a crown! Not a word to the wife. Even without a fight at the church, there's still the lawn party for merriment and perhaps mayhem if the ousted Londoner shows up!"

"Want your crown back, eh? What's the odds, think you?'

Sam listened to the two men who stood under the choir loft. Two women joined them and they all left. The crowd thinned. The organist put away his music.

When the vicar asked if anyone knew a reason this man and woman should not be joined, Sam had jumped up to see what Court would do. No one spoke or moved. Unable to believe it, he had dropped back onto the bench.

It was only afterward, as the woman approached the pew where Seamus and Court stood, that she had seen him. His right arm was tied in a sling. His brow sported a dark bruise and a deep, patched cut. Their eyes must have met. Otherwise, she would not have started and grown so pale, nor would Old Swank have pulled her up with such a jerk.

He'd had enough of bells and flowers and music. All them fancy, pointless words. The only part he liked was the organ, how it bellowed and crashed and boomed along like Judgment Day. Like the end of the world.

Sam pushed through the churchyard throng, shouldering and shoving his way. He set off across the common without a backward glance. A man had to know what he wanted, stand up, and take it! He had to cut his ropes and sail alone. No more ties! Freedom! He was done with men who let themselves get run over like dogs. When a real man did things, he did them big. He was bound for London, where he knew the man he had to see.

PART III

August 1893 – September 1895
and beyond...

CHAPTER 19
Uncertain, but Resolved

Court brushed Mr. Bert's coat. He inspected the bottoms of a pair of riding boots. It was mid-August. None too early to deal with items that needed repair in Mr. Bert's hunt wardrobe. There were other articles of clothing to get ready for autumn. Since Mr. Bert passed the bar, he and Miss Barron had moved their wedding to the week before Christmas. There was much to do.

It was a bare little room where Court worked and slept, but he liked it. When his head hurt, it had a peaceful, monastic quality that appealed not only to his need for quiet while his temples pounded, but his current frame of mind. He felt more his own man than he ever had, but that could all be over in a moment. He didn't dwell on it.

They had been in town since the end of June, but their routine was still irregular. Mr. Bert had never had a manservant and said that technically, Court was still in Winifred's employ. "You didn't quit, and she didn't release you," he explained.

It was an adjustment for both men. A valet-in-training, the young man called him. "A-gentleman-what-I-can't-train-to-sit-still when 'e's bein' shaved," Court would respond. He had begun to appreciate Jakes' numerous duties back at Holloways, and Mr. Bert tried not to fidget while he had his cuffs fastened. Court absolutely refused to call him by his Christian name, so they compromised on Mr. Bert in private and Mr. Barron and Sir everywhere else.

People called Court Sir, too. It was a bit unnerving. "I'll get the hang of it," he would say, practicing his aitches while he re-tied Mr. Bert's cravat for the third time. "Damn it all to bloody blazes! I can't knot this proper when I faces you!"

"Listen to the mouth on the man!" Mrs. Pettiford had chided when he automatically swore at his errors. Before he knew he'd done so, he cursed again. Mr. Bert laughed.

"We're getting better. We've got time. I intend to keep you around, you know."

Though that prospect had its attractions, Court also tried not to think about what he would do when Winifred came back to town. He tried not to think about a lot of things. It still shocked him that Mr. Bert was not, strictly speaking, a gentleman since he had a profession and that Old Swank, who did not raise a finger for his bread and drained his inheritance, was. There was no comparing them. Of a certainty, whatever the future held, Court refused to live under the same roof as Gentleman George.

Meanwhile, he pulled a chair to the window and sat with the boots and a tin of polish. The light was good. On one of the paneled walls was a set of old engravings Mr. Bert called *A Rake's Progress*. Hogarth had gotten the fellow's story about right. He pushed the window open a bit more. The air was hot and still. Perhaps it would rain.

Below in the quad, men in black silk robes and wigs walked purposefully in pairs or on their own. Having spent so much time avoiding the law, it was strange to be surrounded by its most exalted members. Couriers ran in and out of the arched doors, and he imagined other rooms like Mr. Bert's buzzing like hives. He knew exactly how the man liked his pens and fresh paper laid out on the blotter, and which documents to file. Every day a young messenger arrived with a bundle wrapped in brown paper, impressed with various wax seals and tied with cord. Mr. Bert never discussed the specifics of the bundles' contents, and Court dared not touch them. He fought to suppress his dread that one day, a bundle concerning him would lie on Mr. Bert's desk.

Mostly, he kept to his room while Mr. Bert worked. There was a chair and a small table where he wrote his letters. On it sat a stack of books, among them Thucydides and Herodotus and a copy of *Mrs. Beeton's Household Management*, a flute from Grynt, and a jar for flowers. Next to the table leaned a used guitar. There was also a washstand for his shaving kit and a wardrobe. He'd never had so many clothes. Most of them had belonged to Richards or Mr. Bert and were much nicer than any he'd ever owned. Before he left Holloways, he'd finally sacrificed his beloved purple coat, cutting and piecing it into a small blanket for the colt, Meriwether, in an attempt to practice sewing. He confined his taste for garish colors and wild patterns to the neckwear he donned during his hours off and had amassed quite a collection. Jockey's colors, Mr. Bert called them. Along with books, they were what most tempted him to spend his pocket money in the second-hand stalls he liked to frequent on his way back from the Hampstead house.

At Mr. Bert's suggestion, he visited the nicer men's stores and asked the tailors many questions. The well-to-do achieved their grand appearance at a heavy cost; he had never known there were so many pieces of clothing to worry over and tend; and Mr. Bert had impressed on him that he was by no means rich. Given the cleanliness and comfort of their rooms, Court had to keep reminding himself that they weren't princes.

For the first time in his life, he did not have to haul or heat his own bath water, or empty his slops. A boy called Joe saw to these duties, and there was a spotless new toilet housed at the end of the corridor. Court made their coffee and toast, but Mrs. Irons brought the eggs and charred every day as soon as Mr. Bert left. He and Mr. Greystone often worked late into the night, but if he joined Court for supper, Joe brought their food and took away the dirty dishes. Another young fellow named Perkins was on standby during the evening for errands, and there was a porter, Mr. Griffin.

All of these people treated him with a mild deference that had, at first, made him extremely uncomfortable. In his absence, Mr. Bert explained, they thought of Court as acting in his master's stead. "Be friendly but not over-familiar. Always train as though you're getting ready for the next step up." Court tried to wear his dignity lightly and was polite, but knew better than to become too comfortable with the staff; nor did he associate with those servants whom he met in Hampstead. The atmosphere there wasn't at all like the cozy servants' hall at Holloways.

During the day, he was much on his own. He missed the horses and stables something awful, but had other duties beyond his valeting. Mr. Bert said that he had never been so busy and relied on Court to carry out many errands in regard to his and Miss Barron's wedding. Court was very proud to be so entrusted and did not want to fail in his commissions. It always felt strange, however, when he walked through the enormous entrance hall of Winifred's London house. Remembering the families who'd lived cheek by jowl in the

Whitechapel tenements of his boyhood, it was no wonder Winifred felt she had plenty of room for Mr. Bert and Miss Barron.

Whenever the housekeeper, Mrs. Hogg, or the butler, Standish, led him through the family apartments, Court tried to remain impassive. He was fascinated by the atrium's soaring vault, the rooms' high ceilings and elaborate plasterwork, the unusual or precious objects from Sir Percival's travels, and those from India that had once belonged to Winifred's father. The sumptuous salons where Winifred and George would spend their hours together affirmed what he had always known. He had nothing to offer her.

In talking to decorators and contractors, he found a vent for his feelings. Already, they snapped to attention when they saw him. He went to their places of business, armed with checklists and didn't bother to curb his aggressive side or his Cockney accent, or his deep knowledge of petty graft and theft. If he couldn't protect Winifred from George, at least he could protect her pounds and pence and make sure that these men didn't steal from her as well.

He brushed the tops of Mr. Bert's boots until the leather gleamed, then brushed them again, glad to be occupied. While busy, he was not exactly unhappy, but he was never wholly happy either.

In a way, Winifred was no more or less a part of his life than she had been when he struggled to keep his distance from her at Holloways. The flow of correspondence from there or from Miss Barron, and between Winifred and Mr. Bert kept her name constantly in the air. Will wrote to him about Meriwether's progress and sent well wishes from Richards; Mrs. Pettiford provided news of the staff and clarified Mrs. Beeton's mysteries; and Jakes passed on Struthers' greetings and gave sartorial advice. He'd even been surprised by two letters from Mr. Burns, who turned out to be a much better writer than he was a conversationalist, especially when it concerned equine celebrities and other personalities from local stud books.

While they had morning coffee, Mr. Bert read the newspapers or shared passages from his own letters. The couple's continental tour was scheduled to last until the hunt season started. So far letters and postcards had arrived from the Black Forest and Lake Geneva. *We've left Lake Como and tour Florence. George has added Venice as a treat. From there, we plan to stop in Paris for new clothes before returning home.*

Court didn't give a hang how darling the zimmer had been or how well George looked in hiking togs. It was no concern of his how hot and dusty Florence's streets were or how magnificent George found Michelangelo's unfinished sculptures. He didn't even know what fettuccini was, or why George's attempts to twirl it onto a spoon had met with so much laughter at their albergo.

There was a prattling quality about the writing that did not sound a bit like his cousin, Mr. Bert opined. He flashed the postcards of the Ponte Vecchio and Brunelleschi's dome at Court. "Like George writes the letters, and she signs them. Well, that's what the vicar said. The two shall become one."

"A rake's progress!" Court grumbled and set down their breakfast tray with a clatter in the hall. Mrs. Pettiford had warned him long ago never to show his feelings and certainly not his temper before employers. Such self-control might also come in handy if he ever ended up in the dock. At least he hadn't cursed, though he'd felt like it. He closed the door with unnecessary roughness. Why was it that fellows like George always seemed to know everything, "books and art and such, even when they ain't got brains to stuff up their arses?"

Mr. Bert did not comment. He set Winifred's letter and the postcards on the mantle with her others and handed Court a packet of pictures from the Uffizi Gallery that she had also sent. "I've no end of work to do before I go to Holloways Sunday. Don't stay in here shut up on your own. It's summer! Enjoy some of it for both of us."

With a roof over his head and food always in reach, Court had no pressing needs. Jingling the coins in his pocket, he set off to explore a different side of the city. It all looked very different when a fellow didn't have to peer up at it from so far down.

He went to the natural history museum and looked at the bones and fossils. He sat in a teashop and tried a type of cake he'd never tasted. He mounted the steps of the opera house in Covent Garden and counted the vehicles in the line of cabs and hackney coaches at the curb. His matinée ticket was for one of the cheapest seats. At every moment he expected to be shown the door, but no one disturbed him. The lights lowered, and the conductor struck up the overture.

Each time he went to a concert and heard a new piece of music, he wondered if Winifred knew or liked it. During the intervals, he paid attention to the conversations of those seated around him. He went to museums and stared at portraits and paintings. He sat on benches scouring guidebooks for notes, or listened to the patrons' opinions. He formed his own. At night, he would take another of his or Mr. Bert's books to bed and read until he fell asleep.

He did not over-rate his intelligence but did enjoy the reawakening of wonder, the pure love of learning the likes of which he had not felt since he was a boy at the Methodists' school. He easily understood and remembered much of what he read of natural science and geography. Novels rather lost him, though he liked a bit of poetry, especially the *Iliad* and some of Robert Burns' verses. Mr. Bert even set him some problems in algebra and geometry and showed him how to translate, albeit very slowly, Caesar's Gallic wars with the help of a Latin grammar. As always, Mr. Bert encouraged whenever he was daunted by these puzzling mental tasks. Together, they visited the British Museum and frequented the nearby bookstores. The man made no secret of his delight in Court's quick ability to soak up and recall information.

"Mind you, just keep reading," he advised. "That's what old Greystone said to me when I first took up the law. It didn't make a bit of sense, but the more I read, the more I got on."

Court promised himself that he, too, would get on.

But as he sat in the opera house listening to the opening act, the entrance of the soprano and her first duet with the baritone, Court especially yearned to know more about music. One afternoon at Holloways while he and Oliver brought wood upstairs, he'd been transfixed by the sound of Winifred's low contralto and what he realized with dismay was George's voice. They knew many such duets Oliver said, also stopping to listen, and always played and sang together. Court recognized the song. It was the German tune Hez had said was about a fish.

The next time Court was upstairs, he had shyly touched the pianoforte's keys and its mother-of-pearl inlay, marveling at the intricate marquetry. He looked through the stack of music: Beethoven sonatas, Chopin nocturnes, and even a book of Gilbert and Sullivan. Schubert's Lieder sat on top of the pile. Die Forelle, he read, but could make nothing of the lyrics. The ant-like black marks mystified him, though singing in the choir had taught him the rudiments. With one finger, he picked out the simple tune from his childhood that he had shared with Winifred.

On the stage of the opera house, the soprano and the baritone rushed into one another's arms, raising their voices in the duet's triumphant climax.

His eyes grew wet. Of all he'd seen or heard, read or learned, the ability to make music was the most wonderful. The skill, if not the gift, seemed wasted on such a devil of a man as George. It was small comfort, recollecting how Winifred had praised his voice when he sang to her. After the opera, he went to a pawn shop and bought a guitar.

Acquiring so much new knowledge was mostly pleasant insofar as the effort took his mind off what he couldn't hope to attain. But there were painful revelations, too. The more he learned, the more ignorant he supposed he'd appeared to Winifred the day they first met. Even when he sought to escape his mortification in his beloved books, there were constant reminders of his inadequacies. The dictionary, which lay on its own special stand along with the atlases, was both illuminating and confounding. He felt buried by the number of words in it that he had yet to learn.

Finally, he understood the zeal of the Methodist missionaries, the fervor with which they had tried to instruct poverty's children. What benighted, foul-mouthed little beasts they had been! What a strange recalcitrance that could take pride in ignorance and in resisting those who wanted to throw open the doors to all these wonders. It did indeed seem like they had been possessed by a devilish spirit that roamed the Whitechapel streets and wished for children to remain in its gutters, denying themselves the pleasures of their own minds. With what ardor they had tormented their teachers. He and Geoff had done their best to make the young school master's life a trial.

He thought of Beryl's later painstaking efforts to assimilate the speech and manners of her well-heeled customers. Though he'd always admired her learning, he'd never considered taking such measures. Under Piani's thumb, it seemed futile. Now that he had the opportunity, he felt he would never be able to learn enough. He wanted to serve such a man as Mr. Bert and not cause his employer or himself embarrassment. His former dream of meeting Winifred in Saint James's park shamed him. How could he have thought a flash suit of clothes and a hired horse were what made a man a gentleman? How could he have imagined that would make him her equal?

Yet Mr. Bert never appeared mortified by his still uncouth ways and frequent faux pas. What he had once dismissed as cold formality, he recognized as gentility and even forbearance. Oft times when Mr. Bert could have drawn notice to himself among other men, he did not. This was not from a lack of self-assurance, but because he had it in abundance; and all of it was based on his pride in a father he loved and in his own hard-won achievements. A few servants at the Hampstead house emulated their betters to a degree that bordered on a snobbishness Mr. Bert never displayed; not that there weren't those of his class with an unattractive sense of their place or an indifference to others that amounted to inhumanity. Court saw many examples of such behavior whenever he went out, but he also saw men who quietly acknowledged their inferiors' dignity, like Mr. Bert did.

At home, his employer risked the very familiarity he warned Court about, insisting they dine together whenever possible. It was the only way Court could hope to master Mrs. Pettiford's lessons on table etiquette, he said. Court's initial discomfort was partly relieved by Mr. Bert's display of good humor as they exchanged places. On such occasions, Mr. Bert always ordered some impossible edible to demonstrate how to serve it correctly or how to eat it without acting like a hog at its trough. The young man would roll up his sleeves, make purposeful mistakes, and ask Court how they should be righted. Afterward, as they sat down to their port, he taught Court how to play chess, or they talked.

He didn't question his employer's motives, for he observed that Mr. Bert was consistently kind and genial to his fellow man, an initially startling experience in his dealings with a person of higher social rank. Until he met Winifred, his interactions with the upper sorts had been infrequent and mostly unpleasant. He judged them all to be like Old Swank. It had not been so with Winifred's family. Mr. and Mrs. Burns were wrapped up in their dogs and horses and children, but they were forthright and steady. In their way, they were as trustworthy as Mr. Bert. Miss Barron always took an interest in the servants, and even her mother, though sharper-tongued than Mrs. Burns, was as charitable as she could be.

Mr. Bert's love for Winifred ran deep for many reasons, among them her long devotion to his and Miss Barron's cause. If Court stayed after the couple married, they could be counted on to withstand almost any amount of chaffing from George in regard to Court's daily, though increasingly less noticeable mishaps. Mr. Bert seemed to genuinely enjoy Court's companionship and openly admired what he called Court's good sense. He declared Court's untutored opinions on politics and the news "refreshing." He was determined that on the day Court did leave his service, he would be well and truly trained to become a gentleman's valet and make his way in the world. Court wished that day far off and anticipated Winifred and George's return with increasingly mixed feelings.

He still dreamed of horses, but his fantasies no longer included racing victories. Instead, he'd returned to the bucolic scenes he had envisioned for himself and Sadie. Such a life was a far cry from the one he imagined Winifred leading with George on Hereford's vast tracts. Court reminded himself, as he once had her, that she had her world and he had his. He was determined not to resent it, to move on and make his way in the one Providence had seen fit to place him. But he still questioned that Being's purpose in setting them so far apart. When he lay awake at night, he did his best to thrust aside the vision of her bared skin and bright hair by raising up the sight of her walking down the aisle arm and arm with George. It was usually enough of a sting to make him light the lamp and pull the high stool up to the dictionary. If he couldn't sleep, he could at least use the hours to prepare for a life without her, if not independent of his need for her.

But he could not always be so stoical.

On his Sunday afternoons off as he sat in the park listening to the brass band, his proximity to young ladies in their summer dresses made him more than ever aware of how low Winifred had stooped when she allowed him to remove, piece by piece, all the delicate clothes that represented the carefully crafted and rigorously guarded mystery of Woman. It was not the sacrifice of her virginity alone that she suffered for him, it was the willful casting aside of all that defined a woman of her rank. If he had taken her by force, he would never have understood how precious, how costly, her gift had been. For a few hours she had allowed herself to be, as she lay sprawled naked beside him, his equal. The late summer twilight fell and the stars came out over the bandstand. Court looked up and dreamed. The image of their entwined bodies and the sound of her joyful cries as she called out his name in her pleasure came to him unbidden. At times he pushed the vision aside; other times he lingered over it as the sweetest memory he had. For better and for worse, Winifred had changed his life.

If he made his way in the world, it must be for himself alone and not for some phantom dream of becoming worthy of her. Their one night together was a fairy tale that had disappeared with the rising sun. She had been lucky not to find herself pregnant with his child.

Court set down Mr. Bert's riding boots. He ought to be glad about that, too, for her sake, but sometimes.... For a long while, he stared into space. The air smelled like distant rain.

If Winifred and George had troubles in the future, and Detective Sergeant Peele's note to Grynt about Geoff and the necklace suggested they might, they'd have to resolve them on their own. Even after what she had read in Beryl's letter about George, she had chosen him. Why had he even bothered to share poor Rosie's heartache and shame? Willful and high-spirited, her servants called her. Stupid, ignorant, naïve more like! Now no one could protect her from that man, but someone had to keep an eye on Geoff Ratchet. Well, there was always the police; and George was her husband. It was their job. Let them do it.

⚜

Winifred stood on deck, gripping the rail. Water foamed before the prow, and the wind was sharp. Ahead, the white chalk cliffs shone in the afternoon sun. After all these weeks it would be a relief to see her family and reunited with Bettina. George stood some feet away, smoking and talking to one of the deck hands. He always found someone to talk to wherever they went. The other man laughed at a remark George had just made. Strangers always thought him so charming. She stared at the cliffs again.

In Germany, she and George had been a great deal in the open air. They hiked mountain paths beside cold streams and picnicked on flowering meadows. The dark blue sky and the vigorous exercise had been a tonic to her spirits. England and all that was part of it were far away. As she had once told herself, it must be George, always George, and only George from now on.

For his part, George rose to the occasion. To make up for his subterfuge that ensured Bettina would board early on the wrong boat, he promised to be very attentive. In Triberg he hired a maid, but tended to most of her personal needs. He was a master of all that was pleasant to woman's flesh and vanity. At the end of the day undressing one another became part of their lovemaking. It was all very tender.

In the wood, he was boyish and sang as they walked, becoming once again the George of her girlhood. For days, they rambled and laughed and ate well and made love a great deal. They sat alone in a small chapel and played its organ. They were equally charmed by the mountains and the waterfalls and the adorable guest zimmers. He talked of his plans for more refurbishments to the Hall and of a special surprise he had built for her. Before their return home, he would take her to all the best dress and jewelry shops in Paris. He knew every inch of her by heart and exactly what she should wear. His golden girl would shine.

Once, as they walked alongside a booming cataract, he had forged ahead. Thick firs dripped with moisture. The shadows were cold.

When she caught up with him, she saw he had stopped near a lip of rock and leaned on his stick, staring at the violent torrent that plunged into the maelstrom far, far below. "George, dear, do be careful!" Her voice had barely penetrated the roar of falling water. She fixed her own walking staff into the ground. The sight of the cascading green sheet made her feel strange and giddy.

Finally, he turned. "Darling, come here and see this. It's tremendous!"

Winifred picked her way up the path. Her boots slipped on the wet rocks. George held out his hand and grasped hers. When she looked down, her stomach lurched. "Do let's step back a bit," she gasped. George pulled her close and took a step nearer to the edge.

Winifred stopped breathing. The water disappeared as it fell, transformed into a veil of shifting white, like the manes of many horses plunging beneath a boiling mist. She tore her gaze from it and looked at George.

He stared, and seemed fascinated. Again, he took another step forward.

There was in his face that which sent an icy thrill through her veins. She shook but not from the forest's cold. "George, dearest, come away now." She pulled on his arm.

"'Till death us do part!'" he said quietly, still looking down.

Thoroughly frightened, she pulled harder. He stumbled back with her onto the path. His laughter sounded eerily amongst the dark trees. "Oh, I should toss you over myself!" she cried, slapping at him in feigned playfulness. Still laughing, he let her lead him back down the trail.

They had gone on to the medieval schloss near Lake Geneva and their villa at Como, from thence to the albergo in Florence and the palazzo at Venice, and finally to the hotel in Paris. There had been art galleries and operas and dinners and dancing. Everywhere they went they met people and made friends and received invitations. They were called the Beautiful English.

It was in Venice that George's old ennui began ever so slightly to raise its viperous head. On their way to Saint Mark's basilica, he lost their guidebook. In the church they met a distinguished couple from Poland, who offered to share theirs. Winifred found the woman's dark hair and Slavic features very attractive and estimated her to be in her early forties. The gentleman was much older, but he stood tall and straight. His company was as staid as his wife's was voluble. Together, the four of them spent the hours until early afternoon wandering the halls of the Accademia and then lunched together.

Fired by the extraordinary colors of Bellini's portraits and Tintoretto's lavish figures, George commissioned a young artist named Gianni to paint Winifred's portrait. She protested that there would not be time, but the artist said he could begin his work with a few sittings and easily finish the painting from photographs after she and George left for the rest of their trip.

They went to the artist's house. George and the woman, who also had rooms at the palazzo with her husband, watched while the young man made a series of preliminary sketches and his sister took photographs. George and the woman left Winifred. Though the artist's sister spoke no English, and the young man very little, their company was pleasant. He was not much inclined to speak anyway, as he was working. Winifred gazed at his dark curls and eyes, and those of his blonde sister and missed Bert and Amelie. The Venetian brother and sister both looked like Botticelli angels, and she wondered at their beauty.

That afternoon she and George and the older couple took a boat across the lagoon to visit the glassworks. It had been dreadfully humid, and they stayed too long in the sun touring various island sights. Even under the boat's canopy, the sky pressed down on Winifred like a hot, polished dome. The sulfurous smell of the slapping waves against the rocking boat made her nauseous. At the palazzo, she lay down with a pounding headache and woke from a fitful nap knowing her menses had started. She rang for the maid to change the bloodied sheets. As Winifred washed the blood from her thighs, and wrung the rag over the bowl, she wished she was dead.

The trouble started after she told George why she could not join their party for supper. He went downstairs and did not return until late; when he did, he smelled strongly of brandy and cigars. He'd gone out to play cards, he said, and would rest in his dressing room. The next day it was hot and still. She felt unable to go out, so Gianni painted her at the palazzo. George joined the other couple for more sightseeing. When they returned, George glared at the artist, but said nothing. In an hour, he returned and flung himself onto the couch. He stared at Winifred vacantly, a cigarette burning to ash in his long fingers. His mood was so strange that she thought he must already have been drinking. Gianni's work progressed.

Supper alone in their apartment passed without incident. Again, George did not join her in bed, complaining he had overdone it walking on the Lido. The next day, she rose late and did not see him at all. Gianni came to the palazzo again for her sitting. That evening, a breeze blew over the water, and the heat finally lifted. Winifred felt well enough to join the older couple for a gondola ride in the moonlight. George and Frau Steinwicz took their seats at the back of the boat; Winifred and the woman's husband sat at the front. George had suggested she might feel the roll of the boat less, nearer to the bow. As the gondola slid smoothly along the canal's green water, she could hear but not make out George and the woman's low talk. Their intermittent laughter echoed up the slimy stones of the loggias.

She and the older man fell into more serious conversation. Before long, they glided into the open waters of the Grand Canal. She talked with Herr Steinwicz quite openly, as often happens with strangers who meet while traveling. He also spoke of many personal matters, and described his family's home in Warsaw. His father Bruno was German. It was for him that Herr Steinwicz was named. His mother had been a Jew, as was his wife. Slowly, it dawned on her who her and George's companions were. By the time they returned to the palazzo, she was almost ill.

Winifred confronted George. "How could you bring me to this place when you knew she'd be here? Did you write to her first? Or did she ask you to come?"

"Lottie, you mean?" He laughed as he had at the falls.

They exchanged angry words. Unable to bear the sound of George's laughter, she ran downstairs. The salotto was unoccupied. She sat at the piano but was barely able to play a note. After a while Herr Steinwicz appeared at the door and asked if he could join her.

"Every day I listen to your playing with the greatest pleasure. It is most expressive." The silver-haired man sank onto the couch and wrapped his hands around the pommel of his cane. "You have been crying. They are old friends," he said serenely. "You have not known him long? His behavior surprises you?"

"He and I are old friends, too. So no, it's not that," Winifred said.

"I am sorry to hear it."

Winifred was silent.

"Perhaps you do not understand him," the older man said. "Fear is what drives such people. I have known Carla from a girl. I saw her fears and understood them. That is why she chose me. She saw George's, that they are many, so she did not choose him. Now she has a son. I can give her others."

Winifred felt tears spill down her cheeks and averted her face.

The man ignored them. "Did I know George would be here?" He shrugged. "A little bit no and a little bit yes, but I am not worried. Let my wife have her whim! Carlotta will never leave me or our boy. She would never jeopardize her position as a mother. That, and her son, these are most precious to her. This is a—," he waved his hand, "a late-summer madness, a diversion from her fear of old age. That is what they're really afraid of, both of them, growing old. Not like me," he smiled to himself. "Are you afraid?"

Winifred shook her head. "Not of that."

"You are not made for intrigues, Mrs. Broughton-Caruthers. You are honest. You want children, a family, I suppose?"

There was no point in feigning offense. George's preferred methods of giving and receiving caresses up until the first time they had intercourse had been pleasurable and had the advantage of reassuring her she would not become pregnant before the wedding. Yet sometimes, his inclinations—his requests—had seemed perverse. And still did.

At such times it was as though he was playing out some private scene that he alone could see inside his head. She did not feel that he was truly with her. She might have been some other woman. Pleasure aside, those occasions left her feeling lonely, ashamed, and terribly uneasy.

Herr Steinwicz continued. "This young man Gianni is a very affable person. Not the sort who would trouble a lady after a pleasant afternoon or two. There are many such men in the world."

Winifred was shocked. The Venetian seemed little more than a boy to her, like William. She lifted her eyes to Herr Steinwicz's, unable to hide her misery. "I can't! I couldn't!"

"No. You could not. But in such cases as yours, there is no other way. Forgive my forwardness, but your candor in the boat and my old age excuse it. You are very unhappy now. You may be even more unhappy later. I will pray for you, my child."

George came in late. She heard him lie down on the chaise in his dressing room.

It was the last she saw of Herr Steinwicz, for he and Lottie departed for Warsaw the next day. She sat for Gianni a final time. The young man's demeanor was very earnest. He worked vigorously. She was pleased at how quickly he progressed. His sister joined them, and they lunched together. Their sitting resumed. All day, George left them undisturbed; that night she lay alone again.

The next morning, she woke to find the maid packing. Most of their trunks had already been sent to the station, where George waited. The maid set her breakfast tray on the bed. On it was a note. Thinking it was George's, Winifred opened it and read. On her way to the station, she tore up Gianni's letter and threw its pieces in the canal.

She and George traveled to Paris, hardly speaking the whole way except for necessary reasons. She read and tried not to count the number of times she saw the flash of his flask. In the hotel lobby, he was drunk and verbally scurrilous to her before the staff, then became lascivious once they were alone in their room. As the days passed, to her horror, this game of jealous anger and play-fighting became a pattern. In their carriage, before dressmakers, at restaurants and galleries, George was more or less drunk, indifferent, or lewd. In their room, he picked arguments that turned into fights. Once, he was so offensive about Gianni that she slapped his face.

He struck her back.

In her shock, she hit him once more. George seemed to relish it. A new phase began. Each evening they fought, often physically. He seemed to require it before love making. He encouraged her to drink with him, but she would not. Exhausted and sick of his behavior, she threatened to go home if he did not stop.

She wasn't going anywhere, George said. He was extending their tour. They'd go on to Spain and north Africa, travel up the Levant and back through Constantinople and Greece. "Who knows? Maybe we'll go to India and settle there like you said!" He pulled out a letter and handed it to her. It was already opened. It was from Gianni. Winifred balled it up and threw it in George's sneering face. From that moment, he told her he would not let her out of his sight. "Not ever again, cara mia! You're mine!"

Once George had told her that hell was a pleasure palace. She felt its walls rise around her.

That night they sat in the gaming room. When her nerves could no longer stand the spinning roulette wheel, the winning and the losing, the mounting stakes, and George's increasing, drunken recklessness, she left. It was nearly noon when she woke alone. With some apology, the concierge informed her that Monsieur had left the hotel about three o'clock in the morning.

When he did not return by nightfall, Winifred was frightened and thought of calling the police. All day, she had been so relieved to be left to herself that she did not rise or eat and had hardly noticed his absence; but as the hours wore on, she could not rest. The night staff was too discreet to openly show their concern as she wandered from the salon to the casino entrance, or about the garden and corridors, waiting and wondering what to do. When she rose the second day and ordered a carriage to go out for a ride in the Tuileries, the maître d'hôtel asked her, again with an air of circumspect apology, when—or if—she expected her husband to return.

George had been called away to London on business and could be back at any time. She realized her slip immediately. All communications would be recorded at the desk and would have passed under the concierge's scrutiny.

"Mais bien sur, only the last time we saw Monsieur leave the hotel, it was in the middle of the night—and sans baggage. Madame has only to ask." The maître d'hôtel pressed gently. "I can call the police, or perhaps the embassy." His eyes were full of sympathy. "Or I can arrange a train to Calais pour Madame."

Winifred assured him none of that was necessary and retreated to their room. She ordered luncheon but didn't touch it. She waited for her tears to come. They didn't. When she lay down alone on their bed a third night, she wondered if George was even alive.

Just before dawn, he woke her. He was pale and looked almost as ill as she felt. She'd never seen such dark circles beneath his eyes, and they were bloodshot. But he wasn't drunk. He wore the same evening clothes he'd had on at the roulette table. He kissed her. She kissed him back. They looked long into one another's eyes, and he twined his fingers in hers.

"Now you know what it's like," he said softly, "when someone disappears."

"Where were you?"

"Did you miss me? What did you get up to while I was gone?"

It was his old, teasing way. She sighed and pushed his hands off her. He put them back. She could see he wasn't going to tell her. "Oh, I don't know. I spent all my money on dresses and jewels."

"But did you miss me? Were you lonely for me?" he persisted, stroking her.

"Not a bit!" she said crisply. "I did what everyone in Paris does. I took a lover."

"What was he like?" George kissed her neck. "Was he as good as your last one?"

Winifred felt close to tears. "Even better! A horrible, great hairy man with a bushy red beard like a bird's nest!" She ignored George's caresses and tried to sit up and reach for her hairbrush on the night table. He pushed her back onto the pillows.

"That must have been novel. Tell me."

He unbuttoned her nightdress and slid his hands inside it. His tongue fluttered against her neck, behind her ear. He pulled at his shirt studs.

"He was frightful and depraved. You're a choirboy next to him. We're running away together as soon as—." She did not finish. George was on her, kissing her breasts and unbuttoning his trousers. "Where did you go?" she asked softly. "I was so frightened."

George slumped against her shoulder and spoke into her hair. "I took a walk."

"For two days? Goodness George, do talk to me! I'm your wife!" She grasped his face and held it above hers. "You can't abandon me for two days and then waltz back in here and expect me to be sanguine about it. That's really too much, even for you!"

George looked away. She waited.

"I really can't talk about it."

"George!"

"Winifred! Aren't there things you'd rather not talk about either?"

The chalk cliffs loomed nearer. The boat's crew busied itself for landing. A few yards down the deck from her, George stood at the rail alone. The foam churned and flew before the boat's prow. She saw the waterfall at Triberg, saw herself and George standing near its edge, clinging to one another.

Her thoughts returned to their hotel room in Paris. They had made love that morning. He was horribly dirty and smelled of the streets, the filth of gutters. It brought back powerfully her first time with Court, and she held George to her more fiercely than she ever had. He returned her passion, and she felt a corresponding desperation in him like her own.

The boat's prow pierced the waves. She stared at the water rushing by it. They were both drowning, disappearing, and neither one could save the other.

ↂↂ

"I said cut it all off!"

"There's no need to be so severe!"

Behind Beryl, Horace stood with a pair of scissors poised over the last of her dark curls. Beryl laid down his shaving mirror and dug her fingers into the arms of the chair, her usual seat when they talked in her friend's room. Horace snipped and made unhappy, protesting noises in his throat as he did so.

She was dressed in trousers and a man's white shirt. Her collar lay on his desk, and her coat and cravat were folded over the back of the couch. She had sold all her feminine attire, though Horace had salvaged his favorite of her hats and two of her dresses.

"Everyone knows you're a woman! It's not as though you must be incognito to ride."

"That's not the point," Beryl said.

For several weeks, Barry Stuart, or Stuart as she preferred to be called, had appeared as the official jockey of Sweet Little Banshee. Her disguise had not gone undetected for long. There had been, as they anticipated, an initial uproar. The Banshee had finished a respectable fifth, then third. After that, she never placed below fourth, but had yet to win. Upon the discovery of her sex, Beryl had been scratched from her last race and briefly arrested for fraud. Horace got the charges dropped, but they had to repay the money they won in two previous contests.

What she had proved was that she could ride with the professionals, she told the reporter who visited her in her cell. "Women hunt alongside men all the time," she said to the gossip columnist for Today's London.

Some owners or their jockeys refused to be seen on the same turf with her and the Banshee. Other members of the sporting press, impresarios, and bookies of broader mindsets and wider visions immediately saw the attraction of pitting a female jockey against a field of men. Several of Madam Bess' and her own former clients were ready backers. *Is this the Woman of the Future?* Today's London columnist wrote. In the article, Beryl denied any personal involvement with the suffrage movement but said she supported it. She was less enthused by pieces in the sporting news that compared her to the female acrobats whose equine stunts were wildly popular in P.T. Barnum's American circus or Buffalo Bill's Wild West Show. She was pleased to receive letters from their agents, however, and leaked the contents to the press.

An American told her that she rode exactly like a Negro jockey he had seen in Kentucky, who stood with his knees tucked in under his chest. She would never compete in the Grand National, but there were venues ready to host her. Horace had already been approached by a buyer, but he told them the Banshee was not for sale.

So far Horace had been able to keep out of it. The Banshee's trainer, Norris Sterling, and her groom, Scales, told journalists that Mr. Greystone acted on behalf of Miss Stuart, who was part-owner, and a partner who wished to remain anonymous. This was true to a point. Beryl had used her pay from Horace from their first two races to buy a share in the Banshee, and Horace was the partner who wished his name to remain unknown.

Money flew in.

Since she left Rosie, Beryl had not worked at the Lancaster. Madam Bess made no protest. She, too, was raking in a tidy sum off her former star's notoriety and had not offered Beryl a penny from the reprints of the pornographic photographs, which had taken on a life of their own and were published in France in a special edition book format. Beryl didn't care. That part of her life was finished, she told Horace. They did not talk about what would happen if she got injured or couldn't ride again or what she intended to do about Rosie. "I'll pay the bills," she said, "but that's all." She would not go back to the woman. That was over too.

Rosie was pregnant.

There was no question, she told Horace, about whose child it was.

Horace had broken the news to Beryl. He had taken Rosie to the doctor, fearing she might become ill or lose the baby. She worked harder than ever.

"Are you listening to me?" He pulled the whiskey bottle from Beryl's hand.

Beryl took it back. "I've seen her already."

She had gone to the flat to collect a few more of her books. Rosie sat by the grate, knitting a tiny, frilled bonnet. Beryl moved the table and rug, lifted the floorboard, and dumped the bag of coins in the hole. All their furniture, her old armchair and desk, Rosie's knick-knacks and china—and their bed—looked the same, except that nothing would ever be the same again. She put the rug and table back in their places. Rosie's knitting needles clicked while Beryl cleared out her desk. She threw their old receipts into the rubbish bin. Then she threw away Rosie's old ledgers.

"I'd never get rid of it," Rosie said suddenly.

"I don't ask you to do that. But you could give it up."

Rosie continued to knit. "I knows what you wants. I knows what I wants too. You'd do anythin' for me. But you can't do this. You're not a man. You never will be, but you are me best friend in the world."

"It's not the same as you wanting me like I want you though, is it?"

"We'd be like a proper family, Beryl!"

"We'll never be a proper family!"

"I wants this baby more than I ever wanted anythin' in me life! Try and be glad for me!"

"I want to, but I can't. Only tell me you don't love him," Beryl pleaded quietly. "Swear it!"

Rosie's needles clicked.

Beryl closed her valise and left.

That seemed ages ago. She held up the mirror and considered the effect of his work. Horace's eyes met hers. No, damn it! She would never be a man. She lowered the mirror.

Horace bent to whisk up the last of her fallen curls and surreptitiously folded a few into an envelope. Beryl said she hoped he wasn't going to be morbid and save them for a piece of mourning jewelry. He ignored her and put the envelope in his pocket.

"She's only done what millions of women do to get by," he said. "She's a good girl and would never intentionally hurt you. No matter what she felt—what she feels for that man, she's chosen to stay with you."

"She'd go off with him like a shot if he'd ask her!"

"You don't know that," he said gently.

Beryl thought she did but had no desire to argue.

Horace showed her his latest letter from her prospective landlord. "Mr. Norwood's agent writes that the house is in order. 'Briercliff Cottage, interior repainted. New stove and a pump in the kitchen. Chimneys recently swept, some furnishings.' He's willing to wait until the end of the month. After that, we lose our option. My dear, you're not listening again."

He sat next to her. "Put away this pride! It's making both of you miserable. So, you had a dream, and the reality turned out differently. It doesn't make what could be any less precious. Imagine, a child! Choose to be happy! Don't throw it all away out of hatred for this worthless man. He deserves your anger, but I don't think she does. Rosie wants this baby! She wants to be happy! If you love her, why not let her be? I cannot imagine why you of all people would abandon her when she needs you most."

Beryl shot him a vicious look. He met it, unmoved.

"What am I supposed to do? Live with a woman who doesn't love me back? Should I wait for the bastard to ride up on his white horse and carry her off one day?"

"Yes!" Horace cried. "Imperfect as your situation is, it's far more than I will ever have! You may be afraid of the future. You may be bitterly disappointed, but until that hour, live with your Rosie and love her! You have in your heart a rare, passionate devotion! Many never receive such, let alone are capable of giving it! You must carry on, my dear. Have a bit of faith!"

Beryl stood and brushed herself off. Horace pinned her collar, and she tied her cravat. "I can't see it," she said. "Meet you at the tracks tomorrow."

A block from the Montague, it began to rain. Her room was another block farther. Fat drops pattered on the pavement and awnings. A cabbie pulled near the curb, but she did not heed him and slogged on. She thought of Horace's words. Have faith in what? God, Rosie? She had made many mistakes, but he was right. Loving Rosie wasn't one of them. There would never be anyone for her but her girl. Miserable as her love left her, Beryl could not kill it any more than Rosie could take the life of her unborn child.

In addition to seeing Rosie that one time, she had kept another secret from Horace. Though she still wanted and always would want George dead, she had decided to tell Geoff to call off the job. She had tried before, to no avail.

"None o' that, not 'ere!" Geoff had said that day in his office and nudged her bag of coins. "We'll talk later. There's always a way, never fret!"

He'd come to see her in her room several times. His company left her feeling like she'd waded into a greasy, foul slime washed from the Thames' bottom, or breathed the noxious miasma of a corpse rotting in the mud. He had not touched her, but talked oddly, reading to her from his pocket book of Shakespearean quotations, and going on about how Moses had killed a man and how lots of other fellows in the Bible had as well and were famous for it. None of that had much to do with George, she said. "I was in a passion. Forget all about it!"

Geoff shook his head sagely and rubbed his rings. "It's all part of the larger plan written in our stars. Wheels are turning, me girl! Turning and turning!"

Beryl had fallen silent, not wanting to wind him up any more than he already was. Even when they were children, he had a strange side. It had gotten much stranger of late.

Rosie might get lost in her own world from time to time; Court could disappear inside a book; and she would look for her dreams at the bottom of a gin bottle, but Geoff had always been subject to fantastic notions. More than once she had watched the dismayed and baffled face of the young pastor at the Mission's school as Geoff repeated his twisted version of the Sunday school lesson. She wondered at the wisdom of putting the Bible into the hands of a person like Geoff.

In spite of the pitifully odd or grotesque requests she was used to fulfilling given her particular art, she counted many of her customers as some of the sanest people she had ever met. Other than unusual sexual peccadillos, which they confined to expressing in Bess' dark, velvet chamber once or twice a month, they functioned as quite normal men, several of whom served the public good. Of the workings of Geoff's mind, however, she was not certain; except that no good would come of it. Geoff was not merely a cold-blooded killer, like some of Piani's other straightforward toughs. His violent fantasies spilled out of his head, sticky as blood and blacker than ink, and made mayhem of other people's lives.

If Rosie ever found out what she had asked Geoff to do, it would be the end. Whether Geoff did it or not, he could blackmail her. To keep her secret, he would bleed her dry for the rest of her life or worse. In passing, he asked her if she ever considered modeling. "Just for Bertollini and Ratchet!" He winked, and pulled back his lips to show his teeth. The rain fell harder and splashed onto her trousers.

All that was left to make her get out of bed was the Banshee, the thrill and joy and freedom of riding her. She couldn't think about her life after tomorrow's race. It would only be a wait until the next one. If it were not that she needed the money, she would gladly ride for nothing.

Horace was right. She would take the cottage. Rosie would have George's baby. And then? Once, she had told Court that she made a fool of herself for that girl. It was too late to change her ways. What did it matter if the woman simply wanted security and she simply wanted the woman? There had never been any question of abandoning her. Even if

Rosie left her for George and he later cast her away, Beryl would take her girl back. She would hunt high and low for her darling.

Asking Geoff to kill George had been not only a mad gesture, but a monstrous, wicked one. If she couldn't win Rosie's heart on her own merits, did she really think she could buy the woman's love with George's blood in a devil's bargain?

Horace had taken Rosie to see the doctor again. Beryl still shuddered at the cures they'd learned from other whores for ailments picked up working the streets, caustic douches and wretched powders. All of them witches' brews. When Horace told her Rosie was with child, she was more stunned by the fact than she was by her girl's betrayal. After what they had both endured with men and done to their bodies, she had assumed that neither of them could bear children. The doctor reassured Rosie that she and her baby were both quite healthy, only in need of rest. Rosie's pregnancy was a miracle.

Beryl stood in the rain. It fell harder. A passing cab splashed her. The street bustled with cabs and omnibuses, delivery vans and mail trucks. Pedestrians jostled by with raised umbrellas. From a large downspout, water poured into the gutter. There was so much and it moved so fast it appeared solid. Swirling, it disappeared down a storm drain. She took a gold sovereign from her pocket, the one George left under his handkerchief after his last visit to Rosie.

"... faith!" Horace had said.

Love, she thought.

Rosie.

She flung the coin into the gutter. What she uttered wasn't a wish. It was a prayer.

The coin slid along the pavement, resisting the water's onrush. It tumbled, rolled, and was finally borne by the swift grey current as though it was a leaf. Then it was gone.

CHAPTER 20
Wheels within Wheels

The pub where Detective Inspector Patterson was to meet Seamus Todd was not one of the man's usual haunts. It was far from Southwark, on the northeast side of Hampstead in view of the park. Patterson had never been to that part of London. In fact, the only place he'd ever traveled was to his wife's home near Aberystwyth. He always enjoyed the journey west and associated the landscape with Christmas. It certainly didn't feel like winter that afternoon, even in the shade. The hot, quiet streets that skirted the park's edge had more of a village atmosphere than the city a few blocks south. On his way 'round the park, he'd passed some very large, fine houses.

He hadn't heard from Todd since the day he put him on the train north. As they stood on the platform, he'd told Todd to contact him if he ever returned to London; and bless him, the big bear had! He hadn't expected the man to arrive with an escort, however. The trio sat in the snug room at the back of the pub. Peele, who arrived immediately after the pair entered, took a seat in the front room near the door.

"What brings you to these parts?" Patterson asked.

Todd smiled down adoringly on the woman and pulled out her chair. As she sat, Patterson inspected her. A lady's maid or perhaps a housekeeper by her dress and manner. Simple, well-made clothes; a plain straw hat with a single, thin black ribbon, but she wore these with a certain style. The sort of touches Mrs. Patterson would appreciate. Her wiry brown curls were pulled taut but seemed ready to spring out from their combs; and her watchful, shrewd brown eyes were set in a heart-shaped face with a slightly pointed nose and chin. She looked intelligent, very probably was.

"We met on me travels coming back south." Todd settled beside her.

"The last night of the Midsummer fair," she said in a low, accented voice.

"Not from London, then?" Patterson asked her.

"Non, my mistress and her husband are from Norfolk. We are in town a few days for visiting family. Then we go home."

"They've just arrived from their honeymoon. Paris," Todd said dreamily.

Patterson's skin prickled. "Never been abroad. London born and bred. What house?"

"Monsieur's estate is Hereford Hall."

Patterson was mildly disappointed. "Funny you should mention Norfolk. I've news Mr. Todd will be glad to hear. Friend of his was working up that way this spring. Holloways, I believe it's called."

"Courty!" Todd exclaimed. "Why, that's your Mistress—!"

"My bag! I dropped it. Seamus, could you?"

The man bent under the table. The woman narrowed her eyes at Patterson.

"That's right, Court Furor!" Patterson said into his beer but watched the woman and Todd over the rim of his glass. She sat erect, alert. "I thought you'd be relieved after what happened last February!"

The woman glanced quickly at Seamus, who greeted the news about Furor with what to Patterson seemed extraordinary tranquility. "Well, I never!" was all he said. But then, he'd been with Furor from time to time during these last months. Todd ought to take to the stage, he thought admiringly. After the doctor, or whoever he was, announced Furor's death, the big lummox had bawled like a baby, so inconsolable that Patterson had sat with him all night to make sure he didn't hurt himself or go after Geoff, whom Todd announced he was ready to kill. The first letter that Peele intercepted from Todd to Miss Stuart had announced he'd soon see someone special who she would be glad to know was alive and well.

"Surely Seamus told you he's done a bit of prizefighting? What a knockout that was! We thought he'd killed Furor. Pronounced dead at the scene, he was. I put Todd on the train myself next morning to get him out of town 'til it was all sorted. Funny thing, no one could find

Furor's body after to give him a decent send off. Turns out he was up your way all along, Miss Dupree!"

She turned to Todd. "I'll be late! I must go back to the house."

"But it's your half-day, my dear!" Todd protested. "Plenty of time!"

"Stay a bit. We'll have lunch," Patterson encouraged, hailing the boy who wiped tables nearby. "My wife's mother was in service. Now, what house did you say you worked in?"

"Holloways," Todd said. "Name's the same as the village. Lovely little place, that's where the fair was out on the common."

"Then you've met Furor, maybe," Patterson offered conversationally.

The woman looked steadily at him. "Oui," she said very quietly.

Todd sighed appreciatively as the boy brought ham sandwiches and salad. He ordered a second round for himself and Patterson.

"So, you knew Mr. Furor while he was there?"

"Not much. He was a good groom, very much liked. We were sorry to see him go."

"London lad like me, Furor is. Wonder what took him all the way up there? Relatives, or he knew the family mayhap, or your master. The gentleman comes to London often, does he? Holloways is his house too?"

"No, Miss de la Coeur's." Todd bit into his sandwich. "Well, Mrs. Broughton-Caruthers now." He shook his head. "Courty was awfully cut up about that."

"What do you do, Mr. Patterson?" Miss Dupree asked.

"Policeman," Todd mumbled between bites, "and a good one! Detective Inspector Patterson, Southwark branch."

"Do eat, Miss Dupree, or Todd will have it all! Sergeant Peele's in the next room." Patterson nodded at the door. The woman followed the direction of his eyes, blanching slightly at the sight of the man.

"Peele!" Todd said in delight. He pushed aside his plate. "Good old Peele? He watched out for me while I was in hospital last year. Stayed near as much as Grynt, him. I'll have a word!" He rose and went into the front room.

"You didn't know about that either? Modest, that's Todd! Day the Royal Empire blew. He was there."

"I am thinking there is much I don't know."

Todd clapped Peele on the back. The man fell forward onto the bar.

"Last November, day before Bonfire Night. Saved a clerk on the floor where they think the gas lines went first and a few others too." She did not speak, but continued to watch Seamus and Peele, who laughed together at the bar. "Your mistress was there that day and went missing." The woman gave what he took for a slight nod. "Miss Dupree, if I wanted to get a message to Furor...."

Her face became suddenly animated. "Is Mr. Furor in some sort of trouble? Is Seamus?"

With those eyes, she'd be a match for Peele. "What do you know about your new master? Ever have money problems, gambling, horses?"

"Mistress is generous, but he is always—." She rubbed the fingers of one hand together, like she was turning a coin. "Comment dites-vous? Short! Is that how you say it?"

"Your mistress has a very expensive necklace, one with a big orange diamond."

The woman stared at him.

"Come Miss Dupree. You can see I know a thing or two. I can see you do as well."

"I have seen it, but not recently."

Patterson took out his notebook and wrote a message to Furor. He slid it to her. "You can read it, Mademoiselle. I only need him to contact me or Peele, the sooner the better. In the event he does, I'm also going to need your help and Todd's, and that friend of his, Grynt Spivey's."

She did not touch the paper and looked at the note as though it was poisonous. She spoke very quietly. "The bank, was Mr. Furor there as well? Was Seamus with him?"

"Let's just say Todd was along for the ride."

"But he is not in trouble?" She glanced back at the bar.

"He wasn't the driver, was he? There's a difference."

"If they were together, it is not a very big difference."

Patterson answered in the negative. With a swift motion, she tucked the note in her bag. "Now, this is what I know, Mademoiselle." She listened and appeared increasingly uneasy as he described Mr. Broughton-Caruthers' movements since the return from his and her mistress' honeymoon.

"But why would Monsieur George do this? C'est de la folie! Il est fou!"

"Not to mention dangerous."

"Perhaps he has changed his mind about things because of...." She fell quiet, thinking. "I was not with them on this trip, but I will tell what I see now that they've come home."

What she surmised was the true state of relations between the new couple made much more meaningful information that he and Peele had obtained from a very frightened and extremely forthcoming jeweler named Latimer Kleinfeldt.

Immediately after his quarrel with Mr. Broughton-Caruthers over cutting the necklace's largest stone, Kleinfeldt contacted the police. The young constable at the front desk tried to send the man away. They could not investigate crimes that had not happened, he told Kleinfeldt. The jeweler had become so desperate, the officer thought he might suffer an apoplexy and called for assistance. Peele was in his office nearby and heard the ruckus.

It was a very delicate situation, Kleinfeldt had told them. He sat facing Patterson's desk and jumped at every noise. He was about to be swept into an underworld operation such as his family's establishment had never been exposed to; nor he feared, had the Broughton-Caruthers. "We've had the family's custom for three generations, and never have I heard the like from his father or Mr. Charles." He was suspicious of Mr. Broughton-Caruthers' requests and shocked by the identity of his associate. "He ordered the copy before he went abroad. I had already begun it when he came with this new venture. He introduced me to his partner with such sang-froid that I could only put it down to total ignorance of the nature of the man with whom he is dealing, or complete foolhardiness, or worse!" His voice fell to a whisper. "I made my own small investigation, you see. This Geoff Ratchet is part of a gang that operates in your jurisdiction."

Patterson and Peele left the jeweler alone in the office. The man was scared to death but not stupid, Peele said. Broughton-Caruthers was out of his depth, and they didn't want another Adams affair. The gentleman obviously intended to split up the necklace and sell the stones. Perhaps he owed Ratchet money. Or it might be blackmail.

Or perhaps it's the other way around, Patterson suggested. "His wife is the de la Coeur woman. Maybe he knows what Geoff did to her. Maybe the woman remembers more than she let on and told her husband all about it. If he needs money, he could've hired our Geoff to be his errand boy and plans to let him take the fall if it doesn't work out."

They went back into the office. Kleinfeldt had done right to speak to them, Patterson said. This was a dangerous business, and they would need his help.

The man seemed to shrink. Since his initial inquiries, he had heard not only Ratchet's name whispered abroad, but that of his boss, P. Lili Piani. He could not control his terror that Ratchet, or one of Piani's men, would soon enter his establishment with designs more outrageous than Mr. George's. His need to protect himself and his business outweighed any loyalty he might have felt in the past for the Broughton-Caruthers family. "I take no interest in the man's pecuniary or matrimonial affairs. I'd like to save the family undue embarrassment if possible, but when I am asked to make a reproduction of this!" He produced a drawing of a necklace that included a description of its pearls' diameters, its gold's weight, and the number of carats in its diamonds. "When I am asked to dismember this—and especially this!" Choking with emotion, he spread his hands protectively over the large orange stone. "I begin to suspect—I will not be an accessory to fraud!"

Peele took Kleinfeldt's drawing to the Royal Empire Bank and spoke with Mrs. Broughton-Caruthers' banker, Mr. Buckner. Together with an appraiser, they visited the jeweler. The necklace in his possession was indeed Mrs. Broughton-Caruthers'. Patterson gazed at the fabulous gems and thought of the small amethyst ear-drops and cameo Mrs. Patterson saved for best and Sundays. Kleinfeldt presented what he had completed so far of the reproduction. The appraiser pronounced it very fine work.

Did Mr. Broughton-Caruthers intend to bring his own appraiser when he collected the copy? Kleinfeldt wasn't sure. "Make another one," Patterson said. It didn't have to be so fine or made out of expensive materials like the one Mr. George ordered but "sparkly, and only good enough to fool the eye at a distance, or at a glance."

Back in his office, he'd stared at the threads pinned between Winifred de la Coeur's name and Geoff's, and the one between her name and Furor's. Geoff's was connected to Furor's too. He penciled George Broughton-Caruthers' name onto a card, tacked it to the board, and drew several strings from it to the other names. Peele wrote two letters, both in care of Grynt Spivey. The first was to Seamus Todd. The second was more of a shot in the dark. It was addressed to Court Furor. They'd gotten no replies to either until Todd contacted Patterson.

The fight between Todd and Furor had annoyed Patterson's thoughts like a bee buzzing under his bowler hat. Geoff had certainly set up Furor and would've gotten rid of Todd as well if that Spivey character hadn't gotten them all out of town. Would Furor be willing to step forward if he thought Todd might be in danger again, or if he could help put Geoff away? That seemed too great a risk for the likes of Mick Furor's son to take with so much to lose. He was looking at hard time and lots of it.

The only lead he'd had on the man's whereabouts had dried up. After Todd's letter, Miss Stuart had sent one to Furor in Holloways, Norfolk, during the latter part of June. To Patterson's surprise, Peele found out that this was Miss de la Coeur's country address. The police in King's Lynn confirmed that a man going by the name of Court Furor had worked at the house, but left at the end of June. The housekeeper and the head groom had written him good references, but couldn't say more, nor could the other servants. Also, several men on the force had seen a man who matched Furor's description in an exhibition fight with Mr. Broughton-Caruthers at the Midsummer's fair. It turned into a brawl, the man from King's Lynn wrote. Patterson thought about the date of this fight.

He'd also given the police in King's Lynn descriptions of Todd and Grynt Spivey. Todd was positively identified as having been at the fair, and Spivey was a well-known busker and traveler to those parts. A shopkeeper kept Spivey's mail or forwarded it to his next stop. Peele had traced the rest of the fellow's route easily.

"Also find out when Broughton-Caruthers married the de la Coeur woman," he told Peele. Then he'd written to Grynt Spivey himself but still hadn't heard back.

Todd rejoined them.

"How's Sam?" Patterson asked.

"We ain't heard from him," Todd said glumly.

"Since the day of Madame's wedding. He was upstairs at the church. Then after." Miss Dupree looked a little guiltily at Todd, who gazed adoringly at her. "I do not think he cared very much for me and thinks that I am taking his friend away from him."

"That wasn't it, me love," Todd said. "Sammy's fancied himself me batman these past months. His heart's been broke. First his sister and her bloke run off and left him, then Mr. George took down Courty. Next to Hez, the boy was always mad about him. Sammy never liked Mr. George and liked him even less after the business with Fan at the

Boar and Hart. I didn't tell you about it 'cause it ain't nice for ladies, and he is your master now. I really don't know where our Sammy's got off to." He hung his head. "I wish to heaven I did!"

"Perhaps he went to Fan," Patterson suggested. Not that he thought for a second the boy had, or wasn't in London, if not with Grynt Spivey.

Todd quickly gulped the contents of his pint glass. "Honfleur, it's such a pretty name!" His voice grew husky. "Hope so for his sake, but I got a bad feeling. Sam was that angry after the fight."

Patterson smiled inwardly at Todd's slip about Fanny Merton's whereabouts, but didn't feel smug about it. He had a bad feeling about the lad as well. If he could bring in Furor, perhaps he wouldn't have to bother Hezekiah Boors. As for Todd, he was a lucky man. The woman patted Todd's arm and gave her lover her handkerchief. Todd dabbed delicately at his eyes. Patterson didn't like for men to speak crudely about women, but this one was a corker, full of salt and vinegar. There'd be fire and more than a bit of fun in her; yet more importantly, there would be loyalty and lots of heart. He drank the last of his beer.

"Mademoiselle Dupree, it's been a pleasure. Todd, if there's anything more, you know where to find me."

Todd placed a big paw on the woman's hand. "There will be! Me and the lady has come to an understanding." He beamed proudly. "Soon as we set the date, you'll know!"

"I congratulate you both. Miss Dupree, I hope we've come to an understanding as well."

❧

Faust. The Sufferings of Young Werther. George read the gilded titles on the books. His valet still hadn't cut the pages. He tossed them into a box on top of some of Win's old letters.

In his room at the club in Pall Mall, George sat by himself. It was dreadfully hot, but he had lit a fire and was burning most of his letters and all his unpaid bills. He didn't want to return to Hampstead, nor did he feel like playing cards. He wasn't hungry and hadn't been for days. He didn't even want a drink. All he felt like doing was smoking and watching his past crumble to ashes.

He had never told Win what happened during his absence in Paris. Ever since, there had been moments when none of the past few weeks felt real. Not making love to Rosie or fighting with Furor; nor standing at the altar with Win, or riding in the gondola with Lottie in Venice; or taunting Geoff, or feeling the necklace in the breast pocket of his coat every two seconds! And sometimes, like now, he didn't feel quite real either.

It was as though he was dissolving, turning to fragments, and diffusing like the light that filtered through the long sheer curtains that muffled the street sounds below. Or breaking up like his cigarette's smoke, or falling through the grate like the fluffy grey ashes. It was almost as though he saw himself from the outside, but the person he looked upon was a stranger.

As Win once said, he was always playing, never being serious. He needed a costume, a pantomime role; so long as it was make-believe he could keep laughing. But he wasn't on a stage. He and Win were really married. Memories and regrets that had not disturbed him for years rushed to the forefront of his brain and would not let him rest. What to do? Which way to turn or run, backward or forward? Only let him end up anywhere but Hampstead or Hereford Hall! He thought of old superstitions, of priapic monuments to Hermes where the ways met in Achaean Greece, or the gibbets in Normandy that stood befouled at the windy crossroads. Instead of making a choice, all he could do was twirl 'round and 'round like the village idiot. The glow of bodily possessing Win, beating Furor before the home crowd, and claiming her before his rival, had dimmed. Time to face what he'd done, and he couldn't. He was afraid to stop spinning.

After she left him at the roulette table, he had lost fifty pounds in two turns. Having had enough, he started to follow her. She stood in the archway, and their eyes met. She had turned away with a fluid, regal swirl of skirts and a flash of jewels. The laughter died in his throat. She was superb, but chilling; she was a goddess, terrible and more beautiful to him in her anger than she had ever been before.

So, he fled the hotel. He had walked a few blocks, then a few more, crossing a bridge to the Left Bank. Well-lit streets gave way to darker alleys. Twists, turns, it didn't matter where he went. A man of indeterminate race stepped out of the shadows and stopped him. Did he like to try? George didn't understand the rest of what he said. The man pointed to an open door. An old woman in Oriental dress peered out. Her hand beckoned.

George had never smoked opium. He sat on the mattress with the man he had met in the alley. The fellow lit a pipe, sucked deeply, and passed it to him. Soon, George was drowsy. It was not a woman he desired; it was oblivion. Why hadn't he understood that before? The man smiled. George took the pipe and lay down. The drug seemed to promise he would forget Win's cold, furious expression, that he could forget everything. He would never again suffer the ache that only grew worse whether they were together or if she turned away. He could smoke, drift away, and sleep. It did not take much of the oily, black substance to plunge him deep into dreams.

He was running impossibly fast on a forest path. Through dripping fir trees, he saw Win and Lottie flash by him, running even faster. Their bodies unfurled and lengthened weirdly like parallel skeins of gossamer, or flags caught by the wind. Their tenebrous forms trembled like images cast by a camera obscura. He wanted to stop, to watch, but they were gone. A torrential stream fell beside slick rocks at his feet. Lottie was a bubble on the falling waves. Win stood before him with that terrible look. Ominous, billowing shapes rolled between them. She was gone! A restless sensation in his legs drove him forward, but he was pressed by an insufferable weight. Suddenly, he was at the roaring cataract's edge. The ground crumbled away.

With a start he woke, covered in cold sweat. He felt ill and very thirsty. Centuries had passed, but he was sure he had only slept an hour or two. Blood hammered in his ears. Otherwise the room was silent and dim except for a red-shaded lantern and the occasional flare of a pipe as one of many murky, hunched shapes inhaled the poisonous drug. He struggled from the damp cot and almost crawled into the alley, where he was sick. There was no moon. His sense of time was upside down. Someone had stolen his pocket watch and its chain.

George staggered the streets aimlessly. A cab pulled alongside the curb, the sort of shabby vehicle resorted to by prostitutes and other late-night, louche characters. Its interior smelled foul, of urine, male seed, cheap perfume. They drove along the Seine. After that, he climbed a maze of streets. A forest of scaffolding surrounded an unfinished church and he sank down on a brick pile. His mind spun with the half-remembered specters from his opium nightmare. He laughed aloud, then choked back a sob. The echo unnerved him. He ran until he found the river.

The lights of Paris winked and sparkled on the water like a string of jewels.

It had been the truth when he'd told Win he never loved Lottie. She'd been a trophy to prove to him and his mates that he was more than man enough. That was why he'd written her back and told her to meet him in Venice. He needed to see her one more time. To make sure he was still man enough. Nothing happened between them but talk. It was over. They both knew that.

And what of his darling Rose, stripping off her rags and lace and dirty stockings? He was and would always be in love with that girl, but his promises to her would remain broken ones. He couldn't keep them because she didn't exist anymore. She'd grown up, and Rosie Cartwright had taken her place.

His darling Rose pregnant! That brought him to his knees. The child in her belly couldn't be his. That was the weight he couldn't shift from his heart. When Win told him her menses hadn't come, that she thought she was with child, he'd been incredulous but hopeful—happy even. Then the snake Geoff's words about Furor bit into his heart. Old Dr. Thorne at home, and the army surgeon who'd seen him when he'd had the clap, both told him the same story. Maybe it was what they told every nervous young man. He'd lived through all the normal childhood illnesses: mumps, scarlet fever, some sort of pox. He was healthy as a horse, strong as an ox, the usual blather. But they were wrong. He knew. Lottie eventually suspected. But had Rose? None of the farmers around Holloways and Hereford ever beat on his door threatening to horsewhip him because nothing ever came of his repeated congress with their precious daughters.

As payback for one torment too many, he supposed, Charles had blown up at him. "Poppy Smyth says she never worries about a poke from old Georgie because 'it's like ringing a bell that ain't got no clapper!'"

Without children to hold them together, he didn't know how he and Win would go on. But his urge to run away from her was an empty reflex. In Venice, he told Lottie his dream of the old woman in the desert and the pocketful of glass. She offered no comfort, not even empty advice. They sat on the terrace that overlooked the palazzo garden. Win crossed it in the company of Steinwicz. Sunlight played on her hair. She smiled at her companion. At the sight of her upturned nose, the sound of her laugh, he felt the old, warm thrill. The skin of his stomach tightened. There was a rush of sweetness that effervesced and went right to his blood.

"So, this is the golden girl you always talked about." With her eyes, Lottie followed Win, who disappeared under an archway. "You never needed me. For all your scheming with an old lover or teasing Winifred with the besotted Gianni, it is plain you are mad about her, la regina del tuo cuore!" Lottie smiled ruefully. "Maybe you always were. Ah well, so it did not happen for us. Poor George is in love—and with his wife! Finally, you understand your doom."

He hung his head. How well he did. Didn't Win know him better than he knew himself? Hadn't they always been drawn to each other by a kind of fatal magnetism, a horrified yet amused curiosity to see what the other would do or say? Hadn't they laughed at the same people, often for the same reasons? Weren't they masters at keeping others at a safe distance? They used different methods, of course. She did it openly through her queenly poise and deft ripostes while he achieved it backhandedly through a hail-fellow-well-met bonhomie that was the worst sort of lie. At the ball last year, she had indeed shone on the dance floor like a golden queen. That fellow Archer—everybody thought she was sure to give in. George had worried she might, too. In spite of the man's bad humor on the veranda after her rebuff, he had been terribly keen, too much so.

When George spoke to him, he had no plan. He only knew he could not lose her to that pup! He would eliminate the fellow from the running. Between them, he and Win crushed Archer that night. They both knew how to control the conversations of less quick-witted men than her last suitor, driving others to join their mockery lest they be made the butt of it. Win, not him, was the one who could stop conversation with a raised eyebrow or a sarcastic barb. George had merely admitted a claim where there hadn't yet been one, and the ruse had worked!

That night in Paris he had seen her disgust and feared her derision would follow. He didn't like her exerting that cold, autocratic demeanor in the presence of others, certain as he was of her contempt in private after his behavior with the Italian. Though he'd never much regretted losing at cards, except for the minor inconvenience of the money, he minded losing in front of her.

Sitting on the steps of the church, the rush of his turbulent thoughts finally slowed to a trickle. He had been exhausted. Yet he tried, as he always did, to put Win and Lottie and Rose back into their proper places, to sort through and discard whatever troubled him, to close and lock the drawers of his mind. But he couldn't put himself away.

Win had only gone through with their marriage because she thought she was pregnant and possibly to protect Furor from his threats. If the man was in love with her, he wouldn't be the first and wasn't the only one! The discarded Archer had moped about the club ever since George announced the engagement and doubtless thought his shallow heart suffered. After Geoff's jibe about Furor, his first thought was that Win might have, under duress, struck a fleshly bargain with Furor to release her. He applauded her spirit and despised the man's baseness. Furor's arrival signaled blackmail. The man meant to intimidate Win until his fists showed Furor that he'd gotten more than he'd bargained for and sent him scuttling off with his tail between his legs.

But there might be more to it than that. Before the fight, he had seen fear in her eyes—and love. If she'd said that it was for him, he would've walked away from the ring. And after, when he raised his arms in victory, she looked at Furor. That look! No! It was unimaginable that Furor could be a serious rival to her affections, if only because he trusted Win's consummate taste.

It was at Rose's that he began to consider that he might be wrong. She felt more for her friend than some species of devotion from long association. Rose loved Beryl, whether or not his darling or he understood her need for that perverted bitch. Even if Rose still wanted and enjoyed his caresses, her heart was obviously elsewhere. It pained him, how Rose cried for the cunt. He'd had to be rougher than he'd liked to make her shut up and behave. They talked a bit afterward as they sat at the table, or as much as they ever did. He told her about his engagement. Rose cried, but so had he. Maybe because they both knew he wouldn't see her again.

It was easier to believe the feelings of people like Rose and Furor did not concern him, any more than a fox's when his dogs tore it to pieces. He wished people of Beryl Stuart's tastes and Furor's kind did not exist. In the same way he had always denied Beryl's hold on Rose, he tried to imagine Furor as a temporary source of confusion for Win, not a flesh and blood man, or a real threat to his own happiness. That Win and Furor might have any sort of emotional connection, much less have forged a solid, indestructible bond, was not only repugnant but incredible. Undeniably, one existed between Rose and Beryl, but they were from the same gutter.

He was haunted by Win's and Furor's glances at one another the night he surprised them in Percival's study; the whispered gossip that always connected their names; her tears when Furor went down at the fight. Lottie's words pierced him. "Ah, well, so it did not happen for us!" Why hadn't it ever happened with him, for him? In his self-doubt, he envied them all their passion, or love, or whatever the hell it was.

George had raised his head from his hands. Lights twinkled from the opposite bank and cast limpid stars on the river. He had walked down the steps and crossed to the pavement's edge. Beneath it, water lapped. Black, deep.

When Win gave him her mother's necklace and her body, he had triumphed, imagining he finally enjoyed complete possession of her heart as well. How swiftly she had disabused him of his illusion. Over and over, she proved perfectly capable of giving him one without losing the other. Was this because Furor was not merely his rival but the object of Win's deepest love? George struggled not to believe it, but knew the battle lost. How ashen Win's face had been as she passed Furor in the church. The women he wanted were wholly separate and independent of him; they had existed before he came into their lives and would go on existing without him.

Water slopped against the wall. He inched the toes of his boots over the edge. It would've been so much better if Hez had shot him. His own gun hadn't been loaded. Or that afternoon at the Triberg falls, he'd been so close, ready! Only one more step. But he'd let Win take his arm and draw him back from destruction, like she always had. He still wanted badly to disappear, but was afraid to do it.

He had returned to their hotel room. A train, a boat, then London. And here he was alone in his room, burning all his old letters and wondering what the devil to do next.

His empty heart yearned to be filled. Had Win accepted his confusion that morning in Paris, she could've ruled him for the rest of his life, frightening though the prospect was. He'd clung to her and poured out all his unspeakable longings, all his misery. While they lay together, he had accepted, as he had with Rose, that there were secrets beyond those erotic intimacies Win may have experienced with him—or Furor; or that Rosie might with Beryl—into which neither his wife nor his mistress would admit him. There were mysteries about the human heart into which he had failed to be worthy of initiation. If only Win or Rose had told him how it happened to them, he might understand what was happening to him.

They had learned what he seemingly could not be taught. He'd never known how to open his heart or give himself without restraint. What was conquest, or technique? The tools of a soldier, not a husband. They were not the offerings of love. Like Triberg's tossing cataract, love was a force bearing all away before it, even the boundaries of class that existed between Win and Furor, and the taboos that existed between Rose and Beryl. Why couldn't it bear him away, too?

Maybe what made his heart ache was not only the shame of knowing he could never give Win, or Rose, or any other woman a child. What if the pain was caused by his resistance to that overweening, uncontrollable power? What if it carried him away without Win loving him? He'd have to exorcize his tormentor before it was too late, before he completely lost possession of himself and drowned.

Lottie had needed him; Rosie had loved him. Win had never admitted to either.

Last night he had stood outside Win's room but hesitated to go to her. A sliver of light showed under her door. When it darkened, he turned away. On his bed, he wrestled with his fears, alone.

He would not run away. At least he was that much of a man. Geoff could forget about the jewels and could go hang himself. Damned dog! He'd get him barred from entering the club again. Geoff would never dare go to Hampstead, let alone Norfolk. The filth would be arrested, he'd make sure of that.

On the couch next to him lay his coat. He slid his hand into its pocket and fondled the necklace. There was time before the bank closed to return it, as he'd told Win he would. He'd go out now before he changed his mind.

George closed his hand around the jewels and stared at the ashes falling through the grate.

☙❧

Mrs. Harris sat holding her baby and the card of the young man who had just left her. The hansom pulled away from the drive, and she dropped the curtain. She could not claim never to have met such a person before. Her early days as an actress and her unmentionable childhood had exposed her to characters who could've reeled directly out of Mistress Quickly's inn, and other men who were much worse. This fellow had a rough-around-the-edges quality, but had been beautifully dressed. She read his card again.

Bertollini and Ratchet
Gentlemen's Clothing and Outfitters
Haberdashers

Naturally he claimed to be the owner of the establishment. Perhaps he was.

"You're in business," she said noncommittally.

"An entrepreneur of sorts," he said.

He'd explained his visit by saying he understood she was interested in real estate investment. She had greeted this with wary surprise. "Jarvis Perrot, *Acta Diurna*?" she'd laughed as she read the other card he presented. "Chief Correspondent? My dear, he's the only correspondent! I've known Jarvis for ages. A gossip columnist: he's always stirring up something." The young man was sorry for wasting her time. She asked him to stay. He was rather attractive; dark, mysterious. The way he stared at her was the teensiest bit unsettling, but exciting too. Seductive. She had touched her hair and wished her maid had run some tint through its grey streaks that morning. What could be the harm of asking him to sit with her while she had her tea?

She was angry with the Earl anyway. Whatever people said, it really was his child, and the poor thing had come early, in July. He'd been so stingy, she'd had to stay in London for her accouchement and languish there for the rest of the summer while he lived it up in Paris with his wife on, reportedly, their second honeymoon.

It was too bad that she could not afford a new dress. The light had glittered off the small diamond on the man's signet ring. He wore so many, like a barbarian potentate. Perhaps he had connections to a lady's store and could get her a deal.

It was so unfair! Staff was down to Cook and Mrs. Rutledge and one house maid who had to double as her lady's maid. In the hall, the baby began to cry. Nurse was on the way! Mrs. Harris rang the bell furiously to warn the woman she had a visitor. What was she doing nursing a child at her age? Of course, she hadn't planned it! She'd thought she was beyond all that. It was so inconvenient, and she was sore all the time. But the poor mite was so small it quite broke one's heart. And the wretched Earl hadn't even seen his daughter yet or written to ask how they were. Suddenly, she had felt very lonely and dull. Hardly anyone came to see her anymore.

The man rose and ran his fingers over his homburg.

His suggestion was interesting, she told him, but she would need to speak with her accountant first. Perhaps, she had hesitated, raising her eyes in her prettiest fashion, he could come again. Nurse had entered with the fretting baby and waited at the door. She felt her milk and blushed, but forced her smile to become brilliant, youthful. Soon, about the same time, say after four o'clock? He'd always find her alone and quite free.

The man had grinned like a tiger. "'Ow 'bout tomorrow then?"

❧

Geoff and Sam had played cat-and-mouse for days. Once he realized the boy was watching the shop, or followed him to and from the Boar and Hart and his rooms and Arabella's, he'd begun to lead Sam about in circles. It was after a successful feint into an alley that he'd finally turned the tables and begun to follow Sam. To his surprise, the boy didn't go near the Montague Hotel. Beryl had moved out, but Rosie was still in the flat. Instead, Sam slept in Court's old bolt-hole or at the warehouse where Seamus had trained. He seemed to be on his own.

It also seemed Sam was up to his old tricks. In Court's room, Geoff found piles of spent matches and what appeared to be some of Sam's home-made firecrackers. He didn't trust Fabrizio to trail the boy. The fellow was too nervy. Nor did he trust anyone else. He didn't have time for Sam's games but was determined to find out if Peele's hunch about Piani's arsenal was right. Sam had only been to one other place. Geoff had checked it over, but found nothing except a few scraps of heavy, grit-covered paper. His fingers tingled. He sniffed the paper and coughed. Sam had never gone there again. If he did, Geoff was going to be right behind him.

Until then, it was no use scaring him off. Better to let mouse lead puss to its hole.

Peele watched Geoff Rachet leave the warehouse. He'd been hot on his trail since the morning, and the fellow had done some moving. First, he'd been to the store, then to Bagniolli's for lunch with Piani. Next, he'd taken a cab to a house in Richmond where he stayed almost an hour. Then he took one to Hampstead where he sat outside the Broughton-Caruthers woman's house a bit before driving to Pall Mall and going into her husband's club. Then he drove back to Southwark. He'd gone on foot first to that old tumble-down house and next to the warehouse.

Peele was still there. He followed a pigeon's flight amongst the rafters. Ratchet would be on his way back to the store and would finish up at Signorina Bertollini's before heading back to the Boar and Hart. There was no need to hurry. Except for the new Richmond and Hampstead stops, Ratchet was regular as clockwork, even if he was crooked in every other way.

The boy would be back soon as well. Peele walked up and down. The warehouse was empty, except for some dried up paint pots and the boy's blankets wadded next to an empty tea box nearby. He climbed the ladder to the cat walk, not for the first time, and studied the rafters and then the floor. He'd stomped and sounded its long planks and felt along the walls. There was nothing. The boy's movements were as regular as Ratchet's. He didn't go anywhere else. Where in blazes did the boy get the stuff?

He'd seen the lad sit by himself on the wall out back that overlooked the river, striking match after match. He'd seen the flare and flash, heard the scream and pop of firecrackers in the alley. He'd even seen evidence in the upstairs room at the old house that the boy was making a large one. Hard worker he was, quite intrepid and industrious. Otherwise, he followed Ratchet or sat by the river playing with matches, or stared across the water.

It was probably pointless, but Peele thought he'd go back to the house and check it over.

Winifred sat in bed with her breakfast tray. Bettina set the newspaper, folded to the stock quotes, next to her along with a stack of mail and went to arrange the flowers that the housemaid had placed on the table. When Bettina's back was turned, Winifred touched the single, coral-colored rosebud and the frangipani in the vase next to her toast rack. As he had since the day of their wedding, George still sent flowers to her each morning.

She wasn't sure what time he'd come back from his club last night or if he even had. In fact, he hadn't come to her bed after their last morning in Paris. It ought to be a relief. It wasn't.

At least there was a postcard from Morrant.

"Listen to this. They've been to Philae again. *Temple of Isis Philae, Steamer from Cairo*—'Aswan v. quiet. P. not smoking. Still lies about brandy. Heat at Aswan unbearable. M.' As it is here!" She passed the card to Bettina.

Winifred opened her uncle's letter and read it aloud. "'Philae stunning and always makes me think of you standing between its columns, dressed in white and crowned like Isis. Awful story, Osiris and his murderous brother Set. Chopped up like one of those poor devils in the Tower. Never tire of temple, but do of Colonel Perth's constant grunting about our guide.'

"Oh, he's drawn him again, this time as a spitting camel. They must spend all their time together. Uncle's so perverse! He obviously can't bear him!

"'Col. P. overheated, had to sit out last of our walk. Don't let M. tell you I'm not much better. Progress on book finally, down to one brandy after supper, and chew my cigars. Col. P. smokes like a chimney. It will kill him (finally, HA!). Wish you and G. could have joined us but understand why. You will be all right, and I WILL GET WELL AND COME HOME to see your Little Biscuit once it's done! Package in mail for A. Know she is excited her turn to be a mama is next....'"

"Madame, what is it?" Bettina said.

There was more, but Winifred couldn't go on. She put down her uncle's letter and wept.

The sun shone and the brass band played. Children ran screaming and rolled hoops on the grass. Governesses pushed prams. Court did not hear or see any of it. He sat on the park bench in Saint James's reading Miss Dupree's note. Mr. Griffin had given it to him when he passed the porter's room on his way out. It came very late the prior evening, long after Perkins brought the last set of papers and post for Mr. Barron, the man apologized.

Court was sorry too. He wished he'd never read what the woman had to say.

Trouble for W. & Mr. G. re: G. Rat. & necklace. Be at St. J. bandstand, 4 PM Sun., D.

Court read the line again. He'd been angry at Winifred, but he wasn't anymore. He knew what he should do, what he had to do. He also knew what he risked and his likely fate for doing so. He put the note in his pocket and waited for Mademoiselle Dupree.

Patterson had had to read the note several times before he understood what it meant. *OUTSIDE 3 S.* At 2:55 P.M. by his watch, his constable had handed him the envelope. The note's letters had been cut from a magazine by the look of them. Some rag, for it felt like cheap pulp. The thick brown paper that they'd been pasted to was what got his attention though. It was covered with a fine grit and gave off a sulfurous odor that took him right back his army days. Gunpowder.

Hoping he was not too late, he walked around the building twice and was ready to give up when he heard a shrill whistle. Sam stood at the end of the alley next to the rubbish bins. "Tell your bloke to stop followin' me!" he shouted.

Patterson took a step toward the boy.

From his jacket, Sam whipped a paper-wrapped stick about six inches long that had a short, stiff string attached to it. The boy pulled out a match. He stepped closer to the brick wall of the station house, poising his hand to strike. "I can 'elp you get what you wants, but won't 'less you 'elps me first!"

It might be a firecracker, or nothing. Or it might be something else. "I want to help you, Sam!" Patterson took another step.

Gritting his teeth, Sam struck the match, set the fuse, and threw the stick into a rubbish bin. Patterson fell to the ground and covered his head. There was a deafening bang. Glass, paper, bricks and mortar rained onto the street.

CHAPTER 21
Deus Ex Machina

The mixing of social classes can have humorous or disastrous results, and sometimes both. In the case of a prince stooping to take his pleasures amongst lesser mortals, it may even be instructive or at the very least entertaining.

One was sick of summer, and the first good shooting was weeks away. No one he had any fun with was in town. His cousins were on their yachts; his best card partners were chasing American heiresses; and his favorite mistress was lounging at a spa. The end of August was always a very trying, in-between sort of time.

Bertie was feeling restless.

He looked from Alex, who had already risen from the table and removed with one of her ladies-in-waiting to the other end of the room; then to his mother, who was reading; and back at the photograph in the gossip section of the newspaper. Beryl Stuart sat astride Sweet Little Banshee in her tight jockey's breeches. On his last visit to Lizzie Montague's, the young woman's most recent race was the sole topic of conversation. In spite of her shorn ringlets, he definitely recollected the face of the cunning little vixen as one of the Lancaster's top draws; he had also seen the infamous erotic tableaux. Good old Bess had given him a copy of the French edition. Miss Stuart of the dark eyes and the very, very wicked ways indeed!

"What are you chuckling about over there, Bertie?" his mother asked.

"I think I'll go to the races."

"Whatever for?" challenged that decidedly humorless matron. She lifted her capped head and glowered. "Whom are you going to meet?" She glanced at Alex and sighed. "No, no! Don't tell me."

"There's the most extraordinary woman who rides her horse like a man. She's been doing rather well." He flashed the paper and its photograph at his mother. To his satisfaction, she scowled. Is this the future of Woman? He read. "Let's place a bet on it! What do you say?"

"That we are not amused," quipped his mother, returning to her book.

⚭

Morrant closed the sitting room door. George didn't look up from the racing section while the man fussed with the curtains.

Win hadn't told him her uncle was back, but he hadn't been home for two days. He'd spent the nights at his club. He didn't know what she'd told the servants about his absence and didn't give a damn. There was more than a hint of disapproval behind Morrant's usual diffidence. The man had never liked him, but he wasn't about to kowtow to any servant, especially his wife's favorite lackey. Win was entirely too sentimental about him. The sooner he and Percival were on their way to the country or out of it again, the better. The old man must've returned against doctor's orders and would suffer for it soon enough. He'd speak to Sir Percival but otherwise make himself scarce. There were some good races on today.

Damn, it was hot. He felt for his handkerchief. The necklace was wrapped in it.

For the past couple of days, he'd renewed his promise to himself to take Win's necklace to Mr. Buckner, but each day some diversion kept him inconveniently far from the Royal Empire Bank. He rode on the heath or went out to the tracks. He took a cab by the Boar and Hart and then to the Montague Hotel, but stopped at neither. He caught the train to King's Lynn and drove a trap to Hereford. He didn't go as far as the Hall or tell anyone he was there. Instead, he took a back lane, parked the trap near the dovecot, and sat inside it until dark. Then, he went back to London and slept at his club.

In his pocket he also carried a note to Geoff Ratchet that he'd written the day he and Win disembarked in Dover. *All over. See you in hell. G.* At each post box he passed, he meant to drop the letter, but never did. Since Geoff showed up at the club, George's ears were always half-pricked for the man's grating voice. He was tired of glancing over his shoulder. At every turn, he expected to see him. But he was ready.

On his last visit to Kleinfeldt's, the jeweler had been more nervous than ever. The man had written that the copy of the necklace was ready. The little man held his work in his pincer-like fingers and delicately laid the necklace on a black velvet cushion. Trembling, he set down a second black cushion on which George spread the real jewels. The man turned up his lamp, and its shade slipped. Light flashed along the counter. He adjusted the beam to shine down on the stones.

"What's all that?" George asked. At the other end of the long display case Kleinfeldt's light had caught the sparkle of more jewels. They lay in an open box, a parure composed of a ruby and diamond tiara and many smaller pieces that had belonged to George's grandmother. "What'd you get these out for?"

The man followed George to the far end of the counter. "After working on the piece for your wife, I thought you might consider having these made into copies as well. As you've described her coloring, they'd be very...."

"Hideous and too damned expensive!" George had snapped, but his attention was drawn to a stack of rose gold bangles inside the jeweler's case. "Put these monstrosities back and wrap those for me instead," he said of the bracelets.

While Kleinfeldt bustled about, George stared at the jewels on the cushions. If he hadn't known which necklace he set down, he wouldn't have been able to tell them apart. To his untrained eye they were a perfect match. He put Win's necklace back in his pocket. "Box this," he said of the copy.

"Should I expect Mr. Ratchet to collect it?" the man's voice quavered.

George shrugged. He was out of patience with the jeweler's anxiety. "No, I'll take it now."

Kleinfeldt closed the slender box and rested his hands on it. "This took me many long hours and cost me much worry." He gazed pensively at the other jewels in his display case. "Strange, what we put our lives and our hearts into. I sometimes wonder if it's not all a waste of time and effort."

"I wouldn't know," George said indifferently.

That was less than an hour ago. George patted his breast pocket then felt in his other one for the box. Morrant lingered, facing the fireplace. Why the devil didn't he leave? Surely the fellow had some job to do for old Percival. George stared at the back of the man's dark head and broad shoulders. It was on his lips to order him to get out. The man turned around. It was Court Furor.

"What in hell's name are you doing here?" George asked quietly.

"I usually have errands for Mr. Barron, but not today."

"Well, whatever you're here for, do it and go!"

"My business is with you. We've only got a few minutes." Furor glanced at the clock on the mantle. "Madam and Miss Barron will be back from their ride soon."

Before George could interrupt, Furor went on in a quieter voice. "You've come from a jeweler's named Latimer Kleinfeldt. On your orders, that man made a copy of a very valuable necklace belonging to your wife. There's a policeman outside who's been following you. You've been there before with Geoff Ratchet. You're carrying the copy now."

George sat perfectly still. He was not afraid, but he was startled. "What do you want?"

"While you was abroad, Kleinfeldt contacted Detective Inspector James Patterson of the Metropolitan Police. He was mortal afraid he was about to be involved in a crime. No crime had or has been committed, but you and me both knows Geoff's not a man to be trifled with. The day she got this necklace out of the bank Geoff was there. He took her. She got away, so he missed getting it once. He ain't going to miss his chance at getting those jewels again."

George leaned forward in spite of himself. "What is this to you?"

Furor looked him in the eye. "The police want Geoff for Selway Adams' murder, but they ain't got what they need to hang him—yet. Adams was an earl's son, so there can't be no mistakes. They want to draw Geoff out, and they want your help."

"What if I don't have the necklace?" George asked.

Furor walked to the window and gestured for George to join him.

They stood close to the lace sheers. Furor pointed across the square to a grizzled, leathery little man who sharpened scissors on a grinding stone set up by a tinker's cart. "That man's followed you when the police ain't. According to Miss Dupree, Mistress gave you the necklace, but ain't nobody seen it at the Royal Empire yet. Mr. Bucker ain't recorded it, and he'd know."

He pointed to another man who strolled the pavement. A placard and a tobacconist box hung from his shoulders. "That man's Ratchet's. He's been watching you, too, when Geoff ain't."

"So have a policeman escort me to the bank," George said.

"What about Adams, sir? What about your wife? Geoff Ratchet tried to have me killed 'cause I knew he was there that day at the Royal Empire. Your wife can identify him."

"What do you want of me?" George asked.

Furor held up what looked like a playing card covered in orange foil. "This here's the signal. I flash it at our fellow outside, and we're go. Patterson's men start moving, and you and me move, too. Do exactly as I say, and Geoff'll be inside a jail tonight. He won't bother you or Mistress again."

The card shook slightly in Furor's hand. George's heart beat hard, too. "What about my wife? I want the police to stay here with her until this is over."

For the first time, Furor looked uneasy. "No sir, she's got to come along. Geoff's got to see her and that necklace. Only we can't tell her what's doing, not yet."

"This Patterson thinks nothing of exposing her to danger. It seems an undue risk."

"Long as Geoff's on the streets, Winifred's life will always be in danger," Furor said.

"My wife, Mrs. Broughton-Caruthers, you mean," George said coldly.

Furor said nothing.

George stared at the dim shapes of the tobacco seller and the tinker. "But I take your point. I'll help flush out Patterson's quarry on one condition. My wife is always very frank and honest with me, so speak carefully. I'll know if you're lying. You were also with Ratchet—and her."

"Your wife was and always will be a lady. Whatever she's told you about that is all a man needs to know."

George walked to the mantle and stared at the clock. He rubbed at the breast of his coat. "What about at Holloways?"

"I showed her a letter from home and warned her about Geoff." Furor paused. "I also asked her not to marry you."

George hated that it was so difficult to control his emotions in front of this man. He passed his hand over his eyes. The clock began to strike. In the hall, there was feminine laughter and voices. "Signal your man. Let's get this over with. But after today Furor, you're gone!"

The sun slanted through the windows and flashed off of the many mirrors of Winifred's dressing room. The chamber was stifling and overly bright. George called impatiently from the stairs. In dismay, she inspected the reflection of herself and her mother's necklace. The jewels were ridiculously out of place with the new summer dress he'd bought her in Paris. Bettina took the jewelry box and argued that dusty rose and deep ochre looked well with the stones. "Now I know you've gone as mad as he has!" Winifred said, adjusting her jacket to try to cover most of the stones. "Bring my shawl!" She stuck another pin in her hat while Bettina got her wrap.

"I'm completely outdone with George. It's so hot, yet he suddenly takes it into his head we must go to the races!"

The equestrian sensation, Beryl Stuart, was to race Sweet Little Banshee in the evening's handicap, at some track she'd never heard of. Winifred didn't want to go and certainly didn't want to wear the necklace. There was no point asking why he'd taken it to his jewelers instead of returning it to the bank as she had asked. There was no point asking why George did anything.

His nervous energy and sudden enthusiasm smacked of their worst times in Venice. If tonight was like those evenings, she expected him to become intoxicated and quarrelsome. She only hoped he wouldn't make an ass of himself and dreaded what would happen when they got home. In Paris, he'd been alternately amorous and truculent when she hadn't responded with equal ardor to his advances. In such a mood, he was inexhaustibly passionate and violent by turns.

At the top of the stairs, Bettina grabbed Winifred's shoulders and firmly kissed both her cheeks. "I love you so much, Madame! You must have courage tonight! Be brave!"

She was more than a little astonished by Bettina's uncharacteristic display of affection. "How could I not when this time you'll be with me?" Winifred squeezed the woman's hand and kissed her back. "George won't separate us again. He can hardly stand up to us both! Maybe I'll drink too much Champagne and get drunk as well, if I don't faint first from this heat."

Bettina's firm hand stayed her.

"If you don't like it at the race tonight, come home," she said. "Just go! Poof! I'll tell him."

"I'll be fine!" Winifred rushed down the stairs. George was practically running out the front door, shouting that he wasn't going to miss the start of the race. Bettina followed them.

Court stood by the carriage with the footman. George quickly disappeared inside the vehicle without looking at either man. Winifred wished she could catch Court's eye. She climbed in and sat by George. Bettina followed, then Court, who slammed the door. They set off.

She tried not to stare at Court's profile. He was often upstairs when the decorators were there but never alone. He always left out of one door when she came in another. His black hair was neatly trimmed, though a few errant curls betrayed his former wild locks. When he spoke to Bettina, his scars and crooked nose revealed the roughness of his old life. Yet no one would recognize him as the flashily-dressed, dirty footpad who'd bundled her into a stolen hackney with Geoff Ratchet. In the dark suit of a gentleman's valet, he might have always served in a great household. In contrast to George, who was jumpy as a cat, Court appeared self-possessed and calm. Never had he been so handsome. Never had he looked more distressingly like Morrant. But Court had no kind word for her as her old friend would have.

After Bettina and Court arranged the picnic basket between them, no one spoke. They stared out the windows. Once Winifred's initial shock at seeing Court wore off, it was replaced by a growing outrage. No doubt his presence was George's doing. She'd had more than enough of his perverse game-playing with Gianni and wondered what sordid scene he hoped to instigate to spice the evening's lovemaking. If this was how he intended to end their abstinence, she would lock her door. But if George wanted to fight, she felt more than his equal. He rubbed his fingers continuously over his breast pocket and hummed one of his favorite Schubert Lieder. Winifred drummed her fingers on the seat and stared through the dust at the passing houses.

At the racecourse, the crowd was immense. The sun had lowered, but there was still plenty of time before it grew dark. Court walked ahead to claim their seats. Winifred was surprised to spot Amelie and Bert in the stands. She and George, followed by Bettina, pushed their way through the crowd of both the well-dressed and down-at-heel toward a roped-off, tented area where the horse owners and other important personalities of the turf gathered. Nearby was another private tent for their refreshments.

George headed for the paddock, where the grooms walked the horses. A plump, red-haired man who wore thick glasses and a well-tailored but very rumpled suit stood at the rail. From Bert's description, Winifred supposed the man was Mr. Greystone. George said he represented Miss Stuart and the Banshee's owner, then walked to the other side of the paddock.

A brass band played. The air smelled of grass and horses, whiskey and cigars. Amelie waved at Winifred, and Bert raised his binoculars to the track. George was intent on the horses. Winifred sent Bettina into the stands to fetch her cousins, but excused herself, saying that she wanted to see the Banshee up close when the horses were brought out. Court stood at a little distance from them all, his hands clasped behind his back. Mr. Greystone laughed. George had introduced himself and obviously made a joke. He called imperiously to Court.

"Furor, you're not doing anything. Get us some drinks. Be quick, man!"

Court made his way to the other tent. Winifred's cheeks burned. George's sharp command, Court's silent submission; it was precisely how Court told her his life with her would be. He was a servant; George was his master. All his life, he'd had no chance to win. For the rest of his days, he'd be ordered by the man who had won her. She'd stood by and let George do it. If he spoke to her, she'd strike him.

Beryl Stuart rode the Banshee into the paddock. The crowd murmured in appreciation. Mr. Greystone approached the palings, and he and the woman spoke. The man also spoke to the horse, a lovely bay with a springing walk and gorgeously formed legs. Winifred had only seen Miss Stuart's picture in the papers. Her colors were dark pink and white with touches of silver, and she wore a rose in her cap. Sitting erect and assured on her horse, she looked extremely handsome, like a youth. Like Gianni.

Court spoke to her as she passed. The woman gazed in Winifred's direction. Fierce eyes met hers. Winifred cheeks grew warm again. She wondered if Miss Stuart knew who she was. Miss Stuart nodded and touched her bright cap with a gesture disarmingly like one of her brother's. Tucking her heels against her horse's flanks, she and the Banshee ambled into place on the tracks with the other horses and riders.

Winifred could stand it no longer. She turned on her heel and walked as fast as she could toward the stables. She was done with George. She wished she could be done with herself. How she envied Miss Stuart and her whip and her freedom. What she wouldn't do if she was on that field riding Tulip! It was all she wanted: to ride to the sea, to ride forever! She was going home, to Holloways. She would go this very instant, George or no George. Bettina would handle him. She lifted her skirts and strode to the stalls where the grooms parked the carriages. If she couldn't find theirs, she'd hire a cab and go straight to the station.

Or maybe she'd go to the docks and send Bettina a telegram to join her. Why was there no one about?

She had not paid attention and taken a wrong turn. The sheds she passed were full of maintenance vehicles and hay wagons. She doubled back the way she had come.

"Mrs. Broughton-Caruthers!"

At the sound of the harsh voice and Cockney accent, she stopped. A man stepped from behind a stack of hay bales into her path and removed his hat. Their eyes locked. Geoff Ratchet!

Winifred turned and fled.

He quickly caught up, grabbed her left arm, and pulled her to him. She soundly cuffed his temple. He shook her so furiously her hat fell off. "You got away once! I'll do the job right this time!" Backing her against the stable, he clapped his hand over her mouth. Pinned to the wall by his weight, she could not stop him. He tore open her jacket.

"Ah, you 'ave got it! Just like Peele said you would!" Grinning terribly, he pulled out a gun and pointed it at her head. "Ain't we goin' to 'ave fun tonight, girlie!"

The starting bell clanged. Beryl and Sweet Little Banshee took off in the fourth lane from the inside rail and quickly made their way into the foremost of the group. Horses strained, wild-eyed, nostrils flaring. Beryl crouched in her stirrups, whipping furiously at the jockeys to her right and left. They pressed into the Banshee, trying to cut her off. The Banshee's ears lay flat, and she charged ahead. Hooves stirred the track; clods of earth flew before Beryl's face. The field thundered. The crowd roared. Beryl shouted abuse at the jockeys. She shouted encouragement to the Banshee. Only three horses ahead of her! She pressed to the fore of the crowd. Not too much, love, not yet. They took the first bend.

George could not find Win. Furor still waited for drinks in the tent. Dupree was in the stands. Amelie and Bert stood at the fence with Greystone, intent upon the race. George spoke close to Bert's ear, then pushed through the crowd of owners. Still no sign of Win. George began to run. He reached inside his coat pocket and clutched his regimental pistol.

Court directed the boy who carried the box with the champagne bottles and glasses. He wished George had seen fit to bring his own. He minded less being ordered about in front of Winifred than he did leaving her. But Grynt had his eye on things. Somewhere in the crowd, the little man wore one of his disguises. Sergeant Peele was around, too, though he'd have to take Grynt's word for it, never having laid eyes on the man. In addition to other plainclothes constables, Dupree assured him that Detective Inspector Patterson would be on hand as well, though he'd yet to meet him either. What in thunderation was George thinking? Jesus, Mary, and Joseph!

Dupree and Mr. Bert rushed over to him. Amelie stood with Mr. Greystone, but kept glancing over her shoulder in their direction, clearly worried.

"Winifred's gone. George's looking for her." Mr. Bert's expression was strained. "Dupree's told me about Ratchet! I don't want to frighten Amelie!"

"I know where she is!" Miss Dupree cried. "I told her to go home if she didn't like this!"

Court's heart sank. "Stay in case she comes back. No! Mr. Bert, go check the line of cabs! Miss Dupree, find Patterson, Grynt! Find anybody!"

George had heard what Dupree told Win on the stairs and felt Win's rage from the second Furor handed her into the carriage. Ordering Furor about was the last straw. But he couldn't stop himself. He saw her looking at the man as they rode to the track. Naturally, she'd rather go home, and that was where she belonged. Patterson's plan was as insane as one of Geoff's. Damn the lot of them! He'd find Win, and they'd leave tonight. Tomorrow they'd be at sea, on their way to Egypt or India or wherever the hell Win wanted him to take her. Maybe she'd found a deserted stable. That's where she always went when she needed a good cry.

Winifred's hat lay on the ground.

He slowed, felt for his pistol, and peered around the corner.

Geoff Ratchet held Winifred against the shed wall. Her jacket was torn open, and he pressed a pistol under her bosom. She screamed.

At the sound of George's name, Geoff snarled over his shoulder and pointed his gun.

George held his ready, but didn't draw it. "Let her go! I've got what you want!"

"It's right here!" Geoff clutched the necklace at Winifred's throat.

"Are you sure?" George reached into his other pocket. Geoff put the gun to Winifred's temple. George slowly opened his coat so Geoff could see and drew out the necklace.

The man's eyes widened. He cocked the gun by Winifred's head. "Lemme see! Bring it 'ere. Don't try nothin'.'"

George stepped toward them, holding out the necklace. "It'll be all right Win!"

Geoff's face assumed an expression of profound disgust. "Soft!" he muttered. As George edged closer, Geoff burst into laughter. "Bloody people! Can't you never make up your minds what you wants?" He swung the gun into George's face. Winifred screamed again.

Court ran toward them.

"Court!" she cried. "No!"

George struck Geoff's arm. The gun fired into the air. George flung Winifred at Court and reached for his weapon. Court reached for Winifred.

Geoff took aim at them.

Court yelled at Winifred.

Stumbling on her skirt, she fell to her knees. The pistol's report echoed off the shed wall. George and Geoff fell to the ground beside her, grappling. Under their rolling bodies George's necklace lay in the dirt. Court shouted for her to run. Winifred stared at her blood-spattered jacket. She was dizzy, uncertain whether she had been hit or not. Geoff swung his gun at George's face. George punched Geoff's nose. The gun flew from Geoff's hand and landed near Winifred. She lunged for it.

Beryl was in the lead group. For the first lap, the Banshee had kept up with the top five. It took all her effort to hold back her darling, to save her for the final push. They neared the last bend. Pearl-Handled was to their right, his jockey pumping his arms. The stallion ran neck and neck with her girl. Only Silver Slippers and Fly-By-Night remained out front. Beryl tucked her knees tighter and drew her whip under her arm. Wind whistled by her ears. The track thundered. The crowd was a blur of noise and colors. It was time to win.

She called to her girl. Her Girl. HER GIRL!

The Banshee pulled forward. Pearl-Handled fell behind by a head, a length. They drew close to the inside rail. Silver Slippers pulled ahead then lost momentum. The Banshee pressed near Fly-By-Night's flanks. They were neck and neck. The Banshee pushed her nose forward, stretched her stride, and increased her pace. They left Silver Slippers and Fly-By-Night behind, far behind. It was magic. The other horses seemed to slow down, seemed almost not to be running. They were alone. Beryl felt the Banshee's hooves leave the ground.

They were flying.

Winifred and Court rolled in the dust. Behind them were loud curses. Geoff scrambled to his feet, brandishing his gun. George pointed his. Their faces were bloody.

"You think I'd let my wife wear the real one, you mad bastard! It's a police trick!"

Geoff sprang at the necklace that lay in the dirt.

George ran to her and Court, his pistol raised. "Run, Win!"

"Go! Go!" Court gasped.

"No, Court!"

"Furor!" George yelled.

There was a pop. The sound bounced off the shed wall.

Court's eyes opened wide. "Ah!" he gasped.

No one moved. A dark spot bloomed on his waistcoat. Winifred touched it and drew back red, dripping fingers. Court's knees buckled. She tried to catch him. They both went down.

"No!" Winifred shouted.

Court stared at her, his eyes full of disbelief and regret. "Ah! Winifred, I don't want—! I won't—leave—you!"

His eyes rolled, and their lids fluttered.

Winifred shook him. "No!"

Geoff panted and held up George's necklace. With the other hand, he pointed his gun.

George aimed his at Geoff. "Not another step! You've got what you wanted!"

"Not quite!" With a furious, frustrated snarl, Geoff aimed his gun's muzzle at Winifred's head and almost screamed at George. "Put it down!"

George's gun hand bled and shook slightly. He stared from her to Court.

Very slowly, he lowered his arm and dropped the gun.

Geoff pounced and seized the necklace at her throat, dragging her by the neck. She clawed at Geoff's hands. He yanked again, but the links did not give.

Spots swam before her eyes.

There was a grunt, a thud. Geoff lay on the ground. George fell to his knees and pulled Winifred to him. The necklace still circled her throat. In the distance another shot rang. There was a clang of alarm bells, or maybe it was the signal to begin another race.

Court sprawled on his back a few feet distant. Blood soaked the ground under him.

Winifred sobbed and tried to loosen George's hold.

"Win!" George pulled her closer. "He's gone."

Winifred wailed.

George pressed his forehead to hers.

In the distance, the bells continued their clamor.

George kissed her hair, her cheeks, her mouth. He held her face. His own was streaked with dust and blood. His eyes streaming, he tried to smile. "Don't think too badly of me, my sweet girl. I surely never will of you!"

He let her go.

George pried the necklace from Geoff's hand and tucked it in his breast pocket. One bright flash of his old smile and he ran beyond the sheds. He was gone.

Winifred crawled to Court. He lay on his back, his leg crooked and one arm stretched as though pointing the way that George had run.

There was a cold, metallic click. Geoff was on his feet behind her. "This is what I should've done girlie, the second I saw you!"

A shot rang out.

When Winifred opened her eyes, Bettina was holding her. There seemed to be many people milling around them. Geoff lay on the ground close by, a dark stain under his head. A wizened fellow and a police constable knelt by Court. A group of men with stretchers leapt from a first aid wagon. Standing over all of them was a big, sandy-haired man in a long summer duster and a bowler hat, who thoughtfully wiped his gun.

The face of the fat man seated at the foot of Beryl's bed was familiar. He had slightly protruding blue eyes and a pointed beard. He pulled his chair nearer and took her hand. Here she is, back with us at last! There were other voices besides his. People crowded around, but she couldn't turn her head to look at them. A man took a picture. Beryl grimaced. Someone else took her other hand.

"You must lie still for a very long time per doctor's orders" the fat man said.

"Your Royal Highness!" Beryl struggled to sit up. A searing pain in her ribs stopped her.

"By order of my royal decree, lie still! You're a brave girl, but I'll have no arguments." Though he pursed his lips, his eyes twinkled. "By God Miss Stuart, you amaze me!"

A nurse adjusted her pillows. Even the slight change of position was painful. Her right arm was wrapped in plaster. He explained that she couldn't move her upper body because her collar bone and some ribs had been broken. She supposed her legs were smashed too. The nurse said it wasn't as bad as that. Carefully, she turned her head. Horace held her other hand. Behind the men, several nurses herded the reporters farther down the ward.

The Prince continued. "I've already spoken to Mr. Greystone. I'm sorrier than I can say about Sweet Little Banshee. She was a fine horse and courageous, like her jockey."

Beryl's eyes filled with tears. She tried to swallow her sobs. "She was the very best horse in the world, sir!" Her voice broke.

"That she was," said Horace quietly.

"I want you to know," said the Prince, "that while I had all the confidence in the world the pair of you would win, at the last minute, I...." Again, his eyes grew merry. "Miss Stuart, I hope you'll forgive me. I bet the Banshee would only place. I've made you a present of my winnings. I hope in this small way to express my sincere sympathy for your loss and my admiration for your courage. You may not refuse the gift of your future sovereign, Miss Stuart."

Horace bent near and whispered the amount of the princely gift.

Beryl couldn't speak.

The Prince sat back and looked extremely pleased.

"But how did I...? What happened?"

Horace explained, and Beryl's memories slowly returned.

As they approached the finish line, she had sensed that something was very terribly wrong with the Banshee. They had been flying like heavenly creatures when the horse put down her right hoof and dropped her nose toward it. Her head was up in a second, but she began to drift to her right. With the finish line in their sights, she slowed. Silver Slippers flashed by.

The Banshee had strained forward, still ahead of Fly-By-Night with Pearl-Handled in fourth. Her nose reached the line. She pitched forward and cleared it. Then she swerved to the right, almost cutting off Pearl-Handled as he finished, and crashed to the ground. Beryl was thrown over the palings. She never knew when she hit the earth; nor had she known until she had woken in the hospital ward that Sweet Little Banshee had been put down, her right foreleg shattered to bits and its tendon slipped.

Before Horace could finish, Beryl heaved great, dry gasps. A nurse rushed to them.

The Prince laid his hand on hers. "She was true and beautiful, and worthy of her rider. She gave her heart for you 'til her last breath." The man took his leave and rose. The Prince and his entourage left.

The nurse gave her a shot, but Beryl couldn't stop crying. She wept for the Banshee. She wept for Horace. She wept for herself.

Then she saw Rosie.

Her friend sat down in the Prince's chair. When Horace stood, she reached across Beryl to stop him. "Dearest, dearest Beryl, don't take on so, please! The Prince is right. You did the best you could do, and so did the Banshee.

"'Orace and me 'as been waitin' ages for you to wake. Doctor says if you're good, it won't be long before you're up and about." Rosie placed her hands on either side of Beryl's face. She began to cry as well. "And Beryl, we're goin' to Cornwall, to our cottage, me and you! You and the Banshee did it!"

Beryl looked up at Rosie.

The woman pressed her lips to Beryl's forehead. Then Rosie kissed her mouth.

"It's all over. I love you, Beryl!"

For once, her girl was wrong. At long last, their lives were beginning.

CHAPTER 22
The Truth Will Out

Horace Greystone scratched under his woolen wig, and every newspaperman present in the Crown's courtroom made note of it, Jarvis Perrot among them. After months, the Selway Adams case had finally been brought to trial. The gallery was full and promised to be each day. The current session was only about preliminaries. The real fireworks would start the following morning. The prosecutor had just sat, and Mr. Buckner from the Royal Empire Bank stepped down from the witness box; but they weren't who Perrot had come to see. He and all the other spectators looked at the dark-haired man with the badly scarred cheek who stood in the dock.

The counsel for the defense had recently earned a great deal of notoriety, having been revealed in Perrot's column, *Acta Diurna*, as the former owner of Sweet Little Banshee, the horse jockeyed by the infamous Beryl Stuart, until both horse and rider tumbled spectacularly at the finish line of the Queensacre Handicap. Perrot had seen it all and profited thereby. Before the horse's demise, Greystone and Stuart had also profited hugely and been graced by the Crown Prince's patronage, along with that of other swells. A brief surge of support followed for the suffragists. Miss Stuart was not at their rallies. She disappeared and was, according to Greystone, "recuperating in the country from extensive injuries." She had no plans to return to the turf.

Always considered an eccentric amongst his peers and a frightfully tenacious defender, the mild-mannered Greystone had yet again garnered the public's interest as counsel to a criminal whose association with the hitherto unknown P. Lili Piani gang sent shudders through the newspaper-reading populace. Many local MPs weighed in, speechifying to their constituents about cleaning up London's streets and otherwise sedate neighborhoods like Southwark, whose populace ought not to live in fear of "the threats and machinations of those who would squeeze blood from our working fellowmen for their own aggrandizement," and so forth.

Greystone hummed as he arranged his notes on the table before him. The courtroom was packed and restless, but he took no notice of the hundreds of eyes riveted on him and his client. Though it was late November, the room was stuffy. The judge, Jonas Worthington, peered at the defendant and scowled while Greystone spoke. Worthington was a well-known, hard-nosed Conservative of very strict and somewhat High Church leanings.

Greystone probably wished the man on the other side of the globe as far as his poor client was concerned, but would do the best he could, Perrot thought.

Court stood miserably in the dock, watching Greystone like everyone else, but he wasn't listening. As he had once predicted when this whole business started, he was in for it. He'd been in so many courtrooms for so many hours over the past weeks, being remanded and processed and he didn't know what all, that he was numb. His twenty-sixth birthday would've gone by without his notice if not for Mr. Barron. He had been digging in parish records and found Court's birth notice. "I never thought to ask you your birthdate," he apologized, handing Court one of Sir Percival's books. Though the affairs of the day concerned him, he hardly cared. In spite of the fact that Geoff Ratchet's bullet had gone clean through him and he'd lived to tell the tale, his life was over. No matter what Mr. Greystone tried to do for him, Court knew where he was headed.

He was still weak from his wounds. The prison's hospital ward, while sufficient to his needs, left him lonesome and dull-spirited. Only Mr. Barron and Mr. Greystone called on him to prepare his case, though he'd received many kind letters from the staffs of Holloways and Hampstead. Once, he could've sworn the old orderly who winked knowingly at him from across the ward was Grynt in one of his disguises, but the man and his squeaky cart hadn't returned. Maybe it had been a dream. Mr. Barron spent many additional hours at his bedside in an effort to lighten his heart, reading to him or playing chess. He didn't like to tell the fellow it was to no avail. Beryl also wrote, but he could tell by her letters she struggled, too.

Once the wheels of justice began to turn, Court expected to be crushed by them and sentenced swiftly, given the judge's reputation. Greystone had promised he'd try to get his sentence reduced based on Court's cooperation with the police during the Royal Empire's case, and Mrs. Broughton-Caruthers' admission that Court had not hurt her in any way but seemed to act under Geoff Ratchet's coercion; but Court was resigned to the dangers that awaited him in prison. Geoff had quite a few confederates who were already there, and Signorina Bertollini had some relatives on the inside as well.

Mr. Barron was seated on Mr. Greystone's left. Court couldn't look at his friend. He didn't trust himself not to break down. More than ever, the young man had what Court called the de la Coeur look in his eyes. It was too much to bear. His past had finally caught up with him. Though Mr. Barron wouldn't allow Court to say it, he knew he'd let the fellow, and all those who'd been so kind to him, down.

༚

The old docks were a lonely place, Patterson thought. Gulls flew over the filthy stretch of sand, and the sky was very dull. He'd come back to the abandoned store without Peele. They had already checked out the warehouse where Todd used to stay and the old house where Sam dossed. According to his sergeant, he'd only ever seen the boy go into this building twice—one of Piani's buildings, the old chandler's storehouse. Patterson walked back inside the empty storeroom and around the perimeter of the makeshift ring where Court Furor had trained.

Sad about Geoff. Otherwise, he had no regrets. Neither Geoff nor the feckless Broughton-Caruthers realized that nobody had the real necklace. Soon as Kleinfeldt switched out the real one for the second copy, Mr. Buckner took it directly from the store to the bank. Peele had followed Broughton-Caruthers to Hampstead and kept watch with that crafty old geezer, Grynt Spivey. He liked Seamus' friends, even Court Furor, who he still hadn't met properly but whose interviews he'd read after Peele took them in the jail's hospital ward.

At least Seamus was well out of it. The Frenchwoman Dupree and Grynt had taken care of that. He wondered if he'd ever see Seamus or that odd little man again. He didn't know where they'd gone and didn't want to know.

It was the boy he had to think of. Like Sam, he wanted more than what would be handed down in the courtroom, finer and larger than what lay within the law's scope to achieve. He wanted a better world, the sort that didn't spawn and cast aside people like Geoff, letting them grow up twisted until men like him had to cut them down. If that world was ever going to be, the heroes would have to stand up and fight for it. They couldn't disappoint Sam.

Gently, he tapped the floor with his foot. 'Round and 'round he had gone already, feeling at doors and crevices, sniffing and knocking, but like the other places he had searched, it was tight as a drum. They brought in dogs to the others, but not here. What was that noise? He scanned the empty loft, the broken windows, the big doorway that led onto the loading platform.

Sam leaned against the door's frame, chewing a cigar.

"Got your note." Patterson sat on an empty tea crate and took off his hat. "That firecracker was of great interest to the boys in ballistics. It was exactly like the stuff in Selway Adams' office."

"You 'ad to believe I meant business."

"Oh, we believe you, Sam! But what sort?"

"You 'elp me and I'll 'elp you, like I said. Lemme see Court Furor."

"Can't you talk to me?"

"Your man's still followin' me. I don't like it. All I'll say is, you're warm and 'e ain't!"

Patterson felt in his pocket for a cigar and his clipper. He trimmed it to his liking and felt for his match box. As he was about to strike one, the boy called out.

"Warmer!"

Man and boy stared at one another.

"Piani'll run you and these streets for the rest of your life if you don't say what you know."

The boy shoved his hands in his pockets and left.

Patterson put on his hat and walked outside. Sam sat on the wall overlooking the river. He struck a match and sheltered it with his hand. When the flame reached his fingers, he shook it out. He repeated the procedure. Patterson took a seat beside him. "What'll you do?"

Sam raised a shoulder. "Dunno. Go to sea, China, maybe."

"Nah, that's no good. Pyrotechnics are fine, artistic maybe. But it's not the future. You've got to look ahead. What about those combustion engines we talked on? Did I ever tell you about that fellow I met, works for a chap called Simms? Across the river he's got a mechanics shop in Leadenhall Street. Ever heard of Daimler? I could show you."

The boy struck another match. "It ain't that. I don't mind that Fan and 'Ez went off. I know everybody's got to find whatever it is that's out there for 'em. Seamus with 'is paintin' in Paris, Grynt with 'is road, and Rosie. I don't know where she's gone." He shook out his match.

"Even Geoff," Patterson said quietly.

"It ain't that everybody's left. It's that they didn't stay. We was a gang!"

Patterson took out the postcard from Fanny that he'd found in Seamus' pocket and gave it to Sam. He read it, tore it up, and threw its pieces onto the water. Patterson rested his hand on the boy's shoulder. Sam struck another match. Patterson watched the Thames roll on to the sea.

✺

Thus far, it had been a very busy morning for Jarvis Perrot. Business for *Acta Diurna* was booming. So long as the sun shone, he'd be up and at it and ready to make hay. It had also been a busy, but much less profitable month for the defendant. In point of fact, the sun wasn't actually shining. It was as bleak a November day as could possibly be. Prospects looked even bleaker for Mr. Furor.

Both the Royal Empire Bank and the Earl had brought charges against him. While the main perpetrator of the offenses against both, Geoffrey Michael Ratchet, was dead and his primary accomplice, Hezekiah Boors, was missing and perhaps living in France under an assumed name, the Metropolitan Police in the person of Detective Inspector James Patterson and his sergeant, Detective Nicholas Peele, had produced Court Furor to sacrifice upon the altar of justice in both trials. Seamus Todd, whose involvement in each case was also documented, had had his charges dropped by the bank. Patterson and Peele made it plain that from the first, Todd cooperated with the police. He wasn't entirely competent, Patterson said. This statement was backed by the testimony of Dr. G. Rynte Spivey, who had examined Todd after many boxing matches and produced diagrams of the human brain, whose workings he explained to the rapt court. Mr. Graham Buckner and Mr. Kent Darby, of the Royal Empire Bank, provided additional information that corroborated Todd's heroism on the day of the explosion. Furor was found guilty on charges of conspiracy and accessory to a felony. A disgruntled mew's owner had complained of damage to property, and taking a vehicle and livestock under false pretenses. These charges pended against Furor in magistrate's court.

At the opening of the Selway Adams case, the Earl spoke in the House. He also wished to drop all charges against Todd to show that he had an eye to the public weal. *"There are those less fortunate whose circumstances ... etc. The lack of care for the young male children in London's East End and guidance to youths ...,"* wrote Perrot. *"Society will reap the consequences,"* finished the Earl, tearfully.

Selway Adams certainly had, Perrot thought, and wondered what sort of guidance the Earl had offered "dahling Selly" as he rushed out of the House to make his deadline.

Concurrent with Furor's trial, that of P. Lili Piani also took place. Furor had been called to testify against his former boss, having been present as driver on numerous occasions during which crimes ranging from extortion to murder were committed by either Piani or henchmen under his orders. Along with another of Piani's former flunkeys, Jeb Davis, Furor described in minute detail his involvement in rigged prize-fighting, one of numerous money laundering and betting schemes operated by Piani.

Mrs. Agnes Harris of Richmond, known to be the former mistress to the Earl and one-time show girl at the Gaiety, caused a sensation with her testimony. It involved the lately deceased Geoff Ratchet, who had approached her with an investment deal that involved two Southwark properties, a building formerly used as a dry goods store and a warehouse on the Thames. "He said he already owned a men's clothing store, Bertollini and Ratchet, and was looking for investors in his new import-export business. I was in somewhat straitened circumstances," she glared at the Earl, "and he was so convincing."

The watchful D.S. Peele alerted Mrs. Harris' accountant and solicitor. A title search revealed that Ratchet's deeds were forged. The buildings belonged to Piani. D.I. Patterson testified that Ratchet had indeed intended to expand his horizons based on the assumption he would step in as Southwark's new kingpin once he informed the police of the extent of Piani's double-dealing. He destroyed and forged other deeds to properties that belonged to Piani. As well as unsuspecting feminine investors, Ratchet intended to finance his so-called import-export business with stolen jewels and, it appeared from a raid on his flat, pornography. As for the jewels, Patterson cited the assault and attempted robbery of Mrs. Broughton-Caruthers the previous August during a horse race. After hearing of this, Mrs. Harris reported the loss of a very valuable black pearl necklace the previous February.

"When Mr. Ratchet visited me last August, I'd no idea he'd had his eye on the house since that awful business with Selly. My maid, Whyte— at least that's what we called her—she'd been with me so long I don't remember her real name!" There was laughter in the courtroom. "Whyte took off about that time. I hate to think she might've been in league with him! But Geoff—Mr. Ratchet was so charming!" Mrs. Harris raised her handkerchief and pressed it to her eyes.

Were they lovers? Perrot had scribbled in his notebook.

Horace Greystone still hoped to arrange a plea bargain for Furor based on his cooperation with the authorities. In the Adams case, he was charged as accessory to multiple felonies, unlike the Piani case, where Greystone had been able to argue that Furor was pressed into service against his will. In the bank's case against him, it would be more difficult to gain the jury's sympathy.

Listening to this, Court felt glum. His name and photograph were widely circulated in the penny papers and illustrated gazettes, along with Geoff's and those of other criminals of Piani's league. It was generally assumed he turned on his former compatriots to save his own skin.

Amongst leaders of London's many underworld operations, Furor is both marked and celebrated as the man who is helping to bring down their up-and-coming rival, P. Lili Piani, Perrot wrote. *By more respectable firesides, upstairs and down, Furor's example may be used as a caveat to the young, a proof that the lowest classes, soaked in gin and benighted by poverty, have only a stunted capacity for loyalty, and an illustration of the maxim that thieves will always turn on one another.* That would get some letters to the editor, he chuckled.

At the Lancaster Arms, however, where Furor's sister, the notorious Beryl Stuart, had worked before taking the saddle, the man's reputation was sterling. He was deemed "a poor lamb." Perrot rather agreed, but forbore to utter his personal sentiments. Both Furor and the unfortunate Ratchet possessed the same dark, dangerous good looks. Unlike the ladies of the Lancaster, he'd describe Furor as less mutton and more lupine. Like the unfortunate Mrs. Harris, he could easily imagine succumbing to the charms of one, or preferably, both men. He would give his eyeteeth to get an exclusive interview with the prisoner, but the much called-upon Furor was being held in a heavily guarded private room in the jail's hospital ward, at least until he finished his testimony against Piani and, if the Earl exerted his influence, until they'd done with him in the Adams case.

Every day, there was a general rumor that important personages might be present in the courtroom. Though Adams' death caused little mourning amongst his peers, his life had stirred much salacious interest in the populace. Because of Perrot's and his fellow columnists' efforts, the Earl's public acknowledgement of "Selly" Adams as his natural son by Jenny Blythe, another Gaiety showgirl, now deceased, was assured. The Earl and His Royal Highness the Prince were of an age, had been lads about town, and had shared similar interests during their youth. For instance, they had both been similarly interested in Jenny Blythe. Some speculated that the origin of Adams' short-lived sojourn on the planet owed more to Bertie's caresses than those of the Earl.

The latest sensation to take the witness stand was Winifred Broughton-Caruthers. The woman was an heiress, plantations in India and what not, and the niece of former Liberal MP and memoirist, Sir Percival de la Coeur. She stood witness for the Earl's counsel and was also currently involved in divorce proceedings. As a witness in the Royal Empire's case against Furor, she had already stood firm under Mr. Greystone's cross examination. He had asked her but two questions.

Had his client harmed her in any way? Had she charged his client with kidnapping?

To each she answered "no" and reiterated that her choice not to charge Mr. Furor with abduction was based upon her observance of Mr. Ratchet's behavior toward him, and that Mr. Furor had acted as he did under duress.

Not pretty, Perrot thought, but a graceful figure. Voluptuous or alluring would have been more les mots justes, but this was for the general readership. *Arresting—unconventional,* he wrote in search of the correct words to describe her face. That and *extremely elegant* would suffice for the evening edition. She wore a simply cut suit of chocolate brown accented with black, lattice-like cutouts on the cuffs and hem. A dark, veiled hat trimmed in pheasant feathers obscured her eyes. Under the open collar of her jacket, a jeweled Moghul necklace with a fabulous orange pendant glinted. It was the one Ratchet had tried to steal.

He turned his monocle to the gallery. Seated together were her lady's maid, Bettina Dupree, and her cousins, Amelie Barron and Gretchen Burns, daughter of the late Sir Thomas Carlton, and Natasha Barron, mother of Mr. Albert Barron, acting assistant to Horace Greystone. He would take his own chambers next year. Next to his mother sat another pinch-browed, middle-aged woman Perrot had yet to identify. Perhaps Furor's mother or an aunt. All of the women's fingers were busy with crochet-work, and except for Mrs. Burns, they were clearly much more nervous than the poised woman on the stand.

There were men with them as well, but he wasn't sure who they were. A journalist said one was Mr. Burns and another suggested Mr. Albert Barron Sr. was the second individual. The third appeared to be with the unidentified woman. All clearly knew one another.

Mrs. Broughton-Caruthers' picture had also appeared in the papers, along with her and her family's history. Some of the best bits had not appeared in *Acta Diurna*, however. These were leaked by a former housemaid to the family, Miss Molly Striker. Perrot suspected the girl had been fired. She clearly didn't like Mrs. Broughton-Caruthers. What she said was scurrilous and certainly libelous. Whether there was a rivalry between the estranged husband and the defendant couldn't be proven, but would be a tour de force if it could. Perrot had not had a day off since the trials began, but as soon as he got one, he was on his way to Norfolk to gather any corroborating first-hand accounts of the fight Miss Striker so vividly described. Mrs. Broughton-Caruthers had been abandoned by her husband shortly after their honeymoon. The gent was a well-known man about town and a gambler. Miss Striker, with a very red face, described his other wonted pastimes. Dear, dear! One got the picture quickly. Do dry your eyes, Miss! The man's dashing photograph had appeared in the gazettes. Broughton-Caruthers was a figure of much romantic speculation, though not to Perrot's taste.

Country Casanova, Rural Reprobate, he jotted.

Mrs. Broughton-Caruthers was speaking, repeating much of what she had said at the other trial. She described her business at the bank, her movements and separation from Mr. Buckner, and stated the fact of her subsequent assault and kidnapping at the hands of Geoff Ratchet.

While Perrot waited for her to finish, he consulted his notes. A new hall boy at the woman's Hampstead residence said that he'd heard a "ladies' doctor" had been swiftly called in after Mrs. Broughton-Caruthers' return following the bank explosion. "Gone all night, wasn't she?" There'd been more to Ratchet's assault than a mere pistol-whipping. The results of said attack were rumored to be the point of contention between Mistress and Master, the ultimate cause of their parting. "What she did to get rid of Ratchet's baby ruined her! Master's got to 'ave an heir, ain't he?" The young man whispered, "I mean, 'ow would it look for 'im if she didn't?"

One could hardly expect a Harley Street professional to confirm whether his patient had had an abortion or contracted syphilis or suffered some other unspeakable damage from Ratchet's attentions, so Perrot delicately floated these juicy ideas, along with a generous offer, before Mademoiselle Dupree. They were quickly squashed by a vituperative, free, and extremely short interview. Mostly in French, but one got the message. Miss Striker's and the hall boy's insinuations had leaked into the scandal sheets and simmered in the public's collective brain.

Mrs. Broughton-Caruthers was asked by the Earl's counsel to point to the driver of the hackney which carried her from the bank. There was a palpable sense of anticipation in the room. People craned their necks or stood on tiptoe to see the imposing lady as she identified the accused. The prosecution had no more questions.

Horace Greystone peered at the woman over his glasses while she removed her gloves. She lifted her chin and seemed to take the measure of him as well.

"Good morning, Mrs. Broughton-Caruthers."

She answered in a low, pleasing voice, and lightly touched the rail of the witness box. *No wedding band or any other rings*, Perrot wrote.

"Begging your patience, I will begin by summarizing your testimony. Correct me if I am inaccurate in any detail. On the morning of November 4, 1892, at approximately ten o'clock, you entered the Royal Empire Bank and spoke to Mr. Graham Buckner, the bank's senior officer, about your accounts. In the office were also present Mr. Buckner's secretary, Mr. Selway Adams, and a clerk, Mr. Kent Darby. While you were in Mr. Buckner's office, some twenty minutes after the hour, there was an explosion in Mr. Adams' office. There was a fire and more explosions, this time from the gas lines. During the confusion, you were separated from Mr. Buckner and attempted to return to his office, but entered another where you saw and were abducted at gunpoint by Geoffrey Michael Ratchet, who also struck you unconscious with a pistol in an alley behind the bank and forced you into a hackney, which you have testified was driven by my client, Mr. Court Furor, whom you have identified for my esteemed colleague, Mr. Whitehouse."

"That is correct."

Court Furor's expression was impassive during this narrative.

"About twenty-two hours later, a policeman helped you from Omnibus Number 44 to Metropolitan Station 10 and thence to your home in Hampstead, where you arrived under police care at about 2

P.M." Mrs. Broughton-Caruthers answered that she believed that was correct as well. "You were interviewed on the evening of that same day by Detective Randal Owens of the Yard and Constable Robert Clive of the City. According to Owens' report, which I have a copy of here, you had difficulty with or were unable to answer certain of their questions because you lost consciousness at some point during your abduction."

Mrs. Broughton-Caruthers agreed to his account.

"I also remind the court the prosecution has previously heard the expert testimony of Dr. Frederick Frost concerning the effects of trauma, shock, and concussion, all of which he diagnosed in the witness and included in his medical report and statement to the Yard. Which I also have here." He took a sheath of papers from Mr. Barron and raised it. "To proceed, how is your memory today, Mrs. Broughton-Caruthers?"

"Fine, thank you."

"Now respecting my client, you employed him from, roughly, early March until his arrest late this past August as initially, a groom and then a valet. You remember all this with clarity?"

"Yes."

"Thank you. You are currently involved in divorce proceedings from your husband?"

Chief counsel Mr. Whitehouse stood to object. The witness' private life was not germane. Horace Greystone addressed the judge. "Indeed, nor will I mention the more tantalizing details unearthed by our journalistic brethren. We will stick with the facts."

Perrot wrote swiftly, *Mild laughter in the courtroom.* But not much in the gallery where the woman's family sat huddled together. Their crochet-work had disappeared.

Mr. Greystone continued. "My Lord, I seek to establish witness' relationship to my client."

The judge squinted at Mr. Greystone and frowned. "The witness' character is not on trial."

"Nor do I wish to give such an impression. I speak of their professional relationship. I have details from my client concerning the circumstances of his employment that I wish the witness to confirm or deny as they may act in his defense."

"Be advised we will ask you to desist from this line of questioning if you do not make your point swiftly. Overruled," the judge said to Mr. Whitehouse. The judge turned his eyes upon the woman, who looked steadily at Mr. Greystone.

"Thank you, my Lord." Mr. Greystone resumed. "Mrs. Broughton-Caruthers, to your knowledge, did Mr. Furor ever try to threaten or blackmail your husband?"

"No, nor me neither."

"Thank you. After Mr. Ratchet's abduction, during the hours you spent with my client, did you offer Mr. Furor a job to convince him to let you go?"

"I offered Mr. Furor a job because I didn't like the circumstances under which he lived."

"Very good! That much of your memory of the day's events is clear. Was his service as a groom—this was at your country home, Holloways—satisfactory?"

"Yes, he was well-liked."

"Did you like him?"

"We didn't see much of each other, but he was a good groom."

"You were wed June 27 of last year. Was there a fight between Mr. Furor and your husband on June 24?"

Mr. Whitehouse objected, but the woman was already answering the question. The judge instructed the jury not to consider either what she or Mr. Greystone had just said.

"It was a sort of exhibition fight at a public fair," Perrot scribbled. So that much of what the spiteful Miss Striker said was true. Well done, Mrs. Broughton-Caruthers!

"Mr. Furor appeared unannounced at Holloways four months after your abduction from the Royal Empire Bank. From London to your home, that is a distance of around one hundred miles," Mr. Greystone continued.

"Yes, that sounds right."

"He left Holloways directly after the wedding ceremony?"

"I believe so."

"The day of your abduction, you withdrew the necklace you're wearing and put it in your pocket. Your maid found it, along with your purse full of money, in your coat when the police returned you to Hampstead. Did my client know of the presence of these articles on your person?"

The woman did not speak but looked at Mr. Barron. That man appeared busy at his notes and did not look up. Perrot glanced at Mr. Furor, who stared at Mr. Barron in obvious consternation. Perrot examined Mademoiselle Dupree. She clenched her hands on the balcony rail. The woman whom he had not been able to identify leaned forward, hand on her heart.

Mr. Whitehouse rose to object. "This question invokes a time the witness has already stated she has no memory of. In addition, Dr. Frost's evidence suggests her memories, if any, may be inaccurate."

"The witness has shown that she does have some memory of the time during her abduction. She was able to identify my client's presence in the alley behind the bank, though she could not upon her first questioning by Detective Owens last November."

"Answer if you are able," the judge prompted.

Mr. Whitehouse sat down. Horace Greystone coldly eyed the witness over his glinting spectacles. "Would the witness like for me to repeat the question?"

The woman lightly slapped her gloves against her palm. "I gave him money to buy us food and coal. He wouldn't take more. He found the necklace in my pocket but returned it. I believe he thought I was asleep. We were both afraid Mr. Ratchet would return in the night."

"Very well! Mr. Furor left you in his room in order to buy food. Did he lock the door or secure the entrance to either the room or the house?"

"No," the woman said quietly.

"Did he mean to leave the doors unlocked?"

"I believe so. And he told me how to get back to the City."

Mr. Greystone did not comment on the apparent return of more of the woman's memories. Mr. Barron handed him a sheet of paper. "Geoff Ratchet attacked you at the Queensacre Handicap in late August and tried to take the necklace. In your statement to Detective Inspector Patterson and Detective Sergeant Nicholas Peele of the Metropolitan Police, you state that 'Mr. Furor put himself between me and Mr. Ratchet and was shot by Mr. Ratchet because of it.' The actions of a very loyal retainer, wouldn't you agree?"

Here Jarvis Perrot realized Mr. Whitehouse, who was as engrossed in Mr. Greystone's questions as everyone else, had missed an opportunity, indeed several, to object that his witness was being led about by the nose, but it was too late. The witness had already given her quick answer. "Yes, I would."

"Thank you, Mrs. Broughton-Caruthers. Let us review. You've agreed that my client is very loyal. You've said that Mr. Furor shielded you from Geoff Ratchet's bullet. In spite of the fact that he was well-liked and did a good job, he left his post as groom after your wedding

and a fight that took place with your now estranged husband. Strike that
last bit, my apology!" he said as Mr. Whitehouse finally bobbed to his
feet. "You said that he left you at liberty while he brought you food. You
offered Mr. Furor a job not to convince him to let you go, but because
you did not like the circumstances under which he lived, and that he
acted under Geoff Ratchet's coercion. Furthermore, after your
abduction by Mr. Ratchet, my client did not take an incredibly valuable
necklace or your money, though he was aware of both. Is any of this
incorrect?"

"No."

"You know the charges against my client, that he drove Geoff
Ratchet and Hezekiah Boors in the hackney to the Royal Empire Bank,
etc. You've not stated expressly that he was the driver from the bank,
but your statement today clearly indicates that he was with you in the
alley and during your abduction. A witness identified him in a lineup as
the man who put you on Omnibus 44 in Haymarket. You confirmed
this under questioning by the Metropolitan Police. Mr. Furor brought
you food and watched over you as you slept in order to protect you
from Mr. Ratchet. You seemed comfortable employing him and letting
him into your home."

"All of that is true."

"You have never brought a charge of kidnapping or any other
against my client, correct?"

"No. I mean, I've brought no charges."

"In fact, Mr. Furor is technically still in your employ, is he not?
Though he left Norfolk, he never tendered a formal resignation, and
you never released him?"

The woman looked surprised, then thoughtful. "I suppose that is
correct."

A murmur rippled through the courtroom.

"Mrs. Broughton-Caruthers, I need not remind you that you are
under oath. You seem to forget some details about your current status
as an employer, yet remember clearly others you did not in November
when you spoke to the Yard's representative. Do I misrepresent you in
this?"

Jarvis Perrot sat riveted. Mr. Whitehouse looked uncertain as to
whether he should rise to object or not. The judge stared at the witness.
Mrs. Broughton-Caruthers extended a hand to the rail and lightly
drummed her fingers on it. She seemed to be thinking. "No," she finally
said.

"Or those that prompted your offer of employment?"

The woman did not speak.

Horace Greystone set his fists on the table and leaned toward her. "Mrs. Broughton-Caruthers, has my client ever been or is he now, your lover?"

Before he had finished the question, Mr. Whitehouse was on his feet, trembling with indignation, and objecting vociferously. The usher rose and called for order. He was ignored. Voices cried out in dismay or chattered in excitement or apprehension. There were boos and a few cheers. Not since his days as a Parliamentary reporter had Perrot heard such a commotion in such a hallowed hall. All around him, journalists pressed forward. He feared he might be toppled from his seat. Mrs. Broughton-Caruthers' family was in a state of agonized uproar, except for Mrs. Burns, who swiveled in her seat to speak to the ruddy, pock-marked man behind her. The usher called for order. So did Judge Worthington. Mrs. Broughton-Caruthers stared at Mr. Barron, who wrote furiously. Mr. Greystone bowed his head. His client clutched his brow and raked his hair.

The woman stood perfectly still.

The usher called order until the courtroom was quiet.

"Any person disturbing this courtroom will be removed!" Judge Worthington stared about like a baleful old owl. "Mrs. Broughton-Caruthers, on behalf of the Court, I apologize for exposing you to the impertinence," he raised his voice slightly, "of those assembled. Counsel will withdraw the question!"

"With permission, my Lord," Mr. Greystone said mildly, "and apologies to all ladies who are present, Counsel asks the question not only to clarify the character of Mr. Furor's relationship to Mrs. Broughton-Caruthers, but in order to ask that she be withdrawn as a witness against him based on her answer."

"My Lord," she said, lifting her veil, "I would like to answer Mr. Greystone's question. May he ask it again?"

Jarvis Perrot caught his breath. Photographs did not do the woman justice. Her tawny, amber-colored eyes stared resolutely at Judge Worthington. He stared at her as though she was some exotic, wild animal let loose in his courtroom. Then he glanced around the hushed room. Finally, he turned to Mr. Greystone. "As you wish," he said under his breath. More loudly he stated, "You may proceed with your question, Mr. Greystone."

Even from a distance, Perrot could see her flushed cheeks and quick breaths. The jewel that rested on her bosom winked in the light. She glanced at Mr. Furor in the dock.

"At your pleasure, I will repeat my previous question. Mrs. Broughton-Caruthers, has Court Furor ever been or is he your lover?"

This time, she did not hesitate. She spoke out clearly and looked, Perrot thought with amazement, extremely happy. "Yes, he was! My lover!" She faced Mr. Furor. "I loved him then, and I love him still!"

Mayhem ensued. The prosecutor and his juniors were on their feet. A man grabbed Mr. Barron's wig and threw it into the air. Judge Worthington fell back against his seat. The usher cried out until he was hoarse. The woman smiled at Mr. Furor, though she was close to tears. Mr. Furor stared at her and looked ready to cry as well.

In the gallery, the woman's family climbed over the other spectators, headed for the nearest exit. Their way was impeded by the riotous crowd's enthusiasm. They were beset by reporters. Horace Greystone sat down. The usher helped Mrs. Broughton-Caruthers from the witness stand. The clerk called a recess until after lunch.

Jarvis Perrot ran down the stairs with all the other newsmen, writing as he went. *Though not beautiful in the traditional sense, Mrs. Broughton-Caruthers is a woman to impress one's memory.* Around him men's voices babbled with speculations and ejaculations of appreciation or wonderment at the woman's performance. Her stunning declaration had made her as notorious as her lover's sister, Miss Stuart. But what had it done for Furor's case?

Breaking into a run, Perrot remembered the day he'd gone to the police station to see if anyone would speak with him about Geoff Ratchet. There he'd met D. S. Peele. As the young man handed Perrot Mrs. Harris' card and told him what to do, the man's icy eyes made him shudder. In retrospect, they were even colder than Ratchet's. He didn't like to think about the part he'd played in the string of events that led to Ratchet's demise. He hardly knew what he felt about it and didn't have time to. But he wondered what Mrs. Broughton-Caruthers or Court Furor was feeling. All he was certain of was that it would make damn good copy.

⚜

Morrant closed the door of the sitting room after Horace Greystone and Dr. Frost. Mr. and Mrs. Barron Sr. had left before them. The rest of the family was assembled around Sir Percival, who sat enthroned in a deep armchair; he was wrapped in a blanket and near the fire. Delilah sat in a straight chair by his side, crocheting. John and Gretchen sat together on one couch, and Winifred leaned hand-in-hand beside Amelie on the other. Bert stood next to the window by himself until Morrant joined him. No one but Delilah and Gretchen drank the tea, and nobody had touched any of the food. The chimes of the clock struck ten times.

After Winifred left the witness stand, the clerk removed her to the safety of an antechamber where she was met by Mr. Whitehouse and John; Richards brought her and Bettina back to Hampstead before returning to the Old Bailey. Everyone else had stayed through the afternoon to hear Court's sentencing. According to John, D. I. Patterson delivered the most damning evidence. Among Geoff Ratchet's personal effects was a small book of Shakespearean quotations in which he had scratched, over and over, Selway Adams' name as well as other ramblings, paranoid descriptions of the methods he would use to kill Court Furor and everyone else whom he thought betrayed him, and sketches of the stars and planets circling the sun. "Beyond a doubt, Furor was definitely there and knew, at least in part, what Ratchet intended."

The jury returned their verdict within half an hour. To no one's surprise, Furor was found guilty on all charges and sentenced to five years hard labor in Yorkshire. Greystone had been as good as his word and done what he could for his client. For a quarter of his sentence, Furor would be held in a place of confinement closer by for first-time offenders. Then he would be moved north. The sentence was considered light.

John took the plate of cake onto his lap. "Poor Furor!"

"An officer of the law is still stationed at the corner," Morrant said, "and he sent away yet another reporter. They appear to have mostly dispersed, ma'am. It's bitter cold."

"Have Mrs. Pettiford send someone out with a warm drink for the policeman," Winifred said, "and ask her to come up afterward with you."

Percival closed the late edition of the newspaper. "This is the excitement I've come home for, not only a wedding? We seem as a family to be determined to set propriety at naught."

"There's not going to be any wedding," Amelie said peevishly. "I shall never forgive you, Bert Barron, not as long as I live!"

"He did nothing wrong, Amelie," said Winifred.

"He and horrid Mr. Greystone have ruined your reputation!" she cried.

"My dear," said Delilah, "Mr. Greystone can hardly apologize for doing his job well, and I'm extremely pleased for Bert, even if they did lose."

Amelie looked at her mother in vexed surprise.

"Oh, I don't know." Gretchen gave John a sly smile, "People's memories are pretty short, and the public hasn't any."

"Precisely," said Delilah.

"I agree." Winifred turned to Amelie's mother. "You were right. I was on the road to ruin long before I left the house to go to the bank that day. I'm not like you, Uncle Percival. I've never been much good at public life, nor have I ever liked town, unlike you, dear," she said to Amelie, who blushed. "I hope what I've done won't make a bit of difference for you and Bert. I'm never happy away from Holloways. I'll retire quietly to the country, keep my birds, and ride Tulip. It's no use being angry with him, Amelie. Don't take on so."

"Take my handkerchief," Gretchen said to the young woman.

"She's overtired," Delilah said. "Dear, you're overtired. Winifred, pour her some tea."

"There, she's not angry at him," Percival interjected.

"I've already forgiven you, Bert!" Winifred called to him.

Amelie jumped up impatiently. "It's not my sense of honor that's hurt. I do think it's bad what the newspapers will say about you and Mr. Furor. They've been frightful enough already. And...," she faltered. "You won't be received!"

"I thought you didn't care about such trifles," Gretchen said in mock seriousness, "only romance! Winifred, welcome to the Untouchables! You may be Princess Pariah for a day!" She raised her tea cup in salute.

"Why don't any of you understand? Mr. Greystone has assassinated her character! It's so unfair!" Amelie walked to the other end of the room and sat at the piano. Winifred and Bert exchanged looks. He went to smooth his fiancée's ruffled feelings.

Winifred thought she would wait until she and Amelie were alone to reassure her cousin that, while she hated the inconvenience and embarrassment her diminished social status would bring her family and servants, she was relieved to be permanently rid of those obligations.

"Speaking of honor," Bert said pleasantly, "Furor never told me anything about that night."

"He was too much of a gentleman," Gretchen said.

"What about the necklace?" Winifred asked. "I never told a soul what I saw him do with it. Not even him! He must have told you how he found it in my pocket."

"No, that was all Mr. Buckner and Mr. Greystone's doing. Once Dupree said you had it when you got home and Mr. Buckner confirmed you'd just taken it before the blast, Mr. Greystone contacted Patterson. He'd already been in touch with Mr. Buckner. The rest about you and Furor was pure Greystone conjecture."

"I shall thank him for the rest of my life," Winifred mused.

"You were honest!" Delilah smiled at Percival. "Don't snivel, Amelie. There's nothing wrong with your cousin's character."

"Well, well, my dear," Percival said to Winifred. "I'm very proud of what you did today."

She took his hand, and he kissed hers.

"I'm an old war horse, Amelie. Don't worry! Scandal and publicity shan't hurt me or my book sales a bit. If you want Bert to succeed in politics, you must be ready for far worse. Put him out of his misery soon. Otherwise I won't have any wedding cake for my Christmas treat! I was so looking forward to a big ceremony and lots of flowers in Saint George's."

There was an awkward pause.

Inwardly, Winifred thanked her uncle and all of them for saying nothing more about Court. The days waiting to testify against him at the first trial had been terrible, and she had dreaded the morning's testimony almost more than she had news of Court's health after he was shot. As soon as Mr. Greystone asked her under what circumstances she offered Court a job, she'd realized where his questions might lead. She'd been terribly afraid, but also terrifically excited. She remembered what Gretchen had said about marrying John and jumping off the cliff with him. By the time Mr. Greystone led her to the edge, she'd been ready to fling herself over it.

Only then did she think of the Triberg Falls. She was glad that no one ever talked about George, at least not in her hearing. In spite of her worries for Court, she often missed her husband; and in spite of what Court said that day in the stable about George not being her friend, he was. No matter what he had done that was wrong, or his treatment of Rosie Cartwright, she could never forget what he had done for her. She remembered the old Christmas parties and dances, the sugar crumbs he brushed from her bodice and his reassurances when she felt plain.

"I won't forget you, Win," he'd said. "You'll see. I'll always turn up like a bad penny."

In Paris they'd come as close as they ever had to resting heart on heart, and she would always treasure that hour. She wished he'd taken the real necklace. He'd soon be in debt again. She wondered what would become of him.

In order for the divorce proceedings to move forward, his solicitor had contacted theirs. Mr. Bartles said that Mr. Broughton-Caruthers' correspondence could not have been more emphatic. His letter had only lately arrived and was sent from Naples; but its date showed he had started to write it on the train after they left Venice. He had completed it on the Paris hotel's stationery. George wished to make it plain that he released her, without acrimony, from any obligations as his wife. He would not sue or require a penny of her fortune, nor would he accept her money should the court garnish it, but send it to Sir Percival, who could do with it as he liked. She could charge him publicly with desertion and adultery, if she wanted. He provided the name of a woman named Matilda Lupino, who could be reached at the Lancaster Arms.

The missive's tone was light, but parts bore traces of his old cynicism and a new self-abnegation that filled her with dread. She didn't think George would go in search of Lottie or Rose, and she kept his secret about why. The only person who suspected was Bettina. She also wondered if Charles knew. Before the wedding, he and his wife had written her a very kind letter inviting her to stay with them; and after George left, the offer was renewed. She'd written them back with her refusal and told Charles she would keep George's jewels for their oldest daughter. She was not sure she could bear the sight of Charles' blue-eyed, tow-haired children, at least for now. For the same reason, she'd refused Gretchen and John's offer to go to Ben Venue after Christmas. Delilah even asked if she wouldn't like to go to Bath for a few weeks and keep her company while Bert and Amelie were on their wedding trip.

As soon as the ceremony was over, she and Bettina would travel to Cairo with Percival and Morrant. She didn't want to go to Holloways for Christmas. She wanted to be near Court.

Bert put his arm around Amelie's waist. Her head rested on his shoulder, and she gently tugged at his lapel.

Like Delilah, Winifred was proud of Bert. She wondered at his ability to pick the locks of her and Court's hearts and coolly pass the keys to Horace Greystone so that he might work out his strange code of justice for them both. Bert would make a formidable lawyer, she thought.

Mrs. Pettiford stood before her. "You wished to see me, ma'am?"

"Thank you for coming today. I'm sure it meant so much to Mr. Furor."

"After your testimony, Richards told me that soon after Mr. Furor came, he remembered exactly where he'd seen him, but didn't like to say because he thought that the young man was trying so hard to turn over a new leaf. Can you believe it? Richards, of all people, obstructing the course of justice!"

They all laughed.

"And wasn't it strange when they sentenced him?" Amelie asked John. "Not even Court knew his full name was Courtesian Morrant Furor. He looked so surprised."

John's ruddy cheeks purpled. He coughed, spraying cake. "Damn it, Bert! I clean forgot to tell Morrant!"

"I knew you would! That's half a crown you owe me!"

"When Richards and I got back to the Old Bailey, they were hauling a woman out of the courtroom. Dressed all in black she was and screaming at the top of her lungs at Mr. Furor like the devil's daughter! A young chap was with her, trying to calm her down. A reporter told me it was Ratchet's fiancée and his business partner, or clerk, or maybe her cousin. Italian, I couldn't make heads or tails of what she said. Poor Furor, what a day!"

While John spoke Morrant stood at the window where Bert had earlier, watching the patrolling officer. He did not seem to hear the general laughter at John's expense while the money changed hands, but turned to Amelie. "Indeed, Miss. What else was said of Mr. Furor?"

"Nothing," Amelie answered.

"I found his name in the parish records," Bert said. "I knew his mother was from Shropshire. I had one of your flashes, Amelie!"

Morrant turned back to the window and seemed thoughtful.

Winifred studied her old friend's face. It was thinner and browner from his trip, and his hair had significantly greyed about his temples, yet he reminded her more than ever of another who was even dearer. "Court told me as well that his mother was from Shropshire. I never thought about it. All he knew of her family was fairy tales, like King Arthur's knights, like the stories you used to tell me."

Morrant's eyes met hers.

Percival stared at the fire. "That autumn I was laid up, that's where I was, southwest of the Severn, the hill country! That's where Morrant and I met. Remember the horse that threw me?"

"Pickles was quite a spirited animal, sir. I rode with Mr. de la Coeur until the accident. He was indisposed with a broken collar bone and matters were complicated by fever. I was working at his lordship's house."

Winifred smiled at the old story. She'd heard it many times before, as had the rest of them.

"Blast, it was when you saw that you could beat me at cards that you decided to stay close by, Morrant! He took all my money, so I had to hire him for my valet. At least I could get something out of him."

"Are the family still in Shropshire?" Amelie asked. "Morrant's a Norman name, isn't it?"

"The Morrants have lived in that part of the shire from time immemorial," he answered. "We came with the invaders and stayed once the fighting was over."

"There is an ancient church." Percival stared at the fire. "Morrant took me. You've never seen so many knights in effigy laid out. There's a lovely coat of arms for their family in one of the stained-glass windows. Your people sent half the horses to the Hundred Years War!"

"We were and still are farmers, but our days of owning so many horses are far behind us."

Winifred spoke. "Court's mother went by Sadie Smith. It wasn't her real name. It was Llewellyn, I think. She ran away from home with his father and didn't want to shame her family."

Morrant visibly stiffened. Winifred thought he looked as though she had played him an unkind trick, the way he had the evening he'd seen her tea gown the first time. He glanced involuntarily at Percival then composed himself. "Forgive me if I appear startled. I've not heard Sadie's name uttered by a soul except your uncle since she ran away."

Percival pulled the miniature from his pocket and handed it to Winifred.

Amelie looked over Winifred's shoulder. "My goodness, it looks like...!"

"It's Beryl Stuart!" Bert exclaimed.

Everyone crowded around to look at the miniature except Morrant, who told the story.

"Sadie Morrant was the youngest daughter but one in my uncle's house. Her mother was a Llewellyn, an ancient family and descended from the true kings of the Britons. She was a very beautiful but willful girl, though she wasn't raised to be. It was a large family, and they were good Christians all. Very prosperous, respected folk who owned dairies. I always put what happened down to her age."

Percival handed Winifred the miniature and stared sadly at the fire.

Morrant continued. "A traveling troupe of actors always came to the village after Michaelmas. That autumn a dark fellow came with them, a sort of Irish gypsy. He called himself Mick O'Fury. He hadn't been to our parts before. He was a magician, handsome as the devil and equally wicked. He sang and performed tricks, and made objects vanish into thin air. Sadie disappeared with him one night and never returned."

Winifred passed the portrait back to her uncle.

"Good night, Sadie," Percival whispered. He kissed her image and put it away.

CHAPTER 23
"The Wraggle-Taggle Gypsies, O'!"

Three gypsies stood at the Castle gate,
They sang so high, they sang so low,
The lady sate in her chamber late,
Her heart it melted away as snow.
They sang so sweet, they sang so shrill,
That fast her tears began to flow.
And she laid down her silken gown,
Her golden rings and all her show.
She plucked off her high-heeled shoes,
A' made of Spanish leather, O!
She would in the street, in her bare, bare feet,
All out in the wind and weather, O!
It was late last night, when my lord came home,
Enquiring for his a-lady, O!
The servants said on every hand,
"She's gone with the wraggle-taggle gypsies, O!"
"O saddle me my milk-white steed.
Go fetch me my pony, O!
That I may ride and seek my bride,
Who is gone with the wraggle-taggle gypsies, O!"
O he rode high and he rode low,
He rode through the woods and copses too.
Until he came to an open field,
And there he espied his a-lady, O!
"What makes you leave your house and land?

What makes you leave your money, O?
What makes you leave your new-wedded lord,
To go with the wraggle-taggle gypsies, O?"
"What care I for my house and land?
What care I for my money, O?
What care I for my new-wedded lord?
I'm off with the wraggle-taggle gypsies, O!"
"Last night you slept on a goose-feather bed,
With the sheet turned down so bravely, O!
And to-night you'll sleep in a cold open field,
Along with the wraggle-taggle gypsies, O!"
"What care I for a goose-feather bed,
With the sheet turned down so bravely, O?
For to-night I shall sleep in a cold open field,
Along with the wraggle-taggle gypsies, O!"

Court stopped singing. He sat alone on his cot in his prison cell. Above him was a single window. It was too high to see much except for the change of the light as dawn passed to dusk, or a few stars. It was also too far away for a man to reach, and they didn't let him have a belt. Nor did he feel as industrious as the last fellow who'd had his quarters. He'd tied the sheets together and used part of his bedframe to poke them up and around the bars when he decided to make an end of it, according to the guard.

He thought of Mick Furor's many stories about his time in jail. His father always made light of it, bragging about how he'd taken the piss out of the guards or gotten the better of this or that cell mate. He always started some scheme on the inside, and it was always the one that was going to make him. Even if it never did, it was all a great laugh, a joke. He'd throw a coin in the air, and it would disappear. Court wished he could perform one of his father's tricks and disappear too.

If he could only be philosophical like Grynt, he'd think about what a rum old world it was and how as sure as one scene with its players began, if a fellow didn't like it, there would soon be another change. He imagined the man on the box of his painted wagon far from the city lights. Jasper's reins hung in his gnarled hands, and the open road lay before them. They had all the time in the world, Grynt would say whenever Sam was impatient and wanted to know when they'd be at their next stop.

Court thought of where he'd been the same time the prior year, of Richards and Will, the stables and Meriwether's foaling, of Mrs. Lumley's creamed potatoes and strawberry trifle. He missed drinking tea with Mrs. Pettiford in her room.

He tried not to think of Winifred or what she'd said in the courtroom or how happy and beautiful she'd looked. It was the last time he'd seen her, though she often seemed to be right there in the cell with him. He hoped they never met again. It would be better for both of them.

After his first sentencing, he'd been in the hospital ward of the prison a while longer before being moved into his own cell. The warden told him that it was his privilege to be in solitary and relatively safe until after he gave his second testimony in P. Lili Piani's trial. His stay in the hospital ward was lengthened because he contracted pneumonia. Those days were a nightmare of breathlessness and hallucinations. He thought he would smother or drown in his own lungs' fluid. It seemed a terrible joke that he might die of his illness after surviving Geoff's bullet. The doctor reassured him that his was not a bad case. Court understood for the first time how frightened Rosie had been all those years whenever she was ill and couldn't get her breath.

Once he was better, he'd had several visitors. Zeke Odom had surprised him very much. The man had been questioned by Patterson and Peele, but had nothing to tell except for what he and Davis had done during Court's training. He'd gotten another job in a gym across the river. He knew nothing of Davis' whereabouts since his testimony. O'Connell had been picked up in Liverpool on his way back to Dublin. Zeke was certain the man's involvement was much deeper than what he'd probably say on the stand and was cynical regarding the charges against him.

"They'll get dropped. It's all about politics," he said. "It's so damned hard to stay out of messes." O'Connell had treated Zeke unfairly, and he was the nervous sort and easily put upon. For the rest of his visit they'd played draughts. Zeke left him the board and pieces. The man did not return, but Court hadn't expected him to.

The second unexpected visit was from Detective Inspector Patterson and Sam. It was the first time Court had met the lawman, though he'd seen him in the courtroom. As with Zeke, he was extremely surprised but very pleased to see Sam. Patterson said he'd wait outside and instructed the attending constable to step out with him. "Five minutes," Patterson said, "and we're watching you both!"

"Come to blast me out?" Court had joked. Before he could make another pleasantry or ask the boy about himself, Sam stopped him with an expression so serious Court was afraid the boy had brought bad news of Fan or Seamus. Sam spoke quietly and quickly. "I've got somethin' to tell you. It's big! Don't say nothin'. Listen, when Patterson comes back in 'ere, 'e's goin' to ask you a lot o' questions, and you're goin' to tell 'im everythin' you know."

Court listened very carefully while Sam talked. When Patterson came back into the room, he brought a younger man with him whom he introduced as Detective Sergeant Peele. His eyes were icy grey and set deep in his face. They made Court think of the Thames in winter. Sam waited outside with the constable, and the two men sat. Court hoped Patterson wouldn't leave him alone with Peele.

"Good visit with Sam?" Patterson asked. "That's done. Sam said you had something big to tell us. Start talking. Peele's going to write down what you say. Afterward, you're going to sign it."

In a few days, Court repeated what Sam had told him, but this time he was on the witness stand and P. Lili Piani was in the dock. Court described the location and contents of a cache of weapons and matériel that his former boss had stockpiled in a large, tin-lined bunker beneath the abandoned store where he'd trained when he was boxing for Piani's rigged contests.

Peele's testimony enlarged Court's contribution. It was from this stockpile that the dynamite used in the Royal Empire had come. A similar incendiary device had been detonated in an alley outside the Southwark police station in late August, "during the time D.I. Patterson was investigating several other sites of interest." Ballistics confirmed the device was made of similar components as the remains of the one found in Selway Adams' office. It matched a few others found in Piani's cache.

In the spring of 1892, Piani had begun to store weapons and ship them to Northern Ireland in exchange for hefty payoffs. Billy O'Connell confirmed the presence of a second holding facility in Liverpool but disclaimed any involvement other than carrying messages between Piani and his Dublin contacts. Patterson's earlier testimony had shown that Bertollini and Ratchet was one of many covers for Piani's ill-gotten gains; he also used it to launder his money from Dublin. Geoff had gotten wise to that and kept his own set of books, pilfered cash, and built up his own posse. Piani and Ratchet had not always been at cross-purposes, however. Court was also called on to testify in the murder trial of Jubal Lipmann, a money-lender who'd hoped to make inroads on

Piani's territory. He'd blackmailed Piani after he got hold of some of the man's Dublin correspondence during a collection raid of one of his own clients, who apparently had been yet another of Piani's messengers to the Emerald Isle. Piani was convicted on all charges in the Lipmann case and in two other unrelated murders of competitive loan-sharks.

The third visitor he'd had was Mademoiselle Dupree, who was on her way abroad. She apologized on Seamus' behalf for not coming to see him and explained what happened after they met D.I. Patterson in Hampstead.

"I listened to the man after I sent Seamus away. If he loves me, if he loves you, he must go to his friends, I tell him. Monsieur, I was more than a bit fâchée when the inspector explained what you two had done. You are not as smart as I thought, getting mixed up with a fellow like Ratchet. I know Seamus is not smart. He can't be involved in any more tricks. No more bad company, like the dead Ratchet." She spat. "Alors, I've told Madame adieu and am going to him. I wanted to say goodbye to you, too."

Court asked where they would live. "I will be with Seamus. That is all I can say."

After testifying in Piani's trial he was sent north to work the quarries. Solitude had been dreadful, yet on his arrival at his new prison he had dreaded even more being exposed to, as Miss Dupree put it, bad company. He would've preferred to be alone. As it was, he'd had two bunkmates so far who, like him, preferred to keep themselves to themselves. His current one, a morose man of mixed race and a thief, was outside in the exercise yard. They never talked about themselves, only trivial or prison matters. Most of his companionship was in the form of letters. Some that he answered were from Holloways and London, or Scotland. Even Miss Amelie's mother wrote him a very kind note and sent a Bible. Winifred's letters, which came from Egypt along with Sir Percival's and Mrs. Pettiford's, he did not open but stored carefully in his trunk.

Sam wrote that he worked for a fellow who made engines and that he was training to be a mechanic. He sent a newspaper clipping about Arabella Bertollini's wedding and an advertisement for Bertollini's Men's Store, articles about trials related to Piani's, and others about his company or Daimler. *Patterson got made Chief. He bought a new bowler hat and we drank champagne and went to the Opera Comique, where Rosie used to like to go. We are in Brighton now on holiday because none of us has ever been (postcard of the Pavilion enclosed). In*

July I am going to Paris for Le Concours du "Petit Journal" Les Voitures sans Cheveaux (Horseless Wagons, they are the Future) and will see Seamus! Maybe I'll find F. and H. too, but I am not changing no baby's nappies. Mrs. Patterson says Paris is very wicked. I can't wait!

Many letters were from Beryl. Rosie's baby was born in late February, a boy that they christened Edward Stuart Greystone. Horace wrote GBC's solicitors informing them of his intention to legally adopt and give the child his name. *No one seems to know where G. has gone.* There was more about the baby's and Rosie's good health, the agreeableness of the sea air, the cottage, and the kindness of its owner, Mr. Norwood, and his wife. *Horace will never buy another horse, but we ride when he comes down.*

Other letters came from Mr. Barron concerning his appeal. He felt that Court had a good chance given his record of conduct while in prison, personal statements from Richards and Mrs. Pettiford, as well as staff at Hampstead, and most importantly, his contributions during Piani's trials. Before he turned himself in and agreed to Patterson's plan to snare Ratchet, Court had given all his meager property and the winnings from Beryl's last race into his friend's care. Mr. Barron said he would invest the money, which meant about as much to Court as Sam's impassioned paeans to high-speed petrol engines and spark ignitions. "While you're working the tread mill, your money will be working for you," Mr. Barron tried to explain. They met every couple of months. Court could see that marriage agreed with the man, though he was working very hard in his final year with Mr. Greystone. He and Amelie lived in the Hampstead house and were expecting their first child.

He opened the latest volume of Sir Percival's memoirs, a gift from Mr. Barron, *Night Thoughts on the Nile.* He liked to imagine the moored dahabiya and the Aswan Falls as he had seen them in Mr. Barron's books on foreign wonders. The ibises wading in the reeds, the glow of the low, huddled mud houses as the sun set over the sands, and the winking of the first huge desert stars. Inside the front cover was a copy of a portrait of Sadie Morrant. Mr. Barron explained its significance to Sir Percival. Mistress Amelie had drawn the copy for Court as her gift.

Court pulled up his blanket and read.

We began our journey down the Nile asking several questions. How much of our life is ruled by curiosity and the desire to see what will happen next? How much of our existence is within our power to control, and how much of it is circumscribed by apparent coincidences of fortune or affected by the proximity of personalities, either well-suited or ill-matched and among whom we pass our lives? Or is there some other force at work? Though the reader must finally judge for himself, I offer these observations.

I am an old man. I look through my many notebooks and diaries and make a list of all the people I have ever known and all the acquaintances that have even tangentially concerned me. I encourage my reader to do the same. Write these on a map and get a length of thread and some pins. The lines one lays between the names will be many; some lines may cross often or not at all. For some, these lines will create a tapestry, coherent, perhaps even beautiful.

Most of us will end up with more of a tangle. This web may tell us much; or, its lines may lead to no conclusions. Some of us will find we have but few connections, yet they are precious. Some may choose to break whatever strings attach them to others. They may have good reasons for doing so.

Yet I think that often, those who break their connections do so because they do not want to be tethered. They float above the lives they could have touched, imagining themselves free. Such are doomed to wander like airy spirits over the desert and never solve the mysteries of others' and their own hearts.

⚭

Sir Percival and Morrant walked ahead to the dock, where the felucca waited. The tap of her uncle's stick on the pavement sounded like one of the birds as it knocked a shell against a stone. Mrs. Pettiford gathered the rest of their picnic.

Winifred put away her letter from Rigsby Archer. He'd written several times and had accepted a junior post in the Moroccan consulate. Though she couldn't bring herself to throw the letters away, she hadn't answered them either. Without his saying so, they reminded her that she'd been very unkind to him. There was much more to the man than she'd given him a chance, or the encouragement, to show. He didn't have to allude to his deeper feelings for it to be plain why he wrote. She knew how he felt and wished he'd get over her.

They lingered among the columns while the men boarded. Already the air had grown noticeably cooler. She wrapped her shawl more tightly around her shoulders. Hers and the other woman's spidery shadows wavered on the temple floor.

She still missed Bettina, whose sudden decision to hand in her notice the day before they were to depart for Italy had been a painful blow. "As I told you once, I too am a woman," was the only explanation her tearful friend could manage. They had corresponded since the rupture, but the first weeks without her were very difficult. Winifred had spent New Year's Eve by herself on the train, having decided to go to Egypt alone. From the port of Brindisi, she'd taken the boat to Alexandria, where Morrant met her for the final stage of her journey to Cairo. Her uncle had already left immediately after Bert and Amelie's wedding, whereas she had succumbed to Delilah and Natasha's exhortations and stayed on for Christmas at Holloways.

That Bettina had fallen in love came as a shock. Winifred was as upset and embarrassed by her initial reaction as she supposed Amelie had been by hers after the trial. She'd greeted Bettina's news with angry tears. She'd felt fearfully jealous and put upon, and was nearly as unhappy as she'd been when she was told her father had died. She'd shed a good many petulant tears as she sat alone in her train compartment and sometimes still did. She'd get along on her own, she'd shouted at Bettina. She would not hire a maid to travel with her. True to her word, she'd fought to make herself understood by station agents who spoke only Italian and chased after porters who seemed determined to load her luggage on the wrong carts. Her impatience, even more than the inconvenience of learning to do for herself, left her dismayed and dispirited. When her rage abated, she had time to think about what Mrs. Pettiford had said to her after Bettina left.

"What, did you think that she'd stay forever?"

Winifred said that she knew she ought to be glad Bettina had found an admirer and was going home to France. She did not add that she was deeply ashamed to have been so wrapped up in her own troubles that she'd not even noticed that Bettina had her own interests. "But why does it have to be now when I need her so?" She rested her head on her uncle's desk and wept.

Mrs. Pettiford let her cry it out. "I'm sorry for all your trials, but you'll go on. If Miss Dupree has found the right man, I'm glad she had the courage to do something about it."

Winifred dried her eyes but felt very sorry for herself. Until the divorce proceedings with George were completed, Bert suggested she have nothing to do with Court. Unable to forego some sort of contact, she wrote. He did not write back, nor did Bert bring any messages from him. In her loneliness, she missed George more than ever and worried about him. Neither his solicitors nor Charles had any news. She often feared he had gone back to Triberg or done something equally foolish.

"I'll never marry again," Winifred said to the woman. "I'll remain single like you."

"I don't want to be," Mrs. Pettiford answered quietly. She stood next to the fireplace with folded hands, staring at the Stubbs.

Winifred never liked to pry into her servants' lives, unless they invited her interest or needed her help, but the woman's expression and her position beneath the Stubbs brought back another night the previous spring. So far as she knew, Mrs. Pettiford had come to Holloways from Lincolnshire. She didn't know the woman's age, but she couldn't be much older than George's Lottie. Her boy Jim had been old enough to go to school by the time she arrived, and he'd gone to sea thereafter. Winifred had never known the woman to speak of her husband.

"Sometimes we don't meet the right person at the right time," she offered.

"Oh, I met the right person only he...," the woman hesitated. "I was still married to Mr. Pettiford. We married when I was a little younger than you. I came from a farm, a large family. I didn't much fancy the life, so I worked in a factory. I didn't fancy that either. Gerald came along and seemed fond enough. He wasn't a bad man, nor was he an especially good one. We had that much in common. He'd been in service, a big house near York, and thought he could get me on there as an under-parlor maid. It was a way out. I didn't love him. Not as I should've. But in no time at all, there was Jim to think on. That's why I stayed.

"After I found out about this position, we parted ways. Gerald only died last January."

Mrs. Pettiford hadn't asked for any time other than her regular days off that Winifred could recollect. She didn't think the woman was the sort to carry on with a man and couldn't think how, with all her duties, her housekeeper would have ever had the time. But she had fancied someone and perhaps still did. Her curiosity was piqued.

"I can see what you're thinking, Miss. This past year was a very difficult one in many ways, what with your uncle and Mr. Morrant gone."

Winifred felt like she was having one of Amelie's flashes. She saw Court standing before the Stubbs and remembered how Mrs. Pettiford had taken him under her wing. Bettina had told her, as did Amelie and

Gretchen, how much time and effort Mrs. Pettiford had taken to instruct him. They often sat together in the woman's room, talking like old friends. Winifred assumed Mrs. Pettiford missed her son. She thought how handsome Court had looked, seated in the carriage on their way to the races, the way she'd always imagined a younger Morrant.

"Does he know?" Winifred asked. As she had been forced to with Bettina, she saw Eliza Pettiford in a new light. Morrant had always held the woman in the highest regard. "Is that why he's never married?"

"I often wondered. He's always been attentive but never forward."

"I'm sorry. I've upset you. I shouldn't have asked."

There the matter rested until she wrote to ask the woman to be her maid. It was a step down in position, but she promised a better salary. She didn't know how long she would stay in Cairo and agreed to hold Mrs. Pettiford's position back at Holloways. They would hire a temporary replacement. On those conditions, Eliza Pettiford joined them.

⚜

Paul Morrant's letters were the golden thread which led Court through the labyrinth of his loneliest days and nights during his final months in prison. Once the man realized they were second cousins, he had opened not only his heart but his coffers. Letters from the Llewellyns and other members of the Morrant family arrived, offering cheer. Since Sadie died, except for Beryl, he'd thought of himself as an orphan and was astonished at the number of cousins and uncles and aunts who awaited his arrival in the hill country.

Sir Percival was also generous. He opened an account at the Royal Empire Bank under both their names from which Court was to draw while he stayed in London to buy clothes and other gentlemanly accoutrements. "You may look upon the money as a loan if you wish." Mr. Buckner showed him a payment schedule. The interest was negligible. "Mr. de la Coeur prefers to see it as a gift. My secretary, Mr. Darby, will help you with the paperwork." Mr. Bert presented Court a check for the money he had invested on Court's behalf. Lines of credit were opened for him at several establishments. Letters came from one of Sir Percival's old friends in Shropshire, who offered Court the tenancy of a "small house."

Court emerged from prison with more cash, friends, and family than he had ever dreamed of; the happy days spent buying clothes and riding boots, or the evenings by the fire with Mr. Bert, Mrs. Barron, and baby William had a dreamlike quality. Mr. Greystone took him to Tattersall's, where he purchased Lucky Penny, a three-year-old bay gelding. The crowning moment of his release was a visit with Mr. Bert to the mews from which Piani had hired his horses.

Within the hour, he was Eglantine's new master.

It was early April, 1895, when Court rode into the open, hilly country of his mother's people by Paul Morrant's side. In an attic, Sadie's sister, Annie, pulled dust cloths from furniture and boxes. His mother's personal belongings were his, and he could have Sadie's old bedroom suite. She handed him a small box. "A gift from your mother's suitor, Sir Percival de la Coeur," she said proudly. "He meant it for her sixteenth birthday."

At Easter Sunday services, Morrant introduced him to Lord Beacham. The men explained their families' ancient connection. "We're all distantly related around here," his lordship added. "Not only the Llewellyns and Morrants! Mother knew who married whom. It's written in an old book that used to be kept here. The mice love to chew on it. Vicar's having it repaired. I've a tapestry, family tree, and so forth! I'll show you back at the house after luncheon."

That night Court opened his prison trunk and read Winifred's letters. The private workings of her heart were all there. Their one night together; the shared stories and laughter; her stubborn pride; and her uncertainty. She was a woman; she was a frightened girl. She was demanding; yet she was, as ever, generous. She loved him. Court put the letters away, closed the trunk, and locked it.

Before he left London, Bert tried to assure him. All was over between his cousin and George. "In a week, she'll be here to meet William." Old Mrs. Broughton-Caruthers had died, and Winifred also intended to visit Hereford Hall and pay her respects to Charles. "Except for the solicitors, no one's heard from George."

"Their marriage, or whatever she feels for Mr. George, isn't the issue," Court said. "Good riddance to him and good luck!" He wouldn't begrudge any woman her first romantic friendship, even if he wished the fellow would jump off a cliff. George had been wicked. "But I'm beneath her notice." His upbringing, his crimes, his jail sentence were proof enough. "Facts don't go away!"

Bert held the baby and stared at the hearth rug.

Amelie had told him that he was wrong. "You're too proud, like her!"

"With respect, I saw her at home. She's only human and stubborn and spoiled to boot."

"Then don't worship her like she's perfect. That's not what she wants."

In spite of his good fortune, the prospect of meeting Winifred frightened him. What if his new life wasn't a success? He couldn't disappoint her again.

"Bert doesn't earn my love, hard as he works! I simply love him. And what do I have to give? Nothing much! Bert knows all my faults! But he loves me. Like Winifred loves you."

In his cell, he often argued with Winifred. Her imaginary form sat atop his trunk. By the fireside in his new den, he took up the same habit. He wasn't worthy of her sacrifices. Her chaste person and reputation, precious to any woman, were even more regrettable losses to a lady. He'd never forgive himself for letting her give them up. He should've put her from him the second they met; or protected her from Geoff, even if it meant his life.

Broken as his pride was, he still had its pieces. He couldn't bear to live on her or any woman's largesse. Her family's generosity didn't change who he was, a boy from the Old Nichol, a convicted thief. All he had to offer was himself, and that was too poor a gift. "I don't understand meself, or you," he complained aloud. "I wish you'd let me be!"

Winifred's specter said nothing. Her eyes spoke for her.

Near his house was a small chapel, all that remained of a once great house. After his daily, solitary ride about the hills, he sat among the effigies of knights, considering the image of the Good Shepherd in the rose window over the altar. In spite of frequent visits to and from family, or his lordship's hospitality, sometimes he felt so low he might as well have been in prison. In the quiet chapel, he hid himself and gave vent to his sorrows. He read the names and the dates on the walls and paving stones. They belonged to Sadie's people, his people.

He opened the Bible Mrs. Barron had given him. He had marked the verse with one of Winifred's letters. "Lay not up for yourselves treasures upon earth, where moth and rust doth corrupt, and where thieves break through and steal ... but lay up for yourselves treasures in heaven. For where your treasure is, there will your heart be also."

When he was a boy, those words had been a mystery. He imagined great piles of golden coins, trunks full of precious gems. Yet he put back Winifred's necklace with far less regret than he'd put her on 'bus 44.

What grace had brought her into that alley, or his life? There was a time he would've called it chance or luck. Those words did not satisfy him anymore. Her friends had become his. They had all done their parts for him. But mostly, it began with Winifred. Her love had changed his life. In his heart, unworthy as he felt, he knew his love had changed hers.

He unfolded Winifred's letter. *No matter if you write or not! Whether you come to me or not, my heart won't change. In this world or hereafter, I am yours and you are mine. My only home, my heaven, is with you.*

In the middle of May, Court loaded Winifred's two small trunks into his neat, newly-purchased trap. Eglantine waited under the station awning. They drove into the sunshine, out amongst the rolling hills.

As they rounded the bend that took them past the lake, Winifred gasped. "You said it was a small house!"

A boy called Brian met them and led the trap and Eglantine to the stable. His mother would be along shortly, he said, to lay the tea. His lordship expected Miss for the night. "And Father has almost finished plowing the field."

There were four good-sized rooms downstairs and up, a big attic, and a cellar. The kitchen garden and sheds were out back. The stable had its own yard and storage buildings. Court explained that he was leasing the acreage from his lordship for pasture and fodder. "But this land once belonged to my family, and his Lordship says he'd like it to be a freehold again."

Winifred admired the parlor's bluebell walls and played the pianoforte under the bow window. Wildflowers stood in a vase under Sadie's portrait. Court promised to play a tune on his flute after tea. Porcelain dogs sat on the mantle, and the table held a music box and a china dish. The chairs were covered in flowered chintz. His female relatives helped furnish the house, he said, as though the room's delicacy embarrassed him.

She inspected the dining room and kitchen, with its enormous stove, dresser, and long trestle table. Against his protests, she peered into a paneled den. A wadded blanket hung off the sofa; an open book lay face down on a pillow. On the wall were tacked prints of thoroughbreds and a calendar whose picture displayed a champion horse. Equine equipment strewed the floor. Next to a desk overflowing with papers stood a packing crate full of books. She recognized one of Bert's old fly rods. Mrs. Clark charred for him three times a week. Her day was tomorrow, he apologized.

Only one of the four bedrooms was furnished. Winifred paused before a graceful table, its curving legs and top inlaid with flowers. On it lay the battered jewel box that had once held her mother's necklace. Inside it was a plain gold crucifix on a delicate chain.

Court waited at the foot of the stairs. How lovely she sounded, singing at the pianoforte or asking him about his Lordship's crops and what sort of fish were in the lake. His heart began to beat harder. "I've another place for you to see."

Behind the house, she exclaimed over the chickens, the kitchen and herb gardens, the hutches and beehives. Over a hill and down a path, they crossed a brook. Beyond it lay a chapel. While Court explained the history, she read the inscriptions on the coats of arms. He said nothing about the window near the door, a depiction of Saint George and the Dragon. It was missing a few of its panes.

Winifred wanted to meet Lucky Penny.

"For now, I'm helping in his Lordship's stables. He's got plenty of horses and owns a beautiful hunter, but wants to branch out and raise thoroughbreds for racing."

Winifred stroked Lucky Penny's nose.

"I've got me plans. It ain't much, compared to what you come from...."

"How many acres are there? The one's you showed me." Court told her, and she smiled. "I think I like his Lordship! I'm interested in his proposed venture."

"Now don't you start! I'm not taking anyone's money!"

Winifred pressed her fingers on his lips. "It's my money! You can hardly stop me investing it!" She quickly walked to Eglantine's stall. "Oh Court! I loved you from the moment I first saw you in front of the Royal Empire Bank, in spite of that purple coat."

Court approached her. "I didn't think you was that daft. Then again, maybe you is!"

Winifred darted to the stable door, evading his hands.

For a bit she made him chase her, and he let her get away. At the far end of the stable, he finally caught her. They fell onto the hay in the empty stall.

Court buried his face in her hair. As ever, she smelled heavenly.

"Must I stay at his Lordship's?" she teased.

"I think you'd better," he said.

Winifred reached around his shoulders. "Don't you trust me?"

"Now what sort of question is that? I'd trust you with me life, woman!"

"But do you love me? Because Court Morrant Furor, I love you so much!"

Her amber eyes searched his. She touched the scar on his cheek. How had he thought he could ever live without her?

"I love you too Winifred, body and soul. I always has and always will. I love you. I do."

CHAPTER 24

Harvest

Sandringham

Late summer. Bertie read the racing results. He felt a bit world-weary. Mama had been admonishing him again about his conduct, as though it was any of her business how a grown man behaved! He had lived his life exactly as he wanted for years; but at times, even a Prince wishes for the freedom, if not the anonymity, of lesser mortals. Or that his mother would move permanently to Balmoral. His secretary set his correspondence before him. He signed a document. An envelope addressed in June from Shropshire caught his eye. It was in an unfamiliar, slanting hand.

Your Majesty, we met late one night whilst playing cards at the Lancaster Arms. You won't remember, but it was Important to me. You was quite taken with me half-sister, Beryl Stuart, Jockey for Sweet Little Banshee (she wasn't riding then but did a few months later). That night, I said I'd met a Lady. You knew her because of her Golden Eyes and said you was neighbors. You suggested it was True Love on my part. IT WAS.

You also said you hoped to hear the end of my story sometime, so I will presume upon your interest, Sir, and tell my tale. Maybe one day the Lady will come down a bit and make you happy, you said. She did and married me yesterday in the family chapel. I am the happiest man alive excepting You (I hope), for there ain't a Woman in this world the equal of WINIFRED DE LA COEUR.

Yours respectfully, Court Morrant Furor

In the garden, Alex sat at tea, and the children played tennis. It was still warm, but the leaves would begin to turn soon. Time for the hunt, then Christmas, then the Season, and so on and on. As it always would be, and should be, according to Mama.

Sighing, he set down the letter. Not only did he remember the man and Miss Stuart, he had seen the bride's picture in the papers after her debacle on the witness stand during the Selway Adams trial. What man in his right mind wouldn't respond to a declaration such as the one she made? He also recollected how she looked on her horse when she'd visited Sandringham with her uncle for the hunt. It all seemed so long ago.

Court Furor would be a happy, happy man. The thought left him a bit wistful.

Cairo

Morrant turned down the lamp, cleared away the dishes, but left the brandy bottle and the cigars. "Is there anything else? If not, I'll lock up."

Percival did not need to look at his old friend's face. The man was impatient to be dismissed. He couldn't blame him. Life was very different, now that Morrant and Eliza were married. Not so many late-night chats over cards anymore, but he understood. All things must pass. Rivers flow out to sea. Water under the bridge, what ho!

"I'm fine! Be about your business!" he said in his most genial tone.

"Then good night, sir." Morrant adjusted the mashrabiya screens at the window. He pulled the door to, but not quite shut.

Percival listened for a while to Morrant's and Eliza's voices as they finished closing the rest of the house. Some nights, the sound made him feel even more alone. Other times, he was comforted by it.

The Nile reflected the moonlight. The desert was a dark line beyond. Stars, large and small stars, millions of them, dusted the violet sky. Time slipped by in such a place. It seemed to pass differently, faster. It blew away like sand. But that was part of growing older.

Percival was thankful Winifred stayed as long as she did. When she left, he had understood that as well. He only wished he'd met her young man. Their bridal portrait stood on his desk. Both Furor and his sister looked very much like his darling. Different, too—harder, but the resemblance was clear. Maybe he would visit England once more after the baby was born. Would it be a boy this time, or another daughter? They already had two girls—and the twins!

He eyed the brandy bottle and the cigars. Morrant didn't argue with him about his bad habits anymore. It was his choice, after all. What he did with his life.

Percival picked up his pen and continued his letter to Tristan.

Court lives in the bosom of his mother Sadie Morrant's people, and his own family grows. He has his horses and his Winifred. She has her heart's desire. She misses quaint old Holloways and her friends, but it is a small price to pay for her happiness, which is to love and to be loved by Court, who is all in all to her. Another baby is on the way. Another is expected at Bert and Amelie's as well. Delilah says Winifred will have six like Gretchen before all is said and done.

There are no secrets between her and Court, except the ones that belong to them both. They have many happy days ahead, many embraces, and much for which to give thanks.

"So, they do. Indeed, they do," he whispered.

Percival set the letter aside and removed from a pigeon hole of his desk a packet of letters. George's erratic correspondence was as amusing and indiscreetly detailed as always. Yet it was vague about his own inner life, distant. The real George would probably elude everyone—and himself—forever. Percival often thought he should tell Winifred that George wrote, but did not. He had considered destroying the letters, but couldn't do that either. Someday George's boy might like to read them, or maybe Charles' daughters.

There was so much Percival would've liked to tell the man; but George was, well, George! He was not likely to listen, or would have behaved as though he hadn't afterward. In some foreign bordello there was yet another party, or a man to fleece at the card table, and George was in a rush to get there, the reins either slipping from his hands or being cast aside altogether. Percival placed the letters next to Winifred's. No one but George could risk his neck over and over with such apparent glee. He wondered if George would ever go back to England.

He pulled Sadie's portrait from his pocket and kissed it. The sky was already grey! He took up his pen and began to write in his day book. His last memoir had sold well, and his publisher was pestering him again. So was his rheumatism.

Bert wrote that he would be his amanuensis if he would only come home. It was tempting, but so were his brandy and cigars. Egypt wasn't so bad. Until he made up his mind what to do, he would read the young people's letters about new babies and growing children. He would add their stories to his diaries, recording the lives without which his own would be so sorely empty. It was to Sadie and the young couples that he addressed his thoughts. It was a habit he hoped would preserve for their children (or some other reader) a few of the more intimate details of a bygone world without which they would not exist.

ACKNOWLEDGMENTS

The publication of this book would not have been possible without the help of many people. Thank you to the team at Bellastoria Press, especially Linda Cardillo, for her editorial guidance and encouragement. Without her, this book would not have seen the light of day. I owe so much to Vana Nespor for holding my shaking hands through the publication and marketing process. Natalie Mendik deserves many thanks for her attention to detail and for making me a better writer.

Endless appreciation is due to the readers of the first and second drafts. Kimberly Montague's editorial comments on the original draft were of immense value in setting me on the right track. Kathaleen Chandley, Jenny Johnson, Jerry Spears, and Robert Woessner were generous not only with the gift of their time, but also encouragement. Their astute observations and questions about the characters helped me a great deal with later drafts' revisions.

Thanks go to Jessica Medina, for listening and advice on navigating the waters of the publishing world; to Carolyn Chandley, for giving big doses of perspective; and to Dean Verhoeven, for providing technical support and introducing me to Linda Cardillo and Bellastoria.

To my former students, you taught me that writing is, indeed, rewriting...and rewriting...and rewriting....

When this journey began in 2011, my mother had recently begun a journey of her own, only we didn't know it. She was the first to know of *Treasure* and to hear me read from its chapters. "Are these people real?" she would ask.

"Yes, Mama—to me."

Dear, sweet Mary Lu, thank you. Thank you for everything.

Finally, to my husband Gregg, who has what it takes to live with a woman who is perpetually writing a book, I could not have done this without you.

M. Catherine Bunn

ABOUT THE AUTHOR

M. Catherine Bunn fell in love with Victorian England and its literature before she could read. At the family dinner table her father was rarely without a book. "He read aloud to us. Nothing was off limits. It was everything from his old comic books to National Geographic and the Bible, Twain and Dickens, or Zane Grey and Edgar Rice Burroughs." Those tales ignited her imagination. "There was never a time when I wasn't making up romances and adventures, or exploring a character," she laughs. "I also grew up within walking distance of the downtown library and a great used bookstore." Inheriting her father's passion for storytelling, Catherine began writing her own in a red notebook that her mother gave her.

That devotion to characters and writing propelled Catherine to UNC-Chapel Hill to study English and then to spend a stint working in England. After that she attended North Carolina State University for a master's in English and then North Carolina Central University to prepare for the classroom where she hoped to inspire a love of literature in young readers. For nearly two decades, teaching high school kept her busy. She satisfied her creative urges onstage, writing music and singing with her band, Mister Felix.

Yet her unrealized stories haunted her dreams, crying out to be heard, to be brought to life on paper, and to be shared with the world. When life took a difficult turn, Catherine's characters came to her fully formed, tying her to her computer, as scene after scene spilled out on the page. An unconventional heroine and her dangerous, street-gutter paramour filled the pages with action and passion.

tained

CPSIA information can be o
at www.ICGtesting.com
Printed in the USA
LVHW021125100821
694913LV00005B/948